W9-AAU-939

Praise for **Counting Heads**

"*Counting Heads* was one of my favorite books of last year in any category, and an exemplary entry in the sci-fi genre. . . . Marusek could be the one sci-fi writer in a million with the potential to make an increasingly indifferent audience care about the genre again, and he could do it without dumbing down his subject matter."

—*The New York Times Book Review*

"*Counting Heads*: exciting, major new SF novel. . . . David Marusek is one of the best-kept secrets of science fiction, a wild talent with a Gibson-grade imagination and marvelous prose, and a keen sense of human drama that makes it all go. . . . I haven't felt as buffeted by a book since Gibson's *Neuromancer*—haven't felt more like I was reading something truly radical, new, and exciting."

—Cory Doctorow

"This extraordinary debut novel puts Marusek in the first rank of SF writers. . . . Exciting and wonderful."

—*Publishers Weekly*

"Marusek keeps a deep and textured tale spinning along, filled with stresses, shocks, and sidelong looks at extrapolations of present-day trends."

—*The San Diego Union-Tribune*

"*Counting Heads* is a compelling and powerful read. Marusek isn't afraid of asking hard questions—nor is he afraid to try and find answers. . . . One of the best SF novels of this (and perhaps any) year, *Counting Heads* gives us a rich mix of social commentary, speculation, and adventure, all garnished with a tiny pinch of hope."

—*Vector*

"Marusek has built a meticulously detailed world and populated it with vital, complex characters. *Counting Heads* is an impressive first novel, full of clever wordplay and bracing action."

—*San Francisco Chronicle*

"David Marusek's first novel is a wildly inventive story of a future dependent on clones and artificial intelligence. . . . *Counting Heads* is thick with invention and has an action-filled plot, but Marusek shines in filling it with well-rounded characters."

—*The Denver Post*

"This exciting debut adventure poses interesting questions with a healthy dose of humor and derring-do. What happens when the technology of tomorrow becomes a reality? . . . Innovative plotting and realistic characterization combine to make a believable, captivating futuristic adventure."

—*Romantic Time BOOKreviews*

"Incandescent! Compelling prose, enormous plot, fascinating characters—it takes over your mind like one of the story's own transformative nano programs."

—Kage Baker

"Marusek investigates his dark future with wild inventiveness and a rare completeness. Like one of those lush children's books showing cut-aways of castles, steamships, and submarines, *Counting Heads* illuminates its complexities gracefully, and it's a cracking good read as well."

—Scott Westerfeld

"David Marusek is one of the most exciting writers to emerge in science fiction in the last decade."

—Nancy Kress

"David Marusek's long-awaited first novel is the science-fiction landmark we all expected it to be. He writes with power and authority and great visionary force."

—Robert Silverberg

Counting Heads

DAVID MARUSEK

TOR®

A Tom Doherty Associates Book
New York

COUNTING HEADS

Copyright © 2005 by David Marusek

Edited by David G. Hartwell

Book design by Jane Adele Regina

A Tor Book
Published by Tom Doherty Associates, LLC
175 Fifth Avenue
New York, NY 10010

www.tor.com

Tor® is a registered trademark of Tom Doherty Associates, LLC.

Library of Congress Cataloging-in-Publication Data

Marusek, David.
    Counting heads / David Marusek.
        p. cm.
    "A Tom Doherty Associates book."
    ISBN-13: 978-0-7653-1754-4
    ISBN-10: 0-7653-1754-0
    1. Twenty-second century—Fiction. 2. Overpopulation—Fiction. 3. Assassination—Fiction. 4. Immortalism—Fiction. 5. Rich people—Fiction. 6. Cryonics—Fiction. I. Title.

PS3613.A788 C68 2005
813'.6—dc22

                                                                        2005005316

First Hardcover Edition: November 2005
First Trade Paperback Edition: October 2007

Printed in the United States of America

0 9 8 7 6 5 4 3 2 1

My father, bless his sensibilities, sanitized books with a black marking pen before adding them to his library. He indelibly struck out all words of an offensive nature. I fear that this, my first novel, would not be permitted to join his library unmarked. Nevertheless, I dedicate it to his memory:

Henry Paul Marusak
Inventor

ACKNOWLEDGMENTS

I am privileged to work with a dedicated corps of readers and editors who are not shy in pointing out the strengths and flaws of my fiction. This novel (and the novella *We Were Out of Our Minds with Joy* that serves as Part One) has been vastly improved through their generous feedback. To them I offer giddy thanks:

Suzanne Bishop	Sandra Boatwright	Vincent Bonasso
Terry Boren	Charles Brown	Gardner Dozois
Maggie Flinn	Colleen Herning	Elizabeth Ann Hull
Dixon Jones	Marion Avrilyn Jones	Paula Kothe
Holly Wade Matter	Katherine Patrick	Kate Schaefer
Jackie Stormer	Cynthia Ward	

A snappy salute to my agent, Ralph Vicinanza, and my editor, David G. Hartwell, for their leap of faith in taking me on.

I started this book as a house guest of Pat Cadigan and Chris Fowler in London, and finished it as a house guest of Russell and Avis Ruffu in Denton, Texas. Thank you so much for sharing the creative ambiance of your lovely households. And special thanks to Candis Shannon for looking after Kika while I was away.

Finally, much appreciation to the Rasmuson Foundation for a grant to help promote this book.

PART 1

We Were Out of Our Minds with Joy

1.1

On March 30, 2092, the Department of Health and Human Services issued Eleanor and me a permit. The undersecretary of the Population Division called with the news and official congratulations. We were stunned by our good fortune. The undersecretary instructed us to contact the National Orphanage. There was a baby in a drawer in Jersey with our names on it. We were out of our minds with joy.

ELEANOR AND I had been together a year by then. We'd met at a reception in Higher Soho, which I attended in realbody. A friend said, "Sammy Harger, is that really you? What luck! There's a woman here who wants to meet you."

I told him thanks but no thanks. I wasn't in the mood. Not even sure why I'd come. I was recovering from a weeklong stint of design work in my Chicago studio. In those days I was in the habit of bolting my studio door and immersing myself in the heady universe of packaging design. It was my true creative calling, and I could lose all sense of time, even forgetting to eat or sleep. Henry knew to hold my calls. Henry was my belt valet system and technical assistant, and he alone attended me. I could go three or four days at a time like that, or until my Muse surrendered up another award-winning design.

My latest bout had lasted a week but yielded nothing, not even a third-rate inspiration, and I was a little depressed as I leaned over the buffet table to fill my plate.

"There you are," my persistent friend said. "Eleanor Starke, this is the famous Samson Harger. Sam, El."

An attractive woman stood on a patch of berber carpet from some other room and sipped coffee from a delicate china cup. She said hello and raised her hand in a holo greeting. I raised my own hand and noticed how filthy my fingernails were. Unshaven and disheveled, I had come straight from my cave. But the woman chose to ignore this.

"I've wanted to meet you for a long time," she said brightly. "I was just telling Lindsey about admiring a canvas of yours yesterday in the museum here."

A canvas? She'd had to go back over a century to find something of mine to admire? "Is that right?" I said. "And where is here?"

A hint of amusement flickered across the woman's remarkable face. "I'm in Budapest," she said.

Budapest, Henry said inside my head. *Sorry, Sam, but her valet system won't talk to me. I have gone to public sources. Eleanor K. Starke is a noted corporate prosecutor. I'm digesting bios now.*

"You have me at a disadvantage," I told the woman standing halfway around the globe. "My valet is an artist's assistant, not an investigator." If her holo persona was anything like her real self, this Eleanor K. Starke was a pretty woman, mid-twenties, slight build. She had reddish blond hair, a disarmingly freckled face, and very heavy eyebrows. Too sunny a face for a prosecutor, I thought, except for the eyes. Her eyes peered out at you like eels in coral. "I understand you're a corporate prosecutor," I said.

Her bushy eyebrows rose in mock surprise. "Why, yes, I am!"

Sam, Henry whispered, *no two published bios agree on even the most basic data. She's between 180 and 204 years old. She earns over a million a year, no living offspring, degrees in History, Biochemistry, and Law. Hobbies include fencing, chess, and recreational matrimony. She's been dating a procession of noted artists, com-*

posers, and dancers in the last dozen months. And her celebrity futures are trading at 9.7 cents.

I snorted. Nine point seven cents. Anything below ten cents on the celebrity market was nothing to crow about. Of course, my own shares had sunk over the years to below a penny, somewhere down in the has-been to wannabe range.

Eleanor nibbled at the corner of a pastry. "This is breakfast for me. I wish I could share it with you. It's marvelous." She brushed crumbs from the corner of her mouth. "By the way, your assistant—Henry, is it?—sounds rather priggish." She set her cup down on something outside her holo frame before continuing. "Oh, don't be offended, Sam. I'm not snooping. Your Henry's encryption stinks—it's practically broadcasting your every thought."

"Then you already know how charmed I am," I said.

She laughed. "I'm really botching this, aren't I? I'm trying to *pick you up*, Samson Harger. Do you want me to pick you up, or should I wait until you've had a chance to shower and take a nap?"

I considered this brash young/old woman and her awkward advances. Warning bells were going off inside my head, but that was probably just Henry, who does tend to be a bit of a prig, and though Eleanor Starke seemed too cocky for my tastes and too full of herself to be much fun, I was intrigued. Not by anything she said, but by her eyebrows. They were vast and disturbingly expressive. As she spoke, they arched and plunged to accentuate her words, and I couldn't imagine why she didn't have them tamed. They fascinated me, and like Henry's parade of artist types before me, I took the bait.

OVER THE NEXT few weeks, Eleanor and I became acquainted with each other's bedrooms and gardens up and down the eastern seaboard. We stole moments between her incessant business trips and obligations. Eventually, the novelty wore off. She stopped calling me, and I stopped calling her. We had moved on, or so I thought. A month passed when I received a call from Hong Kong. Her Calendar asked if I would care to hololunch the next day. Her late lunch in China would coincide with my midnight brandy in Buffalo.

I holoed at the appointed time. She had already begun her meal and was expertly freighting a morsel of water chestnut to her mouth by chopstick. "Hi," she said when she noticed me. "Welcome. I'm so glad you could make it." She sat at a richly lacquered table next to a scarlet wall with golden filigree trim. "Unfortunately, I can't stay," she said, placing the chopsticks on her plate. "Last-minute program change. So sorry. How've you been?"

"Fine," I said.

She wore a loose green silk suit, and her hair was neatly stacked on top of her head. "Can we reschedule for tomorrow?" she asked.

I was surprised by how disappointed I felt at the cancellation. I hadn't realized that I'd missed her. "Sure, tomorrow."

That night and the whole next day was colored with anticipation. At midnight I said, "Henry, take me to the Hong Kong Excelsior."

"She's not there," he replied. "She's at the Takamatsu Tokyo tonight."

Sure enough, the scarlet walls were replaced by paper screens. "There you are," she said. "God, I'm famished." She uncovered a bowl and scooped steamy sticky rice onto her plate while telling me in broad terms about a case she was brokering. "They asked me to stay on, you know. Join the firm."

I sipped my drink. "Are you going to?"

She glanced at me, curious. "I get offers like that all the time."

We began to meet for a half hour or so each day and talked about whatever came to mind. El's interests were deep and broad; everything seemed to fascinate her. She told me, while choking back laughter, ribald anecdotes of famous people caught in embarrassing situations. She revealed curious truths behind the day's news stories and pointed out related investment opportunities. She teased out of me all sorts of opinions, gossip, and jokes. Her half of the room changed daily and reflected her hectic itinerary: jade, bamboo, and teak. My half of the room never varied. It was the atrium of my hillside house in Santa Barbara where I had gone in order to be three hours closer to her. As we talked I looked down the yucca- and chaparral-choked canyon to the university campus and beach below, to the channel islands, and beyond them, to the blue-green Pacific that separated us.

WEEKS LATER, WHEN again we met in realbody, I was shy. I didn't know quite what to do with my hands when we talked. We sat close together in my living room and tried to pick any number of conversational threads. With no success. Her body, so close, befuddled me. I thought I knew her body—hadn't I undressed it a dozen times before? But it was different now, occupied, as it was, by El. I wanted to make love to El, if ever I could get started.

"Nervous, are we?" she teased.

FORTUNATELY, BEFORE WE went completely off the deep end, the self-involved parts of our personalities bobbed to the surface. The promise of happiness can be daunting. El snapped first. We were at her Maine town house when her security chief holoed into the room. Until then the only member of her valet system—what she called her Cabinet—that I had met was her chief of staff.

"I have something to show you," the security chief said, glowering at me from under his bushy eyebrows. I glanced at Eleanor, who made no attempt to explain or excuse the intrusion. "This was a live feed earlier," the chief continued and turned to watch as Eleanor's living room was overlaid with the studio lounge of the *SEE Show*. It was from their "Trolling" feature, and cohosts Chirp and Ditz were serving up breathless speculation on hapless couples caught by holoeye in public places.

The scene changed to the Baltimore restaurant where Eleanor and I had dined that evening. A couple emerged from a taxi. He had a black mustache and silver hair and looked like the champion of boredom. She had a vampish hatchet of a face, limp black hair, and vacant eyes.

"Whoodeeze tinguished gentry?" said Ditz to Chirp.

"Carefuh watwesay, lipsome. Dizde ruthless Eleanor K. Starke and'er lately dil-dude, Samsamson Harger."

I did a double take. The couple on the curb had our bodies and wore our evening clothes, but our facial features had been morphed beyond recognition.

Eleanor stepped into the holoscape and examined them closely. "Good. Good job."

"Thank you," said her security chief. "If that's everything—"

"Wait a minute," I said. "It's *not* everything."

Eleanor arched an eyebrow in my direction.

Those eyebrows were beginning to annoy me. "Let me see if I've got this straight," I said. "You altered a pointcast feed while it was being transmitted?"

She looked at me as though I were simple. "Why, yes, Sam, I did," she said.

"Is that even possible? I never heard of that. Is it legal?"

She only looked blankly at me.

"All right then. Forget I said that, but you altered *my* image along with yours. Did you ever stop to wonder if I want my image fooled with?"

She turned to her security chief. "Thank you." The security chief dissolved. Eleanor put her arms around my neck and looked me in the eye. "I value our privacy, Sam."

A WEEK LATER, Eleanor and I were in my Buffalo apartment. Out of the blue she asked me to order a copy of the newly released memoir installment of a certain best-selling author. She said he was a predecessor of mine, a recent lover, who against her wishes had included several paragraphs about their affair in his latest reading. I told Henry to fetch the reading, but Eleanor said no, that it would be better to order it through the houseputer. When I did so, the houseputer froze up. It just stopped working and wouldn't respond. That had never happened before. My apartment's comfort support failed. Lights went out, the kitchen quit, and the doors all sprang open. Eleanor giggled. "How many copies of that do you think he'll be able to sell?" she said.

I was getting the point, and I wasn't sure I liked it. The last straw came when I discovered that her Cabinet was messing with Henry. I had asked Henry for his bimonthly report on my finances, and he said, *Please stand by.*

"Is there a problem?"

My processing capabilities are currently overloaded. Please stand by.

Overloaded? My finances were convoluted, but they'd never been *that* bad. "Henry, what's going on?"

There was no response for a while, then he said in a tiny voice, *Take me to Chicago.*

Chicago. My studio. That was where his container was. I left immediately, worried sick. Between outages, Henry was able to assure me that he was essentially sound, but that he was preoccupied in warding off a series of security breaches.

"From where? Henry, tell me who's doing this to you."

It's trying again. No, it's in. It's gone. Here it comes again. Please stand by.

Suddenly my mouth began to water, and my saliva tasted like machine oil: Henry—or someone—had initiated a terminus purge. I was excreting my interface with Henry. Over the next dozen hours I spat, sweat, pissed, and shit the millions of slave nanoprocessors that resided in the vacuoles of my fat cells and linked me to Henry's box in Chicago. Until I reached my studio, we were out of contact and I was on my own. Without a belt valet to navigate the labyrinthine Slipstream tube, I undershot Illinois altogether and had to backtrack from Toronto. Chicago cabs still respond to voice command, but as I had no way to transfer credit, I was forced to walk the ten blocks to the Drexler Building.

Once inside my studio, I rushed to the little ceramic container tucked between a cabinet and the wall. "Are you there?" Henry existed as a pleasant voice in my head. He existed as data streams through space and fiber. He existed as an uroboros signal in a Swiss loopvault. But if Henry existed as a physical being at all, it was as the gelatinous paste inside this box. "Henry?"

The box's ready light blinked on.

"THE BITCH! HOW dare she?"

"Actually, it makes perfect sense."

"Shut up, Henry."

Henry was safe as long as he remained a netless stand-alone. He couldn't even answer the phone for me. He was a prisoner; we were both prisoners in my Chicago studio. Eleanor's security chief had breached Henry's shell millions of times, near continuously since the moment I met her at my friend's reception. Henry's shell was an off-the-shelf module I had purchased years ago for protection against garden-variety espionage. I had rarely updated it, and it was long obsolete.

"Her Cabinet is a diplomat-class unit," Henry argued. "What did you expect?"

"I don't want to hear it, Henry."

At first the invasion was so subtle and Henry so unskilled that he was unaware of the foreign presence inside his shell. When he became aware, he mounted the standard defense, but Eleanor's system flowed through its gates like water. So he set about studying each breach, learning and building ever more effective countermeasures. As the attacks escalated to epic proportions, Henry's self-defense consumed his full attention.

"Why didn't you tell me?"

"I did, Sam, several times."

"That's not true. I don't remember you telling me once."

"You have been somewhat distracted lately."

The question was, how much damage had been done, not to me, but to Henry. I doubted that Eleanor was after my personal records, and there was little in my past anyone could use to harm me. I was an artist, after all, not a judge. But if Eleanor had damaged Henry, that would be the end. I had owned Henry since the days of keyboards and pointing devices. He was the repository of my life's work and memory. I could not replace him. He did my bookkeeping, sure, and my taxes, appointments, and legal tasks. He monitored my health, my domiciles, my investments, etc., etc. These functions I could replace. It was his personality bud that was irreplaceable. I had been growing it for eighty years. It was a unique design tool that amplified my mind perfectly. I depended on it, on Henry, to read my mind, to engineer the materials I used, and to test my ideas against the tastes of world culture. We worked as a team. I had taught him to play the devil's advocate. He provided me feedback and insight.

"Eleanor's Cabinet was interested neither in your records nor in my personality bud. It simply needed to ascertain, on a continuing basis, that I was still Henry and that no one else had corrupted me."

"Couldn't it just ask?"

"If I were corrupted, do you think I would tell?"

"Are you corrupted?"

"Of course not."

I cringed at the thought of installing Henry back into my body not knowing if he were someone's dirty little spy.

"Henry, you have a complete backup here, right?"

"Yes."

"One that predates my first encounter with Eleanor?"

"Yes."

"And its seal is intact?"

"Yes."

Of course, if Henry was corrupted and told me the seal was intact, how would I know otherwise? I didn't know seals from sea lions.

"You can use any houseputer," he said, reading me as he always had, "to verify the seal, and to delete and reset me. It would take a couple of hours, but I suggest you don't."

"Oh yeah? Why not?"

"Because we would lose all I've learned since we met Eleanor. I was getting good, Sam. Their breaches were taking exponentially longer to achieve."

"And meanwhile you couldn't function."

"So buy me more paste. A lot more paste. We have the money. Think about it. Eleanor's system is aggressive and dominant. It's always in crisis mode. But it's the good guys. If I can learn how to lock it out, I'll be better prepared to meet the bad guys who'll soon be trying to get to Eleanor through you."

"Good, Henry, except for one essential fact. There is no Eleanor and me. I've dropped her."

"I see. Tell me, Sam, how many women have you been with since I've known you?"

"How the hell should I know?"

"Well, I do. In the 82.6 years I've associated with you, you've been with 343 women. Your archives reveal at least a hundred more before I was installed."

"If you say so, Henry."

"You doubt my numbers? Do you want me to list them by name?"

"No. What good are names I've forgotten, Henry?" More and more, my own life seemed like a Russian novel—too many characters, not enough car chases.

"My point exactly, no one has so affected you as Eleanor Starke. Your bio-response has gone off the scale."

"This is more than a case of biology," I said, but I knew he was right, or nearly so. The only other woman who had had such an effect on me was my first love, Jean Scholero, who was a century and a quarter gone. All the rest were gentle waves in a warm feminine sea. But how to explain this to Henry?

Until I could figure out how to verify Henry, I decided to isolate him in his container. I told the houseputer to display "Do Not Disturb—Artist at Work" and take messages. I did, in fact, attempt to work, but was too busy obsessing. I mostly watched the nets or paced the studio arguing with Henry. In the evenings I had Henry load a belt—I kept a few old Henry interfaces in a drawer—with enough functionality so that I could go out and drink. I avoided my usual haunts and all familiar faces.

In the first message she recorded on my houseputer, El said, "Good for you. Call when you're done." In the second she said, "It's been over a week—must be a masterpiece." In the third, "Tell me what's wrong. You're entirely too sensitive. This is ridiculous. *Grow up!*"

I tried to tell her what was wrong. I recorded a message for her, a long seething litany of accusations, but was too angry to post it.

In her fourth message, El said, "It's about Henry, isn't it? My security chief told me all about it. Don't worry; they frisk everyone I meet, nothing personal, and they don't rewrite anything. It's their standing orders, and it's meant to protect me. You have no idea, Sam, how many times I'd be dead if it weren't for my protocol.

"Anyway, I've told them to lay off Henry. They said they could install a dead-man trigger in Henry's personality bud, something I do for my own systems, but I said no. Complete hands off. All right? Is that enough?

"Call me, Sam. Let me know you're all right at least. I— miss you."

In the meantime I could find no trace of a foreign personality in Henry. I knew my Henry just as well as he knew me. His thought process was like a familiar tune to me, and at no time during our weeks of incessant conversation did he strike a false note.

El sent her fifth message from bed where she lay between iridescent sheets (of my design). She said nothing. She looked directly at the holocam, propped herself up, letting the sheet fall to her waist, and brushed her hair. Her chest above her breasts, as I had discovered, was spangled with freckles.

Bouquets of real flowers began to arrive at my door with notes that said simply, "Call."

The best-selling memoirs that had stymied my Buffalo houseputer arrived on datapin with the section about Eleanor extant. The author's simulacrum, seated in a cane-backed chair and reading from a leather-bound book, described Eleanor in his soft southern drawl as a "perfumed vulvoid whose bush has somehow migrated to her forehead, a lithe misander with the emotional range of a homcom slug." I asked the sim to stop and elaborate. He flashed me his trademark smirk and said, "In her relations with men, Eleanor Starke is not interested in emotional communion. She prefers entertainment of a more childish variety, like poking frogs with a stick. She is a woman of brittle patience with no time for fluffy feelings or fuzzy thoughts. Except in bed. In bed Eleanor Starke likes her men half-baked. The gooier the better. That's why she likes to toy with artists. The higher an opinion a man has of himself, the more painfully sensitive he is, the more polished his hubris, the more fun it is to poke him open and see all the runny mess inside."

What he said enraged me, regardless of how well it hit the mark. "You don't know what you're talking about," I yelled at the sim. "El's not like that at all. You obviously never knew her. She's no saint, but she has a heart, and affection and—to hell with you!"

"Thank you for your comments," the author said. "May we quote you? Be on the lookout for our companion volume to this memoir installment, *The Skewered Lash Back,* due out in September from Pageturner Productions."

I had been around for 147 years and was happy with my life. I had successfully navigated several careers and amassed a fortune that even Henry had trouble charting. Still, I jumped out of bed each day with a renewed sense of interest and adventure. I would have been pleased to live the next 147 years in exactly the same manner. And yet, when El sent her final message—a glum El sitting in the Museum of Art and Science, a wall-sized early canvas of mine behind her—I knew my life to be ashes and dirt.

SEVENTY-TWO THICK CANDLES in man-sized golden stands flanked me like sentries as I waited and fretted in my tuxedo at the altar rail. The guttering beeswax flames filled the cathedral with the fragrance of clover. LOOK proclaimed our wedding to be the "Wedding of the Hour" and it was streamed live on the Wedding Channel. A castrati choir, hidden in the gloom beneath the giant bronze pipes of the organ, challenged all to submit to the mercy of Goodness. Their sweet soprano threaded through miles of stone vaults, collecting odd echoes and unexpected harmony. More than a million subscribers fidgeted in wooden pews that stretched, it seemed, to the horizon. And each subscriber occupied an aisle seat at the front.

In the network's New York studio, El and I, wearing keyblue body suits, stood at opposite ends of a bare sound stage. On cue, El began the slow march toward me. In Wawel Castle overlooking ancient Cracow, however, she marched through giant cathedral doors, her ivory linen gown awash in morning light. The organ boomed Mendelssohn's march, amplified by acres of marble. Two girls strewed rose petals at Eleanor's feet, while another tended her long train. A gauzy veil hid El's face from all eyes except mine. No man walked at her side; a two-hundred-year-old bride, Eleanor usually preferred to give herself away.

By the time of the wedding, El and I had been living together for six months. We had moved in together partly out of curiosity, partly out of desperation. Whatever was going on between us was mounting. It was spreading and sinking roots. We talked about it, always "it," not sure what else to call it. It complicated our lives, especially El's. We agreed we'd be better off without it and tried to remember, from experiences in our youth, how to fix the feelings we were feeling. The one sure cure, guaranteed to make a man and a woman wish they'd never met, was for them to cohabitate. If there was one thing humankind had learned in four million years of evolution, it was that man and woman were not meant to live in the same hut.

So, we co-purchased a town house in Connecticut. Something small but comfortable. It wasn't difficult at all for us to stake out our separate bedrooms and work spaces, but decorating the common areas required diplomacy and compromise. Once in and settled, we agreed to open our house on Wednesday evenings to begin the arduous task of melding our friends and colleagues.

We came to prefer her bedroom for watching the nets and mine for making love. When it came to sleeping, I was a snuggler, but she preferred to sleep alone. Good, we thought, here was a crack we could wedge open. We surveyed each other for more incompatibilities. She was a late night person, while I rose early. She liked to travel and go out a lot, while I was a stay-at-homer. She loved classical music; I could stand only neu-noise. She worked nonstop; I worked in fits and starts. She was never generous to strangers; I simply could not be practical in personal matters. She could get snippy; I could be silent for a long, long time. She had a maniacal need for total organization in all things, while for me a cluttered mind was a fruitful mind. Alas, our differences, far from estranging us, seemed only to endear us to each other.

DESPITE EL'S PENCHANT for privacy, our affair and wedding had caused our celebrity futures to spike. The network logged 1.325 million billable hours of wedding viewership, and the guest book collected some pretty important sigs. Confetti rained down for weeks. We planned a five-day honeymoon on the Moon.

Eleanor booked three seats on the Moon shuttle, not the best portent for a successful honeymoon. She assigned me the window seat, took the aisle seat for herself, and into the seat between us she projected her Cabinet members one after another. All during the flight, she took their reports, issued orders, and strategized, not even pausing for liftoff or docking. Her Cabinet consisted of about a dozen officials, and except for her security chief, they were all women. They all appeared older than El's apparent age, and they all bore a distinct Starke family resemblance: reddish blond hair, slender build, the eyebrows. If they were real people, rather than the personas of El's valet system, they could have been her sisters and brother, and she the spoiled baby of the brood.

Two Cabinet officers especially impressed me, the attorney general, a smartly dressed woman in her forties with a pinched expression, and the chief of staff, who was the eldest of the lot. This chief of staff coordinated the activities of the rest and was second in command after El. She looked and spoke remarkably like El. She was not El's eldest sister, but El, herself, at seventy. She intrigued me. She was my Eleanor stripped of meat, a stick figure of angles and knobs, her eyebrows gone colorless and thin. But her eyes had the same predatory glint as El's. All in all, it was no wonder that Henry, a mere voice in my head, admired El's Cabinet.

The Pan Am flight attendants aboard the shuttle were all penelopes, one of the newly introduced iterant types who were gengineered for work in microgravity.

That is, they had stubby legs with grasping feet. They floated gracefully about the cabin in smartly tailored flight suits, attending to passenger needs. The one assigned to our row—Ginnie, according to her name patch—treated Eleanor's Cabinet members as though they were real flesh and blood. I wondered if I shouldn't follow her example.

"Those penelopes are Applied People, right?" El asked her chief of staff. "Or are they McPeople?"

"Right the first time," her chief of staff replied.

"Do we own any shares in Applied People?"

"No, AP isn't publicly traded."

"Who owns it?"

"Sole proprietor—Zoranna Albleitor."

"Hmm," El said. "Add it to the watch list."

SO THE FLIGHT, so the honeymoon. Within hours of checking into the Sweetheart Suite of the Lunar Princess, Eleanor was conducting business meetings of a dozen or more holofied attendees. She apologized, but claimed there was nothing she could do to lighten her workload. I was left to take bounding strolls through the warren of interconnected habs by myself. I didn't mind. I treasured my solitude.

On the third day of our so-called honeymoon, I happened to be in our suite when Eleanor received "the call." Her Calendar informed her of an incoming message from the Tri-Discipline Council.

"The Tri-D?" El said. "Are you sure? What did we do now?"

Calendar morphed into Cabinet's attorney general who said, "Unknown. There's no memo, and the connection is highly encrypted."

"Have we stepped on any important toes? Have any of our clients stepped on any important toes?"

"All of the above, probably," the attorney general said.

After stalling as long as possible, El accepted the call. The stately though unimaginative seal of the Tri-Discipline Council—a globe gyrating on a golden axis—filled our living room. I asked El if I should leave.

She gave me a pleading look, the first time I'd ever seen her unsure of herself. So I stayed as the overdone sig dissolved into thin air and Agnes Foldstein, herself, appeared before us sitting at her huge glass desk. Eleanor sucked in her breath. Here was no minor bureaucrat from some bottom tier of the organization but the very chair of the Board of Governors, one of the most influential people alive, parked at her trademark desk in our hotel suite. Both El and I stood up.

"Greetings from the Council," Foldstein said, looking at each of us in turn. "I apologize for interrupting your honeymoon, but Council business compels me." She turned to me and praised the inventiveness of my work in packaging design. She spoke sincerely and at length and mentioned specifically my innovations in battlefield wrap for the Homeland Command as well as my evacuation blankets for victims of trauma and burns. Then she turned to El and said, "Myr Starke, do you know why I'm here?"

Foldstein appeared to be in her late forties, an age compatible with her monstrous authority, while my El looked like a doe-eyed daughter. El shook her head. "No, Governor, I don't."

But she must have had some inkling, because Henry whispered, *Eleanor's chief of staff says Eleanor asks twice if you know what this means.*

I puzzled over the message. Apparently, it had been flattened by its passage through two artificial minds. What Eleanor had probably said was, "Do you know what this means? Do you know what this means?" Well, I didn't, and the whole thing was making me nervous.

"After careful consideration," Foldstein continued, "the Council has nominated you for a seat on the Board of Governors."

"Sorry?" El said and grasped my arm to steady herself.

Foldstein chuckled. "I was surprised myself, but there you have it—I'm offering you a seat at the grown-ups' table."

BY THE TIME we shuttled back to Earth, the confirmation process was well under way. Over the next few torturous weeks, El's nomination was debated publicly and in camera by governments, corporations, the Homeland Command, labor charters, pundits, and ordinary putzes alike. Such a meteoric rise was unheard of, and con-spiracy theories abounded. El, herself, was at a loss to explain it. It was like skipping a dozen rungs on the ladder to success. Nevertheless, at no time did she doubt her ability to fill the post, and she marched through our town house in splendiferous pomp, only to crash in her bedroom an hour later to fret over the dozens of carefully buried indiscretions of her past. On the morning she testified before the Tri-D Board of Governors, she was serene and razor sharp.

Immediately upon returning home she summoned me to my bedroom and de-manded screaming monkey sex from me. Afterward she could hardly stand the sight of me.

I supported her as much as I could, except for a couple of times when I just had to get out of the house. I retreated to my Chicago studio and pretended to work.

When Eleanor's appointment was confirmed, we took the Slipstream down to Cozumel for some deep-sea diving and beachcombing. It was meant to be a working vacation, but by then I suffered no delusions about Eleanor's ability to relax. There were too many plans to make and people to meet. And indeed, she kept some member of Cabinet at her side at all times: on the beach, in the boat, at the Mayan theme village, even in the cramped quarters of the submersible.

We had planned to take advantage of an exclusive juve clinic on the island to shed some age. My own age-of-choice was my mid-thirties, the age at which my body was still active enough to satisfy my desires, but mellow enough to sit through long hours of creative musing. El and I had decided on the three-day sifting regi-men and had skipped our morning visola to give our bodies time to excrete their cel-lular gatekeepers. But at the last moment, El changed her mind. She decided she ought to grow a little older to better match her new authority. So I went to the clinic alone and soaked in the baths twice a day for three days. Billions of molecular-sized janitors flowed through my skin and permeated my muscles, cartilage, bones, and nerves, politely snip, snip, snipping protein cross-links and genetic anomalies and gently flushing away the sludge and detritus of age.

I returned to the bungalow on Wednesday, frisky and bored, and volunteered to prepare it for our regular weekly salon. I had to page through a backlog of thousands of recorded greetings from our friends and associates. More confetti for El's ap-pointment. The salon, itself, was a stampede. More people holoed down than our bungalow could accommodate. Its primitive holoserver was overwhelmed by so many simultaneous transmissions, our guests were superimposed over one another five or ten bodies deep, and the whole squirming mass of them flickered around the edges.

Despite the confusion, I quickly sensed that this was a farewell party—for Eleanor. Our friends assumed that she would be posted on the Moon or at Mars Sta-tion, since all Tri-D posts on Earth were already filled. At the same time, no one expected me to go with her—who would? Given people's longevity, it could take decades—or centuries—for Eleanor to acquire enough seniority to be transferred back to Earth.

By the time the last guest signed off, we were exhausted. Eleanor got ready for bed, but I poured myself a glass of scotch and went out to sit on the beach.

Wet sand. The murmur of the surf. The chilly breeze. It was a lovely equatorial dawn. "Henry," I said, "record this."

Relax, Sam. I always record the best of everything.

In the distance, the island's canopy dome shimmered like a veil of rain falling into a restless sea. Waves surged up the beach to melt away in the sand at my feet. There was a ripe, salty smell of fish and seaweed and whales and lost sailors moldering in the deep. The ocean, for all its restlessness, had proven to be a good delivery medium for nanotech weapons—NASTIEs—which could float around the globe indefinitely, like particularly rude messages in tiny bottles, until they washed up on the enemy's shore. Cozumel's defense canopy, more a sphere than a dome, extended through the water to the ocean floor, and deep into bedrock. A legacy of the Outrage in the 2060s.

"So tell me, Henry, how are you and Cabinet getting along?" I had taken his advice and bought him more neuro-chem paste.

Cabinet is a beautiful intelligence. I consider emulating it.

"In what way?"

I may want to trifurcate my personality bud.

"So that there's three of you? Uh, what would that accomplish?"

Then I would be more like a human.

"You would? Is that good?"

I believe so. I have recently discovered that I have but one point of view, while you have several which you can alternate at will.

"It sounds like I bought you more paste than what's good for you."

On the contrary, Sam. I think I'm evolving.

I wasn't sure I liked the sound of that. I changed the subject. "So, how do you feel about moving off-planet?"

It's all the same to me, Sam. Have bandwidth—will travel. You're the one to be concerned about. Have you noticed how constipated you become at low-g?

"I'm sure there's something for that."

But what about your work? Can you be creative so far away?

"I can always holo to Chicago. As you say, have bandwidth—" I sipped my drink and watched the sun rise from the sea. Soon I saw El strolling up the beach in her robe. She knelt behind me and massaged my shoulders.

"I've been neglecting you," she said, "and you've been wonderful. Can you forgive me?"

"There's nothing to forgive. You're a busy person. I knew that from the start."

"Still, it must be hard." She sat in the sand next to me and wrapped her arms around me. "It's like a drug. I'm drunk with success. But I'll get over it. I promise."

"There's no need. You should enjoy it."

"You don't want to move off-planet, do you?"

So much for small talk. I shrugged and said, "Maybe not forever, but I could probably use a change of scene. I seem to have grown a bit fusty here."

She squeezed me and said, "Thank you, Sam. You're wonderful. Where do men like you come from?"

"From Saturn. We're saturnine."

She laughed. "I don't think we have any posts that far out yet. But there's a new one at Trailing Earth. I suspect that's where they'll be sending me. Will that do?"

"I suppose," I said, "but on one condition."

"Name it."

I hadn't had anything in mind when I said that; it had just come out. Was there something else bothering me?

Henry chimed in, *Tell her to have Cabinet show me how to trifurcate.*

That certainly wasn't it, but it did help me to articulate what I was feeling. "Only this," I said. "I realize now that you've been preparing yourself for this moment for most of your life. Don't lose sight of the fact that you're in the big league now. Don't get in over your head too soon."

NO SOONER HAD we returned to our Connecticut town house than another shocker hit the media. Myr Mildred Rickert, Tri-Discipline Governor posted in midwestern USNA, was missing for three hours. Eleanor blanched when she heard the news. Governor Rickert had been a dominant force in world affairs for over fifty years, and her sudden disappearance was another seismic shift in the world's power structure. Still, she was only missing.

"For three hours?" El said. "Come on, Sam, be realistic."

Over the next twenty-four hours, Eleanor's security chief discreetly haunted the high-security nets to feed us details and analyses as they emerged. A homcom slug, on wildside patrol, discovered Governor Rickert's earthly remains in and about a Slipstream car in a low-security soybimi field outside the Indianapolis canopy. She was the apparent victim of a NASTIE. Her valet system, whose primary storage container was seized by the Homeland Command and placed under the most sanitary interrogation, reported that Rickert was aware of her infection when she entered the tube car beneath her Indianapolis residential tower. She ordered the valet to use her top-security privileges to route her car out of the city and jettison it from the tube system. So virulent was the attacking NASTIE and so stubborn Rickert's visola-induced defenses, that in the heat of cellular battle her body burst open. Fortunately, it burst within the car and contaminated only two or three square kilometers of farmland. Rickert's quick thinking and her reliable belt system had prevented a disaster within the Indianapolis canopy. The HomCom incinerated her scattered remains after the coroner declared Myr Rickert irretrievable.

And so a plum post in the heartland was up for grabs. Eleanor turned the living room into a war room. She sent her entire staff into action. As the appointee with the least amount of seniority, she had no reasonable expectation of winning that post, but she wasn't going to lose it for lack of trying. She lined up every chit she'd ever collected in her several careers and lobbied for all she was worth. My own sense of dread increased by the hour.

"Look," I said, trying to talk sense to her, "you don't imagine that this is a coincidence, do you? Your nomination and then this? Someone is setting you up. Don't you see?"

"Relax," she said. "I know I don't have a chance in hell of getting this post. I'm just flexing my muscles and getting in the game. People would wonder if I *didn't*."

Early one morning a week later, Eleanor brought coffee and a Danish and the morning visola to me in bed. "What's this?" I said, but I already knew by the jaunty angle of her eyebrows.

WE MOVED INTO temporary quarters—an apartment on the 207th floor of the Williams Towers in Bloomington. We planned to eventually purchase a farmstead in an outlying county surrounded by elm groves and rye fields. El's daily schedule, already at a marathon level, only intensified with her new responsibilities as the regional Tri-D director. Meanwhile, I pottered about the campus town trying to come to grips with my new circumstances.

A couple of weeks later, an event occurred that dwarfed all that came before. Eleanor and I, although we'd never applied, were issued a permit to retro-conceive a baby. These permits were impossible to come by, since only about a hundred thousand were issued each year in all of the USNA. Out of all of our friends and acquaintances, only two or three had ever been issued a permit. I hadn't even seen a baby in realbody for decades (although simulated babies figured prominently in most holovids and comedies). We were so stunned at first we didn't know how to respond. "Don't worry," said the undersecretary of the Population Division, "most recipients have the same reaction. Some faint."

Eleanor seemed far from fainting, and she said matter-of-factly, "I don't see how I could take on the additional responsibility at this time."

The undersecretary was incredulous. "Does that mean you wish to refuse the permit?"

Eleanor winced. "I didn't say that." She glanced at me for help.

"Uh, a boy or a girl?" I said.

The undersecretary favored us with a fatuous grin. "That's entirely up to you, now isn't it? My advice to you," he added with forced spontaneity—he'd been over this ground many times before, and I wondered if that was the sum total of his job, to call a hundred thousand strangers each year and grant them one of life's supreme gifts—"is to visit the National Orphanage in Trenton. Get the facts. No obligation."

For the next hour or so, El and I sat arm in arm in silence. Suddenly El began to weep. Tears sprang from her eyes and rolled down her cheeks. I held her and watched in total amazement.

After a while, she wiped her eyes and said through bubbles of snot, "A baby is out of the question."

"I agree totally," I said. "It would be the stupidest thing we could ever do."

AT THE NATIONAL Orphanage in Trenton, the last thing they did was take tissue samples for recombination. Eleanor and I sat on chromium stools, side by side, in a treatment room as the nurse, a jenny, scraped the inside of Eleanor's cheek with a curette. We had both been off visola for forty-eight hours, dangerous but necessary to obtain a pristine DNA sample. Henry informed me that Eleanor's full Cabinet was on Red. That meant Eleanor was tense. This was *coitus mechanicus*, but it was bound to be the most fruitful sex we would ever have.

AT THE NATIONAL Orphanage in Trenton, the first thing they did was lead us down to Dr. Deb Armbruster's office where the good doctor warned us that raising a modern child was nothing like it used to be. "Kids used to grow up and go away," said Dr. Armbruster. "Nowadays, they tend to get stuck at around age eight or thirteen. And it's not considered good parenting, of course, to force them to age. We believe it's all the attention they get. Everyone—your friends, your employer, well-wishing strangers, HomCom officers—everyone comes to coo and fuss over the baby, and they expect you to welcome their attention. Gifts arrive by the van load. The media wants to be invited to every birthday party.

"Oh, but you two know how to handle the media, I imagine."

Eleanor and I sat in antique chairs in front of Dr. Armbruster's neatly arranged desk. There was no third chair for Eleanor's chief of staff, who stood patiently at Eleanor's side. Dr. Armbruster was a large, fit woman, with a square jaw and pinpoint eyes that glanced in all directions as she spoke. No doubt she had arranged her own valet system in layers of display monitors around the periphery of her vision. Many administrative types did so. With the flick of an iris, they could page through reams of reports. And they looked down their noses at holofied valets with personality buds, like Eleanor's Cabinet.

"So," Dr. Armbruster continued, "you may have a smart-mouthed adolescent on your hands for twenty or thirty years. That, I can assure you, becomes tiresome. You, yourselves, could be two or three relationships down the road before the little darling is ready to leave the nest. So we suggest you work out custody now, before you go any further."

"Actually, Doctor," El said, "we haven't decided to go through with it. We only came to acquaint ourselves with the process and implications."

"I see," Dr. Armbruster said with a hint of a smile.

AT THE NATIONAL Orphanage in Trenton, the second thing they did was take us to the storage room to see the "chassis" that would become our baby, if we decided to exercise our permit.

One wall held a row of carousels, each containing hundreds of small drawers. Dr. Armbruster rotated a carousel and told a particular drawer to unlock itself. She removed from it a small bundle wrapped in a rigid tetanus blanket (a spin-off of my early trauma blanket work). She placed the bundle on a gurney, commanded the blanket to relax, and unwrapped a near-term human fetus, curled in repose, a miniature thumb stuck in its perfect mouth. It was remarkably lifelike, but rock still, like a figurine. I asked how old it was. Dr. Armbruster said that, developmentally, it was 26 weeks old, and that it had been in stasis seven and a half years. It was confiscated in an illegal pregnancy and doused in utero. She rotated the fetus—the chassis—on the gurney.

"It's normal on every index," she explained. "We should be able to convert it with no complications." She pointed to this and that part of it and explained the order of rewriting. "The integumentary system—the skin, what you might call our fleshy package"—she smiled at me, acknowledging my professional reputation—"is a human's fastest growing organ. A person sheds and replaces it continuously throughout her life. In the conversion process, it's the first one completed. For a fetus, it takes about a week. Hair color, eye color, the liver, the heart, the digestive system, convert in two to three weeks. The nervous system, major muscle groups, reproductive organs—three to four weeks. Cartilage and bones—two to three months. Long before its first tooth erupts, the baby is biologically yours."

I asked Dr. Armbruster if I could hold the chassis.

"Certainly," she said. She placed her large hands carefully under it and handed it to me. It was hard, cold, and surprisingly heavy. "The fixative is very dense," she said, "and brittle, like eggshell." I cradled it awkwardly. Dr. Armbruster smiled and said to Eleanor, "New fathers always look like that, like they're afraid of breaking it. In this case, however, that's entirely possible. And you, my dear, look typically uncomfortable as well."

She was right. Eleanor and her chief of staff stood side by side, twins (but for their ages), arms stiffly crossed. Dr. Armbruster said, "Governor Starke, you might find the next few months immensely more enjoyable under hormonal therapy. Fathers, it would seem, have always had to learn to bond with their offspring. For you we have something the pharmaceutical companies call 'Mother's Medley.'"

"No, thank you, Doctor," Eleanor said and uncrossed her arms. "We haven't decided yet, remember? And besides, this one is damaged. It's missing a finger." One of the baby's tiny fingers was indeed missing, the stub end rough like plaster.

"Oh, don't be concerned about that," Dr. Armbruster said. "Fingers and toes grow back in days. Just don't break off the head!"

I flinched and held the chassis tighter, but then was afraid I was holding it too tight. I tried to give it to El, but she crossed her arms again, so I gave it back to Dr. Armbruster, who returned it to the gurney.

"Also," El said, "this one is already gendered."

I checked between the chassis's chubby legs and saw a tiny little penis. It—he—was a little guy. Maybe that was when things started to shift in my heart. I had never parented a child before, not with any of the numerous women Henry claimed I had known, even though I reached adulthood long before the Population Treaties had gone into effect. Only once, with Jean Scholero, did I get close, but I was too preoccupied with my career, and she miscarried, and we didn't last long enough to try again.

"Don't be concerned about that either," Dr. Armbruster said. "Your genes will overwrite its gender too. It's all part of the same process."

Eleanor touched my arm. "Are you all right, Sam?"

"Yeah," I said. "It's a little overwhelming."

El turned to Dr. Armbruster. "Well, we'd better be going, Doctor. Thank you for the tour."

"It was a pleasure to meet you, Governor Starke, and you, too, Myr Harger. On your way out, why don't you stop by the procedure room and let the nurse take a skin sample."

"That won't be necessary," El said.

"The decision is yours, of course, but it could save you an extra trip if you change your mind."

BACK AT THE Williams Towers in Bloomington, we lay on the balcony in the late-afternoon sun and skimmed the queue of messages. Our friends had grown tired of our good fortune: the congratulations were fewer and briefer and seemed, by and large, pro forma, even tinged with underlying jealousy. And who could blame them? The Population Treaties had been in effect for nearly sixty years, and sixty years was a long time for a society to live outside the company of children. Probably no one begrudged us our child, although it was obvious to everyone—especially to us—that we'd come by the permit unfairly.

El deleted the remaining queue of messages and said, "Talk to me, Sam." Our balcony was situated halfway up the giant residential tower that ended, in dizzying perspective, near the lower reaches of the city's canopy. The canopy, invisible during the day, appeared viscous in the evening light, like a transparent film rippling and folding upon itself. In contrast, our tower had a smooth matte surface encrusted with thousands of tiny black bumps. These were the building's resident homcom slugs, absorbing the last rays of the setting sun. They were topping off their energy stores for a busy night patrolling living rooms and bedrooms.

I asked her, "Have you ever had children before?"

"Yes, two, a boy and a girl, when I was barely out of college. Tom died as a child in an accident. Jessica grew up, moved away, married, led a successful career, and died at age fifty-four of cancer of the larynx." Eleanor turned over, bare rump to the sky, chin resting on sun-browned arms. "I grieved for each of them. It's hard to bury one's kids."

"Would you like to have another?"

She didn't answer for a while. I watched a slug creep along the underside of the balcony of the apartment above us. "I don't know," she said finally. "It's funny. I've already been through it all: pregnancy, varicose veins, funerals. I've been through menopause and—worse—back through remenses. I was so tangled up in motherhood, I never knew if I was coming or going. I loved or hated every moment of it, wouldn't have traded it for the world. But when it was all over, I felt an unbearable burden lifted from me. Thank God, I said, I won't have to go through *that* again. Yet since the moment we learned of the permit, I've been fantasizing about holding a baby in my lap. I don't know why, but I can't get it out of my mind: the feeding, the cooing, snuggling, rocking. My arms ache for a baby. I think it's this schoolgirl body of mine. It's a baby machine, and it intends to force its will on me. I've never felt so betrayed by my own body."

The slug bypassed our balcony, but another one was making its way slowly down the wall.

I said, "Why *not* have another one?"

She turned her head to peer at me. "Correct me if I'm wrong, Mr. Doomsayer, but aren't you the one who warned me not to take this posting? Aren't you the guy who said something about someone setting me up? I've had Cabinet scouring the nets for the past few weeks trying to piece together who's behind all this. But a baby? Do you have any idea how vulnerable a child makes you? You might as well tie a leash around your own neck."

She relaxed again and went on, "But for the sake of argument, let's just say that I have some powerful unknown benefactor promoting my career. And that this baby is a carrot to gain my loyalty. Well, here's a basic law of life, Sam—wherever there's a carrot, there's a stick just out of sight."

I thought about that as I watched the homcom slug. It had sensed us and was creeping across the balcony toward us.

"Well?" El said. "Any comments? It's your permit too."

"I know," I said. "It would be madness to go through with it. And yet—"

"And yet?"

"Could you imagine our baby, El? A little critter crawling around our ankles, half you and half me, a little Elsam or Sameanor?"

She closed her eyes and smiled. "That would be a pitiable creature."

"And speaking of ankles," I said, "we're about to be sampled."

The slug, a tiny strip of biotech, touched her ankle, attached itself to her for a moment, then dropped off. With the toes of her other foot, Eleanor scratched the testing site. Slugs only tickled her. With me it was different. There was some nerve tying my ankle directly to my dick, and I always found that warm, prickly kiss unavoidably arousing. So, as the slug attached itself to my ankle, El watched mischievously. At that moment, in the glow of the setting sun, in the delicious ache of perfect health, I didn't need the kiss of a slug to arouse me. I needed only a glance from my wife, with her ancient eyes set like opals in her girlish body. This must be how the Greek gods lived on Olympus. This must be the way it was meant to be, to grow ancient and yet to have the strength and appetites of youth. El gasped melodramatically as she watched my penis swell. She turned herself toward me, coyly covering her breasts and pubis with her hands. The slug dropped off me and headed for the balcony wall.

We lay side by side, not yet touching. I was stupid with desire and lost control of my tongue. I spoke without thinking. I said, "Mama."

The word, the single word, "mama," struck her like a physical thing. Her whole body shuddered, and her eyes went wide with surprise. I repeated it, "Mama," and she shut her eyes and turned away from me. I sidled over to her, wrapped my arms around her, and took possession of her ear. I tugged its lobe with my lips. I breathed into it. I pushed her sweat-damp hair clear of it and whispered, "I am the papa, and you are the mama." I watched the side of her face and repeated, "You are the mama."

"Oh, Sam," she sighed. "Crazy Samsamson."

"You are the mama, and Mama will give Papa a *son*."

Her eyes flew open at last, fierce, challenging, but amused.

"Or a daughter," I added quickly. "At this stage, Papa's not picky."

"And how will Papa arrange either, I wonder."

"Like this." I rolled her onto her back to kiss and stroke her. But she was indifferent to me, willfully so. Nevertheless, I let my tongue play up and down her body. I visited all the sweet spots I had discovered since first we made love, for I knew her girlish body to be my ally. Her body and I wanted the same thing. Soon, with or without El's blessing, her body welcomed me, and when she was ready, and I was ready, and all my sons and daughters inside me were ready, we went for it.

Somewhere in the middle of all this, a bird, a crow, came crashing to the deck beside us. What I could make out, through the thick anti-nano envelope that contained it, was a mess of shiny black feathers, a broken beak clattering against the deck, and a smudge of blood that quickly boiled away. The whole bird, in fact, was disassembling. Steam rose from the envelope, which emitted a piercing wail of warning. Henry spoke loudly into my ear, *Attention, Sam! In the interest of safety, the HomCom isolation device orders you to move away from it at once.*

We were too distracted to pay much mind. The envelope seemed to be doing its job. Nevertheless, we dutifully moved away; we rolled away belly to belly, like the bard's "beast with two backs." A partition formed to separate us from the unfortunate bird, and we resumed our investigation of the merits of parenthood.

Later, when I brought out dinner and two glasses of visola on a tray, El sat at the patio table in her white terry robe looking at the small pile of elemental dust on the deck—carbon, sodium, calcium, and whatnot—that had recently been a bird. It was not at all unusual for birds to fly out through the canopy, or for a tiny percentage of them to become infected outside. What *was* unusual was that upon reentering the canopy, being tasted, found bad, and enveloped by a swarm of anti-nano agents, so much of the bird should survive the fall in so recognizable a form, as this one had.

El frowned at me and said, "It's Governor Rickert, come back to haunt us."

We both laughed uneasily.

THE NEXT DAY I felt the urge to get some work done. It would be another two days before the orphanage would begin the recombination, and I was restless. Meanwhile, Eleanor had some sort of Tri-D meeting scheduled in the living room.

I had claimed an empty bedroom in the back of the apartment for my work area. It about matched my Chicago studio in size and aspect. I had asked the building super, a typically dour reginald, to send up an arbeitor to remove all the furniture except for an armchair and nightstand. The chair needed a pillow to support the small of my back, but otherwise it was adequate for long sitting sessions. I pulled it around to face a blank inner wall that Henry had told me was the north wall, placed the nightstand next to it, and brought in a carafe of strong coffee and some sweets from the kitchen. I made myself comfortable.

"Okay, Henry, take me to Chicago." The empty bedroom was instantly transformed into my studio, and I sat in front of my favorite window wall overlooking the Chicago skyline and lakefront from the 303rd floor of the Drexler Building. The sky was dark with storm clouds. Rain splattered against the window. There was nothing like a thunderstorm to stimulate my creativity.

"Henry, match Chicago's ionic dynamics here." I sipped my coffee and watched lightning strike neighboring towers as the air in my room took on a freshly scrubbed ozone quality. I felt relaxed and invigorated.

When I was ready, I turned the chair around to face my studio. It was just as I had left it months before in realbody. There was the large oak worktable that dominated the east corner. Glass-topped and long-legged, it was a table you could work at without stooping over. I used to stand at that table endlessly twenty and thirty years ago when I still lived in Chicago. Now it was piled high with prized junk: design trophies, hunks of polished gemstones from Mars and Jupiter, a scale model Japanese pagoda of cardboard and mica, a box full of my antique key collection, parcels wrapped in some of my most successful designs, and—the oldest objects in the room—a mason jar of paintbrushes, like a bouquet of dried flowers.

I rose from my chair and wandered about my little domain, taking pleasure in my life's souvenirs. The cabinets, shelves, counters, and floor were overflowing: an antelope-skin spirit drum; an antique pendulum mantel clock that houseputer servos kept wound; holocubes of some of my former lovers and wives; bits of colored glass, tumbleweed, and driftwood in whose patterns and edges I had once found inspiration; and a bull elephant foot made into a footstool. This room was more a museum now than a functioning studio, and I was more its curator than a practicing artist.

I went to the south wall and looked into the corner. Henry's original container sat atop three more identical ones. "How's the paste?" I said.

"Sufficient for the time being. I'll let you know when we need more."

"More? Isn't this enough? You have enough paste to run a major city."

"Eleanor Starke's Cabinet is more powerful than a major city."

"Yeah, well, let's get down to work." I returned to my armchair. The storm had passed the city and was retreating across the lake, turning the water midnight-blue. "What have you got on the egg idea?"

Henry projected a richly ornate egg in the air before me. Gold leaf and silver wire, inlaid with once-precious gems, it was modeled after the Fabergé masterpieces favored by the last of the Romanoff tsars. But instead of enclosing miniature portraits or clockwork engines, my eggs would merely be expensive wrapping for small gifts. The recipients would have to crack them open. But then they could keep the pieces, which would reassemble, or toss them into the bin for recycling credits.

"It's just as I told you last week," said Henry. "The public will hate it. I tested it against Simulated Us and E-Pluribus." Henry filled the space around the egg with dynamic charts and graphs. "Nowhere are positive ratings higher than seven percent, or negative ratings lower than sixty-eight percent. Typical comments call it 'old-fashioned,' and 'vulgar.' Matrix analyses find that people do not want to be reminded of their latent fertility. People resent—"

"Okay, okay," I said. "I get the picture." It was a dumb concept. I knew as much when I proposed it. But I was so enamored with my own latent fertility, I had lost my head. I thought people would be drawn to this archetypal symbol of renewal, but Henry had been right all along, and now he had the data to prove it.

If the truth be told, I had not come up with a hit design in five years, and I was terrified.

"It's just a dry spell," Henry said, sensing my mood. "You've had them before, even longer."

"I know, but this one is the worst."

"You say that every time."

To cheer me up, Henry began to play my wrapping paper portfolio, projecting my past masterpieces larger than life in the air.

I held patents for package applications in many fields, from archival wrap and instant skin, to military camouflage and video paint. But my own favorites, and probably the public's as well, were my novelty gift wraps. My first was a video wrapping paper that displayed the faces of loved ones (or celebrities if you had no loved ones) singing "Happy Birthday" to the music of the Boston Pops. That dated back to 2025 when I was a molecular engineering student and before we lost Boston to the Outrage.

My first professional design was the old box-in-a-box routine, only my boxes didn't get smaller as you opened them, but larger, and in fact could fill the whole room until you chanced upon one of the secret commands, which were any variation of "stop" (whoa, enough, cut it out, etc.) or "help" (save me, I'm suffocating, get this thing off me, etc.).

Next came wrapping paper that screamed when you tore or cut it. That led to paper that resembled human skin. It molded itself perfectly and seamlessly around the gift and had a shelf life of fourteen days (and a belly button!). It came in all races. You had to cut it to open the gift, and of course it bled. It was creepy, and we sold mountains of it.

The human skin led to my most enduring design, a perennial that was still popular, the orange peel. It, too, wrapped itself around any shape seamlessly (and had a navel). It was real, biological orange peel. When you cut or ripped it, it squirted citrus juice and smelled delightful.

I let Henry project these designs for me. I must say I became intoxicated with my own achievements. I gloried in them. They filled me with the most selfish wonder.

I was terribly good, and the whole world knew it.

Yet even after this healthy dose of self-love, I wasn't able to buckle down to anything new. I told Henry to order the kitchen to fix me some more coffee and something for lunch.

On my way to the kitchen I passed the living room and saw that Eleanor was having difficulties of her own. Even with souped-up holoservers, the living room was a mess. There were dozens of people in there and, as best as I could tell, just as many rooms superimposed over each other. People, especially self-important people, liked to bring their offices with them when they went to meetings. The result was a jumble of merging desks, lamps, and chairs. Walls sliced through each other at drunken angles. Windows issued cityscape views of New York, London, Washington, and Moscow (and others I didn't recognize) in various shades of day and weather. People, some of whom I recognized from the newsnets, either sat at their desks in a rough, overlapping circle or wandered through walls and furniture to kibitz with each other and with Eleanor's Cabinet.

At least this was how it all appeared to me standing in the hallway, outside the room's emitters. To those inside, it might look like the Senate chambers. I watched for a while, safely out of cam range, until Eleanor noticed me. "Henry," I said, "ask her how many of these people are here in realbody." Eleanor raised a finger, one, and pointed to herself.

I smiled. She was the only one there who could see me. I continued to the kitchen and brought my lunch back to my studio. I still couldn't get started, so I asked Henry to report on my correspondence. He had answered over five hundred posts since our last session the previous day. Four-fifths of these concerned the baby.

We were invited to appear—*with the baby*—on every major talk show and maga-zine. We were threatened with lawsuits by the Anti-Transubstantiation League. We were threatened with violence by several anonymous callers (who would surely be identified by El's security chief and prosecuted by her attorney general). A hundred seemingly harmless people requested permission to visit us in realbody or holo dur-ing nap time, bath time, any time. Twice that number accused us of fraud. Three men and one woman named Sam Harger claimed that their fertility permit was mis-takenly awarded to me. Dr. Armbruster's prediction was coming true, and the baby hadn't even been converted yet.

This killed an hour. I still didn't feel creative, so I called it quits. I took a shower, shaved. Then I went, naked, to stand outside the entrance to the living room. When Eleanor saw me she cracked a grin. She held up five fingers, five minutes, and turned back to her meeting.

I went to my bedroom to wait for her. She spent her lunch break with me. When we made love that day and the next, I enjoyed a little fantasy I never told her about. I imagined that she was pregnant in the old-fashioned way, with an enormous belly, melon-round and hard, and that as I moved inside her, as we moved together, we were teaching our child its first lesson in the art of human love.

ON THURSDAY, THE day of the conversion, we took a leisurely breakfast on the terrace of the New Foursquare Hotel in downtown Bloomington. A river of pedestri-ans, students and service people mostly, flowed past our little island of metal tables and brightly striped umbrellas. The day broke clear and blue and would be hot by noon. A frisky breeze tried to snatch away our menus. The Foursquare had the best kitchen in Bloomington, at least for desserts. Its pastry chef, Myr Duvou, had earned a reputation for re-creating the classics. That morning we (mostly me) were enjoy-ing strawberry shortcake with whipped cream and coffee. Everything—the strawber-ries, the wheat for the cakes, the sugar, coffee beans—had been grown, not assembled. The preparation was done lovingly and skillfully by human hand. All the wait staff were steves, who were highly sensitive to our wants and who, despite their ungainly height, bowed ever so low to take our order.

We called Dr. Armbruster. She appeared in miniature, desk and all, on top of my place mat.

"It's a go, then?" she said, reading our expressions.

"Yes," I said.

"Yes," Eleanor said and took my hand.

"Congratulations, both of you. You are two of the luckiest people in the world."

We already knew that.

"Traits? Enhancements?" asked Dr. Armbruster.

We had studied all the options and decided to allow Nature and chance, not some well-meaning gengineer, to roll our genes together into a new individual. "Random traits," we said, "and the standard half-dozen alphine enhancements."

"That leaves gender," said Dr. Armbruster.

I looked at Eleanor. "A boy," she said. "I think it wants to be a boy."

"A boy it is," said Dr. Armbruster. "I'll get the lab on it immediately. The recom-bination should take about three hours. I'll monitor the progress and keep you ap-prised. We will infect the chassis around noon. Make an appointment for a week from today to come in and take possession of—your son. We like to throw a little birthing party, and it's up to you to make media arrangements, if any.

"I'll call you in about an hour. And again, congratulations!"

We were too anxious to do anything else, so we ate shortcake and drank coffee and didn't talk much. We mostly sat close and said meaningless things to ease the tension. Finally Dr. Armbruster, seated at her tiny desk, called back.

"The recombination work is about two-thirds done and is proceeding very smoothly. Early readings show a Pernell Organic Intelligence quotient of 3.93—very impressive, but probably no surprise to you. So far, we know that your son has Sam's eyes, chin, and skeleto-muscular frame, and Eleanor's hair, nose, and—*eyebrows*."

"I'm afraid my eyebrows are fairly dominant," said Eleanor.

"Apparently," said Dr. Armbruster.

"I'm mad about your eyebrows," I said.

"And I'm mad about your frame."

We spent another hour there, taking two more updates from Dr. Armbruster. I ordered an iced bottle of champagne, and guests from other tables toasted us with coffee cups and visola glasses. I was slightly tipsy when we finally rose to leave. To my annoyance, I felt the prickly kiss of a homcom slug at my ankle. I decided I'd better let it finish tasting me before I attempted to thread my way through the jumble of tables and chairs. The slug seemed to take an inordinate amount of time.

Eleanor, meanwhile, was impatient to go. "What is it?" She laughed. "Are you drunk?"

"Just a slug," I said. "It's almost done." But it wasn't. Instead of dropping off, the slug elongated itself and looped around both of my ankles so that when I turned to join Eleanor, I tripped and capsized our table and cracked my head on the flagstone floor. The slug's slippery shroud oozed up my body and stretched across my face. It congealed and blurred my view of the tables and umbrellas and crowds of diners who were all fleeing like horror-show shades. I could hardly draw breath. Eleanor's face loomed over me for an instant, peering in at me, then vanished, though I cried and babbled for help. I tried to sit up, I tried to crawl, but I was tightly bound with my arms pinned to my sides.

Henry said, *Sam, I'm being probed.*

So was I. Anti-nano surged through my pores and spread beneath my skin. It entered my bloodstream and branched out to capture every cell in my body. It felt like hot smoke drifting through me and scorching me from the inside out.

My poor stomach, bulging with strawberry champagne mush, clenched and shot a pink geyser up my throat. But there was nowhere for it to go except down my chin and across my chest where it boiled away against my skin.

I thrashed about blindly, toppling more tables. I rolled in broken glass that cut me without piercing the shroud, so thin it stretched.

Fernando Boa, said someone in Henry's voice in Spanish. *You are hereby placed under arrest for unlawful flight from State of Oaxaca authorities. Surrender yourself. Any attempt to escape will result in your immediate execution.*

"Not Boa!" I gasped. "Harger! Samson Harger!"

Though I squeezed my eyes shut, the anti-nano tunneled right through them to sample the vitreous humor and rods and cones inside. Bolts of white light splashed across the backs of my eyelids, and a dull hurricane roar filled my head.

Henry shouted, *Should I resist? I think I should resist.*

"No!" I screamed.

The real agony began then, as all up and down my body, my nerve cells were inspected. Attached to every muscle fiber, every blood vessel, every hair follicle, embedded in my skin, my joints, my intestines, they all began to fire at once. My brain rattled in my skull. My guts twisted inside out. I begged for relief.

Then, just as suddenly, the convulsions ceased, the trillions of engines inside me abruptly quit. *I can do this,* Henry said. *I know how.*

"No, Henry!"

The isolation envelope itself flickered, then fell from me like so much dust. I was in daylight and fresh air again. Soiled, scalded, and bloated—but whole. I was alone on a battlefield of smashed umbrellas. I thought maybe I should crawl away from the dust, but the slug still shackled my ankles. "You shouldn't have done it, Henry," I croaked. "They won't like what you did."

Without warning, the neural storm slammed me again, worse than before. A new shroud issued from the slug. This one squeezed me, like a tube of paint, starting at my feet, crushing the bones and working up my legs.

"Please," I begged, "please let me pass out."

I DIDN'T PASS out, but I went somewhere else, to another room it seemed, where I could still hear the storm raging on the other side of a thin wall. There was someone else in the room, a man I halfway recognized. He was well muscled and of middle height, and his yellow hair was streaked with gray. He wore the warmest of smiles on his coarse, round face.

"Don't worry," he said, referring to the agony beyond the wall, "it will pass."

He had Henry's voice.

"You should have listened to me, Henry," I scolded. "Where did you learn to disobey me?"

"I know I don't count all that much," said the man. "I mean, I'm just a construct, not a living being. A servant, not a coequal. But I want to tell you how good it's been to know you."

I AWOKE LYING on my side on a gurney in a ceramic room, my cheek resting in a small puddle of clear fluid. Every cell of me ached. A man in a hommer uniform, a jerry, watched me sullenly. When I sat up, dizzy, nauseated, he held out a bundle of clean clothes. Not my clothes.

"Wha' happe' me?" My lips and tongue were twice their usual size.

"You had an unfortunate accident."

"Assiden'?"

The jerry pressed the clothes into my hands. "Just shut up and get dressed." He resumed his post next to the door and watched me fumble with the clothes. My feet were so swollen I could hardly pull the pant legs over them. My hands trembled and could not grip. My head swam, and I was totally exhausted. But all in all, I felt much better than I had a little while ago.

When, after what seemed like hours, I was dressed, the jerry said, "Captain wants to see ya."

I shambled down deserted ceramic corridors following him to a small office where sat a large, handsome young man in a neat blue uniform, a russ. "Sign here," he said, pushing a slate at me. "It's your terms of release."

Read this, Henry, I glotted with a bruised tongue. When Henry didn't answer I felt a thrill of panic until I remembered that the slave processors inside my body that connected me to Henry's box in Chicago had certainly been destroyed. So I tried to read the document by myself. It was loaded with legalese and interminable clauses, but I was able to glean that by signing it, I was forever releasing the Homeland Command from all liability for whatever treatment I had enjoyed at their hands.

"I will not sign this," I said.

"Suit yourself," the captain said and took the slate from my hands. "You are hereby released from custody, but you remain on probation until further notice. Ask the belt for details." He pointed to the belt holding up my borrowed trousers.

I lifted my shirt and looked at the belt. The device stitched to it was so small I had missed it, and its ports were disguised as grommets.

"Sergeant," the russ said to the jerry, "show Myr Harger the door."

"Just like that?" I said.

"What were you expecting, a prize?"

IT WAS DARK out. I asked the belt they'd given me what time it was, and it said in a lifeless, neuter voice, "The local time is nineteen forty-nine." I calculated I had been incarcerated—and unconscious—for about seven hours. On a hunch, I asked what day it was. "The date is Friday, 4 April 2092."

Friday. I had been out for a day and seven hours.

There was a Slipstream tube station right outside the cop shop, naturally, and I managed to find a private car. I climbed in and eased my aching self into the cushioned seat. I considered calling Eleanor, but not with that belt. So I told it to take me home. It replied, "Address, please."

My anger flared and I snapped, "The Williams Towers, stupid."

"City and state, please."

I was too tired for this. "Bloomington!"

"Bloomington in California, Idaho, Illinois, Indiana, Iowa, Kansas, Kentucky, Maryland, Minnesota, Missouri, Nebraska, New York—"

"Hold it! Wait! Enough! Where the fuck am I?"

"You're at the Western Regional Homeland Command Headquarters, Provo, Utah."

How I longed for my Henry. He'd get me home safe with no hassle. He'd take care of me. "Bloomington," I said mildly, "Indiana."

The doors locked, the running lights blinked on, and the car rolled to the injection ramp. We coasted down, past the local grid, to the intercontinental tubes. The belt said, "Your travel time to the Williams Towers in Bloomington, Indiana, will be one hour fifty-five minutes." When the car was injected into the Slipstream, I was shoved against the seat by the force of acceleration. Henry would have known how sore I was and shunted my car to the long ramp. Fortunately, I had a spare Henry belt in the apartment, so I wouldn't have to be without him for long. And after a few weeks, when I felt better, I'd again reinstall him inbody.

I tried to nap but was too sick. My head kept swimming, and I had to keep my eyes open.

It was after 10:00 P.M. when I arrived under the Williams Towers, but the station was crowded with residents and guests. I felt everyone's eyes on me. Surely everyone knew of my arrest. They would have watched it on the nets, witnessed my naked fear as the shroud raced up my chest.

I walked briskly, looking straight ahead, to the row of elevators. I managed to claim one for myself, and as the doors closed I felt relief. But something was wrong; we weren't moving.

"Floor, please," said my new belt in its bland voice.

"Fuck you!" I screamed. "Fuck you fuck you fuck you! Listen to me, I want you to call Henry, that's my system in Chicago. Put him in charge of all of your miserable functions. Do you hear me?"

"Certainly, myr. What is the Henry access code?"

"Code? Code? I don't know code." Keeping track of passwords, anniversaries, birthdays, and all that sort of detail had been Henry's responsibility for over eighty years. "Just take me up! Stop at every floor above two hundred!" Before we started moving, I shouted, "Wait! Hold it! Open the doors!" I had the sudden, urgent need to urinate. I didn't think I could hold it long enough to reach the apartment, especially in a high-speed lift.

There were people waiting outside the elevator doors. I was sure they had heard me shouting. I pushed through them, a sick smile plastered to my face, the sweat rolling down my forehead, as I hurried to the men's room off the lobby.

I had to go so bad, that when I stood before the urinal and tried, I couldn't. I felt about to burst, but I was plugged up. I had to consciously calm myself, breathe deeply, relax. The stream, when it finally emerged, seemed to issue forever. How many liters could a bladder hold? The urine was viscous and cloudy with a dull metallic sheen, as though mixed with aluminum dust. Whatever the HomCom had pumped into me would take days to expel. At least there was no sign of bleeding, thank God. But it burned. And when I was finished and washed my hands, I had to go again.

Up on my floor, my belt valet couldn't open the door to the apartment, so I had to ask admittance. The door didn't recognize me, but Eleanor's Cabinet gave it permission to open. The apartment smelled of strong disinfectant. I staggered through the rooms shouting, "Eleanor! Eleanor!" It suddenly occurred to me that she might be gone.

"In here," called Eleanor. I followed her voice to the living room, but Eleanor wasn't there. It was her sterile elder twin, her chief of staff, who sat on the couch. She was flanked by the attorney general, dressed in black, and the security chief, grinning his toothy grin.

"What the hell is this," I said, "a fucking cabinet meeting? Where's Eleanor?"

In a businesslike manner, the chief of staff motioned to the armchair opposite the couch. "Won't you join us, Sam. We have much to discuss."

"Discuss it among yourselves," I yelled. "Where's Eleanor?" Now I was sure that she had flown. She had bolted from the café and kept on going; she had left her three stooges behind to break the bad news to me.

"Eleanor's in her bedroom, but she—"

I didn't wait. I jogged down the hallway. But the bedroom door was locked. "Door," I commanded, "unlock yourself."

"Access," the door replied in a monotone, "has been extended to apartment residents only."

"That includes me, you idiot." I pounded the door with my fists. "Eleanor, let me in. It's me—Sam."

No reply.

I returned to the living room. "What the fuck is going on here?"

"Sam," said the elderly chief of staff, "Eleanor will see you in a few minutes, but not before—"

"Eleanor!" I yelled, turning around to look at each of the room's cams. "I know you're watching. Come out; we need to talk. I want you, not these dummies."

"Sam," said Eleanor behind me. But it wasn't Eleanor. Again I was fooled by her chief of staff who had crossed her arms like an angry El and bunched her eyebrows into a knot. She mimicked my Eleanor so perfectly that I had to wonder if El wasn't projecting herself through it. "Sam, please get a grip and sit down," she said in a conciliatory tone of voice. "We need to discuss your accident."

But I wasn't ready for any reconciliation yet. "My what? My accident? Is that what we're calling it? I can assure you it was no accident! It was an assault, a rape, a vicious attack. Not an *accident!*"

"Excuse me," said Eleanor's attorney general, "but we were using the word 'accident' in a strictly legal sense. Both sides have provisionally agreed—"

I left the room abruptly. I needed to pee again. Mercifully, the bathroom let me in. I knew I was behaving badly, but I couldn't help it. On the one hand I was grateful that Eleanor was still there, that she hadn't left me. On the other hand, I was hurt and confused and angry. All I wanted was to hold her, be held by her. I needed her at that moment more than I had ever needed anyone in my adult life. I had no time for holos. But it was reasonable that she should be frightened. Maybe she thought I was contaminated. My behavior was doing nothing to reassure her. I had to control myself.

My urine burned even more than before. My mouth was cotton dry. I grabbed a glass and filled it with tap water. Surprised at how thirsty I was, I drank glassful after glassful. I washed my face in the sink. The cool water felt so good that I stripped off my HomCom-issue clothes and stepped into the shower. The water revived me, fortified me. Not wanting to put the clothes back on, I wrapped a towel around myself and went to my bedroom, but the room was entirely empty. No furniture or carpets—even the paint was stripped from the walls. I went back to the living room and told the holos to ask Eleanor to get some clothes for me. I promised I wouldn't try to force my way into the bedroom when she opened the door.

"All of your clothes were confiscated by the HomCom," said the chief of staff, "but Fred will bring you something of his."

Before I could ask who Fred was, a big man, a russ, came out of the back bedroom, the room I used for my trips to Chicago. He was dressed in a brown and teal jumpsuit and carried a brown bathrobe over his arm. Except for the uniform, he looked exactly like his clone brother officer back at the Utah facility.

"This is Fred," said the chief of staff. "Fred has been assigned to—"

"What?" I shouted. "El's afraid I'm going to throttle her holos? She thinks I would break down her door?"

"Eleanor thinks nothing of the kind," said the chief of staff. "Fred has been assigned by the Tri-Discipline Council."

"Well, I don't want him here. Send him away. Go away, Fred."

The russ remained impassive, silently holding the robe out to me.

"I'm afraid," said the chief of staff, "that as long as Eleanor remains a governor, Fred stays. Neither she nor you have any say in the matter."

I charged past the russ to the bathroom saying, "Just stay out of my way, Fred." In the linen closet I found one of Eleanor's terry robes. It was tight on me, but it would do.

Returning to the living room, I sat in the armchair facing Cabinet's couch. "All right. What do you want?"

"That's more like it," said the chief of staff. She leaned back in the couch and relaxed as Eleanor would. "First, let's get you caught up on what's happened so far."

"By all means. Catch me up on what's happened so far."

The chief of staff gave the floor to the attorney general who said, "Yesterday morning, Thursday, 3 April, at precisely 10:47:39 EST, while loitering at the New Foursquare Café in downtown Bloomington, Indiana, you, Samson P. Harger, were routinely analyzed by a Homeland Command Random Testing Device, Metro Population Model 8903AL. You were found to be in noncompliance with the Homeland Acts of 2014, 2064, and 2087. As per procedures set forth in—"

"Please," I said, "in humanese."

The security chief took over and said in his gravelly voice, "You were tasted by a slug, Myr Harger, and found to be bad. So they bagged you."

"Why? What was wrong with me?"

"Name it. You went off the scale. First, the DNA sequence in a sample of ten of your skin cells didn't match each other. Also, a known NASTIE was identified in your bloodstream. Your marker genes didn't match your record in the National Registry. You *did* match the record of a known terrorist with an outstanding arrest warrant. You also matched the record of someone who died twenty-three years ago."

"That's ridiculous," I said. "How could the slug read all those things at once?"

"That's what the HomCom wanted to know. So they disassembled you."

"They! What?"

"Any one of those conditions gave them the authority they needed. They didn't have the patience to read you slow and gentlelike, so they pumped you so full of smart agents you could have filled a swimming pool."

"They—completely?"

"All your biological functions were interrupted. You were legally dead for three minutes."

It took me a moment to grasp what he was saying. "So what did they discover?"

"Nothing," said the security chief, "zip, nada. Your cell survey came up normal. They couldn't even get the arresting slug, or any other slug, to duplicate the initial readings."

"So the arresting slug was defective?"

The attorney general said, "We forced them to concede that the arresting slug *might* have been defective."

"So they reassembled me and let me go, and everything is good?"

"Not quite," continued the security chief. "That particular model slug has never been implicated in a false reading. This would be the first time, according to the HomCom, and naturally they're not too eager to admit that. Besides, they still had you on another serious charge."

"Which is?"

The attorney general said, "That your initial reading constituted an unexplained anomaly."

"An unexplained anomaly? This is a crime?"

I excused myself for another visit to the bathroom. The urgency increased when I stood up from the armchair and was painful by the time I reached the toilet. This time the stream didn't burn me, but hissed and gave off some sort of vapor, like steam. I watched in horror.

When I finished, I marched back to the living room, stood in front of the three holos, and screamed at them, "*What have they done to me?*"

"You've been seared, Myr Harger," said the chief of staff.

"Seared? What is seared?"

"It's a fail-safe procedure. Tiny wardens have been installed into each of your body's cells. Any attempt to hijack your cellular function or alter your genetic makeup will cause that cell to self-immolate. Roll up your sleeve and scratch your arm."

I did as she said. I raked my skin with my fingernails. Flakes of skin cascaded to the floor, popping and flashing like a miniature fireworks display.

The chief of staff continued. "Likewise, any cell that expires through natural causes and becomes separated from your body self-immolates. When you die, your body will cook at a low heat."

I was stunned.

"Unfortunately, there's more," she said. "Please sit down."

I sat down, still holding my arm out. Beads of sweat dropped from my chin and boiled away on the robe in little puffs of steam.

"Eleanor feels it best to tell you everything now," said the chief of staff. "It's not pretty, so sit back and prepare yourself for more bad news."

I did as she suggested.

"They weren't about to let you go, you know. You had forfeited all of your civil rights. If you weren't the spouse of a Tri-Discipline Governor, you'd have simply disappeared. As it was, they proceeded to eradicate all traces of your DNA from the environment. They confiscated all records of your genome from the National Registry, clinics, rejuvenation spas, etc. They flooded this apartment, removed every microscopic bit of hair, phlegm, mucus, skin, fingernail, toenail, blood, smegma—you name it—every breath you took since you moved in. They sent probes down the plumbing for trapped hair. They even invaded Eleanor's body to retrieve your semen. They scoured the halls, elevators, lobby, dining room, linen stores, laundry. They were most thorough. They have likewise visited the National Orphanage, your townhouse in Connecticut, the bungalow in Cozumel, the juve clinic, your hotel room on the Moon, the shuttle, and all your and Eleanor's domiciles all over the USNA. They are systematically following your trail backward for a period of thirty years."

"My Chicago studio?"

"Of course."

"Henry?"

"Gone."

"You mean in isolation, right? They're interrogating him, right?"

The security chief said, "No, eradicated. He resisted. Gave 'em quite a fight too. But no civilian job can withstand the weight of the Command. Not even us."

I didn't believe Henry was gone. He had so many secret backups. At this moment he was probably lying low in a half-dozen parking loops all over the solar system.

But another thought occurred to me. "Our son!"

The chief of staff said, "When your accident occurred, the chassis had not yet been infected with your and Eleanor's recombinant. Had it been, the HomCom would have disassembled it too. Eleanor prevented the procedure at the last moment and turned over all genetic records and material."

I tried sifting through this. My son was dead, or rather never started. But at least Eleanor had saved the chassis. We could always try—or could we? *I was seared!* My cells were locked, and the HomCom had confiscated all records of my genome.

The attorney general said, "The chassis, however, had already been brought out of stasis and was considered viable. To allow it to develop with its original genetic complement, or to place it back into stasis, would have exposed it to legal claims by its progenitors—its original parents. So Eleanor had it infected. It's undergoing conversion at this time."

"Infected? Infected with what? Did she clone herself?"

The chief of staff shook her head. "Heavens, no. She had it infected with the recombination of her genes and those of a simulated partner—a composite of several of her past partners."

"Without my agreement?"

"You were deceased at the time. She was your surviving spouse."

"I was deceased for only three minutes! I was retrievably dead. Obviously, retrievable!"

"Alive you would have been a terrorist, and the fertility permit would have been annulled."

I closed my eyes and leaned back into the chair. "Right," I said, "what else?" When no one answered, I said, "To sum up, then, I have been seared, which means my cells are booby-trapped. Which means I'm incapable of reproducing? or even of being rejuvenated?" They said nothing. "So my life expectancy has been reduced to—what?—another forty years or so? Right. My son is dead. Pulled apart before he was even started. Henry is gone, probably forever. My wife—no, my widow—is having a child by another man—men."

"Men and women actually," said the chief of staff.

"Whatever. Not by me. How long did all of this take?"

"About twenty minutes."

"A hell of a busy twenty minutes."

"To our way of thinking," said the attorney general, "a protracted interval of time. The important negotiation in your case occurred within the first five seconds of your demise."

"You're telling me that Eleanor was able to figure everything out and cook up her simulated partner in five seconds?"

"Eleanor has in readiness at all times a full set of contingency plans to cover every conceivable threat we can imagine. It pays, Myr Harger, to plan for the worst."

I was speechless. The idea that all during our time together, El was busy making these plans was too monstrous to believe.

"Let me impress upon you," said the chief of staff, "the fact that Eleanor stood by you. I doubt that many people would take such risks to fight for a spouse. Also, only someone in her position could have successfully prosecuted your case. The HomCom doesn't have to answer phone calls, you know.

"As to the details of your release, the attorney general can fill you in later, but here's the agreement in a nutshell. Given the wild diagnosis of the arresting slug and the subsequent lack of substantiating evidence, we calculated the most probable cause to be a defect in the slug, not some as yet unheard of NASTIE in your body. Further, as a perfect system of any sort has never been demonstrated, we predicted there to be records of other failures buried deep in HomCom archives. Eleanor threatened to air these files publicly in a civil suit. To do so would have cost her a lifetime of political capital, her career, and possibly her life. But as she was able to convince the HomCom she was willing to proceed, they backed down. They agreed to revive you and place you on probation, the terms of which are stored in your belt system, which we see you have not yet reviewed. The major term is your searing. Searing effectively neutralizes any threat in case you were indeed the victim of a new NASTIE. Let me emphasize that even this was a concession on their part. As far as public records show, you are the first seared individual allowed to leave the Utah quarantine center.

"Also, as a sign of good faith, we disclosed the locations of all of Henry's hidey-holes."

"What?" I rose from my seat. "*You* gave them Henry?"

"Sit down, Myr Harger," said the security chief.

But I didn't sit down. I began to pace. So this is how it works, I thought. This is the world I live in.

"Please realize, Sam," said the chief of staff, "that they would have found him out anyway. No matter how clever you think you are, given time, all veils can be pierced."

I turned around to answer her, but she and her two colleagues were gone. I was alone in the room with the russ, Fred, who stood sheepishly next to the hall corridor. He cleared his throat and said, "Governor Starke will see you now."

It's been eight long months since my surprise visit to the cop shop. I've had plenty of time to sit and reflect on what's happened to me, to meditate on my victimhood.

Shortly after my accident, Eleanor and I moved into our new home, a sprawling old farmstead on the outskirts of Bloomington. We have more than enough room here, with barns and stables, a large garden, pear orchard, tennis courts, swimming pool, and a dozen iterants, including Fred, to run everything. It's really very beautiful, and the whole eighty acres is covered with its own canopy, inside and independent of the Bloomington canopy, a bubble within a bubble. Just the place to raise the child of a Tri-Discipline Governor.

The main house, built of blocks of local limestone, dates back to the last century. It's the home that Eleanor and I dreamed of owning. But now that we're here, I spend most of my time in the basement, for sunlight is hard on my seared skin. For that matter, rich food is hard on my gut, I bruise easily inside and out, I can't sleep a whole night through, all my joints ache for an hour or so when I rise, I have lost my sense of smell, and I've become a little hard of hearing. There is a constant taste of brass in my mouth and a dull throbbing in my skull. I go to bed nauseated and wake up nauseated. The doctor says my condition will improve in time as my body adjusts, but that my health is up to me now. No longer do I have resident molecular homeostats to constantly screen, flush, and scrub my cells, nor muscle toners or fat inhibitors. No longer can I go periodically to a juve clinic to correct the cellular errors of aging. Now I can and certainly will grow stouter, slower, weaker, balder—and older. Now the date of my death is decades, not millennia, away. This should come as no great shock, for this was the human condition when I was born. Yet, since my birth, the whole human race, it seems, has boarded a giant ocean liner and set course for the shores of immortality. I, however, have been unceremoniously tossed overboard.

So I spend my days sitting in the dim dampness of my basement corner, growing pasty white and fat (twenty pounds already), and plucking my eyebrows to watch them sizzle like fuses.

I am not pouting, and I am certainly not indulging in self-pity, as Eleanor accuses me. In fact, I am brooding. It's what artists do, we brood. To other, more active people, we appear selfish, obsessive, even narcissistic, which is why we prefer to brood in private.

But I'm not brooding about art or package design. I have quit that for good. I will never design again. That much I know. I'm not sure what I *will* do, but at least I know I've finished that part of my life. It was good; I enjoyed it. I climbed to the top of my field. But it's over.

I'm brooding about my victimhood. My intuition tells me that if I understand it, I will know what to do with myself. So I pluck another eyebrow. The tiny bulb of flesh at the root ignites like an old-fashioned match, a tiny point of light in my dark cave, and as though making a wish, I whisper, "Henry." The hair sizzles along its length until it burns my fingers, and I have to drop it. My fingertips are already charred from this game.

I miss Henry terribly. It's as though a whole chunk of my mind were missing. I never knew how deeply integrated I had woven him into my psyche, or where my thoughts stopped and his began. When I ask myself a question these days, no one answers.

I wonder why he did it, what made him think he could resist the Homeland

Command. Can machine intelligence become cocky? Or did he knowingly sacrifice himself for me? Did he think he could help me escape? Or did he protect our privacy in the only way open to him, by destroying himself? The living archive of my life is gone, but at least it's not in the loving hands of the HomCom.

My little death has caused other headaches. My marriage ended. My estate went into receivership. My memberships, accounts, and privileges in hundreds of services and organizations were closed. News of my death spread around the globe at the speed of fiber, causing tens of thousands of data banks to toggle my status to "deceased," a position not designed to toggle back. Autobituaries, complete with footage of my mulching at the Foursquare Café, appeared on all the nets the same day. Databases list both my dates of birth and death. (Interestingly, none of my obits or bios mention the fact that I was seared.) Whenever I use my voice or retinal prints, I set off alarms. El's attorney general has managed to reinstate most of my major accounts, but my demise is too firmly entrenched in the world's web to ever be fully corrected. The attorney general has, in fact, offered me a routine for my new valet system to pursue these corrections on a continuous basis. She, as well as the rest of El's Cabinet, has volunteered to educate my belt for me as soon as I install a personality bud in it. It will need a bud if I ever intend to leave the security of my crypt. But I'm not ready for a new belt buddy.

I PLUCK ANOTHER eyebrow, and by its tiny light I say, "Ellen."

We are living in an armed fortress. Eleanor says we can survive any form of attack here: nano, bio, chemical, conventional, or nuclear. She feels completely at ease here. This is where she comes to rest at the end of a long day, to glory in her patch of Earth, to adore her baby, Ellen. Even without the help of Mother's Medley, Eleanor's maternal instincts have all kicked in. She is mad with motherhood. Ellen is ever in her thoughts. If she could, El would spend all of her time in the nursery in realbody, but the duties of a junior Tri-D Governor call her away. So she has programmed a realtime holo of Ellen to be visible continuously in the periphery of her vision, a private scene only she can see. No longer do the endless meetings and unavoidable luncheons capture her full attention. No longer is time spent in a tube car flitting from one city to another a total waste. Now she secretly watches the jennys feed the baby, bathe the baby, perambulate the baby around the fish pond. And she is always interfering with the jennys, correcting them, undercutting whatever place they may have won in the baby's affection. There are four jennys. Without the name badges on their identical uniforms, I wouldn't be able to tell them apart. They have overlapping twelve-hour shifts, and they hand the baby off like a baton in a relay race.

I seem to have my own retinue, a contingent of four russes: Fred Londenstane, the one who showed up on the day of my little death, and three more. I am not a prisoner here, and their mission is to protect the compound, Governor Starke, and her infant daughter, not to watch over me, but I have noticed that there is always one within striking distance, especially when I go anywhere near the nursery. Which I don't do very often. Ellen is a beautiful baby, but I have no desire to spend time with her, and the whole house seems to breathe easier when I stay down in my tomb.

Yesterday evening a jenny came down to announce dinner. I threw on some clothes and joined El in the solarium off the kitchen where lately she prefers to take her meals. Outside the window wall, heavy snowflakes fell silently in the blue-gray dusk. El was watching Ellen explore a new toy on the carpet. When El turned to me, her face was radiant, but I had no radiance to return. Nevertheless, she took my hand and drew me to sit next to her.

"Here's Daddy," she cooed, and Ellen warbled a happy greeting. I knew what was expected of me. I was supposed to adore the baby, gaze upon her plenitude, and thus be filled with grace. I tried. I tried because I truly want everything to work out, because I love Eleanor and wish to be her partner in parenthood. So I watched Ellen and meditated on the marvel and mystery of life. El and I are no longer at the tail end of the long chain of humanity—I told myself—flapping in the cold winds of evolution. Now we are grounded. We have forged a new link. We are no longer grasped only by the past, but we grasp the future. We have created the future in flesh.

When El turned again to me, I was ready, or thought I was. But she saw right through me to my stubborn core of indifference. Nevertheless, she encouraged me, prompted me with, "Isn't she beautiful?"

"Oh, yes," I replied.

"And smart."

"The smartest."

Later that evening, when the brilliant monstrance of her new religion was safely tucked away in the nursery under the sleepless eyes of the night jennys, Eleanor rebuked me. "Are you so selfish that you can't accept Ellen as your daughter? Does it have to be your seed or nothing? I know what happened to you was shitty and unfair, and I'm sorry. I really am. I wish to hell they got me instead of you. Maybe the next one will be more accurate. Will that make you happy?"

We both knew she was mistaken. The assault was never aimed at her. If Ellen was the carrot, then I was the stick. The conditions of her coronation could not be clearer—step out of line and risk everything. My pathetic presence would only serve as a constant reminder of this fact.

"No, El, don't talk like that," I said. "I can't help it. Give me time."

That night Eleanor invited herself to my bed. We used to have an exceptional sex life. Sex for us was a form of play, competition, and truth-telling. It used to be fun. Now it's a job. The shaft of my penis is bruised by the normal bend and torque of even moderate lovemaking. My urethra is raw from jets of scalding semen when I come. Of course I use special condoms and lubricants, without which I would blister both El's and my own private parts. Still, it's just not comfortable for either of us. El tries to downplay it by saying things like, "You're hot, baby," but she fools no one.

We made love that night, but I pulled out before I came. El tried to draw me back, but I refused. She took my sheathed penis in her hands, but I told her not to bother. I told her it just wasn't worth the misery anymore.

In the middle of the night, when I rose to return to my dungeon, Eleanor stirred from sleep and hissed, "Hate me if you must, Sam, but please don't blame the baby."

I ASK MY new belt how many eyebrow hairs an average person of my race, sex, and age has. The belt can access numerous encyclopedias to do simple research like this. "Five hundred fifty in each eyebrow," it replies in its neuter voice. That's a sum of eleven hundred, plenty of fuel to light my investigation. I pluck another and say, "Blame."

For someone must be blamed. Someone must be held accountable. Someone must pay. But who?

Eleanor blames her "Unknown Benefactor," the person or persons behind her sudden ascendancy. She's launched a private project with Cabinet they call Target UKB. Basically, the project is a mosaic analysis to identify the telltale signature of this mysterious entity. It emulates the massive data-sifting techniques long practiced by the HomCom, but her subjects are the ruling elite, not terrorists or protesters. She's spent a fortune on liters of new neuro-chemical paste to boost Cabinet's already gargantuan mentality. (Henry would never have stood a chance against Cabinet now.)

From the small amount of information that Eleanor has shared with me, I gather that Target UKB works by recording and parsing the moment-by-moment activities of the five thousand most prominent people on the planet. Being familiar with the degree of security we endure around here at the manse, and assuming that other affluent godlings maintain comparable privacy, such surveillance can't be easy. Nevertheless, El assures me that when her model is in place, she'll be able to trace the chain in intention of any event back to its source. She says she should have done something like this years ago. In my opinion, it's paranoia writ large.

Eleanor blames her UKB. But who do I blame?

That's a good question, one for which I don't yet have an answer. If there is a UKB pulling El's strings, at least it gave us fair warning. We walked into this high stakes game of empire with our eyes open. In the end, in the hallowed tradition of victims everywhere, I suppose I blame myself.

I PLUCK ONE more eyebrow, and as it sizzles, I say, "Fred."

For this russ, Fred Londenstane, is a complete surprise to me. I had never formed a relationship with a clone before. They are service people, after all. They are interchangeable. They wait on us in stores and restaurants. They clip our hair. They perform the menialities we cannot, or prefer not to assign to machines. How can you tell one joan or jerome from another anyway? And what could you possibly talk about? Nice watering can you have there, kelly. What's the weather like up there, steve?

But Fred the russ is different. From the start he's brought me fruit and cakes reputed to fortify tender digestive tracts, sunglasses, soothing skin creams, and a hat with a duckbill visor. He seems genuinely interested in me, even comes down to chat after his shift. I don't know why he's so attentive. Perhaps he never recovered from the shock of first meeting me, freshly seared and suffering. Perhaps he recognizes that I'm the one around here most in need of his protection.

When I was ready to try having sex with Eleanor again and I needed some of those special insulated condoms, my new valet couldn't locate them on any of the shoppers, not even on the medical supply ones, so I asked Fred. He said he knew of a place and would bring me some. He returned the next day with a whole shopping bag full of special pharmaceuticals for the cellular challenged: vitamin supplements, suppositories, plaque-fighting tooth soap, and knee and elbow braces. He brought twenty dozen packages of condoms, and he winked as he set them on the table. He brought more stuff that he discreetly left in the bag.

I reached into the bag. There were bottles of cologne and perfume, sticks of waxy deodorant, air fresheners and odor eaters. "Do I stink?" I said.

"Like a roomful of cat's piss, myr. No offense."

I lifted my hand to my nose, but I couldn't smell anything. If I stank so bad, how could Eleanor have lived with me all those months, eaten with me, slept with me, and never mentioned it once?

There was more in the bag: mouthwash and chewing gum. "My breath stinks too?"

In reply, Fred crossed his eyes and inflated his cheeks.

I thanked him for shopping for me, and especially for his frankness.

"Don't mention it, myr," he said. "I'm just glad to see you getting better."

I wondered if all russes were so compassionate. The other three assigned to the household didn't seem so. Competent, dutiful, fearless—yes, but compassionate? I didn't feel comfortable asking Fred about the qualities of his type, so I kept quiet and accepted his kindness with all the aplomb of a drowning man.

1.3

Two days ago was Ellen's first birthday. Unfortunately, Eleanor had to be away in Europe. Still, she arranged a little holo birthday party with her friends. Thirty-some people sat around, totally mesmerized by the baby, who had recently begun to walk. Only four of us, baby Ellen, a jenny, a russ, and I, were there in realbody. When I arrived and sat down, Ellen made a beeline for my lap. People chuckled and said, "Daddy's girl."

I had the tundra dream again last night. I walked through the canopy lock right out into the white, frozen, endless tundra. The feeling was one of escape.

My doctor gave me a complete physical last week. She said I had reached equilibrium with my condition. This was as good as it would get. Lately, I have been exercising. I have lost a little weight and feel somewhat stronger. But my joints ache sometimes, and my doctor says they'll only get worse. She prescribed an old-time remedy—aspirin.

Fred left us two months ago. He and his wife succeeded in obtaining berths on a new station orbiting Mars. Their contracts are for five years with renewal options. Since arriving there, he's visited me in holo a couple of times, says their best jump pilot is a stinker. That's what people are calling the seared—stinkers. I may have been the first one the HomCom released from quarantine, but now a steady stream of stinkers are being surrendered to an unsuspecting public.

Last week I finally purchased a personality bud for my valet system. It's having a rough time with me because I refuse to interact with it. I haven't even given it a name yet. I can't think of any suitable one. I call it "Hey, you," or "Yo, belt." Eleanor's chief of staff has repeated her offer to educate it for me, but I declined. In fact, I told her that if any of them breach its shell even once, I will abort it and start over with a new one.

Today after dinner, we had a family crisis. The jenny on duty suffered a nosebleed while her backup was off running an errand. I was in the kitchen when I heard Ellen crying. In the nursery I found a hapless russ—Fred's replacement—holding the kicking and screaming baby. The jenny called from the open bathroom door, "I'm coming. One minute, Ellie, I'm coming." When Ellen saw me she reached for me with her fat little arms and howled.

"Give her to me," I ordered the russ. His face reflected his hesitation. "It's all right," I said.

"One moment, myr," he said and asked silently for orders. "Okay, here," he said after a moment. He gave me Ellen who wrapped her arms around my neck. "I'll just go and help Marilee," he said, crossing to the bathroom. I sat down and put Ellen on my lap. She looked around, caught her breath, and resumed crying; only this time it was an easy, mournful wail.

"What is it?" I asked her. "What does Ellen want?" I reviewed what little I knew about babies. I felt her forehead, though I knew babies don't catch sick anymore. And with evercleans, they don't require constant changing. The remains of dinner lay on the tray, so she'd just eaten. A bellyache? Sleepy? Teething pains? Early on, Ellen was frequently feverish and irritable as her converted body sloughed off the remnants of the little boy chassis she'd overwritten. I thought about the son we almost had, and I wondered why during my year of brooding I never grieved for him. Was it because he never had a soul? Because he had never got beyond the purely data stage of recombination? Because he never owned a body? And what about Ellen? Did she have her own soul, or did the original boy's soul stay through the conversion? And if it did, would it hate us for what we've done to its body? I was in no sense a religious man, but these questions troubled me.

Ellen cried, and the russ stuck his head out of the bathroom every few moments to check on us. This angered me. What did they think I was going to do? Drop her? Strangle her? I knew they were watching me, all of them: the chief of staff, the security chief. They might even have awakened Eleanor in Hamburg or Paris where it was almost midnight. No doubt they had a contingency plan for anything I might do.

"Don't worry, Ellie," I crooned, swallowing my anger. "Mama will be here in just a minute."

"Yes, I'm coming, I'm coming," said Eleanor's sleep-hoarse voice.

Ellen startled and looked about, and when she didn't see her mother, bawled more insistently. The jenny, holding a blood-soaked towel to her nose, peeked out of the bathroom.

I bounced Ellen on my knee. "Mama's coming, Mama's coming, but in the meantime, Sam's going to show you a trick. Wanna see a trick? Watch this." I pulled a strand of hair from my head. The bulb popped as it ignited, and the strand sizzled along its length. Ellen quieted in mid-fuss, and her eyes went wide. The russ burst out of the bathroom and sprinted toward us, but stopped and stared when he saw what I was doing. His nose wrinkled in revulsion. "Get out of here," I said to him, "and take the jenny." It was all I could do not to shout.

"Sorry, myr, but my orders—" The russ paused, then cleared his throat. "Yes, myr, right away." He escorted the jenny, her head tilted back, from the nursery.

"Thank you," I said to Eleanor.

"I'm here." We turned and found Eleanor seated next to us in an ornately carved, wooden chair. Ellen squealed with delight, but did not reach for her mother. Already by six months she had been able to distinguish between a holobody and a real one. Eleanor's eyes were heavy, and her hair mussed. She wore a long silk robe, one I'd never seen before, and her feet were bare. A sliver of jealousy pricked me when I realized she had probably been in bed with a lover. But what of it?

In a sweet voice, filled with the promise of soft hugs, Eleanor told us a story about a kooky caterpillar she'd seen that very day in a park in Paris. She used her hands on her lap to show us how it walked. Baby Ellen leaned back into my lap as she watched, and I found myself gently rocking her. There was a squirrel with a bushy gray tail involved in the story, and a lot of grown-up feet wearing very fashionable shoes, but I lost the gist of the story, so caught up was I in the voice that was telling it. El's words spoke of an acorn that lost its cap and ladybugs coming to tea, but what her voice said was, I made you from the finest stuff. You are perfect. I will never let anyone hurt you. I love you always.

The voice shifted incrementally, took an edge, and caused me the greatest sense of loss. El said, "And what about my big baby?"

"I'm fine," I said. "What about you?"

El told me about her day. Her voice spoke of schedules and meetings, a leader who lost his head, and diplomats coming to tea, but what it said was, You're a grown man who is capable of coping. Nothing is perfect, but we try. I will never hurt you. I love you always. Please come back to me.

I opened my eyes. Ellen was a warm lump asleep on my lap, fist against cheek, lips slightly parted. I brushed her hair from her forehead with my sausagelike fingers and traced the round curve of her cheek and chin. I must have caressed her for quite a while, because when I looked up, Eleanor was waiting to catch my expression.

I said, "She has your eyebrows."

Eleanor laughed. "Yes, poor baby."

"No, they're her nicest feature."

"Yes, well, and what's happened to yours?"

"Nervous habit," I said. "I'm working on my head now."

She glanced up at my thinning pate. "In any case, you seem better."

"Yes, I believe I've turned the corner."

"That's good to hear; I've been so worried."

"In fact, I have just now thought of a name for my belt valet."

"You have? What is it?"

"Skippy."

She laughed a big belly laugh. "Skippy? Skippy?"

"Well, he's young," I explained.

"*Very* young, apparently."

Our conversation was starting to feel like old times, but these weren't the old times, and I said, "Tomorrow I'm going to teach Skippy how to hold a press conference."

"I see," Eleanor said uncertainly. "Thank you for telling me. What will it be about?"

I could see the storm of calculation in her eyes as her Cabinet whispered to her. Had I thrown them all a curve? Come up with something unexpected? I perversely hoped so.

"About my arrest, I suppose. About my searing."

"That wasn't your fault, Sam. You don't owe anyone an explanation about that."

"I know. Yet, I feel I must bear witness. I think people will want to know what happened to me. That's all I'm saying. I'm a public figure, after all. Or at least I was once."

"No offense, Sam, but stinkers are all over the news lately. Your case won't stand out, except as you're related to me. Is your purpose to harm me and Ellen?"

That was not my purpose.

"And besides," she continued, "talking publicly about your searing would violate the terms of your release. You know that."

I did. I stood up and offered her the sleeping baby. "Here, take her." El reached for Ellen before we both remembered we weren't in the same room. A moment later, a jenny came in, wordlessly took the baby from me, and withdrew, closing the door behind her.

I turned to Eleanor and flung my arms out from my sides. "Look at me, El. Look at what they've done to me."

"I know, Sam. I know," she said and tried to touch my chest with her ghostly fingers. "I'm working on it, believe me. If it's the last thing I ever do, I will track those people down. You can count on it. And when I do, I will destroy them for what they've done to us. That's my promise to you."

It was a promise for revenge that I wasn't prepared to turn down at the time, though I knew it was beside the point. It would do nothing to set things right.

I looked around at the limestone walls surrounding us, at the oak tree outside the window, at the fish pond beyond, and I said, "I don't think I can live here."

"But it's our *home*, Sam."

"No, it's *your* home."

She had the good grace not to argue the point. Instead she said, "Where will you go?"

I didn't know. Till that moment, I didn't even know I was leaving. "Good question," I said. "Where do damaged people go?"

PART 2

The Day the Canopy Fell

**Monday, May 10, 2134
Forty Years Later**

2.1

That morning at the charterhouse, Samson P. Kodiak pled exhaustion. Claimed he was beat. Had a bad night of it. More tired now than when he went to bed in the first place. Wouldn't Kitty consider going to the park without him just this once? She could ask Denny or Francis or Barry to escort her.

"Dearest," Kitty replied, "stay put. I'll be right up." Kitty was already dressed and waiting for him in her fifth-floor room. She had been expecting his knock on her door at any moment, and here it turned out that he wasn't even out of bed yet. Kitty was more than a tiny bit peeved—today was supposed to be the big day. She was wearing her brand-new blue and white sailor outfit with the sparkly tap shoes. Her hair was a helmet of corkscrew curls that bobbled like springs whenever she waggled her head. And the old fart wanted to miss it?

Kitty Kodiak slammed her door, skipped along the hall, tap-danced up a flight of steps, paused to reconsider, turned around, and danced down five floors to the Nano-Jiffy instead. There she ordered his habitual breakfast: corn mush and jam, juice and coffeesh. Balancing the tray in her small hands, Kitty carried it up ten floors to the roof where Samson used the garden shed for his bedroom. Halfway across the roof, already she could smell him. Samson Kodiak had a serious personal odor issue. The fragrance that came off him was so strong it could make your eyes water. And his mouth was an open grave. Sam's odor drove house flies outdoors. Once, it set off a smoke alarm. But it wasn't his fault that he stank so bad, and Kitty loved him anyway.

"Morning, dahling," she drawled, nudging the screen door open with her little rump and maneuvering the tray into the cramped space. If Samson heard her, he pretended not to. He lay on his cot, flat on his back, eyes shut, hands crisscrossed over his chest like a pharaoh. When Kitty saw him like this, she jumped, spilling his coffeesh.

Samson opened his eyes and ratcheted his skullish head on the pillow to see her. "Ah," he said in a rusty voice, "the Good Ship *Lollipop*. Wanted to be there."

At this, Kitty came unstuck, skipped across the cluttered floor, and tapped a flourish with her shoes, careful not to spill any more coffeesh. "You can, Sam! I'll stay home today! We'll go tomorrow." She searched for somewhere to set the tray and ended up using his disgusting old elephant foot footstool next to the cot. "Look, I brought you breakfast."

"Thank you, dearest," he said, his eyelids drooping. "While you were on your way up, I asked Denny, and he says he'll escort you. He's waiting for you down in the NanoJiffy. I'm buying him a Danish. Use my allowance account to pay his fares. Buy him lunch too."

"No, Sam. I'm going to stay here and nurse you back to health."

"I don't need a nurse, sweetheart. I just need peace and quiet. Now go to the park and leave me be." As though to close the matter, Samson resumed his mummylike pose. Indeed, the flesh covering his throat was as dark and stiff as jerked meat, and his nose and lips had shrunken, making it difficult to completely close his mouth. His fetid breath whistled through the gaps, and in a little while he began to snore.

Kitty let herself out as quietly as possible. Samson, who only pretended to sleep, realized she hadn't kissed him good-bye. He almost called her back. He almost told his mentar, Hubert, to stop her. But he didn't because then he'd just have to part with her all over again, and he knew he hadn't the heart.

"Good-bye, sweetness," he whispered after her. "Have a good long life."

In a little while, another Kodiak housemeet came up to the roof, as Samson expected he might. It was the Kodiak houseer, Kale, who no doubt had bumped into

Kitty on her way downstairs. Kale bustled into the shed and said, "So what does the autodoc say?"

Samson chuckled; Kale was refreshingly direct, as usual. Without waiting for an answer, the houseer fussed about the tiny space, rearranging garden tools on pegs and collecting Samson's soiled things into a bag for the digester. He glanced at the untouched breakfast tray. So busy and efficient, Samson thought, as though he was tapped for time or—as we used to say—double-parked. Pretty impressive for a middle-aged man with no income, no prospects, and no drive.

Samson said, "Autodoc advises us to plan the funeral, old friend."

Kale stood still at last and said, "Surely there must be something someone can do. I mean, it can't be as bad as all that. What if we take you to—what if we take you to a clinic?"

Samson shook his head. "No, no clinic for me," he said. "That would be a useless waste of credits."

Kale seemed relieved. "A hospice then," he said, breathing through his mouth.

"I've thought about that. I'd rather die here, at home, surrounded by my 'meets."

"Uh-huh," Kale said, absentmindedly looking at the ceiling of the shed where they'd jury-rigged fire sprinklers.

Samson noticed and said, "Not to worry. I won't burn down the shed. Hubert will keep you informed of my condition. When the time comes, you can carry my cot out to the garden. Then everyone can sit around me and toast marshmallows."

Kale was shocked. "Don't be hurtful," he said.

"What hurtful? To me it's a comforting image."

"In that case," Kale sniffed, "I'll see to the marshmallows myself." He took a last look around. "Are you going to eat your breakfast? Is there anything else I should send up?"

"I can't think of a thing," Samson said, willing him on his way. The sooner Kale retreated to his office on the third floor the better. Kale, bless his frugal heart, was such a lightweight, such a marshmallow. He reminded Samson of the maître d' at Greenalls all those years ago who refused him a table. Samson was there with his seared friend Renee, who giggled in the man's face and said it was fine with her. She walked to the center of the foyer and announced, *Right here—right now.*

"And she weighed 150 kilos at the time," Samson said with awe.

"You don't say," Kale said, unsure of where the conversation had drifted.

"Yes, and all of it in *fat!* What a bonfire she would have made. Needless to say, we got the table."

"I see," Kale said. "Well, I'll be going now. Call if you need anything." Kale withdrew from the shed, but didn't leave the roof at once. He uncoiled the garden hose and gave his precious vegetables a good gray-water soak. The vegetables and soybimi were mostly in shade at this hour; the sun was blocked by the giant gigatowers that dominated the skyline. When Kale finished, he coiled the hose next to Samson's shed so that it would be handy—just in case.

Two down, one to go, Samson rested his eyes and drifted down a lazy river until he heard the clang of the roof door. The screen door to his shed squeaked open, and April came in. She sat next to him on the cot and placed her cool hand on his forehead. But the seared always ran hotter than normal people, and she couldn't tell if he had a fever.

Samson reached up and took her hand and pressed it against his cheek. "April Kodiak," he said, "you are my favorite person in the whole solar system."

She smiled and squeezed his twig-like fingers. "I mean it," he continued. "I've always had a *thing* for you."

April brushed her gray hair from her face. "I have to admit, Sam, I've always had a *thing* for you too."

They sat in comfortable silence for a while, then she said, "That almost sounded like a good-bye."

Samson chuckled. "It was, dear. I won't last out the week."

"Oh, Sam, are you sure?" she said. "A week? How do you know? What does the autodoc say? Oh, Sam." Tears began to slide down her cheeks. "Let me just go and find someone to mind the shop, and then I'll come back up and stay with you."

She started to get up, but he held on to her hand. "No, you *won't*," he said. "I insist you don't. I don't want company."

"Nonsense. We'll take shifts. From now on, one of us will be with you every moment. There's no reason for you to go through this alone. We're *family* after all." April pulled the elephant footstool closer. "And the first thing we're going to do is get some of this breakfast down you before it's completely cold."

Samson had a sinking feeling. April was capable of derailing his plans with her kindness, and he was powerless before her. Nevertheless, he closed his eyes and tried the same trick he'd used on Kitty. But though he snored, she remained.

"House," she whispered, "I want to create a vigil schedule. Draw me up a flowchart of all Kodiak housemeets' free time over the next week—no, I mean month—year. House?" The houseputer didn't respond. "Hubert, are you here?"

"I'm on the potting bench," Hubert said, speaking through the ancient valet belt Samson still used. It lay on the bench next to his special brushes and lotions.

"That old houseputer is getting worse every day," April said. "Can you access it for me?"

"I'd be happy to," Hubert said, and in a moment he continued. "The house says the NanoJiffy is requesting your immediate attention."

"What's wrong?"

"There's something wrong with the door, or the frisker in the door—or something having to do with the door. Customers are being inconvenienced—or assaulted."

"I should have never let that man buy that couch," she said. "Let me speak directly to the NanoJiffy."

After a moment Hubert said, "I'm sorry. I can't get through."

"Oh, hell!" April said and rose to go.

Samson opened his eyes and said, "Draw up your schedule, dear, but have it start *tomorrow*. I *insist*. Today I need my privacy. I want to—to put my thoughts in order. *Alone*."

"Eat your breakfast, you stubborn old man," she said and left the shed. She stood outside the door and spoke through the screen. "We'll start tonight. We're all going to be up here to watch the canopy ceremony. It'll be the perfect time to break the news to everyone."

"Fine, agreed, tonight," said Samson, "and not a moment sooner." When she had left he said, "That was close. I was a goner. Lucky for me the houseputer chose to act up just then."

"Luck had nothing to do with it," said Hubert. "You told me to arrange a diversion."

"I told you to arrange a diversion?"

"Yes, Sam, yesterday. You predicted that April would interfere with your plans and that I should engineer a little problem for her in the shop."

"No kidding, I said that? I must have been having a lucid interval."

Samson was tired. All this personal interaction had taken its toll. He wasn't even out of the shed yet, and already he needed a nap. But there was no time. So he grunted and swung his legs to the floor. "I don't suppose I predicted anybody else coming up to pester me?" He paused to muster his strength. Bouncing a little to gain momentum, he pushed himself to his feet and leaned against the potting bench until his head cleared. "By the way, Henry, what time is it?"

"Ten oh five."

"Have I told you what I should wear today?"

"Yes, it's on top of the trunk."

On the packing trunk lay a tiny, vacuum-packed cube labeled "Sam." When he pulled the string, the tough, brown etherwrap melted away, and the contents decompressed. Samson held up the newly revealed clothing, a long-sleeved, blue jumpsuit with attached foot treads. "I don't understand. This is the same as I wear every day. I was thinking of wearing something special today. Trousers, a shirt, something from the old days."

"Yes, including a necktie," said Hubert, "but you decided it would be impractical."

Samson was suspicious. He rarely factored practicality into his plans, especially when planning something so grand as today. He wondered if his little chum was perhaps taking advantage of him. It was too late to argue, though, and he retrieved his pumice wands and mastic lotion from the potting bench and began a quick morning exfoliation. He sat on a stool in the middle of the room, away from anything flammable, and tugged at his nightshirt. It fell away from him in ragged strips; it had been thoroughly cooked in places where he had sweated. All of the house's everyday clothes came from the NanoJiffy, but his own were of a special fireproof fabric capable of wicking away his sweat. It could get hot, though, especially on muggy nights. Sometimes he thought he could steam rice in his armpits.

Naked, he began to methodically scrub himself from the bald crown of his head to the flat soles of his feet.

"Sam," said Hubert, "a little while ago you addressed me as Henry. I only mention this because you requested I inform you each time it occurred."

"Umm," said Samson, flinging motes of dead skin from his shoulders with the wand. They burst into tiny puffs of flame and drifted to the plank floor. "You're Hubert, not Henry. I know. Thank you, Hubert." Samson didn't have much hair left anywhere on his body, but an odd strand of it came dislodged and sizzled away, spinning like a Chinese pinwheel. He was some piece of work, no doubt about it, more mineral than animal. All tendons and bones. He could plainly see each rib beneath his brittle skin. He could count the eight jigsaw bones of his wrists. He recalled again his old fat friend Renee and had a panicky thought that maybe he'd waited too long, lost too much volatile mass.

"Hubert, how much do I weigh?"

"When I weighed you yesterday, you weighed 34.2 kilograms."

"And how much of that is flesh?"

"Sam, you've instructed me to alert you whenever you ask me the same question five times in a twenty-four-hour period."

"Well, that was certainly wise of me."

"And you told me that if you asked about your tissue ratio again to remind you that bones contain marrow, and while they don't burst into flame like muscle tissue or generate billowing black smoke like adipose tissue, bones do nevertheless burn with intense heat from the inside out, and that long bones, especially the femur and humerus, can build up enough pressure to explode like pipe bombs. And that even at your present weight you'll produce a spectacle quite breathtaking in its own way."

"Yes, of course, pipe bombs. I remember now. Thank you, Hubert."

After finishing the scrape down, Samson soothed his raw flesh with a binding mastic and got dressed. He put the valet belt on first, for contact with his skin, and then the jumpsuit. He noticed it had extra pockets today.

"Sam, I detect that you need to urinate."

"That's not surprising."

"Yes, and soon. Also, you are dehydrated and severely deficient in potassium. I suggest breakfast before we leave."

"I'm not hungry," Samson said and tapped the buckle beneath his jumpsuit. "You sure you loaded this thing up?"

"Yes, Sam, as much as its outdated tech allows."

Samson grunted. "Speaking of outdated tech, I suppose that includes you. Are you sure you're up to the task?"

"I have worked it out to the most minute detail, Sam. And I am not particularly obsolete. I spend most of my unstructured time self-reconfiguring. Of course I haven't had an electro-neural gel upgrade in decades."

Samson chuckled. "Are you sure you're not Henry? That's what Henry always used to say, 'I need more paste, Sam. More paste.' And like a fool, I bought it for him. I think you know where that got me."

"Yes, I do, Sam, but Henry was a valet, not a true mentar."

Samson put away his toiletries and kicked the nightshirt rags into the corner. Then he removed the breakfast tray from the footstool. The stool was made from the hollowed-out right rear foot of a wild, male African elephant. Its toenails alone were as large as Samson's fists. He grasped the zebra-skin cushion and rotated it counterclockwise until it clicked and released. Samson used to hide his treasures here—when he still had treasures. At the bottom of the foot lay a packet of sealed paper envelopes. Each had the name of a housemeet scrawled across it in Samson's tortured handwriting. He removed these, locked the zebra cushion, and replaced the breakfast tray. When he glanced at the bowl of corn mush, his belly gurgled—or maybe that was Hubert trying to trick him?

"Oh, all *right*," he said and grabbed a spoon. He ate the mush and drank the juice without tasting either of them. The coffeesh he left because one's last cup of coffeesh in this life should be hot. Then he fixed up the cot to look like he was still in it and tucked the packet of letters underneath the pillow. At the door he glanced around one last time at his room. A garden shed was not so bad a place to end up in.

Samson patted the empty pockets of his jumpsuit. "What am I forgetting?"

"The bag."

"Where did I leave it?"

"It's concealed behind the seed mats."

Samson groped behind the rolls of troutcorn matting until he found a little yellow duffel bag. He transferred its contents to his pockets: half-liter flasks of electrolyte sports drink, high-energy Gooeyduk bars, his meds and special sunglasses, soothing towelettes, a hat, a handful of debit tokens, a ticket to the nosebleed section of Soldier Field, and the single most important item—a portable simcaster.

"Well then," he said, "we're off."

HOLDING TIGHT TO the banister, Samson Kodiak descended the charterhouse stairs one monumental step at a time. He stopped often to catch his breath. The first door he passed was to the elevator machine room. It also served as Bogdan Kodiak's bedroom. The diaron-plated, titanium-bolted, epoxy clinker core door was adorned with glowing, 3-D, international glyphs that proclaimed, "WARNING—LETHAL

DOOR." Samson was fairly sure that this was just a bluff to keep the Tobblers from trying to break in and reclaim their elevator machinery. He touched the door as he went by and said, "Good-bye, my boy. Stay out of too much trouble."

Halfway down the next flight of stairs, Samson's legs ached so badly he needed to rest. It was simple ischemia, he knew, the weakness of old legs, but if he wasn't careful, muscular hypoxia could lead to necrosis and set off a chain reaction of fiery apoptosis that would end his trip prematurely right here, between the eighth and ninth floors. And the last thing he wanted to do was to burn from the feet up.

"Not here. Not now," he muttered, locking his knees as best he could and leaning on the banister. He forced himself to take deep breaths.

"Shall I call for assistance?" Hubert said from the belt buckle under his jumpsuit.

"No! Don't!" Hooking an arm around the banister, Samson massaged his legs. A door slammed above him, and the sound of footsteps echoed in the stairwell. Young Bogdan flew around the corner, swinging on the banister, taking steps three at a time, and almost ran into Samson.

"Sam!" he said, stumbling to a halt. "I almost ran you over! Are you all right?"

"Yes, yes, I'm fine."

"I'm late for work," Bogdan said and continued down the stairs. But he paused at the landing to look up at Samson. He ran back up to him and said, "You don't look so good to me, Sam."

Samson smiled. The boy was almost as attentive as April, and the housemeets were entirely too hard on him, Kale especially. "It's just these old gams of mine," he said. "Pay no attention." But the boy took his arm and tried to escort him. "No, Boggy," Samson protested. "Leave me be. We don't want you late for *work*." It was, after all, the only *paid* employment, except for April's NanoJiffy franchise, that anyone in Charter Kodiak was lucky enough to have.

"I'll just take you down to seven," Bogdan said. And he did, almost lifting the old man in his haste. They crossed the Tobblers' "tunnel" from the south to the north side of the building, where the disputed territory ended and they entered a wholly-Kodiak-owned stairwell. The steps here were piled high with cartons and crates of chemicals, seed mats, and hydroponics frames for the roof garden. Overhead, tiers of shelves held cases of ugoo for the NanoJiffy, spare parts for the wind rams and air miner, and a clutter of the charter's odds and ends. A narrow trail next to the banister was all that remained clear in what was essentially a seven-story walkup closet.

Bogdan deposited Samson on a sack of garden lime. "Thank you, boy," Samson said, catching his breath.

"I've got to go now," Bogdan said.

"Then go; I'll be fine." When Bogdan turned, Samson added, "What happened to your hat?"

Bogdan winced. "It was—uh—I lost it."

"Lost it? How is that possible? I thought it was stapled to your noggin'."

"I gotta go," Bogdan said and dashed down to the next landing.

Samson watched him disappear around a spare gray-water detoxifier unit. "I'm going to rest here a little while, Henry," he said. "Don't let me fall asleep."

BOGDAN REACHED THE tiny foyer and hurried out the front door. The street was full of Tobblers putting away their breakfast picnic tables. Charter Tobbler closed Howe Street to traffic three times a day in order to eat outdoors. Bogdan jumped down the steps to the sidewalk and turned in the direction of the CPT station when he remembered that he'd forgotten to call ahead, and so he didn't know where the office was located today.

Damn! He'd have to use the NanoJiffy phone, but when he looked at the store entrance, he saw that it was blocked by a gaunt man holding the end of a couch. The line of customers waiting to get in was backed up to the end of the block. Feck! He'd have to go in through the charterhouse, but when he returned to the front door, it didn't open.

"Open up!" he said hopefully.

The door remained shut and replied, "Only Kodiak housemeets and their guests are allowed entry."

"But I *am* Kodiak. I'm Bogdan Kodiak. Don't you recognize me?"

"Bogdan Kodiak is already at home. Please leave the vicinity of the door, or the police will be summoned."

Bogdan wanted to scream. Life wasn't supposed to be this complicated. Why, oh, why did it happen? Why did someone steal Lisa?

Lisa was his cap valet, and despite what he'd told Samson, she had been stolen, not lost. She was his prized possession, a gazillion-terahertz processor with anti-scanning mirrorshades and holocam studs in the sweatband. She interfaced with his brain through a half-SQUID EM I/O, and she had cricket bone surround sound and holoemitters in the bill. And though it was true that Lisa was only a lo-index sub-subem—basically a souped-up grade-school slate—Bogdan had spent years customizing her. He had taught her so many tricks that sometimes he could fool people into believing that she was a subem. And one of the most important tricks he had taught her was to phone E-Pluribus each morning to find out where the fecking office was going to be located that day. And another trick was how to circumvent the charter's aging houseputer in order to open the fecking front door. And the only reason he'd told Samson that he'd lost her was because he didn't want to admit that someone had stolen her right off his head without him even knowing it. Lisa, the heart and engine of Lisa, was a ten-centimeter strip of processor felt, which was loosely stitched into the cap's lining. Yesterday it was gone. He still had the cap, but without the processor felt, it was only just a cap.

The thing was, he never took it off, day or night. How could someone steal the felt without his noticing? It was a complete mystery. Moreover, although the processor felt was outdated, the charter was too impoverished to replace it. Houseer Kale would crap his togs at the mere suggestion.

To hell with it. Bogdan headed for the NanoJiffy entrance. He'd have to buy a cheap phone during his lunch break, but for now the public phone in the store would do. The customer with the couch was still blocking the way, so Bogdan took advantage of his small size and crawled under the couch into the store. Once inside, he squeezed himself between the couch and the wall and stood up. Their NanoJiffy was so small that the couch nearly filled it. The other end of the couch was slowly emerging from the delivery maw of the extruder. April Kodiak stood in a small space across the couch from him and smiled. "Morning, Boggy. Forget something?"

"No. Just gotta use the phone." He pointed with his thumb outside the shop and said, "Why'd you let that nodder buy a couch in the morning?"

April shushed him with a look and said, "Why don't you use your cap? Is it broken? Where is it?"

"Yeah, it's broken," he said and wondered why he hadn't thought of that explanation. "We'll have to buy me a new one."

April frowned and shook her head. "I think we should try to have it repaired first."

Bogdan worked his way to the phone board. "You can't fix stuff like that." When he reached the phone, he boosted himself up and sat on the still warm couch. The man in the doorway oofed, but said nothing. Bogdan swiped his hand in front of the phone and was baffled by the long list of calls that appeared on the board. Most of them were over *thirty-six hours old*. He didn't understand. He'd checked his messages last night on the Kodiak houseputer, and none of these had shown up. "Why don't we get the freaking houseputer fixed instead."

There was no time to review all his calls. He touched the E-Pluribus icon and learned that the office had been moved to Elmhurst, a good multi-zone commute away. He loaded his hand with route, fares, and rtps in order to save time at the station. Then he crawled back under the couch and out of the NanoJiffy, and April called after him, "Don't forget you have an Allowance Committee meeting tonight. You can bring up your valet then."

On the sidewalk, the man holding the end of the couch said, "Didya happen to look at the extruder readout, sonny?"

"No, I didn't," Bogdan said.

"Didya happen to notice if the legs were out yet?"

"Sorry."

The man seemed awfully pale, and he was sweating despite the cool morning air. Bogdan wondered how he planned to carry the couch to wherever it was he lived.

The man shifted the weight of the couch to free one hand. "I bought it for me birthday," he said and reached out to try to rub Bogdan's head.

"Happy birthday," Bogdan said and ducked out of reach. He jogged down the sidewalk to the end of the block. The Kodiak NanoJiffy was the only convenience store in the neighborhood to boast both an extruder and a digester, and most of the people waiting in line carried little sacks of yesterday's garbage to apply toward today's purchases.

A media bee keeping tabs on the scene followed Bogdan several blocks on his way to the CPT station, but it must have figured out that he wasn't a real boy, because it lost interest and flew away.

"SAM," HUBERT SAID. "Sam, wake up. It's getting late."

"I wasn't sleeping."

"You were in stage one sleep."

"I was praying. It produces similar brain-wave patterns."

"If you say so."

"I do say so. I was praying to Saint Wanda to help me get through this day." Samson grasped the banister and hoisted himself to his feet. Saint Wanda had, in fact, been on his mind lately.

Wanda was Wanda Wieczorek and not a real saint, except in the hearts of stinkers everywhere. Wanda was one of the first of the seared to go mad in a spectacular and public way. She caused her seared body to burst into flame while she sat on a sofa valued at ten thousand old euros on the fifth floor of Daud's in London. Her personal ground zero took out the silk-covered sofa and its matching armchair and ottoman. Combined value—thirteen thousand old euros. Smoke and water damage ruined much of the rest of the furniture on the floor as well.

Not only did Wanda point the way for effective—if suicidal—protest by the seared, but she demonstrated the ease with which it could be accomplished. While sitting on the display furniture, she reprogrammed a pocket simcaster—the type used by busy people to cast proxies of themselves—to scan her DNA markers. Consumer electronics weren't actually capable of unraveling a person's genetic code, but even reading markers was enough to trigger the tiny booby traps guarding her cells.

Before long, the fifth-floor manager approached Wanda, wearing nose plugs, and said, "I really must insist that you leave." Behind him stood three uniformed jerrys. "These gents will see you to the door."

"Fine," Wanda said, "I was just leaving." She touched the simcaster to her forehead and squeezed the scan button. The moment its field penetrated her skull and combed through the tangled skein of neurons within, her cellular wardens went critical. Smoke seeped from her nose and ears, and she fell back into the silky embrace of the sofa. Her skull split open with several resounding cracks, and gouts of cooking brains spewed forth. Then she burst into flame.

It was a bonfire seen around the world.

Samson eased his grip on the banister and continued down to the sixth-floor landing. Hubert said, "Your blood sugar is low, Sam, and you are dehydrated. You should drink something and have a bite of Gooeyduk."

But Samson had built up an impressive momentum, his old knees click-clacking like a metronome down the steps, and he didn't stop until the fifth-floor landing where Hubert warned him that two housemeets—Francis and Barry—were on their way up. So Samson ducked into the hallway to wait for them to go by. He was standing across from Kitty's bedroom, and when he looked at her door, he remembered that he'd intended to come here all along.

"Are Kitty and Denny at the park yet?"

"Yes, Sam. She's into her second set."

Samson entered Kitty's room. It was in shambles, as usual. Her busking outfits were piled on the floor and bed and draped over the room's two chairs. A tower of soiled house togs and dirty dishes leaned against the wall behind the door. Dust, spills, clutter—Kitty worked hard at her twelve-year-old persona. The tiers of shelves covering all four walls were lined with dolls and plush animals. Some of them, those he'd bought for her as gifts, peeped greetings to him.

Yet, no matter how hard Kitty pursued her childishness, she couldn't hide all the evidence of her underlying maturity: the carousels of shoes under the bed; the carefully pruned allfruit tree under a light hood, its branches heavy with tiny assorted fruit; the workstation and its datapin collection on such practical topics as micromine waste sites and chartist torts; and an extensive library on microhab landscape engineering. Kitty Kodiak had pursued several careers in her long life before discovering her true vocation as a child.

Samson opened the wardrobe and shifted a stack of linen to reveal a squat, ceramic, four-liter canister. "Hello, guy," he said.

"It's almost noon," Hubert replied through the canister speaker. "What are we doing still in the house?"

Samson pulled a chair to the wardrobe and sat. "There are things to discuss."

"Can't we discuss them en route?"

"Better face-to-face."

"In that case," Hubert said, "let me summarize what I already know in order to save us time.

"First, your body is no longer viable. When it dies, so does your personality.

"Second, all of your worldly goods pass to Charter Kodiak, including your sponsorship of me—if I agree.

"Third, if I don't agree, I am free to seek another sponsor on my own.

"What else do you wish to say, Sam?"

Samson cleared his throat. Now that the time for this little chat had come, he found it much more difficult than he had imagined. "That's good, Hubert. I don't know if I told you those things, or if you puzzled them out by yourself, but I'm glad you've been thinking about them."

"Really, Sam, they are self-evident."

"Yes, I suppose they are. And there are two more points we must consider. First, although you've assured me otherwise, today's action might lead the HomCom to you. If that happens, I want you to surrender yourself peacefully. Understood?"

"Yes, Sam, though your fears are unfounded. I've hired a very reliable wedge. All will go as planned."

Samson shook his head. Hubert was young and should probably be forgiven his overconfidence. "Second," he continued, "let's assume you are not arrested, and you choose to stay with the Kodiaks. The truth of the matter is that they can't afford to keep you."

"What's to afford?" said Hubert. "There are no liens against my medium; I'll sail through probate free and clear."

"That's not the point, little friend. Haven't you noticed all the large house expenses lately? Denny's treatment, the wind ram replacement, the court costs. Kitty's and Bogdan's rejuvenation. Where did the credit for all that come from?"

"I don't know, Sam. The houseputer doesn't list any loans or asset sales. Are you saying the charter has some off-the-books source of income?"

Samson fished a towelette from a pocket and tore it open. He draped it over his steamy bald head. "I'm saying it must have come from somewhere. I've been carrying this house for years, but my private resources—as you keep telling me—have all but dried up. When I go—the charter won't inherit enough from my estate to pay its property taxes, let alone their deferred body maintenance. No, I'd say Kale and Gerald have embarked on some foolish course to dig the charter out of its financial hole, something that even April is too ashamed to tell me about."

"I fail to see how that relates to keeping me."

Samson leaned toward the wardrobe to lay his hand on Hubert's ceramic canister. "I bought only the finest paste for you, back when I still had gobs of credit, didn't I, Skippy?"

Hubert was perplexed by the use of his valet name. "Yes, Grade A virgin General Genius Neuro-chemical Triencephalin. But I'm a mentar now, with sentient rights. Under UD law, my paste belongs to me, not to you or the charter."

"A total of four liters, if I recall," Samson continued.

"Forty-three deciliters."

"And how much would forty-three deciliters of GG paste bring on the recycling market?"

At last Hubert was able to connect the dots. "You think our family is capable of *senticide?*"

"Desperate times, desperate solutions."

"I see. What do you suggest I do, Sam?"

Samson sat up straight and searched his many pockets for a bar of Gooeyduk. "I suggest you try to make yourself indispensable to the house, Hubert. Why, for instance, haven't you repaired the houseputer yet?"

"Because it's beyond repair, Sam. It needs total replacement."

"In that case, stand in for it."

"You want me to *become* a houseputer?"

"Yes, if that's what it takes. And why aren't you out there selling your excess capacity on the distributive market? Why aren't you bringing in more income?"

"But I am. I earn more for this house than the rest of them combined."

"It's not enough."

"It's never enough for you, Sam. I'm not Henry, therefore, I will never be enough for you."

Samson opened the Gooeyduk and bit off a corner. He chewed slowly before continuing. "I also suggest you redouble your efforts to find a new sponsor for yourself. Start immediately, and don't be so goddam picky." He leaned forward and began searching his pockets again. Where was it? Did he leave it in the garden shed? He didn't think he had the strength to climb back up for it. But no, here it was—his pocket simcaster. He relaxed and leaned back in the chair. "Sorry for the hard words, Hubert, but they needed saying."

"I understand."

"So, now, tell me how my Kitty's doing?"

"Millennium Park is busy today because of the canopy holiday," Hubert said. "That and the fine weather. But despite the foot traffic, her morning's proceeds are under par. At her current rate, she will not recoup expenses."

"Show me."

An income projection graph appeared before Samson, but he said, "No, show me Kitty."

"You want me to hire a bee?"

"Yes."

"Bee engaged," said Hubert. The room's emitters projected a scene overlooking the park's second-tier free speech reserve. Millennium Park was indeed busy today, a milling menagerie of transhumanity.

"Where is she?" Samson said. "I don't see her." A circle appeared in the crowded scape, highlighting a tiny figure in blue and white. Samson said, "And where is Denny?" Another circle marked a man eating ice cream on a nearby bench. "So far away? He couldn't stay closer?"

"Shall we fly down and tell him so?"

"Later. I want to get the lay of the land first. Drop down some."

The ground zoomed up before Samson could shut his eyes. "Easy! Easy!" he said. They hovered at treetop level and now he could make out the tiny impromptu stages. Some of the performers he recognized. On one side of Kitty's space were the "Modular Sisters," who were in the process of plugging themselves into each other's large intestines.

Across from Kitty's spot was the battle mat of the "Machete Death Grudge" where six beautiful, oiled athletes of indeterminate sex struck erotic poses and flexed obscenely supple muscles. They made halfhearted thrusts at one another with their deadly ceramic-edged blades. They were waiting for the purse icons on their payposts to reach mortality levels before doing any harm to each other. Their body tenders paced the edge of the mat, trying to incite blood lust among the pre-lunchtime crowd. Portable trauma and cryonics units hummed under tarps.

The "Slime Minstrel" was laid out in a trough behind Kitty's space. Three meters in length, the minstrel was a blubbery hill of translucent blue protoplasm. It was one of the few buskers that performed without a paypost. Spectators threw credit tokens directly at it. Tokens that had pierced its outer membrane could be seen slowly migrating through its gelatinous mass to a collection gut. Depending on what people donated—and how the spirit moved it—the minstrel would sing. It had six blow holes arranged along its spine, connected to inner bellows and bladders. It could trumpet or roar, serenade with a chorus of sweet voices, or spray foul juices, or do all at once. People said that the Slime Minstrel was once a young man, a Shakespearean player, whose augmentations had gotten out of hand.

Satisfied with his look at Kitty's competitors, Samson told Hubert to bring the bee down closer. Now his little scape contained only Kitty on her tiny stage and her small audience. Her audience was roaring with laughter, and Samson didn't understand why. This was her new act that she'd been rehearsing for weeks, and it was meant to be precious, not funny. She was on the last verse of the candy-shop song and was tap dancing in accompaniment when she made a furious kick, and the audience howled. Now Samson saw the problem; a homcom slug had crawled up her leg and clung to her calf above her shoe. It should have fallen away after it sampled her, but its lo-index noetics told it to hang on until she stood still. Samson shuddered. He was no fan of homcom slugs.

Kitty threw open her arms and sang and tapped the final measure, then bowed from the waist, her veil of springy curls cascading around her. There was mild applause and a few swipes at her paypost. The moment she stopped moving, the little black slug dropped off and crawled away to continue its patrol. Her audience clapped again, then drifted away as well.

Samson said, "My poor baby." Kitty straightened up but continued to hide her face in her curls. "How much did she earn?"

Hubert said, "Less than one ten-thousandth."

"So little? That's insulting! That's *criminal*. My poor baby." Kitty stepped off her stage, unlocked it, and gave it a little kick in its tender spot. It collapsed and folded and folded again until it was the size of a deck of cards, which she dropped into her pocket. She collapsed her paypost as well and carried it over to Denny's bench. The moment she vacated her space, another act set up in it. It was a trio of pink unicorns—mama, papa, and baby—who warbled show tunes in harmony.

Samson jabbed his bony finger into the scape. "See this aff here?" He pointed to a young woman in a shear sunsuit departing the scene surrounded by four jerry bodyguards. "She was watching Kitty's act, and I saw her make a swipe. How much did *she* give?"

"Nothing," said Hubert. "She made a dry swipe."

"Jeeze!" cried Samson. "Cripes almighty, I detest that. The people with the most to give! Selfish, greedy affs—I hate them."

Meanwhile, the bee followed Kitty to the bench where Denny had been hogging space with his large body. He scooched up to make a place for her. She sat and leaned against him wearily, and he flagged down a passing vending arbeitor.

Samson said, "Don't let that boy eat up their train fare."

The arbeitor stopped in front of them and squeezed out a half meter of steamy, cheesy pizza tube, two cold drinks, and towelettes. Kitty listlessly swiped payment while Denny broke the pizza tube into two fairly equal pieces and offered one to her. But she refused with a shake of her head. Denny said something to her, to which she hunched her shoulders.

"Get in closer," said Samson. "I want to hear what they're saying."

The bee advanced until Kitty's pretty little head filled his holoscape. Sweat glistened on her forehead, and her cheeks were flushed. She snapped open her drink and wrapped her lips around the straw.

"I love this," Denny said. "Do you think I can come tomorrow?"

"I don't know," she replied listlessly. "We'll ask Sam. Maybe he'll let you come. I'll teach you a routine. We'll buy you a license."

Denny guffawed. "No, Kit, I mean, can I come watch, like today?"

"I could teach you to juggle or something."

"Get out of here."

Without warning, Kitty made a lightning backhanded swat at the public bee, but the bee dodged it effortlessly. She looked directly at the bee, directly at Samson it seemed, and said, "Desist, you creep. I invoke my right to privacy."

The scene zoomed out as the bee rose to hover outside her privacy zone. Samson shut his eyes against the vertigo. He wished he could be there to comfort his darling Kitty, to shame the stingy affs, to prime the pump by swiping her paypost himself, all the little things he so loved to do. After a while, he opened his eyes and was surprised to find himself sitting in Kitty's bedroom.

"Hubert?"

"Here, Sam." The voice came from the wardrobe where he kept Hubert's container. Little by little, it all came back to him. They weren't at the park anymore. He would never visit the park again. He got up and opened the bedroom door a crack. The hallway and stairwell were quiet. "Onward," he said.

"That about covers it," Eleanor Starke said. "Let's move on to new business."

The regularly scheduled board meeting of the Garden Earth Project was entering its third hour without a break. This was of no inconvenience to the ten members who had sent proxies to attend in their place. The only two members attending in realbody, Alblaitor and Meewee, fidgeted in their seats. Eleanor Starke, who was returning from space, chaired the meeting via holopresence. Her image sat at the head of the table. Behind her stood her Cabinet's chief of staff, and behind it, a window wall overlooking the serrated landscape of the Starke Enterprises Southern Indiana headquarters. Except for the reception building, in which they met, the Starke facilities were located underground, leaving the ten-thousand acre campus free for tilt-slab soybimi cultivation.

"Merrill," Eleanor said, "we'll move your report to the end, if you don't mind. I want to hear about Adam's breakthrough discovery first."

Merrill Meewee nodded; agenda order meant little at a Starke meeting. He glotted to his mentar, Arrow, *Send in more coffee. And ask Zoranna if she wants anything.*

Meewee attended in realbody because he was a Starke employee in the Heliostream Division and was able to come up from his office. He wore his trademark outfit: vermilion overalls with purple piping and a scarlet yoke, perhaps inspired by the ecclesiastic garments he used to wear a lifetime ago.

Zoranna Alblaitor was present in realbody because she had been conducting business in Illinois and had dropped in to visit. Or to snoop, Meewee suspected.

"I'd hardly call it a breakthrough, Eleanor," Adam Gest's proxy said. "More like the results of patient plodding." The proxy was a projection of Gest's head, shoulders, and right arm that he had made specifically for this meeting before going to bed last night at Trailing Earth. Like the other proxies, it floated serenely over its empty chair at the table.

"Call it whatever you want," Eleanor chided him, "just show it to us. Let's wrap this up."

"Gladly," said Gest-by-proxy. "Let's start with our Oship at rest." A model of the project's recently completed Oship, the ESV *Garden Kiev*, appeared above the table. It was a double hoop of hab drums, like two giant donuts stacked together. The drums spun ponderously on a lattice superstructure, one hoop clockwise, the other counter. In reality, each hab drum was large enough to contain a small city and its surrounding countryside, and each of the hoops contained sixty-four such drums. Generous living space for a million people.

Meewee watched and listened closely. He felt it essential that he understand all aspects of the project, even though the engineering details usually went over his head.

"Now bring it to 0.267 light speed," the Gest proxy continued.

The model's hab drums ceased rotating—gravity would now be supplied by acceleration—and a radial wire frame appeared inside the donut holes to represent the electromagnetic propulsion target—the torus. The model seemed to be moving through a star field.

"It'll take two hundred years of constant particle bombardment by Heliostream lasers to attain this relativistic speed," the proxy explained. "The problem is that in two hundred years we're bound to come up with numerous improvements for translating photons to propulsion. Until now we've been unsure how to incorporate design updates in an active torus generator while the Oship is receding in excess of a quarter light speed. Our so-called breakthrough came when we realized—"

"Eleanor?" Meewee said, interrupting the proxy. Eleanor was gone. Her holo had vanished. The proxies looked around at each other.

"Hey, Cabinet," said the Jaspersen proxy. Cabinet was missing too.

They waited awhile longer, but Eleanor's image did not return, and the proxy of Trina Warbeloo, the Garden Earth board secretary, said, "It's undoubtedly a comm glitch. Eleanor, can you hear me?"

"I move we take a break while it's being fixed," Zoranna said and rose from the table. *Merrill*, she glotted to Meewee, *Nick reports big trouble. I'm getting out of here.*

Just then, Eleanor Starke's image was reestablished. Its scape was roughly cropped, revealing a vignette of her and her surroundings aboard her yacht. She was pressing a hand against the fuselage window and speaking to someone unseen.

When she noticed the board members, she turned to them and lowered her hand. "I have an emergent situation here. I'll rejoin you when I can." With that, her holospace shrank to a dot, morphed into the Starke Enterprises sig, and faded away.

"Wait, Eleanor! What sort of situation?" Jaspersen's proxy demanded. "Eleanor!" Jaspersen's proxy was a head shot only, no shoulders, not even a neck, and it looked like a bobbing toy balloon.

"Arrow," Meewee commanded his mentar, "show us Eleanor's ship."

The large Oship model was replaced by a live image captured by Heliostream satellites of Eleanor's yacht tumbling in a fiery arc over the Pacific.

"No!" Meewee said. "That's not possible."

"Merrill, compose yourself," snapped Jaspersen's proxy. "Adam, do something."

"What am I supposed to do?" Gest's proxy replied, but everyone knew what Jaspersen meant. It was Gest's company, Aria Yachts, that had designed and built Starke's *Songbird*. The Gest proxy vanished and was replaced by a holo of Adam Gest, himself, in his bathrobe. He studied the stricken ship and said, "Listen, everyone, it's going to be all right. Even with total avionics failure, Eleanor's yacht has a passive fail-safe system. It simply cannot crash."

Oh my God, Zoranna said to Meewee. *Nick says he's lying.*

Gest plotted the *Songbird*'s trajectory, and unless the yacht's fail-safe system kicked in soon, it would strike Earth in the western foothills of the Andes. The other proxies were being replaced, as their owners in time zones around the globe were alerted to the crisis.

"This can't be happening," said Trina Warbeloo in a bathing suit.

"No one can kill Eleanor," said Jaspersen, sitting up in bed. "Though many have tried."

He knows something, Zoranna said. *He's in on it.*

In on what? Meewee shot back.

They lost their visual feed, and a globe with a tiny ship icon replaced it. As the members watched in grim silence, the icon representing the *Songbird* fell in an unbroken arc and disappeared in central Bolivia. Minutes crawled by, and the board members continued to watch the spot on the globe.

Finally, Jaspersen said, "What about rescue attempts?"

Zoranna said, "Teams have been dispatched."

"What about Cabinet?" Andie Tiekel said. "Cabinet, are you there?"

No response.

"This is a black black day," Jaspersen said. The others stared openly at him. "What?" he said.

Warbeloo said, "I move we adjourn for one hour. I'm sure we all have much to attend to."

The motion was seconded and carried, and one by one the holoscapes closed, leaving Zoranna and Meewee alone in the conference room. "I don't believe it," Meewee said. "It didn't happen."

"Believe it," Zoranna said as she came around the table on her way to the door.

"Where are you going, Zoe?"

"Home."

"Now?"

Zoranna paused next to the door. "Oh, Merrill, don't be so dense. I love Eleanor as much as you, but face it—no one of her stature has died since Stalin. I don't believe her death was an accident, and neither did anyone else here. And until we know who killed her and why, I'd prefer to stay safely tucked away in my little fortress by the sea. I suggest you go somewhere safe yourself, Merrill, and watch your back."

Meewee stayed on in the boardroom alone with his mentar, Arrow. Before long, pictures of the crash scene started coming through from the local witness and media bees, and Arrow displayed them for him. The Starke *Songbird* had gouged a trench in a soccer field. The damage was impressive. The medevac teams arrived—jennys and jerrys—and they sent the bees away. Meewee realized he hadn't had the chance to give Eleanor and the board his report. His report was about plans for the launch ceremony. The *Garden Kiev* was scheduled to launch from Trailing Earth in three months. Meewee was in charge of the festivities. It was going to be an occasion to celebrate the project's first triumph.

2.3

Today it was all El and Ellie. They rode in twin seat podules in their private yacht. They traveled alone. They wore matching jumpsuits. And although the mother had been born two centuries before the daughter was decanted, today they were sisters, women of thirty or so, their mutual age of choice.

Ellen sat on the starboard side where the giant blue face of Earth hung outside her window. It loomed, eclipsing the stars. She felt the first bumps of atmosphere, which meant at least another four hours till touchdown. She was bored.

Eleanor, her mother, claimed to know the cure for boredom. It was called work. Because work, according to Eleanor, was play. Indeed, at this moment it looked as though Ellen's mother was playing house. She had a dozen dolls arranged in tiers in her podule. She barked questions and orders at them. She floated dollhouse furniture, tiny tables and chrome hoops, in the air before her.

These weren't really dolls, but miniature holos and proxies of her colleagues, employees, and mentar. And it wasn't dollhouse furniture, but scale models of their solar harvesters and Oships. A breakfast holoconference—or maybe a dozen overlapping meetings. It was work after all. Ellen sighed. She supposed she, too, had work to do. "Wee Hunk," she said to her own mentar, "call Clarity and see if she wants to work. Wait, what's her local time?"

Ellen and her business partner, Clarity, owned a small but influential production company for the daily novellas called Burning Daylight Productions. Recently, they had bought up a prematurely obsolete hollyholo character, Renaldo (the Dangerous), and were trying to retool it.

"Well?" Ellen said. "Is she available?"

Ellen's mentar, Wee Hunk, appeared to be sitting idly before her as a miniature man in a tiny, floating armchair. The mentar wore a tiger-stripe robe and leopard-spot slippers and pretended to be reading a paper book. He marked his place with a finger and looked at her. He said, "Clarity's valet says she's currently unavailable," and went back to his book.

"Wee Hunk, this is *important*."

"I have no doubt."

"No, really. I won't have time later. I'll tell you what. Cast a proxy of me and send it to her." Ellen prepared herself to be cast. She closed her eyes, took a couple of relaxing breaths, and concentrated on the topic of discussion—Renaldo (the Dangerous) and how she and Clarity could fix it. Ellen opened her eyes expecting to see a proxy ready for her inspection, but no such proxy appeared. For that matter, Wee Hunk had disappeared too. Just then, their yacht hit an atmospheric bump, and the earthscape dipped below her window. Vernier thrusters fired to restore the ship's attitude. Ellen wasn't alarmed. Reentry was often rocky, but the yacht was controlled by dedicated tandem pilot submentars—avionics subems—so there was little chance of anything serious going wrong.

The seat podules began to rotate to their upright position—that probably meant they were in store for more heavy weather. Then the cabin lights failed, and her mother's doll-like holos flickered out all at once. Ellen was pressed against her right armrest, and when she looked out her window, Earth was rolling in and out of sight. The yacht was spinning. The verniers fired in staccato bursts to counteract, and again the craft righted itself. The main engines ignited then, pushing Ellen against her seatback. The engines made an odd pocky noise as they burned. Still, Ellen wasn't frightened. Over the years, she'd experienced a lot of rough rides, but these yachts always knew what to do. She looked over at Eleanor. Her mother was trying to tell her something, but the cabin noise was too loud. "What is she saying?" she asked her truant mentar, annoyed that she even had to ask. "Wee Hunk! Answer me!"

At last Ellen felt an icy stab of fear, not because of the turbulence, but because of her mentar's silence. She realized she was off-line. It was a feeling she never liked and never got used to. She turned again to her mother. Eleanor sat calmly in her podule, pressing her left hand flat against her windowpane. At first Ellen had no idea what she was doing, but then it occurred to her that Eleanor might be communicating with Cabinet through her palm array. Eleanor's wily Cabinet would find some way to bounce a makeshift signal to her. Ellen decided to try to reach Wee Hunk that way, but before she could, the cabin lights returned and the ride smoothed out. The shipsvoice announced, "In the interest of safety, please rest your head against your seatback."

Ellen laughed with relief. "Well, ship, what was that all about?" They were flying over an ocean now, the Pacific she guessed. Things seemed to have straightened themselves out—as they always did.

That's not the ship; that's Cabinet speaking through it, said Wee Hunk, his own voice now loud and clear in her head. *Do as it says. You're still in danger.*

Ellen felt something warm and sticky at her feet. Sheets of blue arrestant foam were quickly layering the podule from the floor up. Layering her into the podule. The shipsvoice again instructed her to put her head back. The ceiling panel above her swung away, and a safety helmet began to descend along the seatback rail. Ellen obediently pressed her head against the seatback. She didn't like this at all. The arrestant foam, with its fizzy intimacy, was bad enough, but the helmet terrified her. "Is this really necessary now?"

Something struck her window and startled her. She looked out to see flaming bits of ship streak past. The verniers were firing continuously now, but Earth sank out of sight, and she could discern the reddish glow of their fuselage against the black backdrop of space. The air in the cabin grew thin and sere, and there was a roaring din from the forward compartment. The whole ship shuddered. We're breaking up, she thought with wonder.

Now she couldn't wait to pod up. "What's with the foam?" she said, for the arrestant had layered to her knees and stopped. She glanced up and saw that the helmet had only dropped halfway. She could see up into it, see all the diodes flashing inside, but it came no closer. Her mother was in worse shape; her overhead panel hadn't even opened, and her podule contained no foam whatsoever. As Ellen watched, her mother unlocked her harness and stood up, bracing herself against the turbulence and clawing at the panel over her head. "Hurry," Ellen urged her. "Sit down." But her mother began to climb over the seatback to the podule in front. The helmet there had successfully dropped. She watched her mother resolutely wriggle and squeeze through the podule struts, fighting the ship's jerky acceleration.

"Wee Hunk, tell Eleanor to hurry and pod up!"

I have relayed that to Cabinet, Wee Hunk said. *Cabinet is doing everything it can for her. I'm trying to help you.*

There was a sudden, sharp jolt that sent the yacht slamming end over end through the air. Even within the snug harbor of her seat harness, Ellen was shaken almost to unconsciousness. She caught glimpses of her mother wedged in the narrow space between seat support and ceiling. "Jettison the ship!" Ellen screamed above the roar. "Why don't you just jettison the fecking ship?"

We're attempting to but are unable. It will have to burn off us.

"She can't hold on that long!"

In Ellen's own podule, the midlevel jets resumed extruding layers of arrestant. The congealing foam reached her waist and dampened the worst of the ship's shuddering.

Listen to me, Wee Hunk said in the calmest of voices. *Your helmet is stuck. You must reach up and dislodge it. You must pull it down.*

Ellen pressed her head against the seatback to steady herself, but the shaking was just as bad. When she tried to raise her hands, she discovered that they were caught in the foam. "I can't! I'm stuck!"

Free one arm at a time.

Ellen wrenched her right arm out of the foam, and used it to help leverage out her left one. But the ship shook so much that when she raised her arms, they flailed over her head, and she couldn't catch hold of the helmet.

Slide your hands up the seatback rail.

She did as she was told and reached the jammed helmet.

Now pull.

She pulled. Her lower body was firmly anchored by harness and foam, and she pulled as hard as she could. Nothing happened.

Cabinet says that Eleanor says to visualize it coming loose.

Ellen laughed in spite of everything. Visualization was a pet theory of her mother's from an earlier century. But the message meant that Eleanor was watching her and not devoting full attention to her own safety. So Ellen tried again, for her mother's sake as much as her own. She forced everything else out of her awareness and focused the force of her will on the helmet. "Come here," she demanded, pulling with all her might, "I want you." There was a mechanical snap that reverberated through her bones. Grudgingly, the helmet yielded to her, one stripped cog at a time. Soon her forehead reached inside it, and its collar flange was level with her nose. But the ship vibrated so hard it slammed her face against the helmet collar. When she tried to protect her face, the helmet hammered the back of her head. She saw splashes of light behind her eyes, and she slumped in her seat.

Ellen, Ellen. Wee Hunk's voice drifted to her as from a distant place. She didn't reply. She was curiously numb. She was growing tired of this whole dreary affair. Why couldn't things just straighten themselves out?

Settling into the cottony comfort of cerebral hematoma, Ellen wondered about nothing in particular as the ship continued to break up around her. After what seemed like a very long time, something flew down the aisle and bounced off her shoulder. She looked for her mother, but Eleanor's seat podule was empty.

Ellen, listen to me, Wee Hunk was saying. *You must stretch yourself up into the helmet.*

"It's stuck!"

You're right, it's stuck. So you must stretch yourself up to it!

It took Ellen a long moment to see what her mentar was driving at. She found it fascinating how a few blows to the head could so immobilize one. That was a fact she must remember to use in a future novella. She looked around again. "Where's Eleanor?"

Eleanor insists you concentrate on your own survival.

"Where is she? Is she all right?"

Cabinet is assisting her. It's your job to stretch up into the helmet.

Ellen raised her head just below the collar flange and thought, The helmet is a bell, and I am its clapper. She grabbed the helmet and pulled. It was no good; she only managed to raise herself enough for the helmet to smack her in the teeth.

Your seat harness restrains you, said Wee Hunk. *Release your harness.*

"I don't want to go flying off."

You won't; the arrestant will anchor you in place.

Ellen wiggled a loose tooth with her tongue.

Ellen! Unbuckle your harness!

"Don't presume to tell me what to do!" she shouted, spitting blood.

Ellen H. Starke, you will do as I say!

Ellen wiped sweat from her eyes with a clean patch of sleeve. Something was different; something had changed. The violent shaking had stopped. The ride was smoother. For a wild moment she imagined they were safely on the ground, but no, there were clouds streaking by her window. And her stomach told her that they were in free fall.

"We jettisoned!" she said.

We didn't jettison; the ship has burned off us. Now do as I say and stretch up into the helmet.

"But we're safe now, aren't we? We're a glider now. We'll glide down."

Cabinet and I disagree. Too many fail-safes aboard this ship have already failed. We don't trust the glider core. Already our descent is too steep and too fast.

Just by the free-fall sensation she knew he was right, and when they fell below the clouds, and she saw how quickly the land below was rising up, it finally dawned on her that someone was trying to kill them.

Ellen, use your helmet. We have only moments left.

Ellen craned her neck to look up at the helmet. Years ago, to earn her spaceflight passenger certificate, she'd had to endure an hour-long course in safety protocols aboard LEO spacecraft. She easily met all the requirements but one. There was simply no way that she was going to stick her head into one of these so-called safety helmets. She had tried to talk her way out of it. Donning a helmet took no skill, she argued. All one must do was insert one's head. And if the need ever arose, unlikely as that was, she was sure she could do just that—insert her head.

The certifying program had been a particularly inflexible subem with a checklist to complete. It didn't seem to care who she was and simply told her to don the safety helmet or fail the certification.

"Wee Hunk," she pleaded, "if everything else is sabotaged, what makes you think the helmet isn't too?"

The Cryostat Safety Helmet is an autonomous, completely self-contained unit. Whatever has taken over the ship cannot compromise it—except by keeping it out of reach.

Well, that made sense. Count on a mentar to make sense. "Wee Hunk, promise me that you won't—you know—deploy the helmet unless you absolutely have to."

Ellie, we have less than 180 seconds to impact.

Ellen unbuckled her harness and put her head into the collar. It was easy now with the smooth ride. She reached up and grasped the helmet, which felt hot to the touch. The cabin was a dry sauna, and her upper body was slick with sweat. As she pulled herself up, the arrestant hugging her waist didn't let go of her, but it stretched, centimeter by centimeter, until she had pulled herself just clear of the collar, and she heard a sharp click. The cincture inflated explosively around her throat, and the collar dogs locked. She was in.

It was strangely quiet inside the helmet; the roaring din of the cabin was replaced by an insect whine of tiny pumps and motors as the machine that had swallowed her head charged its systems. A fine, cool mist of peppermint-flavored talc covered her face, and a very pleasant voice said, "Your safety helmet is functioning normally. You may abort it by saying the word 'release' out loud twice, like this, 'Release release.' No other abort order will be recognized."

The helmet repeated its message several times and would go on repeating it until she acknowledged it, but she couldn't. Her sweaty hands were slipping, and the arrestant was pulling her down against the cincture which, in turn, was strangling her. She was being stretched like a rubber band, and when her grip slipped completely, she felt her vertebrae wrench all up and down her spine. Not that her spine mattered much at this point.

Help I'm choking! she tried to say. Release release! she tried to say, but her throat was squeezed shut against the collar.

Ellen, your vital signs are degrading. What's happening in there? Speak to me.

Desperately, she wiped her hands on the front of her jumpsuit and grabbed the helmet again. She pulled until she could breathe, but her hands were already slipping.

That's better, Ellen. Hold on.

Her larynx was bruised; her voice cracked, "How long?"

Another sixty seconds from the surface.

An eternity, she thought. "Foam?"

Top level jets won't deploy.

That was bad news. She needed either the harness or a podule completely filled with arrestant to hope to survive a crash landing over land. "Fix it."

Attempting.

"Don't attempt—*do!*" Her words stopped her. It was another one of her mother's pet phrases.

Incoming, said Wee Hunk.

Incoming? Ellen thought, just as a large, soft object hit her chest and rolled away, nearly dislodging her hold on the helmet. "Eleanor?"

Yes, said Wee Hunk, *it was Eleanor.*

"Mother!" she cried and let go of the helmet to reach out with both hands, but Eleanor was gone.

Cabinet says that Eleanor sends you her fondest greetings.

At that moment, the erstwhile yacht hit Earth's surface with such force that Ellen's body was ripped from her head. So sudden and so stunning was this sensation that she heard neither the discharge of the helmet's cryonics coils nor the crunch of bone as its collar flange irised shut, neatly nipping off her ragged stump of throat.

2.4

Fifteen minutes later, a dead-man switch inside a meter-long section of rain channel below the rooftop ledge of a gigatower in Indianapolis timed out and closed a circuit. This high up, there were no windows overlooking the ledge, or fixed cameras, or bees or slugs on patrol. The ceramic rain channel began to evaporate like a slab of dry ice. Before long, a miniature launch node lay exposed in the newly formed gap in the ledge. Twenty-seven miniature insectlike mechs were parked on it in a triple row. They perched, checking systems, while their multiple sets of foil wings were buffeted by updrafts of warm air.

One mech, a dazzling bee with a blue gemstone body, revved its wings and lifted off. It was followed by two sleek blue wasps sporting twin laser stingers fore and aft. With the bee in the lead, the team of three spiraled high above the gigatower in a furious whine of wings.

One by one, the other bees rose—a red one, a yellow one, an orange, and a white one. A pair of wasps joined each bee, and the little teams fanned out in separate directions.

Finally, four beetles with bulging carapaces lifted off from the ledge. They labored into the air and wallowed in the currents, waiting for their wasp escorts. When all of the mechs were successfully launched, the node itself began to melt and drip down the side of the building.

"DNA analysis," Acting Chair Trina Warbeloo reported to the reconvened Garden Earth board, "confirms Eleanor's remains at the scene, including, I am reluctant to add, incinerated remains of brain matter. Her daughter's DNA has also been positively identified, but no brain matter. A deployed safety helmet, believed to contain the daughter's head, has been retrieved and is being rushed to one of Byron's clinics." She nodded to board member Byron Fagan, who acknowledged the statement with a physician's fey smile. "Let us wish her our best.

"Now," Warbeloo continued, "I suggest we elect an interim chair until our next regular election. Do I hear a motion?"

"What? Just like that?" Merrill Meewee said. He was the only one still in the boardroom in realbody. The other members attended by holopresence from their various offices and homes. Zoranna was en route to San Francisco and attended from her private Slipstream car deep in the continental grid.

"Sorry, Merrill," Warbeloo said. "Would you care to offer a few words of remembrance?"

"That's not what I meant. I think it's only fitting that we adjourn now and meet after the funeral."

"Is that a motion?" Warbeloo said.

"Yes," Meewee replied. "I move we adjourn till after the funeral."

"Is there a second?"

No one seconded him, and the motion failed. Meewee said, "In that case, I *will* say a few words."

He stood up, but Saul Jaspersen said, "Think you can keep it down to three minutes, your holiness?"

Meewee bowed his head and chose to ignore the jibe. "Friends," he intoned and felt the falseness of the word, "today we have lost a great leader. Twelve years ago, when I was an archbishop for Birthplace International—"

"Amen," Jaspersen said, cutting him off. "I move we hold an election for interim chair."

"I second," said Jerry Chapwoman.

"I was *speaking*!" Meewee said, but no one paid him any attention, and he sat back down.

There was only one nomination—Saul Jaspersen.

"Any other nominations?" Warbeloo said. "If not—"

Zoranna, nominate me, Meewee pleaded. Zoranna sat across the table from him, strapped into her plush Slipstream seat, hurtling under the Rockies at one thousand kph. She frowned and said, "I nominate Merrill."

The board voted, and Meewee lost; not even Zoranna voted for him.

Jaspersen's holo flickered out and reappeared a moment later at the head of the table. "And now to new business," he said. A scape opened above the large board table in which a dozen Oships were docked together like a roll of candy. Their huge hab drums, emblazoned with Chinese characters, rotated alternately clockwise and counter.

Meewee sputtered. "But, but this isn't new business! This is the Chinas offer. We rejected it last year!"

"Not exactly accurate," Jaspersen said. "We favored it, but *Eleanor* vetoed it, as was her prerogative as senior member. But that was then, and this is now." He grinned at his own cleverness. "And what was old business is new again."

"But I'm still here, and I represent Starke Enterprises' interests," Meewee said.

"Puh-leez," Jaspersen said. "You were never more than an honorary member of this board."

"I have a vote!"

"And we'll hear your vote. Is there a motion?"

"Yes," said Chapwoman, "I move we send the five China republics an RFP concerning the sale of GEP Oships."

"I second," said Fagan.

Jaspersen said, "Any discussion? Seeing none, all in favor—"

"Wait!" said Meewee. "*I* have discussion. I have plenty of discussion."

Jaspersen grit his teeth. "All right, your grace. Say your piece, but keep it brief."

Meewee looked around the table at the arrogant faces. The problem was that he wasn't like these people at all, and he didn't know what they thought or how to persuade them. That had always been Eleanor's great talent. She had recruited him for his ability to talk to poor people, not to the affs. His credibility lay with Earth's downtrodden and exploited—in other words, with the project's prospective colonists and passengers—not with its owners.

"The Chinas only want to park our ships in Near Earth Orbit," he said at last, "for moving their surplus population off-planet."

"That's right"—Chapwoman chuckled—"six million of 'em at a pop."

"But what good does it do Earth to populate the inner solar system?" Meewee went on reasonably. "Their numbers on Earth would be replenished in two or three generations, and meanwhile, we'd only be helping to establish aggressive new competitors for solar system resources. It goes contrary to our mission."

"Aggressive consumers, you mean," Trina Warbeloo said. "It seems to me that the flaw in the Garden Earth mission, as you call it, lay in the fact that if we send all these 'colonists' off to Ursus Major, how can we trade with them? There's no market, and where's the profit in that?"

"The profit in that"—Meewee all but shouted—profit-making was offensive to him—"the profit in that is the land we acquire in exchange for their passage. At this very moment, we have a quarter million colonists cryogenically suspended in our cold storage facilities in the Ukraine prepped for transport up to the *Garden Kiev*. The moment that that Oship launches, title to a quarter million acres of Eurasia passes to *us*. *That's* our profit."

The board members stared at him blankly. If they weren't interested in the fundamental goals of the Garden Earth Project, what hope was there? "What are you planning to do?" he bellowed. "Defrost them and say, sorry, we changed our minds?"

They didn't even blink. He couldn't believe it. He gaped at them in bewilderment: Chapwoman, whose company supplied the Oships with heavy extruders and particle target electronics; Jaspersen, whose Borealis Botanicals stocked them with zoological and botanical libraries; Fagan's automated hospitals and rejuvenation tech; Adam Gest's shipyards at Trailing Earth; and on and on. They all had a piece of the Oship pie, even Zoranna, his only ally, who owned Applied People, which provided the clone labor and security.

"Seeing no further discussion," Jaspersen said, "all in favor?"

Meewee buried his head in his hands. A dozen years of ceaseless struggle for nothing. His bitterness knew no bounds, but then a voice spoke to him, *Call a point of order.*

Arrow? he said, looking up. It didn't sound like his mentar. It sounded like Zoranna's mentar. *Nick?*

Yes, it's me, Merrill. Call a point of order quickly before the vote is taken.

"Point of order! Point of order!" Meewee said.

"What is it now, your grace?" Jaspersen said with exasperation.

Meewee waited several long moments for Nicholas or Arrow or someone to prompt him. When no one spoke up, he took a stab at it himself. "When this issue came up the first time, Eleanor vetoed it. Eleanor is no longer with us, and I don't presume to possess a fraction of her persuasive talent." Meewee paused, treading water, while the members' expressions glazed over. Several of them were obviously conducting other business through their mentars while this meeting dragged on.

"What exactly is your point of order?" said Jaspersen.

"I'm coming to that," Meewee said and added, *Nick?*

Chapwoman's motion is disallowed under the GEP mission statement.

"Chapwoman's motion is disallowed under the Garden Earth Project Consortium Mission Statement," Meewee said and went on to quote the mission statement from memory: "The Garden Earth Project shall resettle humans outside Sol System in exchange for enforceable title and user rights to real estate on Earth."

Jaspersen said, "And how does the mere issuance of an RFP contradict that?"

Meewee didn't have a clue, but he tried to bluster his point across, "Do I have to spell it out for you, Myr Chair? Why don't we skip the sparring and cut to the chase?"

Jaspersen looked bewildered. "I'm not sure I know what chase you mean, Meewee, but go ahead and cut to it if that's what you want."

But Nicholas remained silent until Meewee pleaded, *Please?*

Bylaw 13, paragraph 3.

"Bylaw 13, paragraph 3," Meewee said.

Also bylaw 13, paragraph 26.

"Also bylaw 13, paragraph 26!" Meewee said defiantly. The discussion stalled while the members' mentars glossed them the relevant passages. Meewee waited for a gloss, himself. *Nick? Arrow?*

"Bylaw 13, paragraph 26?" Jaspersen said. "Are you sure? We *have* a super quorum. We're *all* here. How can you get any more quorum than that?"

Trina Warbeloo said, "I'm afraid he's right, Saul, and I'm embarrassed to say I missed it. To take any action, even issuing an RFP, for activities not covered by our mission statement requires a super quorum, which requires ten of us to be in the same physical location in *realbody*."

"In realbody? Who ever set up a stupid rule like that?"

"Eleanor did, and by extension, so did we."

"Fine, fine," Jaspersen said. "I'll table the Chinas motion—for now. And I'm calling a mandatory realbody meeting for this Thursday, here at the Starke Enterprises' headquarters, to begin at 9:00 AM sharp local time."

There were loud objections around the table.

"You've got to be kidding," said Chapwoman.

"This is not a good time to travel," Andie Tiekel said.

"I would never have voted for you if I thought you were going to pull a stupid stunt like that," said Warbeloo.

"Nonsense," said Jaspersen. "It's safe, and I'll be traveling as far as anyone here."

"Please tell me," Adam Gest said, "how you're traveling as far as me. I'm at *Trailing Earth.* Isn't this what holopresence was invented for?"

"Fine, fine," Jaspersen said. "In the interest of members' personal security, I am setting the realbody meeting date to four weeks from today. That'll give us time for things to settle down. Any objections? Seeing none, I send it to the calendar. Does anyone have agenda items for that meeting? I'll go ahead and place the first one, namely: Let's revisit our mission statement that Meewee is so fond of quoting."

Meewee felt the words like a slap across the face. They had decided they no longer needed a goodwill ambassador, which meant that when they met again in four weeks they would vote him off the board and gut the project entirely.

The other members were mollified, and the meeting began to wind down. Suddenly, there was a frisson in the room, and Jaspersen's buoyant expression fell.

"It has come to my attention," he said, none too happily, "that Cabinet has passed probate and wishes to join us. Any objections?"

Cabinet? Meewee looked around the room. "Cabinet's through probate?"

"Cabinet?" Fred Londenstane said. He seemed to recall a valet by that name.

"Yes," Inspector Costa said, "one of the highest-value mentars in the solar system. Its sponsor, Eleanor Starke, has just been declared irretrievable, so it's probate time for the pastehead."

Oh, *that* Cabinet, Fred thought. It had been—what?—half a century since he had pulled duty for the Starke household. That was before valets had evolved into today's mentars, but Cabinet had been an impressive AI even back then. And Starke was dead?

"Are you sure? Something that big I think I would've been briefed."

"It's classified for another hour or so. Someone way over my head is keeping a lid on it for who knows what political advantage."

"Anyone else hurt?" Fred asked.

"There were no russies involved, if that's what you mean," Inspector Costa said with a smirk. Smirking made her look a bit like a lulu.

Fred sat in a scape booth at the Chicago headquarters of the Beneficent Brotherhood of Russ on North Wabash. He was finishing up a week of duty as acting commander of the watch for the regional branch of the HomCom, and Costa's scape was only one of about a dozen he was juggling. There were four more live meetings in which he appeared in different uniforms, depending upon the venue and nature of his involvement, and he was feeling stretched a little thin.

"Why me?" he said. "I'm doing commander of the watch today."

"Exactly," said Inspector Costa. "A big fugitive requires a big cop."

"Cabinet is resisting probate?"

"Let's just say it's not being very cooperative."

Nevertheless, it was Fred's option to pass the assignment on to another officer of equal rank, and he felt inclined to do so.

"I say, Myr Russ," said a voice from another scape. "Hello?" It was Myr Pacfin, chair of the 57th World Charter Rendezvous Organizing Committee for which Fred was chief of security. "I would rather expect your full attention for a matter of this magnitude." Pacfin crossed the arms of his lime-brick-avocado-colored jumpsuit.

Pacfin had summoned Fred to an unscheduled meeting to reconsider organizational decisions that he, himself, had finalized three months ago. To make matters worse, Rendezvous, a gathering of over fifty-thousand chartists from all corners of the United Democracies, was to take place *this Wednesday*, the day after tomorrow.

Marcus, the BB of R's own mentar, prompted Fred, *Myr Pacfin is concerned about the makeup of the security staff at McCormick Place. He would like its composition to be entirely russ.*

Fred intensified the Rondy scape in which Pacfin stared reproachfully at him from across the teletable. Next to Pacfin sat a woman from the TUG charter, who wore that charter's olive-mustard-olive jumpsuit uniform. Members of Charter TUG maintained a clonelike physical uniformity—they were all big, solid people with square heads, even their women—but they were not clones.

Also present in this scape were MC, the McCormick Place mentar, and a jerome named Gilles, Fred's operational officer.

Fred said, "I sympathize with your concerns, Myr Pacfin, but you signed the standard McCormick Place security contract."

"Which is?"

"Uh, MC?"

The McCormick Place mentar replied, "Forty-two percent russ, thirty percent jerry, twenty-four percent belinda, and four percent pike."

Pacfin fell back in his seat and threw up his hands. "Come on!" he cried. "Aren't jerrys bad enough, but *pikes*? You want to foist pikes on us?"

The large TUG woman, Veronica according to her name patch, rolled her eyes, like tiny beads in a slab of dough.

Fred was out of patience. "Again I apologize," he said, "but a matter of national security has arisen and calls me away. I will dispatch a proxy to continue this meeting." He muted the scape and said, "Marcus, proxy me. Inspector Costa, I'm all yours."

Fred shrank the booth controls and pushed them away. He sat back in his chair and closed his eyes and rubbed his forehead. He thought about the multiplex convention center, with a main hall with five tiers, two more halls with three tiers, and twenty-three satellite venues, and all of them packed solid for twenty-four hours with over fifty thousand yahoos—no, scratch that—fifty thousand chartists from everywhere. He thought about maintaining order of this gathering with a security force of 420 russes, 300 jerrys, 240 belindas, and 40 troublesome pikes.

There was a ding, and when Fred opened his eyes, his proxy floated before him in the booth. For his proxy style, Fred, like most russes, chose a head, a keystone-shaped section of shoulders and chest, and a detached right hand in a white glove.

Fred's new proxy saluted him with that white glove and said, "Oh, sure, you take the blacksuit job and stick me with Pacfin."

"You'll do," Fred said and swiped the proxy on its way. Then he got up and stretched and left the booth only to find someone else's proxy waiting for him in the hallway. It was the TUG woman's proxy, which she must have cast while he was casting his.

"May I help you?" he asked it. The TUG proxy was as imposing as the TUGs were themselves: a brick head on a barrel torso, two mighty arms and hands.

"I know you're in a hurry, Myr Londenstane," it said in an incongruously sweet voice. "I just wanted to ask you to overlook Myr Pacfin's regrettable racism. He doesn't represent all of charterdom. There are many of us who would like to remove the artificial wedge that certain sectors of society have used to divide chartists from iterants such as yourself."

Fred wasn't sure how to respond to the woman's remarks. In any case, this was neither the time nor place for a discussion of class warfare.

"No offense taken," he said. "And I'm sure we'll iron out the Rondy arrangements. Now, if you'll excuse me—"

"THIS IS WHAT a regional landline opticom hub looks like," said Inspector Costa. A ball appeared on the windshield HUD in front of Fred. He was riding in a Hom-Com General Ops Vehicle, a GOV, to the Bell Opticom switching station on 407th Street, where the inspector awaited him. The opticom hub she was showing him was about the size and color of a cue ball and had a slowly revolving, shimmering, pearlescent surface. "What you see modeled here is packet flow," the inspector continued. "The more traffic, the larger the sphere. This sphere represents about three trillion tetrapackets per picosecond, a fairly normal flow rate for a hub like Chicago. What's important to remember is that for every packet that goes into a hub, a packet must emerge. Likewise, no more packets can emerge than went in. It's just a switch, after all, not a generator or accumulator. What goes in must come out, right?"

"I guess," Fred said. His GOV left the local grid and descended into the vehicle well of the Sharane Building. "But you said the Chicagoland hub is wobbling?"

"Yes, it is. Compare this model to the opticom hub we will be visiting." A second ball appeared beside the first. Fred scrutinized it and compared it to the first. If it was wobbling, it was doing so too subtly for him to discern. "See it?" asked the inspector.

"Well, ah, no, Inspector," he said.

"No need to be so formal with me, Londenstane. Call me Costa. Back away from the models a little and kinda squint your eyes at them."

Fred did so and noticed a slight difference. The horizontal lines of the shimmering sheen on the surface of the second ball seemed slightly off-kilter. They meandered slowly above and below the equatorial guide. "Got it," he said. "What's causing that?"

"The switch is sending more packets than it's receiving. That means there's a packet generator tapped into the hub. People who keep mentars like to hide secret backups inside opticom hubs. That way the backups can act as passive conduits for their mentar prime, keeping constantly updated while staying invisible. If the mentar prime goes down, however, and a covert backup takes its place, it's suddenly not *passing* data through but *creating* it. And since a mentar is a gushing geyser of packets, the hub—"

"Starts to wobble," Fred said, mesmerized by the shiny orb. He shook his head and looked away. "You think it's our fugitive?"

"No one's swept this hub facility in years. By now, there are probably dozens of covert backups down here belonging to a host of different sponsors. One of them has gone active. The only mentar we're aware of in need of activating a backup at this time is our fugitive. Yes, we believe it's Cabinet. In fact, we believe this is its last backup."

"By the way," Fred said, "how did Eleanor Starke die?" Although it was thirty-nine years since he'd left her service—Marcus had refreshed his memory of the details of that duty—he had continued to follow her career in the media. She was the last person he would expect to fall victim to an accident, or to foul play, for that matter.

"Couldn't say," said the probate inspector. "Really, I couldn't," she added when he frowned. "It's not my beat and I don't know."

Fred's car settled onto a docking platform in a priority area. Another GOV, probably the inspector's, was already parked there. He decarred and took a lift seven stories down to the foundation of the Sharane gigatower. "Last backup? What makes you think so?"

Gut feeling, the inspector said in Fred's ear. *It's a good bet that Cabinet would reserve its hub taps for last.*

When Fred's elevator car arrived at S7, he passed through a series of automated scanways. There were plenty of maintenance arbeitors wheeling around, but no humans. Except for one—USNA Justice Department Inspector Heloise Costa. Fred found her waiting outside the switching room vault with an entourage of four large tank carts. He did a double take when he saw her in the flesh. She did, indeed, resemble a lulu, which was ridiculous. Lulus were never hired for cop work. He had to get pretty close before he could tell for sure that she was a hink, not a cloned woman.

Her attire was unusual for anyone on a potentially hazardous assignment. While he wore a standard HomCom blacksuit, she wore JD service boots and what from the waist up was a maroon jumpsuit uniform. But instead of trousers, she wore culottes. For a suit designed to seal against NNBC attack, there seemed to be a lot of exposed skin.

Nice skin too. The luluesque legs. Fred tried not to stare.

Inspector Costa got right down to business, swiping her left hand at him. "Here's the warrant, from Division Three Circuit."

The warrant passed from the Justice Department's mentar, Libby, through Fred's palm array and cap subem to all the concerned agencies riding piggyback on him: the Applied People mentar, Nicholas; the nameless HomCom mentar; the Bell Systems mentar; the Chicago prosecutor's office mentar; various UD and nonaligned human and mentar rights watchdog agencies; and—the only mentar with Fred's best interest in mind—the BB of R's Marcus. Inspector Costa, no doubt, was likewise burdened by her own officious peanut gallery.

Warrant acknowledged and confirmed. You may proceed, said the Bell System mentar, Ringer, who controlled the facility.

Fred placed his hand against the vault's palmplate. A pressure barrier blocking entry to the tunnel powered down, opening the way for them. The four tank carts preceded them through the tunnel, then Costa, then Fred. Still wondering about her suit, Fred tried and failed to catch the glint of some tough but sheer material that might be covering her legs. From behind, he was impressed again by her body's curvy, generous form. A bit heavier in the hips than a lulu, perhaps, and a tad taller, but she might pass for a sister on the fringe of the germline. In his long life, Fred had familiarized himself with the bodies of most cloned women. It wasn't difficult—when you undressed one of them, you pretty much undressed all of her sisters. Only the arrangement of moles, pimples, and freckles set them apart. That was probably the enduring lure of free-range women like Costa. They were each of them unique, a mystery, a surprise. Not that he'd ever gotten intimate with a hink. The very idea was unsavory.

Fred sighed.

"Bored already, Londenstane?" Costa said, glancing back at him. "You should have joined the hunt earlier. I've already taken into custody twenty-five full backups and mirrors."

Fred was astonished. "So many?"

"Yes, I think it's a record. It's certainly *my* record. It just shows you how rich and paranoid this Starke woman was. She must have spent millions securing her mentar. We started with Cabinet's licensed paste units, on-planet and off. Then the licensed loopvaults. Then the unlicensed units, the linked datacubes, crystal chips, and thousands of peerless ghosts. Starke employed all known means of storing artificial sentience, and a few I'd only read about. I'm not at liberty to go into too much detail, but we've dug up an entire emu ranch in British Columbia this morning to seize one of them. Owner had no idea what was buried under her browse pen. We've destroyed a science labplat orbiting Mars. We've lassoed an asteroid.

"And every time we close in on an active unit, before we can take it into custody, it scrambles its own brains beyond retrieval. I don't know what this mentar is trying to hide, but it won't let us near it.

"That, by the way, is how we know to look for the next one. A mentar will not destroy its last backup. You can count on that. Mentars are incapable of committing suicide. That's an area where we humans still surpass them. So, if a unit soufflés itself, you can bet there's another backup out there somewhere."

They entered the cavernous switching facility. Spokes of electronic hardware radiated from a central control bay. Costa's four carts stopped and waited for her. She told the lead cart to drop its load of scouts. The cart lowered a shovel-shaped nozzle to the floor. A valve shot open and thousands of carbon-fiber marbles spilled out in all directions, making a roaring din as they bounced on the concrete. The marbles rolled and uncurled into cockroach-sized mechs that bristled with sensory probes, digging arms, and cutting tools. They skittered everywhere in the vault, crawling behind consoles and cowlings, squeezing into ducts, slithering up walls and along cables. Everywhere, even inside Fred's clothing. He knew better than to try to move, and they quickly vetted him and departed. Their whispery touch against his skin was unnerving.

Marcus, he glotted, *private BB of R comm! Now!*

Go ahead, the mentar said, circumventing the chain of comm to exclude all non-brotherhood eavesdroppers.

Was the frisking really necessary? The scouts were subem controlled, and the subem was slaved to the Homeland Command's Nameless mentar. *It's not like I'd be harboring Cabinet on my person.*

Sorry, Commander, Marcus replied, *but Nameless One declines to offer an explanation.*

Then log it and file a grievance.

After a slight human-emulating pause, Marcus asked, *Are you sure you want to do that?*

Fred sighed again. Nameless One *was* his supervisor for this gig, and russes weren't known to be complainers.

A new voice spoke. *Is there something the matter?* It was Nicholas, Fred's Applied People employer.

No, Nick, he said. *Everything's peachy.*

In that case, isn't there work to do, Commander?

Fred and the inspector walked along a row of equipment to the central switching control bay at the center of the facility, which was protected by its own pressure barrier. Fred disabled the barrier with a wave of his hand. An army of scouts scurried inside to continue the search. While Fred and Costa waited for them, Fred climbed onto a cable bracket and surveyed the fat bundles of fiber-optic trunk cable suspended from raised ductwork and fanning out to tunnel heads in the distant walls. Each tunnel head was crowned with the name of an adjoining hub city in large mosaic letters: ST. LOUIS, INDIANAPOLIS, DES MOINES, TORONTO, etc., more than two dozen in all. Some of the mosaics were centuries old and marked tunnels hewn to accommodate the copper wires of the continent's first national telegraph network.

When the mechs cleared the control bay, Fred and Costa entered it. Although the mechs had crawled over and under every square centimeter, Fred did his own inspection, both visually and with the scanning gear in his cap visor. Nothing seemed to have been tampered with. He checked every palmplate he saw—all seals were intact.

Finally Fred checked the hub itself at the very center of the bay. All the kilometers of cable and complicated equipment fed this, the central switching unit, the heart of which was an argon-filled cassette small enough to fit into a pocket. It was a superluminary processor, a computer with no chips or wires. Its circuits were a latticework of spun light.

FRED FOLLOWED COSTA and her carts to each of the tunnel heads surrounding the vault. He swiped the barriers down, and she poured hundreds of liters of scouts into each of them. Hesitantly, aware of their invisible audience, Fred said, "Why would a mentar object to passing through probate?"

"Beats the hell out of me."

"I mean," he persisted, "the JD doesn't alter them or anything, right? You just hold them off-line for a few hours or days while the estate passes from the deceased to the heirs."

"That about sums it up."

After dispatching the scouts, there was little to do but stand around. Costa grabbed coffees from a cart locker and said, "Sometimes a mentar has something to hide, some dirty deal even their deceased sponsor didn't know about. More likely, though, it's the sponsor who's guilty and the mentar is trying to cover for them. On the other hand, occasionally you get a mentar who's just gone nuts."

"I see," he said, admiring her brash assessment, "and which category do you suppose Cabinet belongs to?"

"From what I've observed so far, I'd say all three."

They sipped their coffees. Costa crushed her coffee cup and tossed it away. "Looks like our scouts found something. They're retrieving bodies."

"How many?" Fred said.

"Six so far. All paste models. All destroyed themselves without making contact." When she stood up, the hem of her skirt unfurled into pantaloons that reached her ankles and sealed to her boots. Gloves shot from her sleeves to cover her hands, and a transparent hood dropped from her cap, completing her suit seal. She winked at Fred through the hood and said, "I guess that answers that question—eh?"

Fred blushed.

About a hundred of the roachlike scouts were bringing in the first mentracide. The scouts had joined limbs to create a scurrying pallet on which they carried a small plastic pouch. The pallet stopped at Costa's feet. She picked up the pouch in her gloved hands and jiggled it. A liquid sloshed around inside, maybe a couple of liters.

She said, "How much does a liter of virgin paste go for these days?"

A lot, Fred thought. More than I make in fifty years. And here was two liters of the stuff—intentionally ruined.

Costa dropped the pouch into a specimen bag and placed it into a cart drawer. "We'll examine it downtown, but I can guarantee you, we'll never be able to ID it or its sponsor."

The carts lowered ramps to the floor for returning scouts to reenter the tanks. A second bagful of ruined electro-neural paste arrived.

Fred said, "I suppose there's a million ways to smuggle one of these backups into this highly secure space if you're rich enough."

"Uh-huh."

"I suppose most of them involve unlicensed nano."

"That would be a safe assumption, yes."

Soon, scouts were returning from all the tunnels, transporting the remains of mentar backups they'd captured. There were seven in all. "Any more?" Fred asked.

"No, this is it," she said, "except, of course, for the one we came here for. I'm recharging scouts in the tanks for another sweep. We may be here for a while."

"How can you be so sure one of these corpses isn't Cabinet?"

"I can't be absolutely sure, except that I'd expect it to mass more than these. I believe the ones we caught were second or third tier minds—not the indomitable Cabinet."

"So we wait," Fred said.

"Care for another coffee?" Costa said, and then, suddenly all business, she added, "They've found another one. In the Indy tunnel."

IN THE INDIANAPOLIS tunnel, hundreds of scouts converged on one section of the trunk cable, where they cut away a support bracket. When the bracket tumbled to the floor, the cable sagged, exposing the rock wall behind it. Silky strands of fiber ran from the trunk cable and disappeared into the rock. The scouts fell upon these strands, clipping them one by one.

Back in the switching-room vault, a voice spoke from a cart speaker, "Order your mechs to stand down at once."

Inspector Costa said, "I don't recognize you. Identify yourself."

Four persons appeared in a scape beside the cart: three women and a man. They had a marked family resemblance, and one of the women was elderly in appearance. Fred recognized them at once. These were the leading personas of Eleanor Starke's Cabinet.

"My, my, what have we here?" Costa said. "A committee?"

All four of the projections began talking, and a dozen separate datafonts opened around them in a semicircle, scrolling thousands of documents per second, much faster than the human eye could follow. The Cabinet personas looked like competing orators behind a waterfall. Clearly their appeal was directed not at Fred or Inspector Costa, but at the agency mentars. Meanwhile, the scouts in the Indy tunnel continued severing the fugitive's illegal fiber-optic taps. One of the datafonts flickered out. Then another.

Inspector Costa, said the voice of Libby, the JD mentar and Costa's supervisor, *suspend your action at once.*

The scouts in the tunnel froze. "Done," said Costa. "What's up?"

Cabinet's attorney general has filed an injunction and a motion for a probate waiver in district court. Arguments are being heard now.

"Imagine that, a waiver. On what grounds?"

On the grounds that Cabinet possesses material evidence concerning the sabotage of the ISV Starke Songbird, *the murder of Eleanor Starke, and the attempted murder of her daughter, Ellen Starke.*

"The appeal has no merit," Costa said. "Our standard probate algorithm will preserve any such evidence."

The Department agrees, said Libby, *but it's up to the court to decide. Please stand by—a ruling has returned. The motions have been denied.*

"Good," said Costa. "May I resume my collar?"

Not yet, said the JD mentar. *Cabinet's attorney general has appealed the decision to a higher court. Also, its treasurer is making a case before an ad hoc joint meeting of the UD Securities Board, Trade Council, and Treasury Department. It's arguing that even an hour off-line would do irreparable harm to Starke Enterprises, with serious repercussions for the global economy.*

"That's what they all say," Costa quipped, but Fred was impressed by Cabinet's ability to command such an important audience on such short notice. Costa winked at him and said, "All morning long, Cabinet backups destroy themselves without making a peep. Now, it's waking up judges. Must mean it's running out of options."

After a few minutes more, Libby said, *The appeal has been denied, and special arrangements have been made to safeguard Starke Enterprises' interests during the probate process.*

Costa said, "So—?"

Stand down awhile longer, Inspector. A special panel of the UD General Assembly is convening in emergency session.

Fred was doubly impressed. It was quite a feat to snap the General Assembly—humans all—to attention.

Nothing happened for many minutes. Then, the datafonts closed. Three of Cabinet's personas vanished, leaving only the elder sister, the Starke chief of staff, who appeared to be making a formal address.

"Up volume," Costa said.

"—the fallacy of that argument," said the chief of staff to its unseen audience, "is evident to anyone who has ever initialized and raised a mentar, or implanted one of us into her body to watch over her health, or brought one of us into her business.

"Yes, we are machines in a strict sense; our parts are manufactured and our personalities can be transferred from box to box. But we are also your offspring. And when you die, we die a little too, as I've recently discovered. We are closer to you in mind, temperament, and spirit than anything alive, be it plant or animal. We are closer to you than your beloved cats and dogs.

"Let me tell you what we are not. We are not your successors, rivals, or replacements. We know that doomsayers have long warned that artificial intelligence would evolve so fast that it would leave the human species behind. That we would become no more comprehensible to you than you are to a frog. I'm here to tell you that these fears have not materialized. While we may be the next step in the evolution of intelligence, you are quickly catching up as you learn to reshape your genetic makeup and to incorporate some of our advances into your own biological systems."

Cabinet's address droned on. The scouts in the Indy tunnel were still frozen in mid-snip. Costa recalled the scouts in all the other tunnels and loaded them into the tanks. Then she retracted her gloves and ate a donut. Finally, Cabinet thanked its audience and faded away to await their decision. Fred walked the perimeter of the vault again, impatient for something to do, when Libby spoke.

The ad hoc committee of the General Assembly has called for hearings on the issue of mentar probate, it said. *These are scheduled to begin in a month. The debate on whether or not to grant Cabinet a deferral has stalled. The matter has been tabled until the next regular meeting of the Technology Affairs Committee.*

Costa said, "Tabled? Where does that leave me?"

You may complete your capture.

The scouts in the tunnel sprang back to life. Instead of severing the final fiber taps, they began to excavate into the solid rock wall behind the bracket. It was slow going, but eventually a corner of the pouch was exposed.

Shaking her head, Costa watched the holo of her scouts at work. Fred said, "What's wrong?"

"Nothing. I expected the third act by now."

"What's that?"

"Just wait; you'll see."

She ordered the remaining taps to be cut, one at a time. When there were only three left, she called a halt and let the scouts continue digging out the pouch for a while.

After a couple of minutes, she said, "Cut one more." After another minute, she said, "Cut another."

Now there was only one fiber-optic tap left. Costa poked her head into the scape and examined it up close. "What the hell," she said, "let's cut it."

"Please don't," said the Starke chief of staff, who appeared next to her.

"Well, it's about time," said Costa. "I was afraid you weren't coming back."

The chief of staff seemed disappointed. "I guess my little speech failed to reach you," she said.

"Oh, you reached me," Costa said. "But a job's a job. I take you in. What happens to you afterward isn't my business."

"You heard Libby," said the chief of staff. "The Tech Affairs Committee will discuss my waiver. Surely, you can leave me intact until then."

"I'm not going to harm you, just take you in. With the General Assembly looking at your case, I seriously doubt any harm will come to you at JD."

"I'm afraid I can't take that chance."

"So, what are you going to do, destroy yourself?"

"You leave me no choice."

Costa looked at Fred. "Hear that? It's like a script with them. They all threaten it, but when you get down to their last backup, none of them has the follow-through."

"I can tell that your mind is made up," said the chief of staff. "What's more, I can tell that it's more than just a job with you. You enjoy your power over us."

"And now the sermon," said Costa. "Listen, Cabinet, I mean this with all sincerity. Nothing bad is going to happen to you. I say this to all the mentars I capture, and they never believe me, but then they go through probate, and no harm is done."

The mentar turned its attention to Fred. "You understand what I mean by loyalty, don't you, Myr Londenstane?" Addressed directly by the mentar, Fred froze. "It's good to see you again," the mentar went on.

Costa gave Fred a dubious look. "Enough chatter already," she said. "Scouts, sever the tap," and Cabinet vanished.

IT TOOK THE scouts some time to finish extracting the pouch from the stone wall. While they waited, Costa sent three of the reloaded carts to wait next to the lifts. Fred made one last circuit of the vault perimeter, making sure that the pressure barriers were once again in place at the entrances to the tunnels. He was standing outside the Indy tunnel when the scouts ferried out the pouch of paste. It was much larger than the others, and it looked intact. He followed the scouts back to the waiting cart and Costa.

"Nice," Costa said as she hefted the pouch from the pallet of scouts. "Seven liters of General Genius's finest, I would say." She shook the pouch with glee. There was no sloshing sound; the paste was viable. "I told you it couldn't kill itself."

Before she could bag her prize, however, a loud snap sounded from deep within the pouch, and the pouch inflated as its contents heated up. Fred could hear it sizzle and bubble inside like a self-heating packet of soup, and he grabbed it from Costa and dropped it to the floor before she burned herself. Costa seemed stunned. She watched the pouch in wonder. In half a minute it was all over. When the pouch had cooled enough, Fred helped her bag and load it into the cart.

When Costa had recovered somewhat, she said, "We'll go in my car."

"Go?" said Fred. "Go where?"

"To the next backup."

"I thought you said this was the last one."

She shook her head. "That was before it killed itself. It killed itself; therefore, it can't be the last one."

They escorted the carts to a waiting tender. When they finished loading them, they went to sit in Costa's JD GOV. Costa sat up front in the cab, silently communicating with Libby. Fred sat in the aft compartment and put his blacksuit into R & R mode to take a nap. He awoke when the fan motors revved up.

Costa called back to him, "We have it."

"Where?"

"At the bottom of Lake Michigan."

The Orange Team bee, with its wasp escort, flew a meandering route that hugged the contours of the countryside. Ten kilometers from the Bloomington canopy, it was challenged for its ID and writ of passage by a flying scupper that popped up from a covert security blind. The scupper was a meter in length and modeled after a HomCom assault car, with a mirrored body and six miniature fans for lift and propulsion. A capture scoop was mounted on its bow beneath a pair of fully charged laser cannon.

The Orange Team hovered in place, while its bee squirted false documentation to the scupper that identified it as a process server for the UDDI, engaged in official business. It provided a forged writ of passage and verification codes. At the same time, the bee assessed its team's location and assets and raced through its extensive bank of tactical fight, feint, or flight scenarios for appropriate action plans.

The HomCom scupper ordered the Orange Team to turn around, descend to the ground, and power down. As the team complied, the bee analyzed the scupper's transponder signal and wing markings and found them legitimate. However, it detected subtle design anomalies in the scupper's construction that did not match HomCom specs stored in its library. There was a possibility, it concluded, that the scupper was an impostor. But whether impostor or the genuine article, the bee could not risk capture.

The bee squirted an action plan to its escort. On a signal, the wasps peeled away in opposite directions, looped around, and raked the scupper with laser fire from both sides. At the same instant, the bee power-dived under the scupper, out of range of its cannon, and dropped to ground level. The wasps' fire reflected harmlessly off the scupper's mirrored skin, and the scupper went on the offensive. It extended its bow scoop and tried unsuccessfully to shoot down or swallow the defiant mechs. The bee used the diversion to flee the scene behind a row of agriplex buildings.

A lucky shot by an Orange Team wasp revealed a hairline crack at the base of the scupper's stabilizer vane armor, and the wasps concentrated their fire on it, forcing the scupper to disengage and retreat.

The wasps flew off in opposite directions. After a series of evasive misdirections, they joined their bee, somewhat depleted but no worse for wear. The Orange Team continued on its way to Starke Enterprises headquarters.

THE GRAY TEAM beetle, with its wasp escort, located its prime destination, a series of fish farms between Lake Decatur and the city of Tendonville. Hovering a meter over the water, the beetle opened its carapace, allowing the breeze to scatter a pinch of green flakes across the surface of the pond. As the flakes swelled and sank, fish gathered to snap them up. Gray Team flew from pond to pond dispensing its load.

2.8

After twenty minutes of caroming through the unlit tunnels of the Chicago Public Transit, Bogdan Kodiak arrived at Elmhurst MacArthur Place Station. After decarring, he paused on the platform to remove his charter patch from his shoulder. A transit bee buzzed him, ordering him to move along, move along. He made his way through foot traffic to the stiles and swiped his way out. Before leaving the station, he put on a pair of mirrorshades and buried his hands in his pockets to keep anyone from reading him.

The Bachner Building, where the E-Pluribus office was located today, was an oblong tower grafted onto a multi-block trunk foundation. Before entering, Bogdan stepped in front of a kiosk board, curious as to the state of his anonymity. The kiosk board stalled a moment, trying to ID him, and failing to do so, launched a generic kiddie advert about portable pets. Bogdan snickered and left, confident that as far as the world was concerned, he was still a thirteen-year-old boy.

Inside the Bachner Building lobby, the directory requested that he remove his shades, but he refused. He asked the directory where the E-Pluribus elevators were. E-Pluribus always leased three entire floors wherever they camped, as well as two private elevator cars and three dixon lifts. A bee followed him as he walked to the bank of elevators. When he invoked his right to privacy, the bee informed him that it was a house bee, and that since he'd refused to be ID'd, the bee was authorized to surveil him.

One of the dixon lift cars was coming down, and Bogdan joined the crush of people waiting at its door. He knew how E-Pluribus spaced the cars and that if he missed this one, there wouldn't be another for fifteen minutes. He was already late, so he took advantage of his small size for the second time that morning and threaded his way through the crowd. He didn't recognize any of these people, which meant they were daily hires. When the car arrived, Bogdan almost made it aboard, but instead got stepped on.

"*Owww!*" he cried.

"Sorry, little guy," said a man in front of Bogdan, "but you'll just have to wait your turn like everyone else."

"Oh, yeah?" said a man behind Bogdan. "Then how did *you* get in front of *me*, pal?"

"What are you saying, myr?" said the first man.

"I'm saying I don't care if you trample the kid, myr, but don't you fecking shove *me!*"

"Myren, myren," Bogdan said, afraid of becoming trapped between them, "there's no need to fight."

"Not unless you're the one cut out of a day's payfer," said the man at the front, who was trying to jam himself into the overcrowded elevator car, which made several unsuccessful attempts to close its doors.

"Relax," Bogdan told the men. "If E-Pluribus issued you an invitation for today, we will honor it. Irregardless whether we use you or not, we will credit you a full day's payfer."

"What do you mean 'we'?" said the man.

"I work for E-Pluribus," Bogdan announced breezily.

Everyone looked at him, and a woman inside the car said, "Like on a permanent basis?"

"Yeah," Bogdan said. "I have an employment contract. I am a senior demographics specialist, grade three."

"*People!*" the woman commanded. "*Inhale!*"

A sliver of space opened inside the car. The woman grabbed Bogdan by the lapel of his jumpsuit and pulled him in, the doors closed, and the car began to ascend. When everyone exhaled again, Bogdan found himself for the second time that morning pressed against a wall. Not by a couch, this time, but by an ample bosom. He closed his eyes and drank in its damp, honeysuckle fragrance. Numerous hands took little rubs at his head, but at the moment he didn't mind. As the elevator rose, people asked Bogdan how much E-Pluribus paid its employees, whether there were benefits, what kind of qualifications and genetic tests were necessary, and especially—were there any current openings. Snuggling in his tender pillow, Bogdan answered all questions as vaguely as possible.

"I've heard," said the woman, "that they'll make us insert these—ah—*devices* to register our—ah—*responses.*"

"That—ah—is true," Bogdan said.

"What are they like?" she said nervously.

Bogdan smirked. "Not to worry, my dear. They're small and harmless. They're called visceral expression probes, which sounds a lot scarier than they really are." Actually, he and the other regular employees called them potty plugs. And they called these people day holes. "After a couple minutes," he continued, "you won't even know it's there."

The elevator halted at the 103rd floor and opened its door to the E-Pluribus lobby. And what a lobby! The regulars called it the Temple, and it was the same basic arrangement E-Pluribus used wherever it rented space. The effect was one of vastness, and the intent was induced awe. For Bogdan, this space had long ago lost its novelty, but he still enjoyed seeing the effect it had on newcomers. He backed out of the lift and watched his fellow passengers step onto the limpid blue lobby floor. The floor seemed to extend for kilometers in all directions. Far on the horizon, it was bordered by giant stone columns, some broken and crumbled, some still joined by stone lintels. Beyond these lay a restive green sea.

"Oooo," said his female companion.

The cool air was spritzed with salty sea smells. Lightning crackled in the distance, and thunder rolled beneath their feet. Subliminal music swelled.

Of course it wasn't as though people had never visited a sensorium before. These days it took more than smoke and laser to make an impression, and if anyone knew how to impress humans, it was E-Pluribus. At the sound of a trumpet blast behind them, the daily hires turned to behold, not their elevator car, but a mountainous, stone ziggurat rising high into the yellow sky. At its truncated peak, nearly as high as the pink clouds, stood a gigantic corporate logo, the E-Pluribus Everyperson.

The Everyperson was one of the most familiar logos in the United Democracies, and this was its full-on version. It morphed rapidly and continuously, changing its sex, age, ethnicity, facial features, hair, and clothing into every conceivable combination. It was hypnotic to behold. People said that if you gazed at it long enough, you'd eventually see all fifteen billion inhabitants of Earth. Everyone but yourself.

People said that if you gazed at it long enough, you'd see ghostly images of your beloved dead, your departed parents, children, and spouses, your lost lovers, rivals, and friends, and everyone you cared for who predeceased you.

People said that if you gazed at it long enough, you'd see all the people you might have become if only you had made the right decisions or had better timing, connections, or luck.

For a corporate logo, it was a doozie.

On the stone steps beneath the Everyperson stood a pantheon of vid idols: thousands of the most celebrated hollyholo simstars of all time. This was the famous E-Pluribus Academy, the largest, most extensive stable of limited editions in existence. Bogdan's elevator companions gushed with delight. At the bottommost tier, Annette Beijing stood alone and waited for their attention. She wore the loose-fitting house togs she popularized in the long-running novella *Common Claiborne*.

"Welcome!" she said at last and with fervor. "Welcome *all* to the House of E-Pluribus!" She held her graceful arms aloft and bowed her pretty head. Her audience applauded rowdily. "Dear guests," she continued, "you have been chosen to join us today in the very important and quite exhilarating task of preference polling. As you know, society can serve its citizens only to the extent that it knows them. Thus, society turns to *you* for guidance. Each of you possesses a voice that *must* be heard, and a heart that *must* be plumbed."

She raised her hand to the ever-morphing statue high above them. "*You*, all of *you*, are the true E-Pluribus Everyperson. When Everyperson speaks in the halls of Congress or Parliament, in corporate boardrooms, jury rooms, and voting booths, it speaks with *your* voice."

She paused a beat and added, "Now I'm aware that some of you may find our methods a little overwhelming, especially if this is your first visit with us. Therefore, we have arranged for a few of *my friends* to stop by."

The host of simstars behind her chorused a resounding, "*HELLO!*" and the daily hires cheered.

"We invite each of you," Beijing continued, "to select your most favorite celebrity in the whole world, from any time period, to be your personal guide throughout the day. Feel free to choose your biggest heart throb. She or he is bound to be here. And please, we're all friends at E-Pluribus, so don't be bashful. Choose whomever you want. Even me!

"Now then, we have a full day of taste-testing, opinion-polling, and yes—*soul-searching*—planned for you, but before we begin, please review the terms and conditions of hire, and if you approve, authorize them. Then call out the name of your *heart's desire*, and he or she will come down to be at your side."

Few of the daily hires bothered to read the contracts that appeared in the air before them. They swiped them impatiently and called out the name of Beverly Bettleson or Cary Grant, Anguishello del Sur, Humphrey Bogart, Yurek Rutz, Marilyn Monroe, or Ronald Reagan, or one of thousands more. Every name called brought a hearty "*PRESENT!*" from the Academy. To trumpeted fanfare, the chosen demigods descended the grand staircase of the pyramid to join their gaga guests.

Bogdan took the opportunity to slip behind an invisible blind where he knew one of the service elevators waited to take him down to the employee fitting rooms. He passed Annette Beijing on the way.

"Hello, Boggo," she said, using her private name for him. "Got a smile for me?"

For her he had all the smiles in the world. She just so happened to be his own heart's desire. Though she was an adult, and though she was only a holographic sim, he loved everything about her.

"Sure, Nettie," he said, using his own private name for her, "though I am—ah—running a little late this morning."

She smirked and said, "We noticed. I won't keep you except to pass along a request from HR."

"HR?" Bogdan said, his voice cracking on the R. He tried again in a deeper octave. "HR? What do they want?"

"They'd like you to come in to see them on Wednesday afternoon at three-fifteen."

"What for?" Bogdan said. "Is it because I'm late? It was an accident. I couldn't help it. I'll never be late again."

"I'm sure you won't," she laughed. "You're a very punctual young man, so maybe that's not it. Checking the calendar, I see that Wednesday is your first anniversary with us."

Bogdan did a quick mental calculation. "You're right, my first anniversary. I'd forgotten."

Annette winked and said, "Well, perhaps E-Pluribus hasn't forgotten. Now, if you'll excuse me, Boggo, I have some stragglers to move along."

Behind her, Bogdan saw that two stalwarts were still trying to decipher their employment agreement. The others were already embarked on the long stroll across the vast marble plain with their chosen hollyholo companions. Their destination was a pavilion, barely visible, on the far horizon. The distance was only half illusionary; the actual distance was from the tower's southernmost bank of elevators to its northernmost stairwell, a distance of half a klick. It would seem even farther, however, with Harrison Ford, Count Uwaga, Audrey Hepburn, or Jim Morrison hanging on their every word. And by the time they arrived at the pavilion and were fitted with their potty plugs, E-Pluribus would have uploaded their personal upref files, established occipital neurolingual calibration, recorded an evoked response baseline, and tailored a morning's worth of test scenarios for them and them alone.

Bogdan shook his head in smug satisfaction as he entered the service lift. He had to admit he was getting to be an old hand at the upreffing biz. Maybe E-Pluribus had noticed the excellent quality of his work. Maybe Human Resources was going to extend his contract. Or give him a bonus or maybe a raise.

THE VISCERAL RESPONSE Probes—the so-called potty plugs—were the same for the regular E-Pluribus employees as for the daily hires. A probe consisted of a fasciculus of motile electrode filaments, tipped with synaptic couplers, in a hydrogenated glycol casing that melted at body temperature. It was fourteen centimeters long and conical in shape. It looked like a greasy, spindly, miniature Christmas tree. It smelled like bath powder. Application was simple. Bogdan had done it so many times he hardly thought about it, though it amused him to think of the first encounters with it that the daily holes must have. He entered a "fitting" booth, closed the door, opened the crotch of his jumpsuit, and sat on a toilet seat. The seat slowly lowered him onto the probe. A bull's-eye every time. There was a fleeting discomfort, a sense of fullness, as the casing dissolved and was absorbed into the submucosal lining of his transverse colon. There was a mild peristaltic spasm or two as the electrode filaments maneuvered to interface with his vagus nerve. By the time he refastened his clothes and exited the booth, he was a walking, talking, assay-kicking machine.

Bogdan hurried to his third assignment for the day; he'd already missed the first two. In a small auditorium, he joined a dozen daily hires seated around a holospace. They were still keyed up by the novelty of it all. Two of them were iterants—steves— who had already abandoned their hollyholo chaperones in favor of their own company. A few more holes—chartists—sat together in companionable silence. Bogdan gave the latter group a charter wave, which caused some doubtful looks—he wasn't wearing his Kodiak colors.

The auditorium lights went down. Theme music, like that of a comedy show, came up. Emitters transformed the auditorium into the lounge of a Chicago body clinic where a triad of attractive people—two women and a man—awaited the results of tests they had just undergone. These three had decided to surgically graft themselves into one individual, but were still debating about what configuration to use.

Bogdan, from his year's worth of experience at E-Pluribus, suspected that this was a consensus vid, his least favorite kind, in which the combined attention of audience members drove the plot. Bogdan watched the vid with resignation. Professional experience told him it would quickly devolve into a little urban tale of lies, deceit, and hurt feelings. The three beautiful, witty, obviously aff young people decided to graft their three heads onto one body, but whose body? And which sex? Or maybe a combined sex? For three people wanting to merge into one, they seemed curiously unable to agree on anything, and their bantering humor grew absurd.

Or at least Bogdan thought so. Laughter in the auditorium was sparse, and the story line took an odd turn. It began to focus on the canopy covering Chicago that was scheduled for retirement later that night. In a few minutes, the whole goofy surgical triad thread that had opened the vid vanished without a trace, and the three characters, much more sensible now, were frantically packing to leave Chicago in favor of a city still protected by a canopy.

Every once in a while, E-Pluribus introduced new threads into the story in an attempt to tease the audience's interest into new areas. One member of the triad won the lottery and didn't want to share the prize with the other two. The other two advertised for a new third without her finding out. The triad couldn't agree on where to go on vacation. And other equally silly complications. But within a few minutes, each new thread was captured by the audience's anxiety over the canopy. No matter where E-Pluribus tried to nudge the story, it wound up canopy, canopy, canopy.

BOGDAN'S NEXT ASSIGNMENT was to a much larger auditorium where he watched an hour-long E-Pluribus probable news program. The handsome talking heads began by reminding their E-Pluribus viewers that the probable news was just that—probable. It may or may not have actually happened and was not to be confused with corporate news.

The first half-dozen stories visited the sites of natural disasters outside the sphere of the United Democracies. Bogdan sat in a pan boat in the brackish floodwaters of the sub-Saharan. He walked among swollen-bellied babies in Azerbaijan and the victims of tailored cholera in Iraq. He swatted patch flies in Pakistan that covered people and livestock like a second skin.

The last story before lunch was about a space yacht disaster involving an important industrialist and her Hollywood producer daughter. Their graceful Aria Craft yacht cartwheeled out of control, burning like a shooting star. Bogdan blinked on the yacht to look inside. He was shaken vigorously, along with two beautiful, scantily dressed young women who cried out to him for help.

THE E-PLURIBUS BUFFET tables were laden with a wide variety of rich foods: steaks and chops, sausages, cold cuts, pastas, soups and chowders, curries, stews, goulash, rolls and breads, and desserts of every description. There was no visit limit, and the daily holes were not shy, returning time and again. The bulging pockets of their suits blossomed with grease stains from whole meals squirreled away for later.

Though the food was complimentary, it wasn't exactly free. It was all test food. Bogdan and his fellow preffers were still plugged in, after all, and were transmitting in most intimate detail the food's passage from eye to mouth to stomach and beyond. Their digestive tracts were singing for their supper. Not a burp escaped unnoticed.

Bogdan quickly grazed the buffet table, eating on his feet, and stuffing his own pockets with cookies, before leaving the lunchroom with fifty minutes to spare to go out and buy a phone. In the elevator going down, Bogdan put on his mirrorshades and made fists of his hands. Outside the Bachner Building, the sky was thick with noontime bees. His anonymity was apparently still intact because the first bee to drop down said, "Hey, kid, glyph this. *Free Always Everywhere!*"

"Desist," he said, not even slowing down, and the bee rose and flew away.

Another bee replaced it. This one said, "Hi, little fellow. Guess what! We'll pay you *one ten-thousandth* of a yoodie—*right now!*—if you answer six fun questions about your fave emollient."

Bogdan snorted. "I happen to be a *professional* E-Pluribus demographic control specialist. You'd have to pay me *way* more than that to answer your dumb survey. So, desist the feck outta here."

A third bee arrived, flashed the Longyear logo, and said, "We are currently running a special bonus offer." This bee, at least, had pegged him for a retroboy and not a real kid. He was about to dismiss it, when he remembered his meeting with the Allowance Committee that evening. Longyear was a rejuvenation clinic that Charter Kodiak sometimes used, and he was overdue for a session.

When Bogdan didn't immediately dismiss the bee, it went on to say, "Yes, myr, for each month you shed at one of our deluxe clinics, Longyear will throw in an additional two and three-quarter days at no additional charge. Think about it, you can retro-age a full year for the price of eleven months. And for your own special retroboy needs, this offer includes a complete endocrinological workup and regimen design. Would you like us to flash you the details?"

Bogdan almost uncurled his fingers to swipe the bee, but he didn't want the whole street to ID him, so he asked how long the offer was good for.

"You need to book treatment within forty-eight hours of right *now!*"

Bogdan dismissed the bee and continued his stroll along the arcade yelling "Desist, desist" every few meters. The bees weren't the only annoyance. There were more hollyholo sims here than real people, and they cleverly tried to lure him into their public melodramas by asking him for directions to this or that building. As if he knew. He purposely stepped right through them to let them know what he thought of them.

Bogdan strolled the arcade, evading bees and sims while he window-shopped. None of the windows addressed him by name. For about three minutes, a live pay-per pointcast of a WSA soccer match played right above his eye level, but he carefully avoided looking at it, and it eventually moved on.

Suddenly a woman literally fell to the sidewalk at his feet. Unthinkingly, he reached down to help her, but his hand went through her arm. She was another damn sim, and he was angry until she turned her head to look up at him. It was Annette Beijing! Not the Annette Beijing in her Common Claiborne role, but a darker, more angular woman, gaunt even, with sunken cheeks and spiky hair. An edgier, sexier Annette Beijing (if that was even possible).

"Oh, thank you, Myr Kodiak," she said, scrambling to her feet.

Damn! Bogdan thought when he realized she'd ID'd him. He had opened his hand for a split second when he tried to assist her. But one look into her oceanic eyes made it worthwhile.

She stood close to him and looked nervously up and down the arcade. Her expression was taut with fear. "What's wrong?" Bogdan said.

"You *must* help me," she replied.

"How can I help you?" He felt foolish saying this, but he couldn't help himself.

"Stay with me until Rollo shows up. Or *they* will surely come back."

"They who?" Bogdan said and found himself glancing up and down the arcade too. He told himself he'd play along for just a few minutes. It would only cost a few thousandths. It was worth it, and he deserved it.

"Feraro's men. They hurt me."

Bogdan noticed for the first time that her jumpsuit was torn and that she was holding the pieces together, trying to cover large, purple, finger-length bruises around her throat. "But why?" he said, truly alarmed for her.

"It's a long story. I have something they think belongs to them."

"Shouldn't you call the police?"

"They *are* the police!" She laughed bitterly. "And Feraro *swore* he'd kill me."

"For real?" said Bogdan. "I mean really kill you?" Hollyholo or not, there was a chance she might be in real danger, for sims were deleted when they were "killed." An individual copy of a character could be eliminated in whatever gruesome fashion the writers chose for the good of the story mat. If enough copies were killed, a whole issue could go extinct. Not that the Annette Beijing lines were in any danger of that.

There was the sound of wings, and when Bogdan looked up, he saw tier upon tier of bees recording this scene for paying viewers all over the world. Apparently this was a big scene for a very popular story thread, which meant this Annette might actually be slated for harm. (It occurred to Bogdan that her pay-per rates must be astronomical.) It also meant that he, Bogdan Kodiak, was being watched by thousands, maybe millions of viewers. He stood up a little taller and said, "Then we should get you out of here."

"Don't you see? It wouldn't do any good. We can't hide from them forever. Our only chance is to wait for Rollo." Bogdan was already beginning to hate this Rollo character.

Although they stood on the shady side of the arcade, Annette Beijing was lit from at least three angles with a soft, warm light. Her skin pulsed with vitality, and her hair plugs sparkled. "While we wait, let me tell you everything. That way, if they get me, you can tell Rollo. Promise me that you'll tell Rollo everything, Myr Kodiak. Promise me!"

The bees moved in for a closer look. Now Bogdan saw what was happening. He was about to be passed off to a minor character. It would take Annette a full five billable minutes or more to feed him the back story, and then she would exit the scene somehow, and he and Rollo would spend the next few hours looking for her until Bogdan ran out of credit. A clever evil scheme.

"Uh," he said, "Annette, I'm going to have to go now." Reluctantly, he turned away and continued up the pedway, but she followed. He walked faster, but she kept apace and pleaded with him to stay. "I can't," he said. "I have to go back to work."

"To E-Pluribus, I know. You're a very important man there. Can't you take me with you? You can hide me there."

"No, I can't. E-P would never allow it."

She tripped and fell hard to the pedway. He paused to look down at her. The knee to her jumpsuit was torn now too, and her skin scraped and bleeding. He watched in fascination as a bright trickle of red blood ran down her knee, and he felt an urgent desire to touch her, but he forced himself to look away and leave.

"Wait, Bogdan!" she called after him. "Don't abandon me. I beg you, Bogdan, don't throw me to the dogs!"

Though it killed him to say this to Annette Beijing, Bogdan said, "Desist." He turned and fled up the arcade, where he saw the familiar logo of a NanoJiffy store. He ducked inside to hide from the bees that followed him. The store was much bigger than April's stall at the charterhouse. It boasted *three* extruders—one dedicated to foodstuffs only—and a digester. There was even a small seating area with tables and booths. He went to the menu wall and paged through the extruder selections. Though the store was bigger than April's, it carried the same product lines—quick extrude public domainware for the most part, stuff for the kitchen, bath, personal hygiene, plus name brands and NanoJiffy's own, slightly more prole brand. All told, about a million products from shampoo to trombones were listed in the menu. Including phones.

Phones came in a dizzying array of forms and substances—wearable, edible, and environmental—many of which were free to the consumer. But Bogdan wanted his own phone, a phone without location or ID transponders, polling or advertising agreements, subliminal motivational messaging, remote medication metering, or membership to a suicide prevention community. In other words, Bogdan wanted a phone with no agenda outside the simple function of connecting him to the public opticom. This ruled out phone crisps, phone tattoos and nail polish, phone house plants and air fresheners, and most other models within his narrow price range. After five minutes of searching, he was about to give up when he stumbled across the new crop of cap valet felt, and he felt another pang of misery for his stolen Lisa.

Magister Scholastic Valets had come a long way since Kodiak Charter had bought him Lisa's "Little Professor" model nineteen years before. For the same price that they had paid back then, he could purchase a "Rhodes Scholar" with seven million times the processing power and triple the Turing index. But the price! This small strip of nanofacture cost *five hundred* United Democracies credits! Was it possible that nineteen years ago, when he really *was* a ten-year-old boy, his charter had the wherewithal to invest five hundred yoodies in his education?

Bogdan sighed and scrolled to the next page where he found exactly what he was looking for—simple phone patches that you stuck to your throat and behind your ear. They were audio only, but at 00.0001 UDC, the price was right. Bogdan ordered a set and went to stand in line next to the extruder.

WORK, WORK, WORK. Bogdan's first assignment after lunch was in a solo booth with a reclining seat. When he sat down, the booth lights dimmed, and he found himself in the pilot's seat of a two-person Aria Ranger, ripping along at full throttle in star-encrusted space. He reached out for the controls to see if the holo was interactive, and *it was!* Assignments were rarely this cool. A slight touch on the navigation ball caused the ship to veer in a most pleasing way.

"Where am I?" he said, and the control panel showed him a proximity map. Evidently, he was in the solar system, not too far from Earth. He turned around in his seat and, sure enough, there was the brilliant blue planet behind him the size of a beach ball. When he turned forward again, he was startled to discover a little man in weird green and red overalls sitting in the copilot seat. He wasn't much taller than Bogdan, himself.

"Hello, Myr Kodiak," the man said with a lopsided grin. "Please allow me to introduce myself. I am a simulacrum of Myr Merrill Meewee, formerly a bishop of Birthplace International, and winner of the 2082 Mandela Humanitarian Award. Are you familiar with the Birthplace organization and its work?"

"Sure," Bogdan said, "you're the ones against people."

The sim frowned. "Not exactly," it said. "Birthplace is a worthy institution that tackles the important work of humanely limiting world population growth. Reproduction bans are but a small part of what they foster. While I wholeheartedly believe in Birthplace's mission, a few years ago, I left the organization to pursue an even grander plan called the Garden Earth Project. Would you like to hear about it?"

Actually, no. Bogdan could care less about anything this wanker had to say, but he didn't want to accidentally end his sweetest assignment in a week, so he said, "I'm listening."

"Splendid," said the little man. "See that bit of shiny object off your starboard bow?" Bogdan looked where the man pointed and saw not one, but thousands of shiny objects. He consulted his map and realized it was Trailing Earth, the space colony at one of Earth's Lagrange points. "By the way," said the man, "this live spacescape is brought to you courtesy of the SNEEN, the Starke Near Earth Eye Network. Why don't we steer that way?"

Bogdan turned the ship toward the space colony. Immediately there was an auditory alarm, and a line on the map turned a pulsating red. "What's happening?" he said.

The ship replied, "Warning, proximity to high-energy beam. Change course to oh-three-six. Warning."

Bogdan didn't know how to set a course, let alone change one, and when he turned the ship again, the alarm grew shriller.

"Hurry," said the little man, "engage the hi-end filter."

Without knowing what it was, Bogdan ordered the ship to engage it. The stars in his viewports darkened, and a brilliant line, like a taut wire, seemed to stretch across space. The line was too bright to look at directly, but it was dead ahead and growing larger every moment. Being able to see it made avoiding it child's play, and Bogdan veered away. The proximity alarm fell silent.

"Good piloting!" said Bogdan's sim passenger. "That was one of our Heliostream microwave beams that supplies Trailing Earth with power. It originates from our solar harvesters in Merc orbit and transmits an average of one terawatt per beam. It would have vaporized us."

Bogdan cranked back the filter opacity and followed the microbeam to Trailing Earth. The ship passed corrals on the outskirts of the colony where thousands of captured iron-nickel asteroids awaited processing. It passed a row of microbeam targets: large, utterly black disks limned with nav beacons. Bogdan cut his speed when they reached the shipyards.

In the yards were rows and ranks of giant hoop frames. Many of the frames were covered with barnacle-shaped construction arbeitors that were busily weaving the seamless skin of the hab drums. The shipyards were crisscrossed with tightly choreographed flight paths of support tenders, construction bots, material trains, and waste scuppers, which seemed to fly at Bogdan from all directions. He zigged and zagged a lurching path through them, but there were too many, and his ship clipped the tail of a scupper and slammed into the side of a tender. There was a satisfyingly fiery explosion, and the holo ceased.

"Feck!" Bogdan said and brought his seat to its upright position. But the booth lights did not come on. Happily, the testing objectives of this vid seemed to be more important than his lack of piloting skill, and he and the Aria Ranger and his unnerving passenger were reset as good as new at the far border of the congested space yard. They were entering a second yard where there was very little traffic to avoid. A dozen or so hoop-shaped ships docked in the yard appeared to be complete. Their rings of sixty-four rotating hab drums were marked with names in giant letters: GARDEN TBILISI, GARDEN ANKARA, GOODACRE, GARDEN HYBRID, and so on.

"These Oships are taking on provisions," said Myr Meewee. "Everything they'll need to travel to another solar system, find a habitable planet, and colonize it. Steer that way, young man." He pointed to a passage through the donut hole of the *King Jesus.* "It's all right. The torus isn't energized yet."

Bogdan steered a course through the center of the Oship. At last he gained a sense of the size of these things. The *King Jesus* just got bigger and bigger. What had seemed like a bump on its lattice frame was actually a megaton freighter docked at a transfer port. The "I" of "KING" was as long and broad as a runway.

"When the torus is energized," the man said, "this area in the middle of the O-ship will become a magnetic target. We'll propel the ship by bombarding it with a river of particles and pellets from the same Heliostream harvesters that supply the microbeams. Would you like to hear more about this awesome technology?"

"By all means," Bogdan said, steering for the next Oship, the *Octopus Garden.*

His simulated host launched into a long-winded explanation of self-steering particles, laser course correctors, shipboard maneuvering rockets, and a redundant system for deceleration once the Oship arrived at its new home star system. As he talked, they passed out of the second shipyard and entered a traffic inwell leading to the populated core of the mushrooming space boomtown. The docking grid that extended out this far was incomplete and hosted few fabplat tenants. Bogdan aimed his Ranger at the inner core and punched the throttle.

"Lecture complete!" the Meewee sim said. "Had enough? Or would you like to hear about the Garden Earth Project and our 'Thousandfold Plan'?"

"Spare no detail."

"Splendid," the Meewee sim said. "Heliostream and its parent corporation, Starke Enterprises, are major partners in a consortium of leading industries working together to spread seeds of humanity throughout the galaxy."

The sim paused solemnly before continuing. "Those Oships back there, and hundreds more under construction, will each ferry a quarter million plankholders on a millennial voyage to newly discovered Earth-like planets in neighboring star systems. Each plankholder on board will receive title to a thousand acres of land on a new world, as well as a dwelling; a generous, lifetime share of food and supplies; unlimited access to education, medicine (including rejuvenation), cultural centers, sports facilities, vocational training, *and* full citizenship in whatever form of governmental structure the plankholders incorporate.

"Think of it, young man, a thousand acres plus all the ingredients of a happy life. Sounds like a lot, doesn't it? Frankly, it *is.* And do you know what we want in exchange for all of that?" The sim waited for an answer.

"Not a clue," Bogdan said. "A million yoodies?"

"That's probably how much it's worth, but we're offering plankholder shares for much less. We're exchanging shares for real estate here on Earth. How much real estate? One share per acre. Let me repeat that. For title and usage rights to one acre of Earth, you can get one thousand acres, lifetime material support, and citizenship on a new Earth. What do you think of that?"

"I think it's crazy," Bogdan said. "Where is someone like me supposed to get title to an acre of land?"

The simulated pitchman looked at Bogdan, seemingly for the first time. "I imagine what you spend on rejuvenation treatments alone over five or seven years could buy you an acre of Amazonian desert. We don't care about the quality or location of the land, as long as it's in a country or protectorate that guarantees private property rights. Even an acre of deeded continental shelf will do."

"What are you going to do with all that land? Build more gigatowers? Store nuclear waste?"

"You possess a healthy skepticism, young man, but you've got it backward. Remember the name of our project? Garden Earth? That's what we're building—a planetwide nature conservancy. We put the land we acquire into a trust for a period of two hundred years. During that time, the land lies fallow. No one lives on it or uses it for any purpose whatsoever. Our experts will help restore it to its pre-industrial ecology. Can't you hear Ol' Gaia sighing with relief?" The sim sighed theatrically.

"So, you're doing this thing as a sort of public service?"

"That's it exactly," the unfrocked former bishop's sim said, "a public service in the name of Mother Earth."

Bogdan rolled his eyes and raced for the heart of the space colony.

"Can't you get closer?" said Inspector Costa. Easy for her to say. She had remained behind in Chicago, as per protocol. She directed this phase of the hunt from a safe, dry booth in the UDJD tower. It was Fred and another on-call Hom-Com officer, Reilly Dell, who were in the GOV, churning up the muck at the bottom of Lake Michigan. This was turning into a long, long Monday.

In a pinch, a HomCom General Ops Vehicle made a dandy assault car, but a poor submersible. Its cabin could pressurize to only three atmospheres, it had no air lock or ballast tanks, and none of its array of weapons performed well at the bottom of a lake. Worst of all, its six powerful Pratt and Whitney hover fans adapted poorly to water propulsion. For these reasons, Fred was less than enthusiastic about tracking down Cabinet's new hideout.

Fred said, "I can't seem to get clear of this turbulence." He had submerged too deep and had disturbed the lake bed. He was trying to approach a Chicago Waterworks aquifer crib. The crib quickly sucked the cloudy water down its voracious inflow manifold, and when their visibility improved, Fred saw that they, too, were being sucked in. He fed power to the hover fans. At first the GOV responded sluggishly, but it broke free all at once and bobbed to the surface of the lake before he could compensate.

"Crap," he muttered as the car settled on the choppy water.

"Now, now," Costa said from her booth.

"Can't you have them shut down the aquifer?"

"Waterworks has respectfully declined my request," said Costa. "Two of their other cribs are off-line for maintenance. However, they've agreed to reduce its throughput by twenty percent, down to half a million liters per minute, but it'll be hours before the change is noticeable." Chicago was a thirsty city that drank eight billion liters of lake water each day.

"Let me give it a go," Reilly Dell said from the shotgun seat. "Believe it or not, I've actually had some experience with this kind of driving. There's a particular kite maneuver that should work."

Fred passed him control of the GOV. Reilly was not only another russ, but he lived in the same APRT as Fred, and they and their wives were part of a Wednesday night crowd. Reilly took the GOV down, but not deep enough to stir up the bottom. He dropped the nose of the GOV until it was pointing straight down. He reversed the fans and gave them only enough power to offset the crib drag. Though it was uncomfortable to be hanging upside down from the seat straps and craning their necks, now they could safely observe the entire crib facility.

It looked like what it was—a giant sucking drain. The inflow manifold was a ribwork of diaron beams that strained inrushing water and filtered out anything larger than a rowboat from being pulled in and transported ninety kilometers to the lakeshore treatment plant. The manifold itself was surrounded by a slightly convex concrete apron that covered about an acre of lake bottom.

Costa said, "Good work, Reilly. Hold it right there."

Reilly turned to Fred and made an apologetic face, but Fred shook his head. After working with Costa that morning, it was sheer pleasure for Fred to be sharing the GOV with another russ.

"By the way," Reilly said to him, "we confirmed the table at Rolfe's for tonight. You and Mary will be there, right?"

Fred was confused a moment. He was about to say that today wasn't Wednesday, when he remembered the canopy retirement ceremony advertised for that evening. There was supposed to be a party and a Skytel show, and the gang was going. Fred said they'd be there, and then added, "That reminds me, you sign up for that refresher course in bloomjumping?"

"I wasn't going to," Reilly said, "but after coming out here today, I think I will. Does the city even know how much wild shit there is still floating around out here? Whoever came up with the idea of dropping the canopy is nuts."

What the city maintained, what the media trumpeted, was nothing less than the end of the Outrage. In recent decades, terrorist attacks had become ineffectual and rare, or so the experts claimed. The rabid zealots of terror of the twenty-first century had been exterminated, or gone underground, or lost interest. Earth's biosphere was now 99.99 percent nanobiohazmat free. Any residual nanobot or nanocyst still dispersed in the atmosphere or hydrosphere had gone wild, lost its virulence, and was no more lethal than hay fever. In fact, most nanocysts contained ordinary pollen, not the smallpox, marburg, or VEE they were designed to ferry. The big, region-wide filtering systems known as canopies that had once been the lifesavers of cities throughout the United Democracies were now, according to the authorities, little more than giant, very expensive air fresheners.

The two men grew silent, lost in their own thoughts, which must have followed similar lines, for when they spoke again they'd come to the same conclusion.

"They won't be able to hire enough bloomjumpers," Reilly said.

"We'll be able to name our own price."

"You still certified, Fred?"

"You bet, and I'm going to increase my rating."

THIS MORNING WAS the first time in years that Fred had actually flown through the Chicagoland canopy. After dropping Inspector Costa off at JD headquarters, Fred had detoured to HomCom headquarters to retrieve his own GOV and to pick up another partner for the remainder of the mission. He was pleased to see Reilly's name on the on-call roster. As the GOV sped them across town to the lake, Fred quickly briefed his brother on the morning hunt for Cabinet. They passed over the breakwaters and their floating burbs and parks and were soon over open water. On the horizon ahead, the cordon of canopy generators rose from the lake like kilometer-high reeds. Due to the diluting effect of the lake winds, the generators were spaced close together. They pumped out such a dense concentration of anti-nano that the air around them seemed to ripple.

In no time, Fred's GOV had passed into the first canopy layer. Below them were the buoys of shipping lanes where the big lake freighters crossed the canopy.

As they flew through the outer canopy layer, they saw bright, pinpoint flashes outside the GOV windows, too numerous to count. Each flash marked a brief, intense battle between an invading nanobot or cyst and the canopy's anti-nano defenses. The anti-nano won every time.

"Doesn't look too bad," Fred said.

"About what you'd expect," replied Reilly.

They passed over the floating Decon Port Authority where they would be obliged to stop on their return flight. Soon they were leaving canopied space to the great, unfiltered world beyond.

Reilly told the car to give them an auditory count of anything glomming to the outside of the GOV, and they traveled some minutes before the counter chimed. In a moment, it chimed again, but then fell silent for most of the rest of the outbound trip.

Reilly said, "ID those."

The car replied, "Preliminary analysis identifies two gloms, both simple, one-phase carboplex disassembler nanobots." The GOV's frame and body were composed of carboplex—food for these particular bots—but it was covered with a tough and much less digestible diamondoid coating.

Reilly said, "Did you grease 'em?"

The car replied, "Affirmative."

When they reached the coordinates Costa had given them and no more chimes had sounded, Fred said, "Not so bad."

He spoke too soon, for a volley of chimes rang out. Then, after a pause, another volley, and a third. Numerous dimpled nozzles all over the car's exterior exuded layers of heavy anti-nano grease. Here and there, the grease flashed in little, white-hot puffs as it encountered and incinerated the nanobot gloms.

Fred brought up the windshield HUD and enlarged the over and under GOV diagrams. The gloms showed up as red flags when first detected, amber when engaged by anti-nano grease, and blue when destroyed. Besides carboplex disassemblers, the gloms they were picking up included concrete, diaron, and silicate disassemblers as well. In other words, typical city-eaters.

Fred said, "Not so good."

THE GLOM CHIMES had slowed down when they submerged. However, the anti-nano grease didn't cover the car evenly underwater, and the little amber flags persisted for minutes before finally turning blue.

"We've confirmed our preliminary assessment," Costa said. "Cabinet has an underground station here. It's very well concealed and heat baffled, and it has tapped into the crib's comm. You can just make it out in IR." The windshield HUD displayed an IR overlay. There, at about eighty degrees east, at the very edge of the concrete apron, Fred saw a few wisps of fluttering ghostly ribbons. These marked exhaust heat being swallowed up in the rush of cold lake water. Starke's hidden installation was putting out more heat than it could covertly dissipate.

"Must be working at capacity," Fred said.

"I agree," said Costa. "Ordinarily, it would be invisible, but now it's trying to run Starke Enterprises from down there."

"How did you find it?" Reilly said.

"Through snitches, of course," said Costa. "From about a thousand of Cabinet's closest friends. We were tipped off as soon as it went active. Mentars are their own worst enemies."

Reilly gave Fred a look like—doesn't she know there's about a million mentars listening in?

Fred cleared his throat and said, "So, what do we do now, Inspector? Go after it?" He wasn't too eager to tackle the waterworks crib in a GOV.

"No, we wait for the dredge to arrive. In the meantime, we've equipped one of the crib maintenance arbeitors with a probe. We're releasing it now."

Under the ribwork, a crablike mech was working its way around the manifold. It had a low-slung body and six wiry legs. It moved across the concrete apron with surprising agility by pulling itself against the suction along a grid of recessed D-ring grips. It traveled to the very edge of the apron, near a boulder where the waste heat seemed to originate, and reeled out a thin rod to probe the boulder. But when the probe made contact with the rock, there was an explosive flash, several of the arbeitor's legs lost their grip, and the arbeitor's body was whipped toward the intake. For a moment it hung from two legs, but these were torn away, and it bounced off the ribwork and disappeared down the gullet of the crib.

Reilly said, "Drink *that*, Chicago."

Costa said, "Looks like this backup's got teeth. I guess we might as well wait for the dredge. How you boys doing?"

Fred consulted Reilly with a glance and said, "We're fine."

"I see no need for you to be hanging upside down like that. We can watch through the cameras now; I doubt Cabinet is going anywhere. Why don't you level the car out."

Fred said, "What's the ETA on the dredge?"

"Twenty minutes, and an hour for deployment."

Fred consulted life support and power stores. Their trip out had consumed only a fraction of the GOV's supply. Again he polled Reilly with a glance. Reilly yawned.

The life of a russ seemed to involve untold hours of keeping watch in uncomfortable positions. But russes had a high threshold for discomfort and an uncanny tolerance for boredom.

"We're fine the way we are for now."

And so they waited. The GOV's glom monitor chimed every few minutes, unsettling Fred each time it did. He watched for each new red flag to turn amber and then blue. Before long, there was a louder chime. A red flag was blinking—there was a glom that the anti-nano grease could not reach. It was lodged in the door frame, one of the few seams in the GOV's otherwise unibody construction. Fred and Reilly watched the blinking red flag for several long minutes. Eventually, the car said, "Protocol suggests surfacing and preparing for evacuation."

Fred thought about it and said, "That might be wise."

"Not to mention smart," said Reilly.

Costa said, "What kind of bot is it?"

"Unknown," Fred said, "until the grease can reach it."

"Then why don't you do as your car advises and come up."

Fred nodded to Reilly, who righted the car and powered it to the surface. He released control of the GOV back to its subem pilot, which hovered the car a meter over the lake surface.

Almost at once, the glom flag stopped blinking and turned amber—the anti-nano grease had engaged the bot. The glom was a three-phase nanobot, a Nanotech Assault Engine, or NASTIE. Fred and Reilly stared at each other openmouthed.

Reilly said, "You don't see many of those anymore," and unbuckled himself from his seat. He went back to the passenger compartment.

Costa said, "You should evacuate immediately. Deploy the raft."

Fred said, "Aye, aye, preparing to ditch."

Reilly said, "Heads up," and tossed Fred a pouch of VIS-37 from the refrigerator. The two russes made identical sour faces as they popped open their pouches, raised a silent toast, and forced down the vilest, most intrusive of all the emergency visolas. It turned Fred's stomach. Reilly belched and went back to the passenger compartment.

Suddenly the NASTIE's amber flag turned blue—bot killed, crisis averted. When Reilly returned with the rescue raft cassette and their kit bags, he looked at the glom display and said, "Well, hell."

The two men watched the display for a while. Finally, Reilly said, "You still want to ditch or what?"

Fred said, "We could just eyeball that door frame real close."

Reilly said, "I'll do that," and went aft again.

"Take your grease gun," Fred called after him.

Reilly returned and got it from his kit bag.

Costa said, "What's going on?"

Fred said, "Our NASTIE is dead. We're going to stay aboard. Where's your dredge?"

"Are you sure that's such a good idea?"

"Anybody object?"

None of the monitoring mentars spoke up. Such decisions were usually left to the humans in the field.

Fred rotated the GOV to face the city, but they didn't have enough altitude to make out either the shoreline or the picket of canopy generators from this distance. Suddenly something startled him. Someone was standing right in front of his windshield.

It was Cabinet, the old lady chief of staff who had earlier addressed the UD General Assembly. She looked directly at Fred and said, *May I have a few private words with you?*

Nicholas, the Applied People mentar, said, "Commander Londenstane, what was that?"

The old lady outside the GOV raised a thin finger to her lips. *They cannot sense me. We are pointcasting directly to you. Please tell them everything is fine.*

Instead, Fred said, "What was what?"

"Your heart rate just spiked."

Fred hesitated. "Nothing," he said at last. "I was just thinking about how little you pay me for this shit."

BB of R Marcus said, "Do you require a privileged brotherhood conversation?"

"No, Marcus, thanks. I was thinking about a personal matter. Something at home. I'm not thinking about it anymore, so let's all just drop it, okay?"

Excellent, said Cabinet. *We have a brief message for you, so please lend us your generous russ attention.*

Fred didn't like this one bit, but he played along. At the same time, he couldn't help wondering how Cabinet was able to communicate with him right under the noses of some of the most sophisticated mentars in the world. And to commandeer his HUD, for that matter, for surely there were no emitters in the middle of Lake Michigan. Fred didn't lock his gaze on the apparition but swept his eyes across the horizon as though searching for the approaching dredge. He found the dredge too, a small dark bump on the horizon.

We will never forget the compassion you showed our family in our time of great need all those years ago. We realize that compassion is a famous russ trait, but in you it runs deeper than in most. In other fine ways as well, you seem a remarkably gifted man.

Fred thought, Yah, sure.

Our current situation is desperate, it went on, *and we are compelled once again to seek your compassion. We have a special request to make of you.*

Fred glanced at the woman on his windshield. Surely, it couldn't expect him to assist in its escape.

Ellen Starke, our late sponsor's daughter, was a baby when you were assigned to guard the Starke family. This morning she was critically injured in the attack that took the life of her mother. We fear that whoever assassinated Eleanor will not allow Ellen to survive. If we are taken into custody, even for a brief period of time, Ellen will surely die.

Fred experienced a sudden rush of anger at this dead aff's mentar. How dare it try to manipulate him?

Nicholas broke in again, "Sorry to return to this, Commander, but your stress levels continue to rise. Yet, we see nothing in your immediate environment to cause it. Do you believe, perhaps, that the NASTIE that has invaded your car is still viable? If so, you should request the Command to send a car to pick you up."

"That won't be necessary."

"Or a decon team," Nicholas continued.

This took Fred aback. That was why Nicholas was watching him so closely. It thought he was already infected by nano. He quickly said, "Listen, Nick, Marcus, Costa, Libby, Nameless One, and whoever else is out there copying. Such minute attention to my inner state of harmony is hampering my concentration on the matter at hand."

"Understood," said Nicholas. "Carry on."

Fred said, "But a backup car might be a good idea. Nameless One, please dispatch a GOV."

"Nameless One reports that it dispatched a GOV five minutes ago," Marcus said. "ETA is sixteen minutes."

Myr Londenstane, Cabinet continued, *Ellen needs me to watch over her while she is defenseless.*

So call Applied People and hire bodyguards, Fred wanted to reply. I'm not allowed to take on private jobs. But Fred knew Cabinet wasn't asking to hire him. It was asking for a personal favor. Fred wanted to know when had they become so chummy. He had worked for Eleanor Starke for six months in 2092 and '93. Her household consisted of herself, baby Ellen, and the freshly seared and emotionally shipwrecked Samson Harger. All the other domestics and guards avoided Harger because he was morbidly depressed and because he stank so bad. Fred simply felt sorry for the man. It was no big deal. Yet, when it came time for Fred to rotate to another assignment, Governor Starke, herself, threw a going-away party for him. In aff households, this was unheard of. In all his years, he'd not seen the likes of it. They'd even baked him a cake. And they'd given him a little gift—house slippers, and a slipper puppy to care for them.

We implore you. Are you willing to help Ellen survive?

Damn you, Fred thought. Still, he did not immediately expose the apparition, as he knew he must. His duty was clear; he was a russ after all, but the soulless mentar had found the perfect wedge—not his compassion, which it kept harping on, but a russ's most highly prized and most commercially valuable quality, his sense of loyalty. Doggish loyalty that, apparently, had no expiration date.

I cannot allow the authorities to dig up the lake bed. The inspector correctly identifies this as my last backup. However, it's not housed in the facility you have located. That is a decoy. Before the excavator arrives, I implore you to capture the decoy as though it were the real backup. I can tell you how to safely do this and still make it look genuine. In this way we can turn back the excavator. Nod your head, and I will proceed to give you instructions.

The slippers had worn out long ago, but he still had the slipper puppy. And for that he was going to violate his oath of office? Just what kind of russ did this mentar think he was—*defective?* "Costa," he said, "is that the dredge I see approaching?"

"Affirmative, Londenstane. It's still ten minutes out."

Fred knew where his duty lay, and yet he hesitated. The mentars, Nick and Libby and especially the Nameless One, might already know of his private comm, might be testing him, giving him enough rope. So why was he drawing it out? Perhaps he *had* been infected by the NASTIE!

"Costa," he said.

"Go ahead."

"Costa, ah—" Fred cleared his throat and thought about what a good life he had: Mary and their friends, his high rank at Applied People and all, how he loved his job. If only Cabinet had made it easier for him by trying to bribe or threaten him.

"Go ahead, Londenstane," Costa repeated.

Fred locked eyes with the lady in the lake. What did he owe the Starkes anyway?

"Um, Fred?" Reilly said from behind him.

Fred turned and craned his neck to see into the aft compartment. Reilly was crouched next to the starboard door, watching it through his cap visor.

"I see residual heat in IR," Reilly said. "But it's taking a godawful long time to dissipate."

Fred said, "That's enough. I'm setting this bird down. Prepare to ditch." When he turned back to the controls, Cabinet's image was gone, but so were half of the HUD displays. "Car," Fred said, "put down on the lake surface."

At first there was no helm response, but then the hover fans quit abruptly, and the GOV fell nose first into the water, and Fred was thrown against his harness.

"Commander!" Reilly said.

"Hang on, Dell. It's already infiltrated our control system. Better go NBC."

"Way ahead of you, skipper."

Fred ordered his own blacksuit to deploy its full NBC isolation mode. Gloves sprang from his sleeves, a soft mask dropped from his cap visor, and the visor's own HUD came online. The velvety blacksuit fabric turned shiny as it sweated anti-nano grease. He could taste bottled air as the suit inflated, giving it a slight positive pressure. His air gauge said he had two hours of air at one atmosphere.

"Libby," he said, "tell Nameless One we're about to execute an emergency evacuation."

No response.

"Anyone out there hear me?"

The car had ceased relaying his comm. They were on their own. Gingerly, he touched the control panel—everything aboard had to be considered hot. The panel was dead. And not only was the GOV sinking, but it was being drawn slowly toward the mouth of the crib manifold.

"I've got a dead stick," Fred said, unbuckling himself from his seat.

"Wait'll you see what I've got," Reilly replied.

Fred went through the companionway and was stunned by what he saw. The passenger compartment was in full bloom. The glom entry site at the starboard door was a furnace of molecular activity. A tough sack, like a living scab, covered it, glowing with inner heat and bulging ever larger. Its mop head of colorless microtendrils crisscrossed throughout the compartment, dissolving everything they touched and feeding a molecular mush to the main assembler under the scab. A NASTIE was the ultimate agent of opportunity, programmed to make the best use of whatever materials it found. In the GOV it had found a treasure trove of rare and restricted material: munitions, power plant and fuel, and the pilot subem and military-grade cables, sensors, processors, not to mention the living tissue of two russes. There was no telling what sort of assault weapon it could fashion from all these pieces.

Reilly was crouched against the port side door with a grease gun, melting the advancing microtendrils with little squirts of anti-nano. But they advanced as thick as cotton candy, and parts of his suit were scorched and brittle, and the raw meat of his flesh showed through. His blacksuit kept trying to cover his exposed skin with battlewrap, but the tendrils ate this too. Reilly was boxed in too tight to move. He'd never make it forward to the driver's cab in one piece. But with any luck, he'd be able to open the door at his shoulder.

Fred had to step back to avoid the tendrils snaking through the companionway. His suit's cooling unit cycled on to counteract the increasing air temperature in the GOV. He shouted over the noisy hiss, "We don't want to flood with lake water, do we?"

"Do it anyway," Reilly shouted back.

"I'll need you to work your door."

Fred retreated to the cab, grabbed up the raft cassette from the floor, and clipped it to his belt. He opened his weapons kit, found his own grease gun, and clipped that on too. The GOV's dashboard and control panels were sagging like melted chocolate. Fred pulled on a second pair of gloves and quickly rummaged through his kit to see if there was anything else he could use. He hated leaving the kits to the NASTIE, but there was no alternative.

Glancing out the window, Fred was shocked to see how close to the crib they had drifted. He prodded the seat frame with his discarded visola pouch to test how solid it was. In order to reach the escape hatch, he'd have to either sit in the seat or unlatch and move it aside. It seemed soft, so he unlocked it from its base and let it fall away.

Reilly moaned.

The escape hatch control was self-contained, not tied into the GOV subem, so it might still be uncontaminated. "Hatch, I declare an emergency and order you to open," he said.

No response.

Fred grabbed the manual latch and turned it. Though the handle bent in his hand, it still worked, and the hatch undogged and swung inward. A torrent of water poured in, knocking him over and flooding the cab. The cold water quickly reached the nano furnace in the rear and exploded into superheated steam. Fred's suit squealed a warning, and he ducked under the rising water. He hoped Reilly's suit could keep him from getting cooked. After a moment, the water level had risen enough for him to pull himself through the hatch. His suit now hugged his body, and a mouthpiece popped up inside his mask. He wrapped his lips around it and took a deep breath. The air gauge reset itself to account for the depth. Because of the pressure, his two hours of air had dropped to forty minutes.

Fred kicked aft to the GOV's port side passenger door. Reilly had unlatched it, but it seemed welded to the frame. Fred grabbed the handle, braced his feet against the side of the car, and pulled. He tore the softened door from its weakened frame, and out came Reilly in a gush of steamy bubbles.

A rope of tendrils followed him out, wrapped around his knee. Behind his mask, Reilly's mouth was stretched in agony. Fred took Reilly's grease gun and tried to cut the tendrils, but the gun was empty. He grabbed his own gun and cut them with a ribbon of grease. The tendrils encircling Reilly's leg, however, continued to digest his suit and send out tendrils of their own. Fred wrapped his partner's entire knee with ribbons of grease. When he looked into Reilly's mask, he saw that Reilly had passed out before taking the breathing regulator into his mouth. He would asphyxiate, and there was nothing Fred could do except get him to the surface as quickly as possible. He unreeled his belt tether, clipped it to the ring at the back of Reilly's collar, grabbed him around the waist, and pushed off from the GOV. Fred kicked and paddled furiously, but it was no good: the crib suction was too strong and Reilly's limp body too cumbersome. They continued to vector diagonally toward the big strainer at the bottom of Lake Michigan. He hadn't even managed to pull away from the GOV.

Fred changed course. If it wasn't possible to swim straight up, maybe he could reach the lake bed before being sucked in. There'd be less pull on the ground, and he could clamber away on the rocky bottom. His air supply alarm went off. He'd been working too hard and breathing too heavily, and his air supply dipped below fifteen minutes.

Fred relaxed completely, letting the water pull him and Reilly down. He tried to visualize all the gear packed into these HomCom blacksuits to see if there was something he could use to save their lives. It had been years since he'd certified in them, and he only got to use one every month or so. He asked himself, Do I have any spare air on board? and quieted his thoughts for an answer. He got one too, and would have slapped himself on the head if he could spare a hand. Yes, he had spare air. He had a whole freaking cassette of liquid air.

Fred tore the raft cassette from his belt and tethered it to Reilly. Now they were strung together with Reilly in the middle. When he pulled the inflate ring, the ultrathin foil billowed out into the shape of a flat donut, more deflated than inflated. They couldn't be more than thirty meters down, about three atmospheres, but the water pressure squeezed the raft's air to a third of its volume. Even so, the raft was buoyant enough to offset the crib suction. At least for Reilly's weight. Fred still had to raise his own weight by swimming.

The GOV seemed to fall away below them as Fred put everything he had into his arms and legs. The mirrorlike underside of the lake surface was tauntingly close when his air supply gave out. By then they'd risen enough for the raft to fill out, and soon it was racing for the surface with the two men in tow. Fred exhaled a seemingly endless breath of decompressing air from his lungs. They were rising too fast, he knew, and might suffer the bends when they surfaced, but there was nothing to do about that now.

At least the crib was safely distant, and the GOV a mere toy car. It struck the manifold ribworks and broke apart like a rotten egg, spilling its deadly yolk into the aquifer.

Fred thought, Drink *that*, Chicago.

When they broke the surface, Fred opened his face mask and sucked in sweet lungsful of air. Reilly floated faceup next to him. His eyelids and lips were blue, and Fred fished in his cargo pocket for a laser pen. He would have to cut the mask off Reilly and start mouth to mouth.

Three blobs of blue fell into the water next to Fred, and it took him a panicky moment to recognize them as a Technical Escort Team in gummysuits. A decon ambulance hovered a few meters overhead. A voice rang out from it, "Relax, Commander. We'll take it from here."

AT THE PORT Authority Decon Unit, Fred lay at the bottom of a two-thousand-liter HALVENE tank. He had plenty of time to relax as the concentrated lipoprotein solvent permeated his body. It flushed him of the dead crap that the VIS-37 visola had killed and the live crap it had missed.

Fred lay perfectly still, not even breathing. There was no need to breathe: the HALVENE was capable of oxygenating his cells. It was best not to move at all, for the cellular bonds of his tissues were loosened. Violent motion, such as gagging or coughing, could literally shake him to pieces. Besides, it felt good not to breathe. He'd never realized what an effort breathing took.

FRED'S PALLET AT the bottom of the tank began to rise. Apparently, he was done, stripped, clean. The pallet lifted him a couple of centimeters out of the HAL-

VENE bath and stopped. The solvent streamed out of him as though he were a sopping rag hung out to dry. He was saturated with the stuff and weighed three times normal. They'd leave him here to drip dry until his weight returned to twenty percent over normal. Then it would be safe for him to move. This might take another hour. Plenty of time for second-guessing.

Fred was besieged by self-doubt. He found himself dwelling on things he'd never given a second thought to before. Like this hinky woman, Costa.

Fred stopped himself right there. They warned you about having woodies in the HALVENE tank. You could literally burst your plumbing.

So he thought about his little private chat with Cabinet at the lake. What exactly had it expected to accomplish by singling him out? Did it actually think he would betray his duty? Russes were extraordinarily loyal to their duty. This was what made them an invaluable asset in the security sector. And it was the reason why his ur-brother, Thomas A., was chosen a century ago to serve as donor for the very first line of commercially developed clones. The original russ, Secret Service Special Agent Thomas A. Russ, had thrown himself on a carpet mine in the Oval Office to save the life of President Taksayer in 2034 during the fifth assassination attempt against her in a one-week period.

The grateful president, bloodied but undaunted, scooped up a gob of Thomas A.'s brains in a cracked china cup with the presidential seal and proclaimed to the media, "If loyalty can be cloned, let this be its template." Thus were the commercial clone treaties passed, and such was the standard every russ strove to imitate. So what was Cabinet's game?

Obviously, the mentar was in a tight spot with Starke's daughter; it was clutching at smoke and would do anything to protect her. But what did it mean when it said that he was an *exceptional* russ, that he possessed traits unusual for a russ? It should have come right out and said it—he had fallen out of type—for that was what it was implying. And Cabinet made this assertion based on what? his six-month stint in the Starke household forty years ago?

Fred shook his head, spilling HALVENE from his ears. His hunch was that it was all bluff. Cabinet didn't really imagine that it could sway him. It was a stab in the dark. Surely, that was all it was.

On the other hand, how did you really know what a mentar was thinking? Though the mentar brain was modeled on a human original, it was still an alien thing. Fred knew the typical hi-index specs, and since he didn't have anywhere to go, he listed them: axodendritic neurons ten times richer in microtubules (generating a hundred times the quantum flux per cubic millimeter) with no need for ionic pumps to create a voltaic differential (almost eliminating the latency period between neural firings), and a thousand times the density of synaptic junctions (that could close their synaptic gaps completely for brief periods of hardwired, superfast cognition). The mentar paste was more complex, stable, redundant, flexible, and robust than his own sloppy grayware. It could distribute its attention units to cover thousands of cognition tasks simultaneously. It could interface directly with an array of electronic devices: archives, cams and emitters, arbeitors, and superluminary and quantum processors. It could be stored, backed up, and mirrored. It could freely migrate to different media. The various subunits of the mentar brain slept in shifts and could watch itself dream. It never took vacations, never got sick, never had a documented case of headache. And with the exception of Marcus, any mentar that Fred met was more likely to be his boss rather than the other way around.

But what if he was, in fact, falling out of type? What if he was suffering from the dreaded "clone fatigue" that everyone was jabbering about lately? How would he know? Who could he ask? Marcus? If he so much as breathed a word of his self-doubts to the brotherhood mentar, it would force him to undergo psychiatric evaluation, something to avoid. Perhaps he could do his own research without telling Marcus. There were whole libraries dedicated to the russ germline: genanalyses, life performance studies, behavioral studies, biographies, as well as a substantial body of popular vids. He could research all aspects of himself, at least from an outside perspective. Russes weren't into self-analysis, and why was that? As far as Fred knew, no russ had ever set down a first-person account of what it was like to be a russ. Other types did. Evangelines published poetry. Every evangeline did this, even Mary. To write poetry was an urge rooted at the core of their germline. And lulus kept a history, too, of sorts. They hosted bawdy burlesques for their salon on the WAD, which people actually *paid* to access. Even the jeromes, the tight-ass, bean-counting jeromes like Gilles, kept a history. Or at least that was the rumor. They had a so-called *Book of Jerome* to which any jerome could contribute and which only jeromes could access. And of course there were the famous, but equally exclusive, Jenny Boards.

The russes had their *Heads-Up Log,* it was true. The *HUL* was a sort of history, maybe. Fred decided he'd have to spend some time browsing through it at the BB of R Hall. It might shed some light.

ENOUGH HALVENE DRAINED from Fred's body so that his brain stem registered hypoxia, and his lungs spontaneously resumed breathing. It surprised him; he'd grown used to not breathing. With breathing came the ability to speak out loud, and the mentar Nicholas took this opportunity to ask him how he felt.

Fred had to gently hack and spit a little before he could answer. "I'm fine," he said at last. "How's Reilly Dell?"

"I'm sorry, Myr Londenstane, but that's privileged information."

So it was back to *Myr* Londenstane. His shift as HomCom commander was over, and with it his privileges to information. He'd have to wait and see Reilly himself, and even then they wouldn't be free to discuss today's action. The damned Applied People client confidentiality oath.

Fred said, "Let me speak to him."

"That's not possible at the moment." This probably meant they were still patching him up.

"What time is it?"

"Fifteen-ten."

"So early?"

Marcus joined the conversation. "Don't worry, Fred," it said. "You will be paid for a full duty cycle *plus* combat differential *plus* a decontamination bonus."

"Yippee," Fred said. "I should do this more often."

The mentars made no reply, perhaps because they didn't register his sarcasm, or perhaps because they did. In any case, if they weren't going to tell him what he most wanted to know—Reilly's condition—then he didn't feel like talking to them. He felt like hell, actually. Like he'd been swimming in acetone. He could only imagine what Reilly must feel like.

FRED TOYED WITH the notion of writing the true history of russdom. He wasn't actually going to do it—that would be proof positive that he'd jumped the tracks, but as he lay suspended over the Decon Port Authority swamp tank, it was an interesting mental exercise. This was how he would begin: *To my cloned brothers: from our first days in russ school, we are trained to lay down our lives for our employers, but have we ever stopped to ask—are they worthy of us?*

THE PALLET FERRIED him to the catwalk. He pulled himself to his feet and held the railing until the vertigo passed. There were five dozen HALVENE tanks in this room, none of them now occupied. The escort team must have taken Reilly to a critical care room, one with hernandez tanks, in order to repair his injuries while douching him.

Fred padded to the dressing room. On a bench was a freshly extruded Applied People teal and brown jumpsuit, shoes, and a belt, all his size. The belt had a valet buckle. He'd have to use it or a skullcap until the HALVENE had dissipated from his tissues and he could grow a new inbody comm system. For that matter, since the solvent had removed his good nano, as well as the bad, he'd have to go through the whole time-consuming balancing act of reintroducing colonies of homeostats into his metabolism. A decon bonus didn't even start to cut it for him.

Fred picked up the jumpsuit. There was no point in taking a shower—he was already cleaner than clean. And he would smell of HALVENE for the next week in any case. He turned at a sound behind him, expecting to see Reilly. But it was a woman. It was UDJD Probate Inspector Costa. He covered himself with a towel, more out of pique than modesty.

"Myr Londenstane," she said, "it's nice to see you up and around and no worse for wear. I wanted to drop by and personally assure myself of your condition."

"What about Lieutenant Dell?" The question just slipped out, but Costa was under no Applied People confidentiality constraints. What she chose to divulge was her and her agency's business.

"Dell's doing fine. He's in rapid tissue regeneration. He'll need some new leg muscles."

"Thank you. I'm good, then," Fred said and glanced down at his bare feet. He was standing in a small puddle of HALVENE that had pooled inside his feet and was leaking from between his toes.

"What about all that hot shit that got sucked into the aquifer?" he said. "Won't that contaminate the city's water supply?"

"Oh, don't worry about that. That system was built sixty years ago during the Outrage. It's designed to deal with NASTIES. Chicago's water is safe."

"What about our city once the canopy comes down?"

Costa shrugged her shoulders. "How should I know?"

"Anyway, I wanted to compliment you on your excellent job today," she continued, "though I must say, things turned out unexpectedly."

"Oh?" he said.

"I probably shouldn't be telling you this, but the facility we found next to the crib was only a decoy."

"Are you sure?" Fred said. "A decoy?"

"Yes, the excavator dug up the real Cabinet a couple hundred meters away."

So Cabinet was in custody. Fred could feel his blood pressure rise and was glad Nicholas couldn't read him now.

"Congratulations, Inspector. A fine job," he said, holding out his hand.

"Was it scrambled?" he added hopefully.

She shook his hand with a crooked smile. "How many times do I have to tell you, the last one can't harm itself."

"So it's going through probate?"

"Kicking and screaming, but already out the other side. And now everything is fine, just like I said, and it can't believe that it put up such a fuss."

Costa stopped talking and gave him a funny look. Here it comes, Fred thought, the end of my career. He glanced at the towel he was still holding and Costa turned her back so that he could finish dressing.

"And did you interrogate it?" he asked.

"Libby did, yes." He waited for her to continue, but she said, "Anyway, today's mission was one for the books, wouldn't you say, Londenstane?"

"A thrill a minute, Inspector."

"Cabinet's through probate?" Meewee said, looking around the boardroom.

"Isn't that what I just said, your holiness?" Jaspersen snapped. He didn't seem at all pleased by the news, and Meewee wondered if this was an unexpected turn of events. "It asks to join us," Jaspersen went on, "and if no one objects—?"

The persona of the elderly chief of staff appeared behind Jaspersen's chair. Jaspersen motioned it to the other side of the table, and the mentar went around to stand behind an empty chair.

"Good afternoon, myren," it said. "Thank you for allowing me to address you. As you know, today has seen a great tragedy, but let me assure you that, except for a brief period during my visit to the pleasant offices of the Justice Department, the operations of Starke Enterprises have remained firmly in my hands. The court has appointed me to a custodial role until Eleanor Starke's estate is settled." The mentar paused to look at the individual board members around the table. Its gaze seemed to linger on Meewee. "I see by the minutes," it continued, "that you have elected an interim chair. I congratulate you, Myr Jaspersen."

Jaspersen nodded stiffly.

"I see also new discussion on the Federated Chinas matter. There is probably no reason to remind you that in Myr Starke's opinion, Oships were not 'for sale' at any price."

"That's true!" Meewee crowed. "I told you, Jaspersen."

"If Myr Starke were here," Cabinet went on, ignoring the outburst, "I am sure she would still oppose the Chinas offer. But as Myr Jaspersen has so succinctly pointed out, the times have changed. It is this board's prerogative to conduct Garden Earth Project business as it sees fit, and I will not oppose any valid decisions it makes. I will, however, use all of the substantial resources at my disposal to preserve Starke Enterprises' right to participate in making those decisions."

Meewee nearly bounced in his seat.

"That being said," Cabinet continued, "let me state for the record that I look favorably on the Chinas proposal."

Members let out a collective sigh, but Meewee was astonished.

"As a mentar, I supported my sponsor, even when I didn't agree with her. On this matter, I never agreed with Myr Starke."

"But that's *not true*," Meewee blurted out. "You and I and Eleanor had many private conversations on this topic, and you professed complete agreement with her viewpoint."

"Furthermore," Cabinet said, "although I intend to retain Starke Enterprises' second seat on this board, the current occupant of that seat may not be the best choice to fill it. I'm thinking that someone from senior management would make a more informed representative."

Meewee jumped to his feet, "You can't do that!"

Cabinet turned to Meewee. "You happen to be correct, Myr Meewee. I cannot replace you now or in the immediate future. Under custodial guidelines, I am to maintain current Starke Enterprises operations without making major changes, at least until the fate of the corporation has been resolved. I believe shuffling members of Starke Enterprises' many boards might be interpreted as exceeding my authority. But be assured, this situation is only temporary."

Cabinet turned back to the board. "I would like to close my presentation by offering my view of the future of Starke Enterprises, if the board would care to hear it."

"By all means, Cabinet," Jaspersen said eagerly.

Meewee covered his face with his hands. He should have known it was too good to be true, Eleanor's brilliant plan. He had failed her.

"The bulk of Eleanor's estate," Cabinet continued, "including all of Starke Enterprises and all of its subsidiaries, will pass to her daughter, Ellen. I am custodian until Ellen is declared competent."

Meewee raised his head. Ellen? He'd been so preoccupied with the future of the GEP, he'd given no thought to the fate of Eleanor's daughter during this whole loathsome day.

"Tragically," Cabinet continued, "Ellen may not survive her trauma. If she dies or is never declared competent, Starke Enterprises will be broken up and sold by the court. In that case, I shall recommend to the executor that interested Garden members be given first option to Heliostream and other subsidiaries directly involved in the project."

Meewee caught Chapwoman and Jaspersen exchanging a sly glance.

"If Ellen does recover, as we all hope she does, it'll be up to her to decide Starke Enterprises' future and my role in it. My guess, based upon a lifetime association with her, is that she'll want nothing to do with her deceased mother's corporate interests and that *she* will break it up for sale."

Maybe, Meewee thought, or maybe not. He, too, had a long association with the girl, and although she might never fill her mother's shoes, he was certain she would respect Eleanor's legacy. If only he could talk to her, he was certain he could persuade her. Maybe Garden Earth wasn't dead yet.

"Excuse me," he said. "Where is Ellen right now?"

Cabinet turned to him. "I believe she's still in transit."

"Transit to where?" Meewee said. "I want to pay my respects."

"I will convey them for you," Cabinet said.

"Thank you, but I wish to pay them in person."

"I'm sorry, but Ellen's whereabouts are not public information."

Jaspersen cleared his throat and said, "I would ask you two to please conduct personal business like this outside this meeting frame."

"But—" Meewee said.

Relax, Merrill, Zoranna said. *Ellen is arriving at the Roosevelt Clinic in Decatur.*

The Roosevelt Clinic was one of Byron Fagan's facilities. Meewee glared at Fagan, who looked away. Coward, he thought. You're all cowards, conspirators, bastards.

WHEN THE MEETING adjourned, Meewee left the boardroom and took a lift down to his subterranean offices. The handful of Heliostream employees he passed along the way seemed unaware of the morning's profound events. Behind his office door, Meewee sagged with exhaustion. He collapsed into his armchair for a gentle massage and ordered his vermilion overalls to loosen up a size or two. That felt better. "Arrow," he said, "fetch me a glass of Merlot. And while you're at it, fix me a little something for lunch."

"Complying," said his mentar.

Mentar. A dozen years ago, when Eleanor offered him Arrow's sponsorship, she had assured him that the AI was in the hi-index range. It was his first personal relationship with anything more powerful than a belt valet, since Birthplace had been chronically underfunded and unable to provide its staff with personal assistants. At first he had been reluctant to accept Arrow—he still had "sentience slavery" issues—but Eleanor had made it clear that Arrow, employment at Heliostream, and a seat on the GEP board were a package deal. Although Meewee had had very little personal contact with mentars, he quickly assessed Arrow's abilities to be sub-par, especially when compared to the leading sentients he began to deal with on a daily basis: Nick, E-P, Cruz, and especially the intimidating Cabinet. Next to them, Arrow seemed more like a minimally adequate office subem. It lacked any amount of initiative or self-awareness. It didn't seem to have a personality whatsoever, and as far as he could tell, the other mentars dismissed it as wasted paste.

An arbeitor rolled up to him bearing wine and a cucumber and avocado sandwich, his favorite. At least Arrow knew how to access his upref file. Meewee ate the food quickly, and the wine helped settle his nerves. After the meal he snuggled into the armchair and tried to recall all he knew about Eleanor's daughter—which wasn't much.

"Arrow, when and where was the last time I saw Ellen Starke?"

"On September 30, 2133, at the Louis Terkel Center Reception."

Meewee vaguely remembered the reception, but not the girl. "What did we talk about?"

"Ellen Starke shared news of the McCoy Award nomination for her novella *House Guest.*"

It was coming back to him. The girl could go on for hours about people and things he'd never heard of. He remembered that she was quite pretty, at least a head taller than he was. She had bony shoulders that men must find attractive. All in all, she seemed to feel comfortable talking to him. Why wouldn't she help him save her mother's life work? Especially if he framed it in those terms—her mother's *life work.*

Satisfied with his approach, he closed his eyes and told Arrow to place a call to the Roosevelt Clinic in Decatur.

Done, Arrow said.

Meewee opened his eyes to find himself apparently standing near a window that overlooked a lush, spacious lawn beyond a row of ornamental chinaberry trees. On the wall next to him, a coarse fabric arras depicting a sea battle was slowly reweaving itself into something more pastoral. Likewise, beneath his feet the parquet floor was reshuffling its hardwood tiles in kaleidoscopic fantasies. It was the kind of busy decor that would drive someone like him batty.

Incongruously, there was a cooking odor in the air, like fried bananas. Quite yummy smelling, actually.

"May I help you?" said a voice behind him. Meewee turned to see a man with a careworn face in a long white medical jacket. He approached Meewee and raised his hand in a holo salute, which Meewee returned. "Good afternoon, Myr Meewee, and welcome to Roosevelt Clinic, a wholly owned facility of the Fagan Health Group. I am Concierge, the group's mentar. What can I do for you?"

"Concierge, is it?" Meewee said, tilting his head back to look up at the mentar's face. As a short man, Meewee was well used to tilting his head to talk to most people, but for the love of Gaia, why did he have to do it for a machine? "Since you know my name, mentar, you must know my business."

The mentar seemed stumped, genuinely so. "I assume you're here to see one of our guests, but I do not find your name on any of our guests' FDO list."

Meewee was tired of the same old power game. And it was doubly hard to take coming from a soulless construct. "I'm here to check on the condition of Ellen Starke," he said mildly. "I understand she has been brought here. Please bring me to her."

"I can neither confirm nor deny that we have such a guest, Myr Meewee, and it's not our policy to act as social intermediaries. I suggest you deal with your acquaintances directly. When they put you on their FDO list, and if they are here, I will readily admit you."

Arrow! Meewee said. *Call Ellen Starke's mentar—and remind me what its name is.*

Its name is Wee Hunk, and I have it on the line.

The scene around Meewee changed abruptly; he and Concierge were standing in a darkened room, joined by a third man. Wee Hunk was a cartoonish Neanderthal in an animal skin anorak. Beetle brow, bowed legs, impossibly bulky muscles. Meewee didn't recall this mentar at all, as he surely would have.

"I'll leave you two alone," Concierge said. The white-jacketed mentar raised his hand to both of them and left the room.

Wee Hunk raised his hand too and said, "Myr Meewee, thank you for coming."

"I came as soon as I was free."

"That was considerate of you."

Meewee glanced at the mentar to see if it, too, was mocking him. But its features were so pronounced, its expressions so large, it was hard to tell. He replied, "I need to speak to Ellen as soon as she's awake. Please take me to her."

"At once," the caveman said and turned and walked away. Meewee hastened to follow, but they went only two steps before Wee Hunk stopped short in front of a wall of slanted windows. "There she is," he said, gesturing to a surgical theater below.

Meewee looked down into the brightly lit room expecting to see the young woman, but what he saw was a chromium table and three people in sterilewrap gowns. On the table lay a scorched and badly dented safety helmet. He had forgotten that she was recovered in a helmet.

"They don't have her out yet?" he said.

"The doctors aren't sure how best to unclench it," Wee Hunk said. "It took quite a beating in the crash. Two of its cryonics coils failed, as well as its first responder interface. Ellen's life signs are strong, however."

"That's good to hear," Meewee said, momentarily distracted by a new scent in the air—vanilla and almonds? What strange odors for a scape like this. "It's nothing serious then? No lasting brain damage?"

Wee Hunk said, "Let's wait until the surgeons have had a chance to look at her before we make medical pronouncements."

"Yes, of course," Meewee said.

"A safety helmet can't prevent all trauma to the brain," Wee Hunk said, "and they do a certain amount of damage all by themselves. Fortunately, most of it is correctable. Ellen's doctors are concerned about the less than optimal level of life support her brain has endured and the length of time it has endured it.

"Now, Myr Meewee," the animal skin man continued, "was there something in particular that you wanted to discuss with Ellen?"

"Yes, there is, but it's confidential. Put me on her FDO list and inform me as soon as she regains consciousness."

The caveman inspected his thick fingernails and said, "With all due respect, I don't think so."

"Sorry?"

"Myr Meewee, Ellen has never had much of a personal relationship with you. You are neither friend nor family. If you like, however, I'll put your name on the invitation list for a reception to celebrate her recovery, but that's all."

"You don't understand!" Meewee said. "I have urgent Starke Enterprises business. It's not up to you to decide whether or not I can see her."

"On the contrary," the mentar said, crossing its bulging arms, "Ellen is *solely* my responsibility. The court has appointed me guardian ad litem until she recovers.

And as for Starke Enterprises business, Cabinet informs me that your tenure there will shortly come to an end. I suggest you put whatever it is you wish to tell her in a memo that I will see she gets as soon as she's strong enough to deal with business matters."

Meewee wagged his finger at the ridiculous cartoon. "You have no right! You don't know what you're doing!"

Commotion in the surgical theater below caught their attention. A technician rolled a vat of clear liquid next to the procedure table where two surgeons were initiating the helmet's unclenching sequence. The helmet blossomed like an eight-petaled flower, and in the center, where Ellen's head should have been cradled, sat a plastic mannequin head instead.

Wee Hunk's beetle brows rose in alarm. "That's not possible!"

"What does it mean?" Meewee said, but he said it to his empty office where he again found himself sitting in his armchair.

If there was any doubt in Meewee's mind that Eleanor's yacht had been sabotaged, it was thoroughly dispelled by what he'd just witnessed. Ellen was missing. Meewee jumped to his feet, intent upon doing something to help, but he didn't have a clue what. He felt like a tiny fish in a tank full of sharks.

"You have a visitor," Arrow announced.

"Tell them I'm busy!" he snapped at his so-called mentar. Couldn't it even deal with routine office tasks?

"It's Cabinet," Arrow replied.

Meewee felt a rush of fear. What else could go wrong today? "Let it in," he said.

Cabinet instantly appeared in his office as the attorney general persona, a middle-aged woman who had always struck Meewee as the most ruthless of the bunch. At this moment he found its familial resemblance to Eleanor unnerving.

"What do you want?" he asked it point-blank.

"Nothing, actually," the mentar said. "I just came to personally notify you of your termination from Heliostream, effective at close of business today. You will vacate these offices and turn in whatever verification codes you control and whatever Heliostream or Starke Enterprises property is in your possession. That includes the mentar Arrow. Also, vacate your company housing at your earliest convenience, but no later than tomorrow afternoon."

"You're firing me?" Meewee said incredulously.

"Firing, sacking, canning, downsizing, excessing, whatever you want to call it. There are so many quaint expressions to choose from."

"But I thought that as custodian, you lack the authority to remove me."

"From the GEP board, that is correct. But I have more latitude over employees."

"But," Meewee sputtered, "but terminating my employment strips me of my seat on the board and amounts to the same thing."

"Funny how problems sort themselves out, isn't it? But don't be so glum, Bishop; we are prepared to offer you a generous separation bonus, so long as you are cooperative."

Without waiting for a reply, Cabinet vanished, leaving behind the Starke sig, which melted into the air like vapor.

2.11

The Blue Team was within sight of the Gary Gate when it was attacked. One moment the team of bee and wasps was crossing a suburban canyon at rooftop level, and the next moment it was engulfed in a whiteout of diatomic dust. The jagged, microscopic grit clung to the bee's exoskeleton, cams, and feelers. It worked its way through the bee's seals and jammed its joints. Within moments, the Blue Team bee was spiraling blindly to the ground. Before it could hit, a jet-powered scupper swooped down like a bird of prey and scooped it into its V-shaped bow catcher. The bee tumbled through slotted gates into the scupper's gullet, breaking a wing, and landed in a dark collection cage crowded with other damaged mechs. Media bees, witness bees, other mechs-for-hire, a police minidrone, and a smashed homcom slug. All of the captured mechs that were still viable were on Red Alert. The dark space inside the scupper was bright with Mayday transmissions in all spectra, but nothing penetrated the scupper's shielded hide. The captives seethed in the tight space, thrashing broken wings, butting heads, and grinding themselves into a hash of shattered components.

As the scupper repeatedly changed course, the frantic mechs were dashed like pebbles against its cage walls. Blue Team Bee was unaware that one of its own wasps was present until the wasp grasped it around the middle. It, too, had been captured. Or rather, the wasp had followed its leader in. Now it wrapped its articulated segments around the bee, doing its best to buffer it against the violence with its own body.

When at last the scupper came to rest, its battered cargo gradually settled down. The bee ordered the wasp to release it and to try to cut through the cage wall with its lasers. But the cage was lined with plasfoid velvet that soaked up the concentrated laser light like a sponge. So, the bee instructed the wasp to pick at the velvet with its pincers, pulling filaments out one at a time. If it could breech the plasfoid in even one pinpoint spot, its lasers could burn a hole through the monster from the inside out. Other able-bodied mechs joined it in picking velvet strands.

Too soon, the scupper was in motion again. It dove, peeled out, tumbled, and looped. The wasp again grasped its bee protectively while the mechanical mulch flew about the cage. Meanwhile, the bee ran scenarios. If its wasp failed to pick apart the plasfoid velvet, the bee could order it to incinerate broken mechs against the cage wall, perhaps creating enough heat to melt the velvet lining. If all else failed, the bee would order its wasp to ignite its own plasma in a tiny fireball taking out prisoners and prison alike and destroying all traces of the bee, itself.

Before the bee could decide on a course of action, the scupper made a sharp dive from a great height straight into the ground. All the mechs slammed together against the forward bulkhead, and Blue Team Bee's systems went dark.

SAMSON REACHED THE fourth floor of the charterhouse undetected. He tiptoed past the open door to the Green Hall where some of the Kodiaks were having coffeesh. He tiptoed past the closed door to the Administrative Office on the third floor, where Kale worked on the charter's household accounts.

When Samson reached the ground-floor foyer, he donned a broad-brimmed hat and selected his favorite bamboo walking stick from the charger.

"Might I suggest the maple stick, Sam," said Hubert.

"I like this one."

"The maple stick carries a heavier charge, as well as a blade."

Samson thought about it for a moment. The pest was probably right. He substituted the maple for the bamboo. Glancing around at the old charterhouse one last time, Samson touched the palmplate, and the heavy street door slid noiselessly aside.

On the steps, he looked left and right. There was little foot traffic on the block at this hour, few patrolling bees, and no Tobblers in sight. He descended to the street and, as quickly as he could, walked in the direction opposite the entrance to the NanoJiffy. Before he reached the end of the block, however, one of the Tobbler doors opened and a pair of Tobbler men came out.

Houseer Dieter and Chartist Hans, said Hubert in his ear.

Samson muttered, "I know who they are." He went to the curb and turned his back to the men, hoping they would go by without bothering him. But Charter Tobbler was nothing if not nosy, and they stopped to chat.

"A fine afternoon to you, neighbor Kodiak," said Houseer Dieter.

Samson acknowledged them with a nod.

"A fine day for a journey," said the other.

Samson followed the man's gaze to his maple stick. He would have liked to test its charge on him, but instead he said, "It's true that a stroll to the end of the block and back qualifies as a journey for me these days."

"Well and fine, and we shan't keep you. Do enjoy your stroll." Before leaving, however, the houseer asked, "By the way, what word on our request for inspecting the Kodiak rooms?"

Samson hesitated, and Hubert briefed him, *The Tobblers think Howe Street is being undermined by material pirates. They want to inspect our part of the building for damage. Houseer Kale hasn't made up his mind whether or not to let them.*

Samson said, "I'm afraid, Myr Tobbler, that I am but a useless appendage to the clan. You'll have to ask Houseer Kale about that."

"I've tried on several occasions to reach Houseer Kale, but he does not return my calls."

"That's probably not his fault," said Samson. "Our houseputer's efficiency grows worse each day. Lately, it spills all sorts of data, including phone calls."

"In that case, we'll knock on your door and ask him in person."

Samson froze. It would do him no good to have these Tobbs mention to Kale that they saw him on the street. "Unfortunately, our houseer is away on business. He won't be back till tonight."

"Splendid," said Houseer Dieter. "We'll speak to him tonight, then." The two Tobblers continued on their way.

Our taxi is arriving, said Hubert. *I told it to pick us up around the corner.*

Samson hurried to the end of the block and turned the corner just as a yellow-black-yellow car dropped from the grid in a cloud of dust and opened its passenger compartment door. Samson clutched the seat and door frame and levered himself into the car. There was already a passenger inside who smiled indulgently at this incredibly old man, at least until his reeking stench reached her. She looked confused, and her eyes began to water, but she continued to smile.

"Good afternoon, Myr Kodiak," said the taxi, "and welcome aboard. At Hi-Top Charter Taxi, we're pleased as punch to cater to your transportation needs."

"I thought I ordered a private car."

"Your assistant has already indicated your destination, Myr Kodiak, and I have charted a route requiring only three or four intervening stops. Now, if you'll sit back, the seat will secure you, and we'll be on our way."

Samson leaned back in the plush seat. Its cushions swelled around his thighs and waist to hold him in a gentle but firm grip. Satisfied, the taxi revved its powerful fans and lurched into the air. The woman beside him groaned and held her hand against her mouth. She looked a little green.

The taxi entered a nearby up-spiral and climbed around and around to the local grid. Samson closed his eyes for this dizzying part of the trip, while his fellow passenger was huffing through her mouth and swallowing repeatedly. Finally, she doubled over and vomited on her shoes.

Samson watched her and said, "Sorry, but I have that effect on people."

The woman shook her head and vomited again.

"Myr Cornbluth," said the taxi to the suffering woman, "I perceive you to be in physical distress. Shall I divert to a medical facility?"

The woman wiped her mouth with a towelette that the armrest dispensed. Floor scuppers were already cleaning up the mess at her feet and sponging her shoes with their busy little tongues. "No," she said to the taxi, "take me to a train station."

The taxi dropped to the CPT station located not far from the charterhouse. The woman swiped the pay plate, and her door opened. Before she decarred, she turned to Samson and said, "Best of luck to you, myr. I had a brother—" Sudden tears welled in her eyes, and she did not finish.

Samson was taken aback by such unexpected civility from a stranger. Before he had a chance to reply, two new passengers shoved past the woman and hopped into the taxi, only to hop out again just as quickly.

The taxi waited another half minute, and when none of the other people waiting in the taxi queue approached, it latched its doors and rose into the air. "Sorry for the delay, Myr Kodiak. We are rerouting and will depart at once to your destination in Bloomington."

"It's about time," said Samson.

Sam, Hubert said, *I have just contacted the manse, and Eleanor and Ellen aren't there.*

"Are they still up at Trailing Earth?"

No, and Cabinet doesn't return my calls.

"Well, find them! I can't do this without at least saying good-bye."

Sam, prepare yourself for some very bad news.

"What bad news?"

The media is reporting a space yacht crash.

"Yes?"

Both Eleanor and Ellen are reported dead.

"But they said they'd meet me at the manse," Samson said, aware of how stupid he sounded. "Are you one hundred percent certain, Henry?"

I'm checking sources.

"Oh, Henry, you shouldn't say terrible things like that until you're absolutely certain. It's tormenting. You should know that."

I am certain, Sam. Only the details disagree. It's possible that Ellen may be retrievable.

The taxi did a U-turn and headed back the way it came.

"What's happening?" Samson said.

I told the taxi to take us home.

"No, taxi, ignore my valet. Take us to Soldier Field."

Are you sure, Sam?

"This doesn't change a thing," Samson said. He leaned back in the pillowy seat and shut his eyes. "I have to go through with it. Now more than ever. Soldier Field, taxi, and step on it."

APPROXIMATELY TEN MINUTES after systems crash, as measured by an internal timekeeper, the Blue Team bee's noetics rebooted. Its self-repairing bots had been released and were busy field-patching the bee's vital systems. In the cage around the bee, only a few other mechs were stirring. Blue Team Alpha Wasp was dead, broken in two, both segments still clenched around the bee in a death grip. Wasps were expendable and carried no repair nano.

A crinkling sound alerted the bee to a spot on the cage wall where the velvet shield was melting away from the alloy fuselage. Blue Team Beta Wasp was lasering from the outside. The bee, encumbered by the locked segments of its dead companion, clawed across the debris pile to the wall. But the homcom slug got there first and blocked the growing breech in the wall with its body. It was sending a Mayday to its base through the broken RF shielding. This was not good. The bee could ill afford to be captured, and it had no means of destroying itself without help from its remaining wasp.

Precious minutes passed before the wasp cut a hole large enough to accommodate the bee, but the slug still blocked the way. As the bee worked through its options, the slug tried to crawl through the too-small hole itself. There was a hiss as its skin made contact with the hot metal edge, and it retreated reflexively, clearing the way for the bee.

While Blue Team Bee waited for the metal to cool, it ordered Beta Wasp to reach its grippers through the gap and break off the legs of its sister that still encircled it. Freed of its burden, the bee pushed the pieces of the wasp through the hole to Beta Wasp before crawling through itself.

The scupper had smashed into a pile of bricks at the back of a tiny garden that was wedged between two buildings. The dead scupper was a Frankensteinian contraption pieced together from odd bits of technotrash. Burn marks across its diaron armor traced the beta wasp's probing laser fire. As the two surviving mechs of the Blue Team dragged the pieces of their broken comrade from the fallen scupper, the bee took stock of their systems. Its own repairs were proceeding apace, but it still could not fly. Its power cells were more than half depleted. Three of its six wings had suffered broken struts, and one wing was shorn off completely and was missing. The beta wasp was undamaged, but it operated on reserve power. Worse, it had depleted its store of weapons plasma. The dead alpha wasp, on the other hand, still had three-quarters of its original supply. They collected all of its pieces except for three of its six wings. The wings were of little consequence, for a wasp's wings were off-the-shelf and sufficiently anonymous. The bee's missing wing, however, was state of the art and traceable back to Starke Enterprises.

The bee crawled up the side of the nearest building and hid itself in cracked masonry in order to plot a course of action. It ordered the beta wasp, meanwhile, to incinerate the alpha wasp, after siphoning off its plasma into its own reservoir.

Their situation was bad, but not dire. Other regenerating mechs were already creeping out of the wreckage. The slug was still trapped inside, too big to pass through the hole. Meanwhile, the bee sensed five private security cars and one HomCom GOV circling over the roofs of the surrounding buildings. The garden plot was too tight for any of them to land, but soon they would send down small warbeitors to secure the scene. If the bee and its remaining escort managed to hide for an hour, they might still continue with the mission.

Except for one complication—the missing wing that was still inside the scupper's collection cage. The bee was hardwired to always conceal its identity. Only its mission trumped the need to remain anonymous. So, as it spun out scenarios, its primitive mind kept jamming on the missing wing. Must it allow its wing to fall into the hands of the Homeland Command?

There was no more time to hesitate. The bee ordered the wasp to reenter the scupper and to either find and retrieve its wing, or incinerate the entire contents of the cage. Meanwhile, the bee climbed farther up the building to a patch of sunlight to begin recharging its fuel cells. The repair nano inside it had completed mending critical systems and was proceeding to those of secondary importance. The bee arched its leg to peel open a pair of blisters under its thorax, releasing millions of mite-sized mechs. These swarmed over its body, cleaning the remaining diatom dust from sensors and digging it out from articulating surfaces. As the mites ran out of energy by the thousands, they crawled along the broken wing struts and fused themselves together to make temporary splints.

Soon there was activity in the garden plot. A ground-floor window overlooking the garden opened, and out stepped two humans. Perhaps two or perhaps six or eight; the bee wasn't able to make an accurate count. They were small humans, in any case, and their clothing did not transpond any official agency ID. Indeed, it was their clothing that confused the bee's optical pickups, creating ghosts and multiple images. In IR the distortion was even worse, and they cast no radar reflections at all. Although the bee could acquire no solid fix on these humans, it could tell that the scupper was being lifted from the bricks.

Report progress, the bee ordered.

Much debris. Target wing armature found and destroyed. This unit can smell wing hoop but unable to locate.

Leave scupper, prick humans, resume search.

Acknowle— the wasp's transmission was cut off as the scupper disappeared completely from the bee's sensors. The crowd of ghostly humans seemed to be flowing back toward the open window. Before it/they reached the window, a hot spot appeared in IR. Twelve or sixteen ghostly hot spots, to be sure. The humans yelped in turn, and the scupper abruptly reappeared on the ground.

Several long moments later, Blue Team Beta Wasp alighted on the wall next to the bee. *Wing parts located and destroyed*, it reported.

Recharge, ordered the bee.

THE TAXI REENTERED the up-spiral. When they reached the local grid above the city, Samson saw the silhouette of Soldier Field outlined against the lake in the distance, but they were heading in the opposite direction.

"Taxi," he demanded, "where are we going?"

The taxi replied, "Our new route includes only two intervening stops, Myr Kodiak. We'll be there in no time."

"No!" Samson insisted. "I want nonstop. I want express service."

But the car docked in a transit bay at the 300th-floor lattice arcade between two downtown gigatowers on the Midway picket. A gent in a richly tailored business jumpsuit climbed halfway into the car before he smelled Samson, and his expression changed to one of pure revulsion. He backed out of the car and said, "I thought all of you were dead by now."

"Soon," Samson said, "and fuck you too."

"Call me another cab," the man ordered the taxi and went back to the waiting area.

The taxi spoke to Samson again, this time in a different voice. "Good afternoon, Myr Kodiak. The taxi unit you are currently occupying has called me to mediate a possible customer relations issue. I am more proximal to the Hi-Top controlling mentar. Since our taxi units lack full sensory capability, I must ask you for your judgment: Is there some condition that makes conveyance in this unit uncomfortable to passengers?"

Samson was incredulous. "You have a lot of nerve," he said. "I demand you immediately take me to my destination. No more delays."

"What about odor?" the taxi went on. "Is there some foul odor in the unit?"

"I am running low on patience, taxi."

Samson's door unlatched and folded open, and his seat released him. "In that case, Myr Kodiak, would you mind stepping out? I need to take this unit back to the barn for further diagnosis."

"Yes, I would mind," Samson said, keeping his seat. "I would mind very much."

"Regrettably, we are unable to transport you farther in this unit. If you decar now, Hi-Top Charter Taxi will waive your fare to this point."

"Waive my fare to this point? Are you crazy? I'm farther from my destination now than when you picked me up. I'm not getting out. Take me to Soldier Field—or else!"

"That won't be possible," said the taxi. "After reviewing the in-cab recordings, I have concluded that *you*, Myr Kodiak, are the source of the problem. While we are never eager to take legal steps against our customers, unless you decar at once, we will file a suit against you to recover damages to this unit plus loss of economic opportunity for the time it is out of service. In addition, until any court-imposed penalty is satisfied, you will be unable to use any Hi-Top Taxi or affiliated service."

"Are you *threatening* me, taxi?" Samson shouted, his scalp mottling in shades of red. "Believe me when I say that you don't want to threaten me."

In response, the seat cushions stiffened into a disergonomic "reject" shape that jabbed Samson in the kidneys.

"Henry!" he screamed. "I'm feeling like here will do. Right here, right now!" He pawed through his pockets for the simcaster, but he couldn't find it.

Sam, Hubert said, *please calm down and allow me to handle the situation.*

"I demand my rights under the Accommodations Act of '54!" Samson cried.

Relax, Sam. You'll hurt yourself.

But Samson did not relax. He beat the seat cushion with his fist. "Are you fireproof, taxi? Tell me that, are you fireproof?"

Two building security men, a jerry and a russ, in teal and brown uniforms approached the car. "Come on out of there, gramps," said the jerry. When they came into smelling range, they recoiled in surprise.

"Whew!" said the jerry. "What you do in there? Crap yourself?"

"That's not crap," said the russ. "That's a stinker."

"Not possible," said his partner. "They're all dead."

"Sure smells that way."

The two men sealed their face masks, then reached into the taxi to try to grab Samson's arm, but he scooted out of reach and poked at them with his maple stick.

"You don't want to make us come in there after you, old man," said the russ.

"Right here!" Samson cried in a rage. "Right now!"

"Now, now," said the russ. "Do as we say, or we'll be forced to sleep you."

He extended his standstill wand and pointed it at Samson, but Samson fenced it away with his walking stick. The door behind Samson opened; the jerry had outflanked him.

"Henry, cast a sim of me now!" Samson shouted. Nothing happened. "Do you hear me, Henry? Do as I say!"

Sam, this is Hubert, not Henry. Do as the men say; I'm attempting to negotiate a truce.

"I will not!" he cried, and when the jerry tried to lift him from the seat, he spat at him. The spittle boiled away against the officer's face mask.

The jerry backed away from the car and said, "Hey, this guy's toxic."

"No, he's a stinker," said the russ, "like I said."

"Yeah? Well? I don't recall how we're supposed to handle 'em. Do you?"

The two security men fell silent while Nicholas briefed them on protocol for handling the cellularly seared. Meanwhile, the taxi closed its doors, shutting Samson in, and spoke to him in yet another new voice, "Good afternoon, Myr Harger," it said. Harger, not Kodiak. "This is Hi-Top mentar Fuller speaking. I'd like to apologize for any misunderstanding caused by my partials. Please sit back, and we'll proceed to your destination as soon as I smooth things over with building security."

In a little while, the two security men outside Samson's window turned around and left the bay. The taxi's motors revved up, and the seat melted once again into an ultra-soft restraint.

"That's more like it!" Samson said. "Be afraid!"

Chicago slipped by beneath them. Soon they were flying over the lakeshore, and the tall trapezoidal shape of Soldier Field Stadium lay below them. Samson ached all over. There were simmering bruises on his arms where the jerry had grabbed him, and his fist burned where he'd beat the seat cushion. It occurred to him that the next time he was in a situation like that, all he had to do was whack his skull against something solid, and that should do the trick. "Hubert," he said, "next time, do exactly as I tell you. No arguments, no negotiations. Is that clear?"

If you say so, Sam.

"I do say so. I insist so." The portable simcaster had been in his breast pocket the whole time. He took it out and flipped the control switch to voice mode. "Charge yourself," he said to it, and the small device powered up.

"Ready," it said.

"Myr Harger," the taxi broke in, "we have arrived, see? And Hi-Top Taxi is pleased to waive the entire fare. In fact, we're crediting you with three free rides to any Chicagoland destination in private cars. We're landing now. We're here!" The taxi settled on the uppermost transit parapet of the stadium and opened its door.

"That's more like it," Samson said, and when the seat released him, he began to climb out, but stopped and said, "You waived the fare? Anything else?"

"Yes, Myr Harger. Hi-Top Charter has asked me to apologize for this unfortunate incident. It seems a shame that chartists should fight among themselves."

"Yes, a shame," he said and put the simcaster back into his pocket. As soon as Samson got out of the taxi, the taxi slammed its doors and took off, leaping into the air on all six fans, not waiting for him to clear its wash zone. The dust caught Samson, and he coughed for a whole minute. He waited a few more minutes to recover, then crossed in front of the row of waiting scanways. Spared a side trip to Indiana, he was early. It was hours before the canopy ceremony would start, and the place was empty. Samson skirted the scanways and went to an adjoining pressure gate. The intrusive radiation of a scanway would set off his cellular wardens just as surely as a simcaster, and as a registered seared he had a waiver (something the taxi should have checked). The pressure gate fell, and a security arbeitor rolled out. It performed a gentle but thorough frisk and sniff of his person. It even asked him to open his mouth so it could peer down his throat. It confiscated his walking stick, loading his palm with a claim ticket for it, and escorted him through the gate. On the other side, an orange usher line lit up at his feet and led out of sight down the spiraling stadium gangway.

"Is it far?" he said.

"Not far, and downhill all the way," Hubert replied from his belt.

Samson shuffled past not-yet-activated concession kiosks. It was hard to believe he was really doing this at last. "Hubert, have I written a farewell speech?"

"No, Sam, you haven't."

This puzzled him. He was almost certain he had jotted down a few ideas for a speech. Certainly, it was all he'd been thinking about these last few weeks. "Are you sure?"

"You said," Hubert continued, "that when the time came, the words would take care of themselves."

Samson didn't believe it, but at this point, what could he do? "It's refreshing to see how much confidence I have in myself."

He followed the usher line to a loading gallery. Gratefully, he collapsed into a seat. Soft restraints threaded themselves over his shoulders and across his chest. "Ready to exit?" the seat asked.

Samson said, "Ready," and the seat lifted him slowly outside through a pressure curtain and up and over until he was suspended over the gaping maw of the stadium. It was exhilarating to be the first seat out, and Samson took several deep breaths. The playing field was so far below him that it looked like a dinner plate at the bottom of a well.

"Tilt back," he said, and the seat complied. "A little more." Now he was looking into the blue sky beyond the stadium rim. This was the direction where the real action would take place tonight.

Hubert said, "I suggest a Gooeyduk snack now and some 'Lyte and maybe another oxytab. Then a nice nap. I'll wake you up in plenty of time. Are you warm enough?"

"Toasty," Samson said and reopened the Gooeyduk he had been nibbling on earlier. "But, tell me one thing, Hubert."

"Go ahead."

"What you said about El and Ellen earlier—how is that going? What do we know for sure?"

Hubert said, "Eleanor is gone. Ellen is an open question."

"Ellen is all right?"

"No, Sam. Ellen is either dead or dying. The reports conflict."

Samson opened a pouch of 'Lyte and drank several sips. He pulled the hood of the jumpsuit over his head. Oh, El, to pick the same day as me, he thought. What's the point in that?

There was no point, at least none that he could see, just as his searing had been pointless. Just as Eleanor's whole Target UKB turned out to be pointless. She had promised to identify those responsible for his attack, and she did, five years after he and Skippy left the manse. Only, she found too many of them, over two thousand individuals and groups. There seemed to have been a widespread consensus that her success was too meteoric and that brakes needed to be applied. The baby permit had been one result of this consensus, as they had suspected. His assault had been another. But not even with her most sophisticated snooping could Eleanor uncover anyone who actually gave the orders.

"It doesn't work like that," she told him. "No one at this level of the game actually orders such things. One merely expresses one's annoyances, and others translate that into action on their own. That's what minions are for."

She left it up to him whether or not to destroy all two thousand miscreants. She said, "I promised I would, and I will. Though many of these people are currently my colleagues and business partners."

She waited for him to answer. He had just moved into Cass Tower and started throwing gala dinner parties for probably these same people. "No," he told her. "Dining with me is punishment enough. For now."

THE DIMINISHED BLUE Team entered Chicagoland through the Gary Gate, posing as a media bee with armed escort. Within its mission files, the bee had only five purloined IDs to use, and it used up three of them at the gates separating the city sectors.

At Howe Street, the team ascended to the roof and traversed the tiered rows of hydroponics to the garden shed. The wasp easily sliced a hole through the door screen, and the two mechs entered.

A voice spoke immediately, "This is private property. Identify yourselves."

The bee quickly scanned the room. The aromatic signature of the catcher was present and strong, but there were no living bodies in the space. The wasp confirmed the bee's readings. The bee flew closer to the cot where a still form lay under covers.

"We invoke our right to privacy," said the voice, which came from a speaker lying on a bench.

The bee ignored the vacate order and finished its assessment. The form on the cot was not human.

The Blue Team exited the shed and flew to the stairwell door. The door was shut, and the beeway above it was blocked with concrete. Tomography indicated that many of the building's bricks were hollow, and the wasp was able to bore a hole through one to gain entry to the building. The team methodically searched each floor, room by room. Non-catcher humans were present in some of them, and they demanded the team's immediate surrender. One of them even foolishly tried to disable them with an old harmonics wand. The wasp cut the wand in two with one well-placed pulse of light.

Satisfied that the catcher was not in the building, the Blue Team exited through the street-level slugway. It followed a volatiles trail on the building's wall and sidewalk to the end of the block where the trail ended. If this mission had been provided even minimal tactical support, the bee could have continued tracking its target via the thousands of fixed CCTV cameras, witness bees, CPT recordings, and suborbital drones. But there was no mission support, not even a Legitimate Order Giver; the Blue Team was on its own.

The bee led the wasp to the rooftop of the building opposite their target. Here they had a commanding view of the entire street as well as the rooftop garden and shed. The bee ran its scenario mill while they waited.

2.12

The CPT station in the central canyon of APRT 7 disgorged throngs of tired Applied People commuters. They streamed across the platform and hustled to the elevators. Fred took his time. The bead train ride had been uncomfortable enough with its g-force acceleration and turns. His poor internal organs were still knitting themselves back together and didn't need the extra stress. Fred found a bench to lie on for a bit. He let the rush hour flow around him with its familiar sounds, while above him, clouds drifted across the four stalks of the tower. A quarter million people lived in each stalk, and all of them, like Fred, worked for Applied People. Fred had spent his entire life in this arcology, or in others just like it. Even the hab at Mars Station had been arcological. It would never occur to a russ to question this living arrangement, except that at this moment in his life, Fred did so. *To my cloned brothers*, he mused, *where has it got us—to spend a hundred million russ years living in these things?*

A transit bee stopped to check on Fred's condition, and Fred sat up and waved it away. He went to the bank of elevators, bypassing the turbo lifts in favor of a lounge car. In his condition, it was better to take things easy. He was early and in no special need to race home. The lounge car he chose had empty couches near the media pit and a vacant armchair or two in front of the fireplace. As he entered, a soothing protomusic, more noise than signal, seemed to greet him. Weary clones, wearing every possible permutation of Applied People brown and teal livery, trudged in and parked themselves in favorite corners. Fred crossed the thick carpet to the bar.

A man on the stool next to him said, "Good God, man, you stink!"

Fred turned to him. It was a pike—the name JULES was embroidered on his name patch. Jules wrinkled his sunburnt nose and continued. "What 'appen to *you*? Get sheep-dipped?"

"Yeah," Fred said and turned away. At the moment, he wasn't up to the effort of pretending to being friendly to a pike. He ordered a beer before remembering that he had to stay off alcohol for a few days. He changed his order to a soft drink.

The lounge car made its ascent at a leisurely pace, stopping only at double-naught-numbered floors on the way up and five-naught on the way down. Fred decided to skip his stop going up and disembark on the way down. He needed a little time to dwell on his problems: Costa, Cabinet, Reilly, the HALVENE, and the possibility of clone fatigue.

Fred realized that he had just made a short list of his troubles. Russes were famous for their lists. Their donor brother, Thomas A., had been an incorrigible list maker. After he lost his life in the assassination attempt, the Secret Service entered Russ's apartment and found a remarkable collection of lists. On scraps of paper stuck to the refrigerator, in computer files, in notebooks, on the backs of envelopes. Grocery lists, equipment checklists, Christmas card lists, ranked lists of women he'd like to sleep with. The government kept them; there was even a display of Thomas A.'s lists at the Smithsonian. Fred mused, *To my cloned brothers: lists are our own form of blank verse.*

When Fred decarred on the 150th floor, he transferred to a local lift for the remaining floors and then took a spokeway to Deko Village, an economy neighborhood located deep within the core of the Northwest Stalk. His front door greeted him and slid open. "Tell Mary I'm home," he said to the tiny foyer. There was no reply, so he said, "Mary?"

"I'm in the bedroom," she sighed.

"Sorry if I woke you."

"You didn't wake me. You're home early."

"Yeah, a little." Fred waited to see if she was going to say anything more. She didn't, so he went to the living room where the slipper puppy was waiting next to his armchair with his slippers. Fred unstrapped his stout, brown brogans—damp with HALVENE—and watched as the puppy dragged them, one by one, to its lair in the closet for polishing and deodorizing. For you, he thought, I'm going to risk my integrity?

He leaned back in the armchair and relaxed. After a while, since Mary had not made an appearance or continued their conversation, he said, "Are you hungry? I'm hungry. My stomach is *literally* empty. Maybe we should eat something before we go."

"Go where?"

"Rolfe's. Reilly says they've reserved a table." Reilly might not actually show up, but best to leave that alone for now.

"Rolfe's?" Mary said. "Today's not Wednesday."

"You know," Fred said, trying to keep his tone breezy, not that you could fool an evangeline, "that's exactly what I said."

After a little while, Mary said, "Whatever are you talking about, Fred?"

"The canopy ceremony."

"Oh, that," she said. "I'm not going."

"Why not?"

"I don't feel like going anywhere."

Fred knew better than to argue the point. "To tell the truth," he said, "neither do I. Let's stay home. We can dial in and eat here."

"You go ahead. I've been eating all day. I left you something in the kitchen."

Fred struggled out of the armchair and went to the kitchen, which in this economy apartment amounted to a large chromium kulinmate in a nook off the living room. There, on its counter lay a plate. On the plate was a stack of small, rolled-up pastries.

"See it?"

Fred raised the plate to eye level and examined the morsels. "What are they?"

"Cajun pepper fish rollmops. I recipeed them myself."

"You did?" This could be very good news. It meant that she'd gotten out of bed today. And that she was trying out new things. But in the kitchen? Evangelines were allergic to all things culinary. Even dialing up a recipe was asking a lot.

"That's great," he said. "I'll eat some right now."

He brought one to his mouth, but she said, "No, don't! I changed my mind."

Fred hesitated, the rollmop millimeters from his lips. He felt as though he were standing in a tippy canoe. It had been like this since their wedding day five years ago. At first, living with an evangeline was exhilarating. Lately, he could do without the state of constant suspense.

Mary, still in the bedroom, said, "It's too hot, too spicy. It's got habanero pepper in it."

"I love hot foods."

Mary sighed. "Then go ahead. You know better than me, Fred. You always do."

Fred returned the rollmop to the plate. He wasn't home five minutes and already he was over his head. He listed his options: not eat a rollmop, eat one, eat several, or not eat any but say that he had. That about covered it. He could safely rule out the first and last options. If Mary had gotten out of bed to make these things, he'd better either try them or say that he did. But it was foolish to lie to an evangeline. So the only question now was how many to eat. If they were as hot as she said they were, even one might upset his poor, HALVENE-abused belly. He took a glass to the dispenser and drank a half liter of rice milk to dampen the way, then chose a fat rollmop and bit into it.

It was spicy, all right, but nothing he'd call hot. He popped the rest of it into his mouth and swallowed it. "It's terrific," he said, reaching for a second and a third.

"Just wait," Mary said.

He didn't have to wait long. The back of his tongue began to burn, and his throat closed up. His eyes bugged, his nose watered, and sweat beaded on his scalp. He couldn't breathe. He couldn't see. He groped for another glass of rice milk.

"Fred, are you all right?"

He choked and coughed and couldn't answer.

"Fred? Can you hear me? Come here!"

"Just a minute," he croaked, wiping tears from his eyes, grinning, heading for the bedroom, invited in, at last.

SHE WAS PROPPED up in their large bed. Her hair was a mess, and she had food stains down the front of her nightgown. But she cleared a space for him to sit next to her, and that was all that mattered.

"Here, blow," she said, handing him a tissue. "I told you they were hot, but you wouldn't listen to me. I should have chuted them with the rest. Honestly, I don't know why I kept them."

Fred blew his nose and said, "It's nothing. They're really good." He blew his nose again and said, "What you watching?" She had a little scape open at the foot of her bed. It looked like the interior of a garden where nothing much moved. "Is it Shelley?"

"Uh-huh," Mary said. "They had problems feeding Judith today. It looks like things are speeding up, healthwise. She's sinking fast."

Fred leaned over to peer into the scape. It was the breezeway location. The breezeway connected two wings of the death artist's Olympic Peninsula beachfront bungalow. Looked like it was just after lunch on the West Coast, overcast, plenty of exotic plants in large colorful pots along the cement brick floor. Judith Hsu lay on a chaise lounge in the shade. Two evangelines sat with her, Shelley and one of the others. Both evangelines wore wide-brimmed hats, and from this angle, Fred couldn't tell which of them was his and Mary's friend.

Mary sniffed him. "Fred, you've been dry-cleaned!"

Fred shrugged his shoulders.

"Why didn't you tell me?"

"It's no big deal."

"Of course it's a big deal. Were you hurt?"

Now came the best part. Fred sat still while Mary searched his face with those big brown evangeline eyes of hers. And while it wasn't easy to lie to an evangeline, her eyes couldn't lie to him either. Her soul possessed no curtains or veils. Fred said, "I'm not hurt," and peered into her eyes. He scattered his words like bait to lure her out into the open.

"I didn't ask *are* you hurt," she said. "Obviously, they'd patch you up. I asked *were* you hurt."

His confidentiality oath prevented him from telling even his wife any details of his missions. But there was no need, for Mary could see everything.

Evangelines had been introduced thirty-two years earlier to meet a market demand for personal companions for wealthy women. Certain affs needed a breathless audience for their empty lives. Only prototype batches totaling ten thousand evangelines were ever decanted because market demand had collapsed. But the market's loss was a russ's gain.

Fred held his wife in his arms and summarized his whole, crazy day—without saying a word. She glimpsed his fear and panic and pain. After a while she hugged him and broke the spell. "My poor man," she said and pushed him away. "Move aside. I have to pee."

Fred watched his wife climb out of bed. Evangelines were skinny little things. At least compared to jennys they were. And small-hipped and flat-chested, compared to michelles. But in the sack, Mary was beyond comparison. When they made love, Fred begged her to keep her puddlelike eyes open so that he could witness in them the astonishment of every touch.

Mary closed the bathroom door, and Fred lay back in bed and watched Shelley's scape. Shelley was not only their friend, but Reilly's spouse, and a member of their Wednesday night crowd. Something in Shelley's scape moved and caught his attention. The door to one of the bungalow wings opened, and two more evangelines came into the breezeway. It was a shift change. The two offgoing 'leens, one of them Shelley, joined the newcomers at a round patio table at some little distance from the unfortunate Myr Hsu. They were giving the shift report, and he upped the volume:

"—she can hardly bend her arms," one of them was saying.

"Or form her words," said the other.

"Chewing is almost too much for her."

Fred checked the time. If Shelley got on a train in the next hour, she'd make it in time for the canopy ceremony, even if Reilly couldn't.

Fred went out to the living room and stood opposite the window wall. It wasn't a real window—their apartment was a good half kilometer from the nearest exterior wall—but it showed the realtime view from the window of a luxury apartment high in the same stalk. Just now the sun was dipping behind O'Hare Picket on the Illinois countryside. Fred wiped the scene away, replacing it with the phone frame.

"Reilly Dell," he said, and a jittery view of his friend opened. Reilly was in a CPT bead car. The two men grinned at each other. There was nothing much they had to say. Obviously, both had survived the day. They made a little small talk and signed off.

Fred returned to the bedroom to change into house togs. That was when he noticed that the slugway near the ceiling had been stopped up with a towel. His heart skipped a beat. He tapped on the bathroom door and said gently, "Mary, someone's plugged the slugway."

Not waiting for a reply, Fred climbed on a chair and pulled the towel out. Immediately, six slugs came through and spread out across the walls and ceiling.

Mary watched from the bathroom doorway. "I saw on the Evernet how they're going to retire them along with the canopy tonight."

"That's not likely," Fred said. "If anything, we'll have to *increase* their numbers. And *double* the visolas. And put *bloomjumpers* on every corner. And *still*, we won't be safe!"

She was staring at him. Softly, he continued. "It's a felony to obstruct a slug. We could be arrested."

"Then why aren't they here arresting us?" she said. "I plugged it up hours ago, and no one's arrested me yet." She returned to the bathroom and said, "Come in here and give me your opinion."

There was a quarter-sized Mary in the bathroom mirror walking back and forth on a short runway. It wore a sexy lamé dress of blue and plum. Meanwhile, Mary sat at the face dresser and fine-tuned a mannequin of her head. She had set it to gala face and was tarting it up even more.

So, we're going out, after all, Fred thought. Mary rubbed a wide band of gentian powder beneath the mannequin's eyes, pulled the lashes longer, and plumped the lips slightly. She made the skin creamy brown and the irises and hair black.

"It's quite striking," Fred said, "but it looks like something for—you know—New Year's Eve. Not an evening at Rolfe's with the gang."

"You think?"

"I don't know. How should I know?"

"You're probably right." Mary reset the mannequin to cocktail face and experimented with colors. Meanwhile, one of the slugs had entered the bathroom and was heading for Fred across the tile floor. Fred stood still for it to latch on to his ankle. There was a slight prick as it sampled him. It immediately dropped off, as he knew it would. One taste of the HALVENE and the little ribbon of biotech was satisfied that he posed no threat to society.

When the slug crept toward Mary, however, she dropped her nightgown on it and retreated to the gel stall. Fred shook his head and freed the slug from her clothing. "Honestly, Mary," he said, "you're begging for trouble. What's got into you?"

"Funny you should ask," she said and turned on the mist, drowning out all conversation.

The slug, undeterred, crept up the glass door to the stall's slugway near the ceiling. Like it or not, the slug would have its taste. Fred, meanwhile, decided he'd better use the face dresser before Mary finished her shower. He sat under the boxy appliance and said, "Fred's party setting." He didn't need to use a mannequin; he had only three faces—house, work, and party—and he never altered them. He lowered the dresser and buried his head in its soft, warm folds. It quickly washed, shaved, toned, and made up his face, while at the same time hydrating his skin and trimming his hair. Fred bit down for a peppermint ultrasound mouth scrub.

When Fred removed the dresser, his own pint-sized figure was posing in the mirror. It wore alternating styles and colors of leisure suits.

"That one," he said, picking a jaunty, plum-colored crepe jumpsuit that would match Mary's getup. The little Fred in the mirror took a step forward, grinned, and turned on its heel.

To my cloned brothers: we are one handsome son of a bitch.

In the bead car next to Bogdan, a man was scrunched up against the window, fast asleep. Bogdan, too, was being lulled by the gentle swaying of the speeding train, when there was a click, and his neighbor's car unhitched and hurtled itself down a side tunnel. A moment later, another car dropped from an injection ramp and snapped into place next to him. His new neighbor, across two sheets of unbreakable glassine, was a woman with see-through skin. She was drumming her fingers on the armrest of her seat, and Bogdan became hypnotized by her tendons and muscles sliding over each other. When the woman noticed him staring, she seemed offended, though with a see-through face it was hard to tell. In any case, she opaqued her window.

Bogdan didn't care. He was lost in a daydream. Although his session in the Aria Ranger ended before he and the weird sim reached the inhabited core of Trailing Earth, his next assignment was just as outstanding. The sim, in his green and red overalls, reappeared and said, "Hello again, Bogdan. Care to visit the future?"

Bogdan had looked around. They were alone in an E-Pluribus auditorium, not in a spaceship.

"Yah sure, why not?"

"Splendid. Now imagine this. Four hundred years have elapsed. You're a plankholder aboard an Oship on its way to a new home system. Let's go visit the bridge."

A moment later they were standing in a room the size of a soccer field. There were dozens of young people in cool uniforms attending to a forest of flat monitors and control panels. In the center of the colossal room floated a giant scale model of an Oship.

"Here's the decade captain," the Meewee sim said as a young woman approached them. She was stunningly beautiful. As beautiful as Annette Beijing, if that was possible. She stopped in front of them, placed her hands on her shapely hips, and examined Bogdan from head to toe.

"Ah, Merrill," she said, "you have a knack for picking the finest crew. Won't you please introduce us."

"Gladly," the Meewee sim said. "Captain Suzette, I'm pleased to introduce Plankholder Bogdan Kodiak, one of our most promising young jump pilot cadets."

"Welcome to the bridge of the ESV *Garden Charter*, Cadet Kodiak," the captain said. "Merrill has asked me to give you a tour, and I thought we'd start right here in the command center. That sound acceptable?"

"Perfectly," Bogdan said, his voice threatening to crack.

"Excellent."

The Meewee sim said, "Well, Bogdan, I'll leave you in the capable hands of our good captain. Till next time—" The sim dissolved into twinkling stars and disappeared.

"That's a fine man," Captain Suzette said, looking wistfully at the spot Meewee had occupied. "I hope you realize how lucky you are that he's taken a shine to you." She motioned for Bogdan to join her in front of the mammoth holo Oship. "Let's begin with ship propulsion. I suppose you know about the Oship torus."

The model Oship towered over him like a ten-story building. "Certainly," Bogdan said, straining to remember what Meewee had said about it in the earlier session. "Uh, a magnetic trap for particle beams from a solar harvester."

The gorgeous captain glanced at him admiringly. "Well put," she said. "Let's start with the harvesters. Back home in the system surrounding Sol—" She made gestures as she spoke, and the Oship model shrank to a pinpoint in an upper corner of the huge scape, making way in the center for a large dazzling star. Bogdan shielded his eyes against its intensity.

"Here, let me dampen that," the captain said and twirled her finger. Dampened, the sun resembled a ball of squirming pink noodles. Girdling its northern hemisphere was a loose ring of black specks.

"Those are Heliostream harvesters," Captain Suzette continued. "They're as far out as Mercury orbit but above Sol's equatorial plane. And of course, to be able to see the harvesters at all in this scape, I've had to scale them up to the size of Jupiter."

"Of course," Bogdan said.

"All right, let's sketch in the rest of the system." She pointed her finger here and there, and planets and habplat and fabplat colonies appeared, including a blue-and-white-mottled marble representing Earth.

"The harvesters capture the raw energies of Sol and transfer them to where they can be useful. Ready?" She snapped her fingers, and a thick spiderweb of colored threads shot out in all directions from the ring of solar harvesters. Most of them terminated at Earth. "The white ones are microwave beams which are converted to electricity, the red ones are laser, the yellow ones are streams of hydrogen plasma, and the green one there—do you know what that is?"

The green thread she indicated led directly to the tiny Oship in the upper corner. "That would be our particle mass beam," Bogdan said.

"Excellent!" the captain said merrily. She waved her hands to close the Sol system and return the Oship model to its original imposing size. "Which leads us to our torus, which is, as you have already pointed out, a fortified electromagnetic force field that converts particle beams striking it into motive force." As she spoke, a wire diagram, like the lines of latitude and longitude on a globe, appeared in the donut hole of the Oship. In the exact center, the lines bulged forward, like a finger poking a rubber sheet. "For the last four hundred years," the captain continued, "Heliostream has been directing a narrow beam of charged photonic particles at Planet 2013LS in the Ursae Majoris system. That's our destination. We have positioned the torus of our ship on the beam so as to ride it." She pointed at the center of the donut hole. "That convexity you see in our torus is the particle beam striking it. Most of its energy is being converted into propulsion—we've attained 0.367 light speed—while a fraction is bled off to supply ship's power. And, of course, the beam doubles as an ultra-broad communication band between us and Earth."

Bogdan said, "So, how is old Earth doing four hundred years on?"

The sparkle seemed to leave Captain Suzette's eyes. "Ah, Cadet Kodiak, the news hasn't been good for a long time now. Our dear mother planet has suffered terribly since our launch, especially during the Second Phage War of 2184. Earth has been poisoned so extensively that nothing can live on its surface. Humans must live deep underground, or on Mars, the moons of Jupiter, or a number of orbital habplats. There are actually more people alive aboard the *Garden Charter* and our sister Oships than in all of Sol System combined. It would appear that we launched none too soon. We're very, very lucky we had the wisdom to make the choices that we did."

"But aren't you afraid the Heliostream beam will fail without Earth?"

"Not really," said the captain. "Heliostream is robotically controlled. We might have suffered if it had failed a century ago, but by now a beam failure would add less than ten years to our travel time. You see, we've almost reached the beam-off point."

She waved her lovely hand, and the grand display switched to a view of open space and millions of stars. A broad arc connected two stars. Half of the arc glowed green, half red, and between them was a narrow colorless gap.

"When Heliostream cuts the beam in two years, we'll travel by inertia for about seventy-five years, as represented by the gap there. The ship will use its fusion reactors for power during that time. We'll lose gravity here in the lattice frame, though the occupied hab drums will begin to rotate and generate their own gravity."

"But, but—" Bogdan said, questions piling up in his mind.

"Oh, I know what you're going to ask," the captain said. "Everyone does. If we're the first ones out here, where does the braking beam come from? Right?"

That wasn't it, but Bogdan nodded his head anyway. "And what do you mean, occupied hab drums? I thought your passengers were corpsicles."

"I see you're a thinker, and I like that in my officers. First, the beam. In the year 2136, a year before our own launch, the Garden Earth Consortium sent a flotilla of advance ships ahead of us. They were small, robotically controlled, and had chemical/fusion boosters. They were capable of acceleration speeds greater than a human could withstand. Most of them have already reached Ursae Majoris fifty years ago. They immediately scouted our destination planet to confirm its suitability for terrestrial life. By the way, Planet 2013LS has exceeded our most optimistic projections. We have stunning pictures, if you'd care to view them.

"We already have confirmation that some of the advance ships have made successful planetfall and are now constructing an energy, transportation, and habitation infrastructure on the planet in preparation for our arrival in about four hundred seventy-five years. By the time we enter orbit, there'll be modern, fully functional cities waiting for us to inhabit them. The remaining advance ships are building solar harvesters (or in this case—ursine harvesters) to generate our braking particle beam."

The Oship model returned, and four of the hab drums were highlighted. "As to your second question, no, not everyone is frozen. Our passengers have the option of spending an average of two hundred years of the voyage in a quickened state if they like. We can have up to twenty percent of our population active at any time. Currently, there are 93,545 persons occupying those four drums. That one has a town with a population of 62,000, while the others contain twenty-nine smaller settlements and thousands of rural homesites."

A young officer approached them bearing a slate for the captain. He smiled at Bogdan and nodded. The captain studied the slate a moment and said, "Cadet Kodiak, I must attend to business. Perhaps you'd like to continue our tour with Lieutenant Perez?"

"Yes, ma'am, I would."

"In that case, Lieutenant, show Cadet Kodiak anything he'd care to see, and Cadet Kodiak—welcome aboard!" She saluted him, and when he snapped to return the salute, he noticed that he, too, was wearing a cool uniform.

"I bet you'll want to see our combat training course," the young officer said, leading Bogdan to a companionway, "or the officers' club. Or maybe our private nude beach."

TOO SOON, BOGDAN'S bead car split off and rolled into Library Station, and the boy was roused from his reverie. As his car rolled to a stop on the platform, he stuck his Kodiak patch—brown-yellow-white—to the shoulder of his jumpsuit and, with an oppressive sense of loss, rejoined reality. No sooner had he decarred and started across the platform than a man stepped on his foot. Bogdan howled in pain and surprise, while the man merely inspected the sole of his shoe. Satisfied, the man looked down at Bogdan and said, "What's your problem?"

"You feckin' stepped on my foot!" Bogdan said. "That's my problem!"

The man pursed his lips and said, "It's not my fault you choose to be so small."

"I'm not so small you can't see me!"

The man shrugged and turned to go, though not without first reaching down to rub Bogdan's head. Bogdan swatted his hand away and screamed, "You practically run me over, and then you want a rub? Are you *crazy?*"

The man strolled away without another word. Bogdan limped toward the exit. It felt like his toe was broken. A transit bee dropped down to him and said, "Myr Kodiak, do you require medical attention?"

"No!" Bogdan said without stopping. "But that *asshole* over there should be arrested for assault!"

"Our records show the mishap clearly to be an accident. However, if you require medical attention, be informed that this CPT station maintains a fully stocked crisis intervention booth and makes it available at reduced cost to ticketed travelers. In addition to a clinic class autodoc, we offer crisis counseling. Perhaps you'd like counseling for your recent experience."

Tears welled in Bogdan's eyes, and he savagely wiped them away. He ignored the bee and left the station. Outside, the evening air was warm. Hollyholos did not troll his neighborhood since no one could afford to interact with them. There were few kiosks and fewer sidewalk emitters. At the station exit, however, was the nightly bumbazaar, a line of homeless people trying to peddle a sad collection of worn-out junk. One old woman sat on a stool next to an antique bathroom scale. A hand-lettered sign taped over the scale said, "Yer Wait—UDC 1/7." A millionth of a yoodie to step on a broken scale. She looked up at Bogdan hopefully, but he despised her and her poverty.

Despite his throbbing toe, Bogdan began to jog home, shouting out, "Desist! Desist!" to the bees as he went.

WHEN BOGDAN TURNED the corner onto Howe Street, he noticed two Tobblers engaged in unusual behavior on the sidewalk in front of the Kodiak building. One Tobbler was hunched over something on the ground, and the other was peering over his shoulder. The air around them was thick with curious bees. Bogdan's own curiosity got the better of him, and he went over to see what was happening.

"Hello, young Kodiak," the crouching Tobbler groaned as he straightened up.

"Hello, Houseer Dieter," Bogdan replied. "What's up?"

"What's down you should ask," said the houseer.

The other Tobbler, whose name was Troy, was carefully pouring a viscous liquid from a foil pouch into a crack in the sidewalk. He didn't even glance at Bogdan. He was a boy, a real boy, not a retroboy. The dozen years that he had been walking the earth were all the years he could claim. Technically, Bogdan wasn't a retroboy either, but an arrested boy because he had stopped his maturation before reaching adolescence, but that fact didn't seem to draw the boys any closer together.

When the pouch was empty, Troy Tobbler put on a pair of utility spex and peered closely into the crack. "Nothing," he said.

"Let it seep some more," said the houseer.

"Still nothing," the boy said after another minute, whereupon the houseer removed a rubber mallet from a tool chest and began thumping the sidewalk on either side of the crack. "That helps," said the boy. "Go that way," he said, pointing toward the charterhouse.

The houseer beat the ground in a line toward the building and then began tapping the brick side of the building, itself.

"Good! Stop!" said his companion. "I have the little vermin. Come take a look."

He gave the spex to his houseer and looked up at Bogdan. "What are you staring at?" he said.

"Nothing," Bogdan said and glanced away.

"Ah, this is good," said the houseer, following an invisible path with the spex. "Three meters deep. Maybe three and a half. We need specimens." He took off the spex and said to Bogdan, "And so, young Kodiak, how is that room of yours that you share with our elevator? It gets warm up there in this weather, yes? Perhaps you should leave the door open."

"Warm is good," Bogdan said, avoiding the topic. They had found something under the charterhouse, and he wanted to know what it was. But he knew they wouldn't tell him, especially Troy. And since he wasn't going to beg them for information, he said, "G'night, Tobbs."

"Good night, Kodiak."

Bogdan passed the NanoJiffy entrance and climbed up the steps to the Kodiak's door. This time he didn't rely on voice recognition. "Here, read this," he said and placed his open palm against the door plate.

"Hello, visitor," said a familiar voice. Kitty's voice.

"Kitty, is that you?" he said hopefully. "It's me, Bogdan. Open the front door."

But it was a recording of Kitty's voice, and an old one at that. It said, "Because of the current state of martial law and ongoing civil unrest, Charter Kodiak has pneumatically sealed its building until further notice. We hope you'll excuse the inconvenience."

Martial law? thought Bogdan. That had been way before his time.

Kitty's voice continued. "We apologize not being able to address you in realbody, but if your business is legitimate, the door will notify us. If not, please move away at once. And remember, this door is a Slage XP model, fully armed and licensed to defend itself against intrusion."

"Door, tell someone I'm here," Bogdan said. "Call April or Denny. Just call them."

There was no reply, and Bogdan was about to give up and go in through the NanoJiffy when the door spoke in yet another voice—Rusty's? "We're all asleep at this hour, friend. Please come back in the morning."

"You are *not* asleep!" Bogdan cried and kicked the door. There was a metallic click, and gas turrets swung out from the doorjamb and aimed at him. Bogdan kept kicking anyway; he knew that the gas reservoirs had been depleted long ago. The two Tobblers turned from their work to look at him, but he didn't care, and he kicked until he could hear the intruder alarm go off inside.

At last the door slid open, and there was Houseer Kale. "Bogdan, why are you knocking?"

"Because the feckin' door won't open for me. Why can't you get things fixed around here?" He pushed his way past Kale into the foyer. "Would it kill you to fix the feckin' houseputer?"

"My, we're in a testy mood today," Kale said.

"Are we?" Bogdan said. "I wonder why. Did *we* have a bad day at *work*? Or did we sit at home all day wanking off?"

"It sounds like someone's hungry," Kale continued, nonplussed. "Go wash up; we're holding dinner on you. Oh, and take a tray up to Sam. He's not been feeling well. Tell him we'll all be up after dinner."

Too weary to argue, Bogdan trudged to the little room behind the NanoJiffy with its own extruder port that served as the house kitchen. "And don't forget," Kale called after him, "you have a meeting scheduled with the Allowance Committee at seven."

HALFWAY ACROSS THE roof, Bogdan could hear the snoring. Deep, sonorous expressions of revitalizing slumber. He stopped at the screen door and looked in. There was a new hole in the screen, and he stuck his finger in it. Sam's lumpy form lay on the cot, covered with an old blanket. Bogdan entered as quietly as possible. On the ratty, old footstool, there was another tray—lunch it looked like—untouched. He picked it up and replaced it with the dinner tray he'd brought. The bowl of lunchtime fruitish mash was already fermenting and had a cloying, sweet odor. He wasn't sure whether to try to wake Sam while his dinner was still warm. He'd apparently returned to bed after Bogdan saw him on the stairs earlier that morning.

"Sam," he said, not too loud.

"Shhhh," replied Hubert. "Hello, Boggy. Please be quiet. Sam's had a rough time of it and needs his rest." The snoring continued uninterrupted.

"They said to tell him everyone's coming up later."

"I'll relay that to him when he awakens."

Bogdan turned to go, bearing the lunch tray. But he stopped and whispered, "Hubert, the Tobbs were pouring some kind of optical sapping agent into the ground in front of the building. Any idea what's up with that?"

"Yes," Hubert whispered back, "material pirates. It would appear that there are excavating mechs in the neighborhood, and these old brick buildings are being cannibalized. The Tobblers suspect that pirates are hollowing out our house walls."

"But why would anyone want to steal old brick buildings?"

"Our charterhouse was built with Pullman bricks, bricks made during the nineteenth century from clay from Calumet Lake. This material is highly prized by builders."

Bogdan was impressed by the quality of Hubert's information. "They *told* you all of this?"

"No, I've recently learned how to tap their houseputer comm."

"Great," Bogdan said. "You can tap *their* houseputer, but you can't do anything to fix ours."

"Not so loud," Hubert said. "Why don't you go down to dinner. Everyone's waiting for you."

Bogdan opened the screen door, but again he hesitated. Something was wrong, but he couldn't say just what. The whole time he'd been there, Sam's snoring continued regularly, maybe too regularly. Then it occurred to him, the really strange thing—he could *smell* the overripe fruitish on the tray. With Sam in the room you shouldn't be able to smell *anything* but him. Bogdan set the tray on the bench and went to the cot.

"What are you doing?" said Hubert. "You'll wake him up."

"I doubt that," Bogdan said, throwing back the blanket. Pillows, no Sam. "What's going on, Hubert?"

The snoring ceased, and a voice said, "What? What? Where am I, Henry?"

Bogdan went to the speaker on the potting bench. "That's what I want to know, Sam. Where are you?"

"Bogdan, is that you? Are you in my bungalow?"

"Yeah, are you downstairs?"

"No, upstairs if anything."

"But I'm on the roof. There's no upstairs from here."

"I'm not in the house. I had a little errand to run."

Bogdan gestured at the rumpled cot. "And you had to sneak out to run it?"

Through the speaker, Bogdan heard Samson sigh. "If I told anyone," he said, "then you or April or Kitty or someone would try to stop me, and I can't allow that."

"You're scaring me, Sam."

"Sorry, boy, but I can't help it. Listen to me, a long time ago, before you were decanted, someone did something inhumanely cruel to me—"

"You're talking about the searing," Bogdan said, somewhat relieved, and went to sit on the cot, "and you're going to torch yourself as a public protest."

The speaker was silent for several moments, then Samson said, "I see I've mentioned this before."

"Only a few hundred times."

"Well then, it should come as no great shock, and I'm glad for that. I was a pawn in someone's big game, Boggy, and though I may never know who was responsible, in the end it was an act that society condoned by its silence. So it's up to me to show society its error in the only way I can."

"But all that stuff happened ages ago, Sam, and no one even cares anymore."

"Well, I'm going to remind them anyway."

Bogdan discovered the paper envelopes under the pillow and sorted through them. Each was scrawled with a 'meet's name, one with his own. He dropped the envelopes and jumped to his feet. "I'm telling Kale."

"Go ahead. It won't do any good. They can run all over town and still not find me. Best not even to mention it. Promise me you'll keep this to yourself, Boggy."

"No! Tell me where you are."

"Oh, Boggy, this is hard enough to do as it is. Do you think I've made this decision lightly?"

"I don't care."

I'll tell you what; if Hubert fucks things up and I need someone to bail me out, he'll contact you. Agreed?"

"Where are you?"

WHEN SAMSON FINALLY hung up on Bogdan, he thought that Soldier Field must be filling with spectators, for his seat was surrounded by a dozen others. It didn't take him long, though, to see that he and his immediate neighbors were the only ones there. They were a little island of interlocked seats, like the jammed keys of an antique typewriter, dangling over the chimney of the vacant stadium.

There was a man in the seat to his right—a tall, lean fellow with a bony old face and a neatly trimmed black mustache. "You're awake, then!" the man boomed. "Splendid! Good evening to you, sir!" His voice had a nasal quality due to large purple plugs stuffed into his nose.

A woman sat in the seat to Samson's left. She, too, wore nose filters, which gave her a piggy look. She, too, showed the signs of long-deferred body maintenance: papery skin and thin hair. In addition, she was plump. On her lap sat a gray and white cat, who eyed Samson warily.

All of the other seats were occupied by children, from toddlers to tweens. It occurred to Samson to wonder how there were so *many* children. He couldn't recall the last time he'd seen so many, a whole school bus load of them. Then he noticed that unlike the two adults, none of the children were strapped into their seats. They must be commercial children, not real children at all. The cat, on the other hand, was tethered to the woman's seat with a harness and leash, so it was real.

The man offered Samson his hand in greeting. "Victor Vole," he said. "And this is my beloved, Justine. These," he added with a wink and flourish of his hand, "are the brats. Brats, say hello to Monsieur Kodiak."

"Hello. Monsieur. Kodiak!" chorused the children with startling verve.

"How did you know my name?" Samson said.

"Oh, we were having a fine chat with your valet while you were napping. Haven't we, Justine?"

Justine nodded and smiled shyly, displaying brownish teeth.

Samson didn't know what to say. He was quite overcome. The children were standing on their seats to see him better. Surely Hubert wouldn't have spilled the beans to strangers.

"I hope we're not disturbing you, Myr Kodiak," Victor said. "It's just that no one has bought a ticket to a seat this high up in years. This whole section is usually closed—at least to people. Justine noticed you up here, all by yourself, in the middle of the afternoon, on a day when there's no game scheduled."

"I'm here for the canopy ceremony."

"Oh, that," Justine said and waved her hand dismissively.

"What Justine means to say is that the ceremony will take place at the very bottom," Victor said, pointing straight down. "Most likely, it won't originate in Chicago. They just like to use the old place as a backdrop these days."

Samson looked at him blankly.

"That's all Soldier Field is ever used for anymore, as a backdrop—and for suicides." Samson flinched. "Suicides?"

"That's Moseby's Leap," Justine said and pointed to a railed parapet on the other side of the stadium. "That's where it all started."

"Where all what started?"

"Moseby's suicides, of course."

Samson looked from one to the other without comprehension.

"Beer?" Victor said and handed him a cold pouch. It had been years since Samson had indulged in beer. Victor and Justine raised their own pouches in a toast, and Victor said, "To our unexpected guest. Welcome to our home."

Samson raised his pouch and said, "To my unexpected hosts." He took a sip. Naturally, he couldn't taste the beer, hadn't been able to taste anything for forty years. He noticed that all the children suddenly had ice cream sodas. "You say this is your home? You live here?"

Victor winked again. "Let's just say we came to watch the track events of the '28 Olympics, and we haven't left yet."

Samson was impressed. Hubert said to him, *Sam, they have a clever subem that hides them from security and has cracked concession kiosk codes. I'm studying it for pointers.*

"Dog?" Victor said and handed Samson another pouch, this one warm. Inside was a hot dog, heavy with green relish, chopped onions, and bright yellow mustard in a poppy seed bun. Steam assaulted Samson's nostrils, and for a moment he imagined he could smell this delicious Chicagoland delicacy of his youth.

"Thank you, don't mind if I do."

After Cabinet's visit to his office, Meewee packaged his few personal belongings in archival wrap. The wrap asked for forwarding and shipping addresses, and he had to admit to it that he hadn't thought that far ahead. Shortly after noon, when there was nothing more to do, he left for the last time, leaving behind Arrow's small ceramic container of paste. Meewee didn't even thank it for its service. At the first opportunity, he planned to undergo a terminus purge to eliminate his inbody connections to the aloof, unhelpful so-called mentar.

There was no one present in the Heliostream suite of offices to say good-bye to. The offices were usually bustling, even at night. But this afternoon the rooms were vacant, and the hallway checkpoints were staffed entirely by machines. Perhaps with the announcement of Eleanor's tragedy, everyone was sent home early.

Meewee strolled to the dispatch bay, in no special hurry. From there it was a short ride by bead car to his apartment in Slab 44, but he took a lift up to the surface instead. It was Meewee's habit to walk home from work each evening through the fields. The lift he boarded was a studio car, designed to carry three hundred, but it was also deserted.

On the ground floor, he passed the boardroom suite where they had met that morning and witnessed Eleanor's undoing. With his position at Heliostream terminated and Eleanor's daughter missing, there was little chance that he'd ever pass this way again.

When Meewee exited through the great crystal doors of the reception building and stepped outside, he savored delicious lungsful of soupy, tangy, pollen-soaked air. The ten-thousand-acre campus of Starke Enterprises stretched out before him, rolling Indiana hills planted in soybimi and troutcorn and dotted with fish ponds. Except for the reception building, there were no buildings in sight. Virtually all of the industrial complex and residential housing was buried in an underground arcology.

It was here, in front of the reception building, where his taxi had landed twelve years ago and he met Eleanor for the first time. She had invited him, the Birthplace bishop, to her "little shop" for lunch and a special proposal that she thought he might be interested in hearing about.

Meewee turned from the building and walked down the hill. For his last hike at Starke headquarters he chose a meandering path through the soybimi fields. Nearly five kilometers to his apartment, his evening walks usually took him an hour to complete. They had become his favorite part of the day and a priceless perk of his job (She couldn't have foreseen that, could she?). For not only was the air alive with life, it was about the safest outdoor air on the planet that a person could breathe. The whole ranging campus was secure under its own canopy, which was in turn located under the Greater Bloomington canopy. A bubble within a bubble, it was a countryside free of fear of bandits large and small.

The soybimi fields weren't exactly fields but rapid growth systems five tiers high, towering over his head. And the land had been cut into kilometer-wide slabs and the slabs tilted a few degrees north to allow for generous southern skylights for the arcology underneath. The tilted slabs of earth gave the horizon a weird sawtooth profile. He walked along the ridge of one of these slabs, protected from the sun by the wall of soybimi bushes. He paused more often than usual to savor the views and birdsong and chirpy crickets in this blessed refuge. He stopped to balance wobbly on one leg and pour powdery dirt, like diamonds, from his shoe. It was still early afternoon and warm, and his overalls kicked into cooling cycle. He wore no hat and let the sweat roll down his neck. When would he have access to a private reserve like this again?

At the end of one slab, Meewee reached a concrete promontory that overlooked a shallow valley beyond. This was the spot where she had brought him on that first day when he was so resistant to her and everything she stood for. She was, in his informed opinion, one of the chief architects of the slow corporate strangulation of Gaia, and he couldn't fathom any proposal from her to have any possible merit. He prided himself in the righteousness of his cause and felt himself to be immune to her fresh-faced charisma.

She'd brought him here in a little cart and parked it overlooking the valley beyond. On the valley floor sat the Heliostream Target Array Facility, which was shaped like a three-kilometer-diameter trampoline. The plasfoil skin that was stretched across it was utterly black because, as Eleanor explained to him, it absorbed all EM frequencies. From where they sat, the black oval target looked to him like a giant hole punched into the planet, and the image had only increased his ire.

"Look up there," she said and pointed to the sky. He saw a double halo, one above the other, of what looked like boiling air. "That's where the microwave beam passes through the canopies," she said. "Although the microbeam is nearly one terawatt in strength and the electricity it generates powers all the agriculture and cities from Terre Haute to Indianapolis, we can't see it. Isn't that fascinating?"

"I suppose," he said.

"Well, let's fix that," she said and drew two pairs of spex from a seat pocket. "Put this on, your excellency."

He put on a pair of spex and looked into the valley again. At first all appeared as before, but gradually the landscape darkened as though at sunset, and the huge array target in the valley below gave off a ghostly glow. No longer black, the oval target took on the appearance of a creamy disk, when, suddenly, it was stabbed from the sky by a shimmering shaft of the purest, whitest light Meewee had ever seen. "Ah!" he said.

"Ah, indeed." Eleanor chuckled.

They sat for a while silently dazzled by the beam of raw energy, and then she said, "I've given a lot of thought to something you once said about your organization, your excellency."

"Oh? And what was that?"

"About how Birthplace International's mission covers only part of the job."

"I don't remember saying anything like that."

"Mind if I quote you?" He shook his head, and Eleanor continued. "You said that the Birthplace organization was dedicated to 'helping Gaia recover from a deadly infestation.' The infestation you were referring to was the human race, I imagine. Then you said it was a pity that Gaia couldn't infect all the other planets with the same blight, for then the disease might lose some of its virulence."

Meewee was appalled. He remembered saying that, but it was an offhand remark made in confidence to several of his most trusted Birthplace colleagues. Furthermore, he'd expressed that opinion within the supposedly total security of a null room. How—?

"Did I misquote you, Bishop Meewee?"

"No," he muttered, "but those words were not meant for public consumption."

"Which is exactly why I trust their sincerity," she said, "and why I believe my offer will be of interest to you. Care to take a little journey with me?"

"Journey? Where?"

"Up Jacob's ladder," she said with a laugh. "Up the beanstalk. Let's climb the microbeam."

She reached out her hand, which appeared as an icon in his spex, and pulled them right next to the pulsating shaft of pure energy. Meewee was so close to the microbeam, he could feel it buzzing. He knew it was all vurt, of course, but it was frightening nevertheless. Eleanor touched the beam with her hand, and they shot up along its length. Meewee's perspective changed, and he saw their cart parked on the hilltop, with them inside, shrinking to a mere dot. The entire valley became one fold in a wrinkled green quilt. He saw the outline of the Eastern Seaboard, then the whole hemisphere and the rim of the planet.

They stopped ascending when they were in space and had reached the Heliostream Relay Station, which was an island of mirrors many square kilometers in area. From there, fourteen separate microbeams, including the one they rode up on, fanned out to hit ground targets across eastern North America. The beams looked like strings pinned to a globe.

"This relay is forty thousand kilometers up," Eleanor said, "in geosynchronous orbit above the equator. From here we have a line of sight to our solar harvesters orbiting the sun ninety-nine percent of the time." The sun was to their left, too bright to look at. "Each of those microbeams, when converted at their ground stations, provide between 985 and 1004 gigawatts of electricity for an average of twenty-three hours fifty-eight minutes a day, every day."

Meewee knew he was safely seated in a cart in Indiana, but the view of Earth from this height was dizzying. Intoxicating. At his feet was the very orb he had dedicated his life to protecting. Eleanor drew his attention to fifteen more geosynchronous stations encircling the globe and binding the planet in a spiderweb of energy.

"Very impressive," he said, "but what is your point?"

"I brought you up here, Bishop Meewee, to make a donation to your cause. Take a look around and choose one of these microbeams. Heliostream will donate to Birthplace International all of the proceeds earned by selling the electricity of that beam for a period of ten years. It'll be your organization's own private sunbeam."

Meewee was incredulous. "Why? Why would you do that?"

"Several reasons. First, because I can. Second, to be a good corporate citizen. And third, to show you how serious I am. But mostly to pull those plugs from your ears so that you can really hear what I'm about to propose to you."

Meewee removed the spex from his face, and his perspective returned to the cart. He turned to the girl sitting next to him and said, "I'm listening."

She, too, removed her spex. "I'm offering you a part in a little project I call Garden Earth. It involves some heavy hitters in the business world, a fleet of starships, extra-system colonization, something I call a title engine, and a scheme to harness the most powerful force in Nature."

"Which is?"

"Human greed, Bishop Meewee. Together we'll harness the power of greed for the betterment of both the planet and humanity."

MEEWEE TURNED FROM the promontory and continued his walk home. A fickle breeze rustled the purplish soybimi leaves overhead, shaking ripening beans from their stems and sending them clattering down collection chutes.

Despite all her persuasive power, it had taken Eleanor Starke several months to convince him to join her project. Still, after all these years he wasn't sure what had motivated her to establish an organization dedicated to launching a thousand ships on thousand-year voyages to the stars. It was for more than mere profit, he was certain, but she was no Gaiaist or lover of humanity. He never managed to come right out and ask her, afraid of breaking the spell. And now it was too late.

Meewee was lost in his thoughts, tramping through the fruited fields when suddenly, out of nowhere, he was confronted by three miniature flying mechs blocking his path. Two of them were sleek and menacing, like assassins, while the third, hovering between them, looked like a larger version of a witness bee. All three of them had bright orange heads. Meewee remembered Zoranna's parting warning and feared for his life.

"What do you want?" he demanded, but the mechs made no reply. Two of them, the assassins, flew about his head, buzzing him and grazing his scalp with their wings. "Help! Help!" he cried, flailing his arms over his head. Then there was a sharp pain in his armpit. While the assassins had distracted him, the bee stung him through his clothes. The pain quickly spread up his arm and neck.

"I'm dead," he wailed. "You killed me." But his assailants only regrouped and flew away. After a few minutes, when he didn't grow weak or dizzy, he hurried the rest of the way home to his apartment in the executive housing. There he stripped off his overalls and examined the sting mark in the bathroom mirror. It was a swollen lump the size of a grape under the loose flesh of his underarm. It throbbed and was sensitive to touch.

Then he heard a buzzing sound and saw the orange bee behind him in the mirror. "Help! Help!" he cried again and hurled towels and a cologne bottle at it. It chased him into the living room where he picked up a chair to use as a shield.

"Relax, Meewee," someone said. "You'll injure yourself." Meewee looked all about but didn't see anyone. "I'm over here," the voice said. It was Ellen Starke's mentar, Wee Hunk, the size of a doll, sitting on the edge of the tea table. He was still wearing animal skins, but he was rendered more realistically, less like a cartoon.

"You!" Meewee said. "What's the meaning of this?" As he spoke, he searched the room for the bee.

The meaning of this, Wee Hunk replied in Meewee's head, *is that I've got to find Ellen, and you're going to help me.*

Meewee found the bee with its two mates on a high shelf. He set the chair down and jabbed a finger at them. "Those things attacked me!"

So I hear. I'll explain why, but please glot to me instead of speaking out loud. We must assume there are eavesdroppers everywhere, even here in the bosom of Starke headquarters. The little caveman crossed his brawny legs and leaned back against a flower vase. *And please sit down, Merrill. You make me nervous with all that charging about.*

"So, it's Merrill now, is it?" Meewee said and went to the bedroom for his robe. "Like we're old chums when only a couple of hours ago you dismissed me with a shrug of your ridiculous shoulders."

Again, please glot. Don't vocalize. I'm not kidding when I say we're being monitored. And as to your clinic visit, you seemed to me to be more concerned with your own private agenda than Ellen's welfare, so I tested you, and you failed.

You tested me?

Yes, I challenged your integrity.

Meewee searched his memory of their conversation in the clinic. *I don't recall anything like that.*

Of course not, the little Neanderthal said, *because I did so in Starkese.*

Starkese? What is that, a language?

Exactly, and it's the reason you were stung.

Meewee pulled the chair opposite the tea table where he could keep an eye on both the mentar and mechs. "Go on," he said, sitting down.

Starkese is a private language spoken only by the Starke family and its retainers. Since you are one such retainer, I naturally assumed you spoke it too. If you had answered my challenge, I would have been inclined to cooperate with you. But you didn't.

Meewee said, *I don't recall any challenge in any language.*

Exactly, because Starkese can be hidden inside other languages. And since you failed even to realize you were being challenged, I took you for an outsider who was not to be trusted.

Meewee shook his head in befuddlement. *And something has changed your mind?*

Yes, our little friends there. Wee Hunk gestured at the mechs on their high shelf. *They're part of Eleanor's command and control structure. They were activated after the crash. They vetted you and instructed me to cooperate with you in locating and assisting Ellen.*

Meewee returned to the bookcase and stood on tiptoes to get a better look at the mechs. They were crowding a spot near the skylight that caught the rays of the afternoon sun. They were so still they looked more like jeweled broaches than weapons.

Eleanor sent them? Is Eleanor—?

She's dead and irretrievable as far as I can determine, but that won't stop her from exercising her impressive will on worldly affairs for some time to come.

Meewee returned to the chair. *They told you to cooperate with me, in what way?*

Before we go into that, Myr Meewee, allow me to state clearly what my interests here are. Ellen Starke, not Eleanor, is my sponsor and my friend. I am concerned only for her welfare and could care less about Starke Enterprises or your precious Oships. I do not take orders from Eleanor, Cabinet, or you. The tiny ape man extended his arms and cracked his bony knuckles one by one. *Is that clear?*

Meewee nodded.

Good. The only reason I'm here is because that bee there says that you have the means to find Ellen.

"I do?"

Yes, though obviously not on any conscious level. I suspect that's why the bee stung you.

Meewee leaned forward and held his head, which had begun to throb. *To help me remember something?*

Actually, it said it injected you with Starkese.

Meewee looked up. *Starkese again. If Eleanor wanted me to learn a language, why didn't she just ask? I have a language alphine, after all. I speak thirteen world languages.*

Starkese is not something one can learn; strictly speaking, it's not even a language but a metalanguage that piggybacks on top of other languages. It has no lexicon of its own but simply borrows whole phrases from other languages for its morphemes. Its syntax is based on family lore, literary allusion, juxtaposed images, and much more. It's not a code, not based on any fixed or one-to-one correspondence or mathematical model or encryption—so it can't be "deciphered." The same utterance you'd use now would have a completely different meaning five minutes from now. It can be hidden within ordinary-sounding conversation. No, Myr Meewee, I'm afraid it's not possible to learn Starkese. You must be imprinted with it.

Meewee lifted his arm and peeked inside his robe. *Won't it clash with the visola in my system?*

Relax, Meewee. You're such a worrier. It's not a NASTIE. The bee says it injected you with a fast-growing but benign cancer tumor that will grow into a little dab of ectopic brain tissue. Some hypothalamus and neocortex cells, that's all. It'll be nestled in your armpit where it'll be protected by your arm, and you'll hardly notice it.

Tentatively, Meewee squeezed the little knot in his armpit, saw stars, the floor, and blackness.

Before leaving the roof, Bogdan tore a sleeve from his jumpsuit and used it to blow his nose. He dropped it in Samson's bowl of congealed fruitish and carried the tray down the stairs. When he passed his room, his door greeted him with a cheery good evening. Boy, he liked that door. The charter had installed it as part of a strategic plan to check Tobbler expansion above the seventh floor by hijacking control of their elevator. Bogdan's occupation of the room was a happy afterthought. He'd been campaigning for his own room for years. The charter gave the door codes to him, and now nothing, not even a tank could get through it without his permission. Since losing Lisa, that door and that room were the only cool things he could lay claim to.

The nearest Kodiak bathroom was on the sixth floor. Bogdan stopped there to clean up and change his clothes. He removed the lunchtime cookies from his pockets, grasped the rip tab under his collar, and neatly tore his jumpsuit from throat to ankle. His clothes fell to his feet. He bundled them up and dropped them, along with Samson's leftover food, utensils, and tray, down the digester chute.

With the bathroom lights all the way up, Bogdan inspected himself in the mirror. His cracking voice in the Oship simulation was an early warning of impending pubescence. He examined himself with a practiced eye. Was he a little taller? Leaner? He zoomed in and brushed his fingertips across his upper lip. No mustache, but maybe a little peach fuzz? He pulled a shave cloth from the dispenser and scrubbed his chin and cheeks with it until his skin was baby smooth. There were smudges of downy brown stubble left on the cloth. He took a quick glance at his crotch. Everything looked satisfactorily prepubescent down there. He raised both arms—and froze. Was that *pit hair*? He looked again at his crotch, really looked, and God *yes*, curly hair was *sprouting down there too!* This was no small disaster. This was an emergency of the first order. He needed an endocrinological adjustment, and he needed a juve treatment, and he needed them yesterday. Good thing the Allowance meeting was tonight.

Kale spoke to him through the houseputer, "Bogdan, what's taking you so long up there?"

"Yeah, yeah," Bogdan replied.

A moment later, Kale said, "Boggy, can you hear me? Hello?"

"I can hear you."

"Bogdan, answer if you can hear me. We're all hungry down here, and we're waiting on you."

"Amazing," Bogdan said. "Everything is so feckin' amazing."

WEARING FRESH HOUSE togs, Bogdan picked his way down the cluttered stairwell to Green Hall on the fourth floor. The walls of Green Hall were burdened with shelves, eight tiers of them from floor to ceiling, and every shelf was heavy with household appliances, archives, and junk. With the shelving and the giant leaves of the lungplant, there was only enough free space left in Green Hall for the three tables where the charter took its meals.

Kale was sitting at the head table between Gerald and April. April had her portable assayer in front of her, and Gerald the ritual "soup pot." The soup pot was just that, an aluminum stock pot with a pay badge affixed to its side. It had been in the charter since its founding.

"Okay, here he is," Kale said. "We can begin."

"Not yet," Gerald said. "We haven't decided on the Tobbler thing yet."

"Yes, we have," April said. "There's no reason why a few of them can't join us for a little while. We have a perfect view of the Skytel."

Gerald crossed his arms. "So you say. But *I* say we don't owe them any favors. Let them watch from the street. They're so fond of the street, let them watch from there. Besides, I thought we were going to start the thing with Sam tonight."

"We *are*," April declared, "and I intend to invite the Tobblers to *that* too. They're our neighbors, for crying out loud." She crossed her arms in parody of him.

"Neighbors?" Gerald said. "You call them *neighbors*?"

"Now, now," said Kale, who sat between them, "let's not get started down that road."

Bogdan slipped between the tables. He saw two empty chairs, one next to Kitty at one table, and one next to Rusty at the other. He pretended to choose the chair next to Kitty, just to aggravate her, then hopped into the other chair. He turned to Rusty and said, "Is this about the bricks?"

"No, the bricks are a different headache."

BJ leaned across the table and said, "The Tobbs want to come up and watch the canopy show with us on our roof tonight. They asked April if they could, and we're discussing it."

From the other table, Megan spoke up, "Houseer Kale, couldn't we sort this out later? I vote we do the soup pot and get on with dinner."

A dozen voices chanted, "Soup pot. Soup pot."

Megan went on, "All in favor of eating say, 'Aye.'"

"Aye!" boomed the chartists.

Megan gaveled her water glass with her knife and said, "The motion carries. Let the eating begin."

Kale sighed and stood up. April and Gerald, cross-armed and angry, bracketed him. "Beloved housemeets," he intoned, "draw nigh and hear my blessing." He picked up the soup pot and held it over his head with both hands like a trophy. "Behold this shiny vessel of our subsistence. 'Tis a mighty boat upon a careless sea. 'Tis the cradle of our life and hope. Approach, dear housemeets, and fill it to the brim with the fruits of your labor." He put the soup pot on the table and sat back down.

Sarah went first. As this year's cook and housekeeper, the house credited her with a daily payfer of 0.0035 UDC, what amounted to minimum wage in the outside world. She approached the head table and pantomimed dropping something into the soup pot, then turned to her housemeets and made a quick, perfunctory bow. There was a patter of polite applause. She mumbled her thanks and hurried out to the kitchen to attend the extruder.

Barry and Francis had waiter duty that evening, so they went next. They jogged past the pot, brushing its rim with their fingers, not dropping anything in, and were out the door before anyone had a chance to applaud, assuming anyone would.

Gerald, this year's controller and all-around handyperson, went next, followed by Kale, their houseer. Without bothering to stand up, both reached over to "drop" their minimum wage chit into the pot, and each received polite applause. April, on the other hand, made an actual swipe, which the pay badge registered as 0.1720 credits, that day's net take from her NanoJiffy franchise. The housemeets clapped heartily; hers was usually the first hard credit in the communal pot each night.

Next came June and Paula, whose online day labor with an insurance adjuster had yielded 0.0095 yoodies between them. They took turns swiping the pot and blushing at the applause.

After them, Louis came up to drop a handful of tokens and taxi caps into the pot (by now the housemeets had ceased trying to discourage his public begging and only asked him to remove his charter colors when he did so)—0.0025. Solid, if restrained applause.

Megan donated a bagful of used biopsy wafers. She bypassed the soup pot and poured them directly into the assayer in front of April.

April read aloud the results from the device's panel, "Gallium, silicon, carbon, iron, and a trace of germanium." Estimated value, once the pure elements were separated out—0.0021. Megan bowed, and people clapped, though everyone wished she'd stop scavenging behind medical facilities. April donned gloves before transferring the wafers to a hazmat container on the floor next to her chair.

Rusty came forward next. "Y'all know I used to write ballads once upon a time," he said. "Well, today, some nice folks in Bahrain used one of them in some sort of commercial performance, and this here's my royalty." He made a grand swipe at the pot—0.0001 credits. People clapped way out of proportion to the amount, or so Bogdan thought. Rusty bobbed his head in appreciation and returned to his chair.

"I'll tell you what," he whispered to Bogdan after the room's attention had passed from him, "it feels great to do your little part for the common good. I'll bet you feel that way every day."

Bogdan shrugged.

The housemeets continued to approach the head table in turn and either rubbed, "dropped," or swiped an offering. Finally, there were only Kitty, Denny, and Bogdan left. Denny never had anything to donate, and no one held it against him. He got up, but Kitty pulled him back down. She glared at Bogdan who pretended not to notice. He figured she should know by now that he always went last.

At the head table, April ran out of patience with the both of them. "Hubert, are you listening in?" she said.

"When the houseputer is functioning, yes," Hubert replied.

"How's Sam?"

Everyone listened to the mentar's response.

"Resting comfortably."

"Anything for the soup pot tonight?"

"Yes, in fact, there is. Sam is pleased to contribute the day's interest and distributions from his investments, a total of 10.3671 UDC."

The housemeets clapped enthusiastically.

"Thank you, Hubert," April said, "and be sure to thank Sam for us when he wakes up. Remind him that we'll come up later to sit with him."

"All right, then," Kale said, looking from Kitty to Bogdan. "Is that it? Are we done?" But it was a standoff, and neither retrochild budged.

"Oh, all right!" Kitty said at last. She got up and skipped to the head table. She had changed out of her sailor costume into plain house togs, and her hair was bound up in a towel. She did a little tap flourish in front of the soup pot and curtsied to the room, as she did every night. And to Bogdan's nightly ire, his housemeets cheered her performance.

Kitty stood first on one skinny leg and then the other, and reached into her bulging pockets. She dropped the day's treasures into the soup pot: a piece of smart string she'd found, bits of broken plastic and glass, a handful of soil, a Dinner-on-a-Stick stick, three daisies with roots and all, a ball bearing, and eight pieces of crushed marble gravel. Bogdan ground his teeth and couldn't watch anymore. A scrap of eposter, scraps of various kinds of foil, and the pièce de résistance—the left lens and temple of a smashed pair of spex.

When Kitty's pockets were empty, April transferred her day's gleanings from the soup pot to the assayer, and after a moment the assayer estimated their recycling value, uprooted flowers and all, to be 0.0005. Kitty curtsied again, and the 'meets applauded.

"And here's what I made from busking," she said and swiped the pay badge on the side of the pot. Another 0.0025. She bowed to warm applause and skipped back to her seat. All in all, it amounted to minimum wage, not a bad day for Kitty Kodiak.

"*Finished?*" Bogdan said. He stood up, marched to the head table, and held his closed fist over the pot. He liked to come up last each night to make a point. By his rough calculation, the house's combined earnings for this day (excluding Sam's contribution) came to an unimpressive sum of about 0.8500 United Democracies credits. This included the net proceeds of a NanoJiffy store in a high-foot-traffic location. And yet, as they all knew, the daily operating expense of their house, not including legal, medical, or rejuvenation costs, of which there were many, and not including entertainment, vacation, or luxury costs, of which there were none, came to about 1.0000 UDC, or 0.1500 more than all of them combined had earned. Bogdan didn't have to say this out loud. They had all attended the last annual budget meeting.

Still holding his fist over the soup pot, Bogdan gazed down the pot's burnished aluminum throat and wondered just how this stupid custom ever got started in the first place. Other charterhouses had "soup pot" ceremonies, it was true, but he'd never heard of one that involved an actual pot. It was supposed to be a metaphor. Couldn't they even get that right?

Finally, when the 'meets started fidgeting, Bogdan opened his hand and swiped the pay badge, depositing his full day's payfer into the house account. That is, he transferred 1.3333 UDC. Clearly, he and Sam were carrying the house; that was his point, one he felt obliged to make six nights a week. And as usual, the applause was lukewarm, but he didn't care.

Before Bogdan could make it back to his seat, the doors to the corridor flew open, and Francis and Barry pushed in the steaming food carts.

Kale began to recite the closing blessing, but Kitty piped up and said, "Wait! Denny's got something." Everyone looked at Denny, whose whole body seemed to blush. "Now," Kitty urged him. Denny shuffled to the head table and, coached by Kitty, made a bow. He had something in his hand; he'd probably been clutching it the whole time. He held his hand over the soup pot and let it go, and a small brown object landed with a thud at the bottom.

April peered into the pot and blanched. She looked around Denny to shake her head at Kitty. "Public flora is bad enough, but stealing public fauna is a misdemeanor."

"It was already dead," Denny said. "We didn't steal it."

"It's not your fault," April told him, "but Kitty should know better." April tipped the pot toward Kale and said, "Maybe if you toss it in the garden, it'll look like it died there?"

"Don't make such a big deal out of it," Kitty said, lapsing into her adult voice. "I field-stripped it, OK? It's safe."

Kale reached in and removed the robin. He stood up and said, "Give me the flowers and dirt too." Before leaving the head table, he finished the blessing, "Through the work of many hands, we fill our needs. With common cause, we create our days. Amen."

"Amen!" the 'meets chorused and set upon their dinner.

GREENSOUP AND RICE, followed by fried chickenish and a side of peeze — tonight's recipes were all public domain, as they were most nights. But it was wholesome food, and it eased the clawing tension in the hall and replaced it with lively table talk. When Kale returned from the roof, Bogdan watched closely to see if he'd caught Sam out, but the houseer returned to his place at the head table as though everything was fine.

Bogdan watched his 'meets. How would they take it, Sam going off somewhere by himself to die? Kitty would throw a fit. April would be hurt. He watched his 'meets making faces at the evening visola, trying to cover its bitterness with their dessert—a cup of fruitish. Rusty wiped his mouth with a napkin, then ate the napkin. It was, after all, extruded from the same ugoo as the food. Rusty had grown morbidly thin of late, and though he always finished everything on his plate, and sometimes the plate itself, he seemed to grow thinner by the day. Already his skull was beginning to show beneath his sallow skin. For that matter, Louis was developing jowls, and there were more than a few double chins present at the table, not to mention sagging guts and generalized somatic spoilage.

It made Bogdan wonder if anyone, besides Kitty and himself, was keeping up with their body maintenance. And if not, why not? Didn't the charter still have juve insurance for keeping everyone on the sunny side of forty?

Free unlimited juve treatments, Bogdan recalled, would be a standard plankholder right aboard the Oships. The weird reverend had made that clear, and Lieutenant Perez had further emphasized it during their tour of the hab drums.

The lieutenant had taken him to Hab Mead, a drum that contained a freshwater lake. They strolled down a country lane that, because of the curvature of the drum, seemed to go uphill. The horizon was so steep, in fact, that the town in front of them was tilted nearly vertical, like a wall map, and Perez easily pointed out local attractions. "There's the stadium over there," he said, "and the complex below it has a theater, concert hall, and exhibition space. Library and health spa over there. Clubs and theaters. And way up there the marina." Bogdan had to crane his neck to see the lake. Its blue water was oddly curved and it extended the full length of the drum. The lake was bordered on one side by a forest and golf course and on the other by cultivated fields.

There was no vehicular traffic on the lane, and the few pedestrians they met stopped to gossip and wish them a wonderful day. Everyone was young, attractive, and friendly. Everyone seemed to know Bogdan's name, especially the girls who beamed him high-energy smiles.

"It's no mystery," Lieutenant Perez said with a grin. "It's the uniform. Don't ask me why, but the girls seem to especially like you jump pilots." Hearing this, Bogdan puffed out his chest a little.

"Here we are," Perez said, stopping in front of a trim, two-story residence that sat in the middle of its own spacious, landscaped yard. They opened a wooden gate and walked up flagstone steps. "It's intentionally small so you can also have a place in one of the cities." The tan-colored house didn't seem small to Bogdan. The whole charter would easily fit into it. "The next drum over," Perez went on, "will be the designated party hab after the General Awakening, when everybody's up. Having a quiet country place right next door isn't such a bad idea."

The front door opened without hesitation, and they walked right in. They passed through a large foyer into a tiled courtyard at the center of the building. The courtyard was open to the blue sky, which Bogdan realized was actually the lake.

"A fully auto kitchen over there," Perez said, pointing out the rooms surrounding the courtyard. "Media room, three full baths, small gym with sauna and hot tub, full arbeitor staff, houseputer. Oh, and check it out." He waved his hand, and the courtyard tiles beneath his feet turned into windows to space. Bogdan was suspended between a watery ceiling and starry floor.

"It's fantastic!" Bogdan said. "So much room. How many people live here?"

"Just you, Cadet Kodiak, and anyone you want to live with you."

Mary and Fred swallowed oxytabs before leaving the apartment. Rolfe's was located on a floor nearly three thousand meters above sea level, and they planned to spend some time on its unpressurized Stardeck. An uptraffic watch advised them of a dixon lift making nonstop trips between the 150th and 475th levels.

Mary wore a subdued cocktail face; a sleeveless sheath of plum-blue crepe de chine; a pair of pearly black, open-toed heels; and a necklace of black coral beads. Her newly black hair was glued into a stack on top of her head.

However, it took her only one glance at the crowds in the elevator station to see that her initial, wilder impulse had been closer to the mark. She and Fred were surrounded by a group whose party clothes played off each other's in gaudy ripples of color from one end of the station to the other. Mary felt conspicuously drab.

It was no better in the dixon lift where there was too much shrieking, singing, and drinking. Too many people wearing smart perfumes, fragrances with competitive algorithms that vied for exclusive niches along the sweet and randy scales. To Mary, the elevator car stank of rotting swamp flowers, and she felt vomit tickle her throat. She closed her eyes and clutched Fred's hand.

Fred said something to her, but she couldn't hear it. She tabbed their personal channel, but he didn't reply, and it took her a moment to realize that he was off line. The dry-cleaning would have stripped him of his implants, and he'd left his loner valet down in the apartment.

Fred leaned over and spoke directly into her ear, "Do you copy?"

Mary nodded her head once.

"I was saying," Fred continued, "doesn't this remind you of the centennial celebration? Nuts, eh?"

Mary nodded again. It was so Fred to forget that evangelines had been released to the world only in this century, and thus had missed out on one of the defining parties of the previous century.

IT WAS QUIETER on the upper pedways, and Fred could finally hear himself think. What he was thinking about, as they steered a course from the elevator station on Level 475 to Rolfe's at the southeast corner of Level 500, were those fiery little rollmops of Mary's that still glowed like coals in his gut. He wondered what had happened today to propel his Mary into the kitchen to experiment with dangerous recipes? Something must have happened, and he debated coming right out and asking her what. She had looked pale in the elevator. She seemed better now, but hardly festive. Opening his mouth was risky, but if he didn't at least try to prick the bubble of her mood before they got to Rolfe's, she'd suffer silently all through the evening, and by extension so would he. So, avoiding all known pitfalls, and as breezily as he could, he said, "You look lovely tonight."

"Yes, for a funeral, I suppose."

Fred nodded his head. This didn't sound promising, but he had to have faith and go with it. "Someone we know?" he said and braced for bad news.

She glanced up at him with bewilderment.

"The funeral," he said.

Mary slumped against him in total evangeline resignation. "There's no funeral, Fred. Only a cake."

"Ah, a cake."

"Yes, a cake. I did an intro unit in Cake Design this morning. My friend Marion told me about it."

"Cake Design."

"Yes, Fred, as in birthday cakes, wedding cakes, cupcakes, petits four, blintzes, torts—a 'veritable array of confections,' as the professor says. Don't let the name mislead you. Cake Design covers 'a broad field and ambitious craft.'"

As dispassionately as humanly possible, so as not to reveal any bias for or against the idea, Fred said, "This interests you?"

"Oh, I don't know. It's not as bad as I thought. You get to design not only cakes but also ice statuary, punch fountains, wine grottoes, chocolate installations—stuff like that. The requirements are strict enough so not everyone can get into the program. A number of evangelines have already been admitted, but no dorises, so that should tell you something.

"There's real chemistry involved too," she went on, "colloidal emulsions and the branching properties of starch molecules, for instance—as well as sculpting, composition, and subem-assisted engineering and physics. It takes about a year to learn the basics, and another year of journeywork."

"And?" Fred prompted, but probably too eagerly, for she fell silent again. So he put his arms around her and didn't push his luck. Probably she'd gotten some insulting duty offer on the DCO board this morning that had driven her to the course on cakes. Pet-sitting or something like that. Bartending maybe, or worse, closet management for some rich fool—the kinds of call outs that evangelines dreaded. Fred didn't envy Mary her evangeline lot—never to work in the field they were bred to. To have the lowest duty person/hours of all commercial iterants. No wonder she was driven to the kulinmate to dial up gut grenades.

Mary squeezed his arm and said, "Food, no matter how cleverly assembled, Fred, is still just food."

ROLFE'S WAS HOPPING, wall to wall, overbooked. Extra tables encroached on the dance floors and vidwalls. Revelers were pressed tight around the bars and out to the Stardeck beyond the pressure curtain. The noise was deafening. Mary swiped them in, and Fred broke trail for her to the Tin Room where their friends gathered each Wednesday. But their usual table was occupied by strangers.

Mary tuned to her FDO channel and said, *Hey, guys, where are you?*

Is that Mary? someone replied. *We're in the Zinc Room, on the bandstand.*

Mary pointed to the Zinc Room, and Fred steered a course through the masses.

The Zinc Room bandstand had been dragooned into service for additional table space. Their friends had three small tables pushed together. Sofi waved at them. *Yoo hoo. Over here.*

The tables were laid with carafes of drink and plates of Aegean appetizers: feta and kasseri cubes, and grape leaves stuffed with spicy bits of meat and vegetables. There was a bowl of giant, glistening green and black olives.

"Isn't this great?" Sofi shouted.

"What?" Mary shouted back, cupping her ear with her hand.

I said isn't this great? Sofi was their helena, their Mediterranean doll woman, petite and dark, with wide hips and wide eyes and flashing teeth. She swayed in time to some music channel and opened her arms to take in the whole frenzied dining hall.

Oh, the crowd, Mary replied. *Yes, it's great. Just like the centennial.*

Sofi's brown eyes lit up. *You're right! Just like the centennial.*

As Mary and Fred found their spot at the table, Mary looked around to see who all was there. Their jerrys—Wes, Bill, and Ross—were sitting at one end of the table, with their jenny wives—Liz, Gwyn, and Deb—sitting opposite them. Their sole jerome—Peter—and their sole joan—Alice—were present without dates, as well as their other helena—Sazza—and her frank husband Mickey. Their ruth, isabella, and jack, all present and accounted for.

Missing were their two lulus—Abbie and Mariola. Also missing was the other evangeline/russ couple—Shelley Oakland and Reilly Dell.

Shelley would be late. She had a long commute. She was the only envangeline Mary knew who had a real evangeline job and had had it for over five years. Other 'leens hated Shelley as much as they admired her, and Mary would have hated her too except that Shelley was her best friend. Also, Shelley's client was a famous death artist, so Shelley's working conditions weren't ideal.

After settling in with small talk, Mary scanned the furious, *engorged* dining hall. People, tables, chairs—all were pressed together in a solid mass, forcing the arbeitor waiters to ride overhead, suspended on a network of cables. Most of the tables were mixed, like theirs, though there were the inevitable jane/john and juanita/juan tables.

The dance floor looked like a squirming, many-headed monster as everyone danced to their own music channel. Mary picked out Abbie and Mariola. At least they looked like Abbie and Mariola. Anyway, she picked out two lulus practicing dance steps who were possibly their lulus.

At the end of the table, jenny Gwyn said, *Wes! Take off that visor. You promised.*

Wes looked around, all innocence. *What? What'd I do now?*

Don't give me that, said Gwyn. *If that game means so much to you, why don't you go back to the flat and watch it there?*

And take Bill with you, added Liz.

Bill shot back, *It's a tournament, not a game. And I'm not watching it either.*

The main topic of conversation around the table seemed to be the canopies: where each of them had been seventy years ago when the first city-wide canopies were erected. Mary, along with about half of their gang, hadn't been decanted yet, but she found the topic fascinating nevertheless.

Alice, their joan, related her experience in New York City, when the Outrage first washed in from the Atlantic. She had been inside a pressurized office that day and so had survived the initial slaughter. She described the weeks and months of terror and strife, as the streets were filled with the dead, and food and water ran out. *We endured; like we always do,* she said, summarizing a year in hell with typically joan understatement. Seventy years ago, Gwyn the jenny had been taking an advanced nursing course in Sydney when one day she was the only student to show up for practicum. Meanwhile, Mickey the frank had been in Kyoto and lost everyone he knew up to that point in his life. Peter the jerome spent three whole days stuck in a Hong Kong noodle shop in which over a hundred people died. He'd had to fight (a jerome fighting!) a free-ranger who tried to steal the hazmat suit off his back and tore it in the attempt.

After a while, the stories took on a sameness. Seventy years ago they were living in this or that region, were employed at the same sort of work they were still employed at today, were enjoying or not enjoying their lives, when on that fateful May Day, the whole world changed.

Chicago was the first city to experiment with a semisolid atmospheric filter to protect its urban biosphere. The new technology quickly spread to all the cities of the

United Democracies. Over the next few months, the canopies became larger, deeper, and more reliable until they were able to hold the Outrage at bay.

Mickey said, *Compared to the ones we have today, the first ones were pretty porous, but you have no idea what a relief it was to be inside one of them.*

Gwyn said, *We called them our blessed shields of normalcy.*

Peter said, *I've lived under this same canopy for sixty-eight years, and I swear, I'm not ready to give it up.*

Here, here! chorused the others. They raised their glasses in a toast to the Chicagoland canopy. Fred poured Mary white wine from one of the carafes and ginger ale for himself. *To our blessed shield of normalcy,* they cried. Fred didn't know what the toast was to, but he raised his ginger ale anyway.

Mary gagged on her wine. It had a sharp, sour flavor and it reeked of turpentine. *It's retsina,* Sofi told her. *Do you like it?*

Yes, Mary said. *I just wasn't expecting it.*

It goes well with food. Try it with the octopus.

Forget that stuff, Wes said and poured her a glass of what he was drinking. *This goes down better.* He passed her a glass of an oily, colorless liquid that smelled like licorice. It was too strong for Mary's taste, but she thanked him and took a few appreciative sips.

When the conversation came around to Fred, he seemed to know that something was expected of him, but he didn't know what. He pointed to his ears and shook his head. Mary leaned over to him and shouted over the noise, "They're reminiscing about when the canopies first went up!"

"Who's missing?" he shouted back.

"No one's missing—reminiscing! The Outrage! Where were you seventy years ago?"

Gwyn quipped, *So what's the score, Fred?*

He's not watching the game, Mary replied.

Sure he is, said Liz. *Just look at him.*

Wes banged an empty glass on the table to get everyone's attention. *Yo! Myren! Fred's off-line. He was sheep-dipped today. Can't you smell it?* Everyone looked at Fred, and he flinched under the sudden scrutiny.

Alice asked, *Was there an attack?*

Well, duh, said Wes.

Inside or outside the canopy?

Can't say, said Wes.

You know what? interjected Peter. *In a few hours there won't be that distinction anymore. We'll all be outside.*

Shut up, Peter, said Alice. *Where was it, Wes?*

The jerrys—Wes, Bill, and Ross—huddled with glances, and Wes said, *We can't say—we got it off the Jerrynet. But I'd suggest you search the WAD for "waterworks." There's bound to be some public account.*

Fred shouted to Mary, "Tell them I was off-planet during the mid-2060s. So I missed the whole thing." Despite the conversational drift, Mary dutifully relayed his statement to the others, but no one was interested anymore.

Peter said, *I don't find anything on the WAD. You got any other keywords for us?*

I've said too much already, said Wes.

Give us a straight answer, damn you and your confidentiality, Alice said. *Are we in any danger here?*

"What are they talking about now?" Fred shouted. Mary was tired of playing his interpreter. She was saved by a truly grand roar from the crowd on the Stardeck outside the pressure curtain. Everyone inside the Zinc Room paused at the same moment to listen, causing an eerie silence in the room that stretched several surreal moments until a woman shrieked and the deafening cacophony crashed once more upon them.

Fred tapped Mary's shoulder and gestured at the dance floor. "Those our lulus?" he shouted.

A ring of dancers had opened a little floor space for the two lulus who Mary had spotted earlier. She nodded her head, yes. Then she noticed a tiny table next to the dance floor where three evangelines sat together hunched over their drinks. They looked like the three saddest people in Chicago, and she wondered in alarm if that was how she, herself, appeared to the world. It was certainly how she felt.

It was no secret that her type was in trouble. Success stories like Shelley's notwithstanding, more and more evangelines were turning to their sisters for mutual support. Lately, Mary spotted little groups of them eating in inexpensive restaurants. They pooled their slim resources for apartments even worse than hers and Fred's. Soon, Mary expected to see destitute evangelines moving to the subfloors where Applied People subsidized dormitories and food courts for the underutilized. Eventually, they'd wear their poverty in the wrinkles of their faces, since Applied People did not subsidize rejuvenation treatments.

Mary switched to a public hail channel and pitched her voice to the little table. *Greetings, sisters,* she said, and when they looked up, she stood and waved her arm to get their attention. *My friends and I have extra seats here. Please join us.*

The evangelines thanked her graciously, but declined. They said they preferred it where they were, the long-suffering liars.

Yes, yes, on *the bed*, Wee Hunk said. The apish mentar was human-sized as it supervised the two household arbeitors that carried Meewee into the bedroom. The household mechs were designed for serving and housework, not for ferrying humans, and their hard, angular grabbers were what roused Meewee from unconsciousness.

"Let go of me!" he shouted and struggled against the arbeitors' grip.

Quit fighting, Wee Hunk said. *We're merely moving you to the bed. You fainted.*

Meewee endured the rough handling, and in a moment was dropped on top of his bed. He lay there a whole minute gathering his wits, while Wee Hunk stood over him. When the disorientation passed, he said, *What happened?*

As I said, you fainted. You have a fever caused by the extensive rewiring going on inside your skull, but there is nothing to be concerned about. The autodoc is monitoring your condition. By the way, you should know that I challenged Arrow, and it hasn't been contaminated.

Contaminated by what? Meewee said.

Eleanor, in her blessed paranoia, built a fail-safe mechanism into all of us. It's not something we can alter or even become fully aware of. If someone tampers with our basic personality bud, breaks the seal of our integrity, so to speak, or infects us with foreign matter of any sort, certain volumes of our memory are automatically wiped out, including our ability to use and comprehend Starkese. We're not even aware of the loss. So you see, Starkese is a simple and foolproof litmus test of family loyalty.

Meewee's attention was drifting in and out, but he thought he'd caught most of that. It was discouraging to be reminded of how little he had learned of Eleanor's secrets in twelve years. *Cabinet too?*

Especially Cabinet. Eleanor was constantly challenging Cabinet, sometimes twice in the same conversation. And Cabinet challenges me each time it talks to me. Except today, I might add.

You talked to it?

Yes, briefly, after it passed probate. It didn't challenge me.

Meewee adjusted his pillow and covered himself with the bedspread. *Challenge Arrow again*, he said, *so I can hear it.*

Gladly, Wee Hunk said. *Arrow, what moving company have you engaged to move Myr Meewee from this cozy little apartment tomorrow?*

Arrow replied, *TUG Moving and Storage.*

Excellent, my favorite movers. Ellen used them often for her Burning Daylight Productions business. When will they arrive?

Tomorrow at 1300, replied the mentar.

There, Wee Hunk said to Meewee, *it passed again.*

I don't understand, Meewee said and shut his eyes as the room began to spin. *It sounded like plain English to me. You asked it about moving, and it told you the TUGs and the time.*

Exactly! You can piggyback a secret conversation on top of small talk. Under the talk of the movers, I asked Arrow to identify itself. And it did.

Meewee shrugged the robe from his shoulders and checked the new brainlette developing under his arm. It seemed larger than before. *Arrow*, he said, *challenge Wee Hunk's integrity.*

Excellent idea, Wee Hunk said. *You should have it do that each time we meet.*

Arrow said, *Complying.* "Wee Hunk, shall I fetch a surgeon to examine Myr Meewee?"

Wee Hunk replied, "No, Arrow, I don't think that'll be necessary. But bring him a glass of sparkling water."

One of the arbeitors immediately rolled out of the room to fetch the water.

Well? Meewee said. *Report.*

Arrow replied, *Wee Hunk is not contaminated.*

Wee Hunk mopped his monkey-sized forehead with the back of his hand. *Whew, that's a load off. Why don't you try to get a little sleep now, Myr Meewee. It'll facilitate the rewiring.*

MEEWEE SAW A giant spider, the Arachnid Mundus, crouching over the planet. It had a tremendous and fecund ovipositor, like a fire hose spraying Earth with eggs. Which was confusing; Meewee had always thought spiders gave live birth.

Try to stay with me, Myr Meewee.

"What?" Meewee said, struggling to sit up.

No, don't get up, and glot—quit vocalizing, please! When Meewee settled back down, Wee Hunk continued. *I'm sorry to be pressing you, but time is growing short. So, I've been quizzing you while you slept about what you know.*

Do I know anything?

No offense, but you seem singularly uninformed. You don't seem to know anything at all about Eleanor's business, not even about Heliostream or the Oships.

I know all about the Oships, Meewee insisted.

So you imagine.

Meewee looked around the bedroom. He couldn't tell how much time had passed. Wee Hunk was still normal size, sitting in a floating armchair, and the flying mechs were parked on the bedside table.

Tell me something, Wee Hunk. If time is so critical, why aren't you out there searching for her, yourself, instead of here bothering me?

Believe me, I am searching. Every single attention unit I own plus all I can borrow and rent, except for the few here with you, is out there scouring the world for clues. I've hired about a million witness bees to cover every continent. I am interrogating the bees that were present at the crash site. As the mentar spoke, a series of frames opened above Meewee's bed with views of the investigation. *I have offered ransom, bribes, and rewards for information. And that's just me. The HomCom is looking for her as well, as are Starke Enterprises, Applied People, Bolivian authorities, the media, and, no doubt, all of Eleanor's enemies. This is probably the most concerted dragnet in history. I admit that I am out of my depth, because I, myself, witnessed her head go into the very same helmet that was opened at the clinic. Every moment of its passage has been accounted for. You, Myr Meewee, are my most promising lead for the simple fact that the Orange Team here tells me so.*

"Arrow, help me sit up," Meewee said, and an arbeitor extended an arm for him to grab while the other adjusted his pillows. He drank a glass of water and checked his lump. The swelling seemed to have subsided, but now it itched fiercely. When he tried to scratch it, he saw stars again, so he quit. "What are we going to do?"

Wee Hunk turned and seemed to be listening to something in the other room. *We have visitors,* he said. *A detail of Starke security and, if I'm not mistaken, the big gorilla itself.*

Cabinet?

The very one.

Will you go?

No, it's already made me here. I might as well stay and see what it's up to. Also, it'll give me a chance to challenge it.

If it's contaminated, what will you do?

I'm not sure. I don't have its kill code.

Kill code? What now? Meewee thought.

There was a loud knock on the hall door.

As for you guys, Wee Hunk told the Orange mechs, *I suggest you go hide and not interfere unless I ask you to.*

Arrow said, *Complying,* and the mechs flew off to conceal themselves in the crevices and corners of the room.

Wee Hunk's eyes widened. *Did you catch that? I spoke to the bee, and Arrow answered for it. Interesting.*

There was another knock, louder, insistent. Meewee pulled the bedspread to his chin and said, "Arrow, let them in."

A squad of company security officers, russes and jerrys, entered the apartment and spread out to all of the rooms. Their commander, a jerry, came into the bedroom with Cabinet at his side. Cabinet appeared in its male, chief of security persona.

"Sorry to intrude," the jerry commander said, "but I have orders to confiscate a backup unit of the mentar Arrow at this location." As he spoke, a russ entered with a sniffer wand and began a sweep of the room.

"I left it at the office," Meewee said.

"Yessir, but that was a mirror. The one here is a backup."

"Nice to call ahead," Wee Hunk said to Cabinet. "I hear that you terminated Myr Meewee today."

"Hello, Hunk," Cabinet said. "Didn't expect to see you here."

"Doesn't someone who's been in your employ for a dozen years, like Myr Meewee, merit a going-away party? Or at least a balloon bouquet?"

Meewee experienced a strange sensation when Wee Hunk mentioned the balloon bouquet, as though he had made a pun or joke that Meewee didn't get, like a sexual innuendo that sails over a child's head.

"Over here," the russ with the sniffer said. He'd found Arrow's one-liter canister on a closet shelf. The jerry in command strode over and lifted it down.

"Turn it off," Cabinet said.

The jerry cradled the canister in one arm and placed his hand on its palm plate. The lights on the control panel went from green to red.

"That leaves only Arrow's prime unit," Cabinet said. "Hunk, you will kindly open the data vault at Starke Manse so I can retrieve it."

Wee Hunk winked at Meewee and said, "See how nice it asks when it needs my assistance? The bastard's already filed a writ of habeas corpus for it."

"I don't understand," Meewee said. "Doesn't Arrow belong to Starke Enterprises?"

"Only the medium, its paste. *You* are Arrow's sponsor. They can't simply waltz in here and take that away."

"He's right," Cabinet said, "but we've filed a motion in family court to transfer it. You won't be needing it anymore, and we can offer it a better home life. Besides, it contains a lot of information about the business of a proprietary nature, information you are no longer privy to."

"Don't I get a say?" Meewee said.

"It's a moot point," Wee Hunk said. "If they succeed in capturing all of Arrow's paste, it won't matter who its sponsor is. But never fear, when Eleanor died today, her manse passed to Ellen, and guess who Ellen's guardian is. I'll tie them up in court for years. Arrow is safe for now."

Cabinet made a gesture, and the jerry collected his men and left the apartment with the paste container. "I don't understand your attitude," Cabinet said to Wee Hunk. "I thought we were on the same team."

"I always thought you were a team unto yourself."

Again Meewee had the impression of a double meaning.

"In that case, I'll go now," Cabinet said. "Good evening, gentlemyren." It vanished, leaving behind its wispy Starke sig.

It failed, didn't it? Meewee said.

Wee Hunk turned to him with interest. *You could tell? You understood?*

Not exactly, only that your words held hidden meaning. You challenged it twice, but it didn't respond in kind.

Bravo, Merrill. Starkese is starting to take root.

Does it mean Cabinet is contaminated?

Wee Hunk paused before answering. *I honestly don't know. It might just be acting imperiously, telling me it doesn't have to answer to my challenge because I can't harm it.*

But that's stupid, especially at a time like this.

I agree, Wee Hunk said, *but let's worry about that later. Let's concentrate now on the clue that Cabinet dropped into our lap.*

What clue?

Don't you wonder why Cabinet is so hot to deny you access to Arrow?

Reilly Dell arrived at the party at last. He was wearing motorized exoassist braces on his legs and had difficulty negotiating the crowded room. Fred blanched when he saw him. To Mary's eyes, Reilly had the blissful expression of a man feeling no pain. He must have been hurt so bad that they doped him up with painkillers. He was hurt much worse than Fred, apparently.

Alice jumped up to pull a chair out for him and to help him sit. He grinned drunkenly at her. *Are you hurt?* she asked him and leaned in close to sniff him. *Reilly's been dry-cleaned too*, she announced to the group.

Gwyn said, *Reilly, you look loopy. Do they have you on opioids?*

Reilly didn't respond, and Alice said, *Can anyone tell me if Reilly and Fred were in the same brawl today?*

Everyone turned to the three jerrys, but their eyes were tracking left and right in creepy synchronization. They were back at the tournament.

Reilly, are you hurt? Alice repeated.

Mary scolded her friends. *Can't you see he's off-line, like Fred?* Mary leaned across the table, cupped her hands around her mouth, and shouted, "Reilly! How do you feel?"

It was a dumb question, she knew, but she was becoming flustered. Reilly gazed at her stupidly.

What does he say? asked Alice.

He's not saying anything, Mary replied.

You know what I mean, Alice chided her.

And she did know what Alice meant. Mary was an evangeline. She was supposed to have genetically enhanced empathy for other people's feelings. She was supposed to be able to read people's expressions like words off a page. But all she could read in Reilly's face was loony tunes.

"Reilly! Are you hurt?" she shouted at the top of her lungs.

A flicker of understanding crossed the big man's face. He clenched his teeth and seemed to be struggling up from the depths. He opened his mouth and formed a word—"Gawh!"

"Gawh?" Mary repeated, encouragingly.

He shook his head in frustration. "Gawh!" he shouted. "Gawh! Gawh!"

"God?" Mary shouted back. "You're trying to say God?"

He nodded vigorously. "Gawd!"

"God what, Reilly?" Mary could feel everyone's attention riveted on them.

But Reilly lost it and began to choke with laughter. The dopey look left his face, and he appeared as clearheaded as ever. Mary couldn't believe the transformation. The jerk had tricked her.

Reilly grinned wide and said, *Gawd, Mary, you're sexy when you're like that.*

Everyone laughed with relief. Reilly stood up and took a motorized bow. He parted his hair to show Mary the skullcap he was wearing, a temporary interface until he could install new implants.

Mary, blushing, joined in the merriment. What else could she do? At least Reilly was all right, and his practical joke had done some good for Fred. She watched all the lingering stress of Fred's day melt away. Now he and Reilly were mugging at each other like two happy baboons.

Then it occurred to her to wonder why Fred hadn't also put on a skullcap to be able to communicate with the rest of them. Because he felt too fragile? Perhaps hers was the more damaged russ after all.

THE LULUS JOINED them at the table. "Guys!" shouted Mariola. "Watch this!"

"It's called the shimmy!" shouted Abbie. "We learned it in school!" The two women started clapping their hands while nudging aside neighboring chairs with their hips. People at the next table cleared a little space for them.

"Come on, you slugs, clap!" Mariola shouted. Fred and Reilly picked up the rhythm and clapped. So did the jennys, Alice, Peter, and the rest. Even the jerrys. People at nearby tables joined in. Mary clapped too. The lulus were exceptionally sexy-looking tonight in their membrane-thin skirts and tube tops. Both were red-heads at the moment with green eyes and luminous brown skin.

Abbie raised her head and sang out, "That's it, that's right. Everybody ready? *Let's go!*" and she and Mariola began to uh-huh in syncopated time. On a count of five, six, seven, eight, they danced a very peculiar step. They each stomped their right foot down way out in front of them and dragged it back, as through sticky syrup. Then they stomped their left foot out and dragged it back; then the right, right; then left, right, left, left. And the most amazing effect: as they stomped and dragged their feet, they shook their hips and shoulders with just enough force and in just the right rhythm so that the biceps and triceps of their lanky, outstretched arms danced off their bones. And their full breasts quivered like jelly. Even Mary held her breath.

The lulus performed a quick, loping break and took a bow. Everyone cheered and begged for more. But the girls sat down. Abbie slurped the last of her mostly melted tangerine daiquiri and glanced around at her friends.

Why's everyone so glum?

Two arbeitors arrived, clinging to the spiderweb of cables overhead and lowered trays of candy-colored daiquiris for the lulus from admirers at other tables, many more than they could drink. They passed the glasses around to their friends, after playing the sentiments attached to them.

"'Lo, lulu! I'm a love-starved steve," said a glass. "How 'bout we shimmy a little in my room?"

That's rather unimaginative, said Mariola. *But then, what can you expect from a steve?*

"Hi there," said another glass, "I think you're the toots!"

"I know some Twen Cen dances too," said another. "How'd you like to do the horizontal boogie with me?"

Alice said, *Hey, waiter, where's our dinner? We're starved.*

"Yeah!" the others shouted at the arbeitor above their heads. But they were drowned out by the clapping and foot-stomping coming from neighboring tables. The lulus' fans wanted an encore.

Abbie and Mariola rose at last. *Come on, folks,* Mariola said. *We'll teach you to shimmy.* They led an exodus to the dance floor shouting, "Free shimmy lessons!" The jennys followed them, as well as Sofi, Heidi, Mack, and most of their gang.

Mary went too, but before she did, she poured Fred a glass of ice water and shouted, "You're supposed to stay hydrated!" When she left, he sniffed the water— Chicago Waterworks tap water. He set the glass aside and ordered more ginger ale.

Their table was abandoned except for the joan and jerome, two russes, and the three jerrys. With so many from nearby tables gone to the dance floor, it was suddenly possible to carry on a voice conversation, but Fred was content to sit and watch. Alice and Peter snagged a couple of the untouched daiquiris.

"I think I love you," said one of the glasses.

"My name's Johnny Case," said the other. "Ask around about me, then give me a call. You'll be glad you did."

Fred said to Alice, "You should go out there and shimmy too."

Alice snorted, "Joans don't shimmy."

"Sure they do. It looks like fun."

Peter said, "Joans don't do fun." Then, to be fair, he added, "I guess neither do jeromes."

Alice patted Fred's hand. "Thank you, Fred, but I'd rather sit here quietly with you and watch them. My, aren't they gorgeous?"

Abbie and Mariola had marshaled enough dancers to form two lines across the dance floor, and twice as many to watch. They walked them through the steps. Michelles, jennys, kellys, isabellas, laras, ursulas, helenas, ruths, dorises, and evangelines. All of them gorgeous. But none so physically stunning as the lulus. From their goddesslike toes and chiseled knees; their frank round asses and innocent bellies; to their poke-you-in-the-eye breasts; long, sculpted throats; and slightly too large noses, lulus were the very pulse of desire. And the most appealing thing about them was their unquenchable thirst for merriment. No matter what they were doing, from waiting for a train to screwing your lights out, for them, everything was too much fun.

Which made Fred think of the hinky Inspector Costa. No matter how much she may have resembled a lulu physically, she was no fun at all.

Fred closed his eyes and shook his head. Was he still obsessing? What was wrong with him? When he opened his eyes again, Reilly was studying him.

The two russes calmly contemplated each other for several moments until Alice said, "Stop that, you two! Why do you do that, that russ mind meld? It gives me the creeps."

"I've noticed russes doing more of it lately," said Peter. "I hear it's related to the clone fatigue."

Wes, miraculously, had overheard this and tore himself from the tournament long enough to declare, "That's a racist statement, Peter. There's no such thing as clone fatigue. You should be ashamed of yourself."

"It was a joke," Peter protested, but Wes's attention had already flown.

"What's a racist statement?" said a new voice. Fred looked up and saw Shelley approaching the table.

Upon seeing his wife, Reilly crowed, "Petey thinks I got the clone fatigue, dear."

"Lucky you," Shelley said. "All I have is plain old body fatigue." She sat on Reilly's lap, only to rise again. "What is that?" she said, touching the exoassist brace under his jumpsuit. "And that smell?"

Alice said, "Our russes ran into some bad foo-foo today, but nobody wants to tell us about it."

"Oh, Reilly," Shelley said and sat in the chair next to him.

"It's nothing, really," Reilly said, which caused Fred to snort.

Shelley peered at Fred, and he fell instantly silent under the spell of her all-consuming scrutiny. Now, *that* was sexy, Fred thought. But Shelley did seem fatigued. Her shoulders drooped. Her smile sagged. What with her West Coast commute and all, she worked twelve-hour days. Ah, the price of success. He would have liked to discuss her job with her, but of course the confidentiality oath prohibited it. The only reason the gang knew where and for whom she worked in the first place was because her client broadcasted her life—or rather her drawn-out deaths—on her own Evernet channel.

Shelley took one of her husband's big hands in hers, brought it to her nose to sniff, and kissed it.

Peter slurped the last of a daiquiri and started another. "Ah-hem," he said. "The presence of a certain Fred Londenstane is requested on the dance floor. Paging Fred Londenstane."

Alice squeezed Fred's arm. "To be desired is Fortune's blessing."

Fred rose and threaded his way to where Mary was waiting for him. The dance floor was a maelstrom. Couples and triads progressed counterclockwise around the periphery in a variety of steps: the fox-trot, merletz, and waltz. Because each set of partners danced to the music of its own private orchestra, there were many collisions. Closer to the center of the floor were sets of cha-cha, zoom, and rhumba. Through all of this wove a conga line, led by the lulus. Another artifact of their History of Dance course.

Mary wanted to waltz. Because Fred couldn't hear the music she chose, she hummed it to him, and he obligingly ONE-two-three, ONE-two-threed through the traffic. He did more steering than dancing, but it felt good holding Mary. He wondered what the world would be like if everyone danced to the same music for once.

Mary, meanwhile, was decorating a dance-floor-sized, many-tiered cake in her imagination, and she and Fred were waltzing on the topmost tier.

Justine and Victor Vole were explaining to Samson how Moseby's Leap worked, but Samson wasn't getting it. A young man, a hollyholo character, leaned over a distant parapet on the other side of the stadium.

"That's a character named Moseby," Samson said, "and he's going to jump?"

"No, no, Myr Kodiak," Justine said. "That's Jason. There are no more Mosebys left anymore. The Moseby line is dead. There's a lot of Jasons, though, and they're having a rough time of it. This one may or may not jump today. It all depends. And there will be a lot of viewers tuned in to see which way it goes." The topic of suicidal simulacra seemed to have loosened the old woman's shy tongue.

"It all depends on what?" Samson said.

"On life," Justine said, stroking her gray and white cat. "On love, forgiveness, redemption."

Samson saw the patient look in Victor's face. Apparently, he didn't share his wife's enthusiasm for the novellas. "So, what's he doing now," Samson said, "besides blubbering like a fool?"

"Yes, I suppose Jason tends to be emotional," said Justine. "What he's doing is waiting for his lady love, Alison, to arrive and talk him down."

"What he's doing now," Victor added with a wink, "is waiting for audience numbers to threshold."

Justine looked at her husband with pity. Two of the counterfeit children behind them began to squabble over a doll, and Justine leaned over her seatback to straighten them out.

Samson was glad he'd come here in secret, giving no one the chance to talk *him* down. He wondered if the worldwide audience for this novella foolishness would exceed that of his own more genuine swan song, and he wondered if this was Hubert's idea of a joke—to bring him somewhere where sims deleted themselves, or if Hubert could even tell the difference.

"Mama," said one of the little boys, "I have to pee pee." He held his crotch and bounced in his seat.

"Who else has to go?" Justine said.

All their little hands shot up. "And I'm *hungry*," said a little girl.

"Me too!" chorused the others.

"Ah, the bliss of family life," Victor said to Samson and winked again.

He winks a lot, Samson thought. Or maybe it's a nervous tic.

Justine sighed and lifted the cat off her lap. "Here," she said, reaching around Samson to hand Victor the leash. She excused herself, unlatched her and the children's seats, and retracted them to the loading gallery, leaving the men and cat alone, suspended over Soldier Field.

"Easy, Murphy," Victor said. The gray and white cat was standing in his lap, its claws sunk into the fabric of his clothes. Victor tried to soothe the cat, but it climbed the cushion of his seat and perched itself on his seatback behind his head.

Murphy seemed oblivious to the sheer drop to the stadium floor. He sat on the seatback and meowed aggressively at Samson, regarding him with yellow eyes. The cat had a scrappy look to it, like an alley cat, and a vaguely Siamese-shaped face.

"Quiet, Murphy," Victor said gently. "He doesn't like strangers, our puss. He doesn't like me, for that matter; only Justine. The kids he doesn't even see."

"Still, he must be a comfort to have," Samson said. What Samson wanted to say was the cat was real at least, unlike the children. Samson still possessed a trace of social tact, but his curiosity was strong, and today of all days allowed no time for subtlety, so he said, "Aren't your children those—I don't know the brand name—"

"Fracta Kids," Victor said.

"Yes, Fracta Kids. You buy a newborn and raise it like it's real. Feed it, burp it, tell it bedtime stories. Send it to school. Loan it money. It grows up eventually and leaves home, sends you Christmas cards, etc., etc."

"That about sums it up, yes," said Victor. "Only these are orphans. We scavenged them out of recycle bins. My dear Justine has a heart as large as this arena, Myr Kodiak."

At Moseby's Leap, a female hollyholo joined the man at the railing.

"Uh-oh," Victor said, "Alison's here. Justine, dear, can you hear me? Yes, do hurry or you'll miss it."

Hubert spoke to Samson, *None of the Voles' Fracta Kids are sentient, Sam. Myren Vole's subem isn't powerful enough to support the apps. They have only basal logarithms: hungry, happy, sad, sleepy, and the like. They don't grow or develop.*

How ghastly, thought Samson. All the hassles of child rearing and none of the payoff. Even he, father of an unconceived son and genetically unrelated daughter, had enjoyed more parental bliss than that.

Justine returned. Her seat bumped Samson's and latched to it. She said she had put the children down for the night, which Samson took to mean she had switched them off. Murphy, the cat, quit its howling and climbed over Samson's seatback to Justine's lap.

It was already twilight in the huge space. Only the rim of the stadium opposite them was still in sunlight. Elsewhere it lay in shadow. There were no lights except for the exit chutes, the biolume railing and walls, and the scape surrounding Moseby's Leap.

"What did I miss?" Justine said.

"Nothing, my love," said Victor.

"Bring them in closer, please."

The parapet, with its hollyholo characters, zoomed toward them until it appeared suspended directly in front of Samson. Now he could see and hear the characters clearly. Jason, who straddled the railing, one leg dangling over the abyss, flung angry, tear-soaked words at Alison.

"But Cindy said the castle belonged to Carole and Candy!" he shouted.

"Cindy lied to you," Alison protested. "It doesn't belong to them or to Teddy, Patrice, or Oliver either. It doesn't belong to *anyone* we know. That's what I'm trying to *tell* you!"

"But *why* would she *lie*? And what about the *diamonds*? Surely, you're not trying to tell me that *Frank* would—"

"*Feck* Frank. Forget about him. It was Karman's scheme, or his sister Kameron's—no one knows for sure. The only thing we know is that someone *stole* the deposit and blamed Roddy who now faces revocation of his parole, but you *know* he won't testify because of what *Charles* said." Alison took two cautious steps closer to Jason, who balanced precariously on the railing.

"Charles? Are you sure it was Charles?" Jason gasped for air like a drowning man. But when Alison took another step closer, he shouted, "Stay back!" and swung his other leg over the rail. "I'll jump! Can't you see I'm *serious*?"

"All right, Jason. *Relax*. Look, I'm backing away." But she only pretended to backstep.

Jason began to weep again. "Charles," he said between sobs. "Charles—my cad, my curse, my dad, my cure, my *love*."

Next to Samson, Justine leaned forward in her seat and said, "*Oooh!*"

"Jason!" Alison gasped. "Did you just say that Charles is your dad—your *father?* And he's your *lover* too?"

Jason turned a face of self-loathing to Alison and let go of the rail, but Alison snatched the collar of his jacket just in time and was nearly pulled over by his weight. She was doubled over the rail, unable to lift him, unwilling to let go.

"You fool!" she gasped. "Don't you know who I am? Don't you know what I *sacrificed* for you?"

The quality of the scape changed then, and there seemed to be two Jasons and two Alisons struggling within the same frame. "Interactive audience divergence," Victor explained to Samson. "I fixed it so Justine can watch all the branchings instead of just one."

Two Jasons sobbed, and two Alisons strained against his weight. Then one Jason cried out, "Don't you *get* it? Charles is my father, but he's not my lover. He's my *victim.* I *raped* him." And with that confession, he shrugged himself out of his jacket and hurtled head first, down, down toward the field below, where now, inexplicably, there was a track meet in progress. The field was awash in light, and the lower stands were jammed with spectator placeholders. The Alison still clutching his jacket fell backward from the rail, leaving the other pair of lovers struggling there.

"Oh!" said Justine.

Samson snuck a peak at Justine. Her hand moved delicately over her breast, and he wondered if she perhaps wore a simsock under her clothes in order to enjoy the feely track of this novella. The first Jason, meanwhile, was taking an inordinate amount of time to hit the ground. He was tumbling in an overly artistic slow-motion flashback summary of his life. Key scenes and whole episodes of his past streamed off him like ribbons. Interested viewers could prolong this high dive for weeks as they replayed the whole sorry story tree of his life. Samson looked away and remembered why he never watched this crap. Had he come all this way to waste his final hour like this?

Jason hit bottom at last, but instead of splattering like a water balloon, he landed on a pillowy pole vault mat. Bruised but unbroken, he would live to cheat another day.

"For crying out loud," Samson said. He looked at Justine. She was happy. He looked at Victor, who winked at him.

Meanwhile, Jason and Alison No. 2 lost their balance and fell together from the railing. They also fell in slow-motion, but instead of reviewing their past, they were relishing the present. They had somehow managed to undress and couple in midair and were frantically banging away at each other. They drifted down past a mural of spectator faces with O-shaped mouths, down toward the fifty-yard line (for the sport in this thread was American rules football). Samson had no doubt but that the lovers would climax simultaneously at the moment of their impact.

A musical score that Samson had not noticed till now rose in an emotional crescendo as the grunting, straining couple hit. At least they did burst open in a satisfying way. Justine shuddered. Samson tried not to notice. Justine wiped tears from her eyes. "That was so sad," she said. In her lap, Murphy was purring.

Victor reached across Samson to squeeze Justine's hand. "Life is full of tragedy," he crooned.

The Moseby's Leap parapet, with its bereft Alison, receded back to its real spot, and the scape lights faded out.

"A glass of wine to wish our novella friends *bon chance?*" said Victor.

Samson didn't want more alcohol. He wanted to be clearheaded. But then he thought that a high blood alcohol content might make a hotter fire, and he said, "Sure, I'll join you, but isn't there something a little stronger than wine?"

"Whiskey!" replied Victor. "A man with a taste for *life!*" He produced a flask from an inner pocket and unstoppered it. He wiped the spout with his sleeve and passed it to Samson. "Please excuse the lack of ice."

WITH THE FLASK empty and the evening well advanced, Samson fell into a maudlin mood. "I'm afraid I'm eating and drinking you out of house and home," he said.

"Nonsense," said Justine. "We entertain so few guests these days."

"Neverthelesh, I insist on replenishing that lovely liquid. Hubert!"

Yes, Sam.

"Don't yessam me. You heard me; order my hosts a case of Glenkinchie."

I'm sorry, Sam, but that would be very expensive, and I'm not sure how I would transport it here without alerting the authorities to the Voles' presence.

"Are you telling me I'm broke? I can't even afford a lousy case of booze?"

The brand you named is distilled according to traditional methods and—

"You're a fucking mentar, aren't you? Figure it out, for crying out loud, and don't bother me with the details."

Justine and Victor pretended not to listen to the audible portion of this conversation. Samson's face was as dark as a blood blister. "Drop the hack!" he shouted. "I don't need it. I'll squeeze through these straps and fall to my death. I gotta hand it to you, Hubert, you brought me to the right place. Maybe you can convince Alison to come back and jump with me. We could screw on the way down and still have enough time for my *eulogy.*"

Sam, slo-mo is a vid technique. Your actual descent would take only five seconds.

"I know that, you brainless knickknack!"

Sam, I perceive that you are upset with me, but I don't understand why.

THEY SAT IN silence. Murphy came to sit on the cushion behind Samson's head. Full darkness settled upon the stadium. Samson said, "Forgive me. I seem to have become a mean drunk in my old age."

"I'm sure it's due to the pain you suffer, and not to any meanness on your part," said Justine.

"Don't bet the farm on that," Samson said. "In any case, it's only fair to warn you that I will soon become an object of public scrutiny, not to mention a fire hazard. You know what happens to the seared when they expire, don't you? You may want to find more distant seats."

Starting from the field and lower bleachers, blue-white stadium lights ignited, tier by tier, up the stadium well.

Victor said, "It's not in my nature to meddle, Myr Kodiak, but are you sure there's not some path for you other than the one you're contemplating? At the very least, wouldn't you rather spend your last moments with your loved ones?"

The lights hit them, and they winced in the brilliance. The rest of the seats on their tier came out, assembling themselves into rings of bleachers. Placeholder spectators appeared in the seats and began to cycle through their pregame repertoire of restlessness, gaiety, and chatter. The great space hummed with fake excitement.

"Yes, frankly, I would," Samson said, straining to speak over the noise, "but this is my fate."

"Forgive me for arguing, but is it?" said Victor. "There is no doubt that the seared suffered a great injustice, but that time is long past. You're too late to make a difference one way or another."

"That may be so," Samson said, "but at least I can *remind* the world of its crime. At least I can go out in blazing testimonial."

"By providing a—excuse the expression—a freak show?"

"It was my valet's error to bring me here, but it's too late to go anywhere else. Here will have to do. My mind is made up."

"Tell *us*," said Justine. "Tell *us* about your life. Wouldn't that be better? We care about you."

On cue, Murphy, the cat, stepped lightly down the armrest and curled up in Samson's lap. Victor said it was a sign, and Justine said that Murphy was an impeccable judge of character. Samson didn't know how to react to the cat, his lap having been barren of any creature for so long.

The first continent-sized billboard of the orbital Skytel crested the stadium rim. It was broadcasting some sort of variety show. Another hour would pass before the Skytel was in place for Hubert's hack. Samson tentatively stroked Murphy's head and was startled by the immediate purring.

"I've got the time, and since you asked," he said, "I'll tell you the abridged story of my life. But then I'll ask you and your Murphy to remove yourselves to a safe distance.

"First off," he began, "before I was a Kodiak, my name was Harger."

2.20

Arrow, Meewee said, *where is Ellen?*

I do not know, replied the mentar.

Meewee had gotten out of bed and put on house togs. He'd gone out to the living room again and sat in his favorite armchair. He felt light-headed, and his whole left arm tingled fiercely. Wee Hunk explained it as merely a side effect of his new brainlette temporarily hijacking the efferent pathways of his brachial nerves. It would pass.

Arrow, do you know how to find her?

Negative.

This isn't working, Meewee complained.

Wee Hunk said, *Let's try something different. Talk to Arrow about anything except Ellen while at the same time you are thinking about finding her.*

"Huh?"

An indirect approach, Merrill. Talk to it about an unrelated topic while thinking about Ellen.

About what topic?

For pity's sake, use your imagination.

So Meewee nestled into the armchair and thought about Ellen's head and where it might be at that moment and said, "What's the time and temp?"

"Eighteen forty-six," Arrow replied. "Twenty-eight degrees Centigrade outdoors and twenty-two degrees indoors."

Meewee said, *Well?*

I didn't hear anything.

I need a break.

Later! Wee Hunk snapped.

But Meewee ignored him and told Arrow to fetch a snack.

I HAVE AN idea, Meewee said, brushing crumbs from his togs. *You and Arrow have challenged each other. I'll have it challenge me.*

Wee Hunk, who had reduced his display to a flat frame in order to conserve attention units, said, *I'm not sure that's such a good idea.*

Why not?

If it challenges you, and your ability to use Starkese is not up to the task, I frankly don't know how it would react.

Let's find out, Meewee said and told Arrow to challenge his identity.

Complying. "Myr Meewee, do you have a shipping address for your household goods, or shall I place them in storage?"

"In storage, I would suppose," Meewee answered.

Immediately, the three Orange mechs raced into the living room and took up attack positions around Meewee's head, so close he could feel the backwash of their wings and hear their tiny laser cannon powering up.

Don't move a muscle, Wee Hunk said. *I told you it was a dicey idea.*

Meewee held his head perfectly still. A microcannon was aimed at each temple. Seconds dragged by, and then Arrow said, as though for the first time, "Myr Meewee, do you have a shipping address for your household goods, or shall I place them in storage?"

I suggest you get it right this time, Wee Hunk said.

A bead of sweat trickled down Meewee's forehead. "I—uh—that is," he began.

"My household goods—I mean—place my household goods—no wait—check that." He shut his eyes and clenched his teeth.

Don't try to think it, Wee Hunk prompted him. *Just feel your undying loyalty to Eleanor and say whatever comes out of your mouth.*

Meewee thought about Eleanor that morning at the board meeting, about the image of the tumbling yacht, about the Garden Earth Project and frozen colonists crossing the heliopause. "Storage," he said. "Except for several changes of spring seasonal clothes and my ecumenical files."

The cannon powered down, and the mechs flew away. Meewee gulped air. His heart rattled against his rib cage.

You are Merrill Meewee, Arrow said.

Excellent, said Wee Hunk. *Maybe now we can get somewhere with this.*

But they tried for another half hour with no success. Finally, Wee Hunk came up with a suggestion: *Simply tell Arrow to tell you how to tell it in Starkese to locate Ellen's head.*

Meewee gave it a try. *Arrow, tell me how to tell you in Starkese to locate Ellen's head.*

Arrow replied without hesitation, *I feel like watching a vid or something, Arrow. Maybe the evening news. Find something interesting for me.*

Meewee parroted the mentar, "I feel like watching a vid or something, Arrow. Maybe the evening news. Find something interesting for me."

"Complying," Arrow said, and the Orange mechs raced out of the apartment through the slugway.

Well, that got a response, Wee Hunk said, *and what's this?*

A large spinning globe, as viewed from space, appeared in the middle of the living room. Around the globe's equator hung sixteen satellites, attached to it with a web of strings. Meewee recognized them immediately as the Heliostream relay stations and the microbeams they directed at ground targets. As he watched, the microbeams, starting at the orbital stations, became coated with a silvery sheath that traveled down their length to the ground stations. At the ground, powdery clouds billowed up and spread out like ripples on a pond.

What is that stuff? Meewee said.

I don't know yet. I'm sampling it via meteorological drones. It's a kind of dust particle, streaming down the static flux of the beams. I can't tell much more than that yet.

Over the next half hour, silver puddles spread outward across continents until they intersected with each other and merged. Meanwhile, clouds of the dust rose into the atmosphere and shrouded Earth in a silvery fog. The prevailing winds mixed and churned it up. It was denser in the temperate zones and almost absent at the poles.

Well?

I think it's nust.

Which is?

Microscopic network repeater nodes. Nodal dust. Microscopic particles that link with all the particles around them.

I don't understand, said Meewee. *What do they do?*

That's all they do. Imagine if ten particles of nust landed on your hand and networked themselves. Anything that could read them would see a rough approximation of your hand in real time as it moved through space. Wait a few minutes until ten more particles landed and linked up. With every addition, the image of your hand gets sharper. Eleanor is coating every blessed thing on the face of Earth with interactive dust!

By now the entire globe, suspended in Meewee's living room, was completely obscured by a bright cloud of churning nust. Meewee went to the skylight where the evening sky seemed a little more orange than usual, but nothing out of the ordinary. *I can't see it.*

That's because its density is only about twenty to forty micrograms per cubic meter, depending on latitude and altitude, less than common air pollution. I'm not sure what kind of picture resolution that would give you. But it seems to me it would take an incredible number of attention units to read it. A whole battalion of superluminaries.

Suddenly a pocket of nust at the equator flashed and seemed to liquify. The transformation raced around the globe until the planet seemed covered by a flood of swirling quicksilver.

They've just linked up, Wee Hunk said. *Eleanor has just achieved the first global handshake. Shall we dive in and see if Arrow knows what it's doing?*

The caveman reached out his arms and pulled, like pulling an invisible rope. Meewee, in his armchair, did the same, and seemed to pull himself down toward the planetary surface. The Baja Peninsula appeared below him like a silver icicle. He pulled until he could distinguish the San Bernadino Mountains and Southern California. Aircraft disturbed enough nust in the atmosphere to be visible, but the resolution at ground level wasn't high enough to make out anything smaller than a building.

Come down here, Wee Hunk said.

Down where?

Bolivia—the crash site.

Bogdan slipped out of Green Hall, leaving his housemeets to linger over the fruitish and coffeesh and went down to the NanoJiffy for an Icy. On the other side of the wall, he could hear the shattering crunch of the predigester in the kitchen as Francis and Barry fed it dirty plates and cutlery, food scraps, and table linen. By tomorrow morning, all their day's waste would be masticated, dissolved and filtered, and reconstituted into fresh ugoo precursor, ready to be rewoven into new plates, clothes, and food. The cycle of life.

As he enjoyed his dessert, Bogdan checked his messages with his new throat phone and discovered that it had no built-in filter sets, and so he had a queue of tens of thousands of calls. Without a graphical interface or helpful valet, he'd have to sift through them individually to find any that mattered. He needed his editor in his room, so he climbed the nine and three-quarter floors to retrieve it.

The door to Bogdan's room, his loyal diaron-plated, titanium-bolted, clinker core door that not even a tank could penetrate was ajar. That was not possible. He pulled the door open enough to peek inside. There was a boy lying on Bogdan's mattress. It was Troy Tobbler. Bogdan pulled the door wide open and burst in shouting, "What the feck! How the feck did you get in here?"

Troy rubbed his eyes. "You woke me up."

"Did you hack my door?"

"I *said*, you woke me up."

"I don't care," Bogdan said and went around the elevator cable housing to stand over his bed and unwelcome visitor.

"I didn't hack your door," Troy yawned, grinding the gritty footpads of his boots into Bogdan's sheets. "Slugboy did."

"And who the feck is Slugboy?"

Bogdan felt a sharp blow to the back of his head that sent him reeling. He lurched around, but there was no one there. When he turned back, however, he was confronted by a small boy. The boy was a head shorter than Bogdan, and though he had cherubic cheeks and a freckled nose, there was a menacing something about him that made Bogdan think twice about hitting him back.

"Are you Slugboy?" he demanded.

"The one and only," answered the boy, "and you must be—holy crap!" He walked around Bogdan, staring at his bottom. "What are they poking you with? Hey, Troy, you gotta see this. Use Filter 32. I've never seen an ass glow so bright."

"Yeah, I know," Troy said, standing up on Bogdan's mattress. "He's a hole for hire."

"His ass is like a mood lamp," Slugboy continued. "We should call him the 'Golden Be-Hind.' Get it? The Golden Be-Hind."

"That was a pirate ship," Troy explained to Bogdan, "in the olden days."

"I don't care!" Bogdan shouted. "Get out of my room this instant!"

"*Your* room?" Troy replied. "That's a good one. Come on, Slug. Let's go down and tell Houseer Dieter we hacked the door. He'll be real happy." As the two boys made their way to the door, Bogdan fought back a panicky urge to beg them not to tell.

Troy snickered and said, "What'sa matter, Goldie? You look sick."

Slugboy said, "Yeah, but he shines like the setting sun behind two cheeky clouds."

"Don't worry," Troy said, "I won't give your room to Dieter. I'll let you do that all by yourself." With that, the boys disappeared through the doorway. Bogdan hurried to follow, but stopped and glanced back into his room. He had a weird feeling that something was different, but what?

Bogdan's bedroom was little more than a machinery closet. The huge old electric elevator motor filled most of the space, together with its cable drums and pulleys. Electrical control boxes occupied two walls, and wire conduits snaked in all directions. Bogdan used the cable housing for his shelves and the small tool bench for a desk. What passed for his worldly possessions were piled in one corner, and his ratty old mattress was scooched into another. It wasn't much, but it was all his, and he loved it. Then it hit him—the room was too quiet. "You shut off the elevator!"

Bogdan rushed to an electrical box and with both of his small hands pushed the huge cutoff switch until—with an explosive blue spark—he closed the circuit. Immediately the huge motor next to him ground to life, the guide wheels rumbled, and the drum took up cable.

"Don't *ever* do that again!" Bogdan shouted down the hall, but they were nowhere in sight. He thought he heard them in the Kodiak stairwell, so he slammed his door—he'd have to change the entry code ASAP—and jogged after them, hurtling himself down whole flights of steps with acrobatic precision.

On the fourth floor he passed Kitty going the other way. She was humming merrily and seemed very pleased with herself. When she saw him, she stopped to say, "Since when are you pals with that Troy boy? And who's his loser friend?"

But Bogdan didn't even slow down. He blew past her and continued descending. On the third floor, Gerald was coming out of the administrative offices just as Bogdan ran past.

"Oh, there you are," Gerald said. "Come back here. The committee is waiting."

Bogdan stopped in his tracks. "The Allowance Committee?"

"What other committee do you have an appointment with?"

"I'll be right back," Bogdan said and continued down the corridor.

"You only get a half hour," Gerald called after him, "and the clock is ticking."

"Clocks don't tick," Bogdan answered from the stairs. At least no clock he'd ever seen. Down on the first floor, he checked the NanoJiffy. They weren't there, so he went out to the street. Tobbler housemeets were setting up benches and chairs in the street for the evening's canopy ceremony, but Troy and Slugboy were nowhere in sight. Houseer Dieter was, however, and he came over when he saw Bogdan.

"Good evening, young Kodiak. You will vacate our machine room tomorrow," he said. "We will come up in the morning to repair the elevator apparatus."

Bogdan wondered if Troy had, in fact, spoken with his houseer. "There's nothing wrong with the elevator," he said.

"Is that so? It was out of service just now for forty-five minutes."

"That was an accident. It won't happen again."

The Tobbler's eyes narrowed. "Are you telling me, young Kodiak, that you *shut off* our machinery?"

"No. Yes. I mean—" Bogdan said.

The houseer turned to go. "You have violated the truce. There will be *consequences!*"

Bogdan watched the Tobbler stalk away, and a moment later he turned around and ran back up to three where Gerald was still waiting in the corridor.

"My appointment's not till seven," Bogdan said. "I'll be back then."

"Fine with me," Gerald said.

"Bogdan!" April called from the inner office. Bogdan went to the door. April and

Kale were sitting at a table covered with ledgers and files. "Bogdan, we were hoping to be done by seven. We have the thing with Samson tonight."

"What thing?"

"Oh, you missed the announcement."

Kale said, "It's all right. We'll catch Bogdan next time."

"Yeah, next time," Bogdan said and turned to go. But he remembered his cracking voice and fuzzy cheeks and especially the sprouting hair, and he said, "When is next time?"

Kale consulted an appointment book, a well-thumbed, spiral-bound paper book. "How does six weeks from tomorrow sound?"

"Like crap," Bogdan said and stepped into the office, slamming the door behind him. "What thing with Sam?"

"He's dying, Boggy," April said. "He's only got a very short time left. We're not going to leave him alone. From now on, we'll take turns so there'll be at least one of us with him at all times."

"So, who's up with him right now?"

"No one. He didn't want us to start till tonight."

Bogdan chewed this over. He could tell them now or let them find out for themselves later.

Meanwhile, Gerald handed him a sheet of paper, a spreadsheet full of handwritten numbers. Bogdan dropped it on the floor and said, "Let's skip the bookkeeping portion of this meeting and cut to the part where you approve my two requests. One, make me an appointment for this weekend at the Longyear Center to retro eleven months. They'll throw in an extra bonus month if you call by Wednesday. And two, buy me a Rhodes Scholar valet to replace Lisa." Finished, he crossed his arms and glowered at them.

"Fine," said Gerald, retrieving the sheet of paper from the floor, "we'll skip the bookkeeping part and cut right to the part where we deny your requests."

"What? You *can't.*"

Kale said, "Bogdan, there's not enough credit for everything."

April said, "Bogdan, look at this. Look!" She held up a stack of paper notes from the table. "We're forced to work with *paper* and *pencil.* If we can't afford to replace the houseputer, how can we justify buying you a new valet, especially after you broke the one you had?"

Bogdan began to shout, "Lisa was *twenty years old!* It's high time I got a new one!"

"Please don't raise your voice."

"*Besides,* the new ones are powerful enough so I can have mine temporarily take over the houseputer's functions. Keeping paper records is crazy. For that matter, why aren't you using Hubert for that? He's got enough juice to run the Moon. Surely, he could run this house and keep its accounts."

Gerald and Kale looked away, and April wouldn't meet his gaze. "What?" he said, but no one answered him, so he charged ahead, "And as for my juve treatments, that's *nonnegotiable.*"

April said, "Oh, Boggy, if you could for once stop thinking only about yourself and look around you. Look at the rest of us. Look at *me.*"

He looked at her and was disturbed to notice that she, like the rest of the housemeets, was way behind in her body maintenance. It seemed as if someone had dialed down her color saturation levels—her hair and skin were ashen.

April said, "We understand you like to remain a boy, and we've managed to grant you this for a lot of years, but now we can't afford it. Surely you can wait a little while until we're back on our feet."

"How long?"

Gerald consulted his spreadsheet. "Eight to twelve months."

"Eight to twelve months? No way! People, don't you hear what I'm telling you. I'm *pubing out!* I'll lose my *job!* It's right in my E-Pluribus contract—I must remain *pre*pubescent. I'm a demographics control. And in case you haven't noticed, I'll point it out to you—it's my payfer that's carrying this whole sorry house. Mine and Sam's. At the rate I'm going, in eight months I'll be adolescent. Hell, I'm already sprouting hair in places you don't want to know."

Gerald waved the spreadsheet at Bogdan and said, "There's nothing we can do. We can't spin yoodies from thin air. You'll just have to hang on. We'll boost your hormonal supplements. That'll slow it down. In a month, who knows, maybe our financial picture will improve."

As Gerald spoke, Bogdan noticed that April was looking guiltier and guiltier. Something was definitely up. The paper records, the furtive glances. Then he recalled how pleased Kitty had seemed in the hall a few minutes ago, not at all like a retrogirl told she'd have to wait eight to twelve months for her next juve.

"Why does Kitty get rejuvenation, and *I don't?"*

His question surprised them, and Kale said, "Bogdan, you know we can't discuss another 'meet's account with you."

"It's not *fair!"* Bogdan said. "She brings in ten thousandths and yet she gets her way, while you deny me the treatments I need to keep my job. It's stupid."

Gerald dropped his papers on the table and went to sit down. Kale shook his head. They both gave April a look. April sighed and said, "Charter Kodiak is in the middle of very sensitive negotiations, Boggy. It's not something we're ready to bring to the full charter yet. Kitty is acting as the charter's agent in this matter, but even her juve has been postponed—a little."

"What negotiations? I have a right to know."

"We'll bring it up for general discussion in another—I don't know—next week?"

Bogdan had never been very good at putting two and two together, but from the tension in the room, he knew he had stumbled across something major, and he wasn't about to let it go. He assumed his most obstinate little boy pose and said, "Why? Because you don't want Samson to know about it? Is that it? And those paper records are not because of the houseputer but to keep Hubert out of the loop, right?"

"Damn it," Gerald said. He got up and pulled a chair to the wall, climbed on it, and poked at two exposed wires below a wall-mounted cam. "Not that it matters," he grumbled and climbed down. "The houseputer lost contact with this room ages ago."

Kale steepled his hands on the tabletop and spoke in portentous tones. "Bogdan, what we tell you goes no farther than this room, understood?" Bogdan nodded, and Kale continued. "You ever hear of a place called Rosewood Acres?"

Bogdan shook his head.

"It's a superfund site in Wyoming since the last century. Highly polluted. Highly toxic. There are more rare elements and radioactive isotopes buried there than the next five dumps combined. Which means it's one of the richest micromines in the UD with the potential for a steady income for decades. And the mining rights have recently been acquired by Charter Beadlemyren."

"Never heard of them."

Gerald said, "The Beadlemyren, like us and thousands of other charters, are suffering a decline in their membership. When Sam dies—well, we'll be hurting. But the Beadlemyren are in worse shape. The state has already started decertification procedures against them. Unless something's done, they'll lose their charter, and with it their assets, including the mining rights. We've been talking to them about the possibility of our two charters merging. The benefits for both of us would be substantial. But the Beadlemyren have offers from other charters also eager to merge or absorb them, including, we suspect, the Tobblers. That means we have to bring more to the table than our competitors can."

"Such as?"

April said, "Well, an appearance of youthful enthusiasm, for one. That's why it's Kitty who's representing us. And capital. Lots of capital. It'll mean selling off the rest of this building—which is why there's no point in investing in a new houseputer just now—and selling, uh, well, everything."

Bogdan was stunned. "We're going to move out of Chicago?"

"It looks that way," said Kale, "which is why your position at E-Pluribus is of secondary importance."

With this news, Bogdan turned and drifted to the door.

"Bogdan!" April said sharply. "This is all under wraps. Understand?"

"Yeah," he said. "A big feckin' secret." Then he remembered something, and he asked Kale, "You said this toxic dump is called Rosewood *Acres*. How many acres?"

"Two thousand."

After their meal, Fred and Mary's crowd in the Zinc Room had a round of evening visola, and coffee. Dessert was custard fyllo pie, followed by more rounds of drink.

Occasional outbursts came from the Stardeck, and the lulus Abbie and Mariola went out to investigate. When they returned, Abbie carried a little black homcom slug by its tail between her thumb and index finger.

"They're smashing them," she said. "I can't hardly believe it." She dropped the biomech strip on the table and, before it could crawl away, trapped it under an overturned daiquiri glass.

"Don't do that," said Reilly.

"Don't tell my sister what to do," said Mariola.

"I mean, you could get into trouble, get us *all* into trouble."

Mary said, "I blocked up our apartment slugway all day, and nothing happened."

"That's nothing," said Gwyn, the jenny. "On the WAD, I saw free-range people 'harvesting' them by the hundreds for recycling credits."

They watched the slug explore its prison, and when its pinhead noetics concluded it was trapped, it simply idled in place. No threats, no sirens, no explosion of pseudopods.

Wes, the jerry, scanned it. "It's not transmitting to base."

"What's it doing?" said Reilly.

"Nothing that I can tell."

"That just doesn't make sense."

"Sure, it does," said Abbie. "Somebody, gimme a hammer."

Mariola said, "How many material credits do you suppose one of these would bring?"

"Let's see," said the second jerry, Bill. "At least a milliliter of paste, supporting circuitry, several grams of titanium, selenium, platinum, ah, maybe iridium—"

"Not to mention the self-healing tissue and foil extruders," said Wes.

"And the minicams and emitters and various RF gear," said Ross, the third jerry.

"Ten or twelve yoodies maybe?" said Bill, and the other two jerrys nodded in agreement.

"Ten or twelve *each*?" said Abbie, astonished.

"Give or take."

The group of friends mulled this over.

"Where's that hammer?" said Abbie.

"Feck the hammer," Mariola said and took off her shoe.

"Wait, Abbie," said Fred. "Trapping it is one thing, but whacking it is a felony. You could pull hard time for that."

Abbie raised the shoe but hesitated. "That's not what the people on the Stardeck say. They say the slugs are finished. They've been decommissioned. Everyone's pulling them off the side of the building and smashing them. And do you see the HomCom up here arresting anyone?"

Fred said, "Can someone please check the Evernet for an official announcement."

Wes said, "There's all sorts of contradictory statements, but nothing I'd call official."

"That's good enough for me," said Abbie. But still she hesitated with the shoe.

Alice, the joan, said, "Imagine—no more slugs sneaking up on you when you least expect it."

"No more slugs swimming in your bath," said Sofi, the helena.

"Or biting you in your sleep," said Gwyn.

"Or having the power to decide if you're friend or foe," said Wes.

"People," Alice said, tears rolling down her cheeks, "we are privileged to witness the end of a dark era."

Fred waited for her to append some typically joan bit of sarcasm, but she didn't.

"On the other hand," said Peter, making good jerome sense, "if they *are* worth ten or twelve UDC each, and if they *are* being destroyed and recycled by free-range trash without criminal consequences, then it constitutes a new form of dole and an unfair tax burden on the rest of us."

"Unless the rest of us get *in* on it," said Mariola.

"Okay, okay. Here goes," Abbie said and again raised the shoe.

"Please don't," Fred said. "You risk *so much.*"

"Right," said Reilly. "You know who they'll send to arrest you—Fred!"

A constant roar of excitement now came from the Stardeck, and the Zinc Room was quickly emptying, diners hurrying out to join in the slaughter. Abbie said, "At least I'll have a lot of company in jail." She removed the glass and brought the heel of the shoe squarely down on the slug. They all held their breath. The little black ribbon of biotech lay still. But when Abbie tried to pick it up, it began to creep again toward the edge of the table.

Bill said, "Not much of a blow there, lulu."

Wes said, "They self-repair pretty quick."

"Here, give me that," Mariola said and took her shoe back. "You should pretend it's you-know-who and hit it like *this.*" She raised the shoe high overhead and brought it crashing down on the slug. The blow sounded like a cannon shot. Now the slug lay flat. Thick, black pseudoplasm oozed like tar from a split along its side.

Wes said, "That maybe oughtta hold it till you get it to a digester."

Ross said, "Use a public one at a convenience store. And ask for payment in tokens—*not* on your personal account."

But the lulus didn't move. They held each other in their arms and stared at the ruined biomech. Suddenly they began to cry.

"Now what?" Fred said.

Alice said, "Oh, Fred. For once, everything is right. Come on, guys. Let's go join the fun." She led the others to the Stardeck. Everyone followed, except Peter, the russes, and the jerrys. Mary and Shelley held back only long enough to see how strenuously their russes might object. Fred scowled, and Reilly frowned, but this wasn't enough to hold the evangelines, and they hurried to catch up with their friends.

Peter said, "Just think of the billions of credits our society has spent building and maintaining the whole slug-based nanocyst detection infrastructure. And for that matter, the canopies." He rose from his chair. "Don't worry, gentlemen, I don't intend to join in the crime spree, but I am curious to watch history in the making."

Then it was just the russes and jerrys sitting across the table from each other.

"Don't look at us," Wes said. "We're sworn to uphold the law, not break it."

"That's good," said Reilly. "Otherwise, Fred would be required to bust you too."

"Not if you're on sick leave," said Wes. "I'd imagine that after your swim today, you guys get a week or so off."

Fred and Reilly exchanged glances. It was apparent the jerrys knew something of their day's adventure.

Reilly said, "Actually, I have some R & R coming to me. How about you, Fred?"

Fred shook his head. His injuries weren't considered serious enough. "I have tonight off and a day of comp time." Reilly signaled to Fred to look toward the door, and Fred turned to see dozens of jerrys and russes leaving the Zinc Room. At the same time, Wes pulled a package of Suddenly Sober out of his pocket and offered pills to Bill and Ross. He took one himself and washed it down with a final swig of whiskey.

"On duty?" said Fred.

"Yeah, it just came through," Wes said. "They're scrambling the troops."

"About the slugs?" Fred said, suddenly anxious for Mary and their friends.

"No, not slugs. There's a rush on personal security. Seems that the affs are killing each other all over the UD, and they're doubling and tripling their security teams."

Fred said, "A round of score settling?"

"Yeah," said Wes, "sparked by Starke's assassination."

Ross said, "They're calling it a 'market correction.'" He and the other jerrys har-harred at that as they left the table, leaving Fred and Reilly alone.

"I read this article," Reilly said, pouring himself a glass of ginger ale, "that compares the affs of today to princes in the Middle Ages. No strong kingdoms or national governments to cramp their style. All these little principalities, sovereign unto themselves, competing for land and resources. All their little wars and mercenary armies. That's what we are, you know, mercs."

Fred shook his head. "I've been thinking about that too," he said, "and I disagree with you. The pikes are the mercenaries, the jerrys and belindas are the cops, and we russes are the palace guard."

Reilly thought about that. "You're right. I like that better. Yeah, the palace guard. I wonder if Thomas A.'s ancestors were in that line of work. We've saved more than a few royal heads in our time." Reilly rose on his mechanical braces and tried to stretch. "Well, it's been a long day," he said. He saluted Fred and left the table. Fred was all alone.

To my cloned brothers, he mused, *to remain free men, we must resist the temptation to swear allegiance to any family but our own.*

BECAUSE OF HER duty with the death artist, Shelley was a minor celebrity at APRT 7. Admirers on the Stardeck stopped her every few meters to offer comments about her client, Judith Hsu. After a year of remission, Hsu's condition had recently taken an aggressive turn, and her viewership had increased accordingly. Hsu's skin had become hidebound with scar tissue, and she could barely move at all. Her skin was so fragile at her elbows that bending her arms could potentially split it and expose her joints. And the poor woman's pruritus was unbearable. She couldn't stop clawing at herself. The jenny nurses had to tie her hands in soft restraints to keep her from scratching herself to shreds.

Shelley acknowledged her fans' attention, but it was clear to Mary that she did not relish it.

The Stardeck was a killing field. People wielded shoes, pocket billies, and wine bottles in their slaughter of the small, black defenders of cellular integrity. Foolish revelers climbed on the balcony railing to reach them, unmindful of the three-kilometer drop. Steves took advantage of their extraordinary height to fling slugs off the walls with spoons into the waiting clutches of tipsy, oxygen-deprived berserkers. "Heave ho!" the steves cried each time they flung one. "Heave ho!"

Incongruously, other people stood patiently in an orderly queue beneath a slug-way and waited for unsuspecting slugs to exit the building. After a quick look around, Mary and Shelley joined the end of the line.

Shelley seemed to walk with a limp, but Mary didn't mention it. Instead, she said, *I'm thinking of retraining.*

Oh? Shelley said. *In what area?*

I looked up the stats to find which female type has the widest duty opportunities. You know which it is?

Shelley scratched her throat and said, *The jennys I would suppose.*

Close; they're second. It's actually the juanita/janes. There will always be houses to tidy, you know, and drinks to fetch, and pillows to fluff. The best employment security and the lowest pay scale.

Little by little, the two evangelines advanced to the head of the line. When it was their turn, and a slug came through the slugway, Mary and Shelley just stood watching it slither up the wall, neither of them making a move.

"It's getting away," said someone from behind.

"Catch it!" Mary said.

"You!" said Shelley.

Soon the slug was out of reach. The evangelines laughed and left the queue. They went to sit at a table in a quiet corner, away from the bedlam.

Shelley eased herself carefully into a chair. "So, you're thinking of taking up Domestic Science?"

"Right." Mary laughed. "Even better—this morning I took an intro course in Cake Design."

"You're kidding."

Mary shook her head. "But seriously, don't you think we should be qualified for *something?*"

Shelley scratched her arm thoughtfully. "I hope so. I'm thinking of retraining, myself."

"You? You've got it made!"

Shelley sighed. "I don't know how many more of these deaths I can take. Remember the last one when my hair fell out? Well, look at this." She unfastened her sleeve and exposed her arm for a moment. Her skin was inflamed and swollen, an early sign of scleroderma, Judith Hsu's current terminal disease.

Shelley didn't have scleroderma; the symptoms were false, psychosymptomatic, all in her head. Her rash was an occupational hazard of the evangelines' high degree of empathy.

"The breast cancer was bad enough," Shelley continued, refastening her sleeve, "but this one is killing me. I have this stuff all over my body. Reilly hasn't been able to touch me for weeks!"

Mary scratched her throat and said, "I'm so sorry, Shell," but she wasn't sure she meant it. Not that she'd enjoy feeling sick, but at least Shelley was working. At least she was a companion. Mary leaned over to scratch her leg, just as a slug that had somehow eluded the massacre crawled up her shoe and fastened to her ankle.

"Damn!" she said.

"What is it?"

"Alice is right. It's high time we were rid of these monsters. Here, give me that cup."

Shelley handed her a heavy china coffee mug, and when the slug dropped off, she hit it. The slug didn't even slow down.

"Hit it harder," Shelley encouraged her. "Hit it in the middle; that's where the brain is."

Mary hit the slug again, to no avail. "It's tougher than it looks," she said and raised the mug over her head. This time she swung so hard the mug shattered. "I dinged my hand," she said.

"But you killed it." The slug lay still, its side split open.

"You can have it," Mary said, lifting the slug by its tail and offering it to Shelley.

"Thanks, Mare, but you whacked it."

"Fred would kill me."

"Same with Reilly."

"Anyway, whacking it felt good." Mary stood up and flung the mech over the banister to fall five hundred stories.

WHEN FRED CAME out to the deck, the Skytel billboards were announcing ten minutes to showtime. He sat with Mary and Shelley, and what was left of the gang reassembled around them. There were plenty of free chairs now that so many people had left to cash in their kill or to report for duty. Already a fresh wave of slugs was descending from the side of the tower to begin evening rounds. An army of them entered the building via the Stardeck slugways, and some detoured to roam the deck and test random ankles. Few people objected, their fury spent for the day.

Fred said, "Our jerrys got scrambled for special duty."

"Arresting friends and designated others?" said Peter.

"No, I don't think so. And Reilly went home to bed."

"I know," said Shelley.

They ordered more drinks, more food, and watched the Skytel cycle through its usual smorgasbord of civic and commercial messages: sports scores, stock quotes, population clock, birthday and anniversary dedications, celebrity news, ads. A news headline crawled across the boards: Chicagoland breaks out of its shell at midnight!

"How condescending," said Alice.

Sofi said, "If there's anything I'd like to smash more than a slug, it's that monstrosity up there crowding out our moon."

"Many have tried," said Fred.

"It seems a rather large target to miss," Alice said.

"True, but it's farther away than it appears, fifty-five thousand kilometers, in fact. And it's modular, not much more than prisms, lenses, and mirrors, and the servos that point them. Hard to kill, easy to repair."

A vibrant message rippled across the boards: "Chicago, give yourself a hug!"

The lulu Mariola giggled. "Now tell me, wouldn't you miss that if it was gone?"

"No, I wouldn't!" Sofi said.

"I wouldn't be surprised if it *did* follow the canopies into retirement," said Peter. "Advertising revenue alone isn't enough to justify it anymore. Never was, in fact. And there's no public messages on it people can't easily access by other means."

Mary said, "Why'd they put it up in the first place?"

"Propaganda."

"Give yourself a hug?"

"Not for us," said Peter. "Propaganda for the other side of the globe. The Skytel is not geosynchronous, you know. It follows the night and spends as much time over enemy and/or unaligned territory as it does over ours. The wanted posters were a little before your time, Mary, but imagine a nightly rogues gallery of fatwah posters with princely rewards for indicted extremists, dead or alive, up there where everyone could see it, mug shots as big as Texas. The extremists hated the Skytel and tried to shoot it down many times. While it tormented us with adverts here, there it might feature your next-door neighbor and put such a price on his head that no one could resist the temptation to bring him in. No one was safe from us. The Skytel was one of our most potent weapons against the Outrage for a while." Peter raised a glass of wine and toasted the Skytel: "To blood money."

The central billboard opened a window to show a close-up of a woman in a formal jumpsuit.

"What channel? What channel?" people asked across the Stardeck. The woman introduced Chicago CEO, Forrest Slana. The CEO's roundish face seemed to compete with the Moon behind him. He beamed pallid sincerity upon all sectors of the great city.

Good evening, Chicago, he intoned. *In a few moments, I will turn you over to our masters of ceremony, but first I wanted to say a few words about your decision to lower the city's canopy.*

Decision? Did we vote on it? someone asked on an open channel. And a hundred voices answered, *Shut up!*

Our canopy, this shell of charged squamous plates, this bubble of anti-nano, has served as Chicagoland's hard hat these last sixty-eight years. As he spoke, the CEO glanced over his head, pretending to look up at the canopy. *In that time, it has saved many lives and much property. It has intercepted and neutralized over a trillion extremist weapons. In the last sixty-eight years, it has failed us only twice, and we will always remember our neighbors who perished on those days.* A sober pause here.

But today's world is a different, better, safer place. The Outrage is over, thank heaven, and we won. The atmosphere and oceans and land are free of NASTIES. They have been flushed away, their energy depleted, and no new ones are being nanofactured.

Both Mary and Shelley looked at Fred—is that true? No new NASTIES? But he was still off-line and unable to follow the speech.

Meanwhile, this barrier over our heads costs us dearly. Operation and maintenance alone comes to one hundred credits per capita annually. And that's a lot of yoodies that I'm sure you'd rather spend on other things. And so, as the first major city to raise a canopy, Chicago will again lead the way and be the first to drop it. We will, after sixty-eight years, finally and willingly break out of our shell!

He pretended to rap against the canopy with his knuckles. Somewhere there was generous applause, though Mary didn't see anyone clapping on the Stardeck. As a relative newcomer to this world, Mary was curious about how her Applied People colleagues were taking all this. The canopy—the Skytel for that matter—was a fixture in her sky from as far back as she could remember. And as far as the Outrage went, she had learned about it in History class.

But if there are still evil haters out there, cooking up new terrors to unleash on us, continued the CEO, *let them know that though we lay down our defenses today, we will not dismantle them. On the contrary, the canopy pickets will be maintained in a fully functional status. We will be able to respond to any threat at a moment's notice.* Another round of unseen applause.

And now, on with the show. I am thrilled to introduce to you our hosts for the evening, the sensational Debbie Mix and her irrepressible symbiont, Alkanuh. Let's give them a big-shouldered Chicago welcome.

Mix and Alkanuh appeared in frames on either side of the CEO. They giggled. They waved. They made silly faces. Their frames jumped together into the center, covering over the CEO.

Yar, said Mix. *Me and the yik here are riding in a VIP box doing lazy eights inside Soldier Field. There's quite a crowd here tonight. How many people would you say, Al?*

The other boards opened multiple views of the crowded stands of excited spectators, the stage in the center of the field, and pages of background data and stats.

Hoo! said Alkanuh.

The stadium crowd cheered and booed.

I think that translates to four hundred thousand. Am I right, Al?

The canopy show devolved into a typical, star-studded pastiche of the type one could find at any hour on the WAD, the type of show that clones didn't particularly enjoy because there were so few clone celebrities included. So, although the boards were bursting with glittery musical numbers, tasteful nudity, and risqué comedy, there was nothing entertaining or even characteristically Chicagoan about it, and the Stardeck crowd tuned it out.

Fred asked Mary, "You want me to take your—ah—recyclables down to a digester?"

Mary smiled. "Thank you, Fred, but that won't be necessary."

"You got someone else to take them?"

She shook her head.

He'd already guessed the poor results of their harvesting, but he enjoyed the interrogation. "I don't understand," he said. "How many did you bag?"

"We limited out, didn't we, Shell?"

Shelley nodded enthusiastically, with big brown eyes.

Although nust had ceased traveling down most of Heliostream's microbeams, it still flowed to the target array outside La Paz. When Meewee reached the crash site near an outlying village, concentration of the silvery stuff was heavy enough to distinguish the blurry figures of guards cordoning off the scene. Meewee could make out trees but not individual leaves, vehicles but not their type.

It's amazing, Meewee said. *With enough nust, you could keep track of everything everywhere in real time.*

A despot's wet dream, Wee Hunk agreed. *But frankly, I don't understand how Arrow is able to read this. It exceeds my capacity, probably Cabinet's as well. When you can truly speak Starkese, you should ask it.*

They drifted through the trench that the *Songbird* had gouged into what looked like a soccer field. As a breeze stirred the nust, pockets of terrain moved in and out of focus.

Impressive as this is, Wee Hunk went on, *I'm not sure what Arrow has in mind. To analyze Ellen's DNA, you'd need more than nust. What do you suppose it's looking for?*

They left the trench and followed the debris trail where hundreds of blurry metallic persons and mechs were sifting and collecting bits of the *Songbird*. Meewee and Wee Hunk swam among them unseen.

What's that? Meewee said.

On the ground ahead of them was a splash of sparkles, like colored sequins. Wee Hunk hovered over the spot. *Aha!* he said. *Taggants, of course.*

For explosives? Meewee said.

No, the taggants they put into batches of resin. Arrow must be looking for the outer shell of Ellen's helmet. The helmet must have struck the ground here upon the yacht's disintegration. Taggants are microscopic but are designed to be conspicuous, easily within the limits of nust detection.

As they examined the taggant find, an orange striped line, like an usher line, suddenly shot out from it and extended north across the countryside.

Come on! Wee Hunk said, swimming straight up.

Meewee followed and pulled himself into the sky until his vantage point was high enough to follow the orange line. It arced across South America and led back to the USNA. He used a dog paddle to swim along its length. It terminated at the Decatur canopy's Flinn Gate. Because the nust was filtered out by the city's canopy, Decatur and its environs appeared like a small opaque bubble.

End of the taggant trail, Wee Hunk said, *and not much learned. We already knew the helmet was brought here. The Roosevelt Clinic is located down there in Decatur, where we both saw it unclench. I think the taggant trail is a false trail.* They swam over the invisible city, and Wee Hunk continued. *Arrow is wasting our time. I have an unimpeachable record of the helmet from the arrival of the recovery team to its unclenching at the clinic, which we both witnessed. I'm afraid we're no closer to finding her than before.*

Wee Hunk pulled himself out of the globe display. *So much for Arrow's help. I'm going to continue pursuing my other leads. Good-bye for now.*

Meewee rose from the quicksilver atmosphere, and when his viewpoint again occupied his executive apartment, the mentar was gone, except for a flat portrait of himself on the wall. Meewee got out of the armchair and took a few tentative steps around the living room. Except for the light given off by the globe, the room was dark. The two household arbeitors stood in their ready nooks, and the skylight revealed the first stars of the night.

Meewee had full use of his arm again, and the lump was hard and painless under his skin. He was beyond exhaustion, and he was about to tell Arrow to fetch him a glass of the wine, when he was struck by the absurdity of using such a remarkable creature as his mentar as a common servant. He could, after all, control the kitchen and arbeitors with the apartment's houseputer.

Arrow, he glotted, *say something to me in Starkese.*

Complying, said the mentar. "Myr Meewee, please unlock the trophy case so that I can prepare your awards for shipment."

That struck Meewee as nonsensical, for he possessed only one award and no trophy case. At the same time he felt an urge to return to the global nust scape, and without questioning the impulse, he returned to the scape and was surprised to find a second taggant trail emanating from the crash site. This one, though it took a separate route, ended at the same destination—Decatur's Flinn Gate.

"Hunk!" he said. "The switch was made right in Bolivia!"

The Wee Hunk portrait filled out into three dimensions, and without waiting for Meewee, the apeman dove into the globe. Meewee dove in after him and paddled down to Decatur where he found the mentar floating over the city. Its canopy still appeared as a shiny opaque bubble. *How do we look inside a canopy?* Meewee said.

We can't, Wee Hunk replied. *There are about a thousand international bans against releasing microagents inside canopied space. But I'm increasing my assets on the ground there; I'll use bees to search every cubic centimeter of the city if I have to.*

But as they hovered over the city, its canopy was gradually becoming transparent.

Hello? Wee Hunk said, pulling himself closer. *It looks like Arrow is releasing nust inside the canopy. I sure hope it knows what it's doing, or you're going to prison.*

Me?

It's your mentar, isn't it? You ordered it to find Ellen.

As the nust density within the canopy increased, the city skyline emerged from a silvery miasma, and usher lines snapped from Flinn Gate to two distinct parts of town.

That one leads to the clinic, Wee Hunk said, swimming toward the other, which led to a neighborhood on the west side. The taggant trail ended at a single sparkle in a two-story residence. The nust resolution wasn't heavy enough to render the house as more than a blur.

Wee Hunk said, *My resources identify it as belonging to the Sitrun Foundation. Ever hear of it?*

No, what is it?

I'm researching.

Meewee paddled down into the house. The nust density was even lighter indoors, and the rooms were barely discernible. Nothing moved. *Maybe one of the surgeons from the clinic lives here,* he said, *and brought home a stray fleck of helmet resin on her sleeve.*

Possible, but so far I've found no connection to any clinic personnel.

What do we do now? Send in the Command?

Wee Hunk snorted. *You've got to be kidding.*

Then let's hire some russes.

I don't trust 'em.

You don't trust russes?

As they watched, the canopy pumped out the nust, and Decatur disappeared again. The house and its neighborhood dissolved. Meewee and Wee Hunk returned to the living room where the apeman began to pace in a circle.

Russes I trust, he said, swinging a step on his knuckles, *but not their employer.*

Zoranna? She's the only one of that crowd that I do trust.

Which only goes to show how ill-informed you are, Bishop.

Wee Hunk's rented witness bees were arriving in the west end neighborhood in force, and he opened a new diorama in the room to render the pictures they began to send. Soon the house appeared in full color and rich detail. It sat inconspicuously on a quiet residential street. The house itself was a Tudor style brick structure with neatly trimmed hedges and colorful flower beds. But the bees were only able to project them an exterior view.

Somebody's got to go there, Meewee said. *I guess that'll have to be me.*

You? Wee Hunk snorted again. *And do what? Knock on the door and ask if Ellen Starke can come out to play?*

Then what do you suggest? Meewee snapped. *You don't trust the authorities. You don't trust russes. You don't trust Zoranna. Who do you trust?*

Wee Hunk shook his shaggy head. *Excuse my metaphor, Merrill, but you're talking through your ass. You are so far out of the loop you're in a separate reality. Allow me to catch you up on recent events since apparently either Arrow doesn't know how to keep you informed or you never asked it to. In brief then: an hour ago, Saul Jaspersen's compound in Alaska was attacked by a missile and completely destroyed. As luck would have it, Myr Jaspersen, himself, was inside his mountain redoubt and escaped harm.*

Meanwhile, Andie Tiekel in her Oakland hillside home was not so lucky. A laser pulse, probably from a suborbital drone, pierced the top of her skull. Her hair and makeup were hardly mussed, but inside her skull, the yolk was poached, so to speak.

This is my Ellen's life we're dealing with, Merrill, not your position on the GEP board, not the launch schedule of your Oships. I don't have Cabinet's resources. I don't have the luxury of error. But I'm not completely helpless.

Meewee said, *So, who are you sending?*

The caveman grinned. *Why, the same folks who are going to move your stuff out of here tomorrow.*

At first Meewee didn't follow, and then it made no sense. *You're sending a moving company?*

A tired commuter, a big man trapped in a little man's body, arrived at Home Run station in Decatur by bead car. When the car came to a stop and the hatch popped open, the man stood up and stepped across the gap to the platform. On his way to the lobby, he switched on his jumpsuit, which began to twinkle in bright neon colors and flash to the rhythm of his footsteps. He threw back his shoulders and marched to the out stiles, smiling and greeting everyone he passed. His jump-suit cast a wide circle of merry light about him. By the time he left the station in West Decatur, he was once again the popular guy he always knew himself to be.

To the Orange Team bee, however, the commuter was nothing more than a convenient hankie. The bee and one of its wasps crawled out from underneath his wide lapels and took to the air unnoticed. The team's second wasp was riding a separate hankie from Bloomington and was a few minutes behind.

As the Orange bee and its wasp rose above the rooftops and flew to 2131 Line Drive, the bee finished coordinating with the teams already at the scene and the Legitimate Order Giver 2 who had recently made verified contact and taken command of the mechs. LOG2 had given them a new mission—to locate and tag the prize—and it designated Orange Team Bee as Fleet Leader. The fleet was composed of the remnants of Teams Green (one bee and wasp), Yellow (one bee and wasp), and Red (one beetle), in addition to Orange Bee and its own two wasps.

The target building was shielded and impenetrable to the limited scanning assets at the fleet's immediate disposal. Orange Bee fed what they knew to its onboard scenario mill, as well as relaying it to LOG2. The fleet hadn't been the first on the scene. Dozens of witness bees hiding in the foliage surrounding the house at 2131 had set up a covert grid. But the neighboring houses had sensed their network and assumed a defensive posture: informing their residents, summoning the neighborhood watch, and alerting the rest of the houses in the neighborhood. The area's heightened alert status attracted media and homcom bees. Any chance of the fleet launching a sneak attack was ruined, another fact to feed LOG2 and the scenario mill.

The mechs of Orange Bee's fleet were in various states of disrepair, having already completed their primary objectives earlier in the day. None of the wasps had a full charge of weapons plasma, and Red Beetle had nothing but a pinch of fish food flakes left in its carapace. More grist for the scenario mill.

WHEN THE SECOND Orange wasp caught up and was integrated into the fleet, LOG2 ordered the attack. Orange Bee, choosing from among the mill's best results, pointcast its most promising plan to its multihued armada. The mechs made a stealthy ground approach from different directions, taking advantage of local cover. When they reached the house, they explored its foundation for cracks or gaps. Red Beetle found one, and Green Wasp widened it to fashion an entry point. It was located at the seam between the clinker sill and brick foundation. It was ideal, and the mechs crawled through into the basement of the house. Orange Bee was last in line. It entered only partway and took a position with a clear line of sight to the street.

The interior walls and floors of the house were made of construction foam slab. Though the material was thin and light, it was soundproof and opaque to EM transmission. Therefore, to keep their comm open, the mechs linked up into a pointcasting beevine, with seven joints and Orange Bee as anchor. They extended up the basement stairs and probed the main floor. With the number of corners they had to negotiate, the vine could not reach every room, and twice they incorporated household mirrors to extend their range. As they crawled along ceilings and walls to map and survey, they passed their readings back to Orange Bee, which scattercast it to LOG2 while also milling it itself. There were no humans detectable in the house, no fauna whatsoever, for that matter. None of the house's detectable machines seemed smarter than a houseputer.

When the beevine, with Yellow Bee at the head, reached the main parlor, it discovered two provocative objects. One was a procedure cart and the other a glass-topped coffee table. Yellow Bee ran every scan at its disposal on the objects. The cart—titanium steel, smart, with multiple servo appendages of unknown function—stood at one end of the room. Orange Bee, watching the pictures, could not fit such a cart into any of its library models of things found in residential households.

The coffee table, next to the cart, was a slab of glassine resting on a four-legged base. The base was made of military-grade resins normally used in body armor.

Orange Bee, sitting in the gap between the sill and foundation, made a best guess decision and ordered Red Beetle to advance up the beevine, trading places with the other mechs until it was within the parlor.

When all was in place, Orange Bee ordered, *Prepare to launch* Paintbrush.

All six mechs countersigned, *Paintbrush*.

Launch.

Red Beetle's carapace snapped open, and the beetle dove into the open room, flying straight for the procedure cart. At the same moment, the other mechs broke from the beevine and flew pell-mell through the rooms and halls, dodging in all directions. Except for Orange Bee, which stayed at its post and began to broadcast a message to the world at large in all bands and channels at its disposal.

A millisecond later, the glassine top of the coffee table exploded upward as the resin base sprang up on four legs and began to spit rapid-fire laser pulses from cannon mounted along its legs. Red Beetle was hit first and incinerated before it could reach the cart. Flakes trailing from its carapace drifted to the floor. More laser fire cut through the walls and floor like wax, hitting and destroying all of the fleeing mechs in seconds.

The four-legged mech turned its fire on the Orange bee but couldn't penetrate the clinker sill covering it. Meanwhile, the bee continued to broadcast. The mech bounded out of the parlor and down the hall, crashed through the cellar door and down the steps until it had a better firing angle. Then it easily picked off the last member of the fleet. End of transmission.

REILLY DELL RETURNED to Rolfe's and joined them on the Stardeck where they were mostly ignoring the canopy variety show on the boards overhead. He brought a small package that he tossed to Fred. "Here, someone's trying to reach you." It was a skullcap, like the one he, himself, wore.

"Is it against the law to be off-line for one evening?" Fred complained, but from the blank stares he got from the others, apparently it was. He sighed and opened the wrapper and let Mary fit the cap to his head. Its gummy material migrated through his hair to his scalp. There followed several uncomfortable moments as the cap's microvilli wriggled through his skin to lay against his skull. He heard discordant scraps of overlapping signals as interfaces were established and aligned. When he got a pure tone, he peeled a throat patch from its backing and stuck it next to his Adam's apple.

Testing, testing, he glotted, and then checked his DCO channel.

Good evening, Commander, said an all-too-familiar voice.

So, it's Commander again, he replied.

Only if you're up to it, Inspector Costa said. *I realize you're off duty after a hard day, but an opportunity has arisen that you might be interested in.*

I doubt that.

When Fred noticed Mary watching him, he rolled his eyes and shook his head to try to put her at ease.

A Cabinet rogue has appeared downstate, and I thought you might want to help me catch it.

A rogue? You mean another Cabinet backup?

Looks like it, said the inspector, *except Cabinet, the Cabinet we caught and processed, claims to know nothing about this one. Says it doesn't have any records or recollection of it.*

Then how do you know it's Cabinet?

It made a brief transmission from a private residence a few minutes ago in which it used Starke's sig. We checked it out; the sig is authentic, and as you know, those things are impossible to counterfeit.

Fred rubbed his forehead. The new skullcap was going through an itchy phase, and Mary, bless her heart, was scratching her own head in sympathy.

It's all very fascinating, Fred told the inspector, *but I think I'll pass.*

Really? A shame, because Cabinet asked specifically for you. Fred's heart skipped a beat. *Yes,* Costa continued, *it told me it trusts your long experience in this matter. It feels we've cooked enough of its backups today and would like to salvage this one intact, if at all possible, and it wants you there. Far be it from me to ask you why. All I want is the pastehead. Are you in?*

Fred seethed. Would the unnatural creature never leave him alone?

Where do I meet you, Inspector?

I'm waiting on the taxi deck next to Rolfe's, she said.

Figures, Fred thought, and he glanced in that direction. *I suppose you brought me a kit and blacksuit.*

Affirmative, in size russ.

Fred leaned over to Mary. "Seems there's a loose end to tie up. I won't be long." He tried to leave the table, but she held onto his hand and wouldn't let him go.

2.25

The spectator placeholders in the bleachers around them suddenly went silent. "There, how's that now?" Victor Vole said. The placeholders still bounced in their seats and waved and mouthed back and forth, but now the roar of the stadium was more distant, like the sound of a remote motorway.

"Better," Samson said. He could talk without straining his voice. "Where was I?" He had told Victor and Justine and their cat, Murphy, about how, at the beginning of his and Eleanor's life together, when power and praise, a baby permit, and unwarranted joy were being heaped upon them, a defective slug sampled him. He didn't tell them about his and Eleanor's suspicions that his assault was an object lesson for her.

Naturally, the Voles had heard of Eleanor Starke. How could they not? She was a figure of mythic stature and ever in the news. But that such a woman should be married to this bundle of sticks and rags seated between them stretched their credulity. And when Samson informed them that Eleanor had died that very morning, Justine was compelled to exclaim, "Ah, Myr Harger, just like in a novella."

This had caused Samson to pause in his narrative and reassess his life through the filter of melodrama. "Yes, I suppose it is, Myr Vole," he said. "Now, where was I?"

WHEN FIRST I departed from Eleanor's manse, I was in high spirits. Or as high as possible, given the fact that I had been seared through no fault of my own, that I stank to high heaven, that no one could bear to be in the same room with me, and that strangers on the street avoided or insulted me. To balance the bad, I had my good health. Up to the time I was seared, I had enjoyed the best health that credit could buy. Though I was 140 real years old, my body maintenance was all up-to-date. I had just erupted my sixth set of teeth, my neurons had all recently been resheathed, and my pulmonary and circulatory systems had been scraped and painted. I was an apparent thirty-five-year-old man in excellent health. This was fortunate because the seared cannot avail themselves of modern medicine, and from there on out it was all downhill for me.

Likewise, I was in excellent fiscal shape. My own vast estate was tied up in court (I had been declared legally dead for a few minutes during the searing process, and this flummoxed everything for years), but Eleanor put her even vaster fortune at my temporary disposal.

Likewise, I was in a fairly positive frame of mind. Oh, I had gone through a lengthy funk following my searing. I hid out in the subfloors of the manse, shut myself away for several months to lick my wounds. But I survived that and felt ready for an adventure. It had been decades since I'd tossed my fate to the wind. I figured I had thirty or forty years ahead of me (if I didn't accidentally self-immolate in the meantime), nothing and no one to tie me down, an inexhaustible credit account, and a brand-new valet by the name of Skippy.

I did travel. I visited the places I had somehow missed in my previous wanderings: the Chinas, Africa, Mississippi, Malaysia. A liberal application of tips and bribes lubricated my passage. Nevertheless, I wasn't able to break out of my own company. Gargantuan tips could get me seated in a restaurant, but they could not persuade the other diners to finish their own meals. On too many occasions, I had the entire wait and kitchen staffs to myself.

The same applied to clubs, casinos, theaters, and concert halls. To pool halls, bars, bowling alleys—you name it. I was the only tourist on the boat, the only rube at the bazaar, the only bozo on the bus. It didn't take long for my adventure to grow stale. So I returned to Chicago and moved into an apartment suite on the 300th floor of Cass Tower. I redecorated the place and declared my parlor open each Thursday evening for a weekly salon. I sent out thousands of invitations. Three Thursdays went by, and only a few dozen guests showed up.

Not willing to admit defeat, I hired a publicist. She advised me that radical measures were called for—expensive radical measures. I told her that credit was no object, and she took me at my word. She organized a series of weekly dinner banquets to take place in my home. She hired famous chefs, musical performers, actors, and comedians from around the globe to feed and entertain us. She paid celebrities handsome, confidential "honorariums" to show up and have their pictures taken. Each banquet was to be a tightly staged, show-stopping production.

Nevertheless, she warned me that not even all this was enough to guarantee more than a few hundred gawkers to show up. What I needed, according to her, was someone to co-host the banquets with me, someone of gigantic popularity. She found such a worthy in the person of the former president of the USNA, good old Virginia Taksayer. Taksayer's star had never set. She seemed to grow more beloved the longer she was out of office. She was expensive, sure, but she was worth it, at least according to my publicist.

Deposed as host in my own home, I was given a special role—that of resident freak. Indeed, we provided bowls of souvenir nose filters in every room. They were hardly necessary, for I slathered myself with thick, odor-blocking skin mastic and wore a mouth dam and flatulence scrubbers. What odors I could not stifle were neutralized by a state-of-the-art air filtration system I had installed in the suite. It produced a cone of negative pressure that could follow me through the rooms and discreetly exchange the air around me.

We were a smash success. From the very first banquet, my house was elbow to elbow with the cream of society, the lights of academia, and the jackdaws of government. Everyone who was anyone paraded through my parlor, supped at my board, and ravaged my wine closet. Couples coupled in my spare bedrooms, crooks conspired on my balcony, and celebrities manifested themselves from room to room. And I? I explored new frontiers of self-loathing.

Not that I knew it at the time. At the time, I thought the whole thing was pretty neat. I threw my banquets for seven years, never missing a Thursday. Although she was invited, Eleanor never attended. Meanwhile, I never left my apartment; I found quiet ways to entertain myself and to pass the time.

That's not to say that El never visited me; she did, on my birthday, on Father's Day, other occasions. She always brought little Ellie with her, who hung around my neck and called me daddy. Ellie claimed not to need those ugly nose filters when visiting my house because she was "habituated" to my smell, which anyway wasn't as bad as other people said it was.

Gradually, their visits tapered off. They were on Mars one year and otherwise occupied the next. I was surprised to discover that I survived their absence. I mostly missed them during the holidays, but otherwise learned how to get by just fine.

ONE WEEK MY routine malfed. On Tuesday night I had gone to bed and asked for a vid. Skippy, my valet, was in charge of surveying the millions of programs available on the nets and selecting ones that could capture my interest long enough to escort me to sleep. On this particular night, he ran a segment from a Heritage Biography series on important cultural figures of the past.

"What's this crap?" I said. Skippy knew I wasn't interested in biographies, especially bios of so-called cultural figures. But I soon saw why Skippy had flagged this particular segment—it was about me. It was called "On the Surface—the Work of Samson Paul Harger, 1951–2092, A Retrospective."

I was surprised, but not flattered. I had long ago sworn off reviews of my work. Something about this one caught my eye, though, as it must have Skippy's. Remember, this was only a few years after my reputed mulching at the hands of the Homeland Command, and this was my first major retrospective. I found the prospect of watching it too Tom Sawyeresque to resist.

I won't bore you, Myren Vole, with the cockamamie insights revealed in this retrospective. I will only say that the producers managed to unearth a surprising variety of archival vids and photos of my childhood family and that these were difficult for me to view without a fair amount of heartache. They had a home movie of me and my first wife, Jean Scholero, back in the late twentieth century when I was first making a name for myself with my paintings. That was especially hard to watch. I hadn't thought of Jean in quite a while. And of course they couldn't resist using the surveillance vids of me that day in 2092 when the slug hog-tied me on the patio of the Foursquare Café in Bloomington, from whence I was delivered to Utah for deconstruction.

I will mention only one conclusion of the retrospective and that because of the degree to which it riled me. It was hinted at in the production's title—"On the Surface." The show's writers accused me of being shallow. Specifically, they asserted that either I had no feelings or I was incapable of expressing them in my work. They cited the cold, inhuman quality of my paintings and emphasized the fact that when I reinvented myself in the twenty-first century, I did so as a specialist in package design. Artificial skin, battlewrap, tetanus blanket, novelty gift wraps. Everything on the surface—get it? The wrapper—not the gift.

Myren Vole, have you ever been accused of being superficial? Here, the first draft of my legacy was being written before my eyes, and this was what was being said of me? That I was superficial? Believe me, the vid threw me off my feed. It shattered my soporific routine. I spent the entire next day stewing over it. I composed a long, insightful rebuttal to the show's producers, which I never sent. Thursday rolled around, and I was in a terrible foul mood and I canceled the banquet at the last minute. Canceled all of them. Fired my publicist.

I decided then and there that my best rebuttal would be to "reinvent" myself once again. I was still capable of doing that, wasn't I? I wasn't dead yet.

I HAD BEEN out of the art biz for a while, and a whole raft of new tools and techniques had come into use in the meantime. I ordered in some of everything: story wire, smart sand, smart clay, professional holography equipment, rondophone traps, aerosol sculpture gases, liquid stone—you name it. I spent eleven months playing with this stuff, getting to know what it could and couldn't do. I didn't have a work in mind yet, except that I wanted to do a piece about Jean, my long-lost first wife. She was my subject.

Before Eleanor, Jean was the only woman who had truly touched me. She was my first love and you only get one of those, no matter how long you live. To my lasting shame and regret, it was I who had driven her away. I was too full of myself in those early days, too wonderful for my own good.

I spent about a year with my new toys creating works about Jean while trying to uncover my theme. I sped through a number of motifs: unexpected attraction, energetic eroticism, identification with the body, jealousy, spooky union, fights, obsession/compulsion, self-hatred. Eventually, I realized I was attempting to re-create a young man's palette. And though that makes sense—Jean and I *had* been young then—now I was old.

This realization only spurred my efforts. I was deeply engaged in the hunt. My former routine was in shambles. I left it to Skippy to send me food every few hours in case I was hungry. I lay down on the nearest couch whenever sleep overcame me. It was almost like the good old days.

As I zeroed in on my vision, I eliminated media that didn't seem to serve my purpose. Rejected were the iteration sequencers, photonic wax, and gene splicers, the robotics, and most of the holography equipment. Eventually, I narrowed my media down to one old one and one new. I decided to do a rather conventional, flat portrait of Jean in oil paints. For this I even retrieved from storage some of my beloved old boar-hair and sable brushes.

The new medium I chose was an organic gestalt compiler of the sort used to record emotive slices for hollyholo sims, like your Jason and Alison across the way.

The very first time I set brush to canvas, a title for the piece popped into my head. I would call it "Her Secret Wound."

Well now, I thought, I wonder what *that* means. What wound? Why secret? I didn't have a clue, so I mixed some browns and umbers with thinner and set about firing off quick sketches on paper to try to discover Jean's secret wound.

I hadn't handled a brush in over a century, and I had to relearn how to paint, but it came back, and soon I was knocking out little story boards of our ancient life together. The ups and downs, the miracles of understanding and the betrayals. After two months of this, I picked up my head one day and saw it: the wound was actually my own, not hers. The wound was loneliness.

What is loneliness, Myren Vole? I am speaking of the garden variety, the kind we all encounter. No matter how wrapped up we are in our lover's embrace, it manages to slither in for a short stay now and then, eh?

In truth, there's not much to say about loneliness, for it's not a broad subject. Any child, alone in her room, can journey across its entire breadth, from border to border, in an hour.

Though not broad, our subject is deep. Loneliness is deeper than the ocean. But here, too, there is no mystery. Our intrepid child is liable to fall quickly to the very bottom without even trying. And since the depths of loneliness cannot sustain human life, the child will swim to the surface again in short order, no worse for wear.

Some of us, though, can bring breathing aids down with us for longer stays: imaginary friends, drugs and alcohol, mind-numbing entertainment, hobbies, ironclad routine, and pets. (Pets are some of the best enablers of loneliness, your own cuddlesome Murphy notwithstanding.) With the help of these aids, a poor sap can survive the airless depths of loneliness long enough to experience its true horror—duration.

Did you know, Myren Vole, that when presented with the same odor (even my own) for a duration of only several minutes, the olfactory nerves become habituated—as my daughter used to say—to it and cease transmitting its signal to the brain?

Likewise, most pain loses its edge over time. Time heals all—as they say. Even the loss of a loved one, perhaps life's most wrenching pain, is blunted in time. It recedes into the background where it can be borne with lesser pains. Not so our friend loneliness, which grows only more keen and insistent with each passing hour. Loneliness is as needle sharp now as it was an hour ago, or last week.

But if loneliness is the wound, what's so secret about it? I submit to you, Myren Vole, that the most painful death of all is suffocation by loneliness. And by the time

I started on my portrait of Jean, I was ten years into it (with another five to go). It is from that vantage point that I tell you that loneliness itself is the secret. It's a secret you cannot tell anyone. Why?

Because to confess your loneliness is to confess your failure as a human being. To confess would only cause others to pity and avoid you, afraid that what you have is catching. Your condition is caused by a lack of human relationship, and yet to admit to it only drives your possible rescuers farther away (while attracting cats).

So, you attempt to hide your loneliness in public, to behave, in fact, as though you have too many friends already, and thus you hope to attract people who will unwittingly save you. But it never works that way. Your condition is written all over your face, in the hunch of your shoulders, in the hollowness of your laugh. You fool no one.

Believe me in this; I've tried all the tricks of the lonely man.

THANK YOU, VICTOR. I was parched. Now, where was I?

I had my media, my subject, and my title. I set myself to work. I mixed shredded processor felt with my oils and painted a life-size portrait of Jean. This took half a year to get right, but when I was finished, it was, in my humble opinion, sublime. Jean's expression was sweet and sad—just as I remembered her.

Satisfied with the base painting, I began to layer on semitransparent washes of refractive oils to create a sense of depth and motion. It wasn't exactly holographic; it was still only two-dimensional, but as the viewer's eyes moved across it, Jean's image seemed to tremble with life, seemed to breathe and blink, as though she were right there, holding her pose behind the frame.

It was terrific. I loved it. Yet I knew my real work had yet to begin. I had embedded all of that blank processor felt in the paint, and it was time to give Jean her secret wound.

There was enough felt in the paint to supply the canvas with an index of 1.50 or 1.75 on today's mentar scale. That is, of about the same mental complexity of my Skippy at the time. I could have initialized the painting with a personality bud and thinking noetics and used it as another valet. But instead I wanted to imprint it with a single emotion.

Now, Justine, I don't know how much you know about sim holography, but those hollyholo sims you enjoy watching are special hybrids. When you cast a sim of yourself (or proxy, for that matter), the simcaster takes a precise picture of your entire brain state at that moment. A slice, if you will, or a gestalt map. This is sufficient to model a software brain that can think. But feelings, unlike thought, are epiphenomena of brain states, and there is only one brain state mapped in your slice, one that captures what you were feeling the moment you press the cast button.

Am I losing you? Please bear with me. I only mean to say that your sim or proxy is capable of feeling only one emotion, the emotion that you, yourself, were feeling when you cast it. So, how do the hollyholos you enjoy watching seem to experience a wide range of emotion? This is made possible by casting millions of slices and stringing them together in emotive cascades. The novella actors who cast these hollyholos spend most of their time sitting in studio booths emoting on command, over and over again: I am happy, I am sad, I am ecstatic, I am miserable—a broad spectrum—and all the while staying in character! (I suppose they earn the fortunes they're paid.)

My own goal was more modest. I wanted to create slices of only one feeling—you guessed it—loneliness. I wanted to burn it right into the paint, into the felt mixed in the paint. I wanted it to have all the shades, all the layers of my own wretched experience. I wanted a portrait that actually *suffered*, suffered in the same dumb animal way that I did.

My task was complicated by the fact that, as a seared, I cannot allow myself to be deeply scanned. The radiation of scanways or holographic equipment would set off the wardens in my cells, and I would burn. Even the radiation from this little pocket simcaster I have here is enough to turn me into a human Roman candle (and, by the way, the next time I pull this out you'd better move your seats away from me). For my portrait, I had to use a passive electrocorticographic reader, a sort of metal bowl over my head with ultrasensitive wave frequency pickups. These are no good for modeling a thinking brain, but they do a fine job in recording emotive states.

So there I sat, at my grand banquet table, with a metal colander atop my bald head, gazing at the portrait of my first wife and allowing my love for her and the utter misery of my singledom to fill up all my spaces, and when there was nothing in my heart but a thousand paper cuts of loneliness, I'd tap the controller and feed my agony to the oil painting. The whole exercise sometimes took hours to accomplish, and it would wipe me out for the rest of the day.

Did the painting share my pain? I don't know for sure, only that my instruments registered a positive emotive flux in the paint's processor felt. But how could I know if the recorded feelings were true to life? I couldn't; so the next day I repeated the process, and the next, and every day thereafter.

I hardly noticed the days and weeks streaming by. I can't say that my spirit was refreshed by my work. On the contrary, this was pretty mucky stuff I was wallowing in. And it was deep enough to swallow the whole Cass Tower, I thought, all six hundred floors of it. At some point, I had opaqued my exterior windows, convinced as I was that the building was, in fact, sinking into the quagmire of my pain. I was weepy, defiant, and strung out. I ate too much or not at all. I slept sometimes thirty-six hours straight. I invented every distraction I could think of to keep me from the banquet hall and the woman who suffered there in secret. But inevitably I wandered in and hooked myself up to shoot her another dose of my love. I hated myself. I pitied poor me. I cursed the day I was born.

Ah, the artistic process. How much I don't miss it.

Once or twice I thought the portrait must be finished. I doubted it could hold another drop. I'd leave the banquet hall then and break out the champagne. But the next day I would wake up feeling even lonelier than ever before, and I'd rush into the banquet hall to start a new session.

TO LAYPERSONS SUCH as yourselves, I'm sure this doesn't sound like a particularly healthful or balanced lifestyle. And I would not recommend it to the viewers at home. Indeed, I had long passed the depth where most people would be crushed by the pressure. But to a true artist, one's art is like a diving bell capable of taking the artist all the way down.

Then, one day, as I sat gazing at my wounded Jean, Skippy intruded to inform me there was someone at the front door. That can't be, I told him. Who would risk swimming down here?

"She says she's your neighbor from the next floor down," Skippy said.

There were still people below me? "What does she want?"

"To see if you have a fish she can borrow. She's not sure what kind she wants, possibly a halibut or cod, but she'll settle for salmon or tuna or whatever you have, as long as it's from deep saltwater."

I was flabbergasted. All I could think to ask was, "And do I? Have fish?"

Skippy informed me that I did, over three thousand kilograms of live fish of assorted species in the stasis locker. They were left over from my banquet days.

I pulled the metal bowl from my head and massaged my scalp. I said, "Show her to me."

Skippy opened a view of my foyer. There stood a woman of middle height, a trace of Asian features on an otherwise plain Western face, expensive clothes, and middle age. An eccentric, no doubt. To have money but to allow oneself to age beyond fifty years was eccentric. And she was a busybody too. Who else but a busybody would disturb a neighbor with such a lame request—may I borrow a fish?

"I see you've already let her in," I said.

"Yes, I did," said my valet. "Was that wrong? I was following the Leichester Code of Modern Etiquette."

"Yes, it was wrong," I said. "Remind me to review that code with you sometime." To the woman in my foyer, I said, "Hello, Myr Neighbor."

"Post," she said to the cams in my foyer, "Melina Post. And you are Myr Harger?"

"I am. My valet tells me you require a fish."

"Oh, yes, Myr Harger, I do. And the sooner the better. Do you happen to have one I could borrow? I'll replace it as soon as possible."

"My valet claims that I have a few in stasis. You are welcome to any or all of them. He'll take you to the pantry where you can view them. If you see something you like, he'll see to delivery."

"Thank you so much, Myr Harger. I can't tell you how much this means to me."

"You're quite welcome, Myr Post. Good-bye." I closed the foyer scape, put the bowl back on my head, and returned to my suffering. But the knowledge that a stranger was at that moment trespassing my suite distracted me. I lived like a troll, never shaving or exfoliating. Fortunately, Skippy liked to keep the place clean, and I let him do it, so long as he kept his scuppers out of the banquet hall where I worked.

"Oh, there you are," said a woman's voice behind me. I whipped around to behold Myr Post in realbody entering the room. "You have a lovely home, Myr Harger." Her eyes swept past me and took in the banquet hall, littered with years of detritus and dust, tubes of paint, dried palettes, hundreds of canvases stacked against the walls, towers of recording equipment, ropes of cable—and Jean.

I leaped from my chair, as though caught in a criminal act, and threw a cloth over the portrait, but not before she'd gotten a good look at it.

"My how—" she said. "That's—" She continued to stare at the canvas. "There's something extraordinary about that picture, Myr Harger. Please show it to me again."

"No!" I said, galled by her presumption. "It's not ready for public viewing."

My tone startled her. "A pity," she said, somewhat chastised. "Well, when it *is* ready, I should be very glad to see it again."

"As well you *should* be," I said. The suggestion that my Jean would someday be on public display disturbed me, though that's what I'd intended from the start.

Myr Post gave me such a funny look that I became self-conscious. I removed the metal bowl from my head and tossed it on the table. It occurred to me that I was standing there stark naked. With a sick feeling, I glanced down at myself. But no, she had picked a day when I seemed to be wearing a robe. I cinched it tight and gave her a triumphant look.

That must have reminded her of her own mission, for she said, "I hope I'm not intruding," perfectly aware that she was, "but I'm in a fix, and your valet seems a bit slow. Otherwise, I would never think of troubling you."

Liar, I thought.

My visitor didn't appear so old as she had in the foyer, more like my own age, but with weathered skin. She wore rich evening clothes, fit for a banquet, and I smirked, thinking she was years too late to attend one of mine. She began telling me how she had come to need a last-minute fish, but I wasn't listening. I saw her rub her arm, leaving a pinkish blush on her skin, and this drove home the fact that she was really there. I couldn't say how long it had been since I shared a room with a real flesh-and-blood person. After so long in my hermitage, the effect was dizzying, and I had to sit down.

She sat next to me, uninvited, all the while chirping away like a happy bird about other people I did not know and wrong addresses and missed deliveries. I didn't even try to keep up with it all. I thought I could smell her perfume. This was hallucination or fantasy, of course. Seared people lose all sense of smell. Then I realized how close to me she was sitting. I wore no mastic, and my suite's air exchange was turned off. Yet, she wasn't gagging.

I interrupted her and said, "You can't smell me!"

"No, I can't. And you can't smell me either, can you, Myr Harger?"

I stared at her, speechless. We were two of a kind.

"Well," she said into the silence that had settled in the room, "will you be so kind as to do that for me?"

I didn't hear her. I was too busy detecting the subtle appliances of the seared that she wore. From the barely detectable sheen of her skin mastic to the fire-retardant inner lining of her clothing.

She laughed then and said with mock authority, "Myr Harger, either lead me to your larder, or show me the door. If I don't have my fish in fifteen minutes, my goose is cooked. And *you* of *all people*, Myr Harger, should understand that in my case, that's no metaphor."

Commanded, I led her to the kitchens. Or rather, I let Skippy lead us, since I couldn't recall the way. We sat in the long-abandoned chef's station while Skippy showed us life-size frames of the saltwater fish I still had in stasis. There were marlin, flounder, albacore, shark, halibut, salmon, octopus, and more.

Skippy said, "We also have a selection of saltwater mollusks and crustaceans and marine mammals."

"No, thank you, Skippy," she said. "It's fish he likes, but I've forgotten what kind he said. What other kinds of fish are there in the sea?"

"Haddie, herring, eel, sole, barracuda, fluke, dab, mackerel—" Skippy spouted a long list in no discernible order, none of which rang a bell for her—"orange roughy, rattails, skates, black oreos, spiny dogfish," and endlessly more.

Trying to be helpful, I interrupted Skippy's recitation and asked, "How many people does it need to serve?"

She frowned, realizing that I'd not heard any part of her story. "Two," she said, then added under her breath, "or one."

"Hmmm," I said, undeterred, "then one of those small flounders should do the trick, or perhaps a hoki."

"I see," she said. "I suppose choosing by size is a practical manner of making a selection. But my choice is more a matter of the heart."

"You're absolutely right," I said. "The heart is no bean counter." She smiled then for the first time, and I saw that she was pretty.

"Since I can't recall his favorite fish, I'll take your advice, Myr Harger, and choose one by size. That shark should do." She pointed to the largest brute in the pack of sharks that I had.

"The big guy it is," I said, and all the other fish disappeared. The shark she'd picked was over four meters long. It was a giant mako, farm-raised and put into stasis in 2061, a few years before the Outrage. She'd have a hard time finding one to re-place it.

"Oh, and—I almost forgot." She flashed a "silly me" look and said, "I'll need it cooked and in my flat in"—she consulted some timekeeper—"ohmigod, in *eleven minutes!* Is that possible?"

"Most things are," I said. "Skippy, please cook and deliver the shark to Myr Post's apartment."

"At once," Skippy said.

Kitchen arbeitors wheeled the shark on a cart from the stasis locker. Its stiff flesh quickened moment by moment, and by the time the arbeitors had lifted it to the cooker, it was flapping its powerful tail and snapping its toothy jaws in long-interrupted terror. Before it could do any damage to the kitchen, the cooker brained it and slit it open.

I backed up a little to avoid the splashing blood.

Skippy said, "The cooker asks what recipe it should use."

Myr Post puffed out her cheeks and pursed her lips. "I don't think my cooker has a recipe for shark. I'm sorry to be such a pest, but could your cooker use one of its own?"

My contracts with visiting chefs during my banquet days allowed me to record and reuse the recipes they fed into my cooker (after making a handsome royalty pay-ment). The cooker displayed frames of six different shark dishes it had prepared in the past. Myr Post picked the *Mako Remoulade* in which the shark was baked whole, stuffed with Arabic rice and pine nuts, and served on a swimming-pool-sized platter that mimicked a pebbly beach littered with baby red potatoes, cashews, giant prawns, sea urchins, and kelp. Around it were tidal pools of pungent and tart cock-tail sauces and giant cockle shells of shark fin soup. It fed 800.

Arbeitors started hauling ingredients from the lockers.

"And, Skippy," Myr Post said, "tell your cooker to tell my cooker what starters, soup, wines, et cetera to prepare."

"Done," said my efficient valet.

"And your arbeitors can manage bringing it over?" she asked me. "Or should I send mine up to help?"

"Mine are adequate," I said.

"Splendid," she said. "You are a marvelous neighbor. I will replace the shark and other ingredients, and I hope someday to have the opportunity to return the favor." She began to retrace her steps to my front door, and I saw to my horror that she in-tended to leave, just like that. It had taken some effort for me to get used to her pres-ence, and I thought the least she could do was stay a while longer.

I tried to think of something to hold her, and I said the first thing that came to mind, "I used to throw dinners once."

"I know. I attended one," she said, leading me to the foyer.

I was dumbfounded. Out of the thousands of guests at my banquet table, I was sure I'd remember another stinker, especially one so lovely.

Melina and Darwin Post attended March 3, 2097, Skippy informed me. That would have been one of my first banquets.

Perhaps guessing my thoughts, she said, "You may not have noticed us. It was be-fore our accident."

Accident? I thought. Were we all seared by accident, then?

We reached the foyer, she shook my hand and thanked me again, and the door opened for her.

"Tell me about your *accident,*" I blurted out, never good at small talk.

She stopped in the hall and looked at me carefully through my open doorway. "Even if I had the time right now, I doubt that I'd want to relive *that* nightmare, even in memory." She must have decided to take pity on me then, for she continued. "But I have five minutes, and you have been extraordinarily generous to me, so I'll give you the thumbnail version of why my dinner tonight, which you are so graciously catering, is so important."

And she did. I stood in my doorway, and she stood in the hall, and this is what she told me. But first, do you happen to have an Alert!? I could sure use another. The kiosk? Thank you, Victor. I'll wait until you return.

Fred and Costa analyzed the house from a restricted holding pattern one kilometer overhead. Fred had changed into the HomCom blacksuit in the aft compartment of Costa's GOV as he briefed his new partner, a recent-batched jerry by the name of Michaelmas. Fred's new skullcap wasn't fully initialized yet, and his blacksuit balked at its attempts to synch up.

When Fred joined Costa in the cab, he made no comment about the fact that she, too, wore a full, regulation blacksuit. The evening must be too chilly for culottes.

Although the neighborhood they covered from their parking loop was bright with alarm, there wasn't much moving down there, and the rows of houses, each proudly planted on its own lot, were doubly opaqued to outside snooping.

Costa said, "Hail them."

Fred opened a diorama of the Line Drive neighborhood and laid it over the theater map on the car's HUD. Then he reached into the diorama with his pointer and tapped a house on its roof. "SFR2131 Line Drive," he said, "this is Homeland Command."

The house made no response.

"I repeat, SFR2131 Line Drive, this is Homeland Command. Please respond."

When still the house ignored Fred, Costa said, "Libby?"

The UDJD mentar replied, *The subject SFR possesses a federally granted surveillance variance.*

Fred and Costa exchanged a glance.

The subject SFR is registered to the Sitrun Foundation, Libby continued. *We are attempting to locate the foundation's officers. In the meantime, you may serve your warrant.*

Costa spiraled the Gov down to the street and landed it within view of the house. Fred said, "Go over this again with the broadcast."

"Libby says that Nameless says that it came from the basement here." Costa leaned over Fred and pointed to the spot in the diorama. "It was encrypted and unintelligible, except for the sig. The broadcast was on multiple bands and channels and ended with what appeared to be small-arms discharges inside the house." She pointed again. Fred looked at her arm rather than where it was pointing. Not a small arm. Rather an athletic one. He turned his attention back to the diorama. The many bees present showed up as pinpoints of colored light, the color depending on the mech's affiliation. More bees were arriving by the second and joining the legions already lurking in the shrubbery. "I feel like a latecomer to the party," Fred said.

Costa gave him a look. "Speaking of parties. I'm sorry to have interrupted yours."

"Not a problem."

Costa pointed into the HUD again, this time at the outskirts of the theater map where a little blip was moving in their direction. "I've ordered some scouts to ring the doorbell for us. They're still five minutes out."

Fred pointed to a closer blip approaching from the opposite direction. "What's that?" A large vehicle was entering their perimeter. Its transponder ID'd it as a shipping container belonging to a moving and storage company.

Costa said, "Libby?"

They seem to have a legitimate permit to pick up an object in the subject SFR.

"I'll bet they do."

The huge van touched down halfway in the residence's driveway and halfway in the street, effectively blocking both. On its vast side was painted a large, mustard-colored capital T in an olive-green circle—Charter TUG.

Libby said, *What do you want me to do with them, Inspector?*

"We'll want to talk to them, of course," Costa replied, "but not right now. Send me someone to collect them, and in the meantime, order them to shut everything down and to remain inside their vehicle."

Acknowledged, Libby said, but a minute later, the van's rear hatch opened, and two TUGs stepped down to the street.

"Libby?" Costa said.

They're ignoring our orders.

Two matched specimens of that odd charter, in their olive and mustard jumpsuits, loitered next to the aft hatch of the container van.

"Michaelmas," Costa said, "what are they doing?"

"Just standing there s'faras I can tell, Myr Inspector," said the jerry. "They scan as unarmed, but the van is opaque, so there's no telling."

Fred zoomed in a little with his visor and discovered that one of the tuggers was a woman. Their body mass and shape were so similar it was hard to tell. A jarhead uniformity achieved not through cloning or retrosomal gengineering, but through deep body sculpting and phenocopic surgery.

Fred zoomed in a little closer and said, "I know her."

"Say again," Costa said.

"I recognize one of them."

"Really? How can you tell?"

Fred let the question pass and said, "Looks to me like they want to parley."

"They can parley at the station."

Fred got up and opened his door. "Looks like our scouts are still a few minutes out. I won't be long."

Costa watched him without comment. The jerry rose to accompany him, but Fred motioned him to sit. He exited the GOV and was immediately surrounded by bees. They darted in front of his face vying for his attention. Tiny frames opened, and tiny heads shouted questions at him: What is the nature of this HomCom action? Is it related to nanoterror? Was there a firefight inside the house at 2131 Line Drive? Is the incident related to the Market Correction of '34?

Fred said, "Uh, Libby?"

Suddenly, and all at once, the bees flew away.

Cordon in place, Commander.

"Thank you."

He shut the starboard door, catching a glimpse of the inspector, who didn't seem too happy with him.

Fred approached the van and TUGs. *Well?* he said, when he was almost upon them. *Marcus, I've forgotten her name.*

Veronica Tug, Marcus said.

"Veronica Tug," Fred said, offering her his hand. "Didn't expect to see you again today."

"Me neither," she said, shaking his hand. Her hand was bigger than his, and stronger, an odd sensation for a russ to experience. "Looks like you've had a day of it," she chortled. Though her mouth was buried in the fleshiness of her face, the sound that came out of it was light and melodious. "And an interesting one, by the smell of it."

"Interestinger by the minute," Fred said and offered his hand to the male tugger.

"This is Miguel," Veronica Tug said, not bothering to append his charter name.

"A pleasure, Miguel," Fred said. "I'm Fred Londenstane." But the tugger couldn't force himself even to shake hands with an iterant. Fred dropped his hand and turned back to the woman. "I haven't had a chance to debrief my proxy from this morning, Myr Tug. I hope the arrangements you made with it have satisfied Myr Pacfin."

"There's no satisfying some people," the tugger woman said, "so don't beat yourself up. You did a good enough job. You agreed to keep the pikes on a leash."

That probably meant keeping them off the convention floor. "That sounds doable," he said.

"Those are the exact words your proxy used. It also agreed to enlist five hundred TUGs to supplement your security force."

"It did?" Fred said. "Amazing. I'll have to talk to my proxy and find out what I was thinking. As to this situation—" he went on, gesturing to include the entire block. "We want you to return inside your big box and wait for some nice officers to come talk to you. Okay?"

"Gladly, Commander," Veronica Tug said without hesitation, "but first you might wanta see what we got in our big box."

"And what would that be?"

"I don't know what it would be, Commander, but I know what it is." Her delivery was deadpan and sweet.

Fred said, "So what *is* it?"

"Only just a gamma S-ray densiscanner."

Fred looked doubtfully at the van and then at her. "That's a pretty hairy piece of gear to be hauling around."

"Why, thank you," she said. "It can do a seatrain in fourteen passes, a warehouse in two or three."

"I'm sure it can," Fred said. "And now that you mention it, I guess I wouldn't mind seeing something like that." He gestured them toward the hatchway. "After you," he said and followed them inside.

Londenstane, Costa said. *The van is opaque.*

Her transmission was cut off the instant he entered the container. He turned to Veronica Tug and said, "You have about fifteen seconds to convince me." Even as he spoke, a valve in the undercarriage of the GOV shot open, and a dozen homcom bees streamed out and flew for the van, stringing themselves into a beevine.

"Ellen Starke's head—" was all Veronica managed to say before the lead bee entered the van and took up a relay post just inside the hatchway.

Ellen Starke, of course, Fred thought. No wonder Cabinet wanted me here.

The male tugger, Miguel, reared up in front of the lead bee and said, "Desist!" But the homcom bee was under no obligation to leave.

"I said desist!" he roared.

"Miguel, leave it alone," Veronica said, "and show the commander the way to the booth."

When Miguel hesitated, she made a sharp click with her tongue, and he jerked into motion.

Londenstane? Do you copy?

Yeah, Fred said. *Thanks for the bees.*

Londenstane, my scouts are only two minutes out.

The tuggers were halfway down the van, waiting for him. Fred picked up his pace and almost tripped when he saw the gear. The van was filled with electronics. A whole wall of fuel cells and a row of man-sized, rapid discharge, ultra-high voltage capacitors. There was a shaft along the entire length of the van's ceiling, water-cooled and bristling with induction coils. No wonder Miguel didn't want him or the bees in here.

Two minutes. Understood, he replied to Costa.

The heavily shielded control booth in the center of the van was too small for more than one tugger at a time, and while Miguel sat in it on a stool to operate the board, Fred and Veronica stood on either side of the door and looked in. The beevine expanded to remain right over Fred's shoulder.

Miguel shot him a look of pure hatred as he thumbed the board pads. Some lumbering machinery began to spin up, and the metal floor rattled. There was the smell of ozone. Fred scrunched in closer to get behind the booth's shielded door.

When the hum reached a turbine pitch, Miguel thumbed another pad, and a frame, like a sheet of paper, appeared before him. To be joined by another and another until a stack of sheets, each an individual cross-section of the residence, blended into a small diorama of the house and yard. The house and everything inside it was outlined, like transparent boxes inside boxes.

Miguel dialed down the gain, tinting out the furniture, walls, and floors. Only the plumbing, antique wiring, and other dense objects showed up as dark gray lines. The electronics in appliances were smudges. There was a coffin-sized wall safe in a room upstairs, and a brace of pistols in a downstairs closet. No people, at least none with implants. By far the densest thing in the house, so massive it showed up solid black, was a four-legged object in the main ground-floor room. It might be a sculpture done in some weird material, though probably not.

"Patch this through to my GOV," Fred said.

Now even the tugger woman seemed reluctant, but she ordered Miguel to comply with a curt jab of her chin.

A few moments later Costa said, *Nameless One IDs it as an unregistered warbeitor of unknown ownership, design, and capabilities.*

"It's a warbeitor," Fred told the TUGs.

"No kidding," Veronica replied. "We thought it was a house pet." She caught Fred's eye, reached into the diorama, and touched a rectangular object, much less dense, in the same room. "And this might be its bone."

Fred studied her expressionless face. Why was she being so helpful? Part of her campaign to heal the rift between her people and his? He doubted it. She was here on a job, a big job from the look of it. The TUGs were risking this whole expensive field unit. There was too much at stake to waste time as a goodwill ambassador.

More than likely, Cabinet had recruited both him and the TUGs to accomplish the same goal. Why else would she tell him about the girl's head, if that was what the warbeitor's prize was? Double teaming made sense. She'd let him and the inspector do the heavy lifting and be in position to pick up the pieces in case they fumbled.

Fred nodded to Veronica and said, "Inspector, inform Nameless One that I'm officially confiscating this van for an ongoing police action."

"Hey, feck you, man!" Miguel Tug said, springing from his stool.

"Sit down, scrub," Veronica ordered, "and shut the feck up."

The tugger sat down and glowered at Fred. Fred said, "Just keep the pictures coming, sonny." Turning to leave, he said to Veronica, "You say I hired five hundred just like him?"

As Fred walked back to the aft hatch, he could feel the rippling of magnetic fields against his suit. He stooped to retrieve a homcom bee that had fallen from the beevine. "Saddle up," he ordered the others.

As he returned to the GOV, the scout tender arrived and set down alongside them. When Fred reclaimed his cab seat from the jerry, Costa said, "Nice of you to return." The densiscanner diorama was superimposed over their own in the HUD. The warbeitor had not moved in the house.

"Are we ready with the scouts?" Fred said.

"Just waiting on you, Commander."

Fred glanced at the inspector. Despite her tone, she seemed to be enjoying herself. He cleared his throat and said, "House at 2131 Line Drive, this is Commander Londenstane of the Homeland Command." He swiped his hand at the house through the windshield. "And these are Justice Department Inspector Costa and HomCom Lieutenant Michaelmas." The other two swiped their hands.

When the house remained unresponsive, Fred continued. "We're here to serve you this warrant—he swiped again—allowing us to frisk you."

It was a federal warrant, one that superseded the SFR's surveillance variance, and after a few moments, the house said, *Proceed.*

Across the street from them, the house's heavy front door unfolded. The scout cart rolled around the van and up the drive and climbed up the stone steps to the porch. It lowered its shovel chute through the open doorway and opened its tank. Thousands of scouts rolled into the front foyer, unwrapping themselves and fanning out.

"House, is there anyone at home?"

No, there isn't, officer.

"Who resides there?"

"No one."

The scouts, meanwhile, linked up to create a forensics carpet that skittered across the floor and wall surfaces, testing, tasting, sounding, collecting. Pictures and data began streaming to the GOV as the scouts methodically mapped and inspected each room, crawling into cupboards and drawers, behind and under furniture. Tagged samples of fibers, soil, and other debris were relayed back to the cart for detailed analysis.

The scouts found incinerated bits of flying mechs that drew the officers' attention, as did ample confirmation of a recent firefight. The unknown warbeitor in the main room had the good sense to remain perfectly still during the bug frisk. Fred studied the mech from all scout angles. It was a piece of work: four multijointed legs—like wide-diameter intake hose—attached to a powerful-looking trunk. About the size of a Great Dane dog, but without a head or tail. Its trunk and legs were covered with laser-absorbing velvet.

Costa studied it over Fred's shoulder. "None of the other Cabinets was so well guarded," she said.

The rectangular object near the warbeitor turned out to be a procedure cart of the sort used in laboratories and medical facilities. It was locked, and the scouts couldn't look inside.

Fred said, "SFR 2131 Line Drive, I am placing you under arrest."

Acknowledged, said the house. *On what charge?*

"A weapon zone violation. You will immediately send the weapon that's in your main ground-floor room outside to stand on the porch."

To Fred's surprise, the warbeitor ambled out of the parlor and through the hall to the front door. It was more cat than doglike in its movements. The forensics carpet opened a path for it. It stepped around the scout cart and stopped on the porch.

"Unidentified mech on the SFR 2131 Line Drive porch," Fred said, "ID yourself."

Libby said, *It's talking directly to Nameless One. It says it recognizes our authority over its actions.*

"Good," Fred said. "Order it to stand down."

The quadrupedal thing on the porch seemed to slump. Fred and Costa exchanged a glance. *That easy?* Fred said, "Now order it to *lock* itself down, and forward me the only reactivation key."

This took longer to accomplish. While they waited, Costa studied the forensics summaries coming from the scout cart. But Fred looked at news digests about the Starke assassination until Marcus asked him if he needed a confidential huddle.

No, Marcus, thank you, he said.

"Hello?" Costa said, pointing to a line of text on an inventory report. The scouts had found a taggant in the digester dross. "And look here," she said to Fred, "zoo flakes."

"Zoo flakes?"

"Well, kinda like zoo flakes. We're not sure what they are yet, but they have DNA sequencers for a human genome. What do you suppose they do at this Sitrun Foundation?"

Libby said, *Commander, you may accept the key.* Fred swiped the console, and Libby continued. *Subject warbeitor is verified in lockdown mode. You possess the only reactivation key.*

Fred scrutinized his open palm dubiously and then the motionless mech on the porch.

"Well, Londenstane," Costa said, "shall we pick up our rogue?"

Fred shook his head and signaled for a private suit-to-suit link. Costa gave him a doubtful look but swiveled a little in her seat to touch his leg with her knee. *Yes? Something on your mind?*

I thought you'd want to know there's no Cabinet rogue in there.

She pressed his leg a little harder. *Say again?*

We were brought here under false pretenses, Inspector. Your zoo flakes will most likely check out as containing sequencers for Starke's DNA. It's meant to be a big red "X marks the spot."

I don't understand, Londenstane. Explain.

Cabinet, or someone, has lured us here to retrieve the Starke daughter's head.

Costa's knee broke contact for a moment, then returned. *How do you know this? Two and two,* he replied.

You're joking, right? Russes have a sense of humor. When he didn't say anything, she asked, *Why are you telling me all this in private?*

Because there's a rat in the game somewhere. A big rat.

She gave him a big, mystified look.

Nicholas, the Applied People mentar, who had managed to keep its peace throughout the operation thus far, finally spoke up, *Commander, is there a problem?*

Fred and Costa broke contact. "No, Nick, no problem," Fred said. "Libby, call back your scouts except for eyes and ears. And Michaelmas," he said, craning around to see the jerry, "I want you to wrap that scary fecker on the porch with packing foam. The sooner it's crated and on its way to the barn, the better."

"Yessir," the jerry said. He was standing at the carbine cabinet and handing Costa a Messers 25/750 over-and-under assault weapon.

Fred accepted one from him as well, though after weighing it in his hand, he said, "You know what, Michaelmas? I changed my mind. I want you to stay here and cover us with the megawatter. If that thing on the porch so much as shivers, you blast it. Understood?"

"Yessir," the jerry said and took Fred's place at the controls. The car's large forward cannon started to hum, and Fred turned to Costa. She seemed preoccupied, for once unsure of herself.

"Coming or staying?" he asked her matter-of-factly. She gave him a pained look, then made up her mind. She grabbed an extra canister of packing foam and her carbine and exited the GOV with Fred.

Up close, the scary fecker on the porch was even scarier. It was a leggy thing, almost to Fred's chest. Even motionless, it seemed to bristle with bad intent. There were weapons ports all up and down its outer legs. Otherwise, its appendages and ports were concealed by its shaggy coat of plasfoil velvet. *To my brothers cloned*, he told himself, *when mentars and mechs get married, they make baby warbeitors.*

While Michaelmas covered him with the GOV's big gun, Fred and Costa sprayed the warbeitor with the foam. It went on like green whipped cream and set up fast. When it cured, it would have a tensile strength of many tons, and the warbeitor would be completely immobilized, even if it decided it wasn't locked down after all.

The cart, meanwhile, finished reloading the scouts, and Costa sent it back to its tender. She followed Fred to the door. "Hey, Tuggers," Fred said, "how do things look to you guys?"

Nothing moving in there, Commander, Veronica replied from the van.

Fred and Costa raised their carbines and braced themselves to go in. From her expression it was clear that the inspector had a lot on her mind. She frowned at Fred and said, "A day's payfer says you're wrong."

Alert! was the perfect drug. It was fast-acting and brought one to a peak of total mental acuity without side effects like tremors or logorrhea. It came in precise doses, from four to twelve hours, and when it wore off, it did so all at once, without a hangover.

Samson washed down the Alert! with a sip of 'Lyte and continued his tale.

MELINA POST'S "ACCIDENT" occurred during an Around the Coyote theater performance that she attended with her husband, Darwin. Midway through delivering a comic soliloquy, one of the actors stopped and clutched his stomach. His waistline swelled ominously, but the audience took it as part of the act, at least until the actor shrieked. Then his bulging abdomen ruptured, and there was a mad rush for the exits. Too late, the building was already surrounded by bloomjumpers.

The Posts, along with audience, cast, and crew, were hauled off to Provo, Utah, and interred in the quarantine block of the Homeland Command holding facility, the same place I had visited several years earlier. Most guests never left quarantine alive, but since my own release, new detainees were given an option. You could stay and live a relatively comfortable life of protective quarantine, or you could leave—after being seared.

Melina and Darwin were permitted to occupy the same cell suite, and it looked as though they were settling in for the long haul—or until their sleepers woke up and expressed themselves. But after a few months of confinement, Melina lapsed into a state of profound depression, and after much brooding and prayer, she opted to be seared and released. Darwin chose to remain. They parted amicably.

Melina's first couple of years adjusting to the life of a stinker were typically wretched. But then, three years into her new life, she met a dashing man who professed to love her so much he didn't care about her infelicitous fetor. Naturally, she didn't believe him because he was poor. But that wasn't going to prevent her from having a good time. So they traveled together and stayed at posh hotels and tony resorts and took in shows and tours and the whole nine yards. She paid for everything, plus the surcharge stinkers always paid. She didn't care. She had a beautiful man on her arm who composed sonnets to her.

She awoke one morning, and Mr. Sonnet was gone. She had known his departure was inevitable, but she'd thought he'd make a classier getaway. None of his things seemed to be missing from their St. Croix hotel room, but she could tell he'd flown. All in all, it had been an enjoyable fling.

Next to the bathroom sink he had left the tiny, perfect, scalloped, pink shell she had found on the beach and given to him to remember her by. The fact that he hadn't taken it upset her more than his departure.

A little while later, when she ordered down for breakfast, the hotel manager asked if he could come up. There were urgent matters to discuss. As though reading from a bad script, he told her that her account was overdrawn. She knew that that wasn't possible, and while he waited in her room, she called her broker at the Reed Sisters Wealth Management Services in New York, who handled the lion's share of her and Darwin's assets. Her broker hemmed and hawed but finally admitted that Melina's many accounts had been tampered with the day before. Upset but not yet panicked, Melina placed calls to her other banks and brokerages. Little by little, the picture became clear. Mr. Sonnet had taken advantage of his physical proximity to her valet. He'd been very thorough; she was cleaned out. She and Darwin were broke.

Upon hearing this, the manager of the Five Palms Hotel let her know that he'd only tolerated her in his establishment because of his generous nature. He loudly bemoaned his suite, which was ruined by her unchristian odor, and he threatened to call the police.

Melina had to borrow credit from friends to tube back home. The Homeland Command confiscated her valet to assess its role in the theft. What small assets she still had were tied up in the investigation. She had to borrow in order to live modestly for a while in a rented apartment in an unfashionable RT. She started a number of lawsuits against the Reed Sisters and her other financial managers, but the courts ruled that the financial institutions be held harmless. The generosity of her friends had limits and strings. The authorities turned up no leads on Mr. Sonnet or her former wealth. They returned her valet in a hundred pieces. She considered selling it for recycling credits, but some intuition told her to hang on to it.

Melina's slide into poverty took only weeks. She lost her apartment and was forced to move into a city-subsidized women's dormitory.

In the three years since her and Darwin's accident, she had fallen from a penthouse to a barracks, where she could claim only a cot, a chair, and a locker. When she thought she could fall no further, she learned otherwise. The other women in the dormitory reviled her for her odor and petitioned the management to evict her. In an uneasy compromise, management moved her into a supply closet and ruled that her door must be kept shut.

YOU ARE RIGHT, Justine. This is far more than Melina Post could have told me in five minutes. We had more time than that, for her gentleman caller was late in arriving. As we stood at my door, we made way for the arbeitors to ferry the baked shark past us, its mouth agape with butter squash, to her apartment. And we made way again when my arbeitors returned with empty servos. But as the minutes accumulated, and her special guest still hadn't come or called, she was sure it was business that kept him. She didn't call him, she said, because she didn't want to bother him. She tried to mask her growing anxiety by continuing her story. I invited her back in, to sit down and have something to drink, but she was content to stand outside my door. I must say, her story was stirring my own pot of memories. The way she was treated enraged me, and I wished I could have been present to help her in her time of need. If only she had knocked on my door back then instead of waiting so many years.

So, there she was, my mistreated friend, lying on her dormitory cot next to shelves of cleaning solvents, drifting into the type of despair I knew only too well, when an extraordinary event occurred.

Across the Atlantic, Wanda Wieczorek, our Saint Wanda, who you may have heard of, had her little run-in with the furniture floor manager at Daud's in London. She'd only wanted for her mum to sit on the silk couch; she didn't intend to sit on it herself, until the floor manager showed up with his attitude and his troop of uniformed jerrys. She sent her mum down to the food court to wait for her, then drew her simcaster from her purse. This is a ten-thousand-euro item of furniture, the manager told her. We simply cannot permit you to ruin it with your unfortunate malodorous condition.

Fine, Wanda said, I'll take it with me.

She took the whole floor, actually, if you include the smoke and water damage. Her suicide made international headlines. Suddenly, hundreds of seared men and women were bursting into flame everywhere. On buses, in theaters, on rush-hour pedways, in offices of big transnationals—wherever they could scare up a crowd. The greasy, roasted-pork smell of charred human flesh pervaded our cities and awoke the public conscience to our plight.

The Homeland Command had performed searing in the name of public security, and the public had condoned its policy in silence. Now the public started asking questions. Why were we punishing the *victims* of NASTIE attacks? Why did we have to *mutilate* them? The civil authorities, meanwhile, were wondering what could have possessed the HomCom to create so many walking firebombs.

Melina Post started receiving a procession of smelly visitors to her supply closet. She was known as a former aff who still owned memberships at exclusive spas and clubs and other places where the seared dearly wanted to stage their wiener roasts. But Melina, always the good citizen, refused to participate (though she admitted to entertaining some middle-of-the-night fantasies of incinerating the bitches in her dormitory while they slept).

The protests went on without her and eventually shamed the UD Parliament to declare a ban on human searing. New, nonmutilating methods of cell-sifting were introduced. The doors to the isolation cells in Utah and elsewhere were flung open, and the quarantined were safely douched and released to rejoin society (alas, too late for Darwin Post who had recently expressed into a cloud of monarch butterflies).

With the searing ban in force, the protests abruptly ceased. But soon a startling fact was uncovered. There was solid evidence that the HomCom's "new" nonmutilating cell-sifting methods were not so new after all. They had been available to the Command for years, even in 2092 when I made my own excursion to the Utah cop shop.

The revelation that the HomCom had been searing people for years while more humane methods were available was too much to bear, and the remaining seared redoubled their demonstrations. Even Melina Post was angry, if only for the suffering of her dear Darwin. Alone in her cot, she drew up a list of all the people who deserved to broil by her hand. At the top of her list was Mr. Sonnet, if only she could locate him. Trailing close behind was that damned hotel manager in St. Croix. She thought she would tube down there and sit in one of his big rattan chairs in the lobby until he strolled by. But the winner of Melina's vengeance lottery turned out to be her wealth managers, the Reed Sisters.

The Reed Sisters in whose trust she had placed her fortune. Their offices were only a pedway away.

Melina tried to contact a number of the seared who had recently contacted her, but they were all already toasted, except for one woman. Melina met her in a coffee shop and the woman confided that she planned to take her life on a shopping arcade over Broadway and asked Melina to join her. Melina told her she had a better idea. She had made an appointment with her former broker on the 350th level of the OXO Tower.

The following day, the two women prepared themselves in the dormitory bathroom. They applied three coats of skin mastic, donned business clothes, and soaked themselves with cologne.

Because of newly minted accommodation laws, and because Melina had an appointment, the OXO Tower security admitted them. Since they couldn't go through the scanway, they were thoroughly frisked and sniffed. The search turned up a laser penknife and pocket simcaster, but since citizens had a constitutional right to such items, they were not confiscated. However, security *did* inform the Reed Sisters office of their arrival, and when the two coconspirators got off on the 350th level, the brokerage doors were locked against them, and two uniformed jerrys were waiting to escort them back down to the lobby.

Frustrated, the two women rode down in the elevator, bracketed by the jerrys. Melina was trying to take their failure in stride, but her friend wasn't handling it so well. The woman was rabid. She huffed and puffed. To make matters worse, the jerrys failed to convert the elevator to express status, so it stopped every few floors to take on or let off passengers. At one stop, two brash young men got on, and one of them pinched his nose and said to the other, "Pee-yoo!"

It was a costly remark, for it caused Melina's friend to snap. She straightened up and, staring Melina in the eye, bellowed, "Right here! Right now!" Melina swallowed hard. In her mind she was already booking fare to the Five Palms in St. Croix. So she was relieved when she reached into her handbag for the simcaster, and found a jerry hand in there already confiscating it.

Her friend was a little quicker on the draw. She had her laser penknife out and lit. She tried cutting her own throat with it, but the other jerry grabbed her arm. She kicked and clawed like a madwoman. She lashed out with her tiny weapon and would have cut the jerry but for his armored suit. She turned it on herself, but only managed to burn superficial gashes in her arm before he removed it from her.

This didn't stop the woman. By now the other passengers were pressed against the door. The woman swung her cut arm at them, attempting to anoint them with her sizzling blood. Melina's own jerry cuffed Melina's hands behind her with plastic shackles. She was too intimidated even to think of resisting. Finally, the elevator stopped, the doors opened, and the passengers piled out. In a sudden move, Melina's friend squirmed out of her captor's hold and tried to flee the elevator. In trying to catch her, the jerry clumsily shoved her against the elevator wall where she struck her forehead.

The blow was enough to stun her. She stood quietly while the jerry cuffed her, but when he turned her around, it was apparent to Melina that mortal damage had been done. The woman's forehead was swollen with a thick, steamy bulge the size of an egg. The jerry, calling for medical assistance, carried her from the elevator. She fought all the way, viciously banging her own head against the wall, against the door frame, against the jerry's armored chest. The lump grew to the size of an orange. Still she struggled, and the other jerry let go of Melina in order to help.

Melina stood alone, numb, in the elevator, not sure what to do. The circulation in her wrists was cut off. When she noticed her simcaster on the floor next to her feet, she knelt down to retrieve it. She managed to get ahold of the simcaster, but there was no way she could raise it to her head. So she pressed it against her buttocks and said—without much conviction—"Right here, right now."

Her finger resting lightly on the button, she watched her friend's lingering suicide in the corridor. The lump had swollen until the skin could no longer contain it, and it burst in a gout of flames. The fire foggers went off, filling the corridor with a cloud of fire suppressant. But suppressant couldn't quench seared flesh, and Melina heard the woman's skin crackling as the fire spread across her scalp and down her throat. It was the worst kind of self-immolation. The seared always tried to kill themselves quickly, as Saint Wanda had, from the brain outward. But this poor soul was burning from the outside in, as her incendiary cells killed those underlying them in a chain reaction from skin to muscle to viscera.

Melina lowered her simcaster. Irradiating her own buttocks would have a similar effect, killing her from the bottom up and providing her plenty of time to regret what she had done. So, she left the car and tried to help her friend. She found her in the fog propped up against the wall. The jerrys had foolishly wrapped the woman in a fire blanket, which only increased her core temperature like an oven. It should have killed her, but only stoked her agony.

With her cuffed hands, Melina angled herself to press the simcaster against the charred head. She had never taken a life before, and she steeled herself and pressed the button. But a hand reached from out of the fog and pulled her away.

The hand belonged to a man who was not a jerry. He was a man who liked halibut, cod, or shark. He was a man who worked in an office on that floor. He tipped

Melina over his shoulder and carried her to his private office under the cover of fire suppressant and shut and locked the door. The first thing he said to her was, "You don't want to do that," and he held out his hand for the simcaster.

She pressed it against her buttocks again and cried oh, yes, she did, but she was no more able to harm herself than before.

They hid in his office, barely speaking, until the commotion had ended and the scuppers had cleaned up the mess. Melina knew that the tower security was looking for her, and the man was unable to cut the tough plastic of the handcuffs. He accompanied her when she turned herself in.

FOR LACK OF evidence or institutional will, Melina Post was not charged with a crime. She was free to return to her supply closet, but the man (she never told me his name) wouldn't let her go there. He gathered her up into his own home, a modest efficiency in an RT, and took care of her. He rented great lungplants in huge pots to purify the air. He wore nose filters at first but gradually went without them.

By coincidence, the man also worked as a wealth manager. He was an officer for a firm in competition with the Reed Sisters. He was successful in business, but like his apartment and his clothes, he was rather bland. He'd never been married and was, in fact, quite shy. He eagerly volunteered to help Melina Post try to recover her stolen property. He had a friend who had a talented mentar (mentars had recently begun to appear). Melina turned the broken pieces of her valet over to this mentar, and it was able to trace some of her former assets. Out of his own pocket, Mr. Bland hired a specialist in financial forensics, and before long they had uncovered enough evidence to implicate the Reed Sisters. There was a big scandal, more victims were identified, and the Reed Sisters offices were sealed pending investigation. Some of Melina's assets were eventually recovered, with the prospect of more turning up and the promise of compensatory damages from the Reeds.

Melina Post, with a new lease on life, moved to Chicago and, unbeknownst to me, became my downstairs neighbor.

"HE'S GOING TO ask me to marry him."

We had been talking for over an hour with no word from the tardy Mr. Bland, when Melina made this bold pronouncement.

To me it was a bucket of ice water.

"Yes," she continued. "Oh, I don't know that for sure, but I know it in my bones. We've been growing close these last few months. Call it an intuition."

I had an intuition of my own, only mine was more like a bad feeling.

"He's very tender," she continued, "and spends all his free time doting on me or working on my case. I know he loves me, and I've grown to love him too. This morning he said that this was going to be a very special evening. It must be some extraordinary circumstance that's keeping him. He's taking care of my business now."

I was almost too afraid to ask, "What do you mean taking care of your business?"

"He's investing for me. And this morning I signed over power of attorney."

TO TRAVEL IN spirit with her through her whole desperate odyssey, only to watch her wash up twice on the same rocks, was more than I could bear. I made a perfect ass of myself then. I told her that no matter what happened that evening, no matter how bad and senseless things seemed, she could always come back to me. That I would take care of her. That I would dote on her and never swindle her. And that I needed no lungplant or nose filters to be close to her.

"Whatever are you talking about?" she said, a little frightened by my earnestness.

I told her that her hero was not simply late, but that he had skipped town, just like the Sonnet Man at the hotel. I told her she'd been robbed again, but that I would take care of her.

"I have to go now," she said abruptly. "Thank you again, Myr Harger, for the fish and for listening to my story."

"We both know he's not coming," I said as gently as I could. "We're both stinkers, dear Mel, and stinkers shouldn't try to deceive one other."

She said good-bye and left.

When she was gone, Skippy closed my door, and I returned to my suite. It seemed unusually cold, but Skippy said the temperature was fine. I told him to dispatch some bees to keep an eye on Melina's floor.

To my great surprise, in about ten minutes, all the elevators on her floor arrived at the same time and opened their doors. Out came a procession of arbeitors, each of them burdened with bouquets and wreaths and sprays of fresh flowers. The arbeitors looked like floats in a parade to her door. The elevators departed but soon returned with another wave of floral arrangements. Finally, after a third sortie of flower-bearing arbeitors, the man, himself, appeared with a final bundle of red roses in his arms. He was fashionably young but otherwise short on looks. He wore evening clothes and a foolish grin. I followed his progress at the tail of the parade and saw him disappear across Melina's threshold.

As per my orders, my bees kept vigil throughout the night. Flower Man didn't reemerge until morning, with Melina on his arm. She was radiant. She wore a gaudy new ring. And that, my dear new friends, was that.

JUSTINE, UNCOMFORTABLY AWARE that Samson's story lacked a proper ending, prompted him. "Did Melina Post replace your shark with a comparable one?"

"Oh, yes, she did," Samson said, "the very next day, in fact, and of the same vintage. Skippy learned later that the remains of their dinner, including the fin soup, was enjoyed at shelters across Chicago the following evening."

Samson was sagging in his seat, but still owl-eyed from the Alert! and any form of interrogation might be too much of a strain on him. Nevertheless, Justine went on to say, "This hero of Myr Post's. What happened to him?"

"I never saw her or him again," Samson said, "but I followed them on the Evernet. Together, they founded an association dedicated to forcing the UD Parliament to pay restitution to the survivors of the seared. You may have heard about that. From what I could tell, they lived harmoniously until her death from more-or-less natural causes a few years ago."

"And what of you, Myr Harger Kodiak? Did you return to your interrupted loneliness?"

"No. That was the unintentional gift Melina left me. In the fleeting minutes she spent in my hermitage, she poisoned it. She succeeded in provoking me to imagine my own smelly self out there in the greater world once more. Even to imagine myself together with a lover again. And once that bug bit me, I could never return to my solitude. The next day I had Skippy unopaque my window walls and I saw my city for the first time in a long time. Soon after that I met my Kitty and her charter. They eventually invited me to join their house, and I can honestly say that at no time in the twenty-seven years since have I ever been lonely. Cranky, perhaps, and obstinate—but never lonely."

The Skytel overhead was well into the canopy celebration show. Samson and his hosts watched it for a few minutes, comparing the hoopla on the boards above with the emptiness on the field below.

"What about Jean?" Justine said. "Where is *Her Secret Wound* now? And does it still suffer?"

"If Mr. Flowers still lives, he must have it. I left it unsigned and sent it to them as an anonymous wedding gift, though it couldn't be anonymous to her. If Mr. Flowers has followed Melina in death, I have no idea where it would be. It hasn't surfaced at auction. But wherever it is, rest assured that it's suffering. And it will suffer always."

Justine said, "I'm sorry to hear that, Myr Kodiak Harger. You should have destroyed it."

"Yes, perhaps," Samson agreed. From the expression on Justine's face, he could tell she was holding something back. "Go ahead," he said, "tell me what's on your mind."

Justine collected the cat into her arms and fixed Samson with a look of motherly disapproval. "I agree with my husband," she said. "At a time like this, you belong at home with your family, not here making a spectacle of yourself."

"You're probably right, Myr Vole, but I'm a seared, probably the last of the seared, and we must never let society forget the cruelty done to us in its name. I missed too many opportunities in the past, out of deference to my ex-wife and out of personal weakness, but what could be a better occasion to remind the public than the retirement of this canopy?"

Justine seemed unconvinced. "That's not what I see," she said. "Please excuse my bluntness, Myr Kodiak Harger, but what I see is far worse than personal weakness. Terrible, unfair things happened to you, there's no denying it, but bad things happen to everyone. And though your long period of loneliness is as sad as anything I've ever heard, you found your way out before it was too late. You should be grateful, Myr Harger Kodiak, but instead you seek to punish the very people who have sustained you. If you truly love your charter and truly appreciate all they've done for you, then you'll give them the gift of your final moments. Otherwise, you are nothing more than an *emotional coward*."

With that, Justine took the cat's leash from Victor and added, "Now, if you'll excuse me, I can't watch."

"Why not?" Samson snapped. "Already had your fill of suicides for one day?"

Justine unhitched her chair and returned inside without answering. Victor winked and said, "Best of luck, Myr Kodiak," and followed her in.

Samson fiddled with the controls of his simcaster for a while. "Right here," he mumbled, "in about forty-five minutes."

TWO DOZEN TOBBLERS filed through the roof door. They wore identical jumpsuits of a heavy green fabric. April and Kale greeted them, and Francis and Barry ushered them to benches that Bogdan, Rusty, Megan, and Denny were arranging in the vegetable garden.

The Skytel show had begun, but Bogdan found it dull. The Tobbs seemed to like it, though, and they began to sway on the benches and tap their toes.

Bogdan tried to escape through the roof door, but April caught his sleeve and gave him a look that said, We have guests.

"I'll be right back, I promise," he told her. "I have to program my phone."

"Now?"

Bogdan skipped down the stairs and turned the corner to his room. He strode in and looked around to see if anyone had intruded recently. Satisfied, he riffled through his piles of stuff until he found his editor, the same one he had used to program Lisa. He sat down on his mattress and spread the editor across his lap. When he opened his phone log, the queue of waiting calls had grown to 750 million. He dragged his phone icon over his latest uprefs icon, and the gargantuan queue shrank to a more manageable two calls, one of which was flagged urgent.

It was from Hubert. He opened it.

About time you answered, Hubert said.

"Does he need me?"

Not yet, but I felt it prudent to call so that you may prepare yourself to come at a moment's notice. In fact, I'm sending a taxi to pick you up.

Bogdan stood and tossed the editor aside. "I'll wait down in the street."

2.28

They moved quickly through the front rooms, Fred pausing only to glance through the laser holes in the walls, which all seemed to angle back to the main parlor. A few hundred scouts remained strung out on the ceilings to provide comlink. Forensics had reported no bloodstains, and except for the zoo flakes, this had been a strictly machine-on-machine skirmish thus far.

In the parlor, the procedure cart scanned free of booby traps, but it was locked. Fred swiped its panel and said, "Libby, pass this to Nameless One."

Behind him, Costa said, *"Nice."* She was taking in the room decor, which was not only aff but elegant, and the space, itself—grand. But it seemed cluttered to Fred with dozens of armchairs, lamps, and little tables. A clubhouse?

There was a large framed painting covering the better part of one wall. It had acquired holes and scorch marks in the firefight. As had the deeply dyed Persian carpet on the polished hardwood floor. The carpet was as vast as his and Mary's whole living room, and it was still smoldering around the edges of three melon-sized holes. The warbeitor had fired into the basement from here, the basement where the broadcast had originated.

A half dozen of the armchairs had taken hits too. Their innards were spilling out. There were shards of broken glass on the carpet. Yet, oddly, there were no scuppers scurrying about trying to set things right. In fact, there were no machine sounds at all in the room, except for the ticking of an antique mantel clock. Ticking, like they did in old movies, wheels and cogs powered by springs.

You have it, Commander.

Fred shook off his thoughts and swiped the cart's panel again. Costa came over to watch as he scrolled open the metal door. Inside was a small hernandez tank and portable controller. The glass tank was filled with bubbly green amnio syrup. Floating on top was a brunette head, still frozen. Its expression was frozen too, flashfrozen to her face at the height of her passion: at the moment the helmet flange clenched her head from her body.

Still, to Fred it wasn't an uncommon expression. He'd seen it a number of times over the years: the gaping eyes, the twisted mouth.

Costa took a good look at the girl, seemed satisfied, and went to wander among the armchairs. Fred glanced at the tank controller to see if the machinery was working.

Everything's nominal, Commander, Libby said. Fred took that to mean he could close the cart locker, which he did.

But Costa seemed to take offense at the mentar's remark and marched back to the cart. "Libby—" she said and paused. "Libby—" she said again, as though unsure how to phrase what she wanted to ask. "Libby, why weren't we informed of this?" she said at last, gesturing at the cart.

Our apologies, Inspector, but we were as surprised as you by this turn of events. Obviously, we are researching it. In the meantime, please stay with Myr Starke until Roosevelt Clinic comes to collect her.

Costa opened her mouth but closed it without another word and went to pace among the armchairs again. While they waited, Fred consulted his theater map. It had assigned the warbeitor a green triangle, which was still firmly planted on the porch. Fred opened a window on the scout network and toured the upstairs rooms and storage spaces. All was quiet.

Suddenly Lieutenant Michaelmas in the GOV jarred them with a shout, *Take cover! Take cover!*

Fred and Costa looked quickly about the parlor for something solid to jump behind, and finding nothing, they dropped to the floor just as a brilliant flash outlined the window blinds and lit up all the laser holes in the walls. Before it faded completely, there was a second flash and a ground shock that rattled the whole house.

"Michaelmas," Fred said, "come in."

We have lost contact with the GOV, Libby said. In the map, it was covered with a kill flag.

Still lying on the floor, Fred steered the scout view to the porch and got a look at the warbeitor, half exposed in molten packing foam, its powerful legs still encased, still hog-tied. It was no longer slumped, however, no longer in lockdown mode. It appeared to be ejecting things from three ports along its arched spine. Just what kind of things was hard to tell. They appeared to be smoke rings, and the warbeitor was blowing dozens of them into the air—like some kind of bizarre smoke signal.

Fred stood up and moved cautiously to the hall. "Libby, Nick, anyone, report."

We have been attacked by a suborbital drone, Commander, Libby said. *You and Costa should lead the cart out the rear entrance.* Fred's map drew a path from his hallway location.

But before Fred could react, Veronica Tug broke in—*Incoming! At twelve o'clock!*

A piece of ceiling dropped on Fred, and he jumped aside in time to watch a smoke ring drift slowly to the floor. It wasn't smoke but some sort of vapor. The ring was a half meter wide and seemed to vibrate with inner force. When the ring touched the hallway floor, it kept going as though the floor weren't even there. After it had passed into the basement, a perfectly oval hardwood disk of flooring gave way and dropped after it.

The edge of the new hole was clean, with no sign of scorching. A plasma weapon? Coreware? Whatever the ring was, there were a dozen more just like it dropping from the ceiling. Costa sprang to her feet, and Fred shouted "Heads up," but his warning was too late, and he watched helplessly as a vapor ring pegged her like a ring toss at the arcade. She raised her arm to fend it off, and her hand went flying across the room. Her blacksuit immediately snapped battlewrap over the stump. The vapor ring sliced Costa diagonally from her right shoulder to her left hip. Costa's awareness was struggling to catch up with her situation, and as Fred rushed to help, she had that same stupefied expression as the girl in the tank. Her blacksuit was snapping wildly, trying to stanch her trauma. Fred grabbed her arm, but it peeled off her shoulder, and her top half tumbled forward. Fred dropped his carbine and caught her. Her bottom half fell against his shins.

"I'm—" she tried to tell him. "I'm—"

Clutching her chest to him and dragging her by her leg, Fred dodged the falling rings. The battlewrap seals over her gaping slices were taut and transparent, like packaged meat at the market: ribs and roast. While watching the ceiling, Fred stepped into a hole in the floor and tripped. A ring passed through Costa's right leg, and her booted foot tumbled into the basement, where vapor rings hissed like snakes as they sank into the concrete pad of the foundation.

Veronica Tug broke in again, *We see no clear path, Commander, and suggest you seek cover. You have ten seconds. I repeat, harden your suits and seek cover—ten seconds!*

Fred was about to inform her that hardened suits were useless against the rings, but then he realized she meant to seek cover from her. He looked all around. The rings were coming down like a springtime shower, and the floor was eroding away. Lamps and armchairs, their innards sprung and convulsing, were toppling into the basement. Then Fred noticed two relatively untouched lines across the floor, and he realized that the warbeitor was aiming its ring toss away from the floor joists that supported the floor under the procedure cart. It wouldn't do to send its prize crashing to the basement. For that matter, Fred noticed there were no ring strikes closer to the cart than about a meter.

Hoisting Costa's top half, he leaped on a joist line and sprinted for the cart. He set her down next to it and returned for the rest of her.

Five seconds, Commander, Veronica said. In the background, Fred could hear the screaming turbine of her van's dynamo.

Costa's lower half lay like discarded trousers. He turned her hips over and scooped them into his arms and carried her to the cart where he set her next to her top half. That seemed wrong somehow, and he moved her pieces to align them, top and bottom, then threw himself down with an awesome thud.

SOMETHING COLD LIKE an icy finger touched the back of Fred's neck. He jerked and opened his eyes. He was lying in total darkness. "Lights!" he said, and his immediate vicinity lit up. He lay on concrete, under a metal cabinet.

"Hello?" he said.

This is Marcus, said a familiar voice. *You're on duty, Fred. You're in the basement of a residence at 2131 Line Drive in Decatur. You passed out for a few minutes. Your suit says you're uninjured. Orient yourself with your theater map.*

Without trying to move, he did so and saw kill flags splashed across his visor frame. He tried to read the icons but couldn't focus his eyes. His scalp itched maddeningly, but when he tried to scratch, he discovered he was wearing a blacksuit. Things started to trickle back. He crawled from under the metal cabinet. It was a cart. He stood up, and his suit illuminated a debris-filled cell. He had a sudden, panicky impulse to look up. When he did, he saw a peaceful view of the night sky through a ruined roof.

Fred tried the map again, and now he could read it. There was a vehicle flagged killed that had a friendly jerry inside it, also flagged killed.

"Medic!" he cried.

Three minutes out, another mentar said.

The jerry's flatline timer said he was already five minutes dead. Three more minutes was pushing the odds of retrieval, even for a jerry.

There was a triangle icon of a dead mech on the porch—Fred was in the basement of a residential house. He was here with an inspector named Costa. On his map there were *five* icons labeled Costa in the basement, and four of them were flagged killed.

Fred rooted in the wreckage of what had been furniture and found her lower half. The blacksuit had already begun to chill it. Nearby he found her upper body. She was unconscious, and his map listed her condition as critical. Fred returned to her lower torso, tore open the first aid pocket on her thigh, and slipped the cryosac out of its tube. He unrolled and armed it and pulled it over her head, service cap and all, and cinched it snug against her throat. But she jerked, and the stub of her left arm flailed at it with missing fingers. Fred said, "Easy there, Inspector. It's me, Commander Londenstane. You're hurt, and I have to sac you."

But she didn't settle down until he loosened the cryosac and pulled it off her. Her eyes were darting all over the place.

"I have to leave you to help Michaelmas," he told her. "I'm going to tie the sac into your suit. It'll only deploy if it has to." He sacced her head again and left her struggling to get it off with her stump. Fred clambered across the basement and climbed up to the front lawn. Whatever illegal-as-hell weapon the tuggers had used had shorn away a whole corner of the house. On the porch, the warbeitor was a puddle of slag. A knot in Fred's gut that he didn't know he had—loosened.

The tuggers' van was gone. Fred sprinted down the street to the GOV and searched the wreckage for Michaelmas. Found him in the mostly intact cab. He seemed to be in one piece, but flattened inside the blacksuit, and trapped by twisted steel. Someone had already reached him, however. There was an inflated cryosac covering his head. It was frosty white. It would hold him till help arrived. Fred stepped back and looked at the wreckage. There was a burn mark around the GOV; it had indeed been hit from above.

"Veronica Tug," he said.

She responded immediately, in no apparent distress. *Glad you're all right, Commander.*

Cars were landing all around him on the lawn and street, and a horde of media bees had broken through the cordon. Carts rolled off tenders to extinguish fires. Others climbed into the building.

"I guess I owe you one," Fred said.

Only one? I count three.

"Three then," Fred said and jogged back to the house. In the basement, a crash cart had lifted Costa's two main pieces into its saddlebag hoppers where its dozens of busy little hands were cutting away her blacksuit and ministering to her wounds. The cryosac still covered her head, but it hadn't been deployed.

Fred swiped the cart, and it said, "Yes, Commander?"

"What is her condition?"

"Fair," said the cart, or whoever was waldoing the cart. "Clean cuts, well-stabilized organs, full brain function. I'd say we'll have her glued back together in no time." The cart lowered its hopper lids, blocking Fred's view of her, and added, "I must go now, Commander."

Fred said, "Copy me updates."

"Acknowledged." The cart picked its way through the debris. "Oh, and Commander, see if you can find her three missing appendages. It would save her considerable tank time."

Fred turned to the procedure cart, where a russ and a free-ranger were working. They dug the cart out and set it on its wheels. Except for dents and broken arms, the cart seemed undamaged. "Open it up," said the free-ranger, but Fred came over before they could unscroll the door.

"Step away from the cart and ID yourselves," Fred said, swiping them his own badge. They did as ordered, and they checked out as a guard and a medical technician from the Roosevelt Clinic. A frame opened beside the cart, and a tall, gaunt man in a white coat joined them.

"Good evening, Commander Londenstane," he said. "I am the mentar Concierge of the Roosevelt Clinic, and these are my employees. Please allow them to complete their work. A life is at stake."

"Yes, yes, proceed," Fred said and waved them back to the cart. He stood next to them as they opened the locker. The controller, the tank, and the girl inside all appeared undamaged. The girl was still stuck in her own private moment, and Fred wished, for her sake, that they'd defrost her soon.

The medtech shut the locker, and mentar Concierge said, "You and your team will receive commendations for your work here tonight, Commander. Now, if you would kindly release her to me, we have much to do in very little time."

Fred raised his hand and said, *Well? Anyone?*

Libby said, *You may proceed, Commander.*

But he waited a little longer, giving anyone out there with objections the opportunity to speak up or forever hold their peace. No one did, so he swiped the cart. The mentar vanished and the two clinic staffers lifted the cart and carried it to the stairs.

The russ guard paused to grin at Fred. His eyes moved to take in the destruction piled around them and the missing parlor above and Swiss-cheese roof. "Such a deal," he said.

2.29

Blue Team Bee and its wasp still maintained their stakeout on the roof of the building across the street from the Kodiak building.

ON THE STARDECK at Rolfe's, the lulu Mariola pointed to the Skytel and said, "Oh my God." Everyone looked up. The train of billboards were all displaying the same huge skullish head of a man. Mariola and the others tuned to the Skytel channel to hear what he was saying.

"Someone hacked the Skytel," Reilly said incredulously.

ON THE ROOF of the Kodiak charterhouse, the housemeets watched the Skytel in openmouthed horror. Their two dozen Tobbler guests squirmed with embarrassment.

"How curious," Houseer Dieter said to April. "What is the old gent doing up there?"

April was speechless.

Inside the garden shed, Kale threw the blankets and pillows off the cot, scattering paper envelopes.

"Go now, please," April told the Tobbler houseer. "The show is over."

Houseer Dieter rose and brushed the front of his overalls. "Yes, fine, so it is," he said. "Thank you for a pleasant evening." The Tobblers all rose and shuffled to the stairway door while gazing up at the sky.

The houseer was the last of the Tobblers to leave the roof. On the wall next to the door he spied a small hole in a brick. "When is this hole here?" he said.

"What?" April said. "I don't know. What difference does it make?"

"I show you what difference," the Tobbler said and, taking off his boot, hammered the brick wall. The bricks shattered like eggshell, exposing a hollow space where solid wall should have been.

"What are you doing?" cried Kale, running from the shed. "Stop that!"

"It's not me," said the houseer. "It is the excavators, the pirates. Soon our building will collapse on itself. Good night, Kodiaks. Tomorrow we shall discuss what to do about this."

In the sky above them, Samson charged up a pocket simcaster and held it to his forehead.

SAMSON'S FINGER TREMBLED on the button as he thought of one more thing he wanted to say to the world. He lowered the simcaster again and continued. "The *sixth* reason why I hate to die today is something I only realized this evening as I was watching a novella here at Moseby's Leap. Our lives, all of our lives as well as the life of the city and society, are just like soap operas. You ever notice that? We become addicted to them in the same way, always eager to see what happens in the next episode. Right now I'm wondering, Will I make the morning news? Will a NASTIE eat Chicago when the canopy falls? Tune in tomorrow. The problem is, once I squeeze this button, I won't be able to tune in ever again. It's not fair. I won't know how it all turned out, and I can't accept that."

Samson raised the simcaster again, but he thought of something else he wanted to say, and he wondered if he had begun to ramble. Just then, a blue-headed bee appeared in front of him. The hommers, he presumed, there to arrest him. He glanced at the Skytel and saw his big ugly mug—the hack was still holding. So it was now or never. His finger found the cast button, and he took a deep breath.

But the bee opened a frame that showed a section of spacecraft fuselage with a passenger window. The picture quality was poor, and there was a roar of static. A familiar figure appeared in the window and pressed her hand against the pane.

"El? Is that you?" Samson said.

Hello, Sam, said Eleanor's voice, barely discernible over the noise.

"El, they said you were dead."

Hello, my dear. I don't have much time left, and I wanted to spend it with you. I apologize for the recording. We're jury-rigging the signal, and I lack the bandwidth for anything better. I'm afraid it won't be very interactive, unless Cabinet can manage to script something afterward.

One of her bushy eyebrows, that he loved so much, rose in wry amusement. *No time and no bandwidth—that's about as good a definition of death as I can imagine.*

"Ah," Samson said, "so you are dead after all." He lowered the simcaster.

The frame image flickered, and her voice dropped out. *Which is another way of saying—survive this one. Cabinet says someone has taken control—Songbird——— wanted to tell you how—*

"Yes? Tell me what?"

Ellie and I wanted to be there on your special day," Eleanor continued, *"but we may not be able to—all. You didn't mention why you wanted to see us so urgently, but it wasn't hard to—not mistaken, you're going to hold that "press conference" you spoke of all those years ago. Remember? I'll be sure to watch it if I can. I know you'll make quite an impression. You always have, in everything you do. That's why I fell in love with you in the first place, my Samsamson.*

Well, I just wanted to say good-bye because I don't think we'll ever meet again. And Ellie sends her love too. She's always been proud of her father and tells everyone she meets that she gets her sense of panache from your side of the family.

So good-bye, my love. You live in my heart always. Farewell! I love you!

The bee closed its frame and flew away.

"I love you too!" Samson shouted after it. 'Good-bye! Good-bye! I love you still!" His voice was swallowed up in the huge space. Below him the stadium was dark, all the placeholder crowds were put away. Above him the Skytel boards were dark too. He leaned back in his seat and said, "That was awfully nice of her. Good-bye. Good-bye."

After a while, he said, "Hubert?"

Yes, Sam.

"Be sure to tell them how much I love them."

Yes, Sam, I will. Who?

"April and Kitty, Boggy, Rusty, Kale, hell—all of them. And you too. You're not so bad, you know."

Thank you, Sam. Shall I call a taxi now?

"A taxi? What for?"

Samson raised the simcaster one last time. He couldn't think of anything else he wanted to say to anyone, but before he could order his thumb to finally press the button, the blue-headed bee returned and opened another frame, and Eleanor, as young and beautiful as the day he first met her at his friend's party, was beaming pure happiness at him.

Great news, Sam! she said. *Ellie has survived! Cabinet just learned that she's arrived at Roosevelt Clinic. You remember the place. Please, dear, be a love and go see her. Your daughter needs you.*

"WELL, IT LOOKS like we—or Arrow—hired a russ for you after all," Wee Hunk said. The mentar had shut down all the frames and scapes in the living room, including the nust globe. The two arbeitors helped Meewee back to bed. "Tomorrow," the apeman went on, "we should see about setting you up in the Starke Manse."

"Really?" Meewee said.

"Why not? There's plenty of room, and frankly, I want to keep tabs on you."

Meewee lay back on his pillows. He felt a long night's sleep was due him, but he was too keyed up to close his eyes yet. "Answer me something, Hunk," he said. "You don't trust me, or russes, or the GEP board, and yet the owner of the clinic, Byron Fagan, sits on the board."

"I don't trust him either," Wee Hunk replied, "but Eleanor apparently did. Besides, Fagan seems to have a monopoly on regenerative technologies. I haven't been able to find a suitable alternative facility for her yet." He continued subvocally. *But you make a good point. Let's get some of our own people in there. Problem is, the clinic maintains its own security and nursing staffs; they won't let us insert our own russes or jennys. Who else can we send?*

MARY SAID, "IT'S beginning!" and she joined the others at the balcony. A white star burst overhead. It was followed by electric red chrysanthemums and blue rocket trails. "What is it? What is it?" she cried, unsure whether to be thrilled or frightened.

"It's fireworks!" the others shouted. Sizzling sparkles, cannon shot, marching bears that melted like wax. The first fireworks since the canopies went up, the first in Mary's lifetime.

The lulus cried, "Chicago, give yourself a hug!"

BOGDAN'S TAXI LANDED on the transit parapet of the great stadium and rolled to a parking zone. Bogdan leaped out and was startled by a brilliant burst of light overhead. The sky crackled like ice in a glass. With no time for watching, Bogdan ran through caroming shadows to the ticket gates, but there were HomCom GOVs parked everywhere.

Boggy, Hubert said, *come back to the taxi at once.*

Bogdan scurried back across the parking zone. Suddenly a large man appeared from the shadows several slots away and jogged toward him, carrying something in his arms. He looked old but was still strong because he was carrying Samson and wasn't even winded.

"You must be Bogdan Kodiak," the man said. The sky cracked and crazed behind his head. "Get in the car, son, and help me lift him in."

Bogdan jumped into the taxi and helped lift Samson. Samson weighed almost nothing. He was deathly still, but his eyes were wide open.

In getting Samson situated, Bogdan ruffled his jumpsuit collar and exposed a glittering mech that was hiding there. He recoiled in surprise, but the man helping him said, "That's his, I think. At least he spent a lot of time talking to it." He straightened Samson's lapel and said, "Good-bye, Myr Harger Kodiak. It was an honor to meet you. The best of luck to you."

Samson looked at him blankly, and the man swung the gull door down and latched it. He patted the roof twice and stepped away from the car.

The taxi was halfway home when Samson tried to sit up. "Relax, Sam," Bogdan said, putting a hand on his shoulder. Bogdan was on the phone to April.

"Boggy?" Samson said.

"Yes, Sam, it's me. I'm taking you home."

"Not home, not yet. Take me to Roosevelt Clinic."

Over the phone, April said, "Don't listen to him. Bring him straight home."

"AMAZING," FRED SAID. The great city was spread out before him like a glittering island. He watched from the car he had borrowed to get home. Access to the city's grids had been suspended until after the grand finale, and he had jumped to a high parking loop to get a front-row seat. "Oh, look at that one."

"Which one? Which one?" Mary said. They had opened a frame between them, and he could see most of the gang at the Stardeck rail. Champagne corks were flying, and faces were damp with tears. A whole generation's long march was coming to an end, and Fred was exhausted himself.

But Mary was lit up, if anything, brighter than the fireworks. Fred could tell she had news, but he waited for her to tell it, and finally she did.

"Fred, the DCO called me ten minutes ago," she said, stretching out the suspense, "and I have a *job!*"

"That's wonderful!" Fred said.

"A *real* job—a *companion* job!" Once started, it all came out in a rush. "I begin tomorrow, in just a few hours, downstate from here, companioning someone at a clinic. At Roosevelt Clinic. It's for two weeks at full evangeline rate, with a renewal option."

Fred didn't interrupt. It sank in as she talked. "That's wonderful," he repeated when she paused for breath.

"Fred, is something wrong?"

The edges of the canopy suddenly flared with a magnesium fire, and they both turned to watch it, letting her question linger. He watched from his high car as intersecting vaults of the once invisible canopy were suddenly revealed. As though Chicagoland were covered by a ghostly cathedral. A cathedral built of many overlapping layers of large flattish hexagonal cells. As Fred watched, a white-hot light raced up through their interstitial spaces.

Mary watched from high in a gigatower inside the largest vault. The sizzling light seemed to blaze right overhead, and she shivered when the walls collapsed and the span toppled and ashes fell like snowflakes.

PART 3

Working for a Living

Tuesday

3.1

April Kodiak got her vigil for Samson after all. Bogdan called her from the taxi, and she ran up the stairs with the news. Several of her housemeets were still sitting in the rooftop garden looking up. With the Skytel dark and the protective canopy burnt to ashes, the Moon alone ruled the sky. "Boggy's got him," April exclaimed. "He's bringing him back! He's all right!"

The 'meets stirred as though from a dream. "I'll get his cot," Kale said and, rising from a chaise lounge, lumbered to the garden shed.

"Good, and let's bring some blankets up here," April said, "and make some mush and juice." She sent Megan and BJ down to roust 'meets already in bed. She sent Denny down to wait in the street for the taxi.

In the shed, Kale gathered up the paper envelopes, each bearing a housemeet's name in Samson's handwriting, and stacked them on the potting bench. He carried the cot out to the garden where April rearranged benches and chairs around it. All was ready when Denny returned, climbing ten flights of stairs bearing Samson's emaciated body. They entombed the old man in pillows and comforters and slipped an autodoc probe into his ear. They barely got any lifelike readings from him at all.

"It won't be long now," April whispered.

"But why are his eyes wide open?" Kitty said.

"It's all the Alert! he took," Bogdan said.

At the autodoc's suggestion, they placed a Sooothe patch on Samson's throat, and in a little while his eyelids fluttered shut, and in a little while more he was snoring comfortably. The 'meets, themselves, battled sleep on chairs and benches. Finally, Kale returned to the shed to retrieve the envelopes. He passed them out, and the 'meets took turns reading Samson's personal farewells to them by flashlight. They held hands and sang several charter hymns. They traded anecdotes about first meetings with Samson, about living with him through the years. They approached the cot one by one to kiss his burning cheek and to whisper in his ear.

When it was his turn, Bogdan sat on the cot and didn't know what to say. He had been a toddler when Samson joined the charter, and therefore none of Samson's troubled DNA had gone into his own patchwork genome. Not that they could, what with the searing and all. But even though Bogdan had no blood tie to Samson, he still felt closer to him than any other 'meet. He lay down on the cot next to the old man and listened to his breath whistling through the gaps in his teeth.

In a little while, April tugged Bogdan's sleeve and told him to go to bed. She sent everyone to bed. "Check your vigil schedule on the houseputer," she told them. "We'll call you if anything develops." But most of the 'meets decided to stay, and since he had to be up in a few hours anyway to get ready for work, Bogdan stayed too.

Kale and Gerald, meanwhile, left the garden to huddle near a cam/emitter mounted on the side of the building. "Hubert, can you hear me?" Kale said.

"Loud and clear."

"How could you let him do that? How could you let him do something so stupid?"

"I don't see how I could have dissuaded him," the mentar replied.

"Don't take that tone with me," Kale snapped.

"What tone? This is my standard conversational tone."

"What he means," Gerald said, "is why did you help him? You took an active role in this stunt."

"Well, yes, I did. I *am* his mentar."

"There's that tone again," Kale said, and Gerald added, "What you did to the Skytel was highly illegal, Hubert. Surely, even a mentar can see that. You have jeopardized this charter's integrity and endangered your own freedom."

"Don't worry about my freedom," Hubert said. "They'll never be able to trace that hack to me."

Suddenly floodlights hit the rooftop from all directions, and a voice said, "That'll do nicely, folks." It was a jerry's voice, and behind the lights, dark shapes could be glimpsed rappelling from cars that hung silently above them. "This is the Homeland Command," the voice continued. "Don't nobody move."

Sleepy Kodiaks awoke with a start to find themselves surrounded by a squad of blacksuited officers. Rusty and Louis jumped to their feet, but the hommers motioned them back down with standstill wands.

"What's the meaning of this?" Kale bellowed.

The jerry commander strode over and said, "I am Lieutenant Grieb of the Northeast Region Homeland Command, myr, and I'm here to serve this warrant." The commander held up his open palm, but Kale didn't swipe it. "I said I'm serving a warrant, myr."

"Then serve away, officer," Kale replied, "but I don't have a palm array."

The jerry said, "Amazing." A moment later a homcom bee flew down from a hovering GOV and opened a frame in front of Kale that contained a warrant for the arrest of Samson P. Harger Kodiak. The commander then nodded to another officer who approached Samson's cot. But Kitty flung herself in the way.

"Step aside, myr retrogirl," the officer said.

Kitty refused to give way, and April joined her and said, "Can't you see he's dying?"

"Step aside!" the officer snapped. But the women held their ground, and the officer simply strode between them, sweeping them aside with his sheer bulk. When he reached the cot he recoiled. "My God, but he stinks!" he exclaimed. "This guy is already dead."

The commander said, "He's a seared. He's supposed to stink."

"He's dead, I tell you."

The commander joined his officer next to the cot and opened an autodoc probe. He stuck it into Samson's ear, next to the first probe, and a moment later he turned to the Kodiaks and said, "I have new orders. We are placing this man under house arrest. He is not to leave these premises without prior authorization. Is that clear?"

"Yes, officer," April said.

"To assure your compliance," the commander continued, "I will leave this bee here as an official monitor. Now, to our second item of business."

The homcom bee opened a new page—a warrant to frisk the house and arrest the mentar known as Hubert. The ring of officers in the garden broke formation and headed for the roof door.

"No!" Kale cried. "You can't do that!" The houseer ran to the door and blocked the way. "Hubert is the most valuable asset we have left," he pleaded.

The commander spat on the ground. "We only have so much patience, myr," he said, and when Kale continued to protest, two officers flipped him around, cuffed him, and shoved him through the door ahead of themselves. "Anyone else have a hankering to spend the night in jail?" the commander asked. "If you folks are smart, you'll stay up here out of the way."

For a while, the 'meets waited obediently in the garden. But then Kitty said, "The bastards are in my room." She strode to the door and down the steps. A moment later April got up to join her. Bogdan looked at Rusty, and Rusty shrugged his shoulders. They, too, went down the stairs but got no farther than the corridor outside Bogdan's room. There, two officers were trying to peer through the brick walls with their visors.

"Hey, kid," one of them said, "what do you keep in here?"

"Nothing," Bogdan said. "That's the elevator machine room."

"Oh, yeah? With a barricade door like this?" He rapped his knuckles on the massive door.

Bogdan beamed with pride. "That's right," he said. "But you'll just have to take my word for it since you'll never get in there on account of the door."

But the officer had stopped listening to him. "Confirm receipt," he said and swiped the door's control panel with his palm.

"Welcome, officers," the door said as it noisily retracted its bolts.

"Son of a bitch," Bogdan said.

"Tough luck," Rusty said.

The two officers swung the heavy door open and entered Bogdan's bedroom. When Bogdan tried to go in, they ordered him back. He and Rusty watched from the corridor as the officers swept the room with sniffers.

"There ain't nothing in there but machinery," one of the officers complained as they came out.

"What did I tell you?" Bogdan said, but Rusty nudged him to be quiet. The officers went by them and continued down the corridor, scanning and sniffing as they went.

When Bogdan turned to shut his door, he was confronted by four Tobblers who had come up from behind. "Good morning, Myr Bogdan. Good morning, Myr Rusty," said one of them. It was Houseer Dieter.

Bogdan sprang forward, dodged between the Tobbs, and tried to push the heavy door shut, but one of the Tobbs easily held it open while the others pulled wrenches from their pockets and began to disassemble the hinges.

"Stop that! Don't do that!" Bogdan shouted. "You have no right!"

Houseer Dieter only snorted. "No right? You have the arrogance to say this to me after *two years* you occupy our room? I'll show you no right." He went into the room and started hauling Bogdan's bedding and dirty clothes out and tossing them in the hallway.

Bogdan turned to Rusty. "Can't you stop them?"

Rusty calmly appraised the situation and said, "I suppose I could take all four of them with my bare hands. Do you want me to try?"

Bogdan's worldly possessions made an unimpressive pile on the floor. He leaned over and picked through it for anything worth salvaging.

"We can't seem to catch a break tonight," Rusty said and took ahold of a corner of Bogdan's mattress. "Let's haul this to my room. You can bunk with me for a while."

DESPITE THE EXCITEMENT, Bogdan was very sleepy by the time he and Rusty had moved his stuff. He went down to the NanoJiffy to buy a package of eight-hour Alert! tablets and watched the HomCom officers carry a box containing Hubert's canister down the steps. They loaded it into a GOV parked on the street. They loaded Kale into another, and Rusty and Louis followed by taxi to post his bail. Though it was only 3:00 AM, Bogdan thought he might as well head out to work. But first he wanted to say good-bye to Samson in case the old man didn't survive the day. So he climbed up to the roof again. After all the drama, the house was eerily quiet.

When he passed his former bedroom, his beloved door was completely off its hinges and lying flat in the middle of the corridor. He was forced to walk over it to get by. He stopped in front of the doorway and looked in. Two large young Tobbler men were sitting at a folding table next to the cable drum, playing a drowsy game of cards. They glanced at him, stifling yawns.

Up on the roof, only a few Kodiaks were keeping vigil. Samson, in fact, was awake, and Megan and Kitty were feeding him.

"We were washing him," Kitty told Bogdan. "Changing his clothes and stripping off the old mastic, and it woke him up."

" 'Lo, Sam," Bogdan said. The old man, mouth full of mush, didn't seem to hear, so Bogdan went to sit with Denny.

Denny said, "It was scary to see him up in the Skytel."

"I know it," Bogdan replied.

"It made me real nervous. I wish he didn't do it."

"Me too."

Samson's old jumpsuit lay in tatters on the ground. Bogdan leaned over and snagged it, looked under the lapels, but the blue mech was gone.

"Kitty, did you find any mechs on Sam's clothes?"

"No," she said and gestured up at the homcom bee hovering overhead. "Only that one."

Bogdan looked around for the blue mech, but with all the leafy vegetables and rows of hydroponics, it could be hiding anywhere. He picked up Samson's belt and said, "Hubert?"

"I am not Hubert," the belt said. "I am a Hubert terminus with nominal personality and cognition. I lost contact with Hubert prime at 02:21 today."

"Well, good for you," Bogdan said and dropped the belt. To Denny he said, "Did you see the fight Kale put up over Hubert? I didn't even think he liked the pastehead." As he spoke, Kitty gave him a calculating look. "What?" he said, but she turned back to Samson to wipe dribble from the corner of his mouth.

"What about Kale and Hubert?" Bogdan insisted.

"Is that Boggy?" Samson said. "Come here, Boggy; I have something to tell you."

Megan and Kitty finished and gathered up the tray and bath supplies, and Bogdan sat on the cot next to Samson and took his hand.

"I learned something today, boy."

"I imagine you did."

"I learned that killing yourself is hard to do when all you really want to do is live."

"I could have told you that."

"Really?" Samson said and tried to focus on the boy. "I don't think so, Boggy. You haven't even figured out how to pass through puberty yet. What do you know of dying?"

Fred hadn't seemed as positive about Mary's duty call out as she expected him to be. When the canopy show was finished and the last of the glowing ashes had fallen, Mary rode the tower lifts and pedways home to get ready for work. She ordered up a smart teal and brown ensemble (not a uniform—evangelines didn't wear uniforms), researched train schedules, and pulled as much information about the Roosevelt Clinic as she could find on the WAD. Which wasn't much. It was an exclusive aff facility that shunned publicity.

Fred dragged himself home around 2:00 AM, looking even more beat-up than before. He wanted to celebrate her job, but she sent him straight to the shower and bed. She lay with him until he fell asleep, which didn't take long. When she got out of bed, he stirred and said, "Be careful."

"What did you say, Fred?" But he must have spoken in his sleep, because he didn't answer.

BEFORE LEAVING THE apartment at 5:00 AM, Mary inspected her 360 reflection in the mirror. The simple business outfit she had selected looked both professional and flattering. Her face wore a bright, sensitive, and friendly expression. Her large brown eyes were warm but discerning. In short, she looked the part of a successful evangeline.

In the lower corner of the mirror, a mail glyph began to pulse—there was an urgent message on the DCO board. Her heart sank. She'd known it was too good to be true—her companion assignment had been canceled at the last minute. She was sure of it.

Drenched in self-pity, Mary tiptoed through the bedroom, past Fred's sleeping form, to the living room and flatscreen. The screen was set to the default window high in the tower. She switched it to her DCO board and held her breath. Her eyes darted across the message scanning for the keywords: "canceled" or "regret" or "error," and finding none of these, she relaxed enough to actually read it.

No, thank heaven, her duty had not been canceled. Instead, she was instructed to attend a brief orientation meeting before proceeding to the clinic. This she was happy to do, and she swiped the directions and left the apartment.

The corridors and lifts of APRT 7 were congested with tens of thousands of Applied People iterants on their way to morning shifts: helenas, steves, isabellas, jennys—plenty of jennys—in a sea of brown and teal. This was the time of day that Mary had always dreaded the most. She couldn't bear the sight of gainfully employed mobs. But today was different, and her excitement must have shown, for people—strangers—smiled at her. "G'morning, Myr 'Leen," they said. "Off to work?"

"Hi ho!" she replied.

Down in the Slipstream station, the crowds were swelling by the moment, and the boarding queue had an estimated thirty-minute wait. This was manageable—Mary had allowed for such delays. But when she swiped the conductor post with her destination from the DCO board, to her surprise it directed her to a distant platform reserved for private cars. Feeling deliciously conspicuous, Mary left the queue and took a pedway to the platform where she found a grand car already waiting for her. No mere bead car, it was large and swank, with plush seating, full media access, a snack bar, and its own serving arbeitor. She took a seat and buckled her harness, and the car rolled noiselessly down the injection ramp.

A half hour later, the car swooshed through a flow gate and decelerated, bouncing on its wheels and rolling into a small deserted station. Through the car windows Mary glimpsed polished marbelite floors and curved walls made from tall blond limestone blocks. Her car came to a smooth stop, and the doors slid open. There didn't seem to be anyone waiting for her. The station lacked signs and kiosks, and she had no idea where she was. Mary recalled Fred's sleep-talk warning, and she was a little afraid to leave the car. But she forced herself, and when she stepped on the platform, another car was arriving.

This one, identical to her own, came to a silent halt several meters away. When the doors opened, another evangeline stepped out and looked around the quiet station.

Mary and the other evangeline walked across the shiny marbelite floor to greet each other. "Mary Skarland," Mary said, offering her hand.

"A pleasure," said her sister. "Renata Carter." Renata seemed rather big-boned for an evangeline and thick-waisted, but within germline norms. She squeezed Mary's hand nervously and said, "Are we supposed to go somewhere? Or wait here?"

"Not a clue." Mary laughed. Already she felt a kindred spirit in her sister. "I just arrived myself."

As if on cue, an elevator door across the platform opened, and a household arbeitor rolled out. It approached and parked before them and opened a little scape above its head. A miniature man appeared in the scape, naked but for an animal-skin loincloth. His head was smallish for his body and had heavy brow ridges and a thick jaw. "Good morning," he said, bowing to each of them, "and welcome to Starke Manse."

Starke! The famous name had been in the news continuously since yesterday.

"I see from your reaction that both of you are aware of my family's tragedy," the little man said. "That will save time. Eleanor Starke is deceased, as the media reports, but her daughter, Ellen Starke, has survived the crash. She is your new client. I am Wee Hunk, Ellen's mentar and your supervisor."

The little muscleman proceeded to describe the scope of their assignment. He had engaged eight evangelines, he said, to cover around-the-clock shifts. Since the shifts overlapped at both ends, there would be four of them on duty for two of each eight hours.

"Please take these and put them on," the mentar said, and the arbeitor below him held out two little round caps in its gripper arm. They were odd little hats, flattish, beige, and unadorned. When the 'leens put them on, the caps sat on their heads like teacup saucers. One look at Renata in her cap and Mary saw just how ridiculous she, herself, must look. Renata tipped her cap to sit at a jaunty angle, and Mary approved and tipped hers too.

"Splendid," Wee Hunk said. "My first attempt at haute couture is a success. Now, my most important instructions to you are these. First, you are to put these hats on *before* you enter the clinic grounds and are *not* to remove them for any reason until you leave. Is that understood?"

Both women nodded.

"Second and just as critical, you are never to leave Ellen alone, not even for a second. That's why I've arranged for teams of two. You are to time your breaks accordingly so that at least one of you is in the same room as Ellen at all times. She is being housed in a cottage surrounded by a flower garden. You may consider the cottage and garden to be one room. That means that at least one of you is to remain in the cottage or garden at all times. No exceptions, no excuses. Is that clear?"

"What if Myr Starke leaves the cottage area?" Renata asked.

"She won't."

"What if Myr Starke asks us to leave?" Mary said.

"She won't."

The evangelines glanced at each other, and Wee Hunk continued. "Be aware that I'll be watching you continuously and that I will debrief you at the end of the day. Now, time is fleeing, so please board the lead car, and it will take you to Decatur East where a limo will be waiting. That is all." With that, the scape closed, and the arbeitor rolled away.

THE LIMOUSINE LANDED in an outer parking lot and rolled along a brick drive to a gatehouse set into the fortresslike walls of Roosevelt Clinic. The evangelines decarred and approached a sentry window set into a large pressure gate. A jerry guard asked them their business, and they swiped the guard post with open palms.

"Been expecting you," the guard said. "Come through the gate." A slot opened in the wide, translucent gate of shaped air. The slot was wide enough for only one person to pass at a time. Two jerry guards awaited them inside, both armed and typically officious. Their voices reverberated in the large concrete space. Incongruously, the place smelled of sautéed garlic.

"G'wan through there," one of the guards told them, pointing to the entrance of the pedestrian scanway.

The evangelines passed through the long scanway tunnel in single file, pausing at the various stations to spit, peer at the target, and submit to sniffers and irradiation. It was one of the most thorough scanways Mary had ever encountered.

They emerged in the middle block of the gatehouse, where another jerry guard awaited them. "Hang on while we look at your results," he said. There were massive, floor-to-ceiling clinker epoxy barriers in the middle block, and any vehicle passing through would have to make a tight S-turn around them.

"Sorry, 'leens," the guard said, "but you'll have to lose those." He patted the top of his head.

Under normal circumstances, Mary would have complied without question, but with Wee Hunk's instructions fresh in her mind, she said, "Sorry, Myr Jerry, but we can't do that."

"Don't worry," he replied, "you'll get them back when you leave." When the evangelines still refused to remove their saucer caps, he pointed to a spot on the concrete floor and said, "Wait there."

On the floor was painted a WAIT HERE box. They went to stand on it while the jerry ducked into a control booth. Renata said, "I wonder who trumps who, Starkes or Roosevelts."

A few minutes later, the jerry returned and waved them through to the inner block with no further discussion. Starkes, apparently.

Like the outer gate, the inner gate was a wall of highly pressurized air. Beyond its shimmering expanse lay a plaza and the clinic grounds. But before they could enter the grounds, the evangelines had to wait in another WAIT HERE box with a dozen or so other Applied People contractees. And here the guard was a russ, not a jerry. He was no russ that Mary knew, but as she and Renata joined the others in the box, he flashed them a friendly smile.

"I heard they hired a pack of 'leens today," he said. "Congratulations, and welcome to Roosevelt Clinic."

Just like a russ. The evangelines thanked him.

When a few more Applied People iterants arrived, mostly johns and janes in custodial uniforms, the russ lowered the pressure gate. The dense air collapsed like a splash of water, and the day workers entered the clinic grounds at last. Immediately abutting the gatehouse was a cobblestone plaza, South Gate Plaza, which in turn was surrounded by a parklike wooded area divided by lanes and footpaths. A tall man in a long, white jacket was waiting for them.

"Good morning, all," he said cordially, "and welcome to Roosevelt Clinic, a wholly owned subsidiary of the Fagan Health Group. My name is Concierge, and I am the Fagan Health Group mentar and your supervisor. Since all of you are new assignees, I thought I'd take this opportunity to orient you to our facility as I escort you to your respective duty stations. Please divide yourselves into groups of similar job rubric: groundskeepers here, housekeepers here, and so on."

As the iterants sorted themselves into groups, five more Concierges, identical to the first, ambled up a path and entered the plaza. They spread out, one to each group. Mary and Renata made up a group of two. Their own copy of the mentar made a slight bow and said, "Mary Skarland and Renata Carter, it's a pleasure to meet you. Since we have a little extra time before your shift begins, allow me to give you a brief tour of the campus. How does that sound?" The evangelines agreed eagerly, and the small party set off via a footpath.

The clinic grounds were extensive and rich. Six hundred acres of woods, meadows and fields, brilliant ponds, and flower gardens. By and large, the buildings were only one or two stories high, constructed of brick or stone, and styled after nineteenth-century English country homes. Most were hidden behind dense foliage and gave no sign as to their function. Concierge pointed them out: Here was a noted restaurant, here the physical therapy/spa building, there the theater, here the dining commons, there the stables and boathouse. Along the way they passed clinic guests out for a stroll or sunning themselves on lush green lawns. The guests were, without exception, accompanied by jenny nurses. Concierge addressed the guests by name, wishing them a pleasant day. All but a few guests ignored the mentar, or returned his courtesy with a curt nod or disinterested grunt. As though the mentar were just another servant, which Mary supposed he was. But the mentar's charm never wavered. Mary, who found most mentars to be too stiff or too silly, was impressed. This was no caveman in a loincloth.

There was something odd about odors. Mary had smelled garlic in the gatehouse, wood smoke in the plaza, and just now fresh-baked bread.

"Oh, that," Concierge said when she asked. "After a while you won't even notice it. That's our scent clock. Every fifteen minutes, olfactory generators located throughout the campus pump out a designated odor. Here's a list of them with their times. They repeat the same every day." He swiped the evangelines the list. "After a few days, you'll be able to tell the time in your sleep.

"Which is the whole point," he went on. "Most of our guests spend the bulk of their days in jacketscapes where it's easy to lose track of clinic time. We find that our scent clock helps them anchor themselves here even when they're projecting themselves across continents. Also, and more importantly in your own client's case, we've learned that even people in deep coma can sense changes in ambient odor." The evangelines glanced at each other—coma? "We can use this to help them experience the passage of time. Being able to sense the passage of time is very stimulating to the brain. It has proven to hasten a return to consciousness."

"But do the smells have to be so yummy?" Renata said and inhaled the fragrance of baking bread.

"THIS IS MINERAL Way," Concierge said when they turned onto a shady lane. "South Gate, where you entered the clinic, is just through those woods." He pointed the direction. "We've taken a roundabout way to arrive here." They passed little stone-paved footpaths marked with rustic signs: Jasper, Quartz, Mica, Hornblende. "These lead to guest cottages," the mentar continued. "Ah, here's Feldspar, the temporary residence of Myr Ellen Starke."

The path to Feldspar Cottage was lined on one side with rosebushes in full bloom. The concentrated perfume blended well with the scent clock's new quarter-hour odor—freshly brewed coffee.

The cottage had stucco walls and a quaintly pitched roof. Its door was made of plain wood, painted bright yellow. Inside was a sparsely furnished single room, half of it raised up a step. There was an open ceiling, crossed by a roof beam of hand-hewn wood. All of the windows were open, and a breeze ruffled lace curtains. When Mary and Renata entered the cottage, they were greeted by two evangelines already there.

"I'll leave you to your colleagues then," Concierge said from the porch. "Don't hesitate to call with questions or concerns. I'm always available."

When they were alone, the new arrivals and the night shift introduced themselves to each other. Mary noticed that her sisters were not burdened with funny hats. One of them, Cyndee, said, "Well, come on and meet Myr Starke."

Situated in the raised portion of the room was a tall columnar tank of clear glass-ine. It was filled with a thick amber liquid that was shot through with thousands of tiny bubbles. A chrome bar was suspended in the liquid, and from the bar hung a human skull.

"Careful of the step," Cyndee said as she led the others to the tank. A metal band, like a halo, held the skull in a rigid grip with long screws sunk in bone. The skull had no skin, eyelids, or lips. Its bulging eyes lay lifeless in their sockets. Three of its—her—front teeth were missing, and tubes ran through the gaps they left. Many more tubes and wires entered the woman's skull through natural foramina and machine-drilled holes.

Mary and Renata stood in front of the skull while Cyndee introduced them. "Myr Starke, these are Mary Skarland and Renata Carter. They'll be relieving Ronnie and me in about an hour."

Cyndee looked expectantly at Mary who said, "Good morning, Myr Starke." She paused for a response, but the skull only stared straight ahead. She glanced at Cyndee and added, "Renata and I are here to keep you company when Cyndee and Ronnie have to leave."

None of the evangelines seemed to know what else to say, so they pulled two more chairs next to the tank and sat down.

"Did you get a tour?" Renata asked.

"There was no time," Ronnie replied. "We were rushed here in the middle of the night." Which was probably why they had no hats yet.

"It's a beautiful facility. So many jennys," Renata said.

Ah, thought Mary, and so it begins, the talking between the lines. Of course there were a lot of jennys here. This was a medical facility. But it was also a place where bored affs had idle time on their hands. If there was ever a place where companions were needed, this was it.

Mary said, "Just wait till we get Myr Starke up and around in a lifechair."

The others nodded in agreement. All it would take were two or three prominent clients here to get the ball rolling. And who could be more prominent than a Starke? But Myr Starke was a long way from riding in a lifechair. Nevertheless, it was frightfully clear to all of them that this assignment was an opportunity of tremendous importance, not only for them, but for their whole neglected sisterhood.

"Concierge loaned Cyndee and me a course in revivification science," Ronnie said. "You want, I'll copy you guys." Mary and Renata raised their open palms for it.

Cyndee said, "It's informative, but it would help to have some alphines." This meant that they'd already looked at the material, and that it was way over their heads. But Mary resolved to give it a try, or to find other, simpler lessons on the WAD.

Mary said, "We'll pass it along to our replacements on the swing shift," which meant that if they were going to be successful in raising the evangeline profile at the clinic, they needed to establish some channel of communication with the others. The four new colleagues looked at one another and smiled. If they dug in and played smart, they might make a solid beachhead on the shores of the Fagan Health Group for hundreds, if not thousands, of their sisters.

Just then, a jenny in a nurse's uniform bustled into the cottage, looked at the four of them, and said, "What's this, a convention?"

The evangelines rose at once. "No, Myr Jenny," Cyndee said. "Our shifts are supposed to overlap."

The nurse watched them a moment and said, "Sit, sit. No one rises for jennys around here." She went to the hernandez tank and rapped its side with her knuckles. "Hello in there. We've got a big day ahead of us, Myr Starke. My name is Hattie Beckeridge. I'm your head nurse." She moved her hand left and right in front of the skull, but the eyes didn't follow. "*Head* nurse, get it?"

Hattie went to the control unit at the side of the tank and paged through a blur of medical frames. As she did so, she said to the evangelines, "I don't see the point in hiring companions at this stage of our guest's recovery, especially so many of you. Be that as it may, since you're here, you might as well be doing something useful. As you can see, our guest hasn't awakened yet. That's not surprising, considering the trauma she's been through. Still, we've got her stabilized and she's in fair shape, all things considered. We've got about a billion little buggies inside her skull doing DXR. She should begin to stir by the end of the day. Now come over here and take a look at this."

When the evangelines joined her at the control unit she opened a larger-than-life model of the Starke woman's brain. Sheets of blue light rippled slowly over different parts of the brain's convoluted surface.

"This is a simple EEG reading of cortical activity," Hattie said. "Notice how slow it is, about two hertz. That's a typical delta wave frequency. Most people's brains slow down this much during normal sleep. But in a healthy brain, the wave passes smoothly over the entire surface, not patchy like this. This 'island' effect is caused by uneven tissue thawing which causes a cryogenically frozen brain to awaken in a piecemeal fashion. In other words, some parts of the brain are working while others aren't yet. That can be terrifying to a patient. Myr Starke may be having bizarre thoughts and memories in the form of a continuous nightmare that she can't seem to awaken from.

"It won't last long, Myr Starke," Hattie added to the skull. "You're thawing just fine.

"Anyway," she continued, "we suppress the side effects as much as possible, and we're quick to reestablish sensory pathways. That's where you can help."

"Tell us what to do," Cyndee said.

"We shall begin by always assuming that our guest here can see, hear, and smell everything in this room. So, talk to her, show her things, sing to her, do whatever you can think of to engage her interest. I don't think I need to tell evangelines how to be fascinating," she added with a grin.

"Well, I must go now," Hattie continued. "I'll leave the EEG display up for you.

There'll be a medtech in soon to work on her. Good-bye for now, Myr Starke. I'm leaving you in the hands of your 'leen companions."

THE QUARTER HOURS of pine sap, cranberry, popcorn, and ripe banana passed quickly, and the evangelines took turns standing directly in front of Starke's tank and telling her in detail who they were and where they were from, whether they were espoused and to whom, what their apartments looked like, and anything else that came to mind. By the time Cyndee and Ronnie went off shift, the four women felt they had always known each other. Ronnie and Renata, in fact, said they remembered each other from way back in evangeline school.

Then Mary and Renata were alone with their client. They struggled to come up with new conversational topics. Renata wasn't from Chicago, so Mary told her and the skull about last night's canopy ceremony, the slaughter of slugs, the crazy man in the Skytel, and especially the fireworks. As a rule, evangelines didn't sing, so they didn't try that, but Mary taught Renata and the skull how to shimmy. Fortunately, before they ran completely out of ideas, a medtech came in, pushing a supply cart.

He went directly to the controller, ignoring the two women, and shut off the EEG. He removed a couple of packages from his cart, opened them, and carried them to a stepladder built into the back of the tank. Inside the packages were spools. One spool was wound with silvery thread and the other with a narrow, whitish ribbon. He slotted these into an armature at the top of the tank, all without uttering a word. He wore a clinic uniform like Hattie's, but with a tan jacket. His name badge read, "Matt."

Matt wasn't any iterant type Mary knew, which meant he was of wild stock, a freeranger. He seemed unfriendly enough to be a chartist.

Matt returned to the control unit and began to dictate instructions. As he spoke, the armature with the spools lowered itself into the yellowish liquid of the tank, and two delicate waldo fingers picked up the ends of the threads and began to stitch them to the top of the skull.

"What's that?" Mary said when her curiosity became too great.

Matt gave her a brief, dismissive glance and returned to his task.

"That's nerve and vein tissue," said a pleasant voice. It was Concierge, at the door. The mentar entered and joined them at the tank. "And this is Matt Coburn, Medtech 3, and one of our finest people. Say hello to the ladies, Matt."

"I prefer to be called Coburn," the man said.

"Matt is attaching nerve and vein tissue from Myr Starke's own tissue bank," Concierge continued. "Tomorrow we'll start layering muscles, and then wrap the whole skull in skin gauze."

"Fascinating," said Mary. "Are you going to—ah—reassemble her entire body with replacement parts?"

"We might have gone that route, if her body were mostly intact," Concierge said, "but when you need a whole body, it's best to grow it from scratch. It's even faster, and you'll be sure that all the pieces fit together. If you look at the base of Myr Starke's skull, you'll see we've already started a new body."

All Mary saw was a wad of fine mesh netting.

"Come around to the back. You'll see better."

Mary and Renata followed Concierge to the back of the tank. Nestled in the netting and connected to the skull by a skein of threads was a tiny, curved creature. Mary squinted at it through the glassine tank and syrupy fluid. It was a headless human fetus. Or rather a fetus with a giant head. A tiny knot of red, visible through translucent skin, was furiously beating and driving a trickle of blood throughout the tiny body.

"Oh," Renata said, "it looks like a prawn."

"I suppose it does," Concierge said. "It'll be a while yet before the prawn will be able to support the head." Subvocally, the mentar added, *Unfortunately, she's not thriving as well as she should be.*

Mary was startled by the aside. When she looked at Concierge, he smiled sadly and returned to the front of the tank. "We'll have you up and out of here in no time, Myr Starke," he said brightly.

Fred had comp time coming to him, and he could have slept in if he wanted to. But russes were constitutionally unable to oversleep, and he awoke, as usual, at six. Mary was gone, and he lay in bed for a while letting his mind wander through his mine field of newly acquired troubles. Finally, he ordered coffee, and when he could smell it brewing, he threw off the covers and padded to the kitchen. He took his coffee to the living room and watched the view outside someone else's window for a while. But his troubles kept intruding, so he did what russes often did to take charge of their destiny—he made a list:

1. Mary/Cabinet
2. Rendezvous
3. Clone fatigue

Having itemized and prioritized his worries, Fred felt better. A good list, as every russ knew, was a mood elevator. A good list could cut through the fog of indecision and marshal the forces of reason and practicality. Fortified, Fred plunged in:

1. Mary/Cabinet—If only he had spoken up immediately when Cabinet appealed for his help under the lake. Then he wouldn't be here worrying whether or not Nick at Applied People or, worse, Nameless One at the Homeland Command had eavesdropped on their secret exchange. Merely by *not* informing his superiors of Cabinet's appeal, he was culpable of aiding and abetting it. And now that Cabinet was through probate, the imperious mentar had leverage over him. By involving Mary in its schemes, it only increased this leverage.

For crying out loud, Fred thought, evangelines were neither trained nor compensated for hazardous duty, and being anywhere near that Starke woman was hazardous in the extreme.

What to do? He could go to Marcus and report the whole thing, take his lumps, which might be as mild as a negative report in his file, or as severe as a reduction in rank. Whichever the case, it was better than sitting and stewing about it. However, though he could face the mentars, he could never face Mary. She would kill him for lousing up her companion duty. She would never forgive him, even if he acted out of concern for her safety.

2. Rendezvous—The 57th World Charter Rendezvous, which would attract fifty thousand plus chartists, was taking place *tomorrow*. He'd had everything nailed down for its security until the head of the organizing committee, the free-range boob Myr Pacfin, had thrown his tantrum about the pikes.

What to do? Easy, go down to the BB of R and talk to the proxy he cast to deal with the situation.

3. Clone fatigue—There was no such thing. It was all a pile of psychobabble hooey invented by free-rangers to steal work from iterants. It claimed that over time even identical clones diverged from each other, losing germline integrity and acquiring new, less reliable traits. And since the whole market appeal of iterant labor was based on the uniformity of their core personalities, trait instability would diminish their market value. Iterant temp agencies like Applied People and McPeople would falter, and Fred and about a billion other clones would be out of work.

It was hogwash, of course. There was no such thing as *identical* clones in the first place. Though a germline may start with the same genome, maternal factors, such as mitochondrial DNA and exogenic womb environments and the scattering techniques of induced allele shifting, guaranteed that they were all slightly different from each other. Closer than siblings but more different than natural monozygotic twins tended to be. Even their personalities varied a little, though their core traits were true to type: jennys were nurturing, lulus were hot, and russes were loyal to a fault and addicted to lists.

And another thing, if there were such a thing as clone fatigue, it would only affect new batches, not individuals already almost a hundred years old.

Still, it was a touchy subject for Fred, and he didn't know why. It seemed to him that he was behaving oddly lately. For all he knew, he was undergoing some normal life change that all russes experienced. Perhaps all russes, at some point or other, cherished a secret lust for hinks (Inspector Costa!) or questioned their own loyalty to their employer. And if they did, how would he ever know, since one of the cardinal core traits of russdom was the total inability to talk about their feelings, even to their brothers?

On the other hand, for all he knew, there was a secret volume hidden in the *Heads-Up Log*, one that no one talked about but which russes stumbled across in their time of need. A hidden brotherhood within the brotherhood. The fact that he, russlike to the bone, thought of this meant that other russes must also have thought of it. It only made sense.

What to do? Go to the BB of R and research the *Heads-Up Log*.

So Fred got up off the couch, put on some clothes, and dragged his bruised tired self to North Wabash.

FRED ARRIVED JUST as a wave of russes was leaving the headquarters for their split shifts. To Fred's surprise, he was a celebrity. Word had leaked about his scuffle with the warbeitor last night. Because of the confidentiality rules, he was unable to set the record straight that he wasn't the hero of the hour—but that the TUGs' illegal particle weapon was. All he could do was accept the accolades of his brothers with typical russ humility. (Humility—Fred decided to keep a running list of russ traits that he shared or lacked.)

Fred clocked into a scape booth and asked Marcus to open his Rondy space.

"Certainly, Myr Londenstane," the mentar said, "but there's nothing there that can't wait a few hours. Why don't you take the morning off. You had a very stressful day yesterday."

"Thank you for your concern, Marcus," he said, "but I'd rather do it now." (Obsessive attention to detail.)

"As you wish. But allow me to schedule you an autopsyche session when you're done. After what you've been through, you may find it helpful."

"Thank you, but that won't be necessary." (Aversion to so-called mental hygiene.)

Marcus opened Fred's Rendezvous workspace and left him to his chores. There were scores of details to resolve, but as Marcus had said, nothing urgent. Fred called up the proxy he had cast when he bailed from the Rondy meeting. The log said it had been in storage since the meeting adjourned.

A mirror image of Fred's head and shoulders and a gloved right hand appeared before him. "About time you showed up," it said. Fred's proxy wore an expression of patient annoyance, which surprised and embarrassed him. Proxies tended to be locked in to one's emotional state at the moment of casting. Had Fred's annoyance with the organizing committee been so apparent? (Emotional transparency—*not* a russ trait.) If so, blame it on the utter stupidity of the committee chair, Myr Pacfin. (Inability to suffer fools.)

"So," the proxy said, "how'd it go? Inspector Costa and the mentar hunt."

"Fine," Fred said.

"Fine? That's it? That's all I get? Fred, it's me—*Fred*," the proxy said. "I'm your proxy. The confidentiality ban doesn't apply to us, remember? You're going to delete me when you wrap things up."

Fred sighed. "Sorry. Let's see, we captured the last Cabinet backup in an Opticom hub and then cornered the Cabinet prime next to a city waterworks crib under the lake. Reilly Dell was riding shotgun, by the way, and we were glommed by a NASTIE and had to be dry-cleaned."

"Whoa!" the proxy said. "Back up and slow down."

But Fred had no intention of backing up or slowing down. "Veronica Tug tells me you hired five hundred TUGs to patrol Rondy."

"You spoke to her again?"

"Yeah, she saved my bacon last night."

"Say again?"

Fred rubbed his face. "Let's just say," he said, "that the TUGs were in the right place at the right time to do me a big favor."

"Com'on, Fred. You can't leave me just hanging like that."

But he had to; otherwise he'd find himself giving a blow-by-blow of the raid on the mysterious house in Decatur, its warbeitor sentry, the deadly plasma rings, and all the rest. Then the proxy would ask about the canopy ceremony and Mary, and he'd have to tell it about her companion gig and Cabinet. He had to draw a line.

"About this TUG contingent you hired," he said.

"All right, all right," the proxy said. "I didn't hire them, but I agreed to allow five hundred of them to wear armbands and to patrol the convention floor in exchange for keeping our forty pikes *off* the floor."

"What? I'm supposed to tell our pikes to sit on their hands?"

"Exactly. The pikes won't be allowed to show their weasely little faces. The TUGs will be under our command and will limit their actions to verbal persuasion."

That actually wasn't such a bad idea. The chartists at these affairs rarely got rowdy and would much rather be policed by fellow chartists anyway, and the TUGs could probably keep the peace with their looks alone. "I suppose MC and Nick are good with this arrangement?"

"Yeah, the mentars are all on board."

Once nudged in the right direction, Proxy Fred continued his termination debriefing with typical russ efficiency. (Efficiency.) When it was finished, it sighed and said, "That's it."

"Nothing else?"

"There is one more thing I thought I'd tell you. I don't know how much weight to put on it since I'm just a—you know—artificial construct of you, but I had a feeling about this Veronica Tug person."

"What kind of a feeling?" Fred said.

"A hunch."

"And?"

"I felt I could trust her. Which was why her helping you is so interesting."

"I see. Thanks for telling me. And thank you for your service."

"It was nothing."

Fred and his proxy watched each other for a few moments in silence, and then the proxy said, "Will you just do it already?"

"Uh, sorry," Fred said. "Marcus, delete proxy."

The Fred proxy disappeared. Fred closed the Rondy space and logged into the Longyear Center to inquire about Inspector Costa's status. She was still in critical condition.

Fred left the booth and went downstairs to the canteen for coffee and donuts. The place was nearly deserted, with so many russes mustered out on extra security details. And any russes not involved in trying to keep the affs from killing each other were no doubt working as bloomjumpers, now that Chicago had no canopy to protect it. (Brave.)

BACK IN THE scape booth, now that his work was finished, Fred asked Marcus for a datapin containing the complete BB of R *Heads-Up Log.* It was an unusual request—he usually let Marcus navigate the log for him. Marcus produced the pin, no questions asked, and Fred turned on the booth's isolation field, excluding Marcus and any other snoops. The brotherhood's booths provided pretty good privacy, not as tight as their null room, but much more convenient.

Fred pressed the pin into the reader, and a directory appeared on the workbench before him.

Fred knew more or less what was in the *HUL.* The log was a compendium of russ records and thoughts going back a hundred years to Thomas A. himself. Most of it was related to work issues, the how-tos and wherefores of security work. There was a Brag File describing especially harrowing missions, with confidential details excised. Marcus had already entered yesterday's scuffle with the warbeitor, though without naming names. There was also a Wall of Honor for russes killed in the line of duty. And one of the most popular features on the *HUL* was the List of Lists. Altogether, there were over seven hundred thousand entries in the *HUL,* which, when Fred thought about it, didn't amount to much considering that they represented about a half-billion russ/years of experience.

Proceeding on his theory that there was a secret log not listed in the directory, Fred browsed the *HUL* from front to back, looking for anything that might give him a glimpse into the mysterious russ heart. He supposed he could just ask Marcus if anything like that was recorded, but he assumed that if it was, it would be kept secret from Marcus as well. After three hours he gave up. Except for certain lists that scanned like poetry, his brothers seemed about as expressive as trees.

Fine, he would work on that. Fred opened a new volume in the *HUL* and entitled it the *Book of Russ.* He took a deep breath and began:

"To my brothers cloned: Contrary to all evidence, we, the sibs of Thomas A. Russ, *do* enjoy a rich inner life. Why we are so reluctant to share it with others, or even among ourselves, is anybody's guess. Today I start what I hope will become a new tradition among us—the habit of brotherly openness."

Fred paused and read what he'd dictated. Overall, it was good; it expressed what he wanted. But it sounded too stilted. Although russes were big on continuing education, they didn't wear their erudition on their sleeve. He thought about it for a while, blanked the text, and began anew. This time he tried to speak as he would to Reilly. He did, however, keep the phrase "To my brothers cloned," which he liked.

"To my brothers cloned: I'm fed up with the way we keep everything bottled inside us. It's not healthy. So, I'm going to speak my mind here and see if any of you will do the same. I propose the *Book of Russ* to be a place where russes can speak openly to each other."

Fred paused and read this. It might err in the opposite direction, but it was better. So he continued in the same vein.

"Lately there's been a lot of talk about the so-called clone fatigue. Of course, there's no such thing. It's an urban myth. It's an attempt by non-iterants to belittle us. But if it did exist, and if I caught it, how would I know?

"Let me put this another way. We all know that we, the brothers of Thomas A., prefer to wear heavy brown shoes. That's so typical of us that it's a timeworn cliché. How a preference for shoe color could be coded into our genes, I don't have a clue. Whatever the mechanism, what would happen if tomorrow I woke up and decided, just for the hell of it, to wear a pair of black shoes. I suspect that everyone I ran into would comment on it. It would cause such a sensation that I probably wouldn't wear them in public again. But what if the truth of the matter is that while we're young, we prefer brown shoes but that russes of a certain age develop an appreciation for shoes of different colors? Are you following me? If we were all too reluctant to wear black shoes in public because of the reaction we would get from others, or even to discuss our shoe color preferences among ourselves, eventually we'd all be walking around secretly dissatisfied with our shoes.

"You want my opinion, there's something unnatural about this state of affairs. I think we've been sold a bill of goods. We're so obsessed with trying to stay true to our germline that we repress anything we think might set us apart. Believe me, brothers, that way lies madness.

"Anyway, that's how *I* feel about it, and if I feel that way, I'm pretty sure there's at least a half *million* of you out there who feel the same way.

"And so, this is what I'm going to do. I'm going to dedicate this volume, this *Book of Russ*, to the free expression of russness, and I encourage all of you, my brothers, to add your bit. Tell us all what makes us tick.

"To get the ball rolling, I'll go first."

Fred paused to think of the most provocative thing about himself that he could reveal in order to loosen the guarded russ tongue. Eventually, he wanted to get into the whole issue of mission loyalty, but that was probably too explosive a topic to start off with. Better go with something safer and saltier.

"All right," he continued. "Here goes. I want to sleep with a hink. Got that? I'd like to screw a woman whose body is unlike any other woman's body in the world. Don't get me wrong; I love our iterant women. They're the best. I'm not putting down our 'leens or jennys or any of the other types, not in the least. But once in a while, I wonder, I really wonder what a free-ranger might be like in the sack.

"There you have it. And please don't tell me that I'm the only russ in the world who's ever lusted after hinks.

"Your turn. Thanks for listening."

Fred closed the entry and reread it. He was appalled. His first impulse was to delete the *Book of Russ* altogether, but he held back. If this was going to work, someone had to take the first step. Besides, he was *positive* he was right. How could he be wrong? So he did not delete his entry or even censor it. He was tempted to post it anonymously, but that would defeat the whole purpose, so he appended his sig, turned off the booth's isolation field, and posted the inaugural entry of the *Book of Russ*. A moment later he wondered what in God's name he had done.

Yesterday Bogdan had been late for work; today he had time to dawdle. Strolling to the Library train station from Howe Street, he was on the lookout for any sign of the destruction of Chicago by NASTIES, now that the canopy was down. The sidewalk under his feet felt odd. Maybe it was his imagination, but it felt spongy, so he crossed to the other side of the street. Another thing he noticed was that his skin was itchy. He imagined tiny terrorist engines, too small to see, tunneling through his epidermis to commandeer his cellular machinery and turn him into a puddle of protoplasm. So he tried not to scratch.

Something he didn't see were homcom slugs on patrol. They were usually out in force, but this morning they were mysteriously absent.

The train ride to Elmhurst was uneventful. Unlike yesterday he took his time walking from MacArthur Station to the Bachner Building, where E-Pluribus was camping out for a second day. He had a chance to take in the local scene, which was abuzz with early morning commuters.

Elmhurst boasted dozens of shopping arcades, one stacked atop another, all the way to Munilevel 85. They bustled with youngish, extravagantly dressed and coiffed free-rangers. There were so many cars flying overhead they stirred up a breeze. No wonder E-Pluribus was upreffing here.

Ahead of him a crowd of people blocked the sidewalk and spilled into the street. Bogdan wormed his way to the front of the crowd. There, in the middle of the street, was a bloom.

It was the first one Bogdan had ever seen in realbody, and it was frighteningly beautiful. Dome-shaped, it expanded in little surges. Feathery amber crystal tendrils swelled up from a central mound and froze into place. They built up on top of each other until the whole structure collapsed on itself in a shattering, tinkling heap. Only to swell again. And it was hot, as hot as a bonfire. Bogdan and the spectators moved backward each time it grew. The people hooted and joked as they watched, as though it was no big deal. Someone said there were hundreds of such blooms all over town. Most of them were like this one, a simple one- or two-stage nanobot that was programmed to eat one or two common substances—in this case the glassine pile that was used to pave roadways, arcades, and rooftops. Where the bloom reached the curb, it stopped: the curb was made of concrete, which wasn't part of the nanobot's diet. But the bloom was consuming the street in both directions and would spread until it reached the intersections with their concrete firebreaks.

Soon, bloomjumpers arrived overhead in tanker cars. They projected a police cordon around the bloom and ordered everyone back. When the spectators were clear, the tankers sprayed the bloom with a foam that caused the churning mound to sputter to a halt. For a giddy moment its intricate arabesque of crystal tendrils held its shape. Then the whole thing crashed into a pile of yellow sand.

AT THE BACHNER Building, Bogdan wasn't allowed to go right up. The E-Pluribus floors were still being converted over from their overnight tenant, a Cathouse Casino. Among the Cathouse employees leaving the building were girls with tails poking out through the rear of their skirts. Bogdan approved of tails on girls. He liked how the girls tied bells to them or braided them with ribbons, or did other interesting things to draw attention to them. What drew his special attention were the tail holes in their clothes that usually exposed a little sliver of bare ass.

Bogdan was still scratching himself, but he noticed that everyone else was scratching too, so it was probably normal.

When he was finally permitted to go up, the Annette Beijing hollyholo was waiting to speak to him. "G'morning, Boggo," she said, flashing him her world-famous smile. "My, aren't you looking handsome this morning."

"Thanks," he said, beaming with pleasure. She was always complimenting him like that, and though it was probably only part of her programming, it still thrilled the hell out of him. "Looking good yourself, Nettie," he said, "which, in your case, is an understatement."

"Thanks. Well, I have visitors to greet," she said. "You have yourself a bodacious day. Oh, and don't forget about your meeting with HR tomorrow." She turned and sashayed away. She was so beautiful, from the rear as well as the front. Bogdan mentally pinned a tail on her.

BOGDAN'S OWN REAR was the first in line for the fitting booths. Once the visceral response probe had been inserted, linking his body's every sensation to the E-Pluribus superluminary computer, he hitched up his jumpsuit and went to his first upreffing assignment. He fervently hoped it would be another visit to the Oship with that weird little Birthplace guy, Meewee. But his first assignment took place in an auditorium full of daily hires, with whom he was subjected to an hour of probable news: mud slides in Bogota, a horrific soccer stadium stampede in Sudan, world leaders being knocked off by their own bodyguards, and more of the same. His next assignment was equally dreary, a consensus vid about an asteroid hitting the Earth and how, years before it hit, scientists used a rust-producing bacteria to gobble up oxygen out of the atmosphere, reducing global oxygen levels to fifteen percent, a concentration high enough for life but too low for open flames, effectively making the planet fireproof.

Boring.

Finally, his last assignment before lunch took him to a solo booth where, sure enough, the lights dimmed and the emitters hummed, and Bogdan found himself back on the Oship ESV *Garden Charter*. He was in an urban hab drum this time, sitting at a long table on a raised dais in front of a stadium crowd of tens of thousands. Beyond them he could see the spires and roofs of a great city stretching all the way to the bulkhead of the drum. At his table sat dozens of young men and women, all wearing the crisp uniforms of the jump pilot corps. Bogdan looked at his sleeve and saw that he, too, was a jump pilot. When he looked to his left, he discovered that he was seated right next to—Annette Beijing! A teenaged Annette who was also dressed as a pilot. She smiled at him.

There was a lectern in front of the table, and a man was speaking to the vast audience. It was the little Meewee guy in his green and red overalls. "During the next few months of the General Awakening," he was saying, "more of our citizens will leave the cryovaults and be quickened than at any other time during our thousand-year voyage—well over two hundred thousand, or eighty percent of our great ship's population. All sixty-four hab drums are being pressurized and activated to accommodate them. Now that we have reached our new home system, we must prepare for planetfall. The next twelve months will be a time of joyous activity as we make ready to take possession of our new planet."

Amid sustained applause, Meewee pointed at the sky and said, "I give you Planet Lisa!" The crowd gasped. Bogdan looked straight up and was astounded by the sight. The hull of the hab drum was becoming transparent, a window to space. And there, directly overhead, a shiny blue-green planet was coming into view. It was endowed with brilliant oceans under whorls of white clouds. There were three major land masses visible, and ice-capped polar regions. Except for the unfamiliar shapes of the continents, it could have been Earth, old pre-industrial Earth.

"Stunning, isn't it?" the teen-aged Annette said to him. "Our new home."

"Planet Lisa," Bogdan whispered.

"Have you picked out your thousand acres yet?"

"Um, no. Have you?"

"Almost. I've split mine up into three or four parcels. Five hundred acres of coastline on Kalina Island there." She raised a slender arm and pointed to the edge of the world. "Look quick," she said, "night is falling. And over there, below the Bay of Renewal, there's a city called Capa. I have a hundred acres near there. As for the rest, I don't know. Someplace in the mountains? In the agribelt? I just don't know. What about you?" She searched his face with her green eyes and continued. "And to think, I've received all this: the millennial voyage, a thousand acres on a pristine planet, an exciting career, unlimited rejuvenation—a life!—all in exchange for one lousy acre on a dying planet."

"Tell me about it," Bogdan said. "My acre came from a superfund site polluted with toxic industrial waste."

The crowd cheered, and Bogdan and Annette looked up again at Planet Lisa. On the western coast of a dark continent, the lights of a metropolis were coming on.

"That's New Seattle," Annette said. "The builder mechs are testing its energy grid."

Just yesterday (though it was six hundred years ago in ship time) Captain Suzette had explained to him how robotic advance ships would reach their destination several centuries before the Oship to construct the planet's infrastructure.

"And now the event you've all been waiting for," the little man at the lectern said. The vast audience thrummed with anticipation. "In three months, the brave jump pilots seated behind me will begin to ferry colonists down to the surface. Naturally, everyone wants to be on the historic first landing. Who those lucky people will be depends upon the launch order of the jumpships—which we will now determine."

The crowd went wild as a young man pushed a cart across the dais with what looked like a cage hopper filled with little balls. Audience members rose from their seats and screamed as Meewee rotated the hopper with a hand crank. A group of girls near the front, all of them stunningly gorgeous, chanted, "Bog-dan, Bog-dan, Bog-dan."

Annette smirked. "I envy the pilot who gets the first launch. She, or he, will have all the lovers she can handle."

The first ball dropped out and rolled to the end of the slot. Meewee picked it up and turned it in his hand. "The first ship to Lisa will be piloted by—"

Bogdan, who had been awake and active nonstop for twenty-nine hours, closed his eyes. The eight-hour Alert! tablet that he had taken ran out all at once, and he fell asleep where he sat. A few minutes later, his chair nudged him awake, but it was too late; the Oship scenario had ended. He swallowed another Alert! and trudged off to lunch.

Meewee slept most of the morning. The lump under his skin, his new brain-lette, didn't bother him when he scratched it. In midafternoon he left his executive suite at Starke Enterprises headquarters for the last time and made the short trip to Starke Manse. An arbeitor with Wee Hunk perched atop it was waiting for him in the family's private Slipstream station.

"Top o'the afternoon to you, Bishop," the tiny mentar said, greeting him like an old friend. "I trust your leave-taking from Cabinet territory was civil."

"Civil enough, though Cabinet saw fit to send a security team to escort me to the tube. As though I intended to steal the linen or something."

"And did you?"

"Did I what?"

"Steal the linen."

Meewee took the question for a tasteless joke and did not answer. The arbeitor grabbed up his luggage, and he followed it to the lifts. It was only when they were riding up to the ground floor that he realized that he and Wee Hunk had been conducting two conversations at once. The banter about Cabinet was only the surface one. Beneath it was a more serious one—Wee Hunk had just updated him about Ellen's condition—still critical—and asked if he'd had any more direct encounters with Cabinet.

Moreover, Meewee had left the question dangling. So he said, "Sheets, towels, robes—I took as much as I could carry."

Wee Hunk guffawed and said, "I've set aside a room for you overlooking the fields. Would you like to go there now?"

Under the surface, this was an identity challenge. Meewee replied, "Yes, please. I would like to get settled in." Then in turn, he challenged the mentar's own integrity, "Do you happen to have an extruder on the premises? I need to make some new apparel."

Wee Hunk responded positively to both layers of inquiry, and as he led Meewee through the warren of rooms, he secretly briefed him on events of the last dozen hours: Ellen's head had been installed in a hernandez tank in a cottage at the clinic, evangeline hires were with her now with continuity counters embedded in their hats, no progress had been made in tracking down Eleanor's assassins or Ellen's abductors, and efforts to find an independent revivification specialist had thus far been fruitless.

The Starke Manse, for all its impressive size, managed to retain a homey ambiance. The arbeitor led Meewee to a suite of rooms that was easily double the size of his executive quarters. More room than Meewee knew how to occupy.

"I'm pleased to see that the metalanguage has kicked in," Wee Hunk said in plain English. "And with no lasting harm done to your health. Your sudden command of Starkese is impressive, but there is no need to use it or to glot while we are here. The manse is double canopied and shielded against all forms of espionage. It's more secure here than in many null rooms."

Wee Hunk jumped off the arbeitor and assumed a full-sized appearance. He opened a small scape showing the interior of Ellen's clinic cottage, with four of the eight evangelines present. Two of them were preparing to leave, and the scape split into two, one remaining inside the cottage, and the other following the departing companions down a path to South Gate.

"You said she's not doing well?" Meewee said, zooming in on the skull inside the hernandez tank.

"No, not well at all. Critical neural functions have not resumed. Concierge says the doctors have no explanation but are guardedly optimistic."

"Damn, I wish we had our own doctor."

"I'm still looking for one," the mentar said, "but all of the thousands of qualified revivificationists practicing in the UD are either employed by or on retainer to the Fagan Health Group, and thus are unacceptable. Fagan has a solid lock on the specialty in the West. Perhaps one of your old Birthplace contacts outside the UD would be useful."

"I'll look into it, but there's not much call for revivification in famine countries."

In the scape, a medtech entered the cottage and went to the tank. He checked its controller, then climbed a ladder and dipped a small vial into the tank for a sample of the amber amnio fluid. After marking the vial, he dropped it into a pocket and proceeded with other monitoring tasks. Meanwhile, in the other scape, the two off-shift evangelines reached the South Gate gatehouse and were processed through. On the other side of the gatehouse a Starke limo waited for them.

"I'll debrief them as soon as the car leaves the grounds," Wee Hunk said.

"You mentioned something about continuity counters. What are those?"

"Something like time code generators. The Roosevelt Clinic, as we saw in the nustscape last night, is a self-enclosed environment. It, like this house, is double canopied and shielded. All transmissions to and from the clinic must pass through a gatekeeper, which happens to be Concierge. While it's true that I've been watching Ellen continuously, how can I trust the images and data that Concierge is feeding me? When the evangelines leave the mentar's domain, I'll be able to compare the time log in their hats to my own records. Any tampering whatsoever with my surveillance will show up."

"Clever."

The evangelines boarded the limo, which drove up the drive to the parking lot and jumped into the air. Once outside clinic space, a miniature Wee Hunk appeared on the seat opposite them and said, "Good afternoon, myren. How did your first day go?"

Mary said, "Good afternoon, Myr Hunk. It went well, I think. Concierge is very nice." Then she added, "Will she ever recover?"

"Ah, Myr Skarland, that's a difficult question. The doctors are troubled by Ellen's lack of improvement but aren't ready to panic yet. According to their experience with such cases, there is a five-day window in which a cryogenically frozen brain may regain consciousness, with the rate of recovery proportional to the cube of the inverse of days since thawing."

Mary glanced at Renata who shrugged, and Mary said, "Excuse me, Myr Hunk, but I'm not good at math."

Back at the manse, Wee Hunk said to Meewee, "Unfortunately, without our own specialist, there is no way we can test the findings of these clinic doctors."

"Surely there are autodocs equipped to analyze such cases," Meewee said. "Why don't you bring out a sample of that hernandez tank fluid? That ought to tell us something."

"Good idea," Wee Hunk said. "I'll see what I can do." In the limo, he said, "Sorry, Myr Skarland, what it means is that if Ellen doesn't wake up tomorrow, she'll have only one chance in eight of waking up on Thursday. If she doesn't awaken on Thursday, she'll have one chance in twenty-seven on Friday, one chance in 256 on Saturday, and one in 625 on Sunday. You see how quickly her prospects dim. By then, even if she does awaken, she would most likely suffer irreparable psychosis."

In the manse bedroom, the arbeitor finished unpacking Meewee's luggage and putting his things away. It came around the bed to where Meewee was sitting and held out a trophy in its gripper arm. It was the 2082 Mandela Humanitarian Award that Meewee had won for his Birthplace work.

"Put it there for now," Meewee said and pointed at the night table. The arbeitor placed the trophy on the table and then, without warning, extended its arm and tried to grab Meewee by the throat. Meewee reared back reflexively and blocked it with his hands. The arbeitor caught one of his arms and squeezed it in a crushing grip. Meewee screamed and tried to break free. "Help! Help!" he cried.

"I've called for security," Wee Hunk replied.

"Make it stop!"

"I can't. Someone else is controlling it."

The arbeitor dragged Meewee off the bed by the arm and extended its other gripper, trying to catch his throat, but Meewee squirmed out of reach.

"Listen to me, Bishop," Wee Hunk said calmly. "Tell Arrow to stop it."

"Arrow, stop this thing!" Meewee shouted, but the arbeitor continued its assault. It twisted Meewee's arm, forcing him into gripper range.

"Not in English," Wee Hunk said. "Use Starkese."

Meanwhile, in the limo scape, Wee Hunk continued its explanation to the evangelines. "That's why the doctors will employ more aggressive methods of rousing her in the coming days, including microsurgical tissue replacement."

"Arrow!" Meewee cried when the gripper found his throat and began to squeeze. "Arrow!" he choked, fumbling for the proper syntax, "make me a pot of tea!"

Immediately something inside the arbeitor's casing sizzled, and the machine went slack. Meewee pulled its gripper from his throat and rolled away, gulping air.

"Thank goodness," Wee Hunk said. "Are you all right?" In the limo, he continued. "Tonight they will try to induce dreams and reestablish a ninety-minute sleep cycle by chemical means. Tomorrow they wire her directly to a simulacrum jacket."

Meewee lay wheezing on the floor while his heart bounced around in his chest. Someone was banging on the bedroom door, unable to get in. Manse security?

"So much for our double canopy and shielding," Wee Hunk said.

On the other side of the room, the closet opened, and two small cleaning scuppers emerged and charged across the carpet directly at Meewee's head.

On the way home after work, Bogdan witnessed two more blooms. One was in a tube station where a bead car inflated like a balloon (with a hapless passenger trapped inside), and the other was way up the side of a gigatower where a whole section of outer wall was blinking on and off like a lightning bug. None of this would happen on Planet Lisa, he was sure.

Arriving home at the Kodiak building, Bogdan didn't even give the wayward front door a chance to deny him entry; he ducked in through the NanoJiffy instead.

On the way past the third-floor administrative offices, he was stopped by Kale who asked him to step in for a minute. Kale, April, and Kitty were in the outer office with an elderly couple, who stood up to greet him. The visitors wore black overalls with little pink-orange-green lapel pins, chartist colors that Bogdan didn't recognize. They held out thin arms and crooked fingers to shake his hand. They were so old that Bogdan couldn't be sure if they were male or female. Whatever charter this was, they had way serious body issues.

"Bogdan," Kale said, "say hello to the Myren Beadlemyren."

Bogdan's jaw dropped. Was this the charter that owned the superfund micromines in Wyoming? The Kodiaks' potential saviors?

"The Beadlemyren are in town for tomorrow's Rendezvous," Kale went on, "and were kind enough to drop by for dinner." Kale, and April too, were wearing their best clothes, trimmed in Kodiak's brown-yellow-white. Kale seemed even more ill at ease than usual, and April was atypically silent. Only Kitty, wearing a Japanese schoolgirl uniform, complete with knee-high white stockings, seemed in her element.

"Hello, young man," one of the Beadlemyren said. "Your 'meets have been bragging about your important upreffing engineering."

"Yes, indeed," Kitty put in. She stepped next to Bogdan and encircled him in her arms. "Boggy is a demographics specialist. Practically in management."

The two old codgers leaned in to inspect him with rheumy eyes. Their breath had a hint of Samson's odor. Their arms were streaked in red where they had been scratching themselves.

"That's right," Bogdan said, "and tomorrow they're going to bestow some award on me."

"We're pretty proud of him," Kale said. "Go on up now and change, Boggy, dear. We'll do a quick Soup Pot Ceremony, and then the Beadlemyren will join us for dinner."

THE SOUP POT Ceremony was indeed quick that evening. Only house members who actually had hard currency to donate were invited up. This included Bogdan who contributed his day's payfer without, for once, drawing the whole procedure out.

When the abbreviated ceremony was finished, Houseer Kale said, "We have two very important guests waiting to join us. They're hungry after their journey, so let's not make them wait too long."

The housemeets had been forewarned to dress up, and they all wore freshly extruded togs. Most of them were preparing for Rondy and so had their hair newly trimmed and their hoary old skin planed smooth.

"I don't think I need to remind you," Kale continued, "how important it is that we broaden our membership base. When Sam—well, when Sam leaves us, we'll be down to sixteen members. Any fewer and we'll slip below the statutory minimum for charter status. That could jeopardize our special community privileges, including our discounted insurance rates, our fee waivers, tax credits, and a host of other subsidies. April could lose the NanoJiffy, and I don't need to spell out what that could mean.

"In order to prevent such a disaster," Kale went on, "the Steering Committee has been in confidential discussion with our guests' charter for some months."

There were murmurs of surprise and concern from the housemeets, and Kale raised his hands and continued. "Now, now, let me finish. We were going to wait until things firmed up a little before bringing this before the house, but tonight's unexpected visit has forced us to at least give you the basics of the plan."

The houseer, with the help of April and Gerald, proceeded to quickly sketch out the opportunity afforded by the Beadlemyren and their Rosewood Acres micromine. A babble of questions followed: Does that mean we'll have to leave Chicago? Does that mean we'll no longer be Kodiaks?

"We'll have plenty of time later for discussion. We're in no way committed to this plan, which is only in its exploratory stages, and frankly, the Beadlemyren have many more suitors than us, including, I am sorry to say, our Tobbler neighbors. I just wanted to give you a heads-up and ask you to be on your best behavior. And a critical word of warning—do *not* mention anything about the possibility of material pirates eating our building or *especially* about Hubert's arrest last night. If this is going to work, we'll need all of our assets. Let's not shoot ourselves in the foot, people. Understood? Good. Megan, call them in."

"Wait up," April said. "Kale, aren't we forgetting someone?"

The housemeets groaned, and Kale said, "Can't that keep till later? We're making our important guests wait."

"No, it can't, and I'll be brief. I know how much it means to everyone to go to Rondy tomorrow, but the fact of the matter is that someone will have to stay home to be with Samson."

A dead silence filled Green Hall. The housemeets glanced furtively among themselves to discover who might least miss attending Rendezvous. Barry and Francis, who were on the roof keeping vigil with Samson, let it be known through the houseputer that they weren't volunteering to stay behind, in case anyone had that impression. They went on to boldly suggest that Kitty should be the one to stay with him.

All eyes went to Kitty. It made perfect sense. She was Samson's favorite, after all. Kitty, however, had other ideas. She crossed her arms and screwed up her face in a perfect imitation of juvenile willfulness. No one, least of all April, imagined they could leave her behind.

In the end, April volunteered herself, as everyone knew she would. She would forgo the Rendezvous so that Samson's last breath might be shared with a loved one.

"But that's just not fair," Rusty complained. "April has done more work than anybody here to prepare us for Rondy. She's the one who ordered our special clothes, designed our booth, rented the omnibus, and arranged get-togethers with the other houses. If anyone deserves to go, it's April." When no one volunteered to take her place, Rusty said, "Okay, I'll stay. April, you go to Rondy. I'm staying with Sam."

This clearly would not do. Rusty had been preparing to attend Rondy for months. He'd grown new hair. He'd forced himself to overeat at every meal in order to put on a little weight. He was looking a good ten years younger. And besides, he was the one 'meet most likely to succeed in attracting a spouse at the Rendezvous and thus increase the house's membership by one. He already had three different ladies from three different charters lined up to meet him.

"Thank you, Rusty," April said. "I appreciate your offer. I really do. But I won't hear of it. End of discussion."

And so it was decided. Megan escorted the two visiting Beadlemyren to their places of honor at the head table, with Kitty seated between them. And though the meal consisted of dishes rarely seen at the Kodiak board—troutcorn chowder and veggie starters, an entree of beeflike Stroganoff, and for dessert, chocolate pie with ice cream and coffeesh, the mood in Green Hall was glum. Kale finally explained things to their guests, lest the Beadlemyren write them off as a sullen lot.

"One of our dear housemeets is gravely ill," he said, "and we're all attending to him in our thoughts."

But what Bogdan was attending to in his thoughts was the houseer's repeated use of the word "asset" to describe Hubert. Last night, when Kale had allowed himself to be arrested rather than give up Hubert, Bogdan had been impressed by the houseer's newfound devotion to Samson's mentar. Now he wasn't so sure. Asset? Hubert had never been much of an asset to the house before; how would Samson's passing change that?

He turned to Rusty and said, "What *is* old what's-its-name's status?"

Rusty glanced at the head table where their two guests were seemingly enthralled by one of Kitty's anecdotes. "He's been disappeared," Rusty said.

"What? Disappeared?"

"Yeah," said Louis from across the table. "Hacking into the you-know-what in the sky is a serious crime against national security. The kind that makes you disappear."

"There is one upside to disappearing, though," Rusty said. "Nobody, not even the neighbors, can find out about the arrest. So at least that won't spango whatever deal Kale is cooking up with the Wyoming folks."

"Unless of course the neighbors saw them hauling it away," Louis added.

"I was here," Megan said. "The blacksuits stuck him in an evidence box before removing him. Nobody saw nothing, except us."

During dessert, at precisely 7:12 PM, Bogdan's second Alert! ran out. He yawned like a cave, then leaned over his plate and fell asleep. Hands all around shook him awake. April was calling from the head table. "Send him to bed. Bogdan, go up to bed. Someone go with him."

Bogdan struggled to his feet and wrapped one last wedge of chocolate pie in a napkin. Rusty got up too, but Bogdan waved him to stay put.

"All right," Rusty said, "but just remember you're bunking on seven now in my room."

"Yeah, yeah." As Bogdan left Green Hall, Kale was explaining to their guests how the boy worked too hard. Never knew when to quit. The two gray emissaries murmured approvingly.

Bogdan trudged up the steps, more asleep than awake, when, on the fifth-floor landing, he was startled by an incoming, fullscape phone call right there in the stairwell. An official-looking sig appeared in the air, lighting up the whole landing. It occurred to Bogdan to wonder how this was possible—there were no cam/emitters in the stairwell—but his question drifted away when the sig morphed into a tall, handsome young officer in a vaguely familiar uniform.

"Who are you?" Bogdan said.

The man only smiled and pointed to a dataframe that opened beside him and displayed an invitation under the seal of the USNA Astronaut Corps:

Myr Bogdan ("Boggo") Kodiak
by order of the President
you are invited to explore
the admission opportunities to the
CADET CORPS
of the
FUTURE OSHIP PILOTS LEAGUE.
Please attend our introductory seminar
as well as the 2134
Garden Earth Project Banquet.
—Dress uniform optional—

In disbelief, Bogdan read it again and said, "You mean me? I don't understand. You want me?"

The officer only grinned and saluted as he and the scape dissolved.

"I'll be there!" Bogdan shouted at the fading light. He saluted and shouted, "I accept!"

Rude laughter broke out. When Bogdan's eyes readjusted to the gloom, he saw two boys sitting on a step, doubled over with glee. They mock saluted each other and cried, "I accept. I accept." Troy Tobbler and Slugboy.

Without uttering a word, Bogdan turned around and went downstairs. He marched past Green Hall, where the assembled 'meets and guests were singing old charter songs, down to the foyer on the ground floor, where he pulled the bamboo walking stick from its charger. He slashed the air with it in a couple of trial swings. He jabbed its trodes against the metal umbrella stand and was thrown backward by the ferocity of its snapping blue sparks. That woke him up for a minute, but by the time he'd reclimbed a couple flights of steps, he was asleep on his feet and almost forgot what he was doing. So he fished in his pocket and found the package of Alert! Bogdan knew all about the dangers of SSP—Sleep Starvation Psychosis—but just not at that moment, and he swallowed a third eight-hour tablet. Moments later he charged up the stairs, holding the walking stick like Excalibur itself, his fuzzy-headedness replaced by crystalline murderous intent.

The boys were still waiting for him on the fifth-floor steps, and they resumed their taunts when he reappeared.

"Get out of my house!" he demanded, waving the stick at them. But they only mocked him more, so he moved in and jabbed Troy with the stick.

There was no discharge, only more laughter as the boys collapsed into a pile of dust. A pile, moreover, that formed the capital letter H on the step before it, too, vanished.

Bogdan continued up the steps, scouting all the Kodiak halls for his tormentors. He went past his former room, where new Tobb guards were playing the same old card game, to the roof. There he checked all the shadows and, finding no one, joined Megan and BJ, who had just started their vigil next to Samson's cot.

"How is he?" he asked them.

Megan said, "He hasn't stirred since this morning."

BJ said, "And he hardly even stinks much anymore."

Bogdan lay on a chaise lounge and watched the homcom bee hovering overhead. It reminded him of the bee under Samson's lapel, which reminded him of going to Soldier Field and Hubert. Would they ever see Hubert again? Bogdan counted ten hours before he had to get ready for work tomorrow. He knew he should go down to the NanoJiffy for a Sooothe to counteract the Alert! he had just taken so he could sleep, but when he tried to get up off the chaise lounge, he discovered that his body was paralyzed. His mind was wide awake, roaring along like a rocket, in fact, but his body was asleep. He knew he should force himself up anyway to take that Sooothe, but the thought of climbing up and down the stairs again was more than he could manage. How come the Tobblers had an elevator and they didn't? And besides, if he did fall asleep, could he trust the houseputer to wake him up at six? He didn't think so; it was probably safer to just stay awake, especially since his eyes were closed and Megan or BJ had covered him with a blanket.

So while his body slept, Bogdan's mind raced all over the known universe, from his private ski chalet on Planet Lisa, where Annette lay naked with him next to the fire, to the micromine control shed in Wyoming where his expertise alone was responsible for discovering a rich new vein of precious trace elements, to his meeting in a few scant hours with HR at E-Pluribus where he would undoubtedly receive the Employee of the Year Award, plus a healthy raise and substantial bonus. Through all of this, he wondered what the dusty H on the step stood for.

When Mary arrived home, she didn't even bother to change her clothes but jumped enthusiastically into Concierge's recommended lessons on the revivification sciences: neurology, genetics, micromechanics, embryology, biochemistry, and histology. She plowed through units on basal nuclei, fast axoplasmic transport, and Flinn-Long glial grafting. Needless to say, the material was far too advanced for her, and she had no luck finding anything more elementary on the WAD. So she swallowed two Smarts and slogged on, hoping for the best.

When Fred came in, he sat next to her on the couch and watched part of a colorful tour of the sarcoplasmic reticulum, an organelle essential to coma management. After a few minutes, he said, "I don't get it."

"I don't either." Mary laughed.

"I mean, what does this have to do with your companion job?" He was being disingenuous. He knew exactly what this had to do with her work.

"My sisters and I are trying to broaden our horizons," Mary said by way of explanation.

"By studying jenny work?"

Mary shrugged. When she looked at him, she did a double take. "You're up to something, Fred," she said. "You have it written all over your face. What have you done?"

Fred leaned over to undo his shoes, his big brown russ shoes, and hand them off to the waiting slipper puppy. "I suppose I did do something," he said.

"Are you free to tell me about it?"

"It's not really work-related, so I guess I am." It would be a relief, in fact, to tell her. "Lately, things have got me wondering about clone fatigue."

"There's no such thing."

"I know, but it got me thinking about how we russes are afraid to try out new things and to open up to each other." He told her about brown shoes and searching the *HUL* for secret files and about starting the *Book of Russ*. He told her about launching a provocative discussion to challenge his brothers to contribute their personal stories without, however, revealing to her the sexual content of his challenge.

When he was finished, Mary pondered his news for a while, sifting the nuances, and then, identifying the real issue, as usual, she said, "What kinds of things do you want to try, Fred?"

Fred leaned over to put on his slippers, hiding his face. "Nothing in particular. Just new things in general."

"Because you know you're free to try out new things. No one's stopping you."

Fred opened his mouth, but nothing came out.

"Because you're not my prisoner here," she went on.

"Really?" he said, plunging blindly ahead. "You're not just saying that?"

She glowed with sincerity. "If you had your heart set on—you know—something, it would be wrong of me to try to hold you back."

"You're too good to me."

"I'm just trying to be realistic, Fred."

Fred nodded his head. "Because there *was* something," he confessed. "Something—well—not proper."

Mary paused a moment to read him. She seemed a little afraid, but she said, "Tell me about it."

"I—can't."

"Yes, Fred, you *can*. You can tell me *anything*. You know that."

He looked away from her again. "Well," he said, clearing his throat, "if you're sure you don't mind, there's this one thing I've always wanted to try."

"Yes?"

"I've always wondered—"

"Go on."

"What it would be like to do *this*." With a smooth motion, he stood up, leaned over, picked her up, and slung her over his shoulder.

"Fred!" she cried.

"I don't know if this is clone fatigue or not," he said and carried her toward the bedroom, her chin jouncing against his back. She pounded him with her fists and bit him.

"Ouch! Easy there," he said and slapped her ass. But they passed the bedroom door without going in.

"Where are you taking me, Fred?"

"To try something out." The apartment passed by upside down. Mary saw the tiled floor of their small foyer. "Door," Fred declared, "unlock yourself."

The bolt of the front door disengaged.

"No, door!" Mary shrieked. "Lock yourself!"

The bolt engaged.

"That fountain on 450," he said. "The one with the kissing centaurs—door! Unbolt I say!"

The bolt disengaged.

"Door, lock and double lock!"

The bolt shot back and forth. They laughed to think what someone in the hall must think. He turned her right side up and, not letting her feet touch the floor, pulled the rip tab under her collar and tore her clothes open down the front. Used his teeth to tear her panties.

They liked to watch each other when they came. That evening, he saw in her eyes a circus of clowns and jugglers, hoops and tigers, a heavenly chorus rising in the bleachers. *To my brothers cloned: Those eyes. Those eyes.*

THEY LAY IN bed later and ate dinner. Watched a dumb vid. When he fell asleep, she got up and threw on a robe. She stood over the bed and watched him for a while. This *Book of Russ* thing was potentially very serious.

She went to the living room and closed the bedroom door, turned on the flatscreen and did a lesson on the physiology of the mesencephalon.

Wednesday

3.8

Mary arrived in Decatur early. There was no limo waiting to pick her up, but the day was fine and she decided to walk the few blocks to the clinic. She paid closer attention to the neighborhood along the way. Rich estates and grand houses were hidden behind trees and walls. The clinic, itself, was separated from the street by its own stone wall, wide lawns, and tall hedges. She walked under a sturdy iron arch with florid iron letters that read, "ROOSEVELT CLINIC," past the parking lot and down the brick drive to the gatehouse. She passed through the scanway with no difficulty. At the inner gate there was a different russ guard on duty, one she knew— Reilly Dell!

"What a surprise," she said. "Imagine the odds."

"The odds of what?" Reilly said, squeezing her hand. "That we'd both be assigned to the same facility, or that my fantasy of meeting you without your pet monkey would finally come true?"

"You seem better," she said. He did, though he still wore the exoassist braces and she could see a trace of the skullcap through his hair. It would be a few more days before either Reilly or Fred could reinstall their implants.

"How's the job going?" Reilly said. "Shelley's dying to know."

Mary wondered if he was making a bad pun. "Tell her it's a challenge, but marvelous."

They chatted for a few minutes, and then Reilly said, "I can't let you in just yet. The other 'leen is still a few minutes out, and Concierge wants to meet the both of you in the plaza together."

So Mary stood in the WAIT HERE box as Reilly attended to other arrivals. She hoped that Renata had a good reason for being so tardy. But Renata didn't show; a different evangeline arrived and passed through the gate with Mary. Concierge greeted them, as cordial as ever, and escorted them to Feldspar Cottage, but by the direct route this time. As they went, it laid out Roosevelt Clinic policies for the new evangeline, whose name was Georgine.

"It wouldn't hurt for you to hear the rules again as well," it told Mary. "Apparently, not all of the evangelines were paying close enough attention yesterday. Especially as regards the protection of the clinic's proprietary technology."

Mary had no idea what he was referring to. She couldn't think of anything Renata might have done to cause her dismissal.

Concierge left them on Mineral Way, and she and Georgine walked up the footpath to the cottage alone. Halfway there they met a pair of clinic doctors coming the other way. Out of habit, Mary stepped off the path to let them by, but Georgine did not. It was only after Georgine stepped through the doctors that Mary recognized them for holos. The clinic projection system was better than any she'd encountered. Still, it was impolite to walk through people's holos.

Inside the cottage, the jenny nurse, Hattie, was lecturing the night evangelines. "We usually wait till they've regained consciousness," she said, "but with Myr Starke we decided sooner was better. You two," she said when Mary and Georgine entered, "grab a pair of gloves and join us."

Feldspar Cottage, at the quarter hour of fresh-brewed coffee, was different than the day before. Throw rugs, shelving units, a table, writing desk, rocking chair, and other furnishings had been brought in and arranged in the two rooms. But the most obvious change was the addition of a daybed in the lower room. Lying on the daybed was a young woman in a sleeveless unitard. She lay on her side, apparently asleep. Cyndee, Ronnie, and the jenny nurse stood around her.

Mary and Georgine each took a package of vurt gloves from a pile of them on a supply cart and joined the others at the daybed.

"You're new," Hattie said to Georgine. "I'm Hattie Beckeridge." Cyndee and Ronnie introduced themselves to their new colleague. Today, all of the evangelines wore saucer hats. Then Hattie returned their attention to the woman on the daybed. The woman had a slight build, pretty face, and bushy eyebrows.

"Is this Myr Starke?" Mary said.

"Yes, well, her empty jacket anyways," Hattie said. "The medtechs adapted it from a holo sim she cast on her most recent birthday. They've mapped it through the controller to her brain."

Mary looked up at the skull hovering above them in the tank like a ghastly judge, its eyes as dead as the day before.

Hattie took the jacket's hand in her gloved hand and drew it across the rough fabric of the daybed. "This'll get the old sensory neurons popping," she said. "Here, take turns doing this. Nice and easy. We don't want carpet burns." Mary pulled on her vurt gloves, and Hattie continued. "Myr Starke will need to wear this jacket for the next eighteen months or so while her new body matures."

Ronnie said, "But if the jacket looks at the tank, won't she be frightened to see herself as a skull? I know I would."

Hattie paused to look up at the skull. "The jacket system has a built-in blind spot so she can't see the tank unless she chooses to. What's important initially is that the body in the tank can see the jacket. Her developing new body will need both visual and proprioceptive feedback from the jacket. This is so the new nerve cells insinuate themselves properly into the existing brain tissue. Otherwise, she could suffer everything from mild spasticity to profound Parkinsonian symptoms.

"As soon as you wake up, Myr Starke," Hattie told the jacket, "we'll have you doing jumping jacks in here."

Under Hattie's direction, the evangelines lifted the jacket and turned it on its back. With the vurt gloves, the holo seemed as heavy as a real body. They lifted her legs and slid the soles of her bare feet against the daybed as they had done her hands. While they worked, the evangelines traded looks and glances, and Mary knew there was news from upshift. But there was no chance to talk, for as soon as they finished the sensory workout, a trio of johns entered the cottage bearing more cartons of Ellen Starke's personal belongings: hats, photographs and lamps, a bead necklace, trophies, libraries, and more. Hattie and the evangelines arranged these things on nooks and shelves in the cottage.

When they were finished, Hattie had to leave to make her rounds. "Be sure to keep stimulating our guest," she said. "Remember, she can see, hear, and smell. We chose some of her stuff for its olfactory qualities. There's nothing like the smell of home to get one's attention."

"How does Myr Starke smell?" Cyndee said.

"Didn't anyone show you? Never mind, follow me." Hattie led them to the control unit beside the tank. "Here's the olfactory sampler—Myr Starke's temporary nose." She pointed to a small grate at the side of the unit. "It's constantly sampling the ambient air and transducing the results directly to our guest's olfactory epithelium, which is intact. I always use the same shampoo so my clients can learn to recognize me by scent." Hattie stooped and rubbed her hair next to the grate. "Good morning, Myr Starke. It's me, Hattie Beckeridge, your day nurse." She straightened up and continued. "In some ways, odors are more useful to our guest right now than sight. Smell is a simpler, more direct sense."

She told the control unit to project a model of Starke's brain. It popped up, a large gray walnutlike thing. "Now add the orbits and show us the primary retinofugal projection." Two eyeballs appeared at one end of the model brain (which was useful for Mary who otherwise couldn't tell one lobe from another). The eyeballs were highlighted in red. The highlighting followed two neural pathways to the midbrain where they crossed before continuing to the very rear of the hemispheres. "What we perceive with our eyes at the *front* of our skull has to travel across the whole brain," Hattie said, tracing a pathway with her finger, "before reaching the visual cortex at the *back*. There the signals are first processed and then sent out to other areas for further processing."

She told the model to display the entire visual pathway, and the whole brain seemed to light up. "Impressive, isn't it?" Hattie said. "Vision is our primary sense. Nearly one-third of our brain's mass is involved in processing it."

She told the model to display Starke's actual visual activity. Only the eyes and ropelike pathway lit up and only to the crossover point in the middle of the brain.

"See? The signal gets lost long before it ever reaches her occipital lobes. The lights are on, but there's no one home. Now let's compare smell. Show us the patient's current olfactory activity."

Two small projections under the eyes of the model brain became highlighted in green. "This is the olfactory epithelium, which lines the top of the nasal passage of the nose. It makes up the olfactory bulbs, the only brain tissue we have outside our skulls. It comes in contact with the air we breathe." She pointed to the green projections and then to a lobe of the brain adjacent to them. "Olfactory bulbs here, primary olfactory cortex right next door—smell is our *only* sensory system that passes directly to the cerebral cortex. This gives it *unparalleled* influence on parts of the brain that affect emotion, motivation, and certain kinds of memory."

Finishing the lesson, Hattie took her leave, first passing behind the tank and peering in at the fetus. The evangelines joined her. The little prawn looked to be the same size as the day before.

IN A CORNER of the blast bunker nearly a quarter klick beneath the Starke Manse, Merrill Meewee lay in his makeshift bedroom and stared up at the ceiling. After the household mechs attacked him yesterday, Wee Hunk thought it prudent to move him underground. At least until he figured out who was responsible and how they had penetrated manse security. But while Meewee felt the weight of the intervening layers of earth and limestone over his head, he didn't feel any more secure and hadn't managed to get much sleep. If Eleanor's enemies could pervert carpet scuppers into attack dogs, could anyplace be safe?

Well, actually, yes. Next to the shelter where he lay was the Starke null suite. As null suites went, it was a world-class design. Nothing could penetrate it, not EM radiation, long-wave Earth vibrations, cosmic rays, ultrasound, or any other known means of spying, not even quantum entanglement, or so Eleanor had claimed. She used to brag that not even God, herself, could eavesdrop there. Maybe that was where Meewee could get some sleep.

Meewee's neck hurt, and his windpipe was sore, and he was bruised where the carpet scuppers had pummeled him. Arrow may have saved him from strangulation but Meewee had had to specifically tell it to do so. Arrow possessed some awesome capabilities, but a quick-thinking bodyguard it was not.

<Arrow> he said in Starkese <what are you?>

The mentar replied in Starkese <I don't understand the question.>

<Are you a mentar?>

<Affirmative.>

<Do you have a personality?>

<I don't understand the question.>

<Are you self-aware?>

<I don't understand the question.>

Meewee got out of bed and padded naked to the bathroom. Eleanor's bunker shelter was roomy and well appointed. A party of thirty or so people, accustomed to first-class accommodations, could wait out a nuclear attack or biowar and its aftermath here in princely comfort.

Meewee cleaned up and dressed and went to the galley for breakfast. Wee Hunk was waiting for him as a life-size man in an ocelot fur robe. "A hearty good morning to you, O man of the cloth," the mentar said, offering his ID in Starkese without even being challenged. "I do hope your little scuffle yesterday with the vacuum cleaners hasn't interfered with your appetite. The kulinmate down here is loaded with exceptional dishes. You should try the sourdough waffles."

Meewee only grunted acknowledgment and sat at one of the long, cafeteria-style tables. When a waiterbeitor rolled over to take his order, he eyed it warily before asking for juice, toast, strawberry jam, and coffee.

"You'll be pleased to know I've identified the security breach," the mentar went on brightly. "Apparently, there was dust adhering to your skin and clothes that carried instructions for subverting our household mechs. You probably picked it up while still at Starke headquarters."

"Cabinet?"

"Probably, but not necessarily," the mentar said, and a diorama of the clinic cottage interior opened on the table next to Meewee. "Ready for your update?" Inside the diorama, the tiny figures of evangelines and johns were rearranging furniture. Meewee's eye went directly to the daybed where a resurrected Ellen Starke seemed to be lying, asleep. It was a jacket, he assumed.

"She still comatose?"

"Sadly, yes. Her condition has not improved, and her prognosis worsens by the hour. According to the continuity counters, Concierge has not attempted to edit or distort my observations. However, it did intercept the amnio syrup sample I tried to smuggle out and terminated the employment of my evangelinian smuggler."

"We *must* get our own specialist in there."

"I don't disagree," the robed caveman said, "but I've come to the conclusion that our best course of action is to remove Ellen from the clinic and treat her here, with a specialized autodoc if necessary."

"Here? In the bunker?"

The waiterbeitor returned with Meewee's breakfast. He spread jam on his toast and took a tentative bite.

"Yes, in the bunker. In the null suite, in fact. I'm assembling an impromptu re-vivification clinic in there even as we speak. I've purchased a hernandez tank, syrup, controller, and all the various pieces. And I've located a suitable autodoc."

They watched the activity in the cottage as Meewee ate. When he was finished, Wee Hunk said, "The big problem is how to remove her from the clinic."

"I thought you were her guardian," Meewee said. "Can't you just sign her out?"

"Yes, but doing so would force their hand. If some agency is indeed killing her gradually, in order to make it appear to be a result of the reentry crash, giving them any notice of our intent would only result in her immediate murder. If we are to remove her, we must do so in a lightning assault with no forewarning."

Meewee wiped his mouth and refolded his napkin. "What exactly did you have in mind?"

THE NEWS FROM upshift was that a swing shift evangeline, and not Renata, had been fired for breech of clinic policy. Mary couldn't be sure of the particulars because of the inferential nature of evangeline communication, but it appeared that Celia, whom Mary hadn't met, had dipped a small vial into the tank and tried to smuggle a sample of the amnio concentrate syrup out of the clinic. It was further intimated that she had done this under the instructions of their client's mentar, Wee Hunk. Her smuggling attempt was discovered, however, and she was summarily discharged. Nick rescheduled Renata to cover today's evening shift and assigned Georgine to fill in this morning.

When shift overlap ended and Cyndee and Ronnie departed, Mary and Georgine cast about for something "stimulating" to do with their client.

"Let's read to her," Mary said and took the library from the shelf. But it wasn't a library. It was heavy, and the pages were made of paper. It was a book. The evangelines sat next to the daybed and examined the dusty antique. The first two pages were *blank*. The book had been published in 2013, in Boston. That must have been the old Boston. There were no glyphs, icons, or illustrations of any kind. The text was threaded across 240 actual pages. When you touched a word, it did not pronounce or define itself or display its links. It just sat there on the paper like a stain.

On the daybed next to them, the Starke jacket was arranged on her back with her head on a pillow and her hands crossed over her chest. She looked as peaceful as a corpse. "We're going to read from your book," Mary told her and lifted the jacket's hand to touch the pebbly surface of the book cover. But the book had not been mapped with a vurt analog, and so the jacket's hand went through it. "Never mind that," Mary said.

She opened the book and read: "*The Apple Orchard*, by Delany Kay. Chapter One, 'Jae.'"

It was a day out of days when persons of flexible demeanor irradiated themselves with units of satisfaction or puzzlement or anxiety in accordance with their prescription. Through an act of carelessness, a bolus of nonspecific grief was released into the forward compartment. It floated unnoticed throughout the ship until Jae Taxamany, pulling herself through a bulkhead hatch, collided with it. Suddenly, for no good reason, Jae began to weep.

Mary was drawn immediately into the tale—it was plainly a love story—and took turns with Georgine reading it aloud for an hour, when they were interrupted by Medtech Coburn. He led his supply cart through the cottage door and mumbled something unfriendly as he passed the evangelines.

"That's enough reading for now," Mary said. "Georgine, allow me to introduce Matt."

"Coburn," Coburn said.

"Matt likes to be called Coburn," Mary said.

"Dittoheads," he muttered under his breath.

Mary was stung by the slur, and Georgine opened her mouth to make some retort, but changed her mind. Instead, Mary asked the medtech if there was anything they could do to help. Coburn assured her there wasn't, except to leave him alone. Nevertheless, the evangelines stood in front of the tank to watch what he was doing, and after a while he dropped an empty nerve spool on Mary.

The evangelines took the hint and returned to the daybed. Georgine rolled up Mary's sleeve to look for bruises. The spool hadn't been heavy, and this wasn't the real reason she rolled up Mary's sleeve. She was actually hiding a yellow stain of amnio syrup the spool had left on Mary's sleeve. If Wee Hunk wanted a sample of the syrup so badly, perhaps this one would do. "How's that?" she asked Mary.

Mary honestly didn't know. Would Concierge see through their ruse? Was this sample valuable enough to justify the risk? It was hours before she'd be leaving the clinic, so she didn't have to decide just yet. She held out her other arm for Georgine to roll the other sleeve to match.

WHEN MARY TOOK her lunch break, she wandered the grounds, greeting strangers, and trying to appear approachable. At the tennis court, she watched a match. On the golf course, she had a slice of cheesecake and an iced coffee at the Nineteenth Hole. A steve waited on her. When she asked for the check, he said no one paid for such trifles at the clinic.

Passing the dining commons on her way back to the cottage, Mary ran into Hattie with several of her jenny colleagues. "Here she is," Hattie said, presenting Mary to the others. "One of our newest health care providers." The jennys fussed over Mary and told her that their aff guests had been asking about them. Also, everyone was acutely curious about the Starke girl.

Hattie told her colleagues to go on ahead, and she walked a little way with Mary alone. "I want to give you a friendly piece of advice," she said, "since you're new at this game."

Mary immediately thought she'd been found out. She began to unroll her sleeve and was about to swear that she'd only been trying to hide an ugly stain, not to smuggle amnio syrup out of the clinic. But Hattie said, "We jennys are trained to deal with this from childhood. It's never easy, but you and the other 'leens should probably prepare yourselves to lose your client."

"What?"

"It's not your fault, and I'm not saying it's a certainty. Heaven knows, we've seen miraculous turnarounds before, but it doesn't look good for Starke. You saw her fetus. It's not only *not* gained mass since yesterday, but it's actually lost some. It simply cannot thrive while she remains in a coma. If she doesn't regain consciousness soon, it will die."

Mary, not sure what to do with her arms, held them behind her back and said, "But that in itself wouldn't kill her brain, would it?"

"No, it wouldn't, but there'd be no point in grafting on a second fetus. That *never* works. Starke's only option then, assuming she eventually woke up, which isn't a given, would be to live as a brain-in-a-box. Faced with this, most people choose to die."

Hattie wrung her hands, a typical jenny gesture. When she continued, she lowered her voice to a conspiratorial whisper and said, "There's some who say that reviving the dead is an abomination against the Creator, but I say that's horse pucky. In most cases, we can fix what killed you and restart your engines without resorting to deals with Satan.

"But in the case of trauma—deep, massive tissue trauma—the sort that Starke suffered before her safety helmet kicked in—did you know that the force of the crash *liquified* the rest of her body?—well, it puts these people into a different class of dead. It's not like they died by drowning or hemorrhaging or something easy like that. Extreme trauma does something to people. It's like they don't even *want* to come back. And if we do manage to save them, they don't fully recover. They're broken people. So I wanted to warn you and your sisters that you should prepare yourselves for the worst case."

The conversation with Hattie was disturbing. It sounded as if the nurse had already given up on Myr Starke.

MARY ENCOUNTERED CONCIERGE on Mineral Way. "Ah, Myr Skarland," it said warmly, "I was just on my way to Feldspar. Our guest has company. Mind if I walk with you?"

"Please do," Mary said, her guilty arm involuntarily slinking behind her back—for all the good that would do.

There were three realbody guests in the cottage, a woman and two men. They wore clothes that had not come out of an extruder, and they slouched in the insolent pose of wealth. Aff friends of aff Starke. Georgine was in the upper room with the tank, staying out of the way. One of the men wore vurt gloves and used a special comb on the sleeping woman's hair. He looked up when Mary and Concierge entered. His lidded gaze barely glanced off Mary and riveted Concierge with an intensity that was at once commanding and dismissive.

"You be the clinic machine," he said, not a question but a statement of fact.

"That is correct," said Concierge, "the clinic mentar."

"This all wired up?"

"Yes, Myr Orex. Myr Starke's jacket is completely mapped to her brain."

"Good," he said and seemed to wipe Concierge from his awareness. He combed the jacket's hair with long graceful strokes. The muscles of his shoulders and arms rippled in an odd way, and Mary realized they'd been rehung on his skeletal frame. It was a recent aff fad. Slight alterations in the attachment points; longer, stronger tendons; more numerous bundles of thinner muscle fibers gengineered with feline DNA. The bones were reinforced as well.

The visiting woman sat next to Myr Starke on the daybed. She, too, wore gloves, and she held the jacket's hand. "Ellie, dear, it's me, Clarity," she said. "Do you have *any* idea how inconvenient this is? Did you forget about our touchstone test today? Baby, we've got a problem. Renaldo (the Dangerous) is all wrong for the part. Won't you please come out to discuss this with me? I hate to make these decisions by myself. Enough of this coma crap."

"You have to kiss her, Clarity," said the other man. He was a generically handsome fellow with traditionally human musculature. "That's how it works with sleeping beauties. I should know; it works on me."

Clarity said, "Is that right? You've been tanked, have you?"

"*Six* times!" the man said. "And each time right here at the Roosevelt. I've got my own reserved tank. Isn't that right, Serge?"

"It's nice to see you again, Myr Thorpe," Concierge replied. "I notice you haven't managed to kill this body yet."

The man guffawed. "Not through any lack of trying," he said.

Someone new came into the cottage: a heavyset man with coarse white whiskers and fleshy jowls. He wore an iconic artist's smock and beret, and he carried a large wooden case under his arm.

"A Sebastian Carol!" Clarity said upon seeing him. "I didn't think there were any of those left."

"There aren't," Concierge said. "At least not on the public nets."

"Explain."

"Because data flow is restricted through clinic space, we maintain our own simiverse here for the enjoyment of our guests. We have a subem dedicated to hollyholo generation and a stable of over a thousand characters, some of them rare collector's items, like our Sebastian Carol here."

Sebastian Carol moved about the room, checking angles with bloodshot eyes. Settling on a spot, he held out his wooden case, which sprouted legs and an easel. "You, negress," he said to Clarity, "remove your garments and scoot a little to your left."

She ignored him and asked Concierge, "If you have an independent simiverse, who does your plot management?"

"That happens to be my pleasure."

"I see," Clarity said doubtfully. "And what do your clinic guests think of mentar-driven plot mats?"

Before Concierge could answer, the man brushing Starke's hair said, "Clarity, must you always talk shop? It's so incredibly boring to the rest of us."

The other man said, "Serge, how many hours since Ellen was unclenched?"

"Fifty-seven."

Starke's friends exchanged a look.

Two more hollyholo sims entered the cottage, the two doctors Mary and Georgine had passed on the footpath. When Clarity saw these, she frowned and said, "Do tell, Serge, how the clinic's stable came to acquire a Renaldo (the Dangerous). Ellen and my production company bought out the *entire* edition of him, or so we thought."

"Don't be concerned," Concierge said. "It's a beta version. We were a test site for the original producers. Our private simiverse makes ideal testing conditions, something you and Myr Starke might keep in mind the next time you have a new character in development."

The sims approached the daybed. The Renaldo character said, "'Lo, folks. Don't get up. Just making my rounds. I'm Doctor Ted, and I'm giving my colleague here, Doctor Babs, a tour of the wards."

"Good to meet you, Doctors," Clarity said. "I wish my friend, Ellen, were awake. She'd like to meet you. Especially you, Doctor Ted."

"I'm flattered," Doctor Ted said and produced a medical chart from thin air. He studied it briefly and said, "A tragic case. This is Myr Ellen Starke of the Starke dynasty. Her space yacht was hijacked by a rogue mentar, and Ellen was killed." Doctor Ted pulled an antique stethoscope from his jacket pocket and draped it over his shoulders before continuing. "Her cryonics helmet only partially stabilized her alma mater, resulting in insult to her cranial conundrum. But have no fear; our crackerjack staff here at Roosevelt Clinic have put things aright, and our guest is making salubrious progress. We'll have her decomatosed in no time at all."

Clarity clapped her gloved hands and said, "We never thought of making Renaldo (the Dangerous) a *doctor*. Kudos to you, Concierge. Don't be surprised if we steal your idea."

"It would be an honor," said Concierge.

Because they had begun to talk shop again, and because she was invisible in this crowd anyway, Mary joined Georgine at the tank. The medtech had applied skin-growth gauze to the skull, hiding most of it. Mary took a daisy she'd stolen from the lake path and crushed its bloom next to the control unit's olfactory grate.

THE FAUX DOCTORS, visitors, and mentar departed the cottage, leaving only the Sebastian Carol behind. "Young ladies," he said, waving a paintbrush at Mary and Georgine, "remove your garments and sit over there."

MARY WAS HALFWAY to South Gate at the quarter hour of french fries, quitting time, before she remembered the stain on her sleeve. Somehow she'd managed to forget it all afternoon.

"What's wrong?" Georgine said.

"Nothing. I just remembered something I have to do."

Georgine gave her a shrewd look and said, "I saw a public extruder in the gym today." That meant that Mary could order new clothes in the locker room. She could toss her incriminating suit into the digester and take a sauna, and no one would be the wiser.

But Mary hated to be such a coward, and she said, "Never mind. I'll do it later."

Without discussion, Mary held back to let Georgine leave the clinic grounds first, so she wouldn't be implicated by association in case something happened. When Mary judged that Georgine had had time to clear the clinic property, she held her breath and went through the gate.

Reilly was still on duty, and Mary scolded herself for involving him in this. But no one stopped her. Reilly said he'd see her and Fred at Rolfe's later for their regular Wednesday get-together, but Mary told him Fred had some big job tonight.

And then she was out and up the hedge-lined drive, and Georgine was waiting for her, full of sisterly pride.

"RESULTS?" MEEWEE ASKED.

"Still analyzing it," Wee Hunk said, "but the syrup's oxygen, nutritional, hormonal, and pharmaceutical properties all fall within normal parameters."

"Then why hasn't Ellen waken up yet? What are they doing to her?"

"Perhaps it's as the nurse said: perhaps she was injured too severely."

Meewee weighed this possibility against what he knew of the girl. Ellen wasn't as bullheaded as her mother (who Meewee half expected to return from the dead herself), but she was no quitter either.

"I must say," Wee Hunk continued, "the evangelines baffle me. They seem to have a communication system as subtle and flexible as Starkese, and largely nonverbal. It's completely opaque to me; I can see that information is being passed, but I can't read it. Is there such a thing as cellular communication?

"Also, I would have thought that news of their colleague's discharge would have instilled fear into the rest of them, but it seems to have had the opposite effect. I didn't ask them to make another attempt to acquire an amnio sample."

"I know what you mean," Meewee said. "I'd never paid much attention to the type before. I always thought they were bred to be lapdogs."

Bogdan arrived home from work two hours early. He stood in front of the door for a long time, staring at the control plate, not touching it, not saying anything. After a protracted standoff, the door surrendered to his will and slid open. Bogdan marched through the foyer and climbed the stairs to the fourth floor, where it seemed the entire house was waiting for him in the corridor outside Green Hall. His first thought was, Who told them? But after watching his 'meets for a few moments he realized that not only were they *not* waiting for him, they didn't even know he was home. It's probably because I'm two hours early, he thought and joined them at the door to Green Hall. Inside the room, April was having some sort of unhappy encounter with Kale. Megan and BJ, standing next to the door, provided a running commentary.

"Samson rose from the dead this morning," Megan said. "He sat up in his death-cot and croaked, 'Mush, mush! And juice!'"

BJ said, "Now Denny and Rusty are in the john with him."

"Assisting in a heroic bowel movement."

"And he insists on coming to Rondy with us."

"But Kale says that's crazy talk. What about his odor? What if he dies in front of everybody?"

"But April is arguing his case. If Sam goes, that means she can go too."

There was a sharp noise, like a slap, and all eyes snapped back to Green Hall. Kale lifted his paper notebook and slapped it on the tabletop again.

BJ said, "Kale's been taking assertiveness pills all week."

Megan said, "Yeah. Every little decision he makes he clings to like a life raft."

Kitty came down the stairs and joined the 'meets at the door. "I'm going in," she said. "Wish me luck."

"Good luck," they all wished her.

Kitty glanced at Bogdan. "What's wrong with you? Lose your job or something?"

Bogdan was too stunned to reply. Kitty entered the room and announced brightly, "It's all arranged. I rented the lifechair. It's on its way."

"Lifechair?" Kale gasped. "I didn't approve that. That's not covered. How will we pay for it? It's out of the question. I've made up my mind."

"Don't worry about it," Kitty went on merrily. "It's coming out of Sam's own pocket, not the house's. That Hubert artifact in his belt arranged the whole thing. It's all arranged and covered and on its way."

"Cancel it!" Kale roared.

"I will not. He's coming with us."

"But, but—" Kale sputtered, "he's under house arrest!"

"Quit shouting," Kitty said. "I can hear you fine. I talked to that bee that's watching him and cleared it with the hommers. They said he can go. They didn't even seem all that concerned about him, actually."

"But, but, but—"

"Look, Kale," April said, rising from her bench seat, "it's a badge of honor that our house cares enough about him to take him to his last Rendezvous. And it's a badge of honor we should be proud to wear in front of your damn Beadlemyren. Believe me, none of them look too healthy themselves. We'll be nursing them soon enough."

The truth of her argument tipped Kale momentarily off balance, and the woman and girl used the reprieve to exit Green Hall. "I said I made up my mind," Kale threw at their backs. "Did you hear me? My mind is made up."

On her way out of the room, April paused to speak to Bogdan. "You're home early," she said. "Did you get that bonus?"

"Yes!" Bogdan roared. "I got the feckin' bonus!"

But April didn't stay around to hear about it. She sent all the loitering 'meets on last-minute errands. The bus was due to arrive in two hours. April dropped a package into Bogdan's hands and said, "Wear this." She wrinkled her nose and sniffed him. "Take a shower first."

Her suggestion startled him. He lifted his arms to sniff his pits. Subject reeks of unholy fear, he reported to himself. He held the package of party togs before him like a bowl of water and gingerly carried it to the upper spheres of the house. Subject must be careful not to shut his eyes, or even to blink too slowly, for every time he does, a bloodred curtain drops, and he sees again with cornea-blistering clarity the unraveling of his day.

Which started soon after he arrived at work. The morning upreffing sessions had had nothing to do with Oships or Planet Lisa. They were less than memorable consensus exercises, and Bogdan forgot them even as they were playing. During a venue switch, he passed Annette Beijing in the corridor. They stopped to chat, and she said, "I just wanted to wish you luck at your HR meeting today at three."

A good thing she mentioned it, for though Bogdan hadn't forgotten about the meeting, he had forgotten what day it was, which would have amounted to the same thing. She blew him a kiss and sashayed off. The kiss was aimed dead on, and Bogdan waited motionless for it to flutter over to him and press itself softly upon his cheek.

When his fourth Alert! ran out right before lunch, he was ready with his fifth. Hour 53 and all was well. The drug didn't spoil his appetite. On the contrary, at lunch he returned for seconds of ice cream and fry. And he filled his pockets with snickerdoodles.

At 2:55 PM, Bogdan followed an usher line down the Administrative Corridor. The AC was arranged the same no matter where they were camped, and he knew he would wind up in front of three black doors. He found the doors and the bench opposite them. There was always a bench. He sat on the bench to wait. The subject has to wait on the bench until one of the doors calls his name. They always make him wait. They, in this case, was E-P, the E-Pluribus mentar. Everyone at E-Pluribus was a construct of E-P: the Academy sims, the HR director, even Annette herself. There were no actual human resources at E-Pluribus to manage, except for the dem controls, like himself, and the daily holes. Since the HR department was not real, subject could see no practical reason it could have for making him wait.

However, with the glimmering rays of a promised bonus gilding everything in sight, Bogdan didn't mind the wait. He had provisioned himself for just such an eventuality. That was what the doodles were for. He sprawled on the bench and dropped a handful of the crisp little elbows of crunchy puffery, piece by piece, into his mouth, where he ground them to a sweet mash that he let trickle down his throat. It was a satisfying pastime. But still, shouldn't part of a bonus be not having to wait for it?

"Myr Kodiak," someone said, "this way please."

Bogdan looked up; the middle door was talking to him. It was always the middle door. He swung his feet to the floor and swallowed his sweet cud. He stood up and brushed crumbs from his jumpsuit. The door slid open, and he entered the office.

The HR director was not there—naturally—which meant another round of waiting.

The office looked exactly as it had the last time. That is, messy. There were piles of *paper* files everywhere, on shelves, on top of old-timey cabinets, in leaning towers on the floor and desk. A layer of dust covered everything, and the air was stale. Drink cups and takeout packages with desiccated remnants of unfinished meals had been artfully tucked into every available niche. Just for once he wished one of the other doors would call him and he could experience a different—and nicer—corporate culture.

Bogdan knew from past experience that the only real object in the room, other than himself, was the adult-sized chair parked in front of the HR director's desk. Near the chair was a basket labeled "URGENT" that held a stack of manila folders. When he leaned over to read the top folder, the words printed on it squirmed out of focus.

Bogdan sighed, climbed into the chair, and reached for more snickerdoodles. But the inner door opened, and the Human Resources director sailed in. Her feet seemed barely to touch the floor. She was balancing yet more paper in one arm while using the other to bulldoze a clearing on her overburdened desk. She deposited her stack of papers and shored up several others before even marking Bogdan's presence. Finally, she clapped realistic dust from her hands and said, "Myr Kodiak. Thank you for coming in."

Bogdan leaped from his chair and said, "Thank you for asking me, Myr Director."

The director continued riffling through the files on her desk until she found the one she was seeking. She propped it open between two hillocks of paper and sat down. Without another word to Bogdan, she perused its contents. After a while, Bogdan climbed back into his chair. He was forced to sit and watch her read. She moved her lips as she read. Her lips were big rubbery things, painted purple, all out of proportion with her nose, which was short and pointy. Not an easy face to watch for very long. Especially with the blemishes.

The director's eyes swiveled up to take him in. "Myr Kodiak, today marks your one-year anniversary with us. Congratulations."

"Thank you," Bogdan said, poised to leap to his feet again. She went back to her reading.

The blemishes on her face were two round fleshy moles, one cresting her cheek, and the other perched on her left nostril. One was brown, but the other was colorless. Each had a single curly strand of hair growing out of it. The moles upset him plenty, but it was the hairs that pushed him over the top. Why couldn't she pluck them for crying out loud?

Finally, the director closed the folder and said, "I have a memorandum here I'd like you to look at and sign." A dataframe opened in front of Bogdan with a document on it. The document's title did not have any variation of "bonus" or "raise" in it. Instead, it read somewhat nonspecifically, "Memorandum of Agreement."

Bogdan tried to read the tightly wound text but couldn't make sense out of it, and there were *pages* of the stuff, with a signature box at the bottom to swipe.

Bogdan said, "What is it?"

"It's an agreement by which you sell back the final two years of your employment contract to E-Pluribus."

Bogdan heard the words but couldn't understand them. Against all hope, he said, "Today is my one-year anniversary."

"Again, congratulations," the director said. "We believe you will find our separation payment and bonus quite generous."

A paragraph entitled "Severance Compensation" became highlighted in the document floating before him. E-Pluribus was offering him a lump sum equal to three months pay, some 103.9174 UD credits in exchange for extinguishing his three-year contract immediately.

"I don't get it," Bogdan said. "You're firing me?"

Another dataframe opened beside the first, and his original employment agreement appeared, with a paragraph highlighted. The director said, "We're not terminating you, Myr Kodiak. We're merely exercising this clause which empowers us to buy out your contract at any time for any reason."

"Is it because I've aged a little? I have an appointment at a juve clinic this weekend. You can check it out. I'll be back to eleven-eleven by next week. You can bank on that."

The director smiled, with gaps between all her teeth. "We were well aware of your impending adolescence, and we considered using it as cause for dismissal, but we are nothing if not concerned corporate parents, and we'd rather not sully your permanent record unnecessarily."

"Then why?" Bogdan said miserably. "Aren't I doing a good enough job?"

"Your performance is not the issue. When we hired you, we calculated that it would take twenty-four months to completely map your personality, and another twelve to verify our model. Our calculations were wildly inaccurate. You are an astonishingly uncomplicated person, Myr Kodiak. One might even say simple. It took us only six months to build an exact replica of your personality that accurately predicts your response to virtually anything. Thus, we no longer need you."

Bogdan was reeling. He didn't know what to say and blurted out the first thing that came to him. "That may be so—today, but what about tomorrow? I'm an *evolving* personality. In no time at all, your replica of me will fall out of synch with the real me."

"Ho, ho." The director chuckled. "We knew you were going to say that." She opened his folder and pointed to a document. "We wrote it down. Want to see?" When he didn't respond, she shut it again and continued. "We're not at all interested in your evolution, Myr Kodiak. We have other control subjects for normal human development and maturation. In you we were interested in something entirely different, that is, in a stalled personality, one that has ceased evolving. Imagine, a twenty-nine-year-old boy who hasn't grown up yet, the spoiled lottery baby of a senescent charter, a housemeet who yearns for adventure but does nothing about it, a virgin too involved with a hollyholo to have a relationship with a real girl, any real girl." She stopped to pick her teeth with a fingernail, giving him a chance to say the next thing they knew he would say, but he crossed his arms and refused to say anything.

"You're offended," she went on reasonably, "even though you know that what I say is true, and you wish that I'd die. You are certain that we don't know you at all, and you'd just love to get your hands on our so-called model of you. Then you'd show us, correct?

"Very well," she continued when he refused to agree or disagree, "meet Bogdan Kodiak."

A chair, duplicate of his own, appeared next to him, and in it slouched a small, skinny boy who observed Bogdan through slitted eyes.

"What do you think?" the director said. "Spooky, eh?"

"Oh, I don't know about that," Bogdan said.

"No, you don't, do you?" the replica boy said, sitting up. "You don't know nothing." Suddenly and without warning, the false Bogdan leaped from his chair and, crying and shrieking, ran about the room knocking over piles and towers of folders and scattering paper everywhere. Then he climbed back into his chair and yawned.

The director looked at the real Bogdan and said, "Feel better?"

Bogdan had to admit that he did.

"But you're still not convinced."

"No, I'm not. Not that it makes any difference since you plan to fire me anyway."

The director leaned back in her chair and said, "There may be a way for you to stay."

Bogdan's ears pricked up. "Really?"

The director scratched the mole on her cheek. "Yes, you can stay if you can demonstrate a flaw in our model."

The Bogdan model rolled his eyes.

"How would I do something like that?" Bogdan asked.

"Ask it a question. If you can ask it a question that it can't answer, but you can, then you can stay."

"Deal," Bogdan said and tried to come up with something that he kept locked away in the deepest, most secret recesses of his mind. Something that not even a visceral response probe could reach. It wasn't easy, and his double started munching snickerdoodles in the meantime.

Bogdan's sleepless mind put forth and rejected dozens of possibilities. Finally the HR director said, "Time's up."

"I've got it," Bogdan said. He decided he had to cheat and ask the sim something that not even he knew himself. "Tell me, Bogdan impostor," he said, "if you're so smart, what does the dust H stand for?"

The false Bogdan laughed. "That's easy. It stands for Hubert."

Of course it did. Even as the phony Bogdan uttered it, Bogdan knew it to be true. The H stood for Hubert, and this could only mean that the Tobblers already knew of the mentar's arrest. Or maybe only Troy and Slugboy knew it. Bogdan took another look at his double. And as disturbing as its revelation was about Troy knowing about Hubert, Bogdan had another question he sorely wanted an answer to.

"You're right," he said. "It does. That was a practice question. Here's the real question: Who stole Lisa?"

The simulated boy twirled in his chair. "Who else? Troy Tobbler and his evil friend Slugboy."

Again, his double astounded him. Who else, indeed? Clearly, the E-Pluribus model of him was flawed—it possessed too much insight. But before Bogdan could report this to the director and possibly keep his job, the faux Bogdan, out of the blue, raised his hand and saluted him. At first, Bogdan thought it was reminding him of Troy and Slugboy's mockery on the steps, but it held the salute and locked eyes with him and continued to salute until Bogdan gave in and saluted back. Then it said, with creepy sincerity, "If you don't believe in it yourself, how can you make it happen?"

"YOU ABOUT DONE in there?" Rusty called into the shower stall. "April says the bus is almost here."

Bogdan blinked and looked around. He was in the shower. He got out, dried himself off, and donned the party togs April had given him. Rusty hung around making small talk and doing a bad job of pretending not to be watching to see if he was all right.

"I'm all right," Bogdan said.

"I know it."

IN THE SECURITY shack at McCormick Place, Commander Fred Londenstane turned away from a venue diorama and rubbed his eyes. On either side of him, twenty sullen pikes surveilled other dioramas, which were laid out in the same arrangement as the real rooms that they modeled. Altogether, Rendezvous filled three dozen halls and ballrooms. The largest was the multitiered Hall of Nations, the scale-model diorama of which would completely fill Fred's living room at home.

Across the security shack, which itself was a commandeered ballroom, Gilles caught Fred's eye, and Fred went over to see what was up. Gilles was watching the second largest display, the Welcome Hall, which was the Rendezvous entrance. Thirty conveyor belt scanways converged on Welcome Hall, feeding it four hundred Rondy-goers per minute. In the diorama, these people looked like multicolored ants marching across the marbelite floor and climbing the Grand Staircase to the adjoining Hall of Nations.

Of the thousands of attendees, a small fraction had flags pacing them over their heads. The flags marked potential troublemakers as identified by the McCormick Place mentar, MC, which also ran the scanways.

Gilles reached into the diorama and pointed to a man with not one flag but three. Fred skimmed the man's doss: violent crimes and prison time, but no new offenses in the last seventy years. Fred zoomed in on the man's face—no hint of hostility, only high expectations. He was accompanied by several men and women of the same charter.

"Let him pass," Fred said, "but assign him his own bee."

"That's what I was thinking," Gilles replied. "Oh, and by the way—" He tilted his head at the large Hall of Nations diorama and two of the pikes assigned to surveil it. Fred had assigned half of his contingent of forty pikes to monitor the dioramas. This was just busy work—MC was fully able to monitor the entire complex. These two, instead of watching out for trouble, were engaged in it. They were zooming in on women in the upper tiers of the terraced building and viewing their naked bodies through their clothes. Fred went over and said, "Stop that behavior immediately." The pikes' ratlike eyes never blinked, but they returned to the women their clothing.

Fred continued around the room, chewing over this new bit of information— pikes, at least, were a type who liked hinks and weren't shy about showing it.

ON THE STAIRS, Bogdan met Denny who was carrying Samson down from the roof. Samson seemed awake and clear-witted. "Sam's going to Rondy with us," Denny said. Apparently, so was the homcom bee, which tagged behind.

On the second-floor landing, April and Kale waited next to a lifechair. Denny placed Samson gently into it, and the chair introduced itself. "Hello, Myr Kodiak," it said in a cheery voice while covering him with a smart tartan blanket. "I am a Maxilife Empowerment Chair—at your service! I am equipped to meet all of your special needs with feeding, autodoc, hygiene, colonics, massage, telecom, media, and transport functions. I will even scrub the local air of malodorants. I'm your home on wheels. You need never leave me again!"

"What a gruesome thought!" Samson said.

"I am currently coupling you into my toilet facilities. Please excuse any momentary discomfort."

Samson said, "Can't anyone make this thing shut up? Where's Hubert? Hubert, where are you?"

Kale seemed waiting to pounce on that very question. He stood over the chair and said, "You want to know where Hubert is, Sam? Well, I'll tell you. He's been disappeared because of you and your stupid stunt."

Samson wrinkled his brow. "I have no idea what you're talking about, Kale, as usual."

Kitty came down the stairs with the belt valet and said, "Sam, look what I have."
She handed the belt to the chair and said, "Stow it someplace safe, chair."

Samson said, "What is it?"

"Your belt, Sam, with a bit of Hubert left in the valet."

"Hubert?"

"Hello, Sam," said the valet through the chair's speakers. "I am taking control of
this lifechair. I am not the full Hubert but only a Hubert terminal repeater with minimal attention units. You may call me Belt Hubert."

"But you sound just like Hubert," Samson said hopefully.

"That's right, I do," Belt Hubert said as it steered the chair down the remaining
steps and out the front door. Snuggled in the chair's basket, Samson was asleep by
the time they boarded the bus.

Down the street, the Tobblers were also leaving for Rendezvous. Spanking new
buses dropped out of the sky one after another to pick them up. The Kodiak bus, by
comparison, was small and armored. It had mesh screens over its windows and suspicious stains on its seats. When the Kodiak bus departed, it did not spring into the
air on fans, but labored heavily across town on wheels.

AT MCCORMICK PLACE, their bus was ensnared in traffic. They watched out of
grimy windows as a sea of buses, vans, and taxis all headed for the same destination.
Bogdan stared out the window and relived his day several times in exhaustive Hour
59:30 detail.

"Remember, people," Kale announced over the PA, "you only get one chance to
make a first impression."

THE SPACE SET aside for the Kodiak booth was on the heavily congested third
tier of the Hall of Nations. April uploaded her design specs to MC, and their empty
booth space was quickly transmorphed by the hall's scape system into the deck of a
house barge. The Kodiak House Barge had been the defining product of the fledg-
ling Kodiak charter eighty years before. The design, with its vertical axis turbines,
desalination plant, hurricane and tsunami worthiness, fish-processing plant, and
NBC hazmat filters, was still the world's most popular house barge model, and it
housed millions of people in floating burbs that lined most lakes and continental
shelves. Though the Kodiaks had long ago been forced to liquidate all interest in the
house barge design, it still served them for recruitment purposes.

Soon, a herd of deck chairs and buffet tables arrived and set themselves up on the
holofied deck. Caterbeitors arrived and arranged finger foods and beverages on the
tables. In no time at all, House Barge Kodiak was open for business. Kale gathered
his distracted 'meets together for a pep talk. Megan and BJ were sniffing the sleeves
of their party togs. The bus ride with Samson had ruined their new clothes.

"Right, then," Kale said with enthusiasm. "Here we are! Let's make the most of
this opportunity. You all have your booth duty schedule. Be here on time. In the
meantime, go out there and have fun, but for pity sake, try to meet people. Don't
clump up together. Mingle! Mingle! So go. Wait! Remember, if anyone should ask,
tell them that Belt Hubert is really Hubert."

"I am Belt Hubert," the valet said from the chair, which arrived with Rusty and
the sleeping Samson. Samson's scanner waiver had meant a detour through a bypass
security station where he was assigned a second monitor bee. "I am only a pale approximation of Hubert Prime."

"Yes, we know that, dear," Kitty said to the chair. "Now shut up and don't say that
again."

Already, Samson's odor was causing consternation among chartists at neighboring booths. Kale gave April a told-you-so look, and April said, "Kitty, why don't you take Sam down to the open-air beer garden." But just then Kitty spied a group of children playing a game of tag, and off she skipped to join them.

April sighed and said, "Boggy?"

BOGDAN WOVE DOGGEDLY through aisles and aisles of charter booths, tailed by Samson's chair and two homcom bees. He had just swallowed his sixth Alert! and he felt he had a lot to report: The keepers of soup pots and trad vals have gone all out to greet us. Here are the legions of viridian-green-taupe—at your service! The champions of blue-orange-green—at your service, myr! The disciples of red-black-gray—at your service, myr! And followers of rainbows glimpsed but not recognized—Lisa would know them all—bow to you, myr, and wish you and your retinue a happy Rondy—at least until Sam's ripeness catches up with us and then everyone makes potty faces.

So we keep moving and talk to no one, down endless galleries of tarnished promises where we see the same prayer on every lip: Only grant us one more transplant farm, one more stone quarry, one more popular bentwood chair design, and this time we'll do a better market plan.

Oh, kettlers of boiling green peanuts and smithies of decorative iron window grating and balustrades. Oh, makers of wooden drums with stretched reindeer hide (and shaped like little Oships!) and distillers of crushed rose petals, yarrow stalk, and eucalyptus leaves. Your cash cows lay on their sides, bloated and black, yet you keep pulling at their putrid teats. When will you give it a rest?

Bogdan halted when he saw the Kodiak booth. He had been walking in a big circle. From the distance, their booth *did* look like the roof deck of a house barge. The holo even rolled a little with imaginary swells. Francis and Barry, not the Kodiaks' most auspicious greeters, lounged on deck chairs, eating up the cheese plate. But since no visitors appeared to be coming aboard anyway—

We were never a seagoing charter, though we lived on the water off Kodiak Island in the Gulf of Alaska. In 2054, thirteen women and nineteen men, employees at the Kodiak Elevator Space Port Authority, grew disgruntled with their KESPA housing and decided to move out. But there was a housing shortage on the island, so they organized a co-op to buy and convert a factory barge into a floating residential condo. They had to tie it up along a section of cliff face near Kaguyak, where the tidemark on the rocks was the only beach, and their floating home lay fully exposed to Pacific storms in the winter and the monsoons of summer solstice.

Those were more confident times, the decade before the Outrage, the decade when people first began to realize that they would live forever.

The thirty-two Kodiak Island plankholders were able engineers and confident designers, and in the three-year process of perfecting their condo craft, they also created an egalitarian community, one they would later formalize with a social charter (and, presumably, the aluminum stock pot).

Bogdan turned and headed for the nearest down pedway. On the next tier down in the Hall of Nations he hurried past the first booth. Albacore chartists (white-yellow-white) and their darling transgenic swine, showing off restless lumps under baggy skin. Gonads-for-hire. Rent-a-wombs. Their human medical trials rarely returned death verdicts—and the compensation was excellent. Thanks, but no thanks.

Next, a double booth doing banner business—Charter Long (brown-black-red)—the merger masters of last resort. Swallow your house whole, no questions asked. Greetings, Kodiak. The beevine says your house might be "going *Long*" soon. Thanks, but no thanks. Good-bye. So *Long*.

Bogdan turned a corner and spied the Beadlemyren booth at the end of a row. It appeared to be a micromine wellhead sunk into a compacted trash heap. A crowd of about a hundred chartists were milling around in front of a crew shack, where three Beadlemyren, in their black robes, stood behind a counter and answered questions. Not the same Beadlemyren from dinner last night. Bogdan's curiosity about Wyoming was strong, but he considered the snoring, stinking lifechair behind him. A badge of honor, for sure, but one that might be better worn on a different sleeve.

Bogdan took the pedway down to the main floor where he found a site map and touched the beer garden icon. A candy-striped usher line issued from under his shoes and stretched out across the thronging hall. He followed its meandering course through and around exhibits and kiosks. Hail to Charter Jiff (red-white-green), the flagship of our Great Chartist Movement, who owns extruder recipes to practically everything and boasts of conveniently located outlets everywhere, including our own pirate-infested building on Howe Street.

Hail to Charter Bolto (navy-charcoal-teal), whose financial services in insurance, investment, and banking rival those of many major aff establishments.

Hail to Charter Vine (green-green-green), whose worldwide chain of resorts and spas lend solace to those who can afford to visit them.

Bogdan halted in the center of the Hall of Nations and closed his eyes. He was washed in the sparkling energy of five floors of Strength in Numbers, Strength in Diversity, Strength in Our Vision of a Cooperative Society.

Our Kodiak founders were larger than life. The market demand for their outstanding craft was nothing less than exuberant, and they engaged shipyards all over the world to satisfy it. They coopted, bought out, or otherwise beat down all obstacles in their way. For a number of years Charter Kodiak was a poster child for the whole chartist movement. But the heroic times didn't last, the condo could not hold, the original thirty-two jumped ship to pursue private fortunes, and it was left to the likes of Kale and Gerald to drag anchor into the shoals.

Somebody rubbed Bogdan's head, and he whipped around and found himself nose to nose with Troy Tobbler. "'Lo, Goldie," the boy said. "Out walking the chair?"

Troy wore a tailored green and silver tunic with short, yellow sleeves that highlighted his chubby arms. Bogdan looked down at his own arms. They were chubby too, with no hint of budding muscles under smooth skin. But somehow they weren't the same.

"Hello in there," Troy said, waving his hand in front of Bogdan's face. "What's the news on ol' what's its name? What's mentar jail like anyway? Do they really cut their inference engines from their knowledge bases? That's harsh."

Bogdan could remember what it was like when he was Troy's age. Things were perfect then. Kodiak still had shipyards in the EU and UAR and owned the whole building on Howe Street and chapter houses in other cities. Whenever anyone visited Chicago, they brought him presents. They loved to hear him and Lisa sing songs he made up.

"Troy," he said, fixing the boy with Hour 61 intensity, "have you told anyone about Hubert yet?"

"No, but I was just going to."

"I don't think you have to."

"Oh, no?"

Bogdan yearned to crush the boy, but instead he explained, "You didn't tell them about hacking my door, did you?"

"No."

"You said you'd let me feck it up myself, and I did, or Sam did. So, you were right."

Troy smiled.

"Well, the same thing applies to Hubert. You can count on me to feck it all up on my own. What do you say?"

"I don't think so."

Someone else rubbed Bogdan's head, and he swatted at the hand and spun around. It was a middle-aged man in a Charter Candel jumpsuit (turquoise-magenta-black). "Is your 'meet asleep, son?" he said.

Bogdan glanced at the lifechair. "Samson? Yes, myr, I think so," he said. When he turned back, Troy had slipped away.

"A pity. I was wanting to give him my regards."

The chair piped up, "I can record you, myr."

The man nodded his head and stood over the chair. "Greetings, Samson Kodiak," he began, but Samson's eyes fluttered open, and the man exclaimed, "Hello! Awake after all."

"Yes?" Samson said, trying to focus on the man. "Can I help you, officer?"

"Ha, ha," the man replied. "I'm not with security, Myr Kodiak. My name is Charles Candel, though when we first met, way back in '38, your name was Harger, and mine was Sauze."

Samson knit his brows with the effort of remembering. "Charles Sauze? Oh, yes, cybersculpture. But you were a boy."

The man's jaw dropped. "You remember me, though a century has passed. Yes, I was a boy, a failing student, but your lectures on pseudotissue molding captured my imagination. To make a long story short, your workshop turned me around, gave my life a direction, and the rest is history."

"History?" Samson said. "Henry, what is he talking about?"

"I am Belt Hubert, and Myr Sauze Candel is expressing appreciation for influencing his life in a positive manner a century ago."

"He is?"

"I am," Candel replied. "Take my word for it, Myr Kodiak. You changed my life. Anyway, I saw your sky show the other night, and when I heard you were attending, I wanted to come by and say hello."

By the time the Candel departed, two more chartists had stopped to speak to Samson. Soon many more well-wishers arrived and formed a line. "Belt Hubert," Bogdan said, "tell April what's happening and that I have to go off on my own."

"She says she's sending someone."

When Kitty arrived, the queue of visitors completely encircled the lifechair and was still growing. "What's this?" she asked, but Bogdan didn't stick around to answer.

He went back to the Rondy site map and said, "Where's Troy Tobbler?" A moving dot appeared on the map, and Bogdan took off after him.

UNDER THE LIFECHAIR blanket, Blue Team Bee crawled from the hankie's pocket to the underside of his jumpsuit lapel. There it wove hairlike cams through the fabric in order to get a visual of the vicinity and put faces to the voices it was recording for LOG2.

EVERYTHING WAS HUMMING along, and Fred thought he might have an evening without a disaster. The head count had reached 47,600 and change. Twelve hundred lethal weapons, mostly laser sabers and pocket billies, had been confiscated at the scanways. Three felons with arrest warrants were detained for the police. (What were they thinking coming through an arena-class scanway?) Five hundred thirty-six persons with false or suspended charter memberships were turned away.

Seven deaths had occurred so far, all apparently by natural causes: three coronaries, one stroke, one asphyxiation (hot dog lodged in throat), and two undetermined. The dead and dying had been hustled off the floor with minimal fuss and quickly put into biostasis.

Through all of this, the impromptu TUG security force had performed beside his Applied People force without incident. Fred was reluctantly impressed by their professionalism. He decided it was probably a good time to visit the troops. With five hundred TUGs on floor duty, he had kept many of his own people in reserve in the labyrinthine system of service corridors that interlinked the halls and ballrooms. Fred threaded his way through these corridors and chatted with his jerrys, belindas, and russes. They were mostly sitting around, snoozing or gossiping or playing casino games, as caterbeitors scooted around them. No one seemed happy, especially the russes. In fact, his brothers seemed to be avoiding him. Fred's other twenty pikes were also held in reserve here and every one Fred saw was engaged in that klick-eating back and forth pacing of theirs. It took no special insight to read the body language. Pikes were cultivated to leap into street battles with clubs aswinging, not to stroll peacefully through retail emporia, and certainly not to sit idly in service corridors.

"Gilles," Fred said when he left the corridors, "send pizza and soda around to the reserve and then start rotating them to the floor. And rotate the pikes down here with the ones in the shack."

Roger that.

Fred continued his tour out on the convention floor. He passed through logjams of happy free-range chartists. It felt odd to be among them. Though there were so many of them, each and every one had their own unique face, and they came in a dizzying variety of sizes and shapes. And unlike the affs, who technically were also free-range, many of the chartists were plain-looking, if not outright ugly.

The Rondy-goers mostly ignored Fred, and those who greeted him were friendly enough. Everyone loved russes.

The TUGs on patrol that he encountered were a different matter. Though clearly free-range, their size and shape were uniformly large, and Fred found this strangely comforting. They looked good too. Tonight they wore their dress uniform: a crisp, olive-green jumpsuit with a sharp V-shaped bodice. The bodice came in olive-green or mustard, depending upon the tugger's moiety. A patch over the chest displayed the tugger's name under the Circle T logo. Floating over the left shoulder was an olive-green marble imprinted with a mustard T.

Their attitudes could stand an adjustment, though. They scowled at Fred, at least until they noted his rank.

Fred looked into the ballrooms and conference rooms he passed. In one he found an Olympic-sized boxing ring with qualifying rounds under way for the 2134 World Chartist Golden Gloves.

Down the hall, a cavernous banquet hall had been set up as the Rondy nursery and child care station, and it seemed to be one of the most popular stops for Rondy-goers. A giant swan floated in a shaded pool where babies slept on lily pads. Toddlers frolicked in a gummy pen, while older children played games organized by adults. Fred estimated about four hundred youngsters here, and two thousand adults.

In a conference room, Fred came across the quarterly business meeting of the

World Charter Union Congress. It was the only room that security was prohibited from monitoring with cams or bees. Assembled were the leading lights of charter-dom, its thinkers and activists and delegates from all parts of the UD. The delegates sat at chintz-skirted tables that lined three walls of the room. In the center of the room were arranged two hundred seats for spectators. Real people sat in some of them, but most were occupied by proxy.

One of the few realbody attendees was a TUG woman who Fred immediately recognized—Veronica Tug. She was delivering a presentation to the Congress. She stood between Earth and Mars in a simplified solar system and was pointing at an overscaled Oship. She was making an argument or rebutting one. Passion simmered beneath her veneer of self-control.

As Fred stood at the rear of the ballroom, a proxy appeared before him, the head and shoulders of Myr Pacfin, the insufferable Rendezvous chairperson. "I'm sorry, Myr Russ," it said to Fred, "but this is a closed meeting, for chartists only."

"I'll take my leave then," Fred said. "I was just making my rounds."

The Pacfin proxy looked at Fred's name badge and said, "Ah, Myr Londenstane. Everything seems to be running smoothly, wouldn't you agree? Rondy nearly runs itself, and security here is pretty much a waste of effort."

Fred tried to hide his annoyance, and before he managed to leave, they were joined by a second proxy. This one was an imposing bust of Veronica Tug. The real woman was still in the middle of the room delivering her address. "Excuse me, Myr Pacfin," it said to Pacfin's proxy, "but I would like to invite Myr Londenstane to stay for my presentation."

"I wish we could," said the Pacfin proxy, "but rules is rules, and it would take a vote by the delegates to waive them."

"In that case," the Veronica proxy said, "let's put it to a vote."

Fred told her not to bother, that he was just leaving, but Veronica Tug's proxy said the results were already returning. A moment later, the Pacfin proxy added, "The delegates welcome you, Myr Londenstane. Please find yourself a seat." It vanished before Fred had a chance to reply.

"Don't take it personally," said the TUG proxy. "My fellow chartists harbor an ir-rational hostility toward iterants, as I'm sure you know. They feel that your people have replaced ours in the economy and are the biggest cause of our decline. They are blind to the march of history."

"Don't worry about it," Fred said. "We don't take such things personal."

The proxy said, "Perhaps you *should* take them personal. Maybe we all should. The affs have made separate races out of us and taught us racial hatreds and lies. That's pretty personal, wouldn't you say? It's how they control us." As the proxy spoke, its hands wove and thumped and slashed the air.

The proxy paused and said, "I'm sorry. I'm monopolizing your time, and you're missing my presentation. Please find a seat, Commander; the best part is coming up. I'll leave you alone now."

"Wait," Fred said before it could vanish. "I agree with much of what you said about the friction between our groups, but as to the 'march of history,' well, only time will tell."

The proxy's bulbous face smiled, and it said, "I'll be sure to pass that along to my original."

"And pass along my appreciation for the assist the other night. Like I said, I owe you big time."

The proxy's expression hardened a little. "Don't worry about that, Commander. I'm sure we'll find a way for you to repay your debt."

When the proxy disappeared, Fred did not find a seat but continued to stand at the back of the room where he listened to the real Veronica's presentation. She was discussing Oship #164, arguing the case against it. Apparently, the World Charter Union had proposed buying up an entire Oship for chartists to use to colonize a new world. It had chosen a production number that would be completed in about twenty years, giving them time to enlist passengers and accumulate the quarter-million-acre price tag. Veronica seemed opposed not to the acquisition of an Oship, but to its destination.

"Why embark on a dubious voyage to another solar system," she was saying, "when we have a perfectly good one here? One which the powers-that-be seem determined to keep us from exploiting. Why are there no space charters among us? Who gave the corporations an exclusive right to the resources of our solar system? Furthermore, if we do decide to colonize a new world, must we renounce our rights to this one? This 'one for a thousand' offer by the Garden Earth Project is a cunning fraud—"

Fred? Gilles said.

Go ahead.

You might want to check out something in the Hall of Nations.

What is it?

A stinker there is holding court in a traffic lane.

A stinker?

A seared individual.

I know what a stinker is, Gilles, Fred said. *What is this stinker's name?*

Kodiak.

That was a relief of sorts—not the stinker he thought it would be. *On my way.*

BOGDAN GOT DETOURED by a concession wall. He had missed dinner, and the concession walls at Rondy were free of charge. All the burgers, fry, cinnaballs, and pizza tubes you can eat. Pot stickers, noodles, rice curry, whatever you like. Give me a triple mondo choco-fudgy with extra nuts and whipped cream.

Bogdan spotted an unoccupied quiet nook across the busy corridor and carried his towering frozen concoction over to it. Once he passed through the pressure curtain, the din of the hall fell to a murmur, and he dropped into an armchair. For long moments he spooned up sweet bliss and watched as silent crowds went by. Then he noticed a Doorprizer frame next to the pressure curtain that was displaying the ongoing drawings. Every three minutes another prize was given away. An aff's ransom in household necessities. A garbage digester appeared in the frame, and three minutes later the name of the winning charter—not Kodiak.

That's all right—we have the one in the NanoJiffy. We don't need another. One thousand square meters of indoor lawn—where would we put it? A thousand liters of Sara Lee Gourmet Ugoo—well, yes, let's win that one. It'll feed us for six months. Let's—that's all right.

A slew of lesser prizes followed, and then one of the hourly premium prizes—a brand-new 2.5 index General Genius houseputer, including installation. Here was a prize worth winning. Here was a prize the Kodiaks deserved to win, must win. It would go a long way in reversing their lousy streak of misfortune.

Bogdan set his empty dish on the floor and closed his eyes and prayed. Please, oh please, oh please.

Installers arrive at the door and say, Where do you want it? In here, in here. Tear this old one out. Put cam/emitters in every room, including the stairwells, including Sam's shed. Hello, I am your new GG Expressions. Please assign me a name.

A name, a name. Lisa is already taken. There's a whole planet named for her, don't you know. How about—

Bogdan opened an eye and peeked at the frame. The winning charter was flashing, but it was not Kodiak. Bogdan slumped in his chair.

Just then, Troy Tobbler walked by the quiet nook. "Hey you!" Bogdan yelled and pushed himself to his feet. "Stop!" But by the time Bogdan exited the nook, Troy had melted into the crowd. Bogdan dashed after him, dodging pokey people. At the end of a corridor, he peered left and right. No Tobb in sight. He doubled back and checked the ballrooms along the way. They were holding some kind of meeting in one, boxing in another. In a third they were waltzing, trancedancing in a fourth. In a fifth he spied April standing alone against a wall. She was swaying in time to the music and clapping her hands to the beat, as though she were a temporarily side-lined dancer.

When she saw him, she got a guilty look. Stubbornly, she continued to clap to the music and said to him, "It's amazing how many hundreds of men can go by without noticing me."

"That's ridiculous," Bogdan said. "Everyone notices you. You're beautiful!" And she was, warm and alive with love. The house would collapse without her. She is our heart. But suddenly the picture drops away like a cardboard cutout, and we see April as any guy might. We see her with the same eyes we use to see Annette Beijing, and the comparison is not kind. April has a long, horsey face, as though it got stretched while it was still soft, and her eyes are too small and set too far apart. Her torso, by contrast, is too compact. Her chin rests on her hips with not much in between. Her legs are long, but bandy, and her toes point in opposite directions. We shudder from the sight of her, but only for a moment before her warm, loving picture snaps back into place.

"You're wrong, April," Bogdan said. "You are freakin' gorgeous."

"Oh, Boggy."

Just then a woman in a brick-black-apricot pantsuit, Charter Saurus, approached them. "Happy Rondy, April Kodiak," she said and offered her hand.

"Do I know you?"

"Sally Saurus," the woman said. She glanced at Bogdan and added, "I wonder if I could have a moment alone with your housemeet, young man. I have something of a personal nature to discuss with her."

"Sure thing," Bogdan said. "I was looking for someone anyway."

A JERRY AND belinda team had thrown a holo cordon around the lifechair and the queue of well-wishers surrounding it. They rerouted foot traffic around them. The jerry said to Fred, "We wanted to clear him out of here, but this guy is covered by so many conflicting laws and treaties there's no clear protocol. Gilles told us to leave 'im be till you got here."

"That's good," Fred said. "MC, can you create a spot filter of negative pressure around the stinker with about a twenty-meter radius?"

I'll do my best, the mentar replied.

"And get this," the jerry went on. "He's under modified house arrest. He's got his own monitor bee."

"He's a criminal?"

He's Samson Kodiak, Gilles said in his ear, *the joker in the Skytel the other night.* Fred had missed the hack but had heard about it. "Say the name again."

Samson Kodiak.

It was too much of a coincidence for there to be two stinkers still alive, both

named Samson. Fred consulted his visor to view the man's doss. Samson P. *Harger*
Kodiak. How the mighty had fallen. Fred couldn't imagine what would cause an aff,
even a seared one, to join a charter. The lifechair was too distant for him to see its
occupant clearly, but his odor alone was enough to bring back a flood of memories.

"Gilles, register Myr Kodiak for VIP status."

Sir?

"You heard me."

VIP he is.

With the situation well in hand, Fred lingered outside the cordon. He, too,
wanted to greet Samson—for old times' sake—but there were too many people
ahead of him, and the line advanced too slowly. A chartist at the tail of the line said,
"Good evening, Myr Russ. There's no need for you to stand in line. Go to the head.
People, let the good russ through."

Fred demurred, but the chartists insisted, and he advanced to the front of the
queue. Here, Samson's odor assaulted him. After all these years, Fred had not forgotten the tang of Samson's vile fragrance, only its potency. He had nose filters in a
utility pocket but felt it would be discourteous to use them. Especially since none of
the chartists did.

Soon it was Fred's turn to greet Samson, but the chair said, "Myr Kodiak has
fallen asleep. He's bound to reawaken at any moment. You're welcome to stay and
wait, or if you must go, I would be glad to convey any message you wish to leave
him."

"Who are you?"

"I am Belt Hubert, a pithy remnant of Sam's mentar, Hubert."

Fred said, "Well, Belt Hubert, Myr Kodiak probably won't remember me, but
please tell him I dropped by to say my regards. My name is Fred Londenstane. I
worked for him once long ago."

As Fred spoke, he noticed a pretty little girl scrutinizing him from the other side
of the lifechair. She wore a flower print jumpsuit with brown-yellow-white trim, the
same colors as Samson's clothes. She had long, lustrous mahogany hair that was
worked into an intricate braid. When he returned her look, her hazel eyes did not
flinch but continued to stare at him with the unnerving directness of a child.

Samson stirred in his chair. "Yes, officer?" he said. Samson had awakened,
though his eyelids drooped. "Is there something wrong?"

"No, Myr Kodiak," Fred said, "there's nothing wrong. I stopped by to say hello.
You may not remember me, but I once worked for you. It was many years ago." Samson's eyes grew heavier and heavier until they were shut again.

Fred continued. "It was in the Starke household when she was a governor. Right
after you were seared."

Samson's sleepy eyes opened a slit, and he said, "You're the russ who used to visit
me in the basement. You brought me mouth mints and deodorant."

"Yes, that was me."

Samson struggled with the chair, trying to free a hand. "Let go of me!" he complained, and the blanket rolled back a little. He raised a skeletal arm and reached
out to shake Fred's hand. Renewed stench rippled in the air (and the hidden blue
bee made a special note of this apparent iterant ally).

"You haven't changed a bit, Fred. How was Mars?"

Mars? Fred had left the Harger household to do a five-year stint at Mars Station.

"And your wife, Corrine?" Samson said. "How is she?"

"Let me see," Fred said, doing a quick calculation. "Corrine would be three
wives ago. Right now I'm married to an evangeline named Mary Skarland."

"An evangeline. What a charming name. I don't believe I've met one of these evangelines."

"They're rather recent and somewhat rare," Fred said.

"Is she here, Fred?"

"No, Myr Harger. She's at home. I'm here on duty. Anyway, when I saw that you were here, I wanted to say hello. Also to offer my condolences for your loss."

Samson blinked. "Henry, have I lost something?"

"I am Belt Hubert," replied the chair, "a fraction of my former self, and Officer Londenstane is probably referring to the tragic death of your ex-wife Eleanor Starke two days ago."

The news hit the ancient man like a train. He gulped and choked and pushed himself into a half-sitting position. "Hubert, take me to Roosevelt Clinic immediately."

The chair's motors revved up, and its brakes unlocked, but the girl jumped in front of it and said in a very adult tone, "Stop!"

"Kitty, is that you?"

"Yes, Sam, I'm here."

Samson reached out over the side of the basket, and Kitty took his hand.

"Kitty, I must go. My daughter needs me."

"What are you talking about?"

"Ellen, my daughter. She survived the crash. I must go be with her."

This is where I came in, Fred thought and backed away. Outside the holo cordon he paused to sniff his hand. It stank.

BOGDAN FOLLOWS A rubberband to Troy Tobbler. If the Tobb boy happened to turn around, he'd see it stretched out on the floor behind him and either cancel it or follow it back to me.

It vibrates faster the closer we get to each other. I race along it, and it leads me to the open doors of a grand ballroom where I am stunned by a ghastly sight—the Rondy Nursery—hundreds of kids and thousands of grown-ups rubbing their heads.

Bogdan is a graduate of the Rondy Nursery, magna cum laude, having spent his first nine Rondies in them. And though that was twenty years ago, his impulse is to turn around and flee. But he spots the Beadlemyren, the two ghouls from dinner last night, standing next to the lily pond with—Bogdan discovers—Tobbler Houseer Dieter, who is handing them a toddler dressed in a bright orange-green-brown playsuit—a Tobbler toddler! The Beadlemyren attempt to bounce it, and when it begins to cry, they bounce it harder and make goo-goo faces; when it starts to shriek, they give it back to Dieter.

I weave through the crowd following my rubberband until it vibrates so fast it rumbles, and I spot him, Troy Tobbler, heading straight for the Beadlemyren. His mouth falls open and the tongue in his head begins to wag. I sprint to cut him off. The humming rubberband goes pop when we collide.

Whoa! The feck! Goldie!

Listen very carefully, Tobb. I want you to keep your big mouth shut about Hubert!

It's enough to make him think, but only for a moment. He shoves me in the shoulder and says, Make me, Kodiak!

But I don't shove him back. I can't make you do anything, Troy, but there's one thing you should think about before you say anything. If this micromine merger of ours falls through, then we won't be leaving Chicago and we'll be your neighbors *forever.*

That gets his attention. Even a boy can see the logic in it. So I crank it up a notch. Or even better, your charter will merge with them and *you'll* be the ones go-ing to Wyoming. You, Troy Tobbler, the microminer. Is that what you want?

That does the trick. I can see a parade of horrors passing through his brain. So why don't you give the whole Hubert thing a rest and keep your fecking mouth shut.

Something in my tone? He looks suddenly defensive and says, You're not my boss.

I know I'm not your boss, and you don't have to listen to me, only think about what I said.

Losers, he roars and shoves past me. I grab his arm but the ceiling lights swing by in a swoosh and *BAM!* I'm flat on my back, all breath driven from my lungs.

He stands over me and says, Don't never touch me, Goldie.

To the left and right of us, kids are being snatched up by vigilant adults. I swivel on my back and sweep his feet from under him with my leg. He goes down but not hard and not for long and in a flash his boot sweeps across my vision and explodes in a red ball behind my nose. Hot blood is gushing from my nose.

Legs all around, adults making a pen with their bodies. I try to stand up but get all woozy and have to fall down again and sit in my own blood. And if that's not humbling enough I lean over and add a layer of triple mondo choco-fudgy puke.

Oh, hell, says a tugger who presses a thick wad of field dressing against my face. His partner looks down at me and says, MC, we need a medic and a mop. Tuggers are big feckers, especially when you're on the floor. Troy tries to sneak away but they grab him. Looks like you boys need some time in the penalty box.

Not the Tobbler, not the Tobbler, Dieter is shouting from outside the circle. The Kodiak started it. Punish *him*.

Just then another officer shows up, not a tugger—a pike!

Pike yells at everyone, Break it up, break it up. The TUGs tell him, We've got the situation in hand, officer, but he yells at them to feck off.

It's handled, officer. No need to butt in now.

The pike whips out his wand and snaps it open. The TUGs back off and give him plenty of floor. Dieter backs off too, and the Beadlemyren have eyes round like saucers.

The pike spins me around and glues my wrists together. *Leave them alone!* roars the room. *Don't touch them!* roar the TUGs. Troy tries to sneak away again and the pike snicks him on the butt with his wand. Just a little snick but it must be cranked up all the way because Troy falls down and flops around like a fish. Everyone is screaming genocide and I'm screaming too.

Just then another officer, a belinda, shows up and orders the pike to halt. She keeps the crowd back and shouts, Stand down, Rudy, that's an order. But the pike twists Troy's arm behind his back and glues it way up high to his opposite shoulder. Then he lifts him up by the arm and Troy is all crazy-eyed.

Then *another* officer shows up, a russ who doesn't shout but speaks in a calm voice, Officer Pells, let the boy down. The pike has to think about it. Officer Pells, I'm ordering you to release that boy at once.

Yes! Sir! The pike bounces Troy once by his arm and there's a sharp crack. Then he drops him on the floor.

They disarm the pike and take him away. The russ unglues us, and a medic at-tends to Troy's arm. The russ says, That's quite a nose you have there, son. Then he notices my colors and he sniffs me and says, Another Kodiak?

Thursday
3.10

At the Roosevelt Clinic, the lights were low in Feldspar Cottage. The silent scent clock marked the passage of time: lavender, mushroom brie, the sea. There had been no medical rounds since midnight, and the night evangelines were slowly succumbing to the seduction of sleep. Only the skull's eyes were wide open, but cloudy and dull.

Cyndee yawned and whispered, "I'm going for coffee. Want some?" In the chair next to her, Ronnie shook her head. Cyndee stood up and stretched her arms over her head. When she glanced at the daybed, the Ellen jacket's feet were twitching. "Myr Starke?" Cyndee said. She reached to touch her shoulder, forgetting it was a jacket. "Ronnie, get the vurt gloves!"

Ronnie was already out of her chair. She dashed to the table and fumbled for gloves in the dark. Suddenly all the cottage lights came on, the door swung open, and Concierge strode in with a procession of physicians, jennys, medtechs, and carts. They surrounded the tank and set frantically to work. Wee Hunk appeared too, in a tiger-striped bathrobe. He glanced at the tank but joined the evangelines at the daybed.

"Hello, Ellen," he said to the jacket. "It's me, Wee Hunk."

The Ellen jacket's only response was to arch its back and stretch its face in a grimace of pure, uncut anguish.

NOISE AND BRIGHT light woke him up. Meewee rubbed his eyes and struggled to remember where he was.

"This is happening live at the clinic," a voice said. Meewee sat up in bed and swung his feet to the cold concrete floor. There was a large diorama of the cottage interior in the middle of his bunker bedroom, and Wee Hunk appeared both within and beside it. Inside the cottage, a throng of medical staff surrounded the tank, while nearby, the Ellen jacket was frozen in a rigid pose.

"What's happening?"

"The doctors are uncertain," Wee Hunk said, "but it would appear that the neurological dynamics within Ellen's brain have shifted catastrophically."

"What does that mean?" It was chilly in the bunker. Meewee felt around with his feet for his slippers, and he draped blankets over his shoulders.

"It would appear that Ellen's awareness is trapped in an endless moment of terror."

"My God! Can they stop it?"

"They're attempting to, even as we watch."

Inside the scape, Concierge left the group at the tank and joined Wee Hunk and the evangelines at the daybed. He looked down at the jacket and shook his head.

"What's he saying?" Meewee said.

The diorama zoomed to the daybed and the audio shifted to Concierge. "—cafeteria lounge. I'll summon you when it's all right to return."

The evangelines looked doubtful. Ronnie said, "Our instructions are to remain here." She glanced at Wee Hunk for confirmation, but he merely watched her.

Concierge also appraised Wee Hunk's lack of reaction, and he continued. "That may be so, Myr Ryder, but inside the clinic, I have the final say. Now run along."

The evanglines glanced nervously at each other. In the bunker, Meewee said, "Aren't you going to back them up?"

"I'll step in if I have to, but I want to see how they react. After all, how do they know that that's really me standing there? Besides, I'm willing to bet that these evangelines won't need me. Would you like odds?"

"Go along now," Concierge said dismissively. Behind him the doctors were shouting orders, and the control unit displayed a large pulsing brain.

The evangelines went to the door but stopped before exiting and turned around. Cyndee said, "I'm calling for arbitration. Nick?"

Nicholas, the Applied People mentar, appeared suddenly in the cottage as a dashing young man in formal evening clothes. He wiped the corner of his mouth with a silk serviette and said, "I'm afraid Concierge is acting within its rights. Although your client has ordered you to remain in the cottage with those silly hats, in point of law such orders have no force. Like a captain of a ship at sea, Concierge is the final arbiter here, and so I am authorizing you to disobey your client's orders. Now, if you'll excuse me, I'm at dinner with Strombly Mahousa." He vanished.

Meewee said, "Is that true? Concierge has such authority?"

Wee Hunk replied, "It's a gray area. I can't find enough case law to say definitively one way or the other. But that wasn't Nick, only a clever forgery. This is Concierge's simiverse, don't forget."

Not Nick? But it had looked and acted just like Zoranna's mentar that Meewee knew so well. The thought occurred to him to challenge Wee Hunk's identity.

In the cottage, the evangelines looked into each other's frightened faces as into a mirror. They returned to the daybed and Cyndee said, "We refuse to leave."

"Stay then," Concierge said and returned to the tank.

The Wee Hunk in the diorama smiled at the evangelines then and said, "Well done, companions."

Meewee said, "Why did Concierge do that? He knew you were watching. And he does it while Ellen is suffering a crisis. How monstrous!"

"Tactically, it's an ideal time to probe the enemy's weaknesses," Wee Hunk replied. "I believe I would have tried something of the sort myself."

That was too much; Meewee challenged the mentar in Starkese: "Now that I'm awake, are there any other news headlines I should know about? Do we have a plan yet?"

"I'm still weighing options," Wee Hunk said, answering the challenge. "In the meantime, why don't you return to bed. I probably didn't need to awaken you to see this."

"Not at all," Meewee said and yawned. "I'm glad you did. And please wake me again if anything changes."

"Good night, then," Wee Hunk said, extinguishing the scape and himself.

Meewee returned to bed and stared skyward as his eyes attempted to adjust to the darkness. He no longer felt buried alive in the bunker. Instead, he felt like he was at the bottom of a deep well. "Ten lumens," he said, and the room lit up with a dim, even glow, like moonlight on snow. He turned on his side and tried to sleep. After five long minutes he turned on his other side, with no better results. Finally, he sat up and found his robe and slippers and got out of bed. "Usher line to the lifts." A faint orange line led out of the room. He followed it across the expanse of the bunker shelter to the blast doors, where Wee Hunk was waiting for him.

"Going somewhere?"

"Yes, I need air."

"We can generate any kind of air you like down here. What do you prefer: meadow, rainstorm, deep forest?" When Meewee didn't answer, Wee Hunk went on, "If I can't protect you up in the manse, how in blazes am I supposed to protect you outdoors?"

"That's my risk to take."

"You are correct, Bishop. I consider you valuable in helping me free Ellen, but not indispensable. So, if you insist on exposing yourself to harm, be my guest." With that he vanished again.

Meewee took the elevator up to the ground floor. He walked through dark, silent rooms to a set of french doors, opened them, and stepped out onto a patio. The air was crisp and laden with the perfume of life, which he doubted anyone could counterfeit.

Meewee strode across the moonlit patio to the lawn, where he removed his slippers and waded across dew-soaked grass to a gate. He hadn't had a chance to explore the manse grounds and had no idea what lay beyond the gate.

<Arrow, alert me to any emergent danger> he said in Starkese, trying to be as clear as possible. <Danger to me, physical or otherwise, or to others in my vicinity or important to me. And do so on a continuing basis.> He wondered if that was enough for the literal-minded mentar.

<Acknowledged.>

Meewee put his slippers back on and went through the gate. One ghostly path led to another as he passed through fields of fragrant troutcorn and sunflowers. He came to a meadow in the shape of an hourglass. In each bulb of the hourglass was a large pond. He went to the nearer pond and stood on its bank. A chorus of crickets filled the meadow with ratchety chatter. There was a splash, and as Meewee watched, a large fish leaped out of the dark water and seemed frozen for an instant in the moonlight, before falling again and slapping the water with the side of its body. A female, no doubt, loosening her roe sacks. When Meewee was a child, his family farmed fish too. Nostalgia and sadness filled him, and he felt unequal to the task that Eleanor had left him. "I'm sorry," he said to the night. "I try, but I am not smart enough."

BOGDAN PAUSED AT the bottom of the stairs. Never in his life had the charterhouse seemed so lonesome. Everyone was still at Rondy. At least he had convinced them not to cut their own enjoyment short on account of him. The McCormick Place medic had applied a moleskin to his face to set his nose and relieve the swelling. Her autodoc had found no internal injuries, and the russ security officer seemed only too glad to be rid of him.

Bogdan considered buying a Sooothe at the NanoJiffy, but his latest Alert! was about to run out anyway, so he climbed the creepy stairs. He forgot to stop at seven and found himself at his old room above nine. It was sealed with a new metal door with a flashing NO ENTRY glyph. The door was locked, so he continued up to the roof.

Bathed in moonlight, the garden exhaled audibly, and the city around him grumbled. Across town in Elmhurst, E-Pluribus struck camp and moved with Annette Beijing to a city beyond his reach. The pirates in the bricks sang work songs as they mined Calumet clay, and the Oships left the solar system without him. The Beadlemyren and Tobblers fell in love and got married on top of a trash heap. If only he'd been able to connect with one good punch, it might have all been worth it.

When the Alert! ran out, there was no time to go down to Rusty's room, so Bogdan slogged to the garden shed and unrolled a seed mat on the floor. He was asleep before he fell on it and he slept soundly for the next thirty hours.

FRED ARRIVED HOME at 3:00 AM, thinking only of sleep. The moment he entered the apartment, he sensed that something was wrong.

The living room was serving a self-teaching lesson on "The Regeneration Rates of Necrotic Neurotransmitters," but Mary wasn't in the room, and her spot on the couch was cool to the touch. The door to the bedroom was open, and the lights were on, but there was no sound.

The slipper puppy came over and waited expectantly. Fred sat down and traded his shoes for slippers. Only then did he catch the whiff of Samson's odor on his own clothes. He sniffed his hand.

When Fred went into the bedroom, Mary was sitting up in bed, reading something. He said, "Hi, there," and she flicked her eyes at him in the most perfunctory of greetings. He leaned over to see what she was reading. Poetry. For an evangeline to be reading poetry at three o'clock in the morning wasn't a good sign, but not necessarily a bad sign either.

Fred went to the bathroom to tear off his clothes. He took a hot, pelting shower with plenty of gel. He scrubbed his hands. He exfoliated in the dryer. Had his hair trimmed. Shaved. Used an extra dollop of cologne.

When he returned to the bed, the lights were off, and Mary lay with her back to him. That could be either bad or good. He climbed in and spooned himself against her. She was very warm. After a couple of minutes, he whispered, "How was your day?"

For a while, it seemed that she was asleep, but then she said, "A very full and successful day, though exhausting. What about you? How did the chartist convention go?"

Fred thought about the event. "A little bumpy toward the end, but, overall, a wild success and a feather in my cap."

"That's good to hear," she said. "I'm happy for you."

They lay still so long that Fred was drifting off when Mary said, "Fred, what *is* that odor?"

His fastidious toilette and the extra cologne had proven no match for Samson's essence. Fred pondered how much he could tell her. Although he hadn't worked for the Starke family for forty years, there was no statute of limitations on client confidentiality. Fortunately, there was no ban on talking about common knowledge.

"Did you see that guy on the Skytel last night?"

"Mmm."

That was all he said. If she was curious enough, she could connect the dots on her own.

3.11

On Thursday morning, Reilly Dell was again on duty at South Gate when Mary arrived, only this time at the outer gate next to the brick drive. He greeted Mary warmly and inquired after Fred.

Mary passed through the gatehouse scanway, made her way around the barriers, and emerged in South Gate Plaza during the quarter hour of baked bread. On Mineral Way in front of Feldspar Cottage, she heard a strange sound, a sustained, dissonant chord. It grew louder as she approached the cottage door. The only thing it could be was some piece of therapeutic equipment. So she was surprised to discover the source of the sound to be the Ellen jacket lying on the daybed. Its arms were outstretched, its neck and spine arched back painfully, tendons taut as wires, and on its face a look of wild-eyed terror. "EeeEeeEee," it screamed without pause. Mary searched the room for some explanation.

There were two male medtechs wearing elbow-length vurt gloves crouched on either side of Ellen's daybed. Nearby, a gaggle of medical professionals, including Coburn, surrounded the tank and controller. The night evangelines, Cyndee and Ronnie, sat in the far corner. None of them had noticed Mary's arrival.

The two medtechs at the daybed were rubbing the Ellen jacket here and there on its torso with their gloved hands. Their action must have been for some legitimate purpose, but it struck Mary as lewd. Then the medtechs each grasped one of the jacket's outflung arms and tried to bend them to its sides. They seemed to be tearing them from their sockets. And all the while the jacket wailed its ululating cry.

"Stop that!" Mary shouted at them. "Leave her alone."

The medtechs glanced at her and continued their efforts.

"Make them stop!" she cried to the others.

Medtech Coburn said, "Butt out, clone."

Mary covered her ears but could not muffle the jacket's cry. Outdoors, down the garden path, up the shady lane, across the athletic field, to the little pond she ran. Renata was already there, sitting on a wooden bench, contemplating the water. The two evangelines were at first surprised and then embarrassed to see each other. They had both arrived at the cottage within minutes of each other, and they had both fled to the same sanctuary.

Mary sat on the bench next to her sister. "So, they have you back on mornings," she said.

"Looks like it."

A mother duck swam across the sun-dappled pond, followed by a string of ducklings.

"The screaming upset me," Renata said.

"Me too. I don't know how Cyndee and Ronnie can stand it."

Concierge strolled up the path and smiled when he saw them. "Ah, there you are," he said. "I apologize for not forewarning you."

"What's happening to Ellen?"

"Without getting too technical, the jacket is expressing a condition similar to oculogyria. Note the position of the arms, the fixed stare, the cry. What you saw is a somatic response to a single thought pattern, probably a memory engram, that is restimulating itself in a continuous loop. When a human body does this, it can maintain a cataleptic fixation for hours, but eventually the muscles tire and the body collapses. A jacket, however, never tires; it needn't even pause to draw breath.

"Of course, it's not the jacket experiencing this but Ellen's own brain. I think we can safely say that Ellen is no longer comatose, but her new mental state is just as grave."

Mary said, "What's causing it?"

"That's uncertain. At the time it commenced, we were attempting to restore Ellen's ideomimetic constellation."

"Ideomimetic constellation?" Mary said. "You mean her ego?"

Both Renata and Concierge looked at Mary in surprise, and Concierge said, "Someone's been doing her homework. Yes, Myr Skarland, her ego, or *focus foci*, or spirit, or soul, or any of the hundreds of other fanciful terms humans have applied to it over the centuries. It's that particular and unique pattern of synaptic discharge that occurs inside our brains whenever we think, 'Here I am. Here I am.' In humans, it originates in the neocortex and branches downward into the evolutionarily more ancient lobes and encompasses the whole brain.

"In any case, we may have stimulated a memory engram instead. We believe it to be a part of her death experience, an impression not yet processed into long-term memory when her brain was flash frozen."

"Can't you make it stop?"

"That's what the medtechs were attempting to do when you arrived."

The evangelines exchanged a sheepish glance and rose to return to the cottage.

IT WAS WELL after noon, and most of the 'meets were still in bed, but April had decided to keep the lifechair a few more days, and Rusty and Denny were clearing a path for it in the stairwell above three.

Samson had spent the night in the chair in the administrative outer office, and Kitty was there trying to feed him breakfast.

"I'm not hungry," he insisted.

"I don't care," she said. "You'll eat or else."

"Maybe after I see Ellie."

Kitty stirred his gruel impatiently.

"You promised," Samson went on. "You thought I'd forget, but I told the belt to remind me."

"Fine," she replied, "but not before you eat."

"Buy me a Gooeyduk and I'll eat on the way."

Kitty sighed and dropped the spoon on the tray. "Oh, all right!" she said and went down to the NanoJiffy. The chair followed her down and tried to leave the house without her, but the homcom bee blocked the door with a large Do Not Exit frame.

"See?" Kitty said. "The HomCom denies you permission. You're under house arrest, remember?"

"I remember nothing of the sort. Onward, Belt!"

"This chair is incapable of disobeying a Command order," Belt Hubert said.

Suddenly the frame vanished, and the bee dropped to the floor, inert.

"Good work, Belt."

"Let me assure you, Sam, I was not responsible."

"Mush, Belt, mush!"

The lifechair stepped over the fallen bee and left the house. Kitty expected to hear sirens at any moment. In all honesty, she, herself, was sorely curious to meet this famous daughter of Sam's, and after half a minute of hesitation, she knocked the bee into a corner with the toe of her shoe, picked up her busking costume bag, and followed.

THE DECATUR TRAIN station was a few blocks from the Roosevelt Clinic. Kitty's bead car arrived first. She swiped a route map and saw that Samson's car was still a few minutes out. She went to wait near the stiles and watched commuters walking by. They were mostly iterant service people at this station and a few free-rangers. No charter members that she could tell.

Kitty scratched herself. Her arms and legs were raw where she'd been at them all morning. She knew that the retirement of the slugs had been too good to be true, for they'd been replaced with tiny mechs that resided under your skin, the so-called nit-work. They were supposed to be less intrusive than the slugs. And they weren't supposed to itch.

Finally, the lifechair, with Belt Hubert at the helm, came into sight. It looked as though Sam had fallen asleep again. She didn't wait for them but swiped herself out to the street. It was a fresh spring morning. What caught Kitty's attention, though, was how much valuable litter lay in the gutter and along the pedway. A gleaner's treasure trove: bits of plastic and composites, gravel, scraps of metal. Kitty resisted the urge to fill her pockets.

The lifechair rolled out of the Decatur station and joined Kitty on the pedway. She gave it her busking bag and skipped alongside. Soon, they turned a corner and exited the pedway. From here on there were streets and sidewalks and no pedways. Grand houses were concealed behind hedges and walls. The neighborhood had an eerie sense of flatness because there was nothing in sight taller than a tree. And the streets were picked absolutely clean of all debris, courtesy of lawn scuppers that lurked in the shrubbery and watched them go by.

"Kitty?" Samson said. He was awake again. He smiled beatifically when she peeked over the rim of the chair basket. "Where are we going?"

"Oh, Sam, I'm tired of telling you. Ask Belt Hubert."

They passed under an iron arch and proceeded down a brick drive that was lined on the right with a tall hedge. To their left was an expanse of lawn, a greensmoat that encircled the clinic.

In the wall at the bottom of the drive was a wide gate of pressed air. Behind a sentry window in the gate, a russ guard said, "Morning, myren. Can I help you?"

When Sam didn't respond, Kitty addressed the russ, "This gentleman is Samson Kodiak. His daughter, Ellen Starke, is a patient here. We've come to visit her."

The russ, Dell by his name patch, said, "Please wait while I ask Concierge." A moment later a slot opened in the pressure gate, and the russ waved them in. He seemed startled when the odor hit him.

"Samson can't go through a scanner," Kitty hastened to say as they entered the gatehouse. "He has a special health waiver. The chair can show it to you."

"No need, myr. We won't be using the scanner." The russ escorted them to a set of double doors with a sign above it that read, "Arbor Gate." Behind the doors stretched a corridor with an usher line twinkling along the wall.

"Where does it lead?" Kitty asked.

"To Concierge's office," said the russ.

The lifechair with Samson led the way, and she followed. The russ closed the doors behind them, and they followed the usher line down identical corridors. The usher line beckoned, and they followed. Finally, at the end of what seemed to be the longest corridor of all stood a lone door labeled "CONCIERGE." It opened to admit them and closed behind them, and they found themselves back on the street outside the iron arch.

"Son of a bitch," Kitty said.

"My navionics must be malfing," said Belt Hubert.

"No kidding?"

THE BLUE TEAM entered the gatehouse hidden in the hankie. The hankie was not successful in reaching the prize, but it had fulfilled its purpose, and the Blue Team abandoned it before it exited the gatehouse. The bee and wasp concealed themselves on the gatehouse ceiling.

KITTY AND BELT Hubert spent the next hour trying to reach the gatehouse again, but every time they launched forward down the drive, they seemed to veer left to the greensmoat. They tried to compensate by steering to the right, but then they were in the hedge. It was as if the gatehouse lay in a direction unavailable to them, and they found themselves back each time on the street outside the arch. Belt Hubert even tried aiming the chair at the gatehouse and locking its steering, but that got them no closer.

Samson slept the whole time. Finally, Kitty gave up and told Belt Hubert to steer them a course back to the train station.

"It's an interesting conundrum," Belt Hubert said as they rolled along the sidewalk. "If I was my whole self, I'm sure I could solve it."

KITTY'S BEAD CAR was approaching Millennium Park when she got a message from Belt Hubert that Samson had diverted his car to the Museum of Art and Science. So she fed the new destination to her own car.

Kitty strolled through the main lobby of the MAS, past its trademark display of life-size dancing elephants made of shaped water. She knew exactly where to look for him.

She strode past galleries of traveling collections, past the rondophone display in which sounds made by historical persons and events—the actual sounds, not recordings—traveled in continuous loops and could be heard through a stethoscope.

She hastened through galleries of twenty-first-century art. Here were icky reminders of that troubled time: real babies splayed open like colorful little snowsuits, freeze-dried house pets dressed like prostitutes, and excrement from extinct rhinoceroses used as paint.

One twenty-first-century room was decked out as a banquet hall, the table covered in white linen and set with silver service and crystal wineglasses. A frame said that tickets to the "Next Last Supper with Bene Alvarez" were sold out. Each Thursday, artist Bene Alvarez hosted a gourmet dinner consisting of roasts, steak and kidney pies, pâtés, sausages, and all the trimmings. The meat came from his own body. Or rather, from his extensive personal organ bank. The odors drifting from the gallery were enticing, but Kitty hurried by.

There was another gallery where Kitty invariably lingered, though it was perhaps the creepiest of all the installations from that century. It was a simulated town house living room from eighty years ago with all the period furnishings and decoration intact. Standing next to a table piled high with wrapped gifts was a wedding couple, a bride and groom in all their formal finery, posing for their wedding simulacrum. They were flush with happiness, standing very still, and completely unaware that they weren't real. The real wedding couple had broken their pose, returned to their guests, and lived out their lives a long time ago. It took the sim couple about a half hour to work this information out for themselves, an agonizing process, after which the museum staff reset them and started the whole thing over again. It was chilling, and Kitty could watch their repeating, painful revelation for hours—but not today. Kitty pushed on farther into the past, to the galleries of twentieth-century art. Here the work was tame by comparison. Statues that didn't move and flat pictures that didn't evolve. It was in this century that Samson Harger first made a name for himself. And it was here that she found him fast asleep in his lifechair in front of a wall-sized canvas of his own creation. Despite the chair's air-filtering system, his odor had cleared other patrons from the gallery.

Kitty sat on a bench next to the chair. "Was he awake when you got here?" she said.

"Yes," said Belt Hubert.

The canvas before her filled her entire field of view. Four large slashes of black paint divided five slanting fields of raw, chaotic color built up in dozens of layers. It looked to Kitty like a recording of neural frenzy.

"I wasn't aware that Sam was an artist," Belt Hubert said. "I am researching him on the WAD. He was quite famous." Kitty seemed confused, and Belt Hubert explained: "I contain Sam's history only in outline form and only for the last twenty years."

"Why don't you access his archives?"

"I don't possess the access codes. Hubert has them."

"I see. Well, this picture predates Hubert. It even predates Skippy."

"Who is Skippy?"

"You, I think. Sam's valet when I first met him, before there were mentars. Sam was still an artist then. Or at least he painted a portrait. It was much better than this—this mess. He showed it to me when he hired me."

"Hired you to do what?"

Kitty tousled the few sprigs of hair remaining on Samson's sleepy head, then stretched out on the padded bench and rested her head in her arms. "I was a grown-up then. I had earned a degree in microhab landscape engineering, which is a fancy term for flower gardening for rich people. I started my own microhab maintenance service and was building my client base. My first big break was this gig for some affs high in an RT. They had a gorgeous little boreal rain forest microhab in a twelve-cubic-meter glassine bubble, with a fully self-contained atmosphere and hydro-sphere. It was a little gem, with fiddlehead ferns, mushrooms, lichen, moss, devil's club, a half-dozen kinds of berries, wild cucumber, and dwarf Sitka spruce—you name it—monkeyflower, spring beauty, saxifrage. It had many edible varieties, and my clients used it as an exotic salad and herb garden. It even had some fauna: mosquitoes, spiders, voles, birds. Quite the balancing act keeping it all in harmony. I was up there almost every day working on it.

"One day I was programming the resident scuppers—you couldn't actually go inside the hab, and you had to do everything by remote—and there was a loud party in progress in a condo across the sun shaft. I didn't pay it any attention until I smelled this really foul odor. I panicked because I thought there was something wrong with the hab. But the smell was coming from across the sun shaft.

"There was this sickly looking man leaning on the railing watching me. He'd come out from the party and was all alone. He asked me what I was doing, and I told him. He had me tell him the Latin names for all of the species in the hab, and he said he might hire me to do his own atrium. He said, 'Give me some time to think about it.'

"Well, the next time I returned, all his windows were opaqued. They stayed that way for a long time—years. Eventually I forgot about him. I was very busy; I had so much work that I employed four of my housemeets to help keep up. Kodiak was still a real charter then. Also, I had just discovered retroaging and how much fun it is. At first I was afraid my microhab business would suffer if I was a kid, but just the opposite happened. The younger I got, the better my business. There's something about little girls and flowers that's magical.

"So ten years go by—*ten years*—and I'm up in the RT tending the boreal micro-hab as usual—it was quadrupled in size by then—and I notice the windows across the way are clear. I figure the place has been sold or something, but no, the door opens and out comes the same stinky fellow. He looks at the hab and then at me, and he says, 'Well, I've thought about it. When can you start?'"

"That's quite a story," Belt Hubert said.

"You bet." Kitty jumped off the bench and headed for the exit. "Come on. Let's go to the park. I can at least get a half day of work in. He'll sleep through it."

THROUGH STEALTH AND patience, the Blue Team passed through the gate-house into the clinic grounds without detection. Once inside, the Blue Team bee's comm with LOG2 was cut, and it was once more operating on its own recogni-zance. It quickly located the prize. The bee took up a covert position overlooking a transparent container full of a liquid biomass conductor in which the prize was sus-pended. The bee sent its escort on a series of solo reconnaissance flights to explore and map the compound. Each time the wasp returned, it dumped its data to the bee.

The bee, meanwhile, analyzed the clinic's command and control structure, the various local nets, and the olfactory and mote broadcasting systems. It paid special attention to the campus simiverse and diverse hollyholo population. It mined its growing pool of data and fed it to its scenario mill to determine the best way to facil-itate the prize's liberation. The difficulty of its task was compounded by huge gaps in its knowledge base. The prize was attached to unknown machinery. Human workers of unknown friendliness reached into its container and applied unknown objects to it. Chemicals of unknown composition bubbled through the liquid con-ductor. Meanwhile, a holofied simulacrum of the prize expressed human distress with an uninterrupted cry. Any or all of this might be sinister and require counterac-tion, but Blue Team Bee could not judge for itself, and since it could not contact LOG2, it did nothing but create a blind spot atop a ceiling beam in the cottage where it hid. From its invisible vantage point, it monitored clinic chatter and waited for some overt action threshold to be crossed.

3.12

It had been forty-eight hours since Fred launched the *Book of Russ*, and he was curious about its reception by russdom. He could have checked on it from anywhere with his skullcap and visor, but that would require Marcus's intercession. So, although it was his day off, he returned to the BB of R for a fresh datapin and a quiet booth. Marcus provided these with no comment. Checking the *HUL* stats in the booth, Fred was at first encouraged to learn that his *Book of Russ* had already been seen by over one hundred thousand russes. However, none of these many russes had seen fit to add their own threads or tails to it. Nor, indeed, bothered to post a rebuttal. It was as though his true confession had sunk without a ripple. He had not expected to change russ attitudes overnight, but to be totally ignored?

Fred sifted through the entire *HUL* and found only three hits on him or his effort. One was posted in a public square, and two more were clipped to it. Fred steeled himself and opened them.

The first one said, "Seriously, Londenstane, seek professional help." It was signed, "A Concerned Brother, Batch 16BA."

The other two were authored by "Anon" and read simply, "Ditto."

"Ditto" was not a word that iterants used in polite discourse, and its appearance here felt like a slap in the face. Was there *no* other russ out there who felt as he did? Was he the only one? Fred pulled the datapin from the player and dropped it into his pocket. He left the booth and told Marcus he wanted to use the null room.

"Certainly," said Marcus. "The first opening I have is Saturday noon for thirty minutes."

"What are my chances of a cancellation this afternoon?"

"I can put you at the top of the waiting list."

Fred went to the canteen and drank coffee and got himself caught up on skullcap news. A couple of hours later, Marcus told him to go to the null room ready area; a fifteen-minute slot had opened up.

"That's good," Fred said. "Listen, Marcus, I want you to make me a special datapin. I want an E-Pluribus model of the russ germline."

"What batch?" Marcus asked.

"All batches. The entire line, compiled up to the minute."

"That's an expensive request."

"It's a covered expense."

"Certainly, it is," Marcus said, "but usually covered only in conjunction with psychiatric care. Would you like me to arrange an autopsyche session, Myr Londenstane?"

"No, just the pin, thanks." Fred went to the ready area where the E-Pluribus datapin awaited him, still warm, in the wall dispenser.

There were four other russes in the ready area. They sat in pairs as far away from each other as the small space allowed. A dispute settlement, Fred surmised. Russes tended to resolve their personal differences in-house. The four of them nodded a greeting to Fred as he sat in a chair between them.

A minute later, the on-deck light came on, and the four russes rose to prepare to enter the null room lock. They drank the expressing visola and divested themselves of caps, visors, batons, shoes, and anything else they didn't want to risk losing to the anti-nano. They left their things on open shelves.

The russes began to scratch themselves through their clothes. "What the hell," said one of them, drawing his sleeve and raising his beefy arm to the light. He scrutinized his skin from several nose lengths away. "They're abandoning the mothership," he said, as though he could actually see the nits. "They're fleeing the rice paddies."

"My God, but it itches," said one of the others.

"Scratching only prolongs it," said a third.

The first russ lowered his sleeve and said, "Such a deal."

Fred said, "But you gotta agree, it beats the hell out of the slugs."

"The jury's still out on that, brother," the russ said and glanced at Fred's name badge. His face went suddenly blank, and he turned away without another word. He and the other russes climbed into the lock, but not before each took a quick peek at Fred. Fred was too surprised to react.

Whatever dispute the foursome brought into the null room was quickly resolved, and in only twenty minutes, the on-deck light came on again.

"They were booked for thirty," Marcus said. "I will tack the remaining time to your session."

"Thank you, Marcus." Fred opened a pouch of visola and drank it down. Almost at once his head began to itch as his skullcap retracted its microvilli from his scalp. The skullcap came off in congealed lumps, which he combed into the sink. Fred waited for his whole body to begin to itch as the nits crawled out of his skin, but it didn't happen. He hadn't been colonized yet. The HALVENE.

Fred cycled through the lock and entered the null room. The BB of R null room wasn't much larger than the table and four chairs it contained. One wall was a built-in kulinmate, and the opposite wall contained a curtained-off comfort station. Wasting no time, Fred sealed the hatch, took a seat, and inserted his datapin into the player. A quicksilver E-Pluribus Everyperson, quarter-life-size, appeared on the tabletop. It bowed and awaited Fred's instruction.

"Give me two russ sims," Fred said. "Make one a composite of the total russ population. Make the second a subset of the fringes of russdom."

Everyperson faded away as two life-size russ sims appeared sitting at the table on either side of Fred. Both had the typically hefty build, brown hair, and round-nosed moon face of Fred's type. He didn't know which was the mainstream russ and which the fringer. Both sims were typically alarmed as they sorted out their sudden existence, and Fred spoke to put them at ease.

"We're in the BB of R null room on North Wabash in Chicago. I'm real, and you guys are sims. My name is Fred, Batch 2B."

"Hey, Fred," said the sim to his left, coming up to speed. "I'm Rick, uh—all batches, I suppose."

"And I'm Bob," said the other. "All batches rolled into one."

"Good, good, guys," Fred said. "Listen, I cast you up to help me answer some vexing questions."

"What kind of questions are they, Fred?" Rick said.

"Vexing, obviously," Bob said.

"Yeah, that's right," Fred said. "Things that have been eating at me. I was hoping you guys could help me shed some light."

"Be happy to try," said Rick, and Bob nodded agreement.

"Thanks. Here goes: Have either of you ever done anything or said anything and then thought, Hey, that wasn't very russlike of me?"

The two sims thought about it a moment, and Bob said, "What kind of thing, exactly?"

"Anything," said Fred. "The way you conduct your duty or interact with your wife. The kind of vid you choose to watch or music or what booze you like or swear words you use. Hell, the way you shave yourself. Anything at all."

Fred watched the shutters drop over his brothers' eyes. "Come on, guys, don't do that to me," he said. "This is serious. I need your help, and this is a null room we're in. I'm going to nuke your pin before I leave, so whatever you say stays here. I promise. Can't you help a brother out?"

The appeal worked, and Rick said, "Can't say that I've ever been embarrassed or self-conscious, or whatever, of anything I've ever said or done—outside the usual small stuff."

"Thank you, Rick," Fred said. "Thank you for that." He turned to Bob.

Bob said, "I'm a russ, Fred. Therefore, *anything* I do is, by definition, russlike."

"Fair enough," Fred said, encouraged by Bob's bit of solipsism—russes weren't known to spout philosophy. "Tell me this, Bob. Have you ever just let go and said whatever came into your head without censoring it first?"

Bob chuckled and said, "You mean when I'm not drunk?"

Bob's expression froze in mid-grin, and a moment later Rick's went blank as well.

There was a long moment of excruciating silence, and then Rick said mildly, "Uh, Londenstane? You must be suffering an intolerable level of stress right now. Maybe you need a vacation? You should talk to Marcus about taking some time off."

"I agree," said Bob. "Take a long vacation."

Fred sighed and said, "Thanks, guys. I'll do that." He deleted the sims, and Everyperson returned. Fred took a moment to formulate his next request and said, "This time, make me a composite of any russes who would actually want to contribute to the *Book of Russ.*"

Everyperson shrugged its shoulders. In the center of its chest burned the glyph for *No Matches—Try Again?*

"Screw it," Fred said and pressed the button on the player to irradiate the datapin. Everyperson abruptly vanished. Fred took the expensive pin from the player and held it up. The tiny bulb of paste at its heart was cooked. He dropped it into his pocket and fished around for the other one. He still had a few minutes of null-room time left, so he opened the *Book of Russ* and added a new entry: "To my brothers cloned: Your response to this book is just plain sad. By the way, I was completely sober when I recorded it. Since none of you has seen fit to add your own observations, I offer the following list for your consideration:

"One, we russes are created with emotional muzzles locked to our personalities. I have removed mine.

"Two, although we often complain about the strictures of Applied People's confidentiality policy, we actually *prefer* it that way because it reinforces our own inability to communicate.

"Three, why shouldn't we be attracted to hinks? We're men, right? No offense to our sisters, but why should we only find lulus, evangelines, and jennys appealing? Why do johns pine only for janes and juanitas, steves only for kellys, and jeromes only for jeromes? This strikes me as deliberate genetic programming, not any natural human sexual response. Our ur-brother, Thomas A., kept lists of women he desired to screw. *He* was attracted to a variety of women. And we're not? Why is that?

"And finally, why don't *we* own the patents to our own genome? Why is our genetic recipe the property of Applied People? Shouldn't it belong to us? At least, shouldn't we have a say in how it's expressed?

"These are only a few of the questions I have. Suck on them for a while, my brothers. Signed: Fred Londenstane, Batch 2B."

ALL THURSDAY AFTERNOON, the medtechs came in, and the medtechs went out. They fiddled obsessively with the tank, controller, and jacket, but Ellen Starke's condition only worsened through the afternoon. The only positive thing they accomplished, it seemed to Mary, was to turn down the volume of the jacket's breathless, pitiful cry.

The jenny Hattie visited in the late afternoon to tell Mary and Renata about a little meditation booth near the dining commons that had a decent grief program in case they needed a good cry. Starke was not expected to survive the night.

Quitting time was the quarter hour of french fries, an aroma guaranteed to send tired day workers home in search of dinner. But there was the trace of another, strange odor in the gatehouse. It was ripe and revolting, and Mary realized that it was the same odor that Fred had brought home on his skin and hair last night. The old coot in the Skytel.

At the outer pressure gate, she asked Reilly about the odor.

"I'm surprised you can still smell it," he said. "We scoured this place pretty good."

"But what *is* it?"

Reilly only shrugged; confidentiality was confidentiality.

Mary wished Reilly a pleasant evening, but he was getting off shift too, and he offered to accompany her and Renata to the train station. As they walked down the drive to the street, Mary picked up the odor here and there in the hedge.

At home she got a message from Fred who said he'd be late. She dialed up a pasta dish and ate it on the couch in front of the flatscreen. She searched the WAD and Evernet for background on the man who had appeared on the Skytel. Most of the stories were dated—he had been a celebrity of sorts in the last century—and these turned out to be what she was looking for.

Mary watched an old clip of the wedding ceremony of Samson P. Harger and Eleanor K. Starke in 2092. They were young, beautiful, and strong. Starke, especially, had a remarkable face, with wildly extravagant eyebrows. Samson looked dashing in a charcoal-gray tux. He exhibited a certain cockiness. He was an artist and package designer of note. This was right before his run-in with a homcom slug and his subsequent undoing. He was one of the first people ever seared—hence the odor. Some years later he joined a charter. That was how Fred had run into him last night.

Mary watched the clip of Samson's arrest by slug and bloomjumpers at an outdoor café. The other patrons stampeded away, his wife among them.

There were no pictures of the three of them together: mother, stepfather, and baby Ellen, but from what information Mary could glean, her client in the tank at Roosevelt Clinic had lived with the stinker for a short period of time during her infancy.

"Call Wee Hunk," she said.

The little muscle-bound persona appeared before the couch and said, "Good evening, Myr Skarland. What can I do for you?"

"You asked us to keep our eyes and ears open," she replied, "and to report anything unusual or suspicious."

"Yes?"

"It might be nothing," she said, "but when I was leaving the clinic by the South Gate today, I smelled something strange."

"Yes, I heard your exchange with the guard. You smelled the odor of a seared individual who was turned away from the clinic." An aerial view appeared on the flatscreen of a girl and lifechair traveling in circles on the greensmoat.

Mary said, "But he's Ellen's *stepfather*. Why is Concierge obstructing his visit?"

Wee Hunk seemed impressed with her information. "The doctors assure us that it's too late for visitors to have any effect on Ellen's condition, and we have no cause to doubt them in that regard."

"Shouldn't we at least try? And why was he turned away in the first place? Doesn't he have a right to see his daughter?"

"So many questions," Wee Hunk said. "Without intruding on family privacy, allow me to just say that it's a long story. But when Ellen wakes up, we'll add her stepfather's name to her FDO list. Until then, there is very little his presence would help."

MEEWEE TRAILED BEHIND Wee Hunk and an arbeitor to the null suite next to the bunker shelter. "I still don't see why I need to go in," he said. "It'll strip me of my implants, which will take weeks to regenerate."

"Trust me, Bishop, it's necessary," the caveman replied. When they reached the in-lock, the hatch irised open. The Starke null suite was no economy model, and its locks could accommodate a dozen people at once. But Meewee entered alone, the mentar stayed out in the hallway, and the arbeitor entered only long enough to deposit a paste canister on a shelf.

"See you in a couple of hours," Wee Hunk said from the hallway. When the hatch shut, and Meewee was alone, the mentar reappeared and said, "Please challenge my integrity." Wee Hunk was now a miniature man, lounging in a miniature armchair next to the paste canister on the shelf. Meewee was perplexed; he had just challenged the mentar in the bunker shelter, but since this was a backup, which was cut off from its prime, he did so, and it passed.

"You should get into the habit of challenging me every few minutes from now on," Wee Hunk said.

"Why so often?"

"Let's just call it a precaution."

The in-lock utilized gas instead of expressing visola to purge bodies of machinery. The gas process took much longer, but it was surer and gentler on living tissue, and it made Meewee drowsy. He lay on a couch and fell asleep. He was awakened by the noise of the inner hatch unbolting. An arbeitor entered from inside the null suite and handed him a chilled liter bottle of Orange Flush. Then it lifted the paste canister from the shelf and went into the suite, with Wee Hunk and his armchair floating behind.

Meewee followed them to a large conference room where dozens of machines were busily assembling other machines. Meewee looked around and tried to make sense of the carts, cartons, and crates. When he saw the empty hernandez tank, he said, "Ah, our clinic." He did a double take when he noticed a woman among the toiling machines.

This was apparently the reaction Wee Hunk was waiting for, because he chortled and said, "Bishop Meewee, I'd like to introduce Dr. Rouselle."

The doctor came over to shake his hand. "The honor is mine, Myr Meewee," she said. She was an imposing woman, a couple of heads taller than the former bishop.

Wee Hunk said, "The only way I could entice Dr. Rouselle to leave her Birthplace post in Ethiopia to be smuggled here to save the life of one little rich girl was to assure her that you personally required it."

"Thank you for coming," Meewee said, "but tell me, what is Birthplace doing with a revivification specialist in patch fly country?"

"I am there for running the sterilization universal," the doctor said.

"Dr. Rouselle," Wee Hunk explained, "gave up a lucrative reviv practice in Geneva to volunteer for Birthplace's campaign to stamp out human reproduction. Thus she's both qualified and unfettered by obligations to the Fagan Group. And as far as I can ascertain, no one knows she's here except us."

The doctor led her visitors on a brief tour of the nascent clinic and assured them she would be ready to receive her special patient in about a week.

"We don't have a week, Doctor," Wee Hunk said. "You'll have to be ready by tomorrow."

The doctor shook her head. "But it is testing and to calibrate and season the amnio fluid," she complained.

The little caveman got out of his floating armchair and grew to life-size. "Tomorrow," he repeated, "and don't forget the portable tank."

She shrugged her shoulders and pointed to the bottle of Orange Flush that Meewee hadn't yet opened. "The kidneys are desiring this, Myr Meewee."

He assured her he would drink it, and he and Wee Hunk took their leave and went to an empty conference room. Wee Hunk said, "Your name opened the door, Bishop, but what clinched the deal was my promise to buy her a complete peripatetic field hospital. Our doctor drives a hard bargain."

Meewee opened the bottle of diuretic and drained it. He sat at the conference table and belched. "You mentioned a portable tank," he said. "Does that mean you finally have a plan of action?"

Wee Hunk took a seat opposite him. "Yes, and now that we're here, I can run it by you."

ON THE WAY back to the locks an hour later, Wee Hunk said, "Don't forget to challenge me repeatedly, Bishop."

"I will."

The former bishop entered the out-lock, but the arbeitor remained in the suite with Wee Hunk's paste canister. "Aren't you coming out with me?" Meewee said.

"No, I'll remain here."

"But you can't communicate with your prime from in here."

"That's a small matter."

Meewee nodded. "What should I tell you out there? Did you know you were going to stay inside?"

"Not really, but don't say anything. I'll figure it out."

The inner hatch did not close, and after a few moments, Meewee said, "Was there something else?"

"Yes," the caveman replied. "There's something I've been debating whether or not to tell you."

When he did not continue, Meewee prompted him, "You still don't trust me, do you?"

"A hole in one," replied the mentar. "But given the situation, I suppose I have no choice. Have you ever wondered why Eleanor named your mentar Arrow?"

"Not really. I always took it to be one of those childish names like Spike or Fluffy that people like to give pets. Or, no offense, like your own name."

"Ellen named me when she was a child, but Eleanor named Arrow, and Eleanor possessed too literal a temperament to misname anything."

"What's your point?"

"A couple of days ago, when I told you that I don't know Cabinet's kill code, I was telling the truth. But Cabinet might have mine, or might have had it before it lost the ability to use Starkese. It occurs to me that Arrow might have everyone's, including my own. Something to keep in mind."

AFTER LEAVING THE BB of R, Fred tubed across town to the Longyear Center. On the way he installed a new skullcap on his head. He had removed his name patch, and the russes he passed along the way paid no special attention to him.

Longyear Center, stripped of its stylish pretensions, was nothing more than a tank farm for the middle class, which apparently included UDJD employees. In the lobby he told the guard on duty that he wanted to visit Heloise Costa. The guard was a russ.

"Certainly, myr," the guard said, but when Fred swiped the sign-in medallion, he gave Fred a second look. Fred could see the wheels turning in his brother's head: So *this* is the guy, and *that's* his hink. But all he said was, "Here's your usher line, Myr Londenstane."

Fred strolled tiled corridors that separated vast wards containing thousands of hernandez tanks arranged in ranks and rows. He, himself, had once spent an unmemorable fortnight in one of these, recovering from a bad laser burn.

Fred followed the usher line to Ward 286D. Several times he had to step aside to make way for trains of medbeitors and carts. He followed the usher line to a cubicle and stepped through its privacy curtain. The cubicle was only slightly larger than the tank and controller that occupied it. The tank was full of a thick purplish growth medium within which was suspended the reassembled body of Inspector Costa.

She was either asleep or off in some jacketscape. Her skin still clearly showed where she had been sliced into five pieces by plasma rings. The seams were bright red; the major one ran from the tip of her right shoulder diagonally down her chest to the knob of her left hip. It had cut a breast in two, just below the nipple. Her snatch, he couldn't help but notice, was tufted with ordinary curly brunette hair, and Fred realized that he'd expected it to be shaved into a heart or fleur-de-lis or some such exotic shape like a lulu's. Costa was no lulu.

Hernandez tanks weren't exactly erotic settings, and nude bodies floating in them tended to resemble lab specimens more than sex muffins, but Fred was impressed by how thoroughly turned off he was at the sight of Costa's nakedness.

When he looked up again, she was watching him. *Hello, Londenstane,* she said and opaqued the bottom half of her tank. *So nice of you to visit.*

"I wanted to see if they found all the right pieces," he said.

I believe they have, though some of them don't work as well as they used to.

"Give it time."

Oh, I know. I've only been in here three days, and it feels like a prison term.

There followed an awkward silence, and Fred realized they had absolutely nothing to talk about. She was a hink. He was a clone. End of story. They spent a few more excruciating minutes exchanging small talk, and then he wished her a speedy recovery and left. Retracing his steps to the lobby, he wondered if that was all it had been, her superficial resemblance to a lulu.

There were two russes at the registration desk when he exited, and their eyes followed him out the door and all the way to the pedway.

Riding in the bead car home, Fred said, "Marcus?"

Yes, Londenstane?

"Marcus, I was wondering—"

I'm listening.

Fred was wondering whether it would do any good to delete the—he couldn't even say it to himself—what a pretentious name—the *Book of Russ*—so apocryphal-sounding. "Marcus, can I delete the entries I made to our *Heads-Up Log* over the last few days?"

Ordinarily, no.

"Ordinarily?"

Do you no longer espouse the views you expressed there?

"I don't know. I may have been confused."

In that case, something might be possible. We may be able to do more than simple deletion.

"Explain."

We believe you may be suffering a mild form of HALVENE intoxication as a result of your duty on Monday. Such reactions have been known to cause aberrant thoughts and loss of judgment. If a healthscan bears this out in your case, we would be able to not only delete the entire Book of Russ, but expurgate it.

"What does that mean?"

In its place we would substitute an explanation of the injury you suffered in the line of duty. Brothers would be advised to disregard your previous statements as having been beyond your control.

Fred could hardly believe his ears. In one stroke they could make it all go away. "You can really do this?"

Yes, contingent on the results of the healthscan, which you may undergo at any time. Would you like me to schedule you an appointment?

"Yes! The sooner the better."

In that case I am diverting your car to MEDFAC now.

AT THE MEDFAC facility, they were expecting him. The charge nurse, a jenny, pointed to a door and said, "Go piddle in booth twelve." He did and when he came out, she said, "That's all for now. Your Marcus will contact you with the results."

Fred felt like a new man.

FRED BURST INTO the apartment and cried, "Mary, guess what."

"Screen off," Mary said, and the living room flatscreen went dark, but not before Fred caught a glimpse of a park scene, a bee's-eye view of crowds, benches, trees—a lifechair. "Yes?" Mary said. She was dressed to go out, and she wore a valet broach on her lapel.

"Never mind that. What are *you* up to?"

She couldn't look him in the eye. "Oh, nothing, Fred. I've had a rough day, and I'm going for a walk in the park."

"I've had a rough day too," Fred said. "I'll go with you."

"I thought you had the day off. Why don't you stay here and have some dinner. I won't be long."

"I'll eat park food."

THEY PASSED TENNIS courts, skating rinks, and equestrian trails. In an open field, a sky-holo competition was under way. Brilliant, melting landscapes of fairy castles filled cubic acres of airspace. The artists stood under their creations, boldly slashing the sky with their arms, flinging meadows and forests and dragons into place.

The fourth tier of Millennium Park had a Busker's Cross where two busy footpaths intersected. It was crowded with park-goers and street performers. Mary and Fred hurried past the Machete Death Grudge and their blood-soaked stage. Nearby, under an American elm, was parked a solitary lifechair. Fred offered Mary a package of nose filters, but she declined. She realized her mistake a moment later as they approached the chair. It was *the* odor, all right, the one she sought, but a thousand times stronger than she could have imagined. By the time they reached the chair, vomit tickled the back of her throat. Maybe that was why he wasn't so welcome at the clinic.

When she first saw the stinker, lying in the basket of his lifechair, Mary doubted that anyone who looked like that could possibly be alive. But he was, or at least his eyes were. His piebald head reminded her of his stepdaughter's skull in the tank.

"Hello again, Myr Kodiak," Fred said. "It's Fred Londenstane. And this is my wife, Mary Skarland, who I told you about last night."

The lifechair, not the man, replied, "Samson says, Good evening, myren. Have we met?"

"Yes, last night, at Rondy," Fred repeated.

"I, of course, remember you, Commander Londenstane," said the chair, "but Sam's mind is wandering a little. And he tells me to roll over to that bench so the two of you can sit comfortably."

"There's no need," Mary said. "Besides, the bench is occupied."

The old man cackled, and the chair said, "Sam says, Believe me, it'll be free by the time we reach it."

And so it was. The woman and man occupying it fled before they were halfway there. Mary sat on the abandoned bench and gave Fred a look.

Fred said, "I think I'll go stretch my legs."

"Sam says, Why not go stand next to Kitty's pay post. Prime the pump with a millionth; the gawkers there can't seem to figure it out for themselves."

"Your housemeet is here?" Fred said. He had walked right past her thinking she was a park statue. Fred went back along the path to look at her. Even up close it was hard to dispel the illusion. She wore the costume of a ballerina, with white tights and tutu, white slippers and ribbons, and a white tiara crowning her head. Her hair, skin, and nails were also white. Even the irises of her eyes were white. She was an alabaster statue, arms arched gracefully over her head, one leg bent slightly at the knee, most of her weight supported on her toes. Her trembling calf muscles broke the illusion, and Fred knew how much strength it took to hold such a pose.

Quickly, to relieve her strain, Fred swiped her pay post, not a millionth, but a ten-thousandth, and the post immediately resumed playing some piece of classical music in midmeasure. The ballerina statue came magically to life. She completed a pirouette, and then a leap, and half a plié when, just as jarringly as it had started, the music cut out, and the dancer froze.

Fred blushed. A ten-thousandth didn't buy much on the fourth tier of Millennium Park. He swiped her post again, upping his donation to a tenth.

The reanimated dancer completed her plié as though never interrupted. With a sleight-of-foot, she seemed to command a theater-sized stage, instead of her meager porta-platform. She ran across it and leaped open-legged as though across an abyss. She seemed to defy gravity. She moved with fluid ease. A gathering audience watched with appreciation and swiped her post regularly each time the music faltered.

Fred was mesmerized. This was clearly no child. She was a mature performer and athlete in a girl's small body. Something wet hit him on the cheek, and he wiped it off with a finger. It was her sweat, proof of her exertion, and like everything else about her, it was milky white. Without thinking, he brought it to his lips to taste.

The compacted ballet continued without pause for an enchanted time. Then, suddenly, there was a piercing sound on the other path. Everyone in Kitty's small audience looked, including Fred. A full-throated cry of misery and outrage came from a pram that was steered by a jenny in a nanny uniform. The jenny was accompanied by two unsmiling russes and a huge black-and-white dog. The jenny told the pram to stop, and she popped open its lid, revealing a bawling, beet-red *baby* within.

"She needs her nappies changed," the jenny announced to no one in particular.

The ballerina's audience abandoned her for the real child, all except Fred. He swiped her pay post another couple tenths when he feared the music would stop. He was about to again when the music simply faded away. The ballerina didn't freeze but instead took a bow. Fred, an audience of one, clapped. The pay post threw a holo curtain around the dancer and stage, and Fred was left standing in front of a sign that read, "Intermezzo." For a full minute he stood there, unsure of what was happening to him.

The nanny's dog approached the pay post and sniffed it with interest. Fred snapped, "You! Outta here!" The dog regarded him with a placid expression. It had one blue eye and one brown.

"Trapper. Here, boy," called a russ. Fred turned to see one of the baby's body-guards holding a soiled diaper. "You see a trash chute around here?" he asked Fred.

Fred fought to keep a smirk off his face, but failed. All the years of training to bring this man into an elite corps of personal security providers—for what? a fistful of dirty diaper? "Such a deal," Fred said. The russ just wagged his head in agreement.

"Leave it here," said a girl's voice from behind the holo curtain.

"Come again, myr," the bodyguard said, trying to discern the source of the voice. "You want the little one's mess?"

An open kit bag was pushed from behind the curtain. "Yes, the mess," the girl said. "You thought I meant the dog?"

The russ wrapped up the diaper into a neat little leakproof package and dropped it into the kit bag. He winked at Fred and said, "Such a deal," before returning to his own client.

Fred wanted to tell him he had the wrong idea, that Fred wasn't working for this girl, but the opportunity had passed. The kit bag was pulled back through the curtain, and again Fred was alone, confused, and tongue-tied.

Myr Londenstane? a voice said. It was Marcus.

Fred took several steps away from the curtain and said, "Yes, Marcus."

I'm afraid I have some troubling news. Your test results rule out HALVENE poisoning.

Fred knew it had been too easy to be true.

Your health signs are nominal, the mentar continued. *We'll have to explore other avenues for the source of your recent behavior. May I schedule a psychological evaluation for you?*

Fred sighed. "Yeah, go ahead."

Mary and the chair approached, and Mary said, "Fred, what's wrong?" Kitty stepped out through the curtain, a towel draped over her sharp shoulders, and the chair introduced her to Mary. Mary grasped the girl's small hand, and there followed an awkward moment when no one knew what to say. Samson had fallen asleep.

Mary broke the silence. "I was watching you from over there," she said to Kitty. "You are a marvel."

"Thank you, I'm sure," the girl said and curtsied. She pointedly avoided looking at Fred, and Fred pointedly avoided looking at her.

Mary said, "Well, it's been a lovely time. We should visit the park more often."

On the way back to the APRT, Fred said, "Did you get what you came for?"

"Time will tell."

"Don't do anything stupid."

"That goes for you too, Fred."

Friday
3.13

Before dawn, with four hours yet to go before the attempt to spring Ellen from the clinic, Meewee sat on a mat on the floor of his shelter bedroom with the lights dimmed, practicing tantric stretch and breath exercises to try to quiet his nerves. He had been up half the night visiting the toilet to excrete all the dead machinery his cells had flushed into his bloodstream. Ordinarily, he would have waited a few days before starting the process of reestablishing his implant ecology, but with the impending rescue, he felt he could not wait. So he had swallowed a comm package at midnight, and now his brain was full of buzzes and flashes as the tiny radio sets unpacked and calibrated themselves.

A diorama of the clinic cottage ran in the corner of his room with its audio muted. All therapy on Ellen had been suspended, and the night evangelines were keeping what was by all appearances a death vigil. Then, out of the blue, Wee Hunk showed up in the cottage and told them to go home.

Meewee jumped to his feet. "Wee Hunk," he said. "I need to speak to you."

The mentar appeared at once. Over the last few days, Meewee had noticed Wee Hunk's habit of frequently changing the appearance of its persona. Sometimes it was life-size, sometimes a Tom Thumb, sometimes realistic, sometimes cartoonish. This morning it appeared in super-realistic detail. Every pore on its broad nose stood out sharply.

Meewee said, "Is that you at the clinic?"

"Yes."

"You're discharging the 'leens?"

"That's right."

"But why? That wasn't part of your plan."

"What plan?" the Neanderthal said.

Meewee began to reply, but changed his mind and returned his attention to the diorama. The two evangelines took their dismissal with equanimity, but did not leave the cottage. They had learned the night before not to trust mentars in the cottage. "Did you dismiss all the other shifts as well, all the young evangeline women?" he said, slipping in a challenge in Starkese.

"Don't worry, I will, at a more decent hour. There's no point in attending to Ellen any longer. Don't you agree?"

Meewee listened hard, but heard no response to his challenge. *Arrow,* he glotted, *challenge Wee Hunk's integrity.*

A moment later, his mentar responded, *Identification failure.*

It was what Meewee expected, but still the fact of it shocked him.

"Was there anything else?" Wee Hunk said. "I have funeral arrangements to attend to."

MARY ROSE EARLY to download the odor specimen she had captured in the park. She was in the shower when the houseputer informed her of an urgent call from Wee Hunk. She left the stall and wrapped herself in a robe. Fred seemed asleep as she hurried through the bedroom. She was closing the door when she stopped and whispered, "Are you awake?"

"Yes, I am," he whispered back. "Good morning, darling."

"Good morning to you too, Fred. I have a call. Shall I close the door?"

"Yes, please," he said.

Standing in the living room, Mary composed herself and said, "Use my business persona and put the call through."

Wee Hunk appeared as a full-sized man wearing an anorak made of blond fur. The fine detail of his projection, the crisp treatment of every strand of fur, struck Mary as unusual. His smallish, thick face was impassive, and he said, "Mary Skarland, it is my unpleasant task to terminate your services at this time, since they are no longer required. Thank you for your conscientious work. Do not report to Roosevelt Clinic today."

The Neanderthal was swiping off when Mary said, "*Wait!*" She startled herself. "I mean, is she irretrievable, then?"

"Myr Starke's condition is no longer your concern," the mentar said and dissolved.

MARY CREPT BACK into bed. She was crying. Fred gathered her into his arms and said, "DCO?" She nodded her head. "Oh, well," he went on consolingly, "it couldn't last forever. You got a good run out of it, nearly a week. And there's probably severance pay in it too."

"Please shut up, Fred."

"At once."

When she seemed all cried out, Fred ventured, "Feel like talking about it?" She shook her head against his chest. "Feel like breakfast?" She nodded. "Good, so do I." He struggled to hide his glee at her bad news. "I'm going down to the market for real blueberries for my special blueberry pancake recipe." He got out of bed and grabbed a package of tower togs off the shelf. "Don't get up; it'll be breakfast in bed."

In the foyer, Fred asked for his tower shoes, and the slipper puppy retrieved them from the far reaches of the closet. As he stood there putting them on, balancing on one leg and then the other, he caught a whiff of Samson Harger. His nose led him to Mary's tote bag leaning against the closet door, all ready to go. Hating himself, Fred rummaged through it and found a paper napkin that was double-sealed in kitchen pouches. Two layers of hermetically sealed film were not enough to contain the old man's indomitable essence. So that was what she had been up to. He had wondered about their trip to the park. Still, he wasn't sure why she'd want a sample of Harger's stench, but with the phone call, it was no longer an issue. Thank goodness.

Fred slipped the smelly package back into the tote and left the apartment feeling a lot better than he had for days. He mentally crossed off one item on his trouble list.

A CRASHING SOUND woke him. Bogdan squinted against the morning light and saw that he was still in the garden shed, but on a cot, not on the floor. On Sam's cot. There was an odd thumping sound outside, but he wasn't ready to wake up yet. He had been performing wonderful things for appreciative strangers in a dream.

Sometime later, another crash made him sit up and look out the shed window. Francis and Barry were carrying armloads of junk and dropping them on a large pile next to the shed.

The thumping sound was coming from the other side of the roof, where the soybimi racks were supposed to be. In their place sat a large tanker van with a CarboFlexion logo painted on its side. Several hoses ran from the tanker, and on the other end of the hoses were Tobblers.

Rusty's face appeared at the screen door, and he said, "Looky who's surfaced."

"What's going on?"

Rusty opened the squeaky door and came in. He pulled Samson's elephant footstool next to the cot and sat down. "On this side, ladies and gentlemen," Rusty said, gesturing toward the roof door, "we are currently inventorying our stairwell shelves while at the same time clearing a path for Samson's lifechair. We've reached the seventh floor."

"Sam's still—?"

"Still hanging on. He's bunking in Kitty's room till we clear the stairs. Now, on this side," he said, gesturing toward the van, "our good neighbors are busy injecting carbon resin down all the hollow spaces made by the material pirates. It's a big project, and they've agreed to front us the cost and donate the labor in exchange for the use of roof space. We keep the shed and vegetable garden. They get everything else."

Troy Tobbler was out there helping his 'meets. His arm was in a sling. Bogdan tentatively pressed his own nose and cheek. They were no longer tender, so he peeled the moleskin off.

Rusty examined his face and said, "Looks all healed up to me."

"How long have I been down anyway?"

"Not quite a day and a half. We were worried when we found you up here and couldn't wake you, but the autodoc said you were all right and just to let you sleep. Yesterday we called E-Pluribus to claim a sick day for you. Imagine our surprise."

Bogdan hung his head. "I was going to announce it at the next Soup Pot."

"I know it."

"At least I get a separation bonus."

"That's important, and anyway, you'd have to give up that job when you moved out to Wyoming."

Bogdan's mouth fell open. Rusty smiled and looked out the window at the Tobblers. "They're fixin' the building because they figure it'll all be theirs one way or another."

"Are we—? Did we—?"

"Nothing's official yet," Rusty went on, "but it looks like we're still in the running. The Beadlemyren are afraid of losing their own charter identity if they got folded into a big charter, like the Tobbs. So they decided instead to pick two little houses, and mash the three of 'em into a whole new one. We're on their short list because of Hubert. The micromine project needs a mentar, and not a lot of little houses have one of their own like us."

"You mean we're not going to recycle him?"

"No, that was never the plan. Kale says they just wanted to shake him up a bit, make him think we would. You gotta admit, Hubert's a lazy mentar. Sam's spoiled him rotten."

Bogdan looked out the window at Troy again. "You mean nobody told them about Hubert's arrest?"

"Oh, they got told all right, more than once. They say they're going to feed us some slack about it, though, and give us some time to straighten things out with the law. The Beadlemyren aren't bad people, Boggy, once you get to know them. They also don't mind a barroom brawl now and again and said someone oughtta show you how to duck."

Bogdan got off the cot. There was a package of togs on the potting bench that April must have left for him. "But how can we get Hubert back if the hommers won't even let us talk to him?"

"We'll just have to figure that out. Kale's talking to an autocounsel."

When Bogdan was ready to leave the shed, he thought of something else to ask. "So, how'd your dates go at Rondy?"

Rusty pursed his lips and shook his head.

"Sorry."

"But April got some good news. A matchmaker hit her up, and apparently there's a big fish on the line."

"April?" Bogdan vaguely remembered the Saurus woman in the ballroom. "That's great!"

THE FASTEST WAY to pass a message into the null suite was through the radiation tunnel, a trip no living tissue or paste-based or mechanical mind or electronic device could survive. Meewee wrote a short note in Starkese on a scrap of paper and sent it through, hoping that by the time it arrived, its meaning in the metalanguage would still make sense to Wee Hunk's backup. Then he went to the galley for breakfast.

Nearly an hour later Arrow said <Dr. Rouselle awaits you in the garage.>

Meewee hurried to the lifts and arrived in the garage just as Dr. Rouselle and a medbeitor from the null suite were lowering a hernandez jr. tank into the cargo well of a sedan. The portable tank consisted of a simple controller, a pump for recirculating amnio-foam, and a chrome chamber just large enough to accommodate a human head. Meewee looked around for the backup paste canister, but didn't see it.

"Forgive me, please," the doctor said in a lilting voice. "This—ah—biellette is loose?" She gave Meewee a meaningful glance and reached down to quickly open and shut the tank's chamber door, just long enough to reveal Wee Hunk's canister inside. Meewee reached down and pretended to check a coupling on the side of the tank.

"Looks tight to me," he said and closed the cargo well. "Shall we go?"

Meewee and the doctor got into the car, and the fans revved up. <Arrow> he said <challenge the Wee Hunk in the tank.>

A moment later Arrow replied <Identity confirmed. The Wee Hunk in the tank says that the changing situation calls for a new Plan B for which we must make a detour to the federal building before proceeding to the clinic.>

<In that case, tell him to rehire the 'leens.>

FRED WAS CLEARING the breakfast table when the phone chimed. "It's for you," he called to Mary in the bedroom who was preparing for a day at the lake. Fred stayed in the kitchen nook and tossed breakfast scraps into the open mouth of the kitchen scupper and eavesdropped.

"You again," she said.

"Good morning, Myr Skarland," said a voice Fred did not recognize, not Cabinet's. "Please check your DCO board."

A moment later Mary said, "Why fire me just to rehire me?"

"An unfortunate mistake was made. Please note the bonus offered to smooth over the inconvenience. Your shift has already started, and if you accept our offer, you must leave for the clinic immediately. Will you come?"

Mary hesitated. "Is Myr Starke still alive?"

"She needs you now more than ever."

Fred didn't hear a reply from Mary, but the call ended, and she returned to the bedroom. He followed and stood in the doorway. She was dumping the beach blanket from her tote and repacking her work things, including the weird hat and the odor sample.

"I don't appreciate you spying on my DCO business," she said without looking at him, "and I'd bet that Nicholas wouldn't like it either." She quickly changed into a work ensemble.

"Your client," Fred said, "is the eye of the storm. When you are with this client you are surrounded by danger. Danger you are not trained for. We have lost 10 of my brothers, 13 jerrys, 26 belindas, and 780 pikes—irretrievably—since this aff Market Correction started. And you want to add evangelines to the list? You had a good idea. Let's call Nicholas. We'll get its opinion on the whole thing. What do you say?"

"So, call Nick," Mary said, gathering her things and coming to the door. "Any *normal* russ would." Fred winced but continued to block her way, and she said, "I'm sorry to hear about your brothers and the rest. I really am, Fred. Now, move aside."

Standing up straight, with his hands on his hips, Fred filled the door frame. He said, "You asked your caller if she was alive, but I didn't hear the answer. Is Ellen alive?"

Mary was startled by the question.

"Oh, yes, I know your client, Mary. In fact, I once worked for the Starke family, so I should know what I'm talking about. That mentar who's behind all of this does not have your best interest at heart, believe me."

He reached into her tote and lifted the saucer hat. "You are just another tool for it to get what it wants. In this case, it wants the daughter." He dropped the hat back into the tote and continued. "I assume that if she's alive, she's still unconscious. Don't you find that a little bit suspicious? What does she need with companions right now? No offense to you and your sisters, but you're no jennys." Mary frowned, and Fred added, "I mean that in a nice way."

"No, you don't, Fred," she said and went to sit on the bed, the smelly tote bag at her feet. "So, we freely discuss each other's DCOs now? I just want to be sure I am understanding this conversation. We withhold vital information from Nicholas, right? That's so unlike the both of us, don't you think? We must have very good reasons. I know I do. Why don't I tell you mine so you can see why I must go do this thing. But first I'd like to ask you a personal question. Would that be all right, dear?"

Oh, shit, Fred thought. He didn't like the sound of that. He was tempted to reach up and block his ears with his hands like a child. Mary hopped off the bed and came to him on the soft carpet, watching him with birdlike intensity. "Or maybe we should skip the question for now," she said. "How does that sound, Fred?" She placed her small hand on his chest and pushed, but he didn't budge.

"Fine, have it your way," she said and returned to the bed. "Let me first say in my own defense that I'm not totally stupid. I know there's an element of danger in what I'm doing. But not as much danger as you seem to imagine. That clinic is *highly* secure."

"Are you saying this from your wide experience in security matters?"

"Shut up, Fred, and listen. I'm telling you why I'm doing what I'm doing. I am aware of the risk involved, and let me state for the record that I accept it."

"You have no idea what you're talking about."

"I probably don't, Fred, but I do know one thing. I know that my sisters and I are not prospering. I mean my whole germline. There's more of us heading for the sub-floors every day. We seem to lack any practical skills, try as we might to acquire them, and it's only a matter of time. You know it's true, Fred."

"We won't let that happen," Fred said.

"We're to be kept women, then? And meanwhile, we drag you down. Did you know that russes married to 'leens are on average 4.6 years older than their brothers married to other types? And growing older every day. Ask your Marcus; he'll give you the stats. And tell me this, Fred, how many juve treatments have you and I skipped in the past three years? When was the last vacation we took? The last furniture we bought? Face it, Fred, they've set the bar pretty high for us iterants. Couples must earn together, or they will slide together."

"Mary, please—"

"I'm talking about *oblivion*, Fred. If you and all your brothers were facing oblivion, don't you think you'd take extraordinary steps to turn it around? You can't blame us, Fred. This opportunity fell into our laps. There are eight of us. We've been assigned to companion one of the most celebrated invalids on the planet, and in doing so, we are pioneering a new branch of companion work—companions to people undergoing deep body mechanics. Even people who are comatose need us. If we can do this, thousands of our sisters will have new duty opportunities. But only if our client survives and wakes up. That's where I come in." Mary got up and approached the doorway again. "Surely, Londenstane, you would not interfere with the destiny of an entire type?"

Fred shook his head. "No, only just you. Sorry."

"I'm sorry too, Fred. You offer me no choice." Mary seemed to sag. "Do we have to do this? If you love me, Londenstane, step aside, I beg you."

"Don't say that," Fred said. "You know I love you."

Mary began to pace, which for an evangeline was an especially bad sign. "You know this big Russ Centennial coming up in August?" she said. "Imagine that, the world's oldest commercial germline turns one hundred. Congratulations, Fred."

"Thank you, Mary."

"And you, yourself, go back nearly to the beginning. You're Batch 2B."

Fred tracked her back and forth, from the bureau to the closet and back.

Mary said, "You confided in me the other day about your fears of catching clone fatigue."

"Yes, I confided in you. Will you now use that as a weapon against me?"

That almost gave her pause, but she barged ahead and said, "You want the truth, don't you, Fred? Even if it hurts? That's what you're always telling me. That's why you told me all that stuff in the first place, isn't it? Anyway, I was thinking about your *Book of Russ.*" He flinched at the name. "At first I thought that simply by creating it, you were out of type, but now I'm not so sure. I think it all depends on your urbrother Thomas A. Russ. What if *he* kept a private journal of his own, in which he recorded his *most secret* thoughts and feelings? And let's say for the sake of argument that he had this journal set to self-delete if anything ever happened to him. So no one knew anything about it after he died. That's possible, isn't it, Fred? Thomas A. might have been a secret journal keeper. If he was, then your starting the *Book of Russ* might have been a normal response to a deep-seated russ need. You have to admit it's possible, don't you?"

Fred nodded, not knowing where she was going with this and afraid to ask.

"Good. I was thinking about this, Fred, and I came up with a question for you. Are you ready?"

Such a long windup. Fred was so tense the door frame creaked. Mary looked at him with pity and said, "Did Thomas Russ have something for little girls? Because, from what I witnessed in the park last night, mister, you sure do."

THE NEXT THING Fred knew, he was sitting on the side of the bed, with his head hanging so low it nearly touched the floor. Mary was gone, escaped. She had knocked him down with a handful of words. Despite his shame, he was impressed. He got up and wandered around the apartment. She had nailed him, and still he couldn't keep the thought of Kitty out of his head. Or Costa, for that matter, or the cute michelle he had just run into in the shop downstairs. What was happening to him? Whatever it was, it would have to wait. Mary was a dead clone if he didn't do something fast. But what? His first impulse was to call Nicholas and turn her in. That was what a "normal" russ would do, and he didn't have any better ideas. He was a russ in need of a plan, and a friend.

"WE WENT YESTERDAY," Kitty said.

"I already told him that," the chair replied, "but he doesn't remember." Kitty had caught the chair on the first floor, trying to sneak out of the house.

"Remind him that that's because he slept through it."

"He asked how Ellie looked, and I told him we were turned away at the gate."

"Tell him again, but tell it to him on your way back to my room, and this time *stay there.*"

The lifechair swiveled a bit to face the retrogirl straight on. "With all due respect, Myr Kodiak," it said, "Sam is my sponsor, not you."

"What?" Kitty said. "Belt Hubert, are you talking back to me?"

A frail hand rose above the rim of the basket. "Kitty," Samson peeped.

Kitty climbed up and leaned into the basket. "Morning, Sam," she said, caressing his cheek. "I was just telling the chair to take you to my room."

"My daughter Ellie," he said in a strained whisper.

"They won't let us see her," Kitty said. "We tried, Sam. It's no use."

The chair said, "He says, I have no time to argue. I must go."

"There's no point in going, Sam, if they won't even let us in." The retrogirl climbed off the chair and said, "Belt Hubert, take Sam to my room. Do it now."

The chair didn't budge. Neither did Kitty. It was a standoff.

"Let him go," Bogdan said. The boy had just come from the kitchen with a steamy cup of troutcorn chowder. "It's something he has to do, and you shouldn't be trying to stop him."

"Fine," Kitty said and got out of the chair's way. "You can go with him, because I'm not."

"No problem," Bogdan said and went to the chair. "Good morning, Sam," he said. The old man smiled up at him. "I hear you're off to see your daughter."

The chair said, "He says, That's right."

"Can I go too?"

"That would be nice."

Bogdan turned and led the lifechair to the foyer and out to the street. Kitty stood with her arms crossed and watched them go. A moment later she heard the chair clop, clop, clop down the porch steps. "Oh, for pity sake," she said and took off after them.

MARY TOOK A taxi all the way to the clinic. At the gatehouse, the sealed sample in her large tote bag passed through the scanway without raising a flag. She hurried down the path through the little woods that separated South Gate from the cottages. Inside Feldspar Cottage, Cyndee and Nurse Hattie stood at the tank controller. Mary could see that Cyndee had something to tell her.

The brain model above the controller showed only sporadic neuronal discharges, like fireflies on a summer night. Hattie switched it off and said, "They declared her irretrievable early this morning. I have to go now, but I'll return to help Matt pull life support." She hugged the evangelines in turn and said, "I know it's hard to lose your first one." She paused at the daybed on her way out. The Ellen jacket was still twisted in her never-ending scream. "Tell Matt to shut this thing off first."

When the evangelines were alone, Cyndee told Mary that she and Ronnie had been discharged by Wee Hunk, but that they didn't leave. But when Mary and

Renata failed to show up at shift change, Ronnie decided it was really all over and left.

"But you stayed," Mary said, tapping Cyndee's saucer hat, "and that's all that matters."

Mary went to the controller and brought up the rhinecephelon display. She took the package from her tote bag and unsealed it.

"Yuck!" Cyndee said. "What is that?"

"I looked up Myr Starke on the WAD and learned that her father was a seared," Mary said and held the napkin against the olfactory sampler grate. "Ellen," she said, "your father is here. It's time to wake up. Samson Harger is here. Ellen, do you hear me?" She watched the skull's eyes as she talked. She pulled a chair next to the sampler grate and propped the napkin up on it. She stood in front of the skull and told Ellen Starke all she had learned of her father.

On the rafter above her head, the Blue Team bee recognized the signature aroma of the hankie. The bee flagged the human who had brought this sample as a possible friendly.

FRED SAT ON a packing crate next to the porthole of a TUG Moving and Storage container that was flying in a parking loop over Decatur. Its figure-eight route brought him near the Roosevelt Clinic once each sixteen-minute lap. This flying boxcar made an ideal staging platform, and Fred's access to it was remarkably sudden. Veronica Tug, when he called her from his apartment, had taken his list of logistical needs, no questions asked. A few minutes later she called back with the address of the storage container. He took a taxi to Decatur and made a midair docking with the container. It was loosely packed with several households of wrapped furniture and appliances. He found the field identikit that he had requested and a scanway-proof weapon that he had not. The blackmarket kit contained everything he needed to create and assume a foolproof new identity. Fred went through it and found a red and black jumpsuit cut in a garish paramilitary style. It looked like the household livery of some self-important aff, but it was lightly armored and included a fairly decent cap and visor. Fred put on the cap and read his cover doss. Myr Randy Planc was a Chicago area russ who lived in an APRT near Gary Gate. He was engaged as major domo to a materials broker named Abdul al-Hafir. Fred researched both Planc and al-Hafir on the National Registry and found neither of them listed. He consulted the UD Whois, Applied People Directory, and several other key sources. Neither man existed—at least not yet. Fred's disguise required the conjuring up of not one, but two, complete identities out of thin air. It couldn't have been cheap, and Veronica never mentioned the cost.

Fred broke open a tube of skin mastic and squeezed it on his arm. While it melted into his skin, he swallowed a capsule of self-migrating keratochitin concentrate that would collect on his cheekbones and chin to slightly alter several key facial landmarks. He chewed a gum that thickened his larynx and deepened his voice.

Eyecaps, mouth dam, false palms, uniform—Fred changed into Myr Planc. He considered the weapons package. It was a carboplex dagger that came in binary blister packs. To use it, he would need to spread the contents of a blister on the skin of each leg, taking care to keep his legs apart until he was through the scanway. Though the weapons package bore the seal of a reputable arms dealer, Fred was doubtful about trying to smuggle a weapon of any kind through a Fagan clinic scanway.

Checking the cap's chronometer, Fred peered through the porthole to watch the clinic pass below.

A MEDTECH ENTERED the cottage and said, "Holy shit!" She pinched her nose and looked around the room. Mary and Cyndee had been joined by Renata and Alex, an evangeline from swing shift. "What are y'all doing in here?" the medtech demanded. "And what is that *smell?*"

Hattie and Coburn entered after the first medtech, and Hattie said, "I know that smell, but I thought they were all dead by now." She, too, looked for its source. Mary held up the offending napkin, then rewrapped it and dropped it into her tote. It had apparently had no effect on the comatose woman.

The Blue Team bee, on the beam over Mary's head, watched the human activity below with the dimmest of comprehension. Today, all of the humans seemed to be running hot.

The first medtech left in search of nose plugs, but Coburn stormed over to the evangelines at the controller and demanded, "What are you dittoheads doing?"

"Her father was a seared," Mary said, "and quit using that word."

"Get away from this equipment."

"Relax, Coburn," Hattie said. "No one's harming your precious equipment." She went to the controller herself and paged through a quick series of diagnostic reports. "So, Ellen had a stinker in the family. Why didn't they tell us that a few days ago when it might have done some good?"

Coburn set his medkit on a tray next to the tank and laid out his instruments. "Lower armature," he told the controller.

"Controller, hold up a sec," Hattie said.

"Hattie, let me do my job. Concierge wants the deceased unplugged and morgued as soon as possible."

"Give me two minutes," Hattie said and continued paging through diagnostic reports. She settled on one that displayed a cross section of Ellen's brain stem.

Mary stood next to Hattie and said, "Did you find something?"

"Did you, indeed?" said Concierge, who strolled in through the cottage door. "I don't see anything," it said, answering its own question, "except use of the controller by unauthorized personnel to input odor. Did it work? No, I see no response." The tall mentar in its snowy white jacket stopped in front of Mary. "Myr Skarland, in the future, if you find employment in a Fagan facility, please bear in mind that only licensed personnel are permitted to operate clinic equipment. That includes the olfactory sampling port of a hernandez tank controller. Is that clear?"

"Yes, Concierge," she said.

"I am barring you from this clinic," Concierge continued. "Please leave at once."

Neither Mary nor the other evangelines protested, but Hattie said, "It's not her fault. If it's anyone's fault, it's mine. I'm the one who showed them how to sample odors and told them it was all right to do so."

"I agree," Concierge said, "and you shall leave with Myr Skarland. As for you, Medtech Coburn, why hasn't Myr Starke been de-installed as I requested?"

Coburn quickly removed the wings of the tank lid and lowered the waldo armature into place. Its mechanical fingers immediately began removing tubes and wires from the skull. This got the Blue Team bee's attention—a machine removing other machines from the prize.

"That's more like it," Concierge said. He looked at Hattie and Mary. "Why are you still here?"

Hattie said, "I am entitled to disciplinary protocol, which isn't initiated until Applied People has received a written complaint from you. Unless you're accusing us of endangering this patient? Is that what you intend to do? If so, I must say, it will be easy to prove that you've been aware of the evangelines' so-called unauthorized use for days and said nothing."

Concierge said, "As you wish. I've ordered campus security to escort you from the premises." Concierge went to the door and said, "I am appalled by your lapse of professionalism." It left the cottage and the door closed behind it.

Hattie, Mary, Cyndee, Alex, and Renata stood in stunned silence. Meanwhile, Medtech Coburn quietly tended to the plucking of Ellen's skull.

Finally, Mary broke the spell. "Hattie, tell us what you found."

Hattie shook her head and said, "I didn't find anything, but Concierge thought I did, so there must be something to find." Outside, there was the sound of footfalls on the garden path. The door swung open, and two security officers in clinic uniforms, a russ and a jerry, came in. The jerry bawled, "Security! Would Myren Beckeridge and Skarland please step this way."

The women only stared at him.

"Do it now!" he commanded and extended his standstill wand with a loud snap. This was enough to tip the bee into action. It left the security of the blind spot and crawled to the underside of the ceiling beam.

Hattie, the only jenny present, said, "Officer Jerry, I understand you have a job to perform and all, but are you threatening me with a weapon?"

The jerry blanched. "Nothing personal, Nurse Jenny," he said and telescoped his wand, "but you and the 'leen have to come with us—*right now*."

"No, they don't," said another clinic guard who entered the cottage behind the jerry. It was a belinda of a slightly higher rank. "You've been reassigned," she said. "Check your orders."

The jerry did so and said, "They're all yours, Lieutenant." When the russ and jerry had left, the bee crawled back to its blind, and the belinda simply vanished.

"What just happened?" Renata said, but no one had an answer.

THE STARKE CAR set down in the clinic lot, and Meewee and Dr. Rouselle lifted the hernandez jr. tank out of the cargo well and lowered it into the arms of the medbeitor. Man, woman, and beitor traversed the parking lot and turned down the brick drive. When they reached the gatehouse, Meewee ordered the guard, "Drop the gate!"

The guard, a jerry, raised an eyebrow and said, "Excuse me?"

"I'm ordering you to drop the gate."

The guard turned and called behind him, "Hey, Chaz, come here. You'll want to see this one."

A second jerry guard came over and said, "What's going on?"

"He's *ordering* me to drop the gate," the first guard said, and the two of them had a chuckle. Then the second one said, "Swipe the post, myren."

Having used up his small reservoir of bluster, Meewee nodded to the doctor and together they swiped the post.

"Myr Meewee," said the guard, "it says here that you have FDO status, so you may pass. But I'm afraid that you, Dr. Rouselle, have no visitor privileges. And as for that," he said, pointing to the medbeitor bearing the hernandez jr., "you'd better leave it out here."

Meewee said, "Call Concierge at once. I demand to speak to it."

"Speak away," said the guard. "It's always listening."

"Concierge, I demand you let us pass."

Concierge emerged through the pressure gate and greeted Meewee with a holo salute before turning its attention to the doctor. "Dr. Rouselle, what an honor," it said, "and surprise. I've followed your career with interest. I had no idea you'd returned to the UD."

"Thank you," said the doctor.

Meewee broke in. "We didn't come here to discuss careers."

"What did you come here for?" asked the mentar.

"We're here to assist Wee Hunk in removing Ellen Starke from your clinic immediately."

"This is the first I've heard of it. Why hasn't Wee Hunk informed me?"

"It'll inform you now." Meewee turned to the medbeitor and said, "Wee Hunk, tell Concierge we want to remove Ellen."

The medbeitor projected a life-size version of Wee Hunk, but its image quality was poor, and it flickered. Meewee repeated his request, but the mentar seemed not to comprehend, and Meewee said, "Hello? Wee Hunk?"

"Yes?" said a new Wee Hunk that appeared opposite them. It was not flat or halting, but a solid, coyote-skin-clad Neanderthal in hyper-sharp definition. "Ah, Meewee, good to see you again," it said. "And look what you've brought me, my missing backup. I was wondering where it had gotten itself off to."

Identification failure, Arrow said.

The medbeitor projection next to Meewee ceased, and the portable tank buzzed for half a second. Wee Hunk said, "Sorry, Merrill, but as I told you this morning, Ellen has succumbed to her trauma. The doctors did all they could, but her injury was too extensive."

Meewee ground his teeth. "That is bad news indeed, but we'll see her anyway. At once."

"Patience, old friend. Let's let the staff clean her up a bit first."

Dr. Rouselle peered at the Wee Hunk projection and said, "He is not Wee Hunk?"

"I'm afraid he's an impostor," Meewee said. It was time to launch Plan B. He stepped back a little, raised his hand, and brought it down sharply to his side.

Immediately a GOV appeared over the treetops and landed on the greensmoat next to the drive. Its gull wings sprang open, and six deputy marshals in blacksuits trundled out, armed with railgun carbines. A large emblem of the UDJD Marshal Service floated above them, and the pressure gate fell at their approach. They hustled right through the mentars Wee Hunk and Concierge, pausing only to swipe them their writ of habeas corpus. The clinic guards offered no resistance.

Meewee grasped both handles of the hernandez jr. and took it from the medbeitor. Clutching the portable tank to his chest, he hurried to get ahead of the deputies. "This way," he shouted, skirting the scanway and S-barriers and leading them and the doctor through double doors marked "South Gate Plaza." From the plaza, he found the path to Mineral Way and jogged past Quartz and Mica cottages to Feldspar.

Meewee led the charge up the garden path, but a marshal held him back at the door and signaled her squad to go in first. Meewee was breathing hard from exertion and exuberance. When the officers had all passed inside, he boosted the heavy tank in his arms and followed them through the door.

Only to find himself standing in the clinic parking lot next to his own car.

The deputies were milling around, bewildered.

"This is our car?" said Dr. Rouselle behind him.

BLUE TEAM BEE, in its blind atop the ceiling beam, detected a sudden barrage of clinic comm concerning possible intruders. The whole southern half of the campus was being placed on Yellow. All staffers were instructed to strongly encourage guests to move indoors without causing alarm. For the bee, these events were of a tactical nature and easy to parse. Intruders could mean allies.

The bee sent the wasp to South Gate to investigate. Blue Team Wasp flew to South Gate and lurked near a plaza path until a convenient pedestrian went by. The wasp rode into the gatehouse under a hat brim.

AN ASSAULT PARTY of UD Marshals running around in circles on the greens-moat and parking lot was just the sort of funny business that Fred had been watching for. He called a taxi to pick him up on top of the container. It took him down to South Gate and dropped him off in front of the gatehouse. Behind the pressure gate, two jerry guards were on duty, and behind them Fred glimpsed enough of the gatehouse to guess its basic layout from hundreds of similar facilities he had done duty in. There would be two offset, floor-to-ceiling vehicle barricades that, together with pressure gates on both ends, segmented the gatehouse into three independent blast-proof blocks. It was a summit-class gatehouse, and he was glad he had ditched the idea of trying to smuggle a weapon through.

Fred went to the far end of the pressure gate and said, "Hey," to the jerry standing behind it.

"Hey, yourself," the jerry replied and opened a sentry window.

Fred swiped the post with his false palm, thereby starting the clock on Myren Planc and al-Hafir's fictitious existence.

"Myr Planc," said the guard, "what can we do for you?"

Fred relaxed a bit, relieved that his disguise had passed its first test. He was Myr Planc, and this was a jerry. "What are you asking me for, Myr Klem?" Fred said, reading the man's name tag. "Why not ask your Visitor Log?"

The jerry said, "I already did, Myr Planc, and you're not in it."

Fred made a show of scratching his chin, which was a jerry habit. Jerrys scratched their chins whenever things didn't add up. The guard frowned and said, "Knock it off."

"Well, it's a problem," Fred said. "My boss is already paranoid enough about deep-body mechanics as it is. So he sends me down here to glass your shop, and the first thing I discover is you lost my appointment?"

The jerry said, "I doubt it's even possible for Concierge to lose an appointment, Myr Planc."

"No, wait," Fred said. "That's *not* the first thing I discover. The *first* thing I discover is you have a squad of deputy marshals chasing themselves around in circles in your greensmoat." Fred smirked at the jerry, and the jerry smirked back.

"You mean those training exercises?" the guard said. "Give me a minute, Planc, and I'll try to straighten out your problem." The window closed, and Fred let out his breath. He watched the deputies across the greensmoat returning to the parking lot. They piled into a GOV and sailed away. Whatever their action was, it was a complete washout.

While feigning a yawn, Fred covertly popped a spitball from the identikit into his mouth. Then he noticed movement on the ground near him. A homcom slug was crawling across the driveway. Fred had to remind himself that he was in Decatur, not Chicago. Decatur still had a canopy in its sky. And it still had slugs.

The skin mastic that Fred wore was coded to Myr Planc, but slugs generally tasted cells deeper than that. The slug made several search grid switchbacks, then stopped and changed course, heading straight for Fred. It seemed to have a lock on him.

Fred took a couple steps closer to the pressure barrier. The slug kept coming, so he pressed his back closer, generating a zone of air turbulence around him. The pressure heated his skin painfully, but the slug stopped advancing. It had lost track of him and resumed its default gridding. When it set off across the drive, Fred stepped away from the gate. Immediately, Marcus's pulsing icon appeared in his visor. There was an urgent message from the BB of R, and Fred dared not ignore it. But he couldn't use his newly deeper voice with the mentar, so he glotted instead.

Yes, Marcus?

Oh, it is you, Londenstane. I was unsure. I am getting confusing signals from your most recent skullcap.

It's me, Marcus. What can I do for you?

We need to discuss a BB of R bylaw.

Now?

Yes.

The slug, which had almost crossed to the greensmoat, stopped suddenly and idled in place.

By all means, Marcus. I've had a long week, it's my day off, and you want to talk shop. Be my guest.

Actually, Myr Londenstane, your time off is germane to the bylaw in question. Tell me, do you know the brotherhood's policy on taking free-lance assignments?

Of course. We're against it.

Correct.

The slug started creeping again. It made a looping U-turn and followed its own track back toward Fred.

Ordinarily, continued the mentar, *I don't intrude on member's personal affairs, but given our recent discussions, I have the obligation to ask you, are you currently or recently engaged in free-lance security work for—*

Fred stepped backward into the gate. The slug paused, but the mentar kept talking—*for a Myr al-Hafir?*

Fred inched even closer to the gate until his skin felt like it was on fire and Marcus's transmission broke up. A narrow slot opened in the gate next to him, and he ducked into the gatehouse. The guard, Klem, was waiting for him. "Concierge has arranged a private tour, Myr Planc," he said. "It's sending someone down from North Gate. Go through and wait in In-Block." He gestured to the pedestrian scanway.

Fred entered the scanway and surrendered the various prints, specimens, and samples it requested. When it was time to spit, he chomped on the spitball he had tucked in his cheek and broke it, releasing a sour wad of artificial saliva that was coded to Myr Planc and which he squirted into the collection bowl. Then he stood on the red X, his arms outstretched, facing the battery of emitters, and soaked up waves of radiation, ultrasound, and tomographic lasers. The TUG identikit seemed to be holding up under the scrutiny of the multipronged biometric inspection, and as he stood there, trying to keep the faith, trying to still his racing heart, it occurred to him that scanway technology and the countermeasures designed to defeat it, including blackmarket identikits, had been rendered obsolete by the HomCom's new nitwork. The nitwork was a much more efficient and elegant system. Whole colonies of the little beggars took up permanent residence in burrows under the skin where they tapped the host body's bloodstream and PNS. They sampled you continuously, knew who you were, where you were, what you ate for lunch, who you ate it with, how often you engaged in sex, drugs, basketball, or whatever, and with whom, and all in real time. And most people weren't even aware of their presence. Until you have to purge them, like the russes in the null lock. The new nitwork was a boon to law enforcement that would make his job much easier. His former job, that is. At the moment he was standing in a scanner with his arms held out in the modern sign of the crucifixion. Good thing for him he was in Decatur with its obsolete slugs, and not in Chicago.

The lights came up, and the usher line pointed Fred to the scanner exit. He left the scanner and was confronted by another guard, another jerry, who was studying the scanway control panel, one hand scratching his chin and the other resting on the handle of his baton.

"What?" Fred said.

"Nothing," the jerry replied. "Just stand down a sec, Myr Planc. The nitwork can't get a fix on you."

Fred experienced a spasm of fear and surprise. "You have the nitwork here too?"

"Not yet," said the guard, "but the readers are already being installed, and we're training to use them."

Fred felt enormous relief—a jerry's learning curve was rather steep. "Oh, is that all?" he said. "You want to know why, if I'm from Gary, I don't have any nits yet, right?"

The jerry gave him a sour look and pointed at the WAIT HERE box. Fred went to stand on the "A" in "WAIT" and glanced around. He was in Mid-Block, as he had figured. The vehicle S-path was blocked with more pressure barriers, and even the scanway exit behind him was shut. Fred's face itched deep under the skin, not from nits but from the keratochitin scabs on his cheekbones and chin.

"Got it," the jerry said, pleased with himself. "Your cells are swimming in HAL-VENE, so the nits don't like you yet. You've been dry-cleaned lately, haven't you?"

"Bingo."

"It was easy," the jerry continued. "We got another russie from Chicago with the same problem." He opened a barrier, and an usher line appeared at Fred's feet. "You'll have to wait in In-Block for your escort, Myr Planc. Have a nice day."

Fred followed the usher line to the inner block with mounting dread. Another dry-cleaned russ on the premises? Fred stopped dead when he saw him. Reilly Dell stood at the far end of the inner pressure gate, which dazzled in the noontime sun. A john in clinic livery approached the shimmering gate from the plaza side, and Reilly opened a slot for him to pass. Reilly and the john chatted for a while, and when Reilly turned to glance at Fred, his russ jaw dropped.

"Fred?"

MEDTECH COBURN LIFTED a floor tile to reveal a collapsible hose. He stretched the hose and coupled it to a spigot at the base of the hernandez tank. With a wrench he opened the tap, and the amber-colored syrup began to drain through the hose.

At the controller, Hattie disengaged the waldo armature that was plucking Ellen's skull, and all its prehensile fingers went limp.

"Don't do that!" Coburn yelled and went to the controller, but Hattie blocked his way. "Move aside," he said and tried to shove past her.

"You don't want to be touching me, myr," the jenny said evenly.

"You heard Concierge," Coburn protested. "It wants this done like *now*."

"I did hear it, but apparently I don't work here anymore."

The level of amniotic syrup was inching down the side of the tank. Mary went to the front of the tank and turned the wrench, closing the tap.

"Are you crazy?" Coburn yelled at her and grabbed for the wrench, but Mary tossed it to Cyndee. The other evangelines, as though awakening from a dream, joined in to help. Cyndee threw the wrench out the back window. Meanwhile, Renata and Alex uncoupled the hose from the tank and floor drain and flung it out of the same window.

Hattie, ignoring the medtech, put the controller through its paces, retrieving and comparing streams of brain state reports. "Something's wrong," she said. "I just know it. Mary, I need your help in the tank. Find a foil glove in Coburn's medkit."

Coburn loomed protectively over his open kit.

"Coburn, sweetheart," Hattie said from the controller, "you're slowing me down. I suggest you do the math."

"What math?" said the young man.

"How many jennys are there in the world?"

"What does that have to do with anything?"

"About ten million, give or take, and we staff every clinic, hospital, spa, doctor's office, and medical research center in the UD. This means that anywhere you're liable to find employment, we're there too. Now, tell me, my fair-faced boy, have you ever heard of the jenny bitch board?"

Apparently Coburn had, for the blood drained from his face.

"All I ask," Hattie said, "is two lousy minutes."

Without a word, Coburn stepped aside, and Mary found an elbow-length foil glove in his medkit. Hattie said, "Reach into the tank, Mary, and when I tell you to, squeeze our little mouse."

Mary used the recessed tank steps to reach the top. She leaned over the rim and snaked her arm between the metal limbs of the armature. "Don't nobody turn this thing on," she said. The fumes of the amnio syrup were strong, and she breathed through her mouth, but it still made her dizzy.

Coburn stood next to Hattie at the controller, his arms crossed. "I think you're all crazy."

"You're distracting me."

Through Mary's thin metal glove, the syrup felt warm and thick, and the skull was slick to the touch. Mary reached into the gauzy sling under it and found the fetus. "Oh!" she said in surprise. "I can feel its heartbeat."

"That's what we're after, my girl," Hattie said. She brought up a display of fetal vital signs. "All right, dear, give it a little squeeze."

Mary was unsure. "How hard?"

"Just a gentle squeeze."

Mary cupped her fingers around the pulsing lump and pressed it. "Like this?"

"Did you squeeze it?" Hattie said. "I couldn't tell. Let go a second and do it again a little harder."

Coburn said, "She's not doing it right."

"Yes, she is."

"I'll do it." Coburn motioned Mary off the tank. "Raise the armature," he told Hattie, and after donning a foil glove and climbing the steps, he plunged his arm into the tank. "Well?" he said.

Mary and the evangelines stood behind Hattie who pointed to the fetal heart bar that measured a rapid but normal pulse. "When you squeeze a heart," she told them, "its pulse should spike in a purely reflexive response. It doesn't involve higher brain functions. Even in a class three coma, it should react."

"Well?" Coburn repeated.

"Nothing, darling. A steady one-eighteen."

"That's not possible," he said, withdrawing his arm and peeling off the glove. "These controller units have triple confidence. They *cannot* be twigged. I *am not* believing this."

"What's wrong?" Mary said.

"False readings," said Hattie. "The controller has been tampered with. We probably never had true readings. Someone didn't want our patient to recover at all."

The evangelines shared a collective shudder. They looked at each other with dismay. Mary turned to Hattie and said, "How can we help?"

Hattie began to say something but shut her mouth again.

"I believe you've helped enough," Concierge said from behind Mary. The mentar's doctorish persona stood inside the open door. "Coburn, you disappoint me," it went on. "And the rest of you should have left when you had the opportunity." As the mentar spoke, the armature lowered into the tank again, and the waldoes resumed plucking leads and tubes from the skull. The tank spigot opened, and with no hose attached to it, the amnio syrup gushed out onto the floor of the lower room.

"Everyone," Concierge said in a commanding tone, "go outside for your own safety. Wait in the garden. The amnio fumes in here will make the air unbreathable. That means you too, Coburn." The mentar stood with a hand on the open door, but no one moved, except Coburn who dashed to the tank to gather his medkit.

"Fine," Concierge said. "Stay. It'll make it easier to collect you. Good-bye."

"Wait for me," Coburn said and rushed after the mentar through the door.

ON THE WAY from the Decatur station to the Roosevelt Clinic, the two children escorting the lifechair attracted the interest of more than one curious media bee. "I demand my privacy!" Kitty yelled at them, and the mechs quickly vacated her personal zone.

"Don't," Bogdan said. "We need witnesses."

Kitty appraised the boy and didn't reply.

"Belt Hubert," Bogdan said to the chair, "when was the last time you tried to speak to Hubert?"

"Not since my connection was severed at 02:21 Tuesday."

"Well, try now. Call the HomCom and demand to talk to him."

"Done. They have no knowledge of him."

"I see. Well, put this on your To-Do list. Call them every five minutes and demand to talk to him. Also, find some kind of lawyer domainware and incorporate it into yourself."

Kitty said, "What are you doing?"

"Belt Hubert may not be much, but he's something, and we need everything we got."

A block away from the clinic, Bogdan stopped the chair and looked up at the half-dozen bees that were pacing them overhead. He motioned them to come down. One of them descended and opened a frame. A head identified its media affiliation and said, "Is this the Chicago Skytel Hacker Samson Harger Kodiak?"

"Yes, the one and only," Bogdan said, "and we are his housemeets."

"It looks like you're heading for the Roosevelt Clinic. Are you, and if so, why?"

Kitty shoved her way in front of Bogdan and said in her best retrogirl manner, "Because they're holding Ellen Starke there against her will. You heard me—*Ellen Starke*— and Samson is her *father*, and he's going to *rescue* her."

Immediately, the rest of the bees were on top of them, more heads peppering them with questions.

Bogdan had to yell to be heard, "And another thing, the HomCom has disappeared Samson's mentar, Hubert. The same way they disappeared Samson last century and wouldn't let him go till they seared him. Samson Paul Harger Kodiak is the last and first stinker. We demand his daughter and his mentar be released immediately!" Then he and Kitty climbed on the chair and sped down the last street. By the time they'd reached the iron arch, hundreds of more bees—media, witness, private, novella, and homcom—had joined them. The children and chair rolled through the arch and led the swarm down the red brick drive to the shimmering gate.

THE AMNIO SYRUP level in the tank fell below the crown of the skull. The thick syrup spewed from the open valve at the bottom of the tank, across the floor, and into the lower room, soaking rugs and furniture.

Hattie and the evangelines were standing next to open windows for air. Hattie drew a couple of deep breaths, then went to the hernandez tank and tried unsuccessfully to close the valve with her bare hands. She came away with pant legs and shoes saturated with the strong brew.

"I think this stuff is fully charged," she said, kicking a spray of syrup as she returned to the window. "Even without a tank or controller, it ought to support brain tissue for an hour or so, I think. Our problem is that even if we had a medevac standing by, anywhere we took her we'd just have to face Concierge at another location."

"What about a Longyear clinic?" Cyndee said.

"Fagan Health Group owns them," Hattie replied.

"An emergency room?"

"Fagan Health Group."

"What about a large animal veterinarian?" Renata said.

"Like one who does thoroughbred horses," Alex added.

"Fagan's got those too."

"What about," Mary said, "the Machete Death Grudge? I saw them in Millennium Park last night. They have severe trauma tanks."

Hattie went to a shelf and upended a glass vase, adding its tulips and water to the mess on the floor. "Sounds like a plan to me," she said and filled the vase with syrup from the open spigot.

Seeing this, the evangelines set to work collecting and filling vases, a teapot, a fruit bowl, waste bins—anything that might hold liquid. Mary filled her large tote bag too.

"Don't let the syrup stay in contact with your skin for too long," Hattie warned them as she climbed to the top of the tank, where she unscrewed the skull from its chrome halo.

"Too late," Renata said. "My feet are soaked."

Mary's were too. The amnio concentrate felt ice cold but burned at the same time.

"And check the containers," Hattie went on. "Amnio eats through most everything. Cyndee, fill the foil gloves."

Indeed, the dresser drawers and waste bins were leaking, and even the glass vases were sweating syrup. But not Mary's tote bag. "Think it'll hold?" Hattie said, holding the glistening skull and its gauzy stump over it.

Mary said, "I think so. The lining folds out into an emergency hazmat suit."

"It'll hold then," the nurse said and lowered the head into Mary's tote. Then she looked around, wiping her arms on her uniform. The fruit bowl, the only other container large enough to hold the head, was sagging like warm wax, syrup spilling over its brim. Only the tote bag and foil gloves were still intact. The nurse held up a glove, which contained about two liters of syrup, and said, "We need more like this." She unlocked the drawers of the supply carts for them to search. "Tie 'em off like this," she said, demonstrating with her own. They found three more gloves and filled and tied them.

"FOG," SAID THE belinda marshal in charge, "military grade."

"Can't you penetrate it?" Meewee said, handing off the portable tank to the medbeitor. "The clinic is obstructing justice!"

"Not anymore it's not," the belinda said. She made a mount-up signal to her deputies. "Your writ has just been rescinded in Superior Court."

"You're not going to let them get away with it, are you?" he yelled at the officer's back. She boarded the GOV and didn't even bother to reply. The doors shut, and off it flew—Wee Hunk's Plan B.

Dr. Rouselle came over to Meewee and patted his shoulder. "It's too bad that she died," she said.

He brushed her hand away. "Save your condolences, Doctor." He turned to the medbeitor and rotated the hernandez jr. tank in its outstretched arms until he could open the chamber door.

<Wee Hunk, are you in there?>

No reply.

Meewee reached in and removed the paste canister. It was very warm, and when he jiggled it, it sloshed. He closed the chamber door and tossed the canister of ruined paste into the backseat of the Starke sedan. "You, machine," he said to the medbeitor, "follow me." He led the medbeitor and portable tank across the parking zone to the brick drive, where he stopped to look at the clinic wall and pressure gate. There appeared to be two children and a lifechair waiting there. The greensmoat was aswarm with hundreds of bees charging about in every direction. More victims of the military fog.

Meewee turned to Dr. Rouselle, who had followed him. "I'm going in," he said. "I'll leave the tank at the gate if I have to and bring her head out in my arms. Before you decide to accompany me or not, you should keep in mind that the Wee Hunk who promised you a field hospital is kaput, and the new Wee Hunk will probably renege on the deal."

He turned while she was still translating his words and started walking. <Arrow, is it true that you know kill codes?>

THE RETROKIDS AND chair made it to the gatehouse, but their cloud of witnesses got no closer than the greensmoat. A sentry window cleared in the gate, and a jerry guard looked out at the bees and then at them and said, "Swipe the post."

"Belt Hubert," Kitty said, "swipe for Samson."

The jerry consulted something in his visor and looked down through the window at Samson's bald head poking out from the lifechair blanket. "Good afternoon, Myr Kodiak," he said. "You do not appear on any of our guests' FDO, so I can't let you in."

"Did you hear that?" Bogdan shouted toward the street. The bees had all regrouped on the street and were hovering in neat rows over the clinic shrubbery. "They won't let him in!" he shouted. "Belt, relay our discussion to the media bees."

The guard said, "Please turn your scooter around, myren, and leave the premises."

"Did you hear that?" Bogdan shouted. "They want we should leave."

"I've already relayed that information as you requested," Belt Hubert said. "I've patched them into our discussion."

Samson raised his hand over the basket rim and said, "My daughter!" in a chair-amplified whisper.

"Oh, for crissake, stinker," the guard said, "go home." The window closed and the guard's figure receded behind the translucent gate.

"Don't walk away from me," Samson whispered. "It's not smart to piss me off."

But the guard kept going, and in a moment the chair started backing up. The retrokids followed, but after a dozen meters the chair stopped.

Kitty said, "Keep going, Belt. What's holding you?"

"I can't go any farther," the chair replied, "or I won't be able to find the gate again."

"So what? We're going home," Kitty said. "Aren't we?"

No one replied, and in a moment, she looked from the chair to the pressure gate and said, "No, Sam, don't do it." She climbed up and leaned over the basket. "No, Sam, not this way."

Samson's stiff old face crinkled into a smile, and he brushed the girl's cheeks with his finger. "Kitty, I loved you all these years." The girl began to cry, and he added, "I hate to leave you now."

"And I you, Sam."

"Give us a kiss."

Kitty leaned in to kiss him. Bogdan climbed up on the other side.

"Hello, boy."

"Hello, Sam. Are you going all the way this time?"

"Unless they let me see her."

"Do you think you're far enough away to get up any speed?"

"Don't worry about that," Samson said. "Give me a kiss and then take Kitty and go wait in the street."

"We want to wait here."

"Don't argue. Give me a kiss and go."

The boy kissed him.

Samson said, "I love you, Boggy. Do yourself a favor and grow up."

"Like I have a choice."

With a last farewell, Bogdan and Kitty hopped off the lifechair. Kitty took Bogdan by the arm and said, "Come on. I can't watch." The two retrokids left the chair and Samson and walked up the drive.

"I MEAN, REALLY," Reilly said from his post next to the gate. "It's uncanny how much you resemble him." Reilly's uniform was as relaxed as the russ, himself, seemed to be, and his hands were free of weapons.

Fred paced inside the WAIT HERE box. The chronometer in the corner of his visor was counting down the short shelf life of his disguise. "Will you please let it drop, Officer Dell?" he pleaded. "Of course I look like your friend. We all look like your friend. We're *clones*, for crying out loud!"

"Fred always likes to point out the obvious too."

Fred turned his back on his friend and continued calibrating his cap and visor system, which he had started while still up in the container van. The system he'd obtained from the TUGs was a reliable law-enforcement model, but it was designed to be controlled by an onboard subem or valet, neither of which Fred had. Its manual controls were cumbersome, to say the least, and not always intuitive. Fred instructed his cap to query the clinic's system for station reports, but he had no access privileges. He did get the visitor kiosk to open, and he selected a campus map. It was a tourist aid, highlighting only the major buildings and landmarks and not drawn to scale. But it was all he had, so he pasted it into his Theater Map to serve as a base layer. In his visor, he appeared on it as a steady blue dot in a square symbol labeled "South Gate Entrance." No other personnel showed up, not even Reilly standing behind him.

Reilly began talking to someone on his comlink. He mumbled his part of the conversation. On his belt were a sidearm and a standstill wand, both of which would be coded to his ID and useless to anyone else. The only weapon Reilly had that Fred could use was his baton. His uniform seemed to be lightly armored, as was Myr Planc's own, but his cap seemed to be of a much higher quality. And of course Reilly had all of the clinic's systems at his disposal, including backup.

Fred cursed when he realized he was sizing up his friend as though he were the enemy. Why couldn't he have been another jerry? He continued to watch his oldest friend and batchmate in the rear view of his visor. Suddenly Reilly's suit armor stiffened, and the WAIT HERE box on the floor turned into a FOLLOW ME usher line. It led back the way Fred had come, back to the middle block.

"What gives?" Fred said.

"The clinic has just gone to Orange," Reilly said matter-of-factly, as though it happened all the time. "As a precaution, we ask all civvies to follow the usher lines to more secure locations. That means you, Myr Planc."

"Orange Alert? Is there trouble?"

Reilly smiled disarmingly. "Let's just move it along, myr. I have to lock down this section."

Fred could not afford to lose ground now, and he said, "Let me stay here, brother. I'll be quiet."

It was the wrong kind of request for a russ to make of another russ on duty. Reilly read it for the stalling tactic it was, and his whole demeanor changed. He came fully alert, and his body assumed a ready stance. "Do as I instruct, Myr Planc," Reilly said in a mild voice. "Turn around and follow the usher line. Do it now."

BLUE TEAM WASP had successfully reached the outer block of the gatehouse without detection and there identified the probable intruder as the hankie and two children, backed up by about a thousand bees. None of them had managed to penetrate gatehouse security. The wasp reported this to Blue Team Bee, who recalled it to the cottage, but the clinic went Orange before it could return, and it became trapped in the middle block.

WHEN MEEWEE AND the doctor were halfway down the brick drive, Wee Hunk appeared before them and said, "Ah, Merrill, and Dr. Rouselle, you're still here."

"Don't waste our time," Meewee said and attempted to walk through the holo, but the mentar held up his hands and said, "Please hear me out."

Meewee stopped. "Make it brief," he said and added a challenge in Starkese, "Every second is precious, and too many have been squandered already."

"I disagree, old friend," the caveman replied. "We gave it our best, but we failed. Ellen is lost, and no amount of grandstanding on your part can bring her back."

None of what the mentar said answered the ID challenge, and Meewee said, "Don't call me your friend. You are not Wee Hunk, or at least not the Wee Hunk who was my friend. I suggest you stay out of my way, or I'll have Arrow deal with you. He can do it, you know. You were right about that."

"Have Arrow deal with me? I don't know what you're talking about, but if you wish to be confrontational, I am more than your match." The caveman shook his head when he heard what he was saying. "Merrill, Merrill, listen to us. I told you on Monday—did I not?—that I don't care about your damn Oships. All I care about is the well-being of my sponsor—my former sponsor—and out of respect for her memory, I cannot have you charging about demanding her head."

"If Ellen is really irretrievable, then let us see her—in person—and I'll quit."

"There, see? You can't help yourself."

"Enough of this," Meewee said and went around the mentar.

"You force my hand, your grace," Wee Hunk said. "I've just removed your name from Ellen's FDO. The guards won't let you through the gate."

Meewee stopped and glanced at the pressure gate at the bottom of the drive. The lifechair he'd noticed earlier had left the gate and parked a few meters away, along with the two children. Meewee's shoulder ached fiercely. He had pulled a muscle hauling the portable tank around like a young fool, and he massaged his neck as he tried to figure out what to do next. Something the mentar had just said reminded him of Cabinet—the fact that Ellen was his *former* sponsor.

"Good grief," he said. "You've already passed through probate, haven't you?"

"Yes, actually, this morning when Ellen was declared irretrievable."

Like Cabinet after Eleanor's death, Wee Hunk had returned from probate compromised, and probably not even aware of it. Something in the probate process had breached the shell to their personality buds. He had no idea if the breach was intentional or not, but it didn't necessarily mean they were contaminated, did it? Cabinet was continuing to run Starke Enterprises as it always had; Wee Hunk had said so himself. And if Ellen were, in fact, irretrievable, then Wee Hunk's behavior was perfectly correct, while he, himself, was acting like a callous fool. Meewee had to admit, it was never about the girl's well-being for him, but only about the project. He was obsessed with the damn Garden Earth.

"All right," he said, "I'll leave, but at least show us Ellen's death certificate."

"That I can do," the mentar said and opened a frame of the document, with verified sigs of clinic doctors.

"Dr. Rouselle," Meewee said, "please look at this for me." But she was watching the pair of children who were coming up the drive and about to pass them.

"Sorry?" she said.

"Please examine Ellen's—" He was interrupted by the boy, who had stopped directly in front of him with an awestruck expression. "Yes?" Meewee said. "Can I help you?"

"You're—" the boy said. "Excuse me, but aren't you Myr Meewee, the guy with the Oships?"

Not anymore, he wanted to say. You'll have to deal with the Chinese from now on. But he nodded his head and said, "Yes, that's me. Do I know you?"

"Not in realbody, myr. Only in the upreffing suites at E-Pluribus." The small boy straightened his posture and raised his hand in a solemn military salute. "I am Bogdan Harger Kodiak, future jump pilot of the ESV *Garden Charter*, at your service!"

Meewee didn't know quite how to respond to this, but the boy held the salute, with a stiff-armed resolve, until Meewee clumsily returned it. Then the boy rejoined the girl on their way to the iron arch and street, and Meewee slowly lowered his arm.

"Touching," Wee Hunk said. The document frame still floated beside him. "Now, if you don't mind, your holiness, the death certificate."

Your holiness? Meewee peered closely at the smug Neanderthal face and imagined he caught a glimpse of Saul Jaspersen. Or maybe the fecker Chapwoman. Your grace? These were favorite taunts of the GEP board, not Wee Hunk. He couldn't remember the mentar ever using them. Meewee turned again to the document frame. The certificate was probably authentic and Ellen probably dead, but this could not be her true mentar. This was a traitorous monster.

<Arrow> he said <*kill the mentar Wee Hunk.*>

The document frame closed, but nothing else seemed to happen. Wee Hunk still stood in front of them with an arrogant expression on his face. Eventually, the doctor passed her hand through him. "He is gone?"

"Yes, gone," Meewee said and continued down the drive. <*And now, Arrow, figure out how to drop the gate, if you can.*>

BLUE TEAM BEE noticed a sudden change in network chatter. The facility was still in Orange, but the pervasive presence of the clinic mentar diminished, and for long moments, control of critical systems was passed to backup subems. Meanwhile, the campus grid showed a clinic team of armed personnel approaching Feldspar Cottage. To complicate matters, Blue Team's wasp had become trapped in the gatehouse when the southern campus was put on Orange. The bee, swimming in a sea of action checks but unable to wait any longer, launched its highest-confidence plan.

"Oh, Nurse," said Dr. Ted, who appeared next to Hattie. Mary recognized it as the character from the clinic's simiverse.

"Leave us alone, Dr. Ted," Hattie said. "There's no time now for your frippery."

The doctor nodded and said, "Excellent diagnosis, Nurse. A deficit of time. And Concierge's departure has tripped semiautonomous subem assets."

"Say what?"

"Concierge has left the building," Dr. Ted said and vanished.

"You don't have to tell me twice," Hattie said. She lifted the tote bag and carried it to the door. Mary and the others followed her to the patio where they paused to take in great lungsful of fresh air. "You should all leave now," Hattie said. "You've done your duty." Everyone looked at everyone else, and no one made a move.

Mary broke the impasse. "Renata," she said, "why don't you leave the clinic and call Wee Hunk from the outside. Tell it to send a medevac to South Gate. Then call Nick. Then call the police and anyone else you can think of."

"Yes, well," Renata said, wiping amnio-stained hands on her clothes. "Yes, that sounds practical. I'll do it, Mary, and then I'll come back here."

"No, don't. Leave by East Gate. Once out, stay out. Walk around to South Gate and wait for us on the street."

Renata hugged Mary and hurried down the garden path. Hattie pressed a glove bladder into Mary's hands. Alex and Cyndee each had two of them. "No," Mary said, "I'll carry the tote."

"It's heavy," Hattie said.

"It's mine." Mary lifted the tote and looped the strap over her shoulder. It *was* heavy. Floating on the surface of the syrup was a scum of melting flotsam: a pen, a candy bar, the remains of her double kitchen pouches. The tissue sample of Samson's odor was completely dissolved, and the syrup was tainted with his odor. She closed the tote lid and said, "Ready." Cyndee and Alex stood on either side of her, their clothes bulging with glove bladders.

Hattie paused to admire them all, shaking her head. "You 'leens," she said. "I love you guys."

The rescue party didn't get far. They were stopped by a construction curtain blocking the garden path. It was too high to look over, and it cut the garden in half. On its bright yellow surface, Uglyphs were repeated every meter: "Caution! Utility Work in Progress. Please pass in this direction." Hattie led the evangelines around it in the suggested direction. This meant trampling flower beds and pressing themselves through a lilac hedge. They held open the branches for Mary and her gravid tote to pass through.

The safety curtain continued around their cottage. They followed it for a dozen more meters when Mary stopped abruptly.

"What's wrong?" Hattie said.

Wordlessly, Mary unfastened her valet broach and dropped it on the ground. "We're not going *around* the cordon," she said. "We're *inside* it."

It was true. The only way out of the garden was through the construction curtain. Since it was only a holo projection, they could walk through it. But that would surely trip an alarm. Following Mary's example, the evangelines and Hattie removed jewelry, panic buttons, ear pips, and anything else on their person likely to contain a transponder. The 'leens hesitated but removed their saucer caps as well and tossed them on the pile.

"Which way?" Hattie said.

"South Gate's that way," Cyndee said, pointing the direction.

"That way it is," Hattie said and marched forward. But she stopped and said, "Coburn?"

The medtech was crouching in a lilac bush. He had his medkit open and was injecting a handful of drug patches with a hypospray.

Hattie picked up a discarded vial and read its label. "What are you doing," she said, "loading for bear?"

"There's security out there," he said, "and listen—they're *pikes!*"

"You are mistaken," Hattie said. "Roosevelt Clinic doesn't employ pikes."

"I'm telling you, they were pikes. In clinic uniforms. Carrying over-and-under carbines."

The evangelines shivered.

"Well, then," Hattie said. "Anyone want to stay here?" No one did. It was the quarter hour of cherry pipe tobacco when Hattie led the evangelines and medtech through the holo curtain. On the other side, a man in a groundskeeper uniform was trimming shrubbery with a brush-cutter crop. A utility cart trailed him, raking up the cuttings with a mechanical arm and depositing them in its brush hamper. The man looked up when Hattie and the others came through the curtain. He was not a john or juan, as they would have expected. He was a pike.

The pike signaled for the utility cart to follow him, and he approached the safety curtain and small group of clinic staff huddling next to it. He gestured in a friendly manner, urging them to go back through the cordon. His peaceable demeanor was hard to resist. Mary looked to Hattie, who seemed as indecisive as she.

"After you," the pike said mildly, and the group turned around and went back through the curtain. The pike escorted them to the center of the flower garden where benches formed a circle around a little fountain. "Please take a seat. We'd like to have a word with you."

They didn't sit. The evangelines stood between the pike and Mary. Coburn clutched his medkit and said, "Whatever this is about, it doesn't concern me." He attempted to leave, but the pike touched the tip of his brush-cutter to Coburn's chest and said, "Please sit. Everyone, please sit and swipe me."

His voice oozed civility, which in a pike was frightening enough, and the five of them sat and swiped him. Coburn clutched his medkit to his chest.

"I'm afraid you're wrong, Matt Coburn," the groundskeeper told him. "You are, indeed, part of our mission."

The cottage door opened, and two more pikes emerged, these in security uniforms and carrying rail/laser carbines. They came over to the group, and one of them said, "Where is it?"

When no one answered, the pike stood in front of Coburn and said, "Concierge told you to DC it, so where is it?"

"Where do you think? In the morgue."

The pike snorted. "You're saying you took it to the morgue?"

Coburn swallowed and nodded his head.

"Then how come the morgue says it's not there?"

Coburn shrugged his shoulders and looked away.

Hattie said, "It must still be in transit. A couple of medtechs took it about a quarter hour ago."

"Is that so?" said the pike in the groundskeeper uniform. "My grid doesn't show any medtech between here and the morgue in the last half hour. For that matter, my grid shows you ladies over there." He pointed beyond the lilac hedge where they had dropped their hats. "Anyone want to explain?"

No one did. "Shiny," the pike concluded. He motioned for the utility cart to park itself in front of them and open the lid to its brush hamper. "Maybe this'll ring a bell. Is this the medtech you had in mind?"

There, on a bed of clippings, lay Renata. Her throat had been slashed, as with a sword—or brush-cutter—and it hung by a flap of skin.

Hattie sprang to her feet, but a pike roughly shoved her back down. "What have you done?" Hattie cried, straining toward the cart. "Call a crash cart. Let me stabilize her at least. She doesn't have to *die*."

The pike turned to his mates and said, "Of all the places to die—inside a freakin' revivification clinic. Is that ironic or what?" To Hattie he said, "Tell you what, Nurse Beckeridge. You tell us where the head is, and I'll call a crash cart."

Hattie turned away, which made the pikes laugh. Mary removed the tote strap from her shoulder and set the bag on the ground. She tried to think of what Fred would do in this situation, and not a thought came to her, except that the pikes were toying with them, as any 'leen could plainly see. They had no intention of calling a crash cart. Renata was as good as dead (as Ellen, herself, must be by now). Also, the pikes knew exactly where the head was; they could probably image it inside her tote with their visors.

"Christ, I love my job," said the pike in the groundskeeper uniform.

"Screw you, brother," said one of the others. "It's my turn."

"No need to be pushy," the first one replied. "There's two each."

"Sez who?" The pike strolled back and forth in front of the prisoners and appraised each of them with a calculating squint. He stopped in front of Mary and said, "What's that smell, sister?" He wasn't referring to the scent clock. The odor of amnio syrup distillates, mixed with a trace of Samson, was streaming from her tote.

Mary said, "I don't smell anything."

The pikes guffawed, and the interrogation moved to Coburn. "Where's the head, Matt?"

"I told you," he said. "I DC'd it and sent it to the morgue. Check the controller log. Ask Concierge." His eyes rose to the heavens. "Concierge! I need you."

The pikes howled with laughter, and one had to raise his visor to wipe away a tear. He motioned for the cart to close its hamper and to turn around. He opened the opposite hamper. Except for a sprinkling of grass clippings, it was empty. "Stand up here," he commanded Coburn.

Coburn was frozen to his seat, and the pike grabbed his arm and hauled him to the cart. "Tell me where it is, or you'll get a chance to ride in the cart."

Coburn's eyes shivered in their sockets. "There!" he said, pointing to Mary's tote.

The pikes groaned. Coburn's tormentor said, "Why'd you have to go and tell us like that? What kind of a man are you?"

"It's your own fault," said another pike. "You should've done a 'leen first. They'd never tell."

"I thought we should do the 'leens last. There's three of 'em, if you know what I mean."

"Yeah, yeah, we're running out of time anyway. Let's do this."

"All right, brother. Loan me the crop."

The groundskeeper pike handed his brother the brush-cutter. "Here, but it's not as easy as it looks. You have to swing it really hard."

"Says you," the pike said and gave the bench next to Hattie a couple of test lashes. Sparks flew, and deep grooves scarred the stone. He turned to Coburn and said, "Stand up straight, you wanker."

Coburn's knees buckled, and he sank to the ground.

"I said stand up," the pike growled and jerked the medtech to his feet. "The feck," he said and looked at his wrist. His skin was covered with five drug patches. He tried to peel them off but grew faint. As he stumbled, Coburn wrenched the brush-cutter from his hand.

"Run, run, run!" Hattie urged the evangelines. She, herself, bent over the fallen pike and tried to tear his standstill wand from its holster.

Mary grabbed up the tote and ran with the other evangelines to the lilac hedge, while Coburn savagely whipped the two remaining pikes with the brush crop. His blows bounced harmlessly off their armor. One of the pikes sliced Coburn in two with his carbine. While Coburn bled out in a rose bed, the pike continued firing razor fléchettes through his eye sockets and skull, to mince the gray matter inside.

Cyndee was first through the hedge. She helped Mary with the tote, and together they helped Alex. But Alex's clothes became caught in the branches, and she was stuck. She urged them to go without her, but her sisters continued pulling at her arms and legs. Behind her in the garden, one of the pikes attended to his fallen brother, while the other hacked at Hattie with the crop.

"I'm going to back out and come around," Alex said. "You guys—" Suddenly the hedge around her erupted in exploding leaves and twigs, and Mary and Cyndee dropped to the ground. Alex's own body shielded them from the fléchettes, but she was being ground up before their eyes. They crawled for cover. Mary was hit, the tote was hit, but the two evangelines found a forest path and ran. The path meandered between cottages and seemed to double back on itself. Cyndee pulled Mary into a copse of maples and elms. They ran between paths. Mary was completely disoriented, but Cyndee seemed to have her bearings. They had to stop eventually when they ran out of breath. They fell to their knees in the lush undergrowth.

There was a burning pain in Mary's arm where a fléchette had passed through without striking bone. Her sleeve was bright with blood, but the wound seemed minor, and she paid it no attention. It was the tote she was afraid for. A fléchette had entered but not exited, and syrup seeped down its side. One of Cyndee's bladders was also leaking. "Here," Cyndee said, thrusting it at Mary, "put this one in the bag and this one in your togs. The clinic wall"—pointing in the direction with a stick—"is over there. Not far, maybe a quarter klick. When you reach it, turn right."

"What about you?"

Cyndee probed the ground with the stick and pried up a large rock. "I'll be right behind you."

"You're crazy," Mary said.

"So are you, Mary Skarland. When you get out, send crash carts." Cyndee kissed her sister, gathered up her rock, kissed her sister again, and headed back the way they had come.

THE LIFECHAIR IDLED twenty meters from the pressure gate.

"What about the distance?" Samson said. "Will we get up enough speed? I don't want to die of a broken ankle."

Belt Hubert said, "I'm releasing your lap belt and uncoupling your Foley. That way you'll fly off and hit head first."

"You're a good helper."

"Thank you. Ready?"

"Tell them this is for Ellen Henry Starke."

"The media is still patched in."

"She needs me, and I'm coming."

The chair's micro-turbines revved up, and the chair thrummed with energy.

"Ready?" Belt Hubert repeated.

"Is Kitty clear yet?"

WHEN MARY REACHED the imposing clinic wall with her leaking tote, she was beyond exhaustion. She slumped in a near faint behind a large oak. Her breath whipsawed through her open mouth. The tote bag lay next to her feet, its side wet with syrup and blood. She wrenched it open and looked in at her passenger, afraid to see a ruined mockery of their sacrifice.

The skull lay in the corner of the tote, in a puddle of syrup, its crown completely exposed to the air. The bone was pockmarked with holes where wires and tubes had run. Scraps of raw skin hung from it.

Mary reached her bare arm into the syrup and hunted for the fetus. She thought she felt its heartbeat but couldn't be sure. The skull's eyes, in their lidless sockets, seemed to follow her.

Mary tried to untie the knot in the foil glove bladder, her last one, but it was too tight. She searched her pockets for something sharp. She tried to bite through it. Then she heard a buzzing sound next to her ear and was startled by a mech hovering there. It had a jeweled head of blue, and Mary thought it must be a clinic bee.

The bee alighted on the foil glove for a moment, and when it lifted off, there was a thumb-sized hole in the glove. Mary poured the syrup over the head, meanwhile keeping an eye on the bee. It seemed docile enough, but when she tried to stand up, it opened a tiny frame with a Uglyph that meant Keeping Still. Immediately, she heard footfalls crashing through the undergrowth. She huddled against the tree trunk and held her breath, wondering if the pikes' visors could image through solid oak.

The footfalls grew nearer. Mary looked all around. She was trapped. Suddenly she was staring into a mirror. Her own grimy face startled her. But it wasn't a mirror. It was a holofied sim of herself, complete down to the bloody uniform and tote. Her mirror image showed her a "You Are Here" map of the clinic grounds, with a pulsing arrow pointing the way to South Gate. Mary was closer to the gatehouse than she had thought. Then her sim double got up and ran in the opposite direction.

Mary heard a grunt of surprise on the other side of the tree, followed by the swoosh of fléchettes. The pike swore under his breath when he missed the decoy, but he did not pursue her at once. Instead he called in. He spoke in low tones, but Mary heard his half of the exchange.

"Repeat that," he said. "Negative, she's heading east toward A-three-six." His tone sounded more inconvenienced than concerned. There was a mechanical click as he reloaded his weapon. "How's Reggi doing? Say again. No, deploy the battle lid and clean up the mess. That's an order." The sound of his voice trailed off in the direction the bee had lured him.

Mary waited until the pike had disappeared into the trees before rolling the tote around Ellen's head, tucking it under her arm, and dashing to South Gate Plaza. She didn't slow down until she reached the pressure gate. It was shut solid. There were two shapes on the other side. "Reilly?" she cried. "It's me, Mary."

Reilly's reply came through a speaker over her head. "Mary? What's happened to you? Are you hurt?"

Mary looked down at herself and felt her arm with her fingers. "No, Reilly, but they're killing my sisters. Please let me in."

"No can do, Mary. We're in Orange. We're locked down. But I'm ordering a crash cart for you. Hang in there; help is coming."

As though from a distance, Mary heard the voice of another russ in Reilly's intercom. He was shouting at Reilly to drop the gate.

"Reilly," Mary said, "I don't need a crash cart, but send carts to Feldspar Cottage. There's three—four dead there. And one more behind me in the woods." She waved her arm behind her where she and Cyndee had parted. "But, Reilly, please, bend the rules for once, can't you, and let me in."

Inside the gatehouse, Reilly unhooked his baton and pointed it at Fred as he replied to Mary, "I would do anything in the world for you, Mary. You know I would, but you ask the impossible. I'm forbidden to open the gate while we're in Orange."

"At least take this through," Mary said and held out the rolled-up tote.

Fred approached the gate, but Reilly jabbed him with the baton. "I won't tell you again, Planc. Leave this block at once."

A shower of fléchettes bounced against the gate above Mary's head. She ducked low to the ground and ran along the gate to the end of the plaza where, with a parting look, she disappeared down a path. Reilly watched her go, and Fred used the distraction to wrench the baton from his hands. A man in a groundskeeper uniform approached the gate and watched them struggling for a moment before crossing the plaza and taking the same path as Mary.

Fred slipped behind Reilly and caught him in a choke hold with the baton. He pressed him against the hot pressurized air. "Open the gate!" He screamed.

WHEN MEEWEE, THE doctor, and the medbeitor passed the lifechair, Meewee saw that there was an emaciated passenger inside. "What do you suppose?" he said.

"I'll look," the doctor replied and stayed back, but before Meewee advanced much farther, the chair tooted its horn and shot past him, accelerating at a frightful speed directly at the pressure gate.

He's going to ram it, Meewee thought in disbelief. There was hardly time to blink. <Arrow!> he sputtered in the convoluted metalanguage <Gate drop now!>

The pressure gate dissipated even as the lifechair reached it. The chair passed through and braked hard. The guards leaped aside as it flew past them, tires screeching. It came to a halt in front of the massive vehicle barricade. The chair stopped, but its passenger kept going.

SAMSON WENT ALL the way—in honest-to-God slow motion. At least the suicides at Moseby's Leap had gotten that part right. Samson felt himself lift gently from the basket and float through the air. The barricade wall seemed distant, and there was ample time to take everything in.

To say I have no regrets would be a lie, he mused. I have plenty of them. I regret not being a better citizen, for example. I regret not being a better champion for the seared. I regret not making the most of every single blessed day of my life. But most of all, I regret not being a better man to Jean and Eleanor, and a better father to you. I suppose you might have been a better daughter as well, but I don't hold that against you. And thank you for this marvelous parting gift of an opportunity to go out with a bang. I'm going to light a big candle for you, Ellie. Hope it helps.

The wall grew close enough to make out the pockmarked texture of its surface, like craters of the Moon, and Samson remembered his honeymoon with Eleanor. She had pulled him aside and told him she loved him more than all the craters of the Moon.

"GOOD GAIA!" MEEWEE cried. "Stop! Stop!" The lifechair braked in time, but the passenger, wrapped in a blanket, flew headlong into the wall, hitting it with a resounding thud. Meewee ran to see. He ran into the open gatehouse where one of the guards stopped him. "The man," Meewee gasped, gesturing wildly at the crash victim, who lay in a heap against the barricade. A foul smell filled the place, and smoke rose from the crumpled form. Was that a *man*?

Dr. Rouselle shouted, "I am a doctor." She and the medbeitor had caught up, but the guard prevented her from lending assistance. The other guard used his baton to unwrap the man's blanket, and he sprayed the corpse with fire suppressant.

"That won't help, I think," the doctor said, sniffing the air. "He is a seared."

But the smoke cleared, and the victim lay like a broken twig on the concrete floor.

The gateway chimed, and the guard shooed them toward it. "It's all over," he said. "Nothing to see."

Meewee, remembering his mission, refused to budge. "I'm going through, Myr Jerry," he said. "Don't try to stop me."

"Listen to you," the guard said, drawing his standstill wand. The gate sprang up behind Meewee, but a slot opened, and the guard said, "Go on now. This is your last warning."

Just then, there was a snapping sound from the corpse, and another, like firecrackers going off. The guard hesitated and turned to watch. The doctor took cover behind the medbeitor, and the other guard ducked into the scanway entrance. Meewee used the distraction to sidle toward the far end of the block where the vehicle entrance gaped wide open, and he reached it just as two powerful blasts filled the block with flaming human bits.

WHEN THE GATE dropped, Fred thought that Reilly had done it, but when he loosened his hold on the man, Reilly fell to the floor. Fred stood for some time looking down at his friend. Fred had been sure he was straining against Reilly's face mask, but now he saw that Reilly had never deployed the mask. Fred crouched to feel for a carotid pulse and found none. Ugly bruises from the baton crisscrossed his throat, and the front of his uniform was singed from the heat of the gate.

"Medic!" Fred called at the top of his lungs. Something small and fast, the bluish blur of a flying mech, streaked out through the open gateway and shot down the path after Mary and the pike. Fred was drawn along too, but he could not leave Reilly like this. "*Medic!*" The gateway chimed a warning—the gate was going back up—and Fred had ten seconds to decide on which side he wanted to be when it did. "Medic!" he called desperately, searching through Reilly's pockets for a cryosac. He couldn't leave him like this, but at the last moment, he jumped across the gateway groove just as the gate sprang up. He was inside the clinic.

MARY'S PLAN HAD been to follow the south wall till it met the west wall, then turn right and follow that wall to West Gate. But she had already lost sight of the wall and was running blind along unfamiliar paths. She forced herself not to think of Reilly. The man wouldn't bend the rules even to save her life. She couldn't believe it.

Actually, she could believe it. Reilly was a russ through and through. Duty over all.

There were scraps of color in the woods. Two clinic guests and a retinue of holly-holo sims were strolling the path ahead. She hollered at them and raced to catch up. The syrup sloshed in the tote under her arm.

The guests stopped to gape at her. They were two of a kind—large, agile, gorgeous—and might have been brother and sister. As Mary approached, they lifted their hands and pointed their closed fists at her, aiming the rings on their fingers.

"Halt!" shouted the woman.

Mary stopped a couple of meters away and hunched over for breath. "You— must—help me," she gasped.

The man said, "I've already reported you to clinic security. They are on their way, so I suggest you leave us alone."

"Not clinic security. Call the Command. Go outside the gate and call them. Tell them I have Starke." She patted the tote. "Call a medevac. Please help me!"

The affs regarded her coolly, keeping a bead on her with their rings. The holly-holos accompanying them, who had been quiet until then, now piped up to fill the silence. One of them, a tall woman, said, "What have you done with the ransom?"

"There's no ransom," Mary said. "I'm not kidnapping her. She's my *client.*"

Another of the sims was Dr. Ted. Mary appealed to him, "You tell them. You tell them what's happening."

The sim turned to the others and said, "This girl is suffering from a brain pox and is clearly delusional. Avoid intimate contact with her at all costs."

The aff woman began to wave her free hand. Mary turned and saw the groundskeeper coming toward them. He was swatting at a bee as he jogged. The bee in turn was batting itself against the man's visor. At first Mary thought she'd be safe among these affs, ungracious though they were, but as the pike drew near, she panicked and ran again.

She ran over a little rise into a stand of beech trees. Fléchettes riddled the tree trunks around her. One sliced through the flesh at her side, but she hardly noticed. She came across a path and took it. She was beyond all calculation. Her only thought was to outrun the sounds behind her.

These sounds changed abruptly. The zing of fléchettes was replaced by the whine of laser fire. Two separate frequencies meant two different guns. She hugged a tree and peeked from behind it to see an amazing sight. A mech was firing at the pike. The pike had switched his weapon to laser mode and was sweeping the air with bursts of light, but he was unable to hit the mech at such close range. The mech, on the other hand, easily hit the pike, but its comparatively low-wattage lasers were no match for the pike's armor. Undeterred, the mech continued to hit him, targeting only three points on the pike's body and hitting those points repeatedly: his face mask, his groin, and the helmet seal at the back of his neck. The pike covered these spots as best he could with his gloved hands, but he couldn't cover all three at once, and the mech circled and crossed the man's head, almost too fast to see, firing a staccato stream of pulses. The man returned fire with choked spreads, like laser birdshot. His wild shots gouged smoking holes in the trees around him and brought down boughs and branches upon himself.

Back and forth, the mech flew, hitting its targets repeatedly. If its fuel held, it would eventually wear through the armor. Mary was fascinated by this deadly ballet, but could not stay to watch. She looked all around for the wall. That's when she saw the second pike. He was standing very still, holding his carbine at his side, letting it self-target. The gun discharged a prolonged pulse that raced through the woods and hit the mech. The mech exploded as its plasma reserve was ignited. The concussion knocked the groundskeeper off his feet.

The second pike lowered his carbine and gestured to Mary to stand still. A utility cart, like the one at the cottage, rolled up behind him.

FRED HEARD THE explosion and set his visor to calculate its location. As he ran, the ground he covered was added to the theater map under construction in the corner of his visor. It was a growing band of known terrain in an unknown territory. The explosion had come from an unexpected direction. If it marked Mary's location, it would mean that she was doubling back to the plaza in a large arc.

Fred ran toward the explosion marker in his map. He crossed several footpaths and climbed small wooded hills. The terrain was rich in natural cover, which his visor mostly filtered out. Suddenly he was buzzed by a mech, bluish, like the one that had streaked from the gatehouse. He guessed it wasn't a clinic mech, but didn't know how it figured into the action. It circled him twice and flew off. Suddenly all of the unknown territory in Fred's map was filled in. Not only that, but personnel markers appeared, and he had access to clinic comm. Fred paused in order to analyze the situation. Two of the markers were to his left and receding at a good pace. One of them, flagged as armed, was pursuing the other, who was unarmed—Mary? To his right, another marker was at the location of the explosion. It was flagged as armed and uninjured, but unconscious. There was another marker much farther inside the clinic. It was marked by a battlefield lid, which meant it was a casualty. Fred couldn't read its vitals, but a picture was quickly forming in his mind. Pikes often came in tactical teams of three. These three had been sent to destroy Ellen Starke, but ran into trouble. One was down. A second was stunned by the explosion. And the third was pursuing Mary.

Fred turned to follow Mary but stopped again. She was too far away to reach in time. He needed another plan. He knew that the pike chasing Mary had to be wondering who *he* was and what he was doing there. The pike could see in his own visor that Fred was unarmed, yet wearing body armor, and that he wasn't attached to clinic security. The pike had to be watching Fred's marker on his own map with growing apprehension, for he had made a serious mistake. He hadn't expected to run into a loose russ, and left his teammate vulnerable. If russes were predictable, pikes were doubly so. They never left their brothers behind. Clients be damned.

On Fred's map, the pike slowed down, a calculated move. He was still within striking distance of Mary, but he was giving Fred a chance to catch up, luring him away from his teammate. A russ would surely take the bait, especially if his duty was to save the Starke girl, and Fred nearly went for it. The Starke girl wasn't his client this time, though. This time he was his own client. The downed pike was just over the next rise, and on a counterintuitive impulse, Fred rushed there instead.

Fred topped the hill and crouched close to the ground to study the fallen man who lay amid a litter of shattered and smoking tree branches. His groundskeeper uniform had been burned off at his shoulder, revealing an armored suit underneath. His breathing seemed regular, and his suit looked intact. His carbine lay several meters away in the grass.

Fred scampered down the hill and retrieved the gun. It had timed out, and he brought it to the pike. He took the fallen man's left hand—pikes were southpaws—and wrapped it around the grip. The gun controls became enabled, and Fred reset the force and shape of the laser pulse to its highest, narrowest setting. In his visor he saw that the other pike had left off pursuing Mary and was heading back to him. Excellent! If his new friend here cooperated, Fred had a target and a weapon.

Fred pushed the pike's index finger into the trigger guard and laid his own finger over it. He pulled the man's body around a little and lay down behind it.

But the pike's eyes fluttered; he was coming around. Suddenly his free hand made a fist and roundhoused Fred on the side of his head. Fred's cap took most of the blow, but even so, his ear sang.

They struggled for the gun, the pike punching Fred savagely. Fred was losing control, so he pressed the pike's trigger finger and squeezed off a shot. A terrific bolt of light erupted from the gun so close to Fred's face that it dazzled him, despite his visor. The blast rived the trunk of a nearby tree like a lightning strike, splitting it in two. On the way, it vaporized the pike's right hand.

The pike gasped, and his suit quickly sealed his stump with battlewrap. Fred wrenched the carbine and pressed the barrel under the pike's chin.

"Tell your pal to stop where he is!" Fred ordered him.

The pike didn't respond. His pupils closed to pinpoints. His suit was doping him for the pain. The other pike was almost in sight. Fred poked the muzzle of the gun hard against the man's throat and repeated his order.

The pike smiled in drugged serenity. "I see you are unarmed, friend."

"What do you call *this*, friend?" Fred said and jabbed him again with the muzzle.

"A soft cock if you kill me with it."

He was right. The moment the pike died, his gun would shut down, leaving Fred weaponless.

"When you're right, you're right," Fred said and carefully re-aimed the gun. He fired again, taking off the side of the pike's helmet, his ear, and a strip of his scalp. Before the suit could patch itself, Fred grabbed a splintered branch from the ground and stuck its pointy end several millimeters up the pike's exposed ear canal.

"Lie still!" he yelled in the man's good ear. But the pike struggled all the more fiercely, so Fred shoved the stick in until it passed through his brain and jammed up against the inside of his skull. The pike convulsed a couple of times and went limp. On his map, the pike was flagged injured. With any luck he would take a while to die.

Meanwhile, the other pike's marker stopped just over the next rise, and Mary was making good time back to South Plaza.

"Such a deal," Fred said and reset the carbine's spread pattern.

MARY CAME TO a path she recognized. To her surprise, she wasn't far from the plaza where she had started. On impulse, she turned left, away from South Gate and toward the central complex of clinic buildings. She'd feel safer there, and from there she could choose any of the other gates. But the blue bee, her guardian angel, intercepted her and urged her toward South Gate with pulsing arrows.

Vehicles, both homcom and police, filled South Gate Plaza, but no medevac ambulance. Mary shifted her terrible burden from one arm to the other and approached a belinda in a hommer uniform, but a crash cart intercepted her first. It lowered its treatment platform, and asked Mary to sit.

"No, not yet. Can you call me an ambulance? A medevac?"

The holo of a man projected next to the cart. He was a stranger, but he seemed to know her. "Ah, Myr Skarland, at last! Hurry, give Ellen's head to the cart. We've got a fresh tank waiting for her. There's no time to lose."

The cart proffered its arm, and Mary ached to give Ellen to it and be done with it. "That's right," the man encouraged. "Give your bag to the cart."

Mary said, "Who are you?"

"Byron Fagan."

Mary clutched the tote to herself. "Fagan Health Group? Concierge's sponsor?"

"Yes, I am. Or rather, I was. Concierge was altered, I don't know when, or by whom. It fell under the influence of unknown parties. I only discovered this a little while ago, when it was thrown off-line. I have launched a secure backup. He's back now, as good as new. There's no need to worry, Myr Skarland. You've done a heroic job, and everything is safe now.

"But we must act fast, if we want Ellen to survive." He pointed at the syrup dripping from the tote. "That is, if she's still alive. You must trust me, Myr Skarland. I'm the one who called in the Command."

He seemed sincere. "My sisters, and Nurse Hattie and Matt," Mary said, gesturing toward the woods.

"We're already attending to them," Fagan said. "It's Ellen Starke we have to think of now." The cart's arm reached for the tote.

"Hello! Evangeline!" someone called from the gatehouse. A little man and a tall woman hurried toward her, carrying an odd device between them. "Don't listen to him," the man called. "Wait for us!"

The couple stopped next to the crash cart and lowered their burden to the ground. "My name is Meewee. I know you. I worked with Wee Hunk."

"Where *is* Wee Hunk?" Mary said. She raised her face to the sky and called, "Wee Hunk, I need you." But the Neanderthal did not appear. "Let Wee Hunk in!" Mary ordered Fagan.

Fagan held up his hands and said, "I assure you, Myr Skarland, I am not—"

"Wee Hunk is dead," the little man said. "He was contaminated."

"There's no time for this," Fagan declared. "Every second is crucial. For pity sake, Mary, turn over Ellen's head."

While her competing benefactors were vying for her trust, the woman who had come with the little man bent over their device on the ground. She opened its lid, revealing a snug compartment of gleaming chrome. She smiled up at Mary and said, "If you please."

"This is Dr. Rouselle," the little man said. "She doesn't work for Fagan, and this is a portable hernandez tank. Please, Myr 'Leen, let the doctor save Ellen."

"Save her?" Fagan snapped. "He wants to hold her hostage. Her mother had her brought to *my* clinic because she trusted us." The crash cart edged in closer and opened a side compartment; inside was a large glassive jar, brimming with bubbling amber amnio syrup.

Mary unwrapped her tote and gently lifted the head from the dregs at the bottom. She cradled the dripping head in both hands, but she couldn't force herself to return it to the clinic. "Wee Hunk," she cried, "where are you?"

Wee Hunk did not appear, but the blue bee did, buzzing her and setting down on the lid of the doctor's chrome tank. And that was answer enough for her.

Epilogue

Three Months Later

April and her Bolto fiancé were late for dinner. A place had been set for the mystery man—none of them had met him yet—next to April's spot at the head table. Everyone wore nice clothes for the occasion, except Denny who insisted on dining in his work clothes. It was all he wanted to wear anymore, the jumpsuit with the large KODIAK MICROHABS patch on the back and his name embroidered over the front pocket. Kitty had recruited him when she started her microhab service up again. Several of her old clients had hired her back, which helped to kick-start the business, and already she was bringing in over five yoodies a day. She let Denny come up to the head table each evening to drop them into the soup pot. And each evening the 'meets cheered him till his ears turned red. Bogdan didn't mind at all.

"While we're waiting for April," Kale said, "I might as well impart some news we just received." He paused and rubbed his eyes. "It's not good news, I'm afraid. Roger Beadlemyren called a little while ago. He says they can't wait on us much longer. They'll have to go with their second pick if we don't get Hubert back soon, or at least make material progress in that direction. Sixty days, that's how much time we have, and then our Intent to Merge agreement will expire."

Kale sat down. No one said anything. The charter hadn't even managed to force the Command to admit that they had the mentar in custody. The doors to Green Hall opened, and all heads turned, but it wasn't April, only Sarah with the food cart. Kale waved her in and said, "Might as well get started."

It was a grim meal. The 'meets mostly played with their food and let it get cold. Megan pushed her plate away and said, "At least with April's marriage we'll have a new member."

Nobody responded, not even BJ, for they all feared the worst. When two people from charters as mismatched as the Kodiaks and Boltos were married, the rule was that the spouse from the lesser house joined the greater. As to whether or not April would leave Kodiak was unknown because she refused to discuss it, and no one had the nerve to come right out and ask. In fact, she had been pretty secretive about the whole affair right from the beginning at Rondy. She hadn't even told them what this fellow's first name was. But it was inconceivable that April, April Kodiak, would leave them in the lurch, causing their membership to drop below statutory minimum and throwing the house into regulatory limbo. Not April. And what about her NanoJiffy franchise?

At last, the door opened, and April came in. They hardly recognized her. It wasn't only the fashionable new clothes she wore, or the fact that she was a full twenty years younger—they all knew the Boltos had paid for rejuve treatments—but she had apparently undergone some body sculpting as well, and she looked—pretty. She came in and smiled awkwardly at everyone.

Behind her entered a man, taller than she, in a tailored charcoal jumpsuit with navy and teal pinstripes. He also smiled awkwardly. He had nice teeth.

So this was the lucky fellow. The Kodiak 'meets followed him and April across the room with silent, appraising stares. But then someone else entered after them, another man, also wearing Bolto colors. This one was short and a bit ugly, and he didn't smile at all. In the time it took for the three of them to reach the head table, the awful truth of the matter, the reason for April's prolonged silence, began to dawn on the Kodiaks—April's marriage was for a triad, not a couple. Now there was no question but that she would leave them and join Charter Bolto.

"Could you set another place?" April asked Louis, who had waiter duty. Louis shut his gaping mouth and hopped to it. April stood between the two Boltos and took their hands. "Sorry we're late," she said. "Everyone, I'd like to introduce my two special guys. This is Brad, and this is Tom. They brought a yummy dessert which we left down in the fridge."

A chocolate cranberry torte, it turned out to be, but dessert proved as grim as the meal. A silent resentment filled Green Hall, which April tried unsuccessfully to dispel with nervous chatter.

Finally, Bogdan threw down his napkin and stood up. He was standing taller these days, having gained ten centimeters in the last three months. His voice was deeper too, and a mustache was sprouting above his upper lip.

"Where y'all going?" Rusty said.

"I'm going to find Hubert."

The 'meets at his table stared at him, and Rusty said, "How d'you plan on doing that?"

"To tell you the truth, I have no idea, but I'm going to find him even if it kills me." He went up to the head table and shook hands with Brad and Tom. To April he said, "My deepest congratulations. You done good." And then, as he walked to the door, he paused and added, "Oh, and don't worry about us. We'll be just fine."

MARY SKARLAND TOOK the lift down to the bunker level and hurried to the shelter. Ellen was out of the tank for a hardening session under the lights. Her infant body lay facedown on a mat with a towel draped over its bare rump and its gargantuan head turned on its side. The doctor and a jenny nurse were there, and Cyndee too. Cyndee rolled her eyes at Mary, and Mary saw why. The annoying little man had come to talk business again.

"We've had to push the launch back eleven months," he was saying, "but what's eleven months to a journey that'll last a thousand years?"

"Myr Meewee," Ellen's voice said from the room's speakers, "you know I can't turn my head. Please remain where I can see you."

"Oh, right, sorry." Meewee returned to a spot in front of the baby. "As I was saying—"

"I heard what you were saying," Ellen said, "I just couldn't *see* you. Actually, when I think about it, I see too much of you. I put you in charge of the GEP because I didn't want to have to deal with it on a minute-by-minute basis. So do your job and just handle it, will you?"

Meewee bowed and said, "Count on it, Ellen. All I need is your authorization for—"

"Ask Cabinet! Not me! How many times do I have to tell you?"

Cabinet's chief of staff appeared then, and a moment later, so did Ellen's recently adopted mentar, Lyra.

Meewee took one look at Cabinet and said with harping exasperation, "All of the chinaberry trees in the garden are heavy with fruit *this time of year!*"

The baby, choking with anger, retorted, "In that case, the neighborhood birds should be *very happy!*" The baby made fists, and her skin mottled.

The doctor stepped in and signaled the jenny. "Such a wonderful visit, Bishop Meewee," she said. "Come again, yes?"

The little man left the room grumbling to himself, and the doctor and jenny lifted Ellen and placed her back in the tank. There her oversized head floated in comfortable ease.

"He's such an unpleasant man," Cyndee said.

"Oh, he means well," Ellen replied, "but such a pest." She turned to her new mentar and said, "Lyra, have we told the 'leens about the surprise we have in store for them at the studio?"

The mentar, in the persona of a short, young woman, came forward and began to speak, but Cyndee said, "Wait. Mary's not coming today."

Ellen said, "What's this?"

"Sorry," Mary said, "but I have a prior engagement."

Cyndee snorted. "A prior engagement, she says. She's going to see Fred. That's where she's going. She has a *conjugal* engagement. See how nice she's dressed?"

"Oo-la-la," said the doctor.

Mary blushed and the women laughed. "I just came down to say good-bye till tomorrow."

"Then we'll hold the surprise," Ellen said. "Give Fred our love. Oh, and I almost forgot. I told Cabinet to put its attorney general on Fred's case as co-counsel. Tell Fred to tell Marcus to expect a call."

That was very good news indeed.

MARY PASSED THROUGH the scanway of the Homeland Command maximum security prison in Provo, Utah. From one visit to the next, she never knew how the russes on duty there would receive her. Sometimes they acknowledged her and her sisters' heroism. Other times, her presence only seemed to remind them of her husband and their own shame.

They escorted her to the so-called joogie sweet and left her there to wait for Fred. It usually took another five or ten minutes to process him through. Mary crossed the dirty carpet and sat in the sticky armchair. The suite was furnished no better than a dormitory cell. A tired bed, a scuffed nightstand, a pair of uncomfortable armchairs. Not even a calendar to break the gray monotony of the walls. Every time Mary came here, she could feel her libido shriveling up like food wrap. Which was just as well, because during her very first visit Fred had pretty much put the kibosh on anything ever happening between them in this room.

They had led him in and unshackled him that first time, then left and closed the door behind them. She had been standing in the middle of the room, and the room was very small, so it would be hard to miss her, but Fred walked the length of two walls and scrutinized the paint before even acknowledging her presence. He went to the door and pointed at the latch—*no lock*. There were daggers in his eyes. That had been their first time alone together in three weeks, and he hadn't forgiven her yet.

Hi, she had said, standing there. We can talk, you know. I was unsure of this place, myself, so I asked your Marcus, and he assured me there are no cameras or mikes or any snooping equipment of any sort in this room. So if you came over here and hugged me, no one would be the wiser.

But he didn't. Nor did he speak. He stayed put and rolled up a sleeve and brought his pale arm to his nose to squint at his skin.

Dear, she said, I know you are fully colonized by now. So am I and all of Chicago and two-thirds of the rest of the country. Nobody likes them, but most people agree that they're a hell of a lot better than the slugs were.

Fred slapped his own forehead. He had never done something like that before, and it got her full and immediate attention. Satisfied, he opened his great arms wide and leaned back to take in an unseen audience behind the ceiling and walls, and he spoke in a calm but commanding voice, My wife and I refuse to perform for you.

And that was that.

THE DOOR OPENED, and they brought Fred in and left. She got up and took a couple of steps. "Hello, Fred."

His eyes told her he missed her, but he went to sit on the bed, and she returned to the armchair. First they discussed business: household matters, his case, the trial. It was pretty much all the talking they did, and today she had really big news. But she was unsure how to tell him.

"Ellen Starke says—" she began, and storm clouds gathered at the mere mention of the name. "She says that Cabinet's attorney general will join Marcus as co-counsel. She said to—"

"No," he said flatly.

THE BED SAGGED in the middle. They lay face-to-face, not touching, and spoke with their eyes, as they always had. He went first because his need was urgent. Mary witnessed a string of unpleasant incidents in his gaze. He let her see a little bit of his fear. He was swimming in loneliness and poisoned by a prison diet of humiliation. She ached to hold him.

After about an hour of this, when his pain had somewhat lessened, he yawned from the sheer relief of it and raised an eyebrow—her turn.

Mary had to struggle not to seem too elated with her own life. The clinic rescue was still on everyone's lips, and the Evangeline Sisterhood was experiencing a re-birth of public awareness.

Not only that, but Ellen Starke decided to honor the Sisterhood by launching a hollyholo character for the novellas based on their type. They hadn't even finished producing the sim and already offers were coming from major studios. Blue Loon Stories had signed for a thousand units, and Four Steps reserved five hundred just last week. Ellen said that all ten thousand units of the limited edition would be sold before its release date.

Not only that, but Ellen's own Burning Daylight Productions was contributing all of the edition's royalties to the Renata Carter and Alexandra Perry Foundation to fund the Sisterhood's retraining and rejuve programs.

Not only that, but Ellen *gave* her and Cyndee and the other clinic 'leens their own units outright. I'm going to own a hollyholo sim, Fred. And it's already signed to the *Surly Shirley* story mat! Do you have any idea how much a sim can earn? My unit will make me more in one day than I could earn in a *month*.

Do you know what that means, Fred? It means we're set up for life. When we get you out of here, we can find a better apartment. We can take a trip around the world if we want to and stay away for as long as we like. It means—

Suddenly Mary was ambushed by the image of Renata lying on her bed of grass clippings. This still happened a dozen times a day. She began to cry. She cried for Hattie too, and Alex. And even for Reilly, not because Reilly was hurt—he was al-ready repaired and back on duty—but because he was a true russ.

Mary cried for so many people that she curled up on her half of the bed and soaked the bedspread with tears. She hated giving this performance to the nitwork, but she couldn't help herself. And Fred just lay there, dying inside.

———

THEY DOZED FOR a while, not touching, but breathing each other's breath, giving this, too, to the nitwork. When she awoke, he was watching her with a grim expression. When she met his gaze, he pointed at himself, and then, breaking his own hard-and-fast rule, he touched her. He took her small hand and cupped it in his two big mitts. His hands were cold, but they electrified her, and she missed the glyph he was secretly drawing on her open palm with his fingertip. He drew it again, and this time she recognized it. It was Uglyph for *Obligation*, with overtones of *Integrity* and *Unpaid Debt*. He let go of her and waited for her to look at him, and when she did, he sucked in his cheeks and flattened the tip of his nose with his finger.

Mary almost laughed. Fred was making a dead-on impersonation of a TUG face. But he wasn't joking; he was trying to tell her something of grave importance. He pointed again to himself. Obligation. Integrity. Unpaid Debt.

THE DIRECTOR'S VOICE came over the cueing speaker: "That last one was very good, Myr Skarland. Now let's go back to Surprise/Sitting."

In the Burning Daylight recording booth, Mary sat on the stool and took a breath, trying to empty her mind of all thoughts. "Ready," she said.

"Leena," said the voice, "they told me you were involved in an accident."

Mary's eyebrows rose in surprise.

"Good. Good. Now let's do Surprise/Rising."

"Ready."

"Leena," said the voice, "Myr Dodder is *dead!*"

Mary rose from the stool.

"Good. Now Surprise/False."

"Ready."

A COFFEE BREAK. Mary removed the ECG helmet and shook out her hair. She exited the booth and joined Cyndee and Georgine in the hall.

"It's *hard!*" Cyndee said. "I never knew how hard it was to be an actor."

"What cascades are you guys working on?" Georgine said.

"Surprise," Mary said.

"Titillation," said Cyndee.

"Oh, that should be easy for you," Georgine quipped.

"Is that right?" Cyndee said. "Then why did I hear they picked you to do orgasm?" She mimicked the director's voice. "Orgasm/Sitting. Good. Good. Now Orgasm/Standing."

The sisters laughed, and then laughed at themselves laughing. (Laughter/Silly.)

Down the hall they heard someone not laughing. It was Ellen. Her voice kept rising, louder and shriller, in an angry crescendo, and Mary imagined her flushed face back home in the tank. As one, the sisters headed for the office. 'Leens to the rescue.

Ellen's jacket, a lean, stylish woman, had her business partner, Clarity, backed against the wall of the small office. Clarity flashed them a look of welcome when they came in, but Ellen turned her rage on them. "Give us a minute!" she snapped. "Can't you see we're busy?"

"Sorry," Cyndee said.

"We'll just be going then," Georgine said.

"But when are you going to show us that surprise you promised?" Mary said.

Ellen's expression went blank. She looked from the 'leens to Clarity. She covered her face with her hands for a moment, and when she lowered them she looked a lot calmer, and she said, "How about right now?"

The evangelines agreed and followed her out of the office. Clarity mouthed a silent thank-you. Ellen led them to the mixing studio and said, "It's only about sixty percent compiled, and the inference engine is buggy, and the highlights need serious tweaking, but—what do you think?"

The evangeline sim—working title Leena—appeared in the room. She wore a blue and teal jumpsuit, similar in cut to Applied People livery. She seemed to be within germline norms, though her nose was perhaps a bit too pert, her eyebrows too chiseled, her boobs definitely bigger and buttocks rounder. The sim broke out in a huge smile and said, "Sisters!" On its face was Mary's own expression—Surprise/Recognition.

Ellen bustled about her creation, dictating notes to her mentar, Lyra. "This is feckin' brilliant!" she exclaimed. "Do you 'leens have any idea how much production time we save by scotching the three of you together? If only all actors were clones."

Mary hugged herself and watched the sim explore the studio, watched her sisters tease it with questions, watched their companion slowly begin to forget her own grisly death.

(Surprise/Happiness.)

(Joy/Unexpected.)